BENEDETTI BROTHERS

SALVATORE, DOMINIC & SERGIO

NATASHA KNIGHT

ABOUT THIS BOOK

This trilogy contains the stories of the Benedetti Brothers: Salvatore, Dominic and Sergio.

Please note that although Sergio's story comes first in the timeline of events, I've set it as the last story in the set. I won't give too much away here, but it was released in that order and you will understand why after you read the trilogy.

Killian: a Dark Mafia Romance and *Giovanni: a Dark Mafia Romance* are spinoff standalone romances set in the Benedetti Mafia world. You'll find a sample from Killian at the end of this trilogy.

Thank you for purchasing this collection. I hope you fall in love with the Benedetti Brothers.

SALVATORE: A DARK MAFIA ROMANCE

ABOUT THIS BOOK

Lucia

It all started with a contract signed by him, then by me, while our families watched. While my father sat silent, a man defeated, giving his daughter to the Benedetti monsters.

I obeyed. I played my part. I signed my name and gave away my life. I became their living, breathing trophy, a constant symbol of their power over us.

That was five years ago.

Then came the time for him to claim me. For Salvatore Benedetti to own me.

I had vowed vengeance. I had learned hate. And yet, nothing could have prepared me for the man who now ruled my life.

I expected a monster, one I would destroy. But nothing is ever black or white. No one is either good or evil. For all his darkness, I saw his light. For all his evil, I saw his good. As much as he made me hate him, a passion hotter than the fires of hell burned inside me.

I was his, and he was mine.

My very own monster.

Salvatore

I owned the DeMarco Mafia Princess. She belonged to me now. We had won, and they had lost. And what better way to teach a lesson than to take from them that which is most precious? Most beloved?

I was the boy who would be king. Next in line to rule the Benedetti Family. Lucia DeMarco was the spoils of war. Mine to do with as I pleased.

It was my duty to break her. To make her life a living hell. My soul was dark, I was hell bound. And there was no way out, not for either of us. Because the Benedetti family never lost, and in our wake, we left destruction. It's how it had always been. How I believed it would always be.

Until Lucia.

PROLOGUE

SALVATORE

I signed the contract before me, pressing so hard that the track of my signature left a groove on the sheet of paper. I set the pen down and slid the pages across the table to her.

Lucia.

I could barely meet her gaze as she raised big, innocent, frightened eyes to mine.

She looked at it, at the collected, official documents that would bind her to me. That would make her mine. I wasn't sure if she was reading or simply staring, trying to make sense of what had just happened. What had been decided for her. For both of us.

She turned reddened eyes to her father. I didn't miss the questions I saw inside them. The plea. The disbelief.

But DeMarco kept his eyes lowered, his head bent in defeat. He couldn't look at his daughter, not after what he'd been made to watch.

I understood that, and I hated my own father more for making him do it.

Lucia sucked in a ragged breath. Could everyone hear it or just me? I saw the rapid pulse beating in her neck. Her hand trembled when she picked up the pen. She met my gaze once more. One final plea? I watched her struggle against the tears that threatened to spill on her already stained cheeks.

I didn't know what I felt upon seeing them. Hell, I didn't know what I felt about anything at all anymore.

"Sign."

My father's command made her turn. I watched their gazes collide.

"We don't have all day."

To call him domineering was an understatement. He was someone who made grown men tremble.

But she didn't shy away.

"Sign, Lucia," her father said quietly.

She didn't look at anyone after that. Instead, she put pen to paper and signed her name—Lucia Annalisa DeMarco—on the dotted line adjacent to mine. My family's attorney applied the seal to the sheets as soon as she finished, quickly taking them and leaving the room.

I guess it was all official, then. Decided. Done.

My father stood, gave me his signature look of displeasure, and walked out of the room. Two of his men followed.

"Do you need a minute?" I asked her. Did she want to say good-bye to her father?

"No."

She refused to look at him or at me. Instead, she pushed her chair back and stood, the now-wrinkled white skirt falling over her thighs. She fisted her hands at her sides.

"I'm ready."

I rose and gestured to one of the waiting men. She walked ahead of him as if he walked her to her execution. I glanced at her father, then at the cold examining table with the leather restraints now hanging open, useless, their victim released. The image of what had happened there just moments earlier shamed me.

But it could have been so much worse for her.

It could have gone the way my father wanted. *His* cruelty knew no bounds.

She had me to thank for saving her from that.

So why did I still feel like a monster? A beast? A pathetic, spineless puppet?

I owned Lucia DeMarco, but the thought only made me sick. She was the token, the living, breathing trophy of my family's triumph over hers.

I walked out of the room and rode the elevator down to the lobby, emptying my eyes of emotion. That was one thing I did well.

I walked out onto the stifling, noisy Manhattan sidewalk and climbed into the backseat of my waiting car. The driver knew where to take me, and twenty minutes later, I walked into the whorehouse, to a room in the back, the image of Lucia lying on that examining table, bound, struggling, her face turned away as the doctor probed her before declaring her intact, burned into my memory forever.

I'd stood beside her. I hadn't looked. Did that absolve me? Surely that meant something?

But why was my cock hard, then?

She'd cried quietly. I'd watched her tears slip off her face and fall to the floor and willed myself to be anywhere but there. Willed myself not to hear the sounds, my father's degrading words, her quiet breaths as she struggled to remain silent.

All while I'd stood by.

I was a coward. A monster. Because when I did finally meet

those burning amber eyes, when I dared shift my gaze to hers, our eyes had locked, and I saw the quiet plea inside them. A silent cry for help.

In desperation, she'd sought *my* help.

And I'd looked away.

Her father's face had gone white when he'd realized the full cost he'd agreed to; the payment of the debt he'd set upon her shoulders.

Her life for his. For all of theirs.

Fucking selfish bastard didn't deserve to live. He should have died to protect her. He should never—ever—have allowed this to happen.

I sucked in a breath, heavy and wet, drowning me.

I poured myself a drink, slammed it back, and repeated. Whiskey was good. Whiskey dulled the scene replaying in my head. But it did nothing to wipe out the image of her eyes on mine. Her terrified, desperate eyes.

I threw the glass, smashing it in the corner. One of the whores came to me, knelt between my spread legs, and took my cock out of my pants. Her lips moved, saying something I didn't hear over the war raging inside my head, and fucked up as fucked up can be, she took my already hard cock into her mouth.

I gripped a handful of the bitch's hair and closed my eyes, letting her do her work, taking me deep into her throat. But I didn't want gentle, not now. I needed more. I stood, squeezed my eyes shut against the image of Lucia on that table, and fucked the whore's face until she choked and tears streamed down her cheeks. Until I finally came, emptying down her throat, the sexual release, like the whiskey, gave me nothing. There wasn't enough sex or alcohol in the world to burn that particular image of Lucia out of my mind, but maybe I deserved it. Deserved the guilt. I should man up and own it. I allowed it all to happen, after all. I stood by and did nothing.

And now, she was mine, and I was hers.

Her very own monster.

1

LUCIA

Five Years Later
Calabria, Italy

The last time I walked down the aisle of this cathedral had been my confirmation day. I'd been a child. I'd worn a beautiful white dress, and my mother had wound a rosary through my fingers, binding my hands in prayer.

I hadn't prayed, though. Instead, I'd thought of how I looked in my dress. How it was the prettiest of all the girls. How I was the prettiest.

Today, I wore black. And I no longer cared who was the prettiest. Today, I followed my father's casket to the front of the church.

Black lace hid my face, so I could take in the audience without them seeing me. The pews stood empty until we reached the front rows, where ten were occupied. Fifteen mourners on the right—my family's side. Double that on the left. Did soldiers count as mourners, though? Because that's what the Benedetti's had brought.

I ignored them and looked at each of the fifteen faces who had dared show up on my side. My father did not have many friends. In fact, of the fifteen, two were his brothers, my uncles, and one, his sister. The other twelve made up their families. Only the women sat in the pews, though. My male cousins carried my father's coffin.

As the procession neared the front pew, I prepared myself for the moment I would see *his* face. The face of the man who had, five years ago, sat across from me in a cold, sterile room and signed a contract, declaring his ownership of me. A vow, like a marriage vow, perhaps. But the words *cherish* and *love* had been absent from the pages; *take* and *keep* having taken their place.

No, we had a different sort of contract. My life to spare my family. Me as the sacrifice, the payer of the debt. Me to show anyone in the DeMarco family who had any fight left that the Benedetti's owned their daughter. The Benedetti's owned the DeMarco princess.

I hate the Benedetti family. I hate every single one of them.

The procession halted. My sister, Isabella, stood close enough behind me that I felt her there. At least she wasn't crying. At least she knew not to show weakness. In fact, no sound came from her at all.

Seeing her today, it had surprised me.

Seeing my niece, Effie, for the first time, it twisted my heart, reminding me of yet another thing that had been taken from me.

Six pallbearers laid my father's coffin down on the table arranged to receive it. It would be a closed-casket funeral. No viewing. He'd blown half his head off when he'd shot himself in the mouth.

My cousins turned to me. Luke, who was the adopted son of my uncle, looked just beyond me, though. Beyond me and to my sister. His eyes, a soft, pale blue I remembered from childhood, had hardened to steel. I watched, wishing I could turn back and look at my sister, see what her eyes said. But then his gaze shifted to me. He looked very different from the boy I'd grown up with. But he *was* very different or had become so over the last five years. We all had. Through the lace shielding my face, I met his eyes. Could he see the rage simmering inside me? He gave me a quick, short nod. An acknowledgment. I wondered if anyone saw it. He could be killed for it. The Benedetti's took no prisoners. Well, apart from me. But a woman. What could a woman do?

They would see.

A man moved into my periphery and cleared his throat. I knew who it was. Standing up straighter, steeling myself, I forced my heart to stop its frantic pounding and turned to face him.

Salvatore Benedetti.

I swallowed as my gaze traveled from the black silk tie he wore upward. I remembered him. I remembered him clearly. But the suit seemed to stretch tighter over muscle now, his chest broader, his arms thicker. I forced my gaze higher, pausing at his neck, willing myself to slow my breathing.

I could not show weakness. I could not show fear. But that day, when they'd forced me onto that table—I still shuddered at how cold it had felt against my naked thighs—he hadn't spoken. Not a single word. He had looked at me, watched my struggle, watched me bite my tongue as they shamed me.

But I also remembered something else, and that gave me the courage to raise my eyes to his. He'd turned away first. Was it that he hadn't been able to look at me? To witness my degradation? Or could he not stand the thought of me *seeing* him for what he was?

Our families had decided. I'd had little choice. I wondered for a moment what choice he'd had, but I wouldn't consider that. It didn't matter. Salvatore Benedetti would one day rule the

Benedetti family. He would be boss. He would become what I vowed to destroy five years ago.

I masked any emotion as I turned my gaze up to his. I'd learned to hide my feelings well over the last few years.

My heart stopped for a single moment. Everything seemed to still, as if waiting. Something fluttered inside my belly as cobalt-blue eyes met mine.

Not steely but soft.

I remembered how I'd thought that five years ago too. How, for just the briefest moment on that terrible day, I'd thought there was hope. That he'd stop what was happening. But I'd been wrong. Any perceived softness, it only deceived. It hid behind it a coldhearted monster, ready to take.

And what happened in that magical garden a year ago, when before I'd seen who he was, I'd placed my hand inside his. Danced with him.

No. I couldn't think about that night now or ever again. I would need to remember that. To not to allow myself the luxury of being fooled.

Salvatore blinked and stepped aside, gesturing for me to enter the pew. His father and brother stood watching me, his father's expression screaming victory. He gave me a cruel grin and held out his hand to the space beside him. I moved, my legs somehow carrying me even as I trembled inside.

I would turn my fear to hate. I would make it burn hot.

Because I would need it to survive what lay in store for me. I'd been sixteen when I'd been made to sign that contract. I knew well the true terror of what it meant was only about to begin.

I took my place beside his father. Salvatore resumed his seat to my right. I had the feeling he took as much care not to touch me as I did not to touch either him or his father. I didn't turn to look at my sister when she was ushered into a pew across the aisle. I paid no attention to the Benedetti soldiers lining the perimeter of the church just as I hadn't paid any to the army the Benedetti's had assembled outside. Instead, I watched Father Samson. He'd been old when I'd been confirmed. Now he looked ancient.

He blessed my father, even though he had taken his own life. He prayed for his soul. After all this time, I didn't think I cared anymore. But that kindness, it gave me some small comfort.

No one cried. How strange that no one would cry at a funeral. That fact impressed itself upon me, and it felt wrong.

The service ended one hour later. My cousins once again circled the casket and lifted it. Once it passed us, Salvatore stepped out of the pew. He waited for me to go ahead, and I did, stiffening when I felt the slight touch of his hand at my lower back. He must have felt me stiffen because he removed his hand. We emerged from the darkness inside the church out onto the square, the bright Italian sun momentarily blinding. My father would be buried in Calabria. It was his wish, to be returned to his place of birth. Both the Benedetti and the DeMarco families were well-known here, and for once, I was grateful for the soldiers holding the press at bay, even as camera's clicked in quick succession, capturing everything from a distance.

I stood to the side and watched as they set the casket inside the waiting hearse. The Benedetti men flanked me with Salvatore standing too close for my comfort. Some commotion caught my attention, and I watched as four-year-old Effie escaped from her nanny's grip and ran toward her mother, my sister, and wrapped her arms around Isabella's legs. All of us turned, in fact, and I took that moment to break away from the Benedetti men and walked toward them, toward my family.

"Lucia."

Isabella greeted me, her eyes reddened, her cheeks dry. She

looked different than the last time I'd seen her. She looked harder. Older than her twenty-two years.

She took a moment to look at me, to take in how five years had made the difference between the sixteen-year-old girl she had known and the woman who stood before her now. She then surprised me by pulling me in for a tight hug.

"I missed you so much."

I let out some sound, and for a moment, allowed my body to give over to her embrace. We'd been so close for so long, but then she'd left. She'd turned her back on me and walked away. I knew why. I even understood. But it hurt all the same, and my anger over everything wrapped even her up into this neat little world of hate I'd created for myself.

The thought that it should have been her, that it would have been her, blared inside me, even though I wanted it to go away. It wasn't her fault. None of this was her fault. In fact, she was the only one not to blame.

"Mama," came Effie's voice.

Isabella released me from her embrace but squeezed my arms as if willing upon me strength. Did she see my weakness in that moment? Could they all see my fear?

"Mama," Effie repeated with the impatience of a child, tugging at Isabella's skirt. Isabella picked her up.

"Why did you come back?" I asked, my voice sounding foreign. Cold. "Why now?" It was that or falling apart, and I would not allow the latter.

She looked taken aback. Her little girl watched me while I tried not to look at her. It was impossible, though. Pretty, blue-gray eyes watched me, seeming to bore right through me. I wondered if they'd come from her father, but Isabella had always refused to tell anyone who that was.

"This is Effie," Isabella said, choosing to ignore my question. "Effie, this is your Aunt Lucia."

Effie studied me for a long moment, then gave me a quick smile, a small dimple forming in her right cheek when she did.

"Hi, Effie," I said, touching her caramel-colored curly hair.

"Hi."

"Why are you back?" I asked again. I felt so much anger, and I wanted to burn everyone up with it. Everyone who had abandoned me. Who had so easily given me up.

"Because I should never have left. Forgive me." She glanced at the hearse. "Life is too short."

I knew she'd not had a choice. When my father had found out she was pregnant, he'd freaked. Firstborn daughter to the boss of the DeMarco family pregnant out of wedlock. As modern as my family was, there were some things that did not change. I still wonder if my father regretted his decisions. It had cost him two daughters.

But then again, we seemed to be easy to give away. If he'd had a son, perhaps things would have been different.

"I'll come see you next week."

"Why? Why bother now?"

She lifted her chin, a stubborn gesture I remembered from when we were little.

The sound of a car backfiring made us all jump. The soldiers circling the square all drew weapons until we all realized there was no threat. Before I turned back to her, though, I noticed Salvatore, who stood by his car, tuck the shiny metal of a pistol back into its holster beneath his jacket.

These were violent men. Men to whom killing was part of life. Part of business. Even having grown up in their world, it still made me shudder.

Salvatore shifted his gaze to me. From this distance, I couldn't see his eyes, but he watched me while standing beside the sedan ready to drive us to the cemetery. "I have to go."

"Lucia," my sister started, this time taking my hand. Hers felt warm, soft. It made me want to cry for all we'd lost.

"What?" I snapped. I could not cry. I would not. Not here.

"Be strong. You're not alone."

"Really?" I tugged my hand free. "That would be a first."

Anger flashed through her eyes. Did she want to slap me, I wondered? Would she? Would Salvatore allow it? For a moment, I thought of him coming to my rescue, of him punishing my sister for laying a hand on me. But then, I remembered who I was. Who he was. *What* I was to him.

"I have to go." I took a step back.

Isabella's eyes filled with tears, sadness replacing the momentary anger, and I turned away.

Show no weakness. Not an ounce of it.

I faced Salvatore, the man who owned me. Surely the contract we'd signed wouldn't hold up in any court of law. But it wasn't the contract that dictated my life. I knew what would happen if I didn't do as I was told. I knew who would pay.

I glanced at Isabella and her daughter again. At my uncles and aunts and cousins.

No, they wouldn't need a court of law to ensure I cooperated. The contract was simply another means of humiliation, like the examination had been.

No. Block that memory. I would not have it.

Salvatore straightened to his full height, standing nearly a foot taller than me at six feet four, and opened the sedan door. Even from across the square, I could see he waited patiently, and I thought he might be trying to be civilized, polite. For the sake of the gathered reporters? Surely not for my benefit. I wondered for a moment if he wanted this. If he wanted *me* like this, knowing it was not my will.

But then again, *owning* another person? That had to be the ultimate high.

I glanced back once more at Isabella. I couldn't help it. For the last five years, I'd been shut away at school. I'd lived at St. Mary's and received private tutoring to earn my high-school degree before attending the small college there, studying, free—to a point. But now, it was time to enter the den of the wolf. My schooling was complete, and it was time for me to assume my place as Salvatore Benedetti's *possession*. For one moment, I tried to imagine that it wasn't true. That it was all a dream, a nightmare. That I could look at my big sister and know she'd make it all okay, like she always did. Just one moment, then I'd be able to do this. To go to my enemy, to enter into his house, knowing I would be an outsider forever. Hated. My presence like a living trophy of their victory over my father, my family.

What would Salvatore expect of me?

I steeled myself and faced him, determined to hold his gaze as I crossed the square. Eyes burned into my back, and the crowd hushed, watching me go to him. He didn't smile as I neared. Nothing changed. His face seemed to be set in stone. I reached him and stopped just inches from him, our eyes locked on each other.

"Lucia."

Salvatore said my name, his voice low and dark, making me shudder.

I didn't know what to say, even though I'd practiced this moment in my mind for months. Years. Now, I simply stood like a mute thing.

But then his father, Franco Benedetti, head of the family and a man I thoroughly despised, approached. He didn't even try to hide his enjoyment of the situation.

I cleared my throat, finally finding my voice. "Why are you here? You have no right." I heard my question, knew it was the same one I'd asked my sister.

"I came to give you my condolences."

Franco leaned in, looking around as if we were somehow coconspirators.

"Actually," he started, his tone lower, "I wouldn't miss it for the world."

I didn't think. I didn't do anything but feel the anger, the hot rage as it bubbled over inside me. My hands clenched into fists, and I spat at his shoe. Except he moved at the last moment, and I missed. When I looked up, Salvatore's face showed his shock, and Franco's was quickly reddening, showing his fury. Although I stood my ground, my heart jackhammered against my chest. I wasn't sure he wouldn't hit me. Hell, between this and my comment to Isabella, maybe that's what I was going for.

Salvatore gripped my arm. "Apologize."

"No," I replied, my eyes locked on his father's black gaze.

Dominic, Salvatore's brother, who'd stood watching from a few feet away, approached. He had a smile on his face as he put his arm around his father's shoulders. Salvatore tensed beside me.

"We're getting some attention. Come on, Paps. Let's go."

I met Dominic's gaze, and I would have sworn he was enjoying the spectacle.

"Apologize." Salvatore's grip tightened around my arm.

I cocked my head to the side. "I'm sorry I missed," I said, a grin spreading across my face.

Dominic's eyebrows shot up, and Salvatore muttered a curse under his breath.

"Let's go," Dominic said just when I thought his father would explode.

"In." Salvatore's other hand gripped my waist as he pushed me into the sedan.

"Get your hands off me," I said, trying to force him off.

He climbed in beside me and pulled the car door shut. The driver started the engine. Salvatore transferred his grip to my knee, his eyes burning a hole through me. "That was a very stupid thing to do." His fingers bit into my flesh.

I had nothing to say. In fact, all I could do was shake violently. I wrapped my arms around myself.

"Turn down the air conditioning," he told the driver, his gaze still locked on mine.

I wished it were the cold that had me shivering.

"Yes, sir," the driver said.

Being so close, seeing him again, it was too much, too intense. It brought too many memories back and foretold a future I did not want.

"You're hurting me."

Salvatore blinked, as if processing each word I spoke one at a time. He shifted his gaze to where his hand gripped my knee. I held my breath, feeling powerless, knowing I was entirely at his mercy.

Knowing this was only the beginning of my hell.

2

SALVATORE

I looked down to where I held her, how hard my fingers were squeezing her. It took some effort, but I released her and sat back in the seat, my gaze still on her, on this rebellious, courageous stranger.

Courageous. Lucia was courageous.

She was also a stranger.

I knew nothing about her. Only her name and her face. Her signature on a stupid piece of paper.

I had never seen a woman stand up to my father like that. I'd never seen a man do it either—or, I should say, when I had, it had been the last time I'd seen that man alive.

I looked out the front window. "Don't antagonize my father. He always wins."

"Everyone loses sometime." She turned away and folded her arms across her chest, watching the streets pass by as we drove to the cemetery.

The black veil of her hat had shielded her face from me in the church, but her whiskey-colored eyes had shone through, bright, strong, angry. Very angry. I refused to let the image of how those eyes had looked at me the last time occupy my mind. I would know only this new, angry Lucia.

The one I needed to control.

Her interaction with her sister had been stiff. I'd seen it even from the distance in the courtyard. I knew she hadn't seen either her sister or her father—even once—in the last five years. The day she'd signed the contract, she'd been sent away to finish her schooling. A year-round, all-girls Catholic school chosen by my father. A small institution hidden away in the suburbs of Philadelphia, where she'd lived comfortably but was under strict supervision. Her movements had been monitored, and at least one bodyguard had accompanied her wherever she went. For the most part, at least. Apart from our surprise meeting at Hollister's gala. I had monthly updates on her comings and goings, and not once had her family come to visit her. Well, her father had tried, but she'd refused to see him. She'd chosen to spend the holidays at school.

I glanced at her, wondering if she regretted that now.

"I'm sorry for your loss."

Her body stiffened, and the only sign that she might be crying was when she moved her hand toward her face, pretending to scratch her cheek after swiping it under her eye.

"Are you?" she asked, her voice strained, her face still turned toward the window.

"I know what it's like to lose someone you're close to." I knew firsthand, in fact. My brother, Sergio, had been my best friend. It had never once, not even in the world we lived in, occurred to me that he could die. My mother had died soon after him. Her death, thankfully, not as violent as Sergio's. Although cancer brought its own sort of violence, snuffing out a human life as efficiently as a bullet did.

She turned to me and lifted her veil, tucking it behind the small hat fitted on top of her head. She was stunning. When I'd first met her in person, she'd been sixteen. She'd been pretty, but now, she was no longer a child. Her features had sharpened, her lips fuller, her cheekbones even more prominent. Her eyes... even more accusing.

She studied me, a slow, steady perusal from head to toe. When her gaze met mine, I swallowed, uncertain. Uncertainty was not new to me. I lived with it daily. But this? This was new, this was something—someone—I knew not at all.

The day we'd signed the contract, the day I'd stood by and allowed her to be humiliated, something had happened to me, some obligation had formed, some bond between us. Maybe it was the disgust I felt for myself for standing by and letting it happen. At the time, I told myself, I'd had no choice, but I tried not to lie to myself. Not anymore. After that day, something had changed. I owed her something. What that thing was, I did not know. An apology? Seemed stupid, a waste. My protection? She would have that, she already did. But she was my enemy and the spoils of war. My father had tried very hard to drill that into my head, but he hadn't seen that look in her eyes that day—the desperate, terrified plea inside them—nor did he see it every time he lay his head down to sleep.

I wondered if my father lost sleep over anything at all, actually.

You were twenty-four. What could you have done?

No, not good enough. Not anymore.

"You know what it's like to lose someone close?" Her tone dripped sarcasm. "My father and I weren't close."

I studied her, feeling my face tighten, my eyes narrow infinitesimally.

I did not speak.

"But let me ask you something. Do you know what it's like to watch people you love killed before your very eyes?"

I did, but still, I remained silent.

"To have everyone taken away from you? To become the *property* of your enemy?"

Oh yes. Yes, I did.

"To be sent to live on your own among strangers with not a friend in the world? Under constant watch. I don't think you know those things, Salvatore, because if you did, you would *feel*. You would have some compassion. Be human." She gave me another once-over. "But there is one thing you do know, isn't there? You know how to stand by and do nothing at all."

My hands clenched into fists, and a sudden, hot anger burned inside me. I saw the driver's eyes flash back at us in the rearview mirror, but he kept driving, slowing down as we passed through the cemetery gates.

"Be careful," I warned, my tone low and quiet. But it was true, wasn't it? What she said was true.

Lucia's eyes narrowed, and she tilted her head to the side, one corner of her mouth rising into a smirk. "Did Daddy give you his seal of approval that day? Did he pat you on the back later? Call you a 'good boy?'" she taunted.

My fingernails dug into my palms, and I made it a point of looking out the window as the driver parked the car.

"Is that it, Salvatore?"

She misunderstood my silence, mistaking it for weakness.

The driver killed the engine. "Give us a minute," I said. He stepped out of the car and closed the door, standing just outside.

I turned back to her.

"Are you Daddy's little puppet?" she asked.

Her eyes spewed hate. Did she know she toed a very dangerous line? That she broached a truth that had kept me in a state of constant struggle these past few years?

I gave a little snort and relaxed my body, smiling, leaning just a little closer. I could see the pulse at her neck working, telling me her heart pounded hard, telling me that on the inside, she wasn't so sure.

"Lucia." I said softly, raising my hand.

Her gaze shifted to it, then back to my eyes.

I touched her face with the backs of my fingers, caressing that soft, creamy skin. "So pretty," I said, my eyes on her lips when I gripped her chin. "But such a big mouth."

She swallowed, her eyes widening.

I leaned in close enough to smell her perfume, something soft and light and somehow, even now, erotic. I inhaled deeply before drawing her to me, my eyes still on those lips. She held her breath. "So, so pretty." My other hand traveled to her chest, to the soft swell of one breast, coming to rest on her pounding heart. She knew I knew I affected her.

I turned her face to the side, rubbing the scruff of my jaw against it before bringing my mouth to her ear. "Be careful," I whispered, feeling her shudder when I ran my tongue over the ridge of her ear before sliding it inside.

She gasped. Her hands came up to my chest, but she didn't push.

"When you try to bite the wolf," I said, "he just might bite back."

To make my point, I took her earlobe into my mouth and gently drew my teeth over it, drawing it out. Beneath the hand that rested against her heart, her nipple hardened.

A moment later, I released her and sat back, victorious. I tapped my ring against the window, absently glancing at the family crest. The driver opened the door.

"Let's go put your father in the ground," I said, climbing out. She emerged a moment later, the net of her hat back in place. I buttoned my coat jacket. "Fucking stifling here." I gestured for her to go ahead. She did, refusing to meet my gaze or make a comment. I smiled, putting one tick on my side of the column marking my win for this round.

———

WE STAYED in my family's home in Calabria, sharing a suite of rooms—a bedroom for each of us and a common sitting room. Our flight to New Jersey left the next day. Lucia would move into my home tomorrow. She'd finished her studies, graduated with honors, and now that she'd turned twenty-one, it was time for me to take possession of her.

A knock at the door announced the delivery of dinner. As a kindness, I'd ordered our meal in our room rather than making her eat with my family. A girl I didn't know set the table in the living area and left. The scent of the food made my stomach rumble. I knocked on Lucia's bedroom door. I wouldn't force her to share my bed. Not just yet.

"Dinner's ready," I said through the door.

"I'm not hungry," she replied. "I already told you that."

"Well, you need to eat. You haven't eaten anything all day."

"What are you, my mother?"

"Open the door, Lucia."

"Go away, Salvatore."

"I'm only asking once."

"Then what? You'll huff and you'll puff and you'll break my door down? Isn't that what the big bad *wolf* does?"

I smiled. Clever.

But I was cleverer.

I slid my key into the lock and pushed the door open. She gasped, turning from where she sat at the vanity.

"No need to exert myself huffing and puffing. I have the key. It's my house." I held it out for her to see before tucking it into my pocket.

Even air-conditioned, the rooms felt sticky, and her bedroom more so. I'd taken off the heavy jacket and tie I'd worn earlier, and now I unbuttoned the top few buttons of my shirt.

"You mean your father's house," she goaded. She already knew the buttons to push.

I forced a grin and went to her suitcase, flipping it open. After rifling through her things, I found a pair of lace panties and lifted them out.

"Don't touch my things! Get out!" She lunged to take the underwear out of my hand.

I raised it above my head and out of her reach, really smiling now. "Dinner's ready."

"You are one stubborn son of a bitch!"

She jumped to reach the lacy slip. I stepped back and lowered it, inspecting the little pink thing. "Pretty."

"Screw you!"

I allowed her to grab it this time, and she shoved it into her suitcase and attempted to zip it. With a snort, I took her by the arms and turned her, holding her so I could look at her and she at me.

"Let me go!"

She had already changed into a nightie, a simple, long, almost sheer white cotton dress that reached to just above her knees. She wore no bra, and her small, round breasts swelled beneath the fine fabric, her dark nipples pressing against it.

"You're finished with school, and you're twenty-one now, Lucia. You know the contract. You will come live with me. You belong to me, like it or not, and you will do as I say."

"Oh!" She made an incredulous face. "Oh! I will *do as you say*?"

"Yes."

"Or what?"

She attempted to free herself from my grip, but I shook her

once, holding her tighter. Her fingers curled around the fabric of my shirt.

"So many options," I said, slowly dropping my gaze to her breasts while I brushed a thick strand of hair over her shoulder. "So many possibilities."

Before I'd even turned my gaze up to hers, she raised her free arm in an attempt to slap me. My grip hardened, and I tossed her onto the bed. Before she could right herself, I climbed on top of her and grabbed her wrists. They were small and delicate and vulnerable. I dragged them out to either side of her, pinning her with my weight, my gaze traveling down over the mounds of her breasts to where her nightie rode up her thigh, exposing white lace panties.

She liked lace.

I liked lace.

In fact, I'd like to lick her cunt through that lace.

My cock stiffened. Lucia stilled, her eyes wide on the crotch of my pants for a moment before they met mine.

The fun was suddenly out of it for me. I released her.

"Don't make this harder than it already is," I said, climbing off the bed, turning my back to her momentarily until I adjusted the crotch of my pants.

"How is it hard for you? I'm the one whose father we just put in the fucking ground. I'm the one who's lost everything. I'm the one who pays when I didn't have anything to do with anything!"

Her hand shook as she wiped away the tears that streamed down her face. She looked at me with puffy, red eyes, and I realized she'd probably been in here crying.

Fuck.

She turned away and, pulling two tissues out of the box on the nightstand, wiped her face clean.

"How is this hard for you?" she asked again, her voice quivering as her chest heaved with a heavy breath.

The way she looked at me—did she think I wanted this?

I raked my hand through my hair, feeling like an asshole. "I meant it earlier, when I said I know what it's like to lose someone you love."

She remained silent, watching me.

"Even if you weren't close with your father, he was your father."

I knew on the one hand that I needed to control this, control her. I knew how my father would do that. Knew he'd call me weak if he saw me now. But I couldn't do it. Not yet. Not today.

"Look, it's been a really long day. A long fucking week. We're both tired. Just eat something. I'll leave you alone."

I left her room without looking back and walked out the door of the suite, trying to shake off the image of her anguished face. It was impossible.

"You look like shit, boss," Marco said as I walked out into the hall.

Marco was my private bodyguard and my friend. One of the very few in the world. Maybe the only one I had left.

"I feel like shit. Make sure she doesn't go anywhere, okay?"

Marco nodded.

I headed for the stairs. The house had four floors, of which my room took up half of the third. My father's rooms were on the top floor, and Dominic's were down the hall from mine. The second floor housed more guest rooms, but we didn't have any other overnight guests apart from Lucia tonight.

Before reaching the first-floor landing, I heard the loud voices of men talking. I followed the sound into the dining room, where a large group had gathered around the table, my father at its head. He looked at me, his gaze flat. I wondered what he thought of me right at that moment. If he was surprised to see me downstairs. Dominic, my younger brother, sat beside him with that stupid grin he always wore. The one that made me want to smack the living shit out of him.

I didn't miss the fact he sat to my father's right. My seat.

He didn't make a move to rise. Instead, my uncle and family advisor, Roman, who sat to my father's left, got up. He was my mother's brother, and one of the few men my father trusted.

"Salvatore."

He offered me his seat. I thanked him and sat down.

Dominic picked up his beer and leaned toward me. "Thought you'd be busy with your shiny new plaything."

"She just buried her father, asshole." I signaled for a beer, which the waiter brought a moment later. They were all jumpy, eager to serve. Probably more eager to get us the hell out of there. I hadn't been back in a few years but knew when we were in town, the house became a target. The Benedetti family was a sort of legend here. We owned southern Italy and were moving in on the Sicilian territory. Another war brewed, one we'd win, like we'd won over the DeMarcos. Wherever we went, violence followed. The girl upstairs was testament to that.

Her words played back in my ears.

"I'm the one who pays when I didn't have anything to do with anything."

She was right. She was an innocent; her fate decided when she hadn't been more than a child. Her sister's pregnancy had placed Lucia at the heart of a decades-old war.

"She is a sweet little thing," Dominic continued, sipping his beer. "Nice piece of—"

"Shut the fuck up, Dominic," I said, my hands fisting.

"Salvatore's right. Girl just buried her father," my father admonished my brother, his gaze locked on me.

I didn't trust this, didn't trust him. My father had always been better at cutting me down. Certainly not defending me.

"You just make sure she knows who the boss is, son. I don't

ever want to see another incident like this afternoon again, you understand?"

Ah, there they were, my father's true colors.

I nodded without looking at him, swallowing half of my drink.

"Good. Let's eat."

3

LUCIA

Salvatore surprised me. I expected violence. I'd prepared myself for it. But this, this kindness? His attempt to understand? Was that what it was? I didn't like it. And I didn't like how my body reacted to having him so close.

When I heard him leave, I went to the outer room. My stomach growled. I hadn't eaten all day, and as appealing as a hunger strike seemed, when you were actually hungry, it lost some of its appeal.

I took the lid off one of the two dishes to find a thick steak, potatoes, and mixed grilled vegetables. I swallowed, salivating already, and sat down. Picking up the knife and fork, I glanced at the door before I dug in. If he returned, I'd be ashamed at having given in. Even if he kept his word and stayed away, when he saw I'd eaten, wouldn't it just be a second victory to him?

I placed a piece of the meat in my mouth. So buttery and delicious, it melted on my tongue. God, that made me not care what he thought. I took a second bite, then tasted the grilled potatoes spiced with rosemary and more butter. A bottle of wine stood open on the table. I poured myself a glass, sipping it before returning to the meat. I finished nearly my entire plate and took the wine with me to my room, locking the door behind me even though I knew he had a key. Of course he had a key. It was his house.

I sat on the bed and poured myself another glass. That comment had gotten to him, just like what I'd said in the car had. I didn't know much about Salvatore's relationship with his father, Franco, but I had felt Salvatore tense when Franco approached us at the church. I'd been guessing when I taunted Salvatore with my comment about being his father's puppet but didn't realize I'd hit the nail on the head. When I'd said it was his father's house, not his, I'd seen it again, that I'd gotten under his skin. I would learn more, watch their interactions, find and exploit their weaknesses. Maybe it was a matter of pitting son against father.

Then there was Dominic, his younger brother. I knew his relationship with Salvatore was strained, and I didn't like the way Dominic looked at me, but maybe I could use that too.

Salvatore had mentioned knowing how it felt to lose someone close. I knew he'd lost his older brother, Sergio, and his mother, both within a year of each other. I assumed they were who he meant. I felt like a jerk for a minute. I picked up my glass, drained it, and poured some more. Was he trying to connect with me over our shared pain or something? Why? What would be the point?

I lay my head back on the headboard and closed my eyes. I was tired, overwhelmed with emotion, jet-lagged, and exhausted. I'd cried over my father after the funeral once I'd been left alone here. Why hadn't I talked to him when he'd called? Why had I refused to see him when he'd come to the school? I knew he regretted what he'd done, selling me to buy his and our family's lives, but what choice had he had? I was a peace offering, in a way. An olive branch. The white flag of surrender to keep everyone else safe—my sister, my niece, my cousins, aunts, and uncles. It was the deal: no more bloodshed. We surrender. You own us.

I just happened to be the sacrifice.

Whose idea was it, I wondered, my father's or Franco's?

I swallowed two sleeping pills and finished the second glass of wine. Setting it on the nightstand, I pulled back the sheets and climbed into bed. I wanted to sleep, to stop thinking about everything.

Darkness fell when I switched off the lamp, and I closed my eyes. My thoughts moved from Salvatore and Franco and my father to Izzy. The pregnancy had saved her, or she'd be the one here in this bed right now. They'd wanted her, the firstborn. I'd heard my father and my sister arguing, yelling like I had never heard him yell before. Not at us, anyway. That's how I'd found out she was pregnant. That was when Izzy had run away, leaving me to a fate that should have been hers.

I couldn't blame her, though, not when I thought of Effie. She was protecting her baby. But it didn't absolve her for leaving me without a good-bye. Without telling me the truth herself. She knew what would happen to me.

Those few words we exchanged at the funeral were the first we'd traded in the last five years. Maybe it was time to forgive her. I needed at least one ally, didn't I?

———

MY HEAD HURT the next morning. Probably a combination of too much crying, too much fighting, and too much wine.

A knock came on the door just as I zipped my suitcase.

"Come in," I said, expecting Salvatore but finding someone else.

"Car is ready," the man said. He was the same one who'd stood at the door after accompanying us up here yesterday. He moved toward my suitcase. I'd only packed one. It was a brief trip, and we'd be going back to the US today. I'd be going to my new home—Salvatore's home—in New Jersey.

"Where is Salvatore?"

"He was called to a meeting, left earlier this morning."

"What's your name?"

"Marco."

"What meeting, Marco?" I asked, my curiosity piqued.

The man simply looked at me, letting me know he chose not to answer.

"Fine."

I walked out the door carrying my purse, leaving him behind to follow me with the suitcase. I went downstairs with my head held high, hoping most of all I wouldn't run into Franco Benedetti. As much as I hated to admit it, he scared me.

The front doors stood open, letting in the bright sunshine and already too hot temperatures. I refused to glance around and kept my eyes on the car waiting outside, the driver standing beside it. Marco's footsteps followed.

I was almost out the door when I heard a small clicking sound and instinctively turned my head. There stood Dominic, leaning against the doorway to another room. He watched me, and I took a moment to look at him, to *see* him. He and Salvatore couldn't be more different in appearance. Salvatore was big and thickly muscled, whereas Dominic stood maybe an inch taller but not as wide, his build leaner. Salvatore had dark hair and olive skin. Dominic was blond and lighter skinned. His eyes, though, were a piercing, steely blue-gray so cold, they chilled me through.

But then he smiled a big smile. The change in his features became suddenly disarming.

Marco cleared his throat behind me.

I glanced back to find Marco's eyes locked on Dominic. Dominic only shook his head and disappeared back into the room he'd come from. I walked out the door and got into the backseat of the car. After loading my suitcase in the trunk, Marco climbed into the front passenger seat, and the driver started the engine. I glanced up at the mansion as we drove off, irritated that Salvatore hadn't come with me, wondering if I was being sent away again on my own, hating knowing I was a prisoner to his will.

I had a hundred questions but refused to ask Marco. I wouldn't let them know I felt unsure, uncertain. Instead, I sat in the backseat of the car and watched the small Italian villages roll by on the hour-long drive to Lamezia Terme International Airport. I would connect through Rome, and the combined flights would take over fifteen hours to get back to the US. Getting to Calabria was a pain in the ass. I remembered hating the flights when we'd come here as kids, and that hadn't change. I still hated the long trip. At least Salvatore wouldn't be on the flight with me. Although would Marco then accompany me?

At the airport, Marco opened my door, and I climbed out, the heat coming off the asphalt stifling after the air-conditioned car. The driver unloaded my suitcase. Marco gestured for me to go ahead, guiding me toward the check-in counter. The man seemed to know Marco. I noticed their small exchange when he handed over my passport and ticket, neither of which I'd been allowed to hold on to, as if I'd skip out on my own father's funeral and fly home. The desk agent took my bag and handed my passport and ticket back to Marco.

"This way," Marco said.

"You didn't check-in. You won't be allowed past security," I said.

Marco smiled. "I will hand you over to one of my...colleagues in a few moments."

Marco's Italian accent was distinct. Raised in the US, although I spoke fluent Italian, I had no accent. Neither did Salvatore.

"He will travel with you."

I would have been surprised if they let me go alone, honestly.

Used to having guards nearby since I was a little girl, I went along, ignoring Marco and the other man, whom Marco introduced me to and whose name I instantly forgot. We boarded our flight within the next half hour, and I settled in. I read the coverage of my father's funeral in the newspaper reports, saw my face in the photos along with Salvatore's and numerous others plastered across page after page of both local newspapers I'd picked up. We made big news here. The reining Mafia family, coming to bury their biggest rival. The daughter of the fallen man, now on the arm of the opposing family's son. Most of the articles actually told the story of how we'd met and fallen in love. That would be Franco Benedetti's work. It wouldn't look good to tell the public the truth.

I folded the paper and tucked it into the pocket of the seat in front of me. I closed my eyes. I felt my bodyguard's gaze on me, but I ignored him as best as I could.

With a three-hour delay in Rome, by the time we arrived in New Jersey and then drove the hour and a half to Salvatore's home in Saddle River, I was exhausted. Evening fell, and it took an effort to keep my eyes open, to take in the surroundings of my new home. I was grateful it was Salvatore's house and not the Benedetti family home.

Salvatore's estate was large and very private. Tall iron gates opened upon our arrival. Only moonlight illuminated most of the grounds, until we drew closer to the house, and I got my first glimpse of the mansion with its huge garage, outbuildings, and extensive and various types of landscaping lights. The grounds, from what I could make out, were expansive, with woods circling most of the property. It seemed to me that the driveway was at least a mile long before it finally circled at the main entrance to the residence. A woman came outside and waited for us. As soon as the car stopped, I climbed out on my own, needing to stretch my legs after so many hours of sitting. I'd grown up surrounded by wealth, but I'd never lived in a house this grand. It seemed pretentious of Salvatore, maybe another weakness. I walked toward the woman.

"Ma'am."

"Just Lucia," I answered, attempting to give her a warm smile. I'd need allies. I didn't want to be hated.

The woman smiled back and nodded. I turned to the guard who'd flown with me. He looked as tired as I felt.

"When will Salvatore arrive?" I asked, wanting information.

"I'm not sure."

"Come inside," the woman said.

I followed her in, looking around the house—my new home —for the first time. The large circular foyer led off in several directions, one of which had to be the kitchen, considering the delicious smell coming from that direction. I could see the living room through a large archway. At the far end stood a wall of glass, and large doors led to a patio. Dim, colorful lights shone off the glass-like surface of the swimming pool, inviting even now. The rest of the interior doors stood closed. I turned my attention to the large marble staircase leading to the upper floor.

"Are you hungry?"

I shook my head, stifling a yawn. "I'm just very tired."

She nodded. "I'll take you to your room."

I touched her elbow to stop her before she turned. "What's your name?"

"Rainey."

"Rainey. That's a pretty name."

"Thank you."

I figured her to be in her early forties. It felt strange to have her wait on me. I'd always hated that, actually. I felt uncomfortable and awkward even with servants. I didn't mind a house-keeper or cook, but a servant felt different.

I followed Rainey up the stairs and toward the double doors at the end of the hall. I assumed that was the master bedroom. My heart thudded as we approached, knowing he'd expect to have me in his bed. Of course he would. Why not? What sense would it make for him to *take possession* of me but not fuck me?

But before we reached the foreboding doors at the end, we turned to the right, where Rainey opened a single door.

"This one's yours," she said, switching on a light and gesturing for me to enter.

The room was huge and richly decorated with heavy dark curtains draped from each of the windows. Exposed brick made the space appear darker and gave it a masculine flair, but I liked it, especially the large fireplace I wouldn't have need for just yet. Rainey pointed out the bathroom, which I barely glanced at, because my gaze had fallen on the large, four-post, king-size bed in the room with a thick duvet and overstuffed pillows at the head.

"Shall I help you unpack? We've already moved your other things into the closet."

"Other things? Oh." I'd forgotten. Salvatore had had my things packed up and brought here a few days ago. I didn't have much, hadn't needed much at a Catholic school, but what I had was neatly organized in the open walk-in closet Rainey stood at the entrance of. "I'm actually tired. If you don't mind, I think I'll just have a shower and go to bed."

"Of course."

She closed the closet doors and moved over to turn down the bed—another thing I didn't like. I could turn down my own bed.

"Thank you, Rainey," I said, dismissing her.

Once she left, I went over and peeked inside the closet. Huge. The racks were full and contained my clothes as well as items that did not belong to me. I checked the size of a dress. Four. He'd probably bought them for me. Or had them bought. I couldn't see Salvatore Benedetti shopping.

Apart from the bathroom, there stood another door Rainey hadn't pointed out. I walked over to it, but when I tried to open it, I found it was locked. I'd ask about it tomorrow.

I went into the bathroom and saw the separate shower as well as a bathtub set in the middle of the large space. It was old-fashioned, one with copper feet and fixtures. All surfaces were sparkling clean, and on one of the shelves stood several of my favorite brands of shampoos and body washes. Even bubble bath. I hadn't had a bubble bath in years. I decided I'd have one instead of a shower.

I turned the taps on in the bath, checked the temperature, and poured in the soap, watching as champagne-pink bubbles began to appear almost instantly. I found a hairclip in one of the sink drawers and piled my hair up on top of my head. The deep auburn mass would fall to the middle of my back when I let it down. As I undressed, I checked out the rest of the space. Every-thing was high-end, from the gold-veined marble on the floor and countertops to the copper fixtures on the taps. A stack of towels stood on a shelf. I touched them. Soft and luxurious. Brand-new.

The bath filled. I turned the water off and dipped a toe inside. I caught my reflection in one of the two mirrors. I'd lost a few pounds in the last two weeks. I ran almost daily, and at 5 feet five and 120 pounds, I was healthy with long, lean muscle, small but pert breasts, and a bubble butt. That was the yoga. The sisters at the college actually allowed a woman to teach classes three evenings a week, and I never missed a single one. It was that and the running that kept me sane, that kept me from tearing my hair out in frustration at how life had turned out for me.

I sank slowly into the bath. Steam rose off it, but the warmth felt good compared to the relative coolness inside the house. They must have had the air conditioner cranking, since it was July and the heat outside was stifling, with the evenings offering only the slightest relief. I wadded up a small towel and lay my head back against it, closing my eyes. Between the heat and my exhaustion, I must have dozed off, because the sound of someone clearing his throat startled me awake.

My eyelids flew open, and I caught my breath when I saw Salvatore standing just inside the bathroom, watching me.

"Jesus!" I sat up, instinctively covering myself, although it wasn't necessary. The bubbles created a barrier between us. "You scared the crap out of me!"

"I knocked, but there was no answer."

He wore dress slacks and a button-down shirt he'd undone to where I could see the gold chain circling his neck. A small cross hung from it. It took me back five years, seeing that. I remembered noticing it, concentrating on it when I couldn't bear to look him in the eye.

I flushed and glanced away.

"I fell asleep, I guess."

"It's dangerous to do in the bathtub."

"Yeah." I pulled my knees up, making sure the bubbles still hid me. When Rainey had told me this was my room, I'd assumed we weren't sharing it. I'd assumed the double doors had led to the master. Had I misunderstood? "What do you want?" I tried to keep my voice friendly. Salvatore seemed to process the question slowly. He looked like he had a thousand things on his mind. Was it the meeting he'd been called to?

He opened his mouth to speak, but instead shook his head and ran a hand through his thick, dark hair. It made me think of his brother, of how different they looked, and thinking about his brother made the water suddenly feel cold.

"I wanted to check on you, see if you needed anything," Salvatore finally answered.

"I'm fine." I wanted to ask if we were sharing the bedroom, if it was his, but couldn't bring myself to just yet. "Where were you? Marco said you had a meeting."

"I did."

A wealth of information.

"How close are you to your cousins, Lucia?" he asked, coming a little farther inside the bathroom and leaning back against the counter, ignoring my question entirely.

"Odd question. Why?"

"I'm curious."

"I don't know. Not particularly, at least not in the last five years." I wasn't going to tell him that Luke had been keeping me in the loop with the goings-on of my family while I was at school. Besides, it wasn't like he told me anything Salvatore would be interested in.

"So you didn't talk to Luke once a month over the last five years?"

"Am I being interrogated?"

He folded his arms across his chest and studied me closely. "Do you need to be?"

"What are you talking about? Luke is my cousin, we talked, so what?"

"You didn't talk to any other member of your family, not even your sister."

"Christ, you were keeping tabs?"

"I was keeping an eye on my property, yes."

"Oh, right, your *property*." I glared at him. "You do know I'm a human being, right? That we typically aren't referred to as property."

"I don't think there's anything typical about our relationship."

He stepped over to the tub, and I leaned back, covering my breasts. He didn't touch me, though. Instead, he sat on the edge and dipped a hand in the water.

"You and Luke good friends? I saw the way he looked at you at the church."

"He's my cousin."

"Not by blood."

"What are you implying? What, are you jealous?" The moment I said it, I knew there was truth to the statement. I saw it in the slight shift of Salvatore's eyes. In his momentary hesitation before answering.

"I want to be sure you realize you're as good as a Benedetti now. Want to be sure your loyalties are where they belong."

"Just because I was forced to sign that stupid contract doesn't mean my loyalties suddenly shifted. I am not a Benedetti."

He snorted, shaking his head. "Water's cooling." He rose to stand. He wiped his hand on a towel. "Get out of the tub," he said, without looking at me.

"I'm not getting out with you here."

"I want to have a look at what I own." He said the words purposefully and unfolded one of the plush bath towels. He held it out before him but remained several feet away, so that I'd have to walk toward him to reach it, giving him a full view.

"What exactly is this? What do you want, Salvatore?"

"Just what I said. I want to see you. Naked."

"You want a look at what you can't have?" Flimsy words, and I knew it. He could take whatever he wanted. I just, for reasons that had no basis in reality, didn't think he would. And I was determined not to give him this particular power over me. My heart pounded against my chest as I slowly rose, suds clinging to me as I stood. "You want to see?" I asked again, seeing how his eyes darkened as they raked over me before returning to mine. His attraction to me, mine to him, this cruel sort of push-pull between us, I would use it. I would be stronger than it, and I would use it. I climbed out onto the bath mat and stood before him. "Have a look, then. Get your fill," I bit out.

Salvatore's throat worked as he swallowed. Without a word, he stepped toward me, held my gaze, and wrapped the towel around me. His hungry eyes held mine, meeting my challenge, posing his own as he dried me, his handling of me rough, the soft towel now scratching at my breasts, my sex. Once he finished, he stepped back, letting the towel drop to the floor.

"Now I can have a proper look."

He did, gaze pausing at breasts and belly, hovering at my naked sex. Again, he swallowed, then met my eyes once more.

I stood still, watching him. Watching his eyes. They burned, the blue darker now, sparkling like blackest onyx. Something raged behind them, inside them. Something that screamed for release even while it reduced me to flesh alone, to a thing, an object possessed.

Was this some sort of contest, some game? If it was, I lost, because I blinked first, looking away, unable to maintain the contact.

"Go to bed." He turned to leave the bathroom but stopped at the door.

I swooped down to grab the discarded towel and held it against myself, shielding my body from his view.

"And Lucia," he said, turning to look at me and taking a step back inside, back toward me. "Don't do anything stupid."

He rubbed his hand across his mouth, that rage behind his eyes burning now.

"I *will* punish you if you betray me."

He turned on his heel and walked out the door.

I sat down on the edge of the tub, trembling.

4

SALVATORE

My cock throbbed. I'd had to force myself to leave her room. Fuck, she was so beautiful. Her anger, her hate, it only made her all the more appealing. I wanted her. Wanted to take her. Have her.

The monster inside me screamed to possess her.

My cell phone rang. I tugged it from my pocket and checked the screen. It was Dominic.

Prick. I rejected the call, almost running Rainey over in the hallway on my way to the study.

"Mr. Benedetti! I'm sorry," she apologized, although I was the one not paying attention.

"No, it's fine. It was my fault."

I raked a hand through my hair. What the hell was that upstairs? Why had I gone in there when I'd seen her in the tub? I should have walked away.

"Would you like to eat dinner, sir? Miss...Lucia...wasn't hungry, but—"

It's dangerous to fall asleep in the tub? Christ, what did I think she was, a kid? No. Not with that body. She was certainly no kid.

"No, it's fine. I'm..." I walked into the study, looked around, then walked back out. "You know what, I'm tired. I'm just going to go to bed."

"Oh. All right."

I went back up to my room. It connected to Lucia's, but I doubted she knew that. Once inside, I stripped, headed into the bathroom and turned on the shower.

I didn't understand Lucia. Hell, I didn't understand myself around her. The meeting earlier, it had been last minute and required both myself and my father to be present. Dominic had been pissed to be left out, but that was too bad. I knew what Dominic wanted: anything I had. Including becoming our father's successor. But it didn't work that way. It would have been Sergio, firstborn, as the successor, but he'd been killed, so I was next in line. As little as I wanted to be the boss of the Benedetti family, Dominic taking on the role I wanted even less. My little brother had a mean streak, a violence inside him that when unleashed was terrifying to witness. Some days, I wasn't sure I knew him at all, wasn't sure I wanted to know the depths of his darkness.

I stepped into the shower, the water so hot, it scalded me. I turned it down.

My father, Roman, and I had been the only three of the Benedetti's at today's meeting. There was talk about a new group forming. Luke DeMarco was a problem. Or he could become one. Was it vengeance that fueled him or a lust for power? I'd bet the latter. Given that one DeMarco daughter wanted nothing to do with the family business and the other belonged to the enemy, Luke stood to gain a whole lot if he were able to gather enough support and rouse them to war. Which was exactly what he was attempting to do. And he'd come farther than any of us had expected. He'd gained supporters from the Pagani family, our fiercest opponent of the two Sicilian families.

Was Lucia in any way involved? I'd seen the look exchanged between Luke and Lucia at the church, but that had fueled a different sort of burn. One of jealousy. Why did I feel so possessive of her? Why did I care? I could have any woman I wanted, as many as I wanted. Our contract bound her to me with no restrictions on me. My father had orchestrated it, enjoying the idea of having a living trophy under his thumb he could torture as he pleased.

Thoughts of my father made my stomach turn. I switched off the shower and grabbed a towel. My eyes locked on the door connecting my room to Lucia's. I bypassed it, climbed into bed, and laid there with the sheet tossed aside. I closed my eyes and gripped my cock, the image of her standing before me, naked, suds sliding off her creamy skin, her hard little nipples, her shaved cunt. I wanted to see all of her, to take my time. To lay her out and open her. Smell her, taste her. Sink my cock inside her.

Her eyes flashed into my mind, accusing and hard. I pumped faster, imagining her here, watching me, sucking me, squatting over my face while she took my cock in her mouth and fed me her pussy. *Fuck.*

I bit my lip when I came, ropes of cum landing on my chest, my cock throbbing against my palm as I squeezed out the last of it with a groan, knowing it would not be enough, knowing this would not sate me, knowing however many women I fucked, none would give me the release I needed, the one only *she* could give.

I woke a few minutes past five. It was a long, deep sleep, considering my usual two- to three-hour stints. I lay there for a few minutes, hoping if I kept my eyes closed, I could sleep again.

Less hours to get through in the day if I could just sleep them off. But that wasn't happening.

My cell phone buzzed on the nightstand. I picked it up. Dominic. A quick glance told me he was still pissed about the meeting. I decided to delete Dominic's message without bothering to read the rest.

I tossed the covers back, got out of bed, and pulled the curtain aside to look outside. Dawn. The sun would rise soon.

Finding clean running clothes, I put them and my Nikes on, glanced once at the connecting door, and walked out of my bedroom and down the stairs. I used the door in the kitchen, which opened onto a large terrace. I jogged out, crossing it and the swimming pool area, and headed into the woods, running to meet the sun. It only took me a few minutes to realize I wasn't alone.

Gates protected the grounds, and cameras recorded all movement. The sound came from a short distance away: branches cracked underfoot, and I could hear the crunching of pine needles and leaves. Too heavy for a squirrel or bird. Deer sometimes jumped the fence, but it was rare. As I stalked closer, I heard the sounds of shortened breath. My intruder on my morning ritual run was human.

A few moments later, I caught sight of Lucia. She didn't see me. I slowed to her pace, watching her, lean muscle working as she leaped over a tree stump and avoided a moss-covered boulder. She'd bound her long hair in a ponytail that bounced from side to side, and sweat glistened on her bare shoulders. She wore a sports bra and shorts, the white fabric bright against her lightly tanned skin. Earbuds connected to an iPhone secured on her arm told me why I was able to get so close without her hearing me.

I caught up, startling her. She stopped, clutching her chest.

"Stop doing that!" she said, pulling the earbuds from her ears.

"I was behind you for the last five minutes. You should be more aware of your surroundings." The music was loud enough that I could clearly make out the song. Mumford and Sons. "You don't need that anyway, not when you run in the woods." I loved the stillness of this place, the peace I found as soon as I disappeared into the cover of the trees.

She looked me over. "You're running?"

I nodded. "You're up early."

"Couldn't sleep."

"Me either." I glanced up toward the place I ran to, a clearing on a hill that gave the best view of the sunrise. "Come on. I'll show you something."

I turned and ran. It took her a moment, and I imagined her mind working up some snarky comment, but then she followed. I slowed my pace so she could keep up, and we ran in silence for the next twenty minutes, climbing up the slope. Lucia slowed, her breathing coming shorter but her condition obviously good. Used to running.

"Wow."

I heard the awe in her voice as we reached the top of the hill. The sun had just broken through the clouds, and the sky was a wash of orange and pink and red.

"This is...amazing."

She walked a bit farther. I watched, finding myself smiling.

"Beautiful," she muttered.

"It's the one good thing about being an insomniac. I never miss the sunrises."

She glanced back at me, and I realized how easily I'd given away that piece of myself. I imagined the staff at the house knew I slept little, but no one else.

Lucia returned her gaze to the sky. I watched her framed by this show of lights.

"How long have you been like that? Unable to sleep, I mean."

"As long as I can remember." I was twenty-nine now so maybe fifteen years.

We watched the sunrise in silence. When the sun had crested, she turned to me, her whiskey eyes shining bright, the accusations of last night absent this morning, although her gaze remained cautious.

"I don't know what I'm supposed to do," she finally said, her arms folded across her chest, defensive and closed.

"That makes two of us."

She scrunched up her forehead. "I don't understand."

"I'm not a monster, Lucia, but I am my father's son. I am obligated, just as you are." She studied me. "You choose how hard you want to make this on yourself. There are worse things than being in my care."

"In your *care*?"

"Yes, my care. It could have been my brother. Or my father. Where do you think you'd be if it had been either of them instead of me?"

"I don't see the difference."

Her words got to me. "Fine, let me simplify this for you. You're to be obedient."

"I don't even know what that means. Do you expect me to just…" She glanced away, a blush creeping up her neck to her cheeks. "What do you want?" she finally asked, straightening, obviously forcing herself to look at me.

"Your obedience."

She opened her mouth to speak, but I stepped closer to her and placed my finger over her lips.

"Hear my words, Lucia. I *expect* your obedience. I didn't say want. I own you, no matter how you feel about that. I can make this good for you." I couldn't keep my gaze from wandering to the soft swell of her breasts before they returned to hers. "Or I can make it bad. It's up to you how this goes."

"It was supposed to be my sister," she said, a sheen of tears obscuring her eyes.

Looking at her, helpless, alone—and she was alone—only made me want to comfort and reassure her. So opposite what I was supposed to do.

"But she got herself pregnant." She turned her back to me and wiped one hand across her eyes before turning and looking at me again. "I don't know what I'm supposed to do here. Are you..." she floundered again. "Do you... Fuck. Never mind."

Without warning, she bolted back toward the house, her pace faster now. I followed easily, keeping a short distance between us, unsure how to answer her questions, not knowing myself what the hell I wanted from her. Her obedience, what the hell did that mean? That she sit when I say sit and fetch when I say fetch? It was so much more than that. A woman like Lucia DeMarco didn't simply give her submission. A man would have to earn it.

Or break her to take it.

"Lucia," I called out when we drew near the back entrance to the house, the large sliding glass doors of the dining room standing open.

She glanced back but ran into the house. I followed, seeing the blur of a maid setting the table for breakfast.

"Lucia!" I was only a few steps behind her, and when she stumbled over the last stair to the second floor, I caught her around the waist and lifted her, holding her to me. I saw then why she'd run. Tears stained her cheeks, and her eyes were puffy again, her face flushed.

For a moment, I faltered.

For one moment, I was human.

But then I looked down at her. I watched her struggle uselessly as I held her tight.

"Lucia," I whispered this time, snaking a hand up her back, the feel of her body moving against mine making me forget everything else.

I gripped her ponytail and tugged her head back.

"Stop," she said, her voice quiet.

I held her like that, my gaze drifting to her lips, soft and pink, her mouth slightly open, and I kissed her. I just...kissed her. It was our first kiss.

She made some sound, but my mouth muffled it. I walked her backward until her back was against the wall, and I leaned down to kiss her harder, tasting her, her mouth so soft, so inviting, even as she protested, or tried to. But her body gave me this, and she opened, her hands relaxing against my chest, even curling a little over my biceps. I dipped my tongue inside her mouth, the moan coming from me now as my cock stiffened against her belly. It felt like a mutual want heated our kiss. Lucia's fingertips touched my shoulders, drawing me closer, her tongue meeting mine. Hands wrapped around the back of my neck and pulled me in. I relaxed my hold, feeling her surrender, but as soon as I did, she struck. She rammed her knee so hard between my legs that she knocked the wind out of me.

I doubled over, sucking in a loud breath as she stumbled backward, smiling.

"You want my obedience?" she taunted. "You want me to be a good little thing, do as I'm told? Fuck you when I'm told?"

I made some sound, more animal than human as fury fired me from the inside. Lucia backed away, a moment of uncertainty crossing her features before she reached her door down the hall, placing her hand on the doorknob.

"You've got another thing coming, Salvatore." She turned the knob and pushed it open. "If obedience was what you wanted, you chose the wrong woman to fuck with."

She ran into her room and slammed the door shut. I straightened, my balls fucking killing me, and reached for the key on top of the door frame. I'd installed the special lock on her bedroom door before her arrival for exactly this reason. She would not lock me out. Not in my own house. I imagined her in there right now, frantic when she discovered the missing key. I slid it into the lock and turned it, locking her in from the outside.

"Obedience is what I'll have," I said. "I don't mind teaching it to you. Remember what I said last night?"

She tried the door, jiggling the handle.

I smiled at her muttered curse.

"If you betray me, I'll punish you. This will be your first punishment."

I LEFT her to stew while I showered. She'd fooled me with that kiss. I'd thought she felt it too, thought she liked it. I think she had, at first. But then, maybe her own sense of duty made her attack.

Regardless, I grinned as I pulled on a pair of jeans. The thought of punishing her aroused me.

Drying my hair roughly with a towel, I went to the door between our rooms and turned the key in the lock on my side. Lucia sat on her bed, her hair wet from a shower, dressed in a pair of shorts and a silk tank, her knees tucked against her chest, a letter opener in her hand held like a knife. The look on her face told me of her shock to see me enter from this door. I locked the door behind me and pocketed the keys.

Her eyes raked over me, from the top of my wet head to my

bare feet. I wore only a pair of jeans, wanting her to see what she was up against. I stood a foot taller than her and outweighed her by probably seventy-five pounds. I wouldn't hurt her, but I wasn't above a little intimidation. It would be good for her to learn her place and learn it fast.

When I stepped toward her, she got up on her knees in the middle of the bed and pointed the letter opener at me.

"Put that down."

She shook her head. "What are you going to do?"

I stalked closer. "I said put it down." I didn't give her a choice this time. Instead, when she scrambled backward on the bed, I placed one knee on top of it and caught her wrist, dragging her down on her belly until I relieved her of her weapon, tossing it away. I released her. She climbed back up on her knees and glared at me.

"Get undressed, Lucia."

"No."

"Come on. I've seen it all before. You showed me last night, remember?"

She jumped off the other side of the bed. I liked this. Always liked cat and mouse.

"Go away, Salvatore."

"Strip, Lucia."

She'd cornered herself by now, but I gave her space to bolt, just because I didn't like the game to end too quickly. She ducked under my arm and did just as I knew she would. I turned, watching her try the door.

"Leave me alone!"

"Where are you going to go?" I asked, following her as she ran to retrieve the letter opener. I have to admit, she was faster than I thought, but I caught her around the middle and squeezed her wrist, taking the weapon from her a second time.

"Please leave me alone. Please."

"What would be the fun in that?"

"I hate you! I hate you!"

With her back to me, she shoved against me, but I had her locked in my embrace. She was trapped. We both knew it. "I'll tell you how this is going to go. I'm going to release you, and you're going to do as you're told and strip. Once you're naked, I'll take it from there."

"I'm sorry, okay?"

I shook my head. "No, not okay." I grinned a wicked grin, my cock hard already at her back, growing harder with anticipation.

"What are you going to do?"

"I haven't decided yet."

She glanced back at me, and I knew she felt me pressing against her back. She couldn't not feel my hardness.

"I'm not going to fuck you." From the look on her face, I surprised both of us with that. But it needed to be said. Hell, she had every right to be afraid of me.

I eased up, giving her a little space. "Do as you're told, and I'll go easy on you, but if you make me strip you, your punishment will be worse, understand?"

After a moment, she nodded.

I released her, this time tucking the letter opener into a nightstand drawer. I took a seat on the chair at her desk and watched while she stripped off her clothes layer by layer, first her blouse, then the white shorts. She wore a matching set of white lace panties and bra beneath.

"Go on, Lucia."

She unhooked her bra and let it fall to the floor, that look of innocence now replaced by the same thing I'd seen last night: defiance.

That was good. I preferred defiant.

I'd work that out of her. Slowly, though. No sense in rushing the fun.

I waited for her to slide off her panties. Then she stood before me naked, her hands fisted at her sides.

"Come here."

Reluctantly, she walked over to me. I took her hips in my hands and looked her over, my gaze on her breasts, those nipples hardening beneath my perusal, the slight hint of arousal making the air musky.

I swallowed and rose to my feet, my hands moving up to her waist. She remained where she stood, turning her face up to keep her eyes on mine.

I walked her to the bed, sitting her on it when the backs of her knees hit it. "Lie back, and open your legs."

She stared up at me, and I worked my knees between hers, widening them a little, keeping my gaze locked on hers.

"I told you I'm not going to fuck you. I just want to see. Now lie back, Lucia."

She did, slowly, watching me as I took her in. I knelt between her legs. She let me spread them and presented me with the beautiful sight of her pussy opening to me, the pink lips glistening, gaping, her clit swollen.

She was aroused.

I inhaled deeply, my cock ready to tear free from my jeans. I pressed one hand against her chest, covering a breast with my palm so I could hold her down as well as play with the nipple. I brought my mouth to her, felt her gaze on the top of my head as I dragged my tongue along her length, the sound of her sucking in a breath music to my ears. Her hands came to my head, and she pushed then pulled.

I looked up. "Spread your arms out to the sides."

She obeyed, and I dipped my head back down to her pussy. She tasted as good as I imagined. Better. Fuck. She thrust herself against me, her cunt dripping as I sucked her clit, then licked her length, dipping my tongue inside her.

She moaned, twisting her body. I looked at her face while I worked the tight little nub. She squeezed her eyes shut and bit her lip. I circled my tongue around the clit, and she opened her eyes, her face flushing pink when our gazes locked. I took her clit in my mouth, watching her, making her watch me until I brought her to orgasm, holding her thighs wide as she bucked beneath me, her hands on the back of my head now, pulling me tight to her until she was spent and begging me to stop, to release her.

"Too much."

I grinned. "This is the punishment part," I said, holding her down and eating her pussy again, making her come twice more, hearing her beg me to go on, plead with me to stop, all while I sucked that clit and licked every drop of juice from her cunt until I couldn't take any more.

I rose to stand over her, my legs still between hers to keep them spread.

I looked down at her, her hair a tangled wet mess all around her, her face flushed, her limbs limp. I unzipped my jeans. When I did, her eyes went wide, and she startled, scooting backward. I caught her thigh and placed one knee on the bed.

"Stay."

She made a sound, her forehead furrowing.

"I'm not going to fuck you," I said again, knowing what she feared. But as I pushed my jeans down and off and began to rub the length of my cock, she stilled, swallowing, her gaze darting from my cock, away, then back. "Watch, Lucia." She wanted to, I could see it on her face, and somehow, the thought of corrupting her innocence made me harder.

I fucked my fist while she watched, her eyes riveted on my hand working my cock. It turned me the fuck on to have her watch me, and I leaned into her, just touching the head of my cock to her folds, making her gasp and bite her lip.

"Fuck," I said. "I love how you look at me, Lucia. And I love how you taste. How you come on my tongue."

"Salvatore," she started, trying to sit up.

I shook my head. "Lie back."

She did, and I pumped harder, my cock swelling, the scent of her, of me, filling the room with sex.

"Have you ever seen a man come, Lucia?" I asked, close now.

She met my gaze and shook her head.

"Have you ever had a man's tongue on your cunt?"

She flushed red and blinked twice before looking away.

"Answer me."

She held her lower lip between her teeth. "No. I've never..." She stopped.

"I'm going to come all over you," I said, pumping faster, gripping harder. "I'm going to cover you in my cum, and you're going to wear it all day long, so you know you belong to me." I jerked, moments away now. "Fuck."

I blew then, my orgasm coming hard and fast, making me grip one of the posts of her bed to keep upright as I emptied on her, covering her in my cum, watching her face, her eyes, as she took it. And when I finished, I leaned down and rubbed it into her skin, her chest and neck, her belly, her cunt. I then straightened, wiped my hand on her thigh, and pulled my jeans back on. Lucia sat up and looked down at herself for a moment.

"Get dressed," I said, buttoning my jeans. "Breakfast is ready."

"I need a shower."

I shook my head. "Like I said, you'll wear it all day." I slapped her hip twice. "Let's go. I'm suddenly ravenous."

5

LUCIA

I hated him.

Salvatore sat across from me with a huge grin on his face, chomping on a piece of sausage. I tore my bread into pieces and glared at him. He was gloating. Fucking gloating.

"I hate you."

I hated myself more. How could I have done what he said? How in hell had I enjoyed it? He'd made me come three times. Three times! I'd felt... Fuck, what had I felt for him? The man had made me come, that was all. Any feelings were physical. Sexual.

"You liked me just fine a little while ago." He bit into a piece of Nutella-smeared toast, a little of the chocolate paste sticking to the side of his mouth. He wiped it with his thumb then made a show of licking it off his finger.

Frustrated, I grabbed an apple out of the bowl of fruit and threw it at him. He caught it like a baseball and bit into it.

"Thanks."

I fisted my hands at my sides at this infuriating man. Rainey came by with a pot of coffee.

"More, ma'am?"

"No," I said, tacking on a "thank you," as I folded my napkin. I forced myself to take a deep breath. "I'm done."

She stepped away, nodding, and I made to rise.

"I'll have more, Rainey," Salvatore said.

I shoved my chair back, scraping the legs along the hard-wood floor.

"Sit, Lucia," Salvatore said as Rainey poured. She avoided looking at either of us.

"I'm done." I set my napkin on my plate.

"I said sit."

His tone made me meet his gaze. He wiped his mouth and pushed his plate back, all joking gone from his expression. For a moment, we battled in silence, me standing, willing my legs to move, the limbs refusing. Him watching me, intently waiting to see what I'd do.

Rainey, who had left with the coffeepot, returned, saw us, and disappeared back into the kitchen. You could slice the tension in the dining room.

Salvatore raised an eyebrow and gestured for me to sit. I thought about my options. I was in his house, in a town I did not know, miles from the next house, without a vehicle.

I sat, folded my arms across my chest, and jutted my chin out.

"Your sister does that."

"What?"

He stuck his chin out to show me. "Stubborn. I guess it runs in the family."

I adjusted my position, sitting up straighter, lowering my stupid chin. He was observant, I had to give him that. He must have seen it at my father's funeral.

"She and I are very different people."

He raised an eyebrow but apparently decided not to pursue

it. He shifted his position, pushing his chair back and folding one leg over the other. He took up a lot of space. Too much.

"Let's go over the rules of the house now that you're finally here."

I waited in silence. I'd hear him out first. Tell him to go fuck himself after.

That thought took me back to an hour earlier, to him standing over me, his big naked body, his thick cock in his hand pumping, pumping...

I shook my head, forcing the image away, and looked at the floor littered with the bread I'd torn up throughout breakfast. I'd made work for Rainey in my anger at Salvatore. I'd pick it up when we were done.

"First rule, you are not to leave the grounds without my permission, and you are never to go anywhere alone."

I snorted. "As if."

"As if what?"

He leaned forward, his expression questioning but also consequential, calling me on my bullshit because he and I both knew I couldn't leave without A) having a car, and B) knowing the code to open the gate.

"I won't be treated like a prisoner." I almost added *in my own home*, but this wasn't my home.

"It's not a prison, Lucia. I want you to be safe. I have enemies, like your father did. They may think getting to me is best accomplished through you. I don't want to see you get hurt."

He sounded almost genuine. He sure looked it. But then again, he'd seemed different earlier too, before he'd used my body's surrender against me.

"You're free to wander the grounds. There are several acres of woods, so take care you don't get lost. The house as well, only my study and my bedroom are off-limits. I'll show you around once we're done. If you need or want anything, all you have to do is ask. You'll have a monthly allowance—"

"I don't need your money." I had my own. My family was not poor, even after the Benedetti's destroyed us. I'd inherited everything but the house after my father died. Although without credit cards, with no way to access that money as long as I was locked away here, I was still at Salvatore's mercy.

"Well, you'll have it anyway."

"I don't want it," I muttered.

"What are you doing, Lucia? What exactly is going through your mind right now?"

"I'm trying to wrap my brain around my new prison. First, you send me away to the fucking nuns for five years—"

"It was part of the agreement—"

"I may as well have been behind bars, and you know it!"

He just shrugged a shoulder.

"Now I'm sitting here in *your* house, where I'm supposed to live as your—what? Plaything?—and I'm being told the rules like I'm a child!"

"Aren't you? Look at how you talk to me. I'm not an unreasonable man, Lucia, but I will be obeyed."

"Obeyed? You want me to bow down to you? You've got another thing coming."

"I think I have a pretty good idea of what I have coming."

"Are we done?"

"No."

I bit my lip, waiting.

"I have a cell phone arriving for you today—"

"I have my own."

His jaw tightened, and he took a minute before responding. "Well, you'll have a new one. When you want your family or a friend to visit, you'll let me know first."

"I don't need to see my family, and I don't have any friends, so I'm well and truly yours. I guess that makes you happy."

"It doesn't, actually."

Why did he have to seem so fucking genuine?

It was my turn to shrug a shoulder and, needing to break eye contact, I leaned down to pick up a few pieces of the bread I'd inadvertently scattered.

"Leave it. Rainey will clean it up."

I shook my head, feeling tears building, refusing to let him see.

"Leave it, Lucia. When I'm talking to you, I expect your undivided attention."

I snorted, wiping my face, angry again. I faced him. "You expect so many things. Maybe what you need to do is check those expectations. You're less likely to be disappointed then."

His eyes narrowed, and his chest heaved as he took a deep breath in.

"Am I irritating you, Salvatore? Because you know what's irritating me? Your...stuff...drying on my skin," I said through clenched teeth. I stood so fast, I knocked the chair over behind me. "You've told me your rules. Well, fine. I have just one of my own. Leave. Me. Alone!" I turned on my heel to march off.

"Sit back down," he hissed. "Now."

"*Fuck. You.* I'm going to take a shower."

I heard his chair scrape back, and I started to run for the stairs, all the while wondering what the hell I was doing. Where I was going. He had the key to the lock. It's not like I could hide. What was I doing?

Salvatore caught up with me. I didn't even really fight him when he took my arm and dragged me up the stairs with him.

"You want a shower? Fine," he said through clenched teeth. "I'll take you to have that fucking shower if my *stuff* is so *irritating*."

"Let me go."

He hauled me to my bedroom and into the bathroom. There he released me. I backed into a corner, his fury suddenly frightening.

"Get in the shower," he said, reaching for the collar of my blouse and tearing it down the middle.

I screamed, trying to push him back, knowing it was impossible.

"You wanted a shower."

"I'll do it," I said as he popped the buttons off my shorts and yanked the zipper down. "Please. Just—"

"In the shower!"

He shoved me into the shower, even though I still wore my bra and panties.

"Let me go. I'll do it, I promise." He stopped and brought his face within an inch from mine.

"You don't have to promise. I know you'll do it."

He switched on the water, and I recoiled from the cool spray that hit one side of my arm.

Tears burned my eyes, and I cursed the drops that fell.

"Take off your bra and panties," he said, pushing his hand through his hair as he stepped back.

"I will. Just go, okay. I'm sorry. I shouldn't have pushed you."

His breath was audible, his lips tight, the look on his face telling me he was trying hard to get himself under control.

"I have to pee. Let me pee." I tried, hoping that would convince him to leave. Using that moment to reason with him. "I'm sorry, okay?"

Some battle raged behind his eyes, and next thing I knew, he had me shoved against the shower wall, one hand wrapped around my throat. I grabbed his forearm, trying to pull him off. He reached over and switched off the water, drenching one side of his T-shirt in the process.

"Piss."

"Wh...what?"

With his wet hand, he pushed my panties down to midthigh. "Piss."

"Salvatore..."

"Fucking. Piss. You want me to leave you alone? I will. But first, you piss."

We stood staring at each other, his eyes dark with anger, mine, maybe the look of a deer caught in the headlights of an oncoming Mack truck? I didn't know what to do, whether or not to try to reason with him. I didn't know him. That fact well and truly hit me for the first time, right here, right now. He was the son of a mafia boss next in line to succeed him. I'd seen he was armed at my father's funeral. This man knew violence, it was his world. What horrors had his eyes seen? What atrocities had his hands committed?

In this moment, he was truly and utterly terrifying.

I let my arms fall to my sides, no longer fighting against tears, and I did what he said. I pissed. He glanced down for a second, then returned his gaze to mine. As warmth trailed down my legs, he released his hold around my throat and stepped back, blinking as if coming out of a stupor, shaking his head. I slid down and sat on the shower floor, watching him as he looked at me, the rage all but dissipated now, as if evaporated into thin air, replaced by...remorse?

Salvatore walked out of the bathroom, and I heard the bedroom door close. I rose and started the shower, stripped off the rest of my clothes, and stood under the warm flow, weeping, a sense of loss so all encompassing, so whole, it physically hurt.

6

SALVATORE

I left.

I walked out of the house and to the six-car garage, a building separate from the main house. Taking the keys from the locked box by the door, I chose the Bugatti and climbed inside. I turned the key, the engine crisp and sharp in the early morning quiet. The gates opened, and the tires squealed as I left the property and drove onto the lonely single-lane road. I opened it up then, enjoying the rush as my body pressed back into the seat, the car's powerful engine roaring, taking the turns tightly, my foot pressing harder and harder on the accelerator.

Who the fuck was I? What in hell had I just done, humiliating Lucia like that? Hurting her. Christ. Fuck.

I was a monster.

I inhaled and exhaled short, audible breaths, my stomach tight, the muscles of my arms clenched as I fisted the steering wheel hard.

She got under my skin. This barely twenty-one-year-old woman whom *I fucking owned* got under my fucking skin every single fucking time. I needed to control her for so many reasons.

But I couldn't do it this way. Fuck. I'd scared the piss out of her, literally. Her eyes—they hadn't accused me. No. They'd been terrified of me.

"Fuck!" I punched the side of my fist against the steering wheel.

A car turned a blind corner, surprising me, his horn honking, waking me from wherever the fuck I was. I jerked the steering wheel, and the Bugatti swerved onto the side of the road, missing the car by inches.

"Shit!"

The man in the other vehicle flipped me off.

"Fuck you!" Not that he heard me. My windows were up. My cell phone vibrated in my pocket as I slowed to a full stop. The display on the Bluetooth said it was Roman. I got out, rubbed my face with both hands, and pressed the heels of my hands into my eyes. The phone stopped, then started again. I dug into my pocket and fished it out.

"Roman," I said after sliding the Talk button. I walked a few steps away to look over the deserted road, the dewy grass sparkling in the sun, the morning quiet apart from the birds chirping in the trees.

"Morning, Salvatore."

"You're calling early."

"I wanted to talk to you. I tried to call last night but couldn't catch you."

"What is it, Roman?" Was this about the meeting? Luke DeMarco?

"Your father wants to be sure you'll be attending his birthday dinner."

"You're calling me about that?" It was at the end of the following week, and of course I'd be there. There was no way for me not to be. Unless I wanted to give Dominic ammunition.

"He wanted to invite you and Lucia to spend the night."

"That won't be necessary. We'll drive home."

"He insists."

I took a deep breath. The party was going to be held at the house in the Adirondacks, but I'd have driven four hours each way rather than spend more time in that house with him.

"Of course," I said, understanding.

"Listen, there's one more thing."

I waited.

"Your brother."

He paused, and I could hear him measuring his words.

"I just thought you should know he met with your father late last night."

My father had gone back to the house in Calabria after I'd left for New Jersey. "So?" I asked, not surprised. He'd been pissed to have been left out of our meeting.

"He's stirring the pot, Salvatore."

"What's new with that?" I'd known my uncle all my life. He was an intelligent man. He was also a businessman. He knew what would happen if Dominic, rather than I, took over the family. And he somehow had a calming effect on my father. Sergio had trusted him. And I trusted Sergio.

"Nothing is new, but now that you're...distracted...with your houseguest, he's suggesting he take care of the DeMarco problem."

"Take care of it how?"

"Take out Luke DeMarco. Make an example."

I shook my head, although Roman couldn't see. "Fucking typical. This is my problem to deal with. Not his."

"He's got your father's ear."

"That's not news."

"It's different this time, Salvatore," he said heavily.

"When are they flying home?"

"Late afternoon. I'm flying with them."

Silence again, but I could tell he had something to say.

"Franco won't give the word just yet, but you need to know what's going on."

"Thank you, Uncle."

I hung up and pocketed my phone. I didn't want to deal with Dominic's jealous aggressions right now. I had other things on my mind. I needed to get back. Talk to her. Explain that I wasn't a fucking monster.

She'd said she had no friends and refused to see her family. Well, we had more in common than she knew. She'd learned to hate my family over the last five years. Learned to hate everyone, maybe. I just, stupidly enough, didn't want her to hate me.

I got back into the car, started the engine, and drove an hour to the cemetery. I came here more often than I probably should. Parking close to the family plot, I got out. The heat and humidity seemed to want to suffocate me after the air-conditioned drive. I stopped and picked up a dozen white Calla lilies from the flower store a block away, my mom's favorite, and headed up the small hill. The ground beneath my feet felt soft here, damp and covered in moss. A small gate surrounded the plot of land housing many of the Benedetti family. I walked my usual path, reading off the names of the dead in my head, noting the number of years each had lived. Too many damn lives cut short.

But this was what we did. We killed. We died. And for what?

I reached the spot where my mother's and brother's head-stones stood side by side. I tossed the dying flowers, the ones I'd brought the last time I'd come, and replaced them with fresh ones. I pulled out some weeds and scraped dirt off the inscriptions on both their tombstones, noting the year of birth and death on Sergio's grave. He'd been a year older than I was now. Married. His wife pregnant when he died. It wasn't fucking fair.

When it had happened, I'd been broken. He was my one ally, my friend. He'd known how to become boss. Our father loved him and yet, Sergio wasn't like him. Not at all. He'd been gunned down at a gas station. A stupid, cowardly drive-by. He'd deserved a better death than that. And he'd deserved a life first.

My father had retaliated, but something didn't sit right with me. In fact, the whole thing stank. They'd blamed a smaller family from Philadelphia, one that was supposed to have been loyal to us. Somehow, evidence had turned up incriminating them. But it didn't make sense, not then, not now. My father had been crazed, though. He'd loved Sergio, and he'd simply reacted, killed off the boss's sons. Effectively ending the family.

I was supposed to have been with Sergio at the meeting he was coming home from, but I'd been sick. In a way, it felt like I'd cheated death, but then, if I had been there, maybe Sergio wouldn't have died. Maybe things would have gone differently.

I never said much when I came to the cemetery and never stayed long. Just showed up. Wanted them to know I hadn't forgotten them. I got back in the car and headed toward Natalie's house. Natalie was Sergio's wife. Apart from her friendship with me, she'd cut off ties with the family after his and my mother's deaths. She hated my father and brother. She hated the life. But she had loved my brother, knowing the cost of that love.

My father hadn't really allowed her to walk away, though. Not with her bringing his first grandchild into the world. Jacob Sergio Benedetti was born six months after Sergio's murder. Natalie had purposely not given him an Italian first name, which had pissed off my father. Jacob was one and a half years old now. I knew she worried about what demands my father would put on her as Jacob grew older, but she kept those mostly to herself. My father supported them financially. As much as I knew Natalie hated it, she needed the money. And as long as she took it, Franco gave her the space she wanted. I guess he figured he owned her anyway.

I dialed Natalie's number on my cell phone. She answered after the fourth ring.

"Hello?"

"Natalie, it's me, Salvatore."

"Hey, Salvatore. How are you?"

"Okay." Not really. "How are you doing?"

"I'm fine. Just playing with Jacob."

"Can I drop by?"

"Are you sure you're okay?"

"Yeah," I said quickly, then added, "you know." Natalie was the one person who knew me for who I really was. I trusted Marco, my bodyguard, but he didn't know this side of me. I didn't trust anyone enough to share this vulnerability. Too many people ready and waiting for weakness.

"Come on over."

"Thanks. See you in twenty minutes."

I drove to her house, a two-story brick home about forty-five minutes from mine. Her parents lived nearby, and she'd moved here specifically to be close to them. When I rang the doorbell, Natalie answered with Jacob perched on her hip. He still wore his pajamas and held the stuffed animal I'd given him on his first birthday. He gave me a huge gummy smile. He only had three teeth, although I could see the fourth one was working its way in.

"Wow, haven't you grown." I took Jacob from Natalie's arms. He wrapped his arms around my neck and planted a wet kiss on my face.

"Nice," Natalie said. "You look...not so good."

She gave me a hug and a kiss on the cheek after wiping off the mark Jacob had left.

"Come in."

I put Jacob down on the floor among his toys, which seemed to be everywhere.

"Espresso?"

"Please." I took a seat on the couch and watched Jacob play while Natalie made espresso and then joined me in the living room.

"How was the funeral?"

"Shitty." I took a sip of the espresso she handed me, dark and rich and bitter as hell, just the way I liked it. "He's got Sergio's eyes," I said, taking the toy Jacob held out to me.

Natalie stroked the little boy's hair. "And his stubborn streak."

"I don't know. I think you may both be responsible for that one."

She smiled. "You could be right on that. What's up, Salvatore?"

"Lucia's home with me."

Natalie nodded, knowing the situation. "How's that going?"

"Well, she's been there less than twenty-four hours, and I think I've fucked it up pretty well." I drank the last sip of espresso.

"Want to talk about it?"

What could I tell her? What could I tell her that wouldn't make me sound like a monster? Like my father. Hell, he would have been proud of me this morning.

"She hates me, as expected. She is battling me at every turn. Stubborn as hell."

"She's only been with you since the funeral?"

I nodded.

"Then you must really be pissing her off." She winked. "Just give her some space. It's a huge change for her, and her father just died. Suicide, right?"

"Looked that way."

"You don't believe it?"

"I don't believe anything unless I see it with my own two eyes."

She studied me but dropped it. "What's she like?"

"Pretty. Young. Scared. She spit on my father at the funeral. Or tried to but missed." I chuckled.

"Tough too, then. I like her already."

"And full of hate for us. Rightfully so. I guess that's where I'm torn. She can't get out of this. Neither of us can." I paused. "Until death do us part."

"That's not too creepy." Natalie looked away for a moment.

"That's the wording in the contract. Like a marriage contract, but different. And if I die before her, Dominic inherits her. Like she's a fucking thing. My father has a sick sense of humor, as you know."

Her lip curled at the mention of his name. "Do you want to get out of it?"

Her question startled me. I answered without hesitation. "No."

"You like her."

I studied Natalie and felt the need to correct what she said. Whether that correction was for my benefit or hers, I wasn't sure. "I feel some obligation to her."

She snorted.

"Besides, even if I wanted to, I couldn't get out of it. And she certainly couldn't. I don't want her to hate me."

"Give her some space and some time, Salvatore," Natalie said, touching my hand. "She just needs to really see you, like I do. She only sees the Benedetti name right now. The Benedetti family, the one that destroyed hers."

She was right.

"Maybe you could..."

Natalie shook her head. "I'm sorry, I can't. I can't be a part of that anymore." Tears welled in her eyes.

"I understand. It's okay. I just think she needs some friends or something."

"I'm sorry, I just—"

I touched her shoulder. "I shouldn't have asked."

An awkward silence hung between us.

"Do you need anything?" I finally asked.

She shook her head. "No, we're fine. We're good."

"You'll call me if you do, right?"

"I promise."

"I miss Sergio." My eyes felt hot.

"Me too." Natalie wiped hers before leaning against my chest. I hugged her, rubbing her back.

"Hey, I'm going to take Jacob to the beach a little later. Why don't you come with us?"

I nodded, not really having to think about it. I didn't want to go home. I'd bury my head in the sand for a little bit longer. "I'd like that."

"Good."

Jacob stood then, holding out two of the farm animals he was playing with. Both were a little wet from drool, but I took them. He stood leaning against my legs, babbling.

"That so?" I asked, not really understanding a word he said.

Natalie chuckled and stood. "More coffee?"

"Sure."

"Hey, Jacob, Uncle Salvatore's going to come with us to the beach. What do you think of that, honey?"

Jacob leaned his face into my leg and smiled, still "talking." I made out the word beach then something sounding like uncle in there before he gave me a cuddle. I cuddled him back.

I'd spend the day here. It would be good for me. And I'd think about what Natalie said about giving Lucia time and space. I could do that. It would help me get my thoughts figured out.

7

LUCIA

I was a prisoner here.

I spent the day in my bedroom. I slept a little, then read and slept some more. Rainey brought me a tray at lunchtime when I told her I wasn't feeling well, and then another at dinnertime. I didn't ask where Salvatore was or what he was doing. Didn't know if he'd just come barging in here and demand things from me. Punish me. Humiliate me. But he never did. When Rainey came to clear my dinner tray, I finally got up the nerve to ask.

"Is Salvatore home?"

"No, ma'am. He called a little while ago to say he wouldn't be home tonight."

So was he spending the night somewhere else? Where? With whom? And why did I care? At least he wouldn't hurt me, not if he wasn't here.

But Salvatore didn't come home the next night either. Unable to hide in my room any longer, I finally left it late the following morning and gave myself a tour of the house, looking around in the corners, behind plants, for cameras. I wouldn't be surprised to find them. He'd said I had free rein of the house apart from his study and bedroom. Of course, the first thing I did was try his study door but found it locked. The bedroom, too, was locked, but when I saw the maid slip out of the room, I tried the door. She'd forgotten to lock it behind her.

I looked around to make sure no one was watching and slipped inside, closing the door quietly behind me. I spent a long moment with my back against it, trying to calm my breathing, knowing if he found out I was in here, that I'd disobeyed, he'd punish me. And yet I felt like a triumphant, defiant kid who'd taken the piece of candy she wasn't allowed to have.

I pushed away from the door and looked around. The room was about twice as large as mine, and the furnishings were all dark wood or metal, the carpet and drapes shades of blue to match his eyes in all his moods. Leather panels covered the whole of the wall behind the four steel frames of the bed, which was perfectly made, all corners tucked neatly in, since he'd not slept here for two nights now.

The connecting door to my room had a key in the lock. Figured it'd be on his side. Another door led to a bathroom similar to mine, just larger, this one containing black towels and bath accessories, nothing feminine about the space.

The final door opened to a closet. I stepped into it, chuckling at the inch of space between each of the black velvet hangers that contained suits, jackets, and pants on one side, dress shirts sorted by color along another wall, and more casual wear, again, grouped by color and perfectly spaced along the final one. Three dozen pairs of shoes filled the neat little show racks, and two shelves contained belts. Ties were rolled on their own cushions, the color coding continuing even there. The drawers held underwear and socks. Everyday items. Things I for some reason could not associate with the man who owned the house.

I ran a hand over the suits, then dragged them a little,

messing up the OCD spacing, thinking it funny for a moment. But then I found myself inhaling deeply. I shook my head and walked back into the bedroom.

It smelled like him in here.

I tentatively touched one of the cool steel posts of the bed as I thought about what I was doing, not feeling quite good about it. I perched myself on the edge of the bed and told myself I needed to do this. To break his rules and invade his privacy like he had mine. To take back some of the power he'd taken from me when he'd made me do what he did.

The surface of the nightstand had just been dusted. I ran a finger over it before opening the drawer and peeking inside. It was empty.

I walked to the other side of the bed. The book lying beside the lamp told me this was the side he slept on. I sat on the edge of the bed and pulled the drawer open less cautiously this time. This one wasn't empty. I reached in and took out a bottle of what I thought was hand cream, but when I read the label, I quickly set it back down. It was a half-empty container of lubricant. Digging deeper, I found a row of condoms and behind that, a set of handcuffs.

Voices outside the door had me quickly shoving the things back inside the drawer, and when the door opened, I dropped to the floor and slid underneath the bed.

The women spoke, and I saw the one come inside to pick up the bucket she'd left in the bathroom before walking back out the door. This time, she didn't forget to lock it behind her.

"Shit!"

I made my way out from under the bed. That was when I saw the leather restraint that hung off the post. Curious, I sat up and pulled it out from behind the cover. I then walked over to the post at the foot and found a similar one, and two more on the other posts.

I grinned. This was a side of Salvatore I hadn't considered, and I wasn't sure how I felt about it.

But now wasn't the time to think about that. I had a bigger problem. I had to get out of his bedroom.

IT TOOK me thirty-five minutes to finally pick the lock and get into my own bedroom. Feeling like some sort of thief, I picked up my cell phone, which I'd been charging since it had run down completely. It showed six missed calls. All from Isabella. No texts, but voice mails after each one.

"*Hey, Luce. Call me when you get this.*"

"*Checking in, Luce. You there?*"

"*Um, I'm feeling like a stalker. You can't still be mad at me. Hell, you can be whatever you want. Shit, I'd be pissed. Okay, please don't be mad at me.*"

"*Fuck.*" Effie's voice in the background, then my sister again. "*No, honey, mommy didn't say a bad word.*"

I smiled.

"*Lucia, if you don't call me back right now, I'm getting in my car and driving over there!*"

"*Fuck. I'm on my way!*"

I checked the time of the messages. The last one was from about an hour and a half ago. Which meant she'd be here any minute.

I pocketed the phone and ran out the door. On my way down the stairs, I heard a voice I recognized as Marco's. I paused on the stairs, listening.

"She's got a visitor."

He must have been talking into a phone because I didn't hear another voice. He mumbled, "Okay, boss," and hung up.

When I heard his footsteps, I headed down the stairs, noting the room he'd come from. He looked up at me.

"Good afternoon."

Marco was always around, but at least he stayed out of my way. "Afternoon."

I heard a car door close and turned toward the front door. From the side window, I spotted my sister taking in the mansion before opening the back door to help Effie out.

"Your sister's here," Marco said, reaching the front door ahead of me.

"I can see that."

"Mr. Benedetti has given his permission for you to see her." He opened the door, but his comment made me stop and turn to him.

"Really? He's given his permission?" Asshole.

Marco faced me and was about to say something, but Isabella spoke first.

"Well, it is remote and it is protected," she said. "I wasn't sure they were going to open the gates for a minute there." She came right to me, looked me over from head to toe, and pulled me in for a hug.

I yielded right away, her warmth something I'd missed, something I cherished. It made me feel protected.

"Izzy." I used the name I used to call her when I was little and couldn't say her full name. It had stuck. I was the only person who called her that.

She pulled back and looked at me. I wiped at my eyes but apparently not quickly enough because I saw the concern in hers. She glanced at Marco, who stood stupidly watching us.

I hated him.

"Mommy." Effie tugged on her mom's skirt. "The gift."

Her high-pitched voice made me smile. She held up a box. I could see from the torn wrapping that it contained chocolates.

"Why don't you give it to Aunt Lucia, and explain why the wrapping's been torn."

Effie turned to me and offered up the box. "I started to open it for you to help you."

"Is that really why?" Izzy asked.

I gave Izzy a look. So did Effie.

I bent down to take the box from her, trying to keep a straight face. "Is this what I think it is? My favorite chocolates?" I asked, picking up an end of the wrapping and peeking inside the torn paper. "Maybe you can help me get the rest of the wrapping off." She happily took the box and tore off the gift wrap.

"Yep. They're my favorite too." She reluctantly held the box out to me.

"You hold on to it. We should probably eat some, though. What do you think?"

"I definitely think we should eat some!"

I straightened and looked around, noticing how Marco hovered. "Let's go into the living room."

With a hand on the top of Effie's head, I followed him to the spacious room adjoining the dining room. The sun shone bright, and the swimming pool glistened blue just beyond the large patio.

"God, it's beautiful, isn't it?" Izzy asked.

"It is."

"Did you bring my swimsuit, Mommy?" Effie asked, her attention focused on the pool.

I looked at my sister, who rolled her eyes.

"I didn't know they had a pool, so no."

Effie gave her a look, which made me cover my mouth to hide the chuckle.

"How would I know? It's my first time here," Izzy protested.

"How about something to drink," I asked just as Rainey walked in. She smiled warmly, and I introduced everyone.

"What would you like? I have some homemade lemonade maybe for the little one?"

"Actually, for me too," Izzy said.

"Homemade?"

Rainey nodded.

"Make it three then, please," I said. Rainey had been my only point of contact over the last couple of days. My world had always been small, but now, it had become miniscule.

Rainey nodded and returned to the kitchen. Marco remained in the room with us. Izzy and I both eyed him while Effie worked on getting the plastic off the box of chocolates.

"Are you just going to stand there?" I asked him.

He looked at me with raised eyebrows.

"I want to have a visit with my sister. Surely you don't have to monitor every word I say. I promise, it won't be that interesting."

Before he could answer, footsteps echoed on the marble floors. We all turned as Salvatore entered the room. He wore a T-shirt and jeans, the V-neck clinging to his sculpted body. His cobalt-blue eyes locked on mine, and my heartbeat quickened, my body suddenly tingling, nipples tightening, every hair standing on end.

A moment later, he released me from his gaze, his posture relaxing as he nodded to my sister and smiled at Effie struggling with the plastic.

"Thanks, Marco. You can go," he said.

Marco nodded and left the room. Salvatore walked over to Izzy.

"I don't think I've met Lucia's sister officially. I'm Salvatore Benedetti."

She took his hand. "Isabella DeMarco."

"Good to meet you. And this is?"

Effie looked up. "Got it!" She held up the plastic

triumphantly, then checked out Salvatore. "I'm Effie," she said, rising to her feet from the floor and holding out her hand.

Salvatore took it. "Nice to meet you, Effie."

Rainey walked in with a tray and set the glasses of lemonade down on the coffee table. We stood awkwardly.

"I'll let you and your sister have some privacy," Salvatore finally said, his tone casual, his gaze wavering. "I'm going to take a shower."

He waited. My body still did that vibrating, tingling thing as the air crackled between us.

"Thank you," I finally said.

He nodded and left the room. We watched him go. Only when he was out of the room did either of us breathe. My thoughts wandered to what I'd found in his room. I wondered if he'd think he'd forgotten to lock the door between our bedrooms, or if he'd know I'd broken in.

"Wow. He's intense."

I exhaled. "Yeah." I couldn't tell Izzy about what he'd done. What I'd done. Hell, I wasn't sure myself what it all meant or how I felt about it.

"Effie, it's polite to offer chocolates to others first before you dig in."

My sister tried to sound strict, but I saw the proud smile she worked to hide.

Effie turned her big, pale blue eyes to her mom, her mouth working on a second piece of chocolate. She rose to her feet and walked over to us.

"Would you like a chocolate?" she asked, turning to me first.

"I'd love one." I chose a dark chocolate and thanked her. Izzy declined, and Effie shrugged a shoulder and helped herself to a third.

"How are you doing? You didn't answer any of my messages. I thought he wasn't letting you use the phone!"

I shook my head with a weak smile. "No, it was just drained. I only checked the messages a few minutes before you got here, actually."

"Well, you're going to have to answer next time. I got worried."

I nodded.

"You okay?" she asked quietly.

I shrugged a shoulder. "I don't know. I don't want to cry." As I said it, the first tears wet my lashes.

"Shh." Izzy dug for a tissue in her bag.

Rainey walked out of the kitchen and toward us just then. I turned my face away.

"I'm getting ready to bake cookies in the kitchen. Maybe Effie would like to help?" she asked Izzy.

Effie's eyebrows rose, and she bounced up to stand. "Oh, can I, Mommy?"

"You sure?" Izzy asked Rainey.

After a glance and a small smile at me, she nodded.

"Sure," Izzy said. "Thank you."

Effie took Rainey's hand easily, and they walked off.

"That was nice," Izzy said.

"I haven't yet figured her out."

Izzy took my hands. "Are we okay, Lucia? This is important. I know we haven't talked about it, about me leaving. I was wrong to just take off. I know that. I'm back now, though, and I'm not abandoning you again, okay? You're not alone, even though it may feel that way right now."

I smiled. More tears fell. "We're okay, Izzy." It felt good to say that. Felt good to have my sister back, actually.

She hugged me tight to her, then whispered into my ear. "Are there cameras? Listening devices?"

Her question surprised me. "I don't know," I whispered back. "I haven't seen any but can't say for sure there aren't."

She pulled back and looked at me. "The pool looks amazing."

I knew what she wanted. "Let's go check it out."

We walked outside and away from the house toward the swimming pool.

"How is he? When no one's around, I mean?"

"Bossy." I couldn't tell her about earlier. About any of it. "And gone, mostly. He just got back from wherever he was, actually."

"He looks at you like he wants to eat you alive."

He scared me, but I didn't want to say that out loud, and not to Izzy. "I can't figure him out. He's horrible one second, then nice. Almost...caring. Like he gives a shit what I feel or think." I picked a single dandelion growing in the otherwise immaculate lawn. "But then he's a jerk again, and then he disappears."

"Is he making you..." she hesitated.

"Sleep with him?" I thought of what I'd found in his bedroom and felt my face heat up.

She nodded.

"Not yet."

"Good. Are you able to come and go?"

"I don't know. Not on my own, I think."

"Okay, that's fine. I'll just come get you. If he wants to send someone to follow us, we'll deal."

"It doesn't matter, Izzy. I'm stuck here."

"Luke and I...We're not going to sit back and let them have everything. Let them have you."

"Luke?"

"Just because we lost one war, doesn't mean we can't start another."

"Izzy." Even in the heat of the day, a shudder ran through me. "You can't. We lost once, and we had an army to back us."

"We don't need an army. We've got access now."

"What?"

Izzy suddenly laughed out loud as if I'd told a joke. It was then that I saw Salvatore standing in the window of his study, watching us. "By access, you mean me."

"It's what you want, isn't it?"

"Well, yes." It was all I'd thought of for the last five years and for good reason. "I want my freedom. And I want Franco Benedetti to pay for what he did to us. For what he made Papa do." I remembered the last time I'd seen my father. It was in that horrible room when I'd signed the contract. Why had I refused to talk to him all these years? He'd tried. He'd come to the college once every month. He'd call once a week. But I blamed him for my fate. And he *was* to blame, but I also understood he had no choice.

I should have been more understanding of the strain he was under.

"And what about him?" she asked, cocking her head in the direction of Salvatore, who'd turned away from the window.

"I want my freedom."

"Well, that's a start. Let's go inside, before he gets suspicious."

"Cookies are ready!" Effie called out as soon as we got into the house.

"They smell amazing," I said.

She watched proudly as Rainey carried a plateful of freshly baked chocolate chip cookies into the living room.

"I'm packing up the house," Izzy said. "Effie and I are moving in."

"You are?" I was surprised. Papa had still lived in the house we'd grown up in. I didn't think she'd want the house but was glad she wasn't talking about selling it. I wasn't ready for that yet. The thought—it was just too final. I wasn't ready to say good-bye to it, ending that chapter of my life so permanently.

Izzy nodded. "I should have come back sooner than this. I should have forgiven him."

"I didn't."

"It should have been me here in your place," she said, her eyes downcast.

"I don't want to think about that."

"If it weren't for me getting pregnant..."

"Do you keep in touch with the father?" I wanted to know who he was. It didn't matter anymore, not now that Papa was gone, and even if he had found out, it couldn't have mattered then either.

Salvatore chose that moment to walk into the living room. "I could smell the cookies from the study." His eyes met mine first, his expression guarded, almost cautious.

"I baked them. Rainey helped," Effie proudly said.

"Did you now? May I?"

She smiled, nodding.

He picked one up and took a bite. "Well, you did a good job. They're the best cookies I've ever had."

Effie gave him a big smile. "They are?"

"Yep. And Rainey's a good cook, so that says something."

Izzy checked her watch. "We should get going."

"You can't stay longer?" I didn't want her to go. I didn't want to be alone with him.

"I've got people coming to help with the house, and we'll be back with bathing suits soon. Maybe you can come help? I'm packing up some things and moving them to the attic, getting rid of some things. Maybe you want to do your room?"

I glanced at Salvatore, hating that I had to ask his permission. Ask him for a ride. Ask him for everything.

"When?" he asked.

Izzy shrugged her shoulder. "Tomorrow or the next day."

"I think we can manage that."

I felt like I went from my father's house, to the nuns, to

Salvatore Benedetti's. I was powerless to decide anything for myself.

"Luce?" Izzy asked.

I nodded, adjusting my expression. "My calendar is free," I said, giving Salvatore a smirk.

He didn't react.

"Great, we'll see you then. Come on, Effie, time to go back home."

"Ugh. Home is so boring," she said, her shoulders slumping.

"No, it's not. We've just got to find your box of toys. Maybe you can pack up a couple of those cookies for home."

I picked up a napkin, tucked the remaining cookies into it, and handed it to Effie.

"Here you go, honey. Don't forget your bathing suit the next time you come, by the way."

"I won't, Aunt Lucia."

She gave me a hug. Again came the thought that I'd missed out on the first years of my niece's life. I didn't know her. I hardly knew Izzy anymore. Or Luke.

Were Luke and Izzy really planning an attack on the Benedetti family? What did that mean for Salvatore?

Salvatore walked with us to the door. Once they had driven off and were out of view, he closed it. We stood in the foyer.

"I'm sorry," he said. "I shouldn't have done what I did."

Shit. An apology was the last thing I'd expected. If he'd locked me in a room, been a beast to me, it would make more sense. I could hate him. But an apology? Him offering to take me to my sister's?

"I hope we can forget it and start again," he added.

I think both of us found it hard to hold each other's gaze, and the last thing I wanted to do was talk about what happened, so I nodded. "Okay."

He smiled a small smile. "Thank you."

"If you ever do something like that again, Salvatore, I will kill you."

His eyes narrowed, and apologetic Salvatore was instantly gone. "You don't have to threaten me with murder. I said I was sorry."

He held my gaze until I blinked and nodded, looking down, my attention absorbed by an invisible piece of lint on my blouse.

"Are you really going to take me to help my sister?"

"You're not a prisoner, contrary to what you think, Lucia. This contract between us, the circumstances of our families, those things bind us, and although I have expectations of you and won't tolerate misplaced loyalty, I'm not interested in keeping a prisoner. Neither you nor I can get out of this, even if we wanted to. We have to find some way to live with it."

Even if we wanted to. Did that mean he didn't want to? And what did I want?

"I feel like a prisoner. I'm constantly watched. I couldn't visit with my sister without Marco standing by. I have nothing to do here. You have a cook, people who clean..."

He looked confused. "You're neither a cook nor a cleaner."

"But I am your property. You said so yourself. I have a degree, I want to work, but—"

His mouth tightened, and he looked away for a moment. "Come into my study, Lucia."

"Why?" I didn't trust him. And as much as I hated to admit it, he scared me.

"So we can talk. That's all."

I didn't move.

"I promise."

After a moment, I nodded. He gestured for me to go ahead and followed close behind me, opening the door to the study once we reached it and letting me inside. Once he'd closed the door, he moved behind his large desk. I looked around the room.

The walls were painted a dark shade of gray, and two windows overlooked the backyard and the forest beyond. The furnishings were made of a dark, heavy wood, and his desk, the focal point, must have been an antique. Directly before it stood a leather sofa, and the shelves along two of the walls contained floor-to-ceiling books. Set apart from the desk and sofa was an armchair, the leather well-worn, with a matching ottoman at its foot. The reading lamp behind the chair was on, and although it was sunny outside, this room remained darker. Masculine. Even the scent here was different, all man.

"Sit down."

I realized he'd been watching me take it all in. I lowered myself to the couch and faced him, the desk looming between us, him sitting behind it, making me feel small. I smoothed the skirt of my sundress down, unsure what to do with my hands.

Salvatore got up and walked around his desk. Surprising me, he joined me on the couch.

It only made me more uncomfortable, though. If only he'd act like I expected him to...

"What do you know about me?"

I studied him, drawn to him, to his eyes. I remembered for a moment how the blue had turned nearly black when he'd been aroused. Remembered how he'd looked at me when I'd lain before him. How he'd taken me in. How he'd gripped his cock...

Then the image of what I'd found in his bedroom flashed across the screen of my memory.

I cleared my throat and focused on the firm set of his jaw instead of his eyes. The scruff along the chiseled line told me he'd probably not shaved in the two days he'd been gone, and it didn't help my wandering mind. I lowered my gaze to his neck, to the exposed flesh there, the T-shirt hugging his powerful chest.

Shit. This wasn't working. I was attracted to this man I

wanted to hate. In spite of what he'd done, the physical attraction was like an energy between us, a living, breathing, scorching thing.

I closed my eyes and willed myself to focus. Opening them again, I forced myself to meet his eyes. But when I did, I saw what he saw. He knew his power over me.

"Were you with a woman the last two nights?" I blurted out.

He chuckled, apparently surprised. "Not like you think."

So that was a yes?

"I felt ashamed of what I'd done. What I'd made you do."

My neck and face heated.

"That's why I left. I wasn't with another woman. I wouldn't be. We have a contract."

"That binds me to you." Nothing in the contract spoke of any obligation on his part, certainly not one to be celibate or faithful. It was not a marriage contract, after all.

"And me to you."

Now I was confused. Salvatore leaned back and crossed his ankle over his knee.

"Let me ask you again, Lucia. What do you know about me? Or perhaps the better question is, what do you *think* you know?"

"I know you're Franco Benedetti's son." I stuck my chin out. "That's all I need to know."

"I think you're smarter than that."

"I know your hand shook when you signed the contract."

He paused, his gaze faltering momentarily. "I'm not firstborn. I was never intended to be in the position I'm in."

"You mean, being your father's successor?"

"Yes."

"So you're stuck with me? If your brother were alive, I'd be his."

"I mean I am obligated to do many things, which I would not choose to do and do not condone."

"Me, you mean. You wouldn't choose me?"

"Stop putting words in my mouth."

"Isn't that what you're saying?"

"Why don't you try listening for a change and remember not everything is about you, Lucia."

Too shocked to retort, I unwittingly did as he said.

"I'm saying I wouldn't have created that contract in the first place. But to be fair, your father agreed. Remember that."

"My father didn't have a choice."

"He should have been willing to die..." he paused and leaned forward, anger marking his words, an anger I did not expect. "He should have been willing to die rather than see you go through what you did."

That last part made me stop.

"He did die." But Salvatore was right. And that was why I'd been so angry with my father all these years. Why I refused to see him. He'd given me up without a fight. Salvatore was right. How could he stand by and watch what they did? How could he have offered his daughter to the Benedetti beasts?

"I don't want to upset you, Lucia."

I wiped the back of my hand across my face, catching the single tear that had slipped from my eye. I shook my head, not wanting to speak for fear I would weep. It would be easier if he were unkind. Damn him, it would be easier.

"All I'm saying is I wouldn't have done what my father did. I would not have required the innocent daughter of my enemy as payment."

Fuck.

I swallowed back tears, knowing he saw right through me all along.

"But we're here now. You and I are both here, and bound to one another. I don't want a prisoner. I don't want someone who fears or hates me in my own house."

"Then I don't understand. Why do you care what I think? I'm your enemy, and you've won. My presence here is proof of that. To your power over me and my family."

"I'm not a monster, whether you believe it or not."

"What do you want from me, then?"

"I've already told you: your obedience. You give me that, and I'll make this easier."

Obedience. I hated that fucking word. "And if I don't, you'll punish me like you did before."

"I'll be creative in my punishments, yes," he said with a wicked gleam in his eye.

Goose bumps made the hairs on my arms stand on end, and my mind wandered to the restraints attached to the posts of his bed. Would he use those? Was that getting *creative*?

Salvatore reached out to softly touch my knee. My mind screamed for me to pull away, but instead, I looked from his eyes to his hand. I swallowed as he stroked the inside of my knee, then my thigh, pushing the dress up as he did so.

"I think you enjoyed at least part of your punishment."

I shook my head, just a small "no," but kept my eyes on his hand, on his fingers as they drew small circles on too sensitive flesh.

He slid toward me, making me look up, forcing me to meet his gaze.

"And it doesn't always have to be punishment."

His fingers left my thigh and touched the top button of my blouse. I watched in silence, unable to speak. He slowly undid the buttons and pulled my top open.

"Look at me."

I did, my breath hitching when I met those cobalt eyes. With both hands, he slid the blouse from my shoulders, leaving it at my elbows. He then explored my exposed chest, my nipples tightening just from his gaze upon them, barely hidden behind the white lace.

Bringing his face to mine, he inhaled, his mouth close to mine, so close, but not touching. He kissed my cheek softly, making my stomach flutter, his breath on my face making my sex throb.

"I can make this good," he whispered by my ear. "I want to make this good for you."

When his fingers traced the border of my bra, I licked my lips, wanting him to kiss me, preparing for him to kiss me. He could make this so good. I knew. I knew how good he could make it.

His fingers slid inside my bra as his mouth neared mine again. This time, I tilted my face upward to meet his and reached a trembling hand to touch the naked muscle of his arm. His kiss was soft, slow, tender almost as his fingers tickled my nipple. But then it changed, building in heat and intensity as one hand cradled the back of my head, and my mouth opened to his tongue, my entire body arching up to meet him, wanting—needing—something more.

"But only good girls are rewarded," he said, his mouth at my ear again, me breathless, blinking up at him as he pulled back. "Bad girls are punished. Have you been bad, Lucia?"

His eyes seemed to dance, and I knew in that instant he knew.

I straightened, trying to tug my shirt up to cover myself.

Salvatore shook his head and smiled, cocking his head to the side. "Tell me, have you?"

"No," I said, my voice cracking.

He reached over, and I gasped when he pushed the cups of my bra beneath my breasts.

"Wh...what are you doing?" I moved to cover them.

"No," he said, taking my wrists and pulling them behind my back.

"Salvatore?"

That smile still plastered on his face, he dragged me forward and laid me facedown over his lap. He kept my wrists at my back while the fingers of his other hand tickled the inside of my thighs as they dragged my skirt up.

"Have you been snooping?" he asked outright once he'd stuffed my skirt beneath my wrists at my waist.

"What? No!"

He smacked my right cheek. I think I was more surprised than pained. "What the..."

"Have you been snooping?" he repeated.

I craned my neck. "What are you doing?"

Smack.

"Ow! Stop!"

"Have you been snooping?"

I shook my head, squeezed my legs together, and wriggled to get free, which was impossible, considering his size and strength.

"No?"

His fingers found the waistband of my panties and tickled the flesh there. "What are you doing? Let me up!"

I knew he heard me, he just was enjoying this. When he began to drag my panties down, I wildly kicked my legs only to have them trapped between Salvatore's hard thighs. The swoosh of his belt made me stop struggling, and he laughed at what I was sure was my deer in the headlights expression.

"Don't worry." He wrapped the belt around my wrists and secured them behind my back. "I'm just planning on using my hand this first time."

"What?"

But he began, smacking one cheek then the next, each slap

screaming at my brain that this was really happening. That I was naked from the waist down being spanked!

"Stop! It fucking hurts!"

A few moments later, he did, rubbing circles over my punished cheeks.

"Let me up," I said, wiping my wet face on his jeans.

"Were you snooping?" he asked again. This time, there was no teasing in his tone.

"Yes!" He knew it anyway; why he had to humiliate me like this to get me to admit it was beyond me.

"Good girl," he said, his touch sliding between my thighs. "Bad girls get punished, but good girls get rewarded."

Then, without any warning, his fingers found my sex, and I sucked in a breath.

I tensed, squeezing everything tight, but Salvatore tickled and stroked until I relaxed my legs and let them fall open, my back arching of its own accord as he smeared my own arousal over and around my clit, rubbing soft, then hard, pinching, making me cry out.

"What did you find in my bedroom?" he asked, still rubbing.

When a moan escaped me, I hung my head, wanting to disappear. How could I be enjoying this? Enjoying this humiliation?

"No..."

"Remember, good girls are rewarded, bad girls punished. Lying would make you a bad girl."

"I hate you," I said, not believing it myself.

"No, you don't. You just feel powerless and are acting out in response."

"I'm not a child."

"I know that. Tell me what you found."

He started on my clit again, rubbing harder, faster. "God."

He chuckled. "God would be a first."

"I'm..."

"Focus, Lucia," he said, the fingers of his free hand taking one of my breasts.

"Restraints," I said, my eyes about to roll to the back of my head when he kneaded my nipple.

"And how did it make you feel to find them?"

He eased off my clit, and I groaned, arching back again, wanting to—needing to—come.

"I...I don't know."

He struck my pussy, and I gasped.

"What did you feel?"

He rubbed again, and I melted into him. "Curious."

Was it possible to hear a smile? Because I did. And then, I came. I came hard in his hand, the sounds I made foreign to my own ears, my body going limp over his thighs, my eyes closing, sleepy. When it was over, I felt him unbind my wrists and lift me, cradling me in his arms and leaning back against the sofa.

"Lucia, Lucia, Lucia. You surprise me."

"You'll still take me to my sister?" I asked, burrowing into his body, my eyes half-open.

"I told you I would. And we need to go shopping to find you a dress."

"A dress? For what?"

"My father's birthday party."

8

LUCIA

Being locked away with the nuns for five years had been easier than this. I didn't have to face anything. I could think about it. I could get angry about it. I could blame everyone and everything, but I didn't have to face them. Now I sat beside Salvatore in his car as he drove me to what should have been considered home to me. Thing was, I didn't know what was home anymore. I didn't know where I belonged, who I was. Who I was meant to be.

I looked at Salvatore, at his profile. At a glance, the set of his jaw told of power, of strength, while his eyes betrayed a depth beneath this outermost layer. Gave a glimpse into the darkness there. He kept his attention on the road while I studied him, wondering who this man was. What was expected of him.

Wondering what the hell had happened between us yesterday.

They'd examined me on the day of the signing. His father had wanted to be certain I was *intact*. A virgin. Was it only to humiliate me? To break my father to the point he could no longer be repaired?

I shook my head, trying to erase the memory of my father's face when I'd finally been able to look at him. How his hands had been fisted, his shoulders slumped. He'd been made to stand by and watch his daughter's degradation. Why?

Yesterday, Salvatore hadn't forced himself on me. He hadn't tried, and he'd had the opportunity. Multiple opportunities. And, he might argue, the right. He *owned* me. But he hadn't taken anything I hadn't given up. And I'd given it. I'd lain there and let him bring me to orgasm. I'd felt his cock pressing against me throughout both the punishment and the reward, but he hadn't taken his pleasure from me.

I fumbled to turn up the AC, feeling too hot suddenly. Our fingers touched when Salvatore adjusted it for me, and it was like a bolt of electricity. Our gazes locked, but I quickly blinked and turned away.

"If you get off at this exit, I can show you a shortcut."

He made his way over. Once we were off the exit, I gave him directions. We weaved our way through the narrow streets near my childhood home.

"Want to get a cup of coffee first?" I asked when we neared my favorite bakery, wanting to put off our inevitable arrival. Afraid Isabella would see right through me. Would I be a traitor then?

He seemed surprised by my offer. "Sure."

"Right here, you can park at the curb. The parking lot is usually full." And I wanted to walk through the streets, see the houses and neighborhood I didn't realize I'd missed. "You don't mind walking a few blocks, do you?" I asked once we climbed out.

"No, it's fine." Salvatore pushed a button to lock the car and looked around. "I'm curious where you grew up. This is very different from what I imagined."

Wayne, Pennsylvania, was a pretty suburb. Quiet. Wealthy. And, apart from the mob family living there, safe.

I slung my purse over my shoulder and glanced up at the sky. Clouds collected thick and heavy with moisture. It had to be ninety degrees already. As much as I hated rain, I'd welcome it today to cool things down.

Salvatore came to my side, his attention still on the surroundings. He wore a navy T-shirt and jeans, and I had no idea how he wasn't sweating his ass off. My tank top and shorts seemed stuck to me.

"What did you imagine?" I asked as I led the way, liking the fact that most of the houses looked just like they had five years ago.

Salvatore turned his blue eyes my way. Would I always become breathless when he looked at me?

"I don't know. A castle with a moat."

I chuckled. "That's your family. We were more...low-key." I thought about it. "My father kept us out of things. He wasn't meant to rule the family, my uncle was. But when my grandfather and uncle were killed, he was forced to take over. I remember it happening. Well, remember all the meetings, all the people who were suddenly in our house all the time. I was maybe ten." They'd told my sister and me that they'd had a car accident, but I knew better. I'd snuck into my father's study and had seen the photos of the bullet-riddled car. Of them inside it. I shuddered. Some things you couldn't un-see, no matter how much you wanted to. "I remember not being allowed to play in the front yard or bike through the neighborhood anymore."

"Your father didn't have control of the family."

I stopped.

Salvatore turned to me.

"He's dead. Isn't that enough? I thought that would have satisfied you, but I guess I was wrong." Tears burned my eyes, but I didn't feel sad. Confused and remorseful, yes, the need to defend my father fierce. The desperation to understand my muddled loyalties even more so.

Salvatore ran a hand through his thick, dark hair and glanced away. He nodded but didn't speak.

"Why don't you just drop me off at the house?" I asked, feeling betrayed after yesterday. But what did I expect? What did I think, that we were building a relationship?

"Which way to the coffee shop?" he asked, ignoring my request.

I pointed and walked just ahead of him. The coffee shop was small and exactly as I remembered it. And it was full.

The entire place quieted when we walked in. I looked around at the faces, not really recognizing anyone, but knowing they must recognize me. Or, more likely, Salvatore. Benedetti were not welcomed in this neighborhood for a long time. That hadn't changed, even though now, they owned it.

"Let's get a table," Salvatore said when I walked up to the counter.

"We can just get a cup to go." I hadn't thought about how people might react to him. To me with him.

"No."

He made a point of meeting every eye in the place, and I was sure he felt it too.

"There's a couple leaving. We can take their table."

I looked to where he pointed, and sure enough, the pair at the table left money on the check, gathered up their things, and walked out.

"We don't have to stay," I whispered, not sure if it was more for him or me. People would know who I was. They'd know either because of my father and the photos of the family after his death in the local paper or because of Salvatore.

"We'll stay."

He pulled out one of the chairs and waited for me to have a seat before he took the chair opposite. I saw how he'd chosen the seat where he could watch the whole of the café, especially the door. It was a subtle reminder of who he was. Who I was.

A waitress came to clear and wipe down the table.

"What would you like?" Salvatore asked me.

"Um, a cappuccino, please. Thanks."

"I'll have a double espresso and one of the éclairs if they're fresh."

"Baked just this morning," the waitress said, her tone unfriendly.

Salvatore excused her with a nod.

Voices picked up as conversation began again, and I wondered how many of them were talking about us.

Salvatore leaned back in his seat and looked at me. "You came here a lot growing up?"

I knew he wasn't oblivious to the stares or whispers, but he acted like he couldn't have cared less.

I nodded, trying to stop from glancing around. "Izzy and I would come every Sunday morning after church. The éclairs were my favorite."

"Why didn't you order one?"

"I don't feel very hungry."

"Take one." He raised his hand to get the waitress's attention.

"No," I reached out to make him take his arm down, to not draw any additional attention to us, but the waitress was already coming over.

"I don't think I can eat anything, Salvatore," I whispered.

He studied me, his eyes curious. Concerned? "Your niece will be there today, right?"

I nodded, glancing up at the waitress who stood quietly, clearly not happy about having to serve a Benedetti. Did they see me as a traitor? Did they know I'd been made to do this? To be with him? It was in that moment I realized they likely did not know about the contract. But even so, wasn't I myself confused?

"Let's get six of those éclairs boxed up to go too," he said to the waitress, then turned to me. "She has a sweet tooth from what I saw."

I smiled. "That's nice. She'll like that, and so will Izzy."

The waitress returned and delivered the coffee and Salvatore's pastry and set the additional box of eclairs up at the register. Salvatore took a big bite, and I chuckled.

"What?" he asked, looking for a napkin.

"You have some cream," I pointed, then reached over to wipe it off when he missed. "Right there." I pulled my hand away and without thinking, licked off the cream. He watched me, and as soon as I realized what I'd done, I pulled a napkin out of the dispenser and wiped off my finger.

"They're very good," Salvatore said, not commenting.

"You don't care that no one wants you here, do you?"

He raised his eyebrows and picked up his espresso. "No. Why should I? Besides, I'm not even sure it's true." He looked around the café. "What happened, happened five years ago."

That was when things had been at their worst. When fighting on the streets had turned this neighborhood from a quiet, safe place to a bloody one.

"And we've kept peace since."

"By killing off most of your enemies."

"Both sides lost people, Lucia. We just won the war *your* father started." He drank the last of his espresso and stood, looking pissed. "You finished?"

I rose to my feet. "I need to use the bathroom."

He nodded and took out his wallet as I made my way to the tiny bathroom. Once inside, I locked the door and gripped the sink, looking at my reflection. I had to find some way to be okay with all of this. This was my life now. I belonged to a man whose name I hated, but who made me question everything I believed. I needed to make sense of it all. To find some way to survive this. I splashed water onto my face and patted it dry, taking a deep breath before walking back out to find him waiting for me, his expression hard.

We drove to the house in silence. Turned out I didn't need to give Salvatore directions. He knew the way, and by the time he pulled up in front of the large, two-story brick home with the wraparound porch and swing hanging from a branch in the overgrown tree in the front yard, my heart was racing.

Salvatore switched off the engine and turned to me. He tucked a strand of hair behind my ear, his thumb resting against my cheek as his mouth moved into a small smile. A sort of truce, maybe.

"Relax," he said.

"It's that obvious?" I asked, holding onto the box of éclairs.

"Yeah." Salvatore's cell phone rang. He looked at the display but declined the call. "I'll walk you in, then I have to make a call."

I nodded, oddly grateful, and climbed out of the car.

"Aunt Lucia!"

I turned to find Effie running across the lawn toward us.

"Effie!" She crashed into my legs. Salvatore's hand at my back kept me upright. "I'm excited to see you too." I hugged her with one arm. "Look what Salvatore brought for you." She pulled back, and I opened the box of éclairs .

"Oh!" She squealed and looked with huge eyes from the box to him then back. "Thank you!"

The front door opened, and Izzy stepped outside followed by Luke.

"Huh?" I didn't realize Luke would be here.

Izzy came toward us, her mouth pasted into a smile. I glanced at Salvatore to find his eyes locked on Luke's.

"What the hell is he doing here?" he muttered. I wondered if he'd meant to say it out loud at all.

"Those look great," Izzy said, her eye on the box Effie held. She took my hand and pulled me to her side, her gaze on Salvatore. "Thanks for dropping her off."

"Oh, I can stay," he said, taking me by the arm and pulling me to stand beside him. "I'd love to see where Lucia grew up."

"Didn't you have to make a call?" I reminded him, unsure where my loyalties should lie.

His smile didn't reach his eyes. "It can wait."

"Luke came by to help. Luke, this is Salvatore Benedetti," Izzy said, introducing them.

The men eyed each other, neither offering a hand. "We know each other," Salvatore said.

I watched Luke, saw how he stood a little closer to my sister than he maybe should, remembered my conversation with Izzy yesterday.

"Mommy, can I have one already?" Effie asked.

My attention went to the little girl. I looked from her to Luke and back. But then Salvatore spoke, interrupting my thoughts.

"Want me to take the first bite, so you can be sure they're not poisoned?" he asked Izzy in Italian while placing a hand on top of Effie's head. I realized he'd spoken Italian so Effie wouldn't understand.

My sister's eyes hardened. "Go ahead, honey," she said to Effie, her gaze never leaving Salvatore.

"Thanks!" Effie, oblivious to the tension, chose the largest éclair and began eating.

"Okay, let's go inside and get started." I tugged my arm free from his hold, took Salvatore's arm, and dragged him with me into the house.

"Did you know Luke would be here?" he asked in a clipped tone.

"No. I'm just as surprised as you." I walked into the living room which, even on a sunny day, was dark because of the wide-covered porch, and today, with the heavy clouds overhead, Izzy had turned on several lamps even though it was early in the day. I stopped just inside the house, the faint but familiar scent of vanilla flooding my mind with memories. I'd forgotten that scent. Mom's favorite candles. Papa had always claimed to hate them, but he'd kept right on buying them even after she died. It was all too many years ago. An entire lifetime ago.

"Is there something going on between your sister and Luke?" Salvatore asked, his gaze on the pair outside, who stood having a heated discussion.

"They're cousins. They're just close, that's all." Was that all?

"I don't like it, Lucia. And I don't like you around him."

I faced him. "He's my cousin too. My parents are both dead now. I need all the family I can get."

"Sometimes family is bad for you."

I paused, trying to read what I saw in his eyes, but Salvatore had a talent for being unreadable. Feeling weak, I sat on the arm of the sofa and took a deep breath.

"Don't take them away from me too," I whispered without thinking, knowing he could do just that. What would happen then? Izzy would start a war. Hell, she and Luke were already planning it.

Salvatore came toward me. He took my hands and made me look at him. "I won't take them away."

"Promise it," I said after a long moment.

"I promise."

That was the second promise he'd made me.

Without another word, I led the way up to my bedroom, where Salvatore helped me pack up the things I wanted to keep, mostly books and old diaries I'd hidden. My bed stood where it had always been, just beneath one of the two windows. My father used to ask me how I could sleep there in the summer months—didn't the light wake me up too early?—but I loved it. I looked out onto the backyard, where he'd put up a second swing like the one in the front yard.

I sat down while Salvatore taped up the last box. It was when I picked up the pillow that I found it. A letter addressed to me, the envelope sealed, the handwriting familiar.

My father's.

I picked it up and stared at it. My father's suicide note had been brief. He'd said he was sorry. He'd said he'd failed everyone he loved.

I ran the pad of my finger over the blue ink before sliding my finger beneath the flap and tearing it. The sound stood out, almost as if it blocked out every other sound, every other person or thing. My heart pounded, and my hand trembled as I pulled out the folded sheet of paper.

Dear, dear Lucia,

I know this comes too little too late, and you won't ever know how sorry I am for the part I forced you to play in this terrible war. I want to say I had no choice. I want to blame anyone else. And for a time, I did. But that wasn't real.

One thing I've learned these last five years is to take responsibility for my actions, for their consequences. For your consequence. And this one, this final one, is the one I cannot reconcile. The single thing that has broken me.

I am so very sorry, Lucia. I am so ashamed of myself. I am a weak man, and I've burdened you with a weight too heavy. I can't live with this anymore. I will fail you again by being absent when the bastard comes to claim you. But you see, I cannot live with this for another moment longer. I cannot live, knowing they destroyed both of my daughters.

I hope you will forgive me. I do love you more than anything in this world.

Papa

A hand on my shoulder startled me, and I glanced up.

"You okay?"

It was Salvatore. I quickly crumpled the letter and threw it into the trash can, then wiped my face with the backs of my hands.

"I want to go." I said, looking around for something, what I had no idea. "I need... I can't."

"Shh."

He wrapped an arm around me and, without another word, pulled me into his chest and held me there, one hand rubbing my back, the other holding tight.

"Shh," he said again.

I choked on a sob and pressed my face into him, for one moment letting his strength support me, lift the weight of all of this from me. But when in response to my surrender he hugged me back, I shook my head and wiped my face before breaking away from him. I couldn't look at him. I couldn't take comfort from him. He was the enemy. And I was betraying my family with every tender moment I shared with him.

I couldn't do this.

"Please..." I started.

With a nod, he ushered me out to the car. "Stay here."

Salvatore went back into the house and a few moments later returned, loaded the two boxes I'd packed into the trunk, and climbed behind the steering wheel. He glanced at me, the look in his eyes strange, cautious, measuring. Then, without a word, he turned the key and started the engine, taking us back to his house, back to my new home.

9

SALVATORE

I knew it wasn't right, but I did what any man would do in my situation. I fished out the letter Lucia had thrown into the trash and read it.

If I hadn't been sure before, I was now. The fucking bastard of a father was too weak to stay alive. Too weak to take responsibility even in this, his final letter to the daughter he betrayed. Did he even know what his letter would do to her? Did he know it would only add to the guilt she already felt with his loss?

Fucking bastard.

I paced my study, phone to my ear, when, finally, Roman picked up on the fifth ring. "I need you to do something for me, Uncle." I rarely called Roman that. Only when I needed to trust him absolutely. "Just for me."

"What is it?" he asked. He was too smart to agree to something without knowing the details.

"I know we have Luke DeMarco under surveillance, but I want more. I want to know where he spends his nights. I want to know exactly how much time he spends with Isabella DeMarco. And," was I really going to do this? "I want a paternity test run on the little girl, Effie. I want to know if he's her father."

"We share the same suspicions."

"And my father? What does he think?"

"He doesn't think she's a threat, so he hasn't looked into it."

"Isabella?"

"Yes." He paused. "Never underestimate your enemy, Salvatore. It will get you killed."

"No one knows that better than me, Uncle."

"I'll keep this between us for now."

"For now. I will go to my father once I have solid information."

"I'll work on it right away."

"Thank you."

I hung up the phone, that last part a lie. If my suspicions were correct, I couldn't go to my father with the details. My father did not need any more ammunition against Luke DeMarco, and something about what Lucia had said, asking me not to take them away, I felt it.

Luke was collecting supporters, that I knew, but was Lucia's sister involved? If so, how deeply? Just how close were she and Luke? And what would I need to do if I what I believed was confirmed?

On top of everything else, I needed to gain Lucia's trust. I needed to be sure she'd do as I said and not act out during the birthday dinner. I needed to make sure my father knew I had control of her.

THE NEXT AFTERNOON, I pulled into Nordstrom's parking lot.

"I don't want to go to your father's party."

We climbed out of the car and went into the department

store. She sounded defiant, but I heard the panic behind her words.

"I'm not going."

I touched her back to lead her inside. "Yes, you are. And you're going to behave while you're there."

"Why? Why can't you just go on your own?"

"Because he's expecting both of us." We stepped onto the escalator, Marco and another man following nearby. A piano played on the second floor. Before we reached it, I saw the sales-girl waiting for us.

"Why?" Lucia asked again.

Once off the escalator, I took her arms, rubbed them, and turned her toward me. There would be no discussion. She would go. Period. Even if it was the last place I wanted to take Lucia, we would both go. "Because I said so. Now be good." I leaned in, and to anyone who watched, it looked like I was planting a kiss on her temple, but instead, I whispered in her ear. "Or else I'll have to get creative again."

Her eyes searched mine when I pulled back, questioning, perhaps trying to gauge how far I'd go. Honestly, I didn't mind if she did push me.

"Mr. Benedetti," the salesgirl said, her high heels clicking toward us.

I turned to her. She couldn't be more than twenty.

"I'm Carla, and I'll help your..." She searched our ring fingers and modified, "I understand you're looking for an evening dress."

I chuckled and kept one hand at Lucia's back. "For Lucia. I'd look rather silly in an evening dress."

The girl laughed nervously and looked Lucia over. "Size four?"

Lucia nodded.

"Any preference as to length or cut?" We followed her as she led the way to the designer dresses.

My phone rang. When I saw Natalie's name displayed on the screen, I excused myself. Lucia raised her eyebrows but didn't question. Marco followed me, and the other guard kept close to Lucia.

"Hello?"

"Hi, Salvatore. It's Natalie. Is this a good time?"

"Yes, of course. Is everything all right?" She sounded tense.

"Dominic came by. He was here when I got home from work."

Natalie didn't trust Dominic. She had never liked him, and I'd seen Sergio have words with him. I never knew the details but suspected it had something to do with Natalie.

"What did he want?"

"He said he wanted to see his nephew. See how he's doing, since I won't take him to the house for visits."

Why in hell did Dominic care about a baby? He never had before.

"Salvatore?"

"I'm listening. How long was he there?"

"Just ten minutes. I wouldn't let him in. Talked to him on the front steps. What does he want, Salvatore?"

"I don't know, but I'll see him at my father's birthday dinner. I'll talk to him then. Do you feel safe? Do you want me to send someone over?"

"No, it's okay. I just...seeing him again...it brought back so much."

"I know." I heard her sniffle. "I'm sorry, Natalie." I heard Jacob fuss near the phone.

"It's okay, it'll be fine. He just surprised me. I'd better go get Jacob's dinner."

"I can come by myself if you want me to."

"You have your hands full. Really, I'll be fine. I feel better already, now that I've talked to you. It's fine."

"Let me at least send someone to keep an eye on the house."

"No. I don't want that for myself, and I don't want it for Jacob. We're out of this life. It's what Sergio would have wanted for us."

I nodded, even though she couldn't see. The salesgirl came around the corner, looking frazzled until she spotted me. I turned my back to wrap up my call.

"Okay, but if you feel unsafe or need anything, you call me, understand?"

"Yes. I will, Salvatore. Thank you."

We hung up, and I walked toward the girl, my mind going a thousand miles a minute, wondering what the hell Dominic was up to.

"She's ready with the first one." The girl sang out and pointed to the dressing room.

I followed her. It was a private room with a sofa and a long mirror with a curtain to separate the changing area. Once inside, the girl closed the door and disappeared behind the curtain.

"It's too low," Lucia complained.

"It looks amazing," the girl retorted.

A moment later, she pulled the curtain aside, and my eyes about popped out of my head. There stood Lucia, her expression annoyed, her long dark hair falling in waves over her shoulders, a cream-colored dress wrapped around her petite frame. The material fell heavy to her feet, which I could see were wrapped in silver-and-gold, high-heeled sandals. They added three inches to her height. The dress was cut low so that the V dipped all the way down to the high belt around her waist. Gemstones circled her waistline and edged the V between her breasts, clinging to her, displaying their small, round mounds beautifully.

"I think the hair should go up," the girl said, piling Lucia's hair on top of her head and forcing her farther out so that she stood before the mirror, her back to me. "To display this gorgeous back." The V of the neckline repeated on the back. "We'll need to alter it slightly here," she pointed out the pins at Lucia's shoulders. "But it'll be ready by tomorrow."

"You look beautiful," I said to Lucia.

Lucia's eyes found mine in the mirror. She looked at herself once more as if not quite believing it was her. I wondered if this was her first time in a dress like this.

"It's too..." she started, looking down at the V between her breasts.

"It's perfect." I stood and went to her, standing close behind her. Our eyes locked in the mirror. I took the clip out of her hair and let the mass tumble down her back. Lucia bit her lip and shuddered.

"Find us something more casual for tonight," I said to the girl without taking my eyes off Lucia. "Take your time."

"Yes, sir." The girl walked out, closing the door behind her.

I turned Lucia to face me. "I want you."

Her hands came up to my chest, and I brushed her hair off her shoulders. The light overhead flickered on and off, then settled for on. Without another word, I leaned in to kiss her. I loved kissing her. I'd seen her naked. I'd tasted her pussy, but this was our most intimate act yet, and I took my time, tasting her, her mouth soft, her tongue shy at first, submissive to mine, then bolder, curious in its exploration as the kiss deepened, drawing a moan from deep inside my chest.

A quick knock and the door opened. Lucia gasped, but the girl remained oblivious. She carried in an armful of dresses and spoke without giving us a glance as she hung them all up.

"And, what do you think?"

I looked Lucia over again, my gaze hovering on the exposed

mounds of her breasts, my cock pressing against the crotch of my jeans.

"We'll take this one." My voice came out hoarse, and I cleared my throat. "You'll be able to deliver it altered tomorrow?"

"Yes, sir."

The girl beamed, and when I checked the price tag, I understood why. She'd probably made more tonight on commission than a month on the floor.

"Let's get that one off and try another," she said, ushering Lucia behind the curtain.

"Out here. I want to see."

She stopped, confused, tilting her head to one side, but then glanced at Lucia who only stared back at me, her swollen lips slightly parted, her eyes a darker burnt caramel as opposed to their usual whiskey-brown.

"Here," I said, pointing to a spot before the mirror, where I could see her front and back.

"Yes, sir." The girl moved Lucia, who only watched me.

I leaned back in my seat as the salesgirl unhooked the belt and slowly slid the dress off Lucia, leaving her standing in panties, a pair of boyshorts like the ones she'd packed to Italy. That seemed so long ago now.

I abandoned looking at Lucia's eyes as I studied her nearly naked body, each time seeming like the first. Narrow shoulders; small, high, round breasts with nipples that tightened beneath my gaze; a flat belly; and long, slender, muscular legs. She was beautiful. Perfect. And my cock twitched in appreciation.

I had her, she was mine. But I wanted her to want it. To want me.

I swallowed as she raised her arms for the girl to slide a short black dress over her head. This one hung loose to the low waist and had long sleeves with slits all the way through.

"Best part," the girl said, turning Lucia so she had her back to me. The back was cut out to the hips, accenting the silhouette of her figure seductively.

I nodded. "I want to see that one." I pointed to another, and the girl quietly obeyed, undressing Lucia and dressing her again. Turning her this way and that, all while my cock grew harder, Lucia's submission turning me on as much as having her naked did.

Once she'd gone through the rest of the dresses, the girl left us.

"What are we doing?" Lucia asked as she stood before me in just her panties and those sandals, her hands over her breasts, the spell broken.

"We're shopping. Don't cover your breasts."

For a moment, she resisted, her eyes questioning. But then, she obeyed and dropped her arms to her sides.

"Turn around."

She did, presenting me with her ass still clad in lace. I stood. She glanced over her shoulder but then faced the wall again.

"Hands up on the wall." I stood close enough to make sure she felt my breath on her shoulder, the heat of my body pulsing against hers. Leaning down, I inhaled the clean scent of her hair, watched her nipples harden and goose bumps rise along the flesh of her arms. "I like looking at you, Lucia." I pressed my erection against her hip. "You don't know how badly I want you."

She swallowed as I ran the knuckles of one hand along her hip, then slid two fingers along the edge of her panties. "I like these." With both hands now, I traced the outline of lace on the soft swell of her ass. I then dragged them upward, exposing more of her cheeks as I set the material in the split between them, then tugged upward.

Lucia gasped.

"I like your ass." I wrapped one hand around to pinch her nipple. "I like your breasts." I slid it down over her belly and into her panties to cup the wet mound of her sex. "And I like your pussy." I rubbed her clit as she leaned against me, softening, a small moan escaping her lips. Wrapping my free hand around her neck, I drew her against me, still playing with the slick folds of her sex as I ground my cock against her back. "I want to bury my cock inside your pussy, Lucia. I want to bend you over here and fuck you so hard, everyone in this damn place knows it. Knows you're getting fucked. Knows you're mine."

She stiffened at my words, resisting, but her body jerked as she neared orgasm.

"Stop." Her voice was weak. A half-hearted plea.

"Give it to me."

"I..."

I pinched her clit, and she fisted her hands, leaning her forehead into the wall.

"Please. Don't. Not here."

"Come."

She shook her head but stayed as she was, not attempting to free herself, to drag my hand from her pussy.

"Come."

"No... Fuck."

Her knees buckled, but I kept her pressed against me, this time gripping a handful of hair and tugging her head backward. "Come, and I'll release you."

"I...said...no."

"Stubborn." I turned her to face me, kissed her, and worked her clit hard between thumb and forefinger. Her mouth opened to mine, and her arms wrapped around my neck, pushing and pulling, so close to orgasm yet resisting with all she had.

She broke away. "I...won't."

But I took her mouth again, and this time, I slid the hand that held her hair down into her panties, parting her ass cheeks, pressing my finger there, rubbing her tight little asshole until her knees gave way, and she cried out, gripping my neck, burying her face in my chest to stifle her moans as she came, her pussy soaking my fingers, my hand, her weight fully supported by me as her body gave out. She sighed, her breathing short, her eyes wet and dark when she turned them up to me. I wrapped my arms around her, smiling, victorious.

"I hate you," she murmured, closing her eyes when I claimed her mouth for the kiss I took, triumphant again.

"I'm not hungry."

"But you are stubborn," I said to Lucia, leaning in closer. "You're eating. Choose something, or I'll choose for you."

She glared but acquiesced. "Fine. I'll have the mushroom ravioli."

"Ravioli it is," the waiter said, giving me a look and taking our menus.

Once the clothes had been paid for, Lucia had dressed in the black backless dress, and we'd headed to a small Italian restaurant for dinner.

"I can't show my face at Nordstrom again. You know that, right?"

"No one saw your face," I said, winking, as I picked up a piece of bread and dipped it into a bowl of olive oil.

"You make me so mad!"

I chewed on the bread. "They have the best olive oil. You know, it's made from their own olives from their groves in Tuscany."

She took a piece of bread and violently dipped it before biting off a chunk, then sat back and gave me a look. "Did you wash your hands?"

I laughed so hard I nearly choked, and the patrons at the

tables around us turned to stare. "I like the way you taste," I said, reaching under the table and sliding one hand up the inside of her thigh.

"You're terrible!" She caught my hand and shoved it away.

"That's not what you were saying in the dressing room."

The waiter brought over the bottle of wine I'd ordered. Lucia dropped her gaze to her lap, her cheeks flaming red.

He popped the cork and poured. "It's fine," I said after tasting it. He filled Lucia's glass first, then mine. "There's nothing to be embarrassed about," I said to her after the waiter left and we picked up our glasses.

"I just had a very loud orgasm in the fitting room at Nordstrom."

I smiled and shrugged a shoulder. I knew this resistance was in part due to her anxiety over my father's birthday party. "You're probably not the first," I teased, then gave her a wink and decided now was a good time to change the subject. "Your niece is cute."

She studied me, slowly sipping from her glass. "She is."

"You're close with your sister?"

"I was. Before...everything."

"What do you think of her moving into your father's house?"

"I'm glad she's moving in there. I don't know if I'm ready to sell it. And I'm glad she's staying nearby."

"Why didn't you see each other while you were at school? You could have. Nothing was forbidden."

She shrugged a shoulder. "You mean like when Marco was standing over us when she came to visit me at the house?"

I gave her my most patient smile. "You didn't want to."

"You don't know me or my family."

"I'm trying to get to know you. Just because you haven't been in touch with them doesn't mean you can't start again. They're your family."

"What about your brother? Are you close?"

"With Dominic?" She nodded. "No. Dominic is...not good."

"But you were close with Sergio?"

"Yes. Very."

Neither of us spoke until the waiter interrupted with our dishes. Once he left, Lucia looked at me.

"I'm sorry I didn't talk to my father before he died. I should have told him I forgave him."

"Do you? Forgive him, I mean?"

She shrugged a shoulder. "I think he was backed into a corner. And you're wrong, he wasn't just saving himself. He gave me up to save all of them. You...your father had murdered—"

"I'm getting bored of this conversation. It was a war. Both sides lost many lives. You and I both know that."

She sighed and pushed ravioli around her plate.

"But you're right. Your father was backed into a corner."

"Thanks for that."

I nodded as I stuffed a forkful of salmon into my mouth. We ate in silence for a few minutes. Every time I looked at her, she'd have her eyes on her plate.

"Your sister isn't married?" I knew she wasn't and suspected what the man I'd assigned to follow her would come back with.

"No."

"If I may ask, who is Effie's father?"

She picked up a ravioli and turned her gaze fully to mine. "You're welcome to ask. You'd just have to ask her." Her mouth spread into a victorious grin.

"Touché."

"Salvatore," she started a moment later. "This party," she put her fork down and wiped her mouth, shaking her head. "I don't know if I can. He hates me, and I feel the same toward him. I don't even know why you're nice to me."

I reached across the table to touch her hand. "I'm not him, Lucia."

She looked at my hand covering hers. It was so much bigger than hers. It swallowed her up. It was almost a physical manifestation of my power over her: I could make her disappear.

"Look." I turned her hand around and traced the lines of her palm with my thumb. "We don't have a choice. We will go to that party. There's no *if* about it, not even for me. You and me...it could be worse. He could have kept you himself or given you to my brother. You don't want that."

I knew she understood by the way her face changed a little, becoming more hesitant, but her expression told me she trusted me, at least more so than any member of my family. It was a start.

"I'm not saying you have to be grateful for any of it, but neither of us have a choice. We just need to go, to get through it. Just do as I say, don't make waves. We'll eat dinner; I'll be beside you the whole time. Keep under the radar, and don't give him any reason to have to prove anything. He will not miss another opportunity, Lucia."

"So do as you say. We're back to that again."

She rolled her eyes, but it was all an act underneath which, she was afraid. "Look at me."

She did, reluctantly.

"I can only keep you safe from him if you do as I say."

"I'll try."

"Are you finished?"

Lucia nodded. She'd eaten half her plate, which was good enough.

"Then let's go." I tossed some bills onto the table and stood. "I want to give you a closer look at those things you found in my bedroom."

10

LUCIA

He didn't try to hide his amusement at my expression when he said that. And if he did it to get my mind off the discussion of the party, it worked because the entire way back, all I could think about was that.

Once inside the house, Salvatore kept his hand at my back and told Rainey and Marco to go to bed. We then went into the living room to grab a bottle of vodka before he led me upstairs to his bedroom.

"Are you still curious?" he asked once we were inside and he'd closed the bedroom door. Uncapping the vodka, he took a swallow then handed me the bottle. Watching him, I did the same, then coughed and handed it back. He chuckled and drank once more before setting the bottle on the nightstand. He dimmed the lights and stripped the bed of its comforter before turning back to me. "Are you?"

"Salvatore—"

He wrapped one arm around my waist and put his forefinger to my lips. "I want you, Lucia. My cock is aching to be inside your warm little pussy." He kissed me, and I yielded, my body already reacting to his touch, wanting him. Remembering how he made me feel. How he made me come.

His fingers touched my shoulders, and I felt the dress dragged down over my arms and to my waist, leaving my bared breasts pressing against his chest. Salvatore stopped for a moment, pulling back, his dark eyes making my nipples tighten. With one hand, he tugged his shirt over his head. I watched, desire hot in my core as I took him in, his body big, muscular, powerful.

Large hands found my hips as he neared to kiss me again, our eyes open. He pushed the dress down and off. Salvatore stepped back, and I watched him strip off his jeans and briefs, wetting my lips at the sight of his thick cock ready for me.

He sat down on the edge of the bed, reached for the bottle, and drank again. When he held it out to me, I shook my head. He put the vodka back on the nightstand and gestured to my panties.

"Off."

My pussy clenched. I slid my fingers into the waistband and slid them down and stepped out of them. Salvatore's eyes went to my pussy, a hunger in his gaze he did not try to hide.

"Come here." He pointed between his widespread legs.

I went to him, and he took my hands, holding me. "Birth control?" he asked.

I was confused for a moment. "Yes. I...I'm on the pill." I'd had heavy periods for years and used the pill to manage the pain.

He nodded, his mouth closing around a breast, suckling first then biting the nipple. I gasped, not sure if the pain or the pleasure was the dominant sensation as he drew it out, all while watching me. He repeated the same on the other breast, leaving each one wet, cool in the air-conditioned room.

"Have you ever had cock in your mouth?" he asked, pushing me to my knees.

I shook my head. I was a virgin, he knew that. Placing my hands on his thighs, I eyed his thick cock and licked my lips, preparing.

Salvatore placed one hand at the back of my head. "Lick."

He drew me forward, and I dragged my tongue over the wet tip, tasting the salty drops collected there. I looked up to find his eyes on me, watching me take him. He guided me down over his length, the skin of his cock soft against the hardness. It made me want, being like this, being made to kneel before him, to pleasure him.

"Good girl, now open your mouth."

He guided his cock into my mouth all the while our gazes remained locked on each other.

"That's good."

He moaned and closed his eyes as he pumped his length slowly in and out of my mouth.

"That's very good."

He stood, kept a tight grip on my hair, and held himself inside me.

"I like looking at you like this, Lucia, on your knees, your mouth stuffed full with my cock. You don't know how badly I want to fuck your face, come down your throat."

As he said the last part, he pumped deeper, making me choke, holding himself there, his fingers tight in my hair when I tried to pull back.

I gasped for breath, pushing against his thighs.

He smiled then pulled out a little.

"Again," he said.

He thrust in deep, calling forth tears from the corners of my eyes as I struggled only to have his grip tighten, hurting me. And when he repeated once more, going a little deeper, all the while smiling, watching me, I had the strange idea he liked my tears, my struggles.

"But I won't come down your throat tonight," he said, dragging me off him by my hair. "Hands and knees," he said, tossing me onto the bed. "Ass to me."

I glanced at him, wondering if I should be turned on by his rough treatment of me, knowing only that I was.

Once in the center of the bed on all fours, I looked over my shoulder, keeping my eyes on his. He looked me over and climbed on the bed behind me, his gaze on my ass, then my face. He reached for the leather cuff to my left and dragged it up onto the bed. Taking my wrist, he pulled my arm and bound it. He then moved to the other side and did the same so I lay with my face on the bed, my arms stretched out to either side, my ass in the air.

Salvatore moved behind me and knelt between my legs. He gripped my ass, spreading me wide.

"Look at me," he said.

I turned my cheek and watched, aroused, embarrassed, wanting. Something slid down my inner thigh. I knew it was my own arousal.

"You're dripping, Lucia."

He leaned his head down. His tongue must have caught the drop. He slid his tongue up all along my thigh until he reached my core.

I made some sound, momentarily burying my face in the mattress as he buried his in my pussy.

"I love to look at you like this, Lucia, all spread and open for me."

The rough scruff of his jaw scratched my tender flesh. He licked me, the tip of his tongue tickling my clit before dipping inside me. But before I could come, he straightened. I craned my neck to look at him again.

"And I love your sexy little asshole."

I tensed when his thumb pressed against it. "I'll fuck that hole too—"

When I protested, he grinned and pushed against the tight ring.

"When I want it, you'll give it to me. You'll get on your hands and knees just like you are right now, and you'll beg me to fuck your ass."

My mewling had his grin widening.

"But don't worry. That's not tonight. Tonight, I want to bury my cock inside your pussy. I'll go slowly at first, but what I want, Lucia, is to pound into your cunt until I feel your very center. Until you beg me to stop and beg me for more all at once. Until you scream my name."

I arched my back, biting my lip, wanting his hands on me, his mouth on me. Wanting him inside me.

"Make me come, Salvatore," I begged, my body shuddering at my request.

"You want it hard, don't you?"

"Mmm."

"Your first time, though?"

He knew that, though he still asked the question while rubbing his cock along my folds. His heat, his hardness, the softness of bare flesh on bare flesh. It all made my eyes roll to the back of my head.

"Yes."

"Are you scared?"

"No."

"Maybe I like you a little scared, Lucia."

The dark whisper made me shudder.

"Maybe I like to hold you down and fuck you hard while you scream. Maybe it turns me on." He lined himself up between my legs. "Keep your eyes on me. I want to watch you."

I nodded, swallowing as the head of his cock pressed against my entrance. "Maybe a little scared." My voice came out hoarse.

"Fear makes your cunt drip."

He pushed in then, more slowly than I expected, stretching me, the invasion feeling strange, my skin too tight, but as he moved in and out of me, I relaxed, closing my eyes, feeling. And it felt good.

"Eyes, Lucia."

I opened them, watching him, his face, as he rocked inside me, going a little deeper, taking more of me, pressing against a barrier that had my eyes go wide. I tried to rise, but he rubbed my back.

"Shh. Keep your eyes on me. It will only hurt for a minute. Then you'll be begging me to fuck you hard."

I fisted my hands, trying to pull my arms into myself. Salvatore leaned over my back, stretching his arms over mine, his cock lodged inside me.

"I want to feel all of you," he whispered, moving slowly. "I want to feel your tight cunt squeeze my cock." He pulled out, then rolled his hips, going deeper. "I want to feel the warmth of your virgin blood."

He thrust then, making me cry out.

"I want to hear you cry out. I like it."

Another thrust, harder this time.

"I like feeling you come."

He slid one hand beneath me, trailing it over my breast, belly, finding my clit. "Oh, G—"

"Hard and soft. I want to fuck you raw."

He withdrew entirely, then pounded into me, kissing my shoulder, then biting it, his breath ragged.

"I'm going to come," I managed, his cock inside me hitting just the right spot, his fingers rubbing my clit hard; It was all too much: too much feeling, too much sensation, too much *him*.

Hearing his labored breathing, feeling him swell even thicker inside me, it overwhelmed me. Moments later, I came, my cry sounding foreign, Salvatore's thrusts harder, faster. I felt raw, like he said, but all I wanted was him inside me, on top of me, having me, his fingers working, making me come.

"Fuck."

It was more of a grunt, and then he stilled, his cock twitching, releasing, filling me. I watched his face from the corner of my eye, his eyes so dark, they were black, and when he stilled, he collapsed on top of me, flattening me to the bed. His cock softened and slowly slid out. A rush of cum spilled over my thighs as he held me there, his face on my back. He undid the cuffs at my wrists before curling one hand possessively over the curve of my hip and kissing me gently at neck and shoulder until my eyes closed and I drifted off to sleep in his arms.

11

SALVATORE

Growing up, I'd loved coming to the house in the Adirondacks, but that felt like a hundred years ago. Now, as we neared the property, Lucia sat beside me in the car, everything about her tense. She looked beautiful in the cream-colored dress I'd chosen, her auburn hair piled high on her head, dark eye makeup accenting the almond shape of her whiskey-colored eyes.

I touched her knee as we pulled up to the security gate.

She startled.

"You'll be fine. I'll stay with you."

She nodded, but the tension kept rolling off her.

I hated this. Knew as I waved to the guard and pulled around back to the garage that she was here to be shown around, shown off, a token of my father's—of my family's—triumph. I also knew my father had not forgotten what she'd done at the funeral. He would punish her for it, and I had a feeling he'd do it tonight.

I just needed to keep her reined in nice and tight. After parking the car, I climbed out and met Lucia on her side.

"I feel sick."

I slid her hand inside mine and squeezed. "You'll be fine. Just breathe."

We were barely inside the front door when a woman's voice called out my name. It was Dalia, Roman's wife.

"Salvatore. There you are. I wasn't sure I'd see you tonight."

She leaned in, and I kissed her on both cheeks, as expected.

"Dalia," I said. I never called her Aunt Dalia. It didn't fit, not when she was only two years older than me. My uncle liked younger women.

She turned eager eyes to Lucia, who stood stiff beside me.

I introduced them. "Lucia, this is Dalia, my uncle Roman's wife. You've...met him." Shit. She'd met him five years ago on the day she'd signed the contract.

Luckily, she didn't register and only gave a faint shake of her head.

"Lucia *DeMarco*, isn't that right?"

Dalia could be a bitch but it only seemed to strengthen Lucia.

"Yes, that's right. Lucia DeMarco," she annunciated her last name slowly, standing up taller, her smile conquering, telling anyone who dared question that she would not be a victim.

I respected her for that, but it also made me worry. If my father saw her weak, if he thought she'd been broken, at least a little, he might lay off.

Dalia clearly wasn't expecting Lucia's response. "Well, lovely to meet you," she managed before excusing herself.

"Be careful," I whispered to Lucia. She gave me a cocky raising of the eyebrows.

"What do you mean? I was simply confirming that she was right."

"Don't make waves, Lucia. Once this night is over, you won't have to see these people again."

"Fuck these people."

I squeezed her hand hard.

"Ow!"

My father's guests turned to us as we moved through the room, not one even trying to hide their interest in Lucia. I let go of her hand to grab two glasses of champagne from a passing server.

"Drink," I said, handing it to her.

She took it and swallowed a big gulp.

"We need to see my father. He's waiting for us, I'm sure."

She downed the glass.

"Be good. Do not antagonize him. Remember what we talked about."

"Fine."

My father stood at the end of the room beside the fireplace. I knew he'd seen us, but he didn't let on and remained in a relaxed conversation with Roman and two other guests. But before we reached him, Dominic stepped into our path, his eyes hungrily sweeping over Lucia, making me wrap a hand around the back of her neck.

She was mine.

"Dominic," I said.

He dragged his eyes away from Lucia, the glimmer of fun disappearing the moment they met mine.

"Salvatore." He turned to Lucia again. "I don't think I've formally met the beautiful Lucia DeMarco."

Lucia shrunk into my hold. Dominic held out his hand to shake hers. It took her a moment, but she extended hers.

"Dominic," Lucia said.

I don't know why but I liked the fact that she didn't say it was nice to meet him.

"Dad's waiting for you. He's peeved you're late."

He took a sip of his beer, his eyes still on Lucia, who looked around the room, defiantly meeting the eye of every man and woman who glanced her way.

"Is he? Better not keep him waiting any longer, then. Excuse us." I made a point of knocking my shoulder against his and guided Lucia toward my father, who now watched our approach. His gaze, like Dominic's, traveled the length of her. It made my skin crawl.

I leaned down to whisper a reminder in Lucia's ear. "Behave."

She didn't reply but kept her eyes locked on my father's.

"Well, well," Franco Benedetti started, checking his watch. "Glad you could make time for us, Salvatore."

"Traffic," I lied, hating how whenever I was around him, I felt like a kid again, that eager–to–please child who never could. He didn't reply to my lie but turned to Lucia, appraising her dress.

"So nice to see so much more of you today than at the funeral," he said to her.

Her hands fisted at her sides, and I squeezed her neck in warning. Even though she tried to hide it, I knew she feared my father. It was just that her hatred of him overrode that fear.

"Another year of your life over," Lucia said, looking at the server who'd just appeared with a fresh tray of champagne. "I'll drink to that."

My father fumed. I stood uncomfortably by her side, wanting to shake her. To ask her what part of *behave* she didn't understand.

I heard Dominic's chuckle behind me. Roman placed a hand on my father's shoulder.

"Well, since my son has finally graced us with his presence, let's have dinner."

My fingers tight around the back of Lucia's neck, I held her while my father disappeared into the dining room. I took her into a corner of the hallway and turned her to face me, held her by the arms, and shook her once.

"If you don't want me to take my belt to your ass here and now, shut the fuck up, understand? Do *not* goad him. He is not a man for you to fuck with. He *will* retaliate."

"You're hurting me."

I looked at my hands wrapped so tight around her arms my knuckles had gone white. I released her, turned away, and ran a hand through my hair. I plastered on a fake smile when someone passed by.

"Why does he have power over you? Why do you care what he thinks?" she asked.

I spun around to face her, making her stumble backward. "Not here. Not now. Just keep your mouth shut. Am I clear?" I squeezed that last words out, desperate. We just needed to survive this dinner. She could go to our room, then, and we could leave early the following morning. But how many nights like this would we have to survive? And what would happen if she didn't do as I said, and she did goad him into action? What would he do?

Take her from me.

Take my place from me.

Give it all to Dominic.

She had no idea what she was doing.

"Let's go," I said.

Her gaze stabbed me, as if by forcing her in there, I was betraying her. In a way, I was. Because I was a coward, I was. But this was the only way.

Twenty-eight sets of eyes turned to us as we entered the dining room, my father's flat gaze locked on Lucia who, for once, didn't challenge him with her own. Instead, she kept her eyes on the intricate patterns of the fresco on the far wall, probably wishing she could disappear into it.

Alice in Wonderland. My mother had loved the story, and my father had surprised her with the fresco. Tenderness was not a trait I associated with my father, but he'd felt it. For her, at least. It was almost as though I never knew that version of Franco Benedetti, though, and in a way, it was sad.

My father pulled out the chair beside him. "Lucia."

Fuck. The only other empty seat stood at the foot of the table, as far from her as physically possible.

Lucia's footsteps dragged, and I had to nudge her forward. As the guests watched, I sat her down between my father and Dominic and, hands fisted, I walked to the empty chair and took it. Lucia's eyes met mine, and I burned my warnings in the look that passed between us, knowing she'd heed none of them.

Servers began to pour wine, and conversation flowed. I watched the lecherous eyes of both my brother and father consume her. She remained between them, eyes on her plate, her face tense as she pulled her arms tighter to herself. I'd come to know those little things she did, small physical movements she may not have been aware of herself, to protect herself. To hide away. Perhaps willing herself to disappear.

I felt powerless as course after course was served. I ate a few bites from each plate, forcing myself to join in the conversation or at least smile and pretend to be listening, but all I could do was watch her. She refused to eat a bite of food but drank glass after glass of wine and, after a glare in my direction, finally turned her attention to Dominic. He gave me a grin and brushed his fingertips over her shoulder.

I fumed, nearly breaking the stem of the wineglass I held. Clearing my throat, I stood and, with my knife clinking against the crystal of the glass, called everyone's attention.

"A toast."

Everyone picked up their glasses. Everyone except Lucia.

"To my father on his birthday."

We waited, the room silent as my father watched her, his fury visibly increasing. I willed her to pick up her glass, to take one last fucking sip, before I could excuse us and take her away, but she wouldn't do it. She was too stubborn to save her own damn neck.

"Happy birthday," I said, hoping to draw attention back to me. "And many more, father."

Everyone joined in, wishing him many more, and, after a moment, my father turned to me, acknowledged my toast with a raising of his glass, and drank, our gazes locked, his angry, dark, and foreboding.

He stood. The guests put knives and forks down and wiped their mouths, rising too. Lucia remained as she was. At least she knew to remain seated. As if the guests understood, they cleared the dining room quietly so only my father, brother, Lucia, and I remained. A server closed the doors.

"Punish her," he said, spitting the words. "Make it good, or I'll do it for you."

A grin played along Dominic's lips. I nodded once. Dominic and my father left the dining room. I looked at Lucia sitting there, her face insolent, her eyes the only part of her betraying her fear.

I took my jacket off and hung it over the back of a chair, then loosened my tie, unbuttoning the top buttons of my dress shirt before it choked me. All the while, my eyes remained locked on hers. I walked toward her, rolling my right shirt sleeve up as I went. I wondered if she knew what was coming, what had to happen now. Why the room adjacent to ours became suddenly so quiet, as if there wasn't an audience just beyond the doors to bear witness.

I reached for the buckle of my belt and undid it.

That was when she understood. She made to rise, but I was too close and caught her halfway up.

"Make this easy on yourself," I whispered, wondering if those in the other room heard the swoosh of my belt as I yanked it from its loops, pulled her up out of her chair, and pushed her to bend over the table that had yet to be wiped down.

"Salvatore," she began.

"Quiet." I shoved her dress up to her waist. She struggled, but I held her flat and pushed her panties down so they slipped from her hips and pooled around her ankles. "Count yourself lucky that he closed the doors."

"You can't mean to..."

I gripped a handful of her hair and leaned down close to her ear. "One fucking sip. You could have been drinking to his death for all I cared, but you couldn't do it. Now, you pay."

I straightened, keeping one hand on the flat of her back while I swung with the other, the sound of leather striking flesh coming instantaneously with the sharp intake of her breath.

"He'll require more than that," I said, lashing her again. "And forgive me, but so will I."

I whipped her hard, knowing I had to, wanting to beat her for her stupidity, her inability to keep one fucking promise. Knowing if I didn't, he would. Or, worse, he'd let Dominic do it while I watched.

It took nearly thirty strokes, her screams becoming hoarse as she wept, lashing my heart as I lashed her flesh, hating myself, hating her for making me do this. Hating him, hating my father for his power over me. For the power I allowed him to have.

I only stopped when the quiet on the other side of the door grew into a soft murmur and the sound of silverware on dishes told me cake had been served. The vultures had been sated or perhaps had grown bored. I hated them all, but hated myself most of all.

When I lifted my hand from her back, she remained as she was, bent over the table, her dress hiked up to her waist, her ass bare. I adjusted the crotch of my pants before sliding the belt through the loops and buckling it. Red welts crisscrossed her ass and thighs, and when I placed the flat of a palm over her hip, heat throbbed against my hand.

I squeezed.

She mewled.

I picked up her panties and pocketed them before lifting her to stand. The skirt of her dress dropped to her ankles, covering her. I turned her to face me and held her tight to me as she wept into my chest, fists pounding against me. Hiccups interrupted her sobs, and I lifted her into my arms and, ignoring the stares of the waitstaff as I carried her up to our room from the server's stairs, I locked the bedroom door behind us. I sat on the bed, cradling her in my lap, refusing to let her go even as she fought me.

"I warned you."

She pounded her fists into my chest, trying to free herself, tears streaking her face black with mascara.

"You liked it!" she screamed as the evidence of my arousal stabbed her hip.

"I didn't like hurting you."

"You're hard, you prick! You liked it just fine!"

"I can't deny the fact I'm aroused." One corner of my mouth quirked upward. "But you deserved that one."

"I hate you!" She clawed her fingernails down the side of my face.

I flipped her onto the bed, gripped her wrists and spread them wide, straddling her hips. "I fucking warned you. You have only yourself to blame!"

"They all heard!"

"That was the point. Humiliation. You're lucky he didn't demand the doors stay open!" During her struggle, her dress had shifted, exposing one breast.

"Let me go! Don't look at me!"

She renewed her struggle, pissing me off when she tried to line her knee up with my crotch. I transferred her wrists into one hand and held them over her head.

"I can look at you whenever I want." Gripping the V neck of the dress, I tore it down, the fabric giving way, the sound of it ripping somehow satisfying.

The harder Lucia fought against me, the harder my cock grew.

"I hate you!" she cried again.

I crushed my lips over hers, and for a moment, she stilled, maybe surprised.

I broke the kiss. "No, you don't." I kissed her again. I undid my pants, slid between her legs, and pinched her nipple with my free hand. "You make me crazy." My words came out angry. I pushed one of her legs open wider and then pulled back to look at her. She watched me, her hands clenched into fists. I lined my cock up at the entrance of her sex. "You drive me fucking insane."

I thrust in hard.

She grunted, her eyes locked on mine in defiance.

"Fuck you."

I thrust again, then again. "Fuck me." I wouldn't last long, but her wet cunt told me she wanted this too. "Your cunt is greedy."

"Harder," she gasped, hoarse from screaming.

"Fuck." I did what she said, fucking her harder, watching her, not feeling like I had had nearly enough of her.

Easing my hand off her wrists, I brought both hands to her face. We were both panting. I pushed the hair that stuck to her forehead away and held her, lost in those eyes that now burned a fiery amber. Her mouth opened, and I kissed it, so close now.

"What are you doing to me?"

"What?" she asked, puzzled.

I must have said it aloud. Lucia's hands gripped my shoulders, her face getting that expression it did just before she came. I loved seeing her like this, watching her in those moments just before her release, her face as she let go. It was the single most arousing thing, that.

"I hate you," she whispered, her nails digging into my shoulders, my neck. She squeezed her eyes shut, coming. "I do."

"Lucia."

Her pussy throbbed around me, and as she came, so did I, stilling deep inside her, filling her, feeling like—for the first time since that goddamned contract—I'd claimed her. Like she was mine. She was well and truly mine.

12

LUCIA

I looked at the window. Sunlight filtered through the crack between the curtains. I blinked, confused for a moment, but the soreness between my legs and on my ass quickly reminded me of where I was.

The clock beside the bed read 7:04 a.m.

I dragged the silk sheet up over my naked body, sat up, flinched, and lay back down. Beside me, the empty pillow lay sideways. I touched it, leaned over and buried my nose in it, then reared back and shook my head.

What the *hell* was I doing?

He'd whipped me, humiliated me, then fucked me.

I'd come.

I'd begged him to fuck me harder.

I hated myself.

No, I hated him. I needed to remember that.

Why was it so hard to remember that?

I got out of bed and went into the bathroom. He must have showered recently. Steam still fogged up the corners of the mirror, and the scent of his aftershave hung in the air.

I found I liked it, felt somehow comforted by it.

The devil you know. That's all that was. I knew Salvatore. I knew his limits.

Fuck. I was fooling myself.

I used the bathroom, not surprised to find blood between my legs even though I wasn't having my period. He'd fucked me raw, like he said he would.

And you'd come.

I turned my back to the mirror, the dark, crisscrossed welts reminding me to hate him. To see him for what he was: a Benedetti. My enemy.

I touched the raised marks, pressed against them, forced myself to remember that he was my fucking enemy. I could not let myself trust him, let myself depend on him. He would hurt me. Wasn't this evidence of that?

This strange emotion—no, it was not emotion. Only confusion. I felt confused, but who wouldn't be if they were me? Isolated from family and under the *care*—more like under the thumb—of Salvatore Benedetti, I needed him for everything. Every fucking thing. And that was why I had any feeling for him whatsoever. Maybe it was a form of Stockholm Syndrome. I mean, this may not be a traditional kidnapping, but it wasn't like I was here by choice. Not my choice, anyway.

I turned on the shower and stepped under the hot stream. I wanted to scrub his touch from me. Wanted to scrub the memory of my reaction to him from my mind.

He'd fucking whipped me, and I'd begged him to fuck me.

I scrubbed my hair with shampoo and my body with soap, gritting my teeth when the hot water hit my ass. When I was finished, I climbed out and dried off. I wanted to be out of here. I'd only been told I had to stay the night. Not any longer. But what if his father made me stay? What if Salvatore had already gone? And left me behind.

Panicked, I hurried into the bedroom, found my cell phone in my purse, and dialed Isabella's number.

"Hello?"

"Izzy?" I was sure I'd woken her. "I'm calling too early. I'm sorry."

"No, no, it's okay. How are you?"

"I don't know. I'm in Franco Benedetti's house in the Adirondacks."

"What?"

Well, that woke her up. "I had to come. It was his birthday. We were required. I just..."

"Are you okay, Luce?"

I only heard concern in her voice now. I felt my eyes heat up, but I blinked hard. I didn't need tears. I hated weakness. Hated it! "I—"

The door opened then, and Salvatore walked inside carrying two mugs of coffee. I sighed in relief.

"Lucia, what's happened?" Isabella asked, likely having heard the sigh.

Salvatore looked at me quizzically and closed the door. He wore a pair of jeans and a T-shirt, his usual uniform, and he'd slicked back his dark hair. He mouthed the word, *Okay?*

I turned away.

"Never mind, I'm fine," I said to Izzy. "I thought he'd left me here," I whispered, hoping Salvatore wouldn't hear.

I heard a male voice asking what was going on in the background.

"Who is that?" I asked.

Isabella sighed. "No one. I'm getting up to come get you now."

"No, it's okay," I said, turning to find Salvatore sipping his coffee, watching me. "He's not going to leave me here," I said, the comment more a question to Salvatore.

He shook his head.

"I'll call you once we're home. Uh, I mean, back at his house." Fuck. What the hell was wrong with me? "I have to go."

"You're sure?"

"Yeah. Sorry to have called so early, sis."

"You're fine. You can call me anytime, day or night, understand?"

I nodded. "Thanks. Love you." I hadn't said that in more than five years.

There was a pause. "Love you."

I disconnected the call and slid the phone into my purse. "I thought you'd left me here."

"I wouldn't do that to you. Come here."

I went to him.

"You okay?"

I shrugged a shoulder, dropping my gaze to shield my eyes. Why did his asking make me feel so fucking needy? Why did him taking me into his arms make me want to sob? Because that's what it did. That's what having his arms around me right now, like he would keep me safe forever, even after last night, that's what they did. They made me want to weep.

The last time he'd held me like this, I'd pulled away. This time, I didn't. I let myself melt into him. Neither of us spoke. I squeezed my eyes shut against his chest, feeling confused and hurt and vulnerable and so fucking grateful he was here. None of it made sense.

"Can we go?" I asked when I could speak without crying.

He pulled back and looked at me, his thumb wiping away some of the moisture around my eyes. "Not yet. I need to go down to breakfast, but I'll make an excuse for you. Get packed. We'll leave as soon as possible."

I nodded and went to sit on the bed but stood again as soon as my ass made contact.

"Lucia?"

I looked at him.

"Does it hurt?" His face told me he knew it was a stupid question.

"What do you think?"

He studied me, his forehead furrowing. He at least had the decency to look away for a moment.

"If it means anything, I didn't want to punish you on my father's order."

"But you did."

"I'm trying to tell you I'm sorry."

"Sometimes sorry isn't enough, Salvatore."

He stood there a moment, his eyes on mine. "Get packed. We'll leave as soon as we can."

He walked out the door and left me standing there in my towel.

His absence filled the space as soon as the door closed, and I hugged my arms around my belly, feeling more alone now than ever. But I forced myself to move. To get dressed. And as much as I hated it, to go down the stairs and face Franco Benedetti head-on.

I couldn't hide, I wouldn't. If I did, it showed that he'd won. That he'd shamed me, and I was hiding from him, afraid of him. Well, the latter was true, but I'd be damned if I'd let that fear get the better of me.

I dressed, packed my things, and pulled my wet hair into a bun before dabbing concealer under my eyes. I picked up my purse and walking out into the hallway. I paused, finding a staircase at either end. I looked over the banister, but all was quiet down below. I chose the stairs to my right and headed down, heard a door open and Salvatore's voice coming from it. I followed his voice, steeling my spine as my heart raced and my belly flipped.

I would not let Franco Benedetti win. I would not.

I reached the door and would have turned the knob but Franco's raised voice made me pull my hand away.

"You know what I expected of you!"

"I would not parade her through that room full of pariahs! She was humiliated enough! This is done. She's mine. I choose!"

Something pounded. I imagined a fist and a table. Was it Salvatore's? Was he defending me?

Then came Franco's laughter. Quiet at first, menacing, slowly growing louder, almost manic. Someone clapped his hands.

"My son, he finally grows some balls."

I fisted my hands, inhaling tightly.

"Fine, Salvatore. She's *your whore*. But remember, I gave her to you. I can as easily take her back. Take care of Luke DeMarco before there are any more supporters. One week, or Dominic will do it. I'm finished with him."

What? What did he mean, take care of Luke?

But then I heard footsteps, heavy and moving fast, and I charged toward the stairs. I bolted up then and ducked down behind the banister. Franco Benedetti stalked out of the room, his face tight with anger, his hands fisted at his sides.

I scurried back to the bedroom and closed the door, thinking, trying to make sense of it all. Should I call my sister and warn her about what I'd heard? Warn Luke? Or should I try to find out more first? See if Salvatore would tell me anything?

When a quick knock came, I jumped up, thinking it was Salvatore and that we could go. The door opened, but it was Dominic who stepped inside. He looked me over, his gaze odd, almost curious, but he remained at the entrance of the door.

"Hey," he said casually. A smile curved his lips upward, his voice sounded almost sweet. Too sweet. "I wanted to see if you were okay. My brother can be a brute and, to be honest, it sounded like he wasn't holding back last night."

I flushed. Was he talking about the whipping or the sex or both?

"I...I'm fine." I faltered.

He nodded and stepped inside. I didn't like him, didn't like the way his eyes shifted around the room and over me.

"I'm glad." Again, his voice soft, his smile gentle. "If you ever need anything"—he grabbed a card out of his pocket—"this is my private number."

"I don't—"

"Just take it and hope you never have to use it. Like I said, my brother can be very physical. Brutal even. I've seen what he's done before, Lucia. I've cleaned it up."

What?

When I made no move, he closed the space between us, took my hand, turned it over, and pressed the card into my palm.

"What the fuck are you doing in here?"

I jumped at Salvatore's sudden appearance, but Dominic only gave him a smirk and picked something out from under his fingernail.

"Just checking in on Lucia. Since she wasn't feeling well and all. She looks good to me, though, considering."

"Get the fuck out of here, Dominic."

Dominic shrugged a shoulder and glanced back at me after taking a step toward the door.

"If you ever need anything, Lucia..."

"She won't be needing anything from you."

Salvatore stalked toward me, the look in his eyes chilling me as he squeezed my wrist and took the card from my hand. He didn't look at it. Didn't need to, I guessed.

Dominic walked out the door. Salvatore kicked it shut behind him, his hand still gripping my wrist.

"You're hurting me, Salvatore."

Anger, frustration, I don't know what it was, but whatever he was feeling, it rolled off him and slammed into me.

"It seems that's all I can do." He dropped my wrist. "We're leaving." He grabbed the suitcases and walked into the hallway.

I followed him out of the bedroom, wanting to be away from this house most of all, yet fearing Salvatore. Uncertain now if would save me or destroy me.

We didn't run into anyone as we left. Salvatore's car waited just outside the front doors. The man who must have brought it around handed him the keys. Salvatore loaded the bags into the trunk and opened my door, not waiting for me to get in before he moved around to his side. He was clearly as anxious as I to leave.

We didn't speak for the first twenty minutes of the ride back. Salvatore's tension literally rolled off him.

"Dominic will fuck with you. You're not to have anything to do with him, understand?" He didn't look at me but kept his eyes on the road.

"Is that an order?"

That made him turn his head toward me. "Yes."

"Or what, you'll whip me again? Doors open this time?"

His grip on the steering wheel tightened, his knuckles going white. "Don't push me, not now."

"What the hell happened back there?" His face tightened even more. "I heard, Salvatore. I heard you stand up for me. I heard your father lose his shit."

"Then you didn't learn your lesson about snooping."

"I wasn't snooping. I was coming down to have breakfast, show my face. Show him he hadn't won."

Salvatore snorted and shook his head, the smile that appeared on his face sad. "You don't get it, Lucia. He always wins."

"I told you before, everyone loses sometime."

"Not Franco Benedetti."

There was such a weight to him, to his words, that it made me sad. Just sad. But I needed to ask one more question. I needed to know one more thing.

"He said something about taking care of Luke."

Salvatore gave me a sideways glance. He didn't answer my question, but he sure knew how to distract me.

"I'm going to let you out of your contract. Once all is said and done, and I'm boss, you'll be free, Lucia."

13

SALVATORE

I couldn't win. No one could. What I said to her, I meant it. Franco Benedetti would win. And everyone else would lose.

Lucia went straight to her room when we got back to the house, and I shut myself up in my study. She hadn't talked to me the entire ride. Probably pissed at me, which I expected. I would deal with that later, though, because as soon as I booted up my laptop, I saw an e-mail from Roman regarding Luke's activities.

Luke had been busy indeed, meeting with various members of the Pagani family in the tristate area. We knew that, though. That wasn't new. It was the next part that intrigued me.

He was spending his nights in Isabella DeMarco's bed.

That's why it so surprised me to learn that I was wrong. That he wasn't Effie's father.

But that wasn't the strangest thing. In fact, what I saw made zero sense.

I picked up the phone and dialed Roman, but before he could answer, the door burst open. Lucia stood in the doorway, looking pissed off.

"So are you just going to lock yourself up in here and not talk to me at all?" She walked inside. "Because you're giving me fucking whiplash."

I put the lid of my laptop down just as Roman answered the phone. "Let me call you back." I got up and closed the door. "You ever hear of knocking?"

"What the hell is going on, Salvatore? What happened this morning? You were fine. We were fine. Then you had that breakfast meeting, and I don't know. It's like you keep pulling the fucking rug out from under me!"

"I told you, I'll give you your freedom as soon as I can. I thought you would want that."

"This isn't about that. You can't just throw that out there. And besides, how long until you're boss? And what if you change your mind?

I resumed my seat behind the desk but pushed away from it and crossed one ankle over my other knee. "I won't."

That silenced her for a second. She just stood there surprised.

"If you want a fight, I'm not in the mood," I said. "Not now."

She shifted her weight and folded her arms across her chest. "How about the truth, then? Are you in the mood for that? What is the Luke DeMarco problem you have to take care of?"

I let my gaze run over her. She'd changed into a pale yellow sundress, and I could see she wasn't wearing a bra underneath. My balls tightened, but I steeled myself. Lucia was fast becoming a weakness. My weakness. I needed to stop this. I meant what I said, that I'd release her from her contract. I needed to take care that when the time came, she wouldn't look back.

The best way to do that was to be a dick.

I leaned forward and placed my elbows on the desk. "How's your ass, Lucia?"

"My ass is none of your concern."

"Show me."

"Screw you."

"You want to know about Luke DeMarco?"

She eyed me warily but nodded.

"Fine. He's stirring up trouble. A lot of it."

"What did Franco mean when he told you to take care of it?" she asked.

"You aren't surprised by what I just told you?"

She shrugged a shoulder. "We'll always be enemies."

That took me a moment to digest. I decided to push further, see how much she knew.

"Why exactly did your father disown your sister?"

"Because she got pregnant."

"Doesn't that seem strange to you? I mean, this is modern day. Women have babies out of wedlock and alone all the time."

She studied me. What did she know? Did Isabella confide in her? How much?

"I don't know. I guess my father was old-fashioned."

"Has your sister ever questioned it? How he was willing to lose her and his grandchild?" I asked.

"My father didn't exactly make the best decisions regarding either of his daughters, did he?"

"No, I guess you're right."

"Why are you asking?"

"Just curious. Why don't you go for a swim. It's nice out."

"Why are you pushing me away? I thought—"

She sat gingerly on the edge of the couch, and the fact that I'd caused her that hurt messed with me. Was she innocent? Or did she know more than she let on? And if Luke wasn't Effie's father, then who was?

"What did you think?"

"You said some things last night."

She shook her head then brought her hands to her face, rubbing it before looking at me again.

"I am so confused. I don't know what I'm supposed to feel. I don't know where I stand, and as soon as I think I understand something, understand you, you strike out then pull back again."

Watching her, I rubbed the back of my neck and loudly inhaled, then exhaled, realizing I couldn't be a dick. Not to her. She deserved better. "It's best if we keep our distance, Lucia." *I don't want to hurt you, and it seems it's all I can do.*

She studied me, and the look inside those wide eyes screamed confusion. I understood it. I understood her comment about the whiplash.

My phone buzzed on the desk, and I glanced at it, seeing a text from Natalie.

"I need you!"

What the...

"Salvatore?" Lucia called me back to the present.

"Go for a swim," I said, standing and patting my pockets for my keys.

"So that's it? Go for a swim?" She snorted, rising too.

Finding them, I heard the phone buzz again.

"Hurry, please!"

"I have to go."

"No!"

She rushed me, gripping my arms before I made it to the door.

"You can't just walk away from this. From me! You can't just leave me here like this! I have a right to answers!"

I pulled her hands away and sat her down roughly on the couch. "I have to go. When I come back, we'll talk. I'm sorry, but I can't right now."

"It'll be too late then!"

My mind was too full with Natalie's frantic messages for Lucia's words to penetrate. I bolted out of the house and to the car that still sat parked in the driveway. I didn't look back, just drove as fast as I could to Natalie's house.

14

LUCIA

I couldn't believe this. He'd just left, walked out! I'd really thought last night, after what had happened in the bedroom, the things he'd said, I thought he felt something. And even as I'd told him I hated him, I didn't. I'd held fast, refusing to let go.

I felt something for him.

Then this morning, when he'd defended me, didn't that mean something? And what about when he'd been so possessive when he'd seen Dominic in our room?

God, I was stupid.

His cell phone buzzed again, and I got up. He'd forgotten it in his rush. The latest text was on the screen.

"Are you getting my messages? I need you!"

The name of the contact read Natalie.

Natalie *needed* him?

And he'd dropped everything for her. In a fucking heartbeat, he'd dropped everything and run out of the house, not even remembering to take his cell phone with him!

Fine. That was fine. She was probably the reason he'd

release me from my contract. He didn't want me. I was a burden on him. He claimed not to have liked humiliating me last night, but he'd gotten hard doing it. He'd used me. He was getting off on it while he could. Probably cheating on Natalie while he was *forced* to keep me.

He made a fool out of me. I was a complete, fucking idiot.

He wanted Natalie? Fine. He could have her. He could fucking have her.

I walked into the bathroom that adjoined his study and dropped the cell phone into the toilet before I ran upstairs to my bedroom. I threw a few things into a duffel bag. I didn't care about anything anymore. I wasn't permitted to leave the grounds? I had to tell him where I was at all times?

He could go fuck himself. Or fuck her.

Fuck!

Flinging the duffel over my shoulder, I made my way to the garage. I knew they kept the keys to the cars there, and I'd seen the code Salvatore had punched into both the box that contained them and to open the gate yesterday. I was out of here. I was done.

Getting into a car was easy. Getting out of the garage easy. By the time I got to the gate, I saw Marco running down the driveway after me. I punched in the code to open the gate, but nothing happened.

"Shit."

I tried again, one eye on the rearview mirror as Marco's form neared. He ran fast.

I tried the code again, and again, nothing. I stopped, squeezing my eyes shut.

"Think. Think! You saw it yesterday!"

I tried again and exhaled in relief as the tall gates finally crept open, slow as fucking molasses. I inched the car forward, too aware of Marco just a few feet away as finally, finally, the gates opened wide enough that I hit the gas, the tires screaming against stones, kicking up dirt and rock and leaving him literally in the dust.

I grinned, seeing him pull his phone out and put it to his ear, no doubt trying to call Salvatore, tell him I'd broken one of his stupid rules. Too bad Salvatore's phone sat in the toilet.

That made me laugh.

I didn't calm down on the drive over to Isabella's house. The opposite, actually. What was the point of all of this? Why take me when he wanted someone else? Why?

Because daddy said he had to if he wanted to be boss.

This was so fucked up. Salvatore's father controlled him. He had to do what he did, or his father would take away what was his right. He'd give it all to Dominic. My life didn't matter. What I felt didn't matter.

Felt. No, I *felt* nothing. Nothing tender, at least.

But I was beginning to trust him.

The devil you know.

At least Salvatore's indifference to me kept me safe. Franco or Dominic, they would do worse things to me. Of that, I had no doubt.

So why did his indifference hurt me? What did I want?

Isabella's house looked empty when I got there. I pulled the car up in the driveway, far enough back that it wouldn't be visible from the street. I wondered if she kept the spare key where we used to in case we locked ourselves out. But as I walked down the long drive back to the house, I saw Isabella's face peer out of the kitchen window. I raised my hand in greeting, but she didn't wave. Her face grew worried. I saw her rush from the window and throw open the back door.

"Lucia?"

I fell into her arms, tears breaking loose, although I couldn't say exactly why. What would I tell her? How could I explain that

I was jealous and hurt? That after all the things he'd done to me, all the things they'd done to me, I wanted him. Because I did. I wanted Salvatore.

"What's wrong? What's happened?"

We walked inside and went right into the kitchen.

"Sit down."

She pulled a chair out and set a box of tissues in front of me. She busied herself making some tea, casting glances my way as I blew my nose and mopped my face, forcing deep breaths in and out, trying to get myself under control. Isabella set a fresh cup of tea in front of me and then took the seat across from mine, taking a sip from her cup.

"What's happened?"

How much should I tell her? I wasn't worried about her judging me. I just didn't want her to think me weak. Or worse, a traitor.

"I'm so confused." I shook my head, picked up the mug of tea, and stared into the swirling dark liquid.

"Did he hurt you?"

Yes. Oh yes.

I swallowed a sip of tea then faced my sister. "I think he's having an affair."

She looked surprised. "Why do you think that?"

"Because we were in the middle of a conversation when he got a text from someone named Natalie and bolted. He was in such a hurry he left his phone behind. I read one of the messages."

"What did it say?"

"For him to hurry. That she *needed* him."

Isabella checked her watch. I went on.

"He just left me there and walked out in the middle of a conversation!"

"Wasn't Natalie the name of his brother's wife?"

"What? Dominic's married?"

"No, Dominic's not married. Sergio."

"Oh." Shit, how had I not remembered that? "He's having an affair with his dead-brother's wife?"

"Why are you jumping to that conclusion? It could be anything."

"Are you defending him?"

She sat back and folded her arms across her chest. "I guess I'm trying to figure out why you care."

I would almost say there was something accusing in the gaze she leveled me with. I rested my elbow on the table and dropped my forehead into my hand. "I don't fucking know."

Isabella's chair scraped away from the table. She got up and went over to her phone on the counter. She typed in what I assumed was a text message then turned back to me. She leaned against the counter and studied me with a strange expression on her face before she walked back over to me and rubbed my back.

"It's natural, I guess, if you're stuck living with someone who basically holds your whole life in his hands, to develop some feelings for that person. You're not in love with him, though."

I shoved her hand away. "In love? Who said anything about being in love?"

She sat back down. "I'm just saying don't beat yourself up over it. Good riddance, and hope he *is* fucking his dead-brother's wife!"

"Izzy!"

"I'm sorry, that came out cold. The most important thing is that you're out of there. And you're not going back."

"Where's Effie?" I suddenly realized the little girl wasn't here.

"She went swimming with her best friend, and they were going to have dinner together after. I should go get her soon."

"You should have seen Marco's face when I drove away."

"I bet that was something."

"Izzy, I overheard something this morning at Franco Benedetti's house. I wanted to talk to you about it."

"What?"

"Salvatore and his father were talking. I'm not sure if Dominic was there or not, but I heard his father say something about taking care of Luke."

She didn't seem surprised by what I said.

"They know you're trying to stir things up, Izzy. You have to be careful."

"That's Luke. Not me."

"Well, then you need to tell him to be careful. What's going on with you and him, anyway? I saw how he looked at you at the church, and he was here the other day. Are you two having an affair?"

"An affair. It sounds so illicit." She picked up her teacup and dumped its contents into the sink. "You're caught up on this affair thing today, aren't you?" she asked, her back to me.

"Is he Effie's father, Izzy? Is that why Papa—"

She snorted and looked off to the side. "Luke is not Effie's father."

"Who is?"

She turned and met my gaze, her expression cooler. "It's not important. What is important is figuring out what we're going to do to keep you away from Salvatore."

Isabella's cell phone rang, and she eyed the display. "I have to take this. I'll be right back."

She walked out of the kitchen and into the living room, surprising me with her sudden secrecy.

"This isn't a good time," I heard her whisper. Then I heard my name before she hung up and returned to the kitchen.

"Who was that?"

"The mom who took Effie swimming."

"Oh. You could have talked to her."

"It's fine. She was just checking in. Are you hungry? I can make you a sandwich."

"No, I'm good. I think I'll go lay down if you don't mind."

"Of course, go ahead."

I stood, feeling this space between us, something strange that hadn't been there before. But then she walked over to me and hugged me.

"You'll be okay, sis. I won't let him hurt you. I'll take care of everything."

An unease settled over me as I made my way up to my old bedroom. Something in her tone or posture was off...wrong. I couldn't quite put my finger on it, though. Maybe it was nothing. Maybe it was the five years between us. She'd changed too, just like all of us. She'd grown a little harder. But maybe that was what she'd needed to do to survive.

AFTER A SHORT REST and a microwave dinner later in the evening, I'd gotten ready and gone to sleep in my old bedroom, the sinking feeling never leaving my stomach. It wasn't too much later when I woke to rain beating against the window and voices arguing. I sat up and glanced at the time on my phone. It was a little after midnight. The display showed eight missed calls, all from—surprise, surprise—Salvatore.

I guess he'd gotten home from Natalie's. Asshole.

I ignored the messages, got out of bed, and cracked the door open. The voices came from downstairs. It was Isabella and a man. Although I knew the voice, I couldn't place it. It didn't belong here.

"You promised me. I don't want him hurt!"

My sister sounded agitated.

"I'm placating. Relax."

"How the fuck can I relax? God, I wish this were over!"

I stepped out onto the landing and crept over to the stairs. Hearing the familiar creak on the third step, I froze, hoping they hadn't heard. They continued arguing.

"You need to go. You can't be here."

I suspected my sister didn't realize she was whispering that loud.

"I took care of what you wanted done. Don't I get a little reward?"

What you wanted done?

"I'm sure Salvatore will be here any minute. He's not stupid, he knows where she'd run to. Get out of here before he gets here."

Salvatore was coming?

"I parked a few blocks down. I'll duck into a room. No worries, babe."

Was that *Dominic*? Calling my sister *babe*?"

Tires screeched to a halt just outside the house. Headlights shone through the windows, and a car door slammed shut.

"Pussy whipped," the man said just as someone leaned on the doorbell.

I turned and ran into my room, pretending to just come out of it when I saw Izzy run to the door.

"Is that the doorbell?" I asked, not wanting her to know I'd overheard anything.

"Here we go," Izzy said.

I walked down the stairs. Izzy opened the front door.

A soaked and furious Salvatore stood just on the other side, his gaze fixed on me.

15

SALVATORE

"It's the middle of the night," Isabella said, standing in the doorway.

I looked over her shoulder and saw Lucia standing on the bottom step of the stairway. "I won't be long," I said, my eyes trained on Lucia. "I'm just here to collect what's mine." I then turned to Isabella. "Move."

"No."

"Move."

"I'll call the police."

"I own the police."

"It's okay, Izzy. Let him in."

Lucia stepped down from the stairs and folded her arms across her chest. She wore a short pink nightshirt that reached to just beneath her ass, and her hair looked like it did when she woke up: a beautiful mess.

"You don't have to listen to him," Isabella said, although she stepped aside.

Lucia's eyes were locked on mine.

"Get your things," I said to her.

"How's Natalie?"

"Natalie? That's why you left?" I'd gotten home to find my cell phone in the toilet. Had Natalie sent another text that Lucia had read? My phone was password protected, but the messages flashed and stayed on the screen for long enough that she wouldn't have needed the password.

Lucia stuck her chin out. She was jealous. She was fucking jealous.

I watched her, and the longer I did, the more nervous she became, shifting on her feet, biting her lip.

"Let's go home. We'll talk about it there."

"This is my home, Salvatore. I'm staying here."

I stepped toward her, dropping my gaze to her bare feet with their pretty pink toenails, before I took her arms and unfolded them. I attempted a smile. I'd been pissed when I'd gotten home to find out she'd run. Marco had tried to get hold of me, but all he'd been able to do was leave messages and assume I got them. But since my phone was in the toilet, I'd only found out about Lucia leaving when I got home around eleven at night.

But now, understanding why she'd run, I wasn't angry. I was surprised.

"You're coming with me," I said in a quiet whisper. I didn't care if her sister could hear or not. I also couldn't have cared any less what she thought of me. I'd talked to Roman about the DNA tests, and I was putting two and two together. "Your home is not here, not anymore. It's with me."

Lucia's eyes widened, and for a moment, I saw she wanted to believe, wanted to do as I said, but then Isabella cleared her throat.

"Luce, you don't have to do anything you don't want to do."

I glanced at her, feeling only disdain as things slowly fell into place, piece by piece. I turned my attention back to Lucia.

"I'll say it one more time. Get your things, and get in the car, or I will carry you out over my shoulder. But one way or another, you will be sleeping in my bed tonight."

I watched Lucia swallow and saw how her breasts tightened beneath the pink nightshirt.

She was turned on.

"What's it going to be?"

"Luce—"

I held a finger up to Isabella, not taking my eyes off Lucia. "This is between us."

Lucia stiffened, looking over my shoulder at her sister, then back at me, defiance in her gaze.

"You can't make me go."

I grinned. "I was hoping you'd say that."

She squealed, surprised I guessed, when I gripped her hips and heaved her over my shoulder, slapping her ass hard when she kicked her legs and pounded my back with her fists.

"I'm calling the police!" Isabella ran into the kitchen.

I ignored her and moved us out the door, sheets of rain soaking us both.

"Let me down!"

"I gave you a choice," I said, opening the passenger-side door and dropping her into the seat. She immediately tried to spring out, but I pressed her back with the flat of my hand against her chest. "You chose wrong." I clicked her seat belt and shut her door, locking it until I got into the driver's seat. I hit the gas, propelling us forward.

"You can't just...take me like that!"

"Put your seat belt back on." She'd unbuckled it. What did she think she'd do, jump out of a car going sixty miles per hour?

I made sure the door was locked just in case.

"I swear, Lucia, if I have to pull over to discipline you—"

"Slow down!" she screamed as I took a turn.

"Fasten your fucking seat belt."

"I hate you."

She fastened it as I merged onto the highway. "You say that a lot. Mostly when you're turned on."

"I'm not turned on!"

I glanced from her face to her nipples and back. "No, obviously not," I said, returning my attention to the road.

She covered herself with her arms. "You have no right, Salvatore."

"I have every right. You signed a contract."

"I was sixteen, and I had no choice!"

"And what's your choice now? Huh? Break it? Risk your family's safety?"

"You wouldn't hurt them."

I glanced at her again, some part of me glad she knew that. But I wasn't the only danger. "I may not, but others would."

"Are you going to threaten me with that for the rest of my life?"

I just shook my head and concentrated on the road. I had more important things on my mind at the moment. Like figuring out what the hell had happened that afternoon.

By the time we pulled inside the gates and up the drive, the silence between us hung like thick, impenetrable fog. Rain still poured down. Since the garage structure was separate from the main house, I parked as close to the front door as possible and climbed out. Lucia had already opened her door and sat measuring the distance between the car and the house.

"Your feet are bare. I'll carry you." I leaned in to lift her, getting soaked for the third time that night.

"I'm fine. Don't touch me."

"Stop fighting me. The stones will cut your feet." With one arm beneath her knees and the other at her back, I lifted her out.

"I said don't touch me!"

Just as I leaned to close the car door, she hoisted herself out of my arms and fell to her hands and knees with a grunt.

"Lucia!"

"Stay away from me!" She scrambled to her feet and made for the front lawn.

"Godamnit!" I chased her, although there wasn't anywhere for her to go. If it wasn't pouring down rain, I'd have left her to it. Although knowing her, she'd tear herself up, trying to climb over the gates.

She ran fast, but the slippery ground beneath her bare feet hindered her progress. She fell twice more before I finally caught up to her. When I wrapped an arm around her waist to haul her up, she kicked out, knocking my legs out from under me so that I fell on top of her.

"Leave me alone! Why can't you just *leave me alone*?"

She fought like a feral cat, scratching and kicking until I lay my full weight on her, caught both of her wrists, and trapped her beneath me.

"Stop! Stop fighting me!"

"I hate you. I hate you, and I will never stop."

I looked down at her, tears and rain soaking her face.

"You will stop."

"Why did you come for me? What do you want from me?"

"What do I want?" I looked at her face flushed with exertion, her mouth open to suck in gulps of air, her dark hair fanned out around her head, stuck to her face, soaked and dirty. "What do I want?" She jerked her body. I touched my forehead to hers, her eyes burning amber now. "This," I said, and kissed her.

She tried to say something, but whatever it was, I swallowed it up. Her soft wet lips yielded beneath mine. Even as she attempted to fight, her body gave itself over, her mouth surrendering. She made a small sound as I deepened the kiss, tasting her, pressing her harder into the earth, my cock like steel against her soft belly.

"I want this," I said, claiming her mouth again while I reached with one hand to take my cock out of my pants. Her nightie had already ridden up to midbelly. "This." I kissed her again, this time softer, on her lips, then her chin, her cheek. I wanted to see her face, her eyes. Slipping my fingers beneath her panties, I drew them aside. She bit her lips, watching me. "I want you." I thrust into her, and she arched her back, closing her eyes momentarily. "You." I drove in again, her tight pussy wet like a glove around my cock. "I want you, Lucia," I said finally, taking her wrists in my hands and pinning them out to her sides, watching her face as I fucked her, just a few more short, hard thrusts before she clenched around me, coming, making that sound she made, crushing my cock until I stilled, squeezing her wrists harder, coming, heart racing, not breathing until I'd emptied.

The rain slowed, finally, as if it matched our moods. I kissed her and slowly slid out, kneeling to zip my jeans before lifting her up. She let me this time. Let me carry her into the house and up to the second floor and through my bedroom to the master bath, where I ran the shower and placed her inside. I followed, still fully clothed, stripping first her and then myself beneath the warm flow of water.

"I want *you*, Lucia," I said yet again, pressing her back against the wall, kissing her. "As wrong as it is, I want you."

LUCIA LAY IN MY BED, the cuts on her knees and palms bandaged, warm beneath the covers. Safe in my arms.

"Natalie is my sister-in-law. Sergio's wife." She had her back to me, so I couldn't see her face. "She has a son who was at daycare while she worked her usual hours. When she got there to pick him up, he was gone. The daycare provider had fucked up, releasing Jacob to someone who claimed to be his uncle."

She turned her head to look at me, then shifted to lie on her back. I kept my arm over her belly, my hand closed possessively around her hip.

"She was frantic, as you can imagine."

"Did they find him?"

I nodded. "It was Dominic, I'm certain. He'd dropped him off at her parent's house but only after a couple of hours."

"Is Jacob okay?"

"He's fine now. He's only a year and a half, so he couldn't tell us much. Dropped off with an armful of toys and an ice-cream cone that had melted all over him. He apparently ran into his grandmother's arms and sobbed, calling for his mom."

"Why would Dominic do that?"

"To show he could." That's what pissed me off the most. This was the one thing that could terrorize Natalie.

"I can't imagine what Natalie must have felt."

I nodded. I'd never seen her like I did today, not even when she'd learned Sergio had been killed.

"I'm the only person she trusts, Lucia. I couldn't abandon her or my nephew."

"You should have told me."

"I know."

"I assumed... I thought she was your... That you were having an affair." She lowered her lashes, her face growing pink with embarrassment.

"I told you I wouldn't do that. The contract—"

"It doesn't say anything about that."

"I'm not interested in anyone or anything else at the moment, Lucia." The words *at the moment* made me pause. I wondered if she noticed them. "Don't worry. I will still release you from the contract when the time comes."

She grew quieter. "I'm tired."

I pulled her tight against my chest and rested my chin on top of her head. "Go to sleep."

LUCIA STILL SLEPT DEEPLY when I woke early the next morning. Kissing her softly on her forehead, I climbed out of bed and tucked her back in, then left a note, and drove to Dominic's house. He lived about forty-five minutes away. When I got there, I saw my father's sedan in the circular driveway. I wondered what he was doing here. If he was meeting with Dominic about the Luke DeMarco situation.

Stop being so fucking paranoid.

If it wasn't for Lucia, would I give a fuck if Dominic became the next boss? Would I care? Or would I take the opportunity and walk away? Although walking away wasn't really an option. Nothing in this life came that easy.

I shook it off. I needed to focus. Parking my car behind my father's, I walked to the front door, my anger from yesterday coming back white-hot as I approached. Lucia had tempered it. She'd cooled the anger, turned it into something else. She'd awakened a different side of me, one I'd tried to keep buried for a very long time. I'd always thought that part of me weak, but it was actually the opposite.

I rang the doorbell. A woman I'd only seen here twice before answered. As soon as she recognized me, I saw the momentary note of panic on her face.

"Mr. Benedetti, was Dominic expecting you?"

"No, it's a surprise visit." She seemed nervous and stood blocking the doorway.

"He's in a meeting, sir, and he said no interruptions."

"Did he?" I glanced behind her. A woman vacuumed the living room, but apart from that, the house stood still. "Well, I need to see him, so please step aside."

"I'm afraid I can't do that, sir."

"What's your name?"

"Patricia, sir."

"Patricia, I need to see my brother. I need you to step aside."

"Sir," she glanced behind her, clearly uncertain what to do. "I'm not supposed to..."

I smiled as wide as I could, feeling the gesture crinkle the corners of my eyes. "I'll take full responsibility, Patricia. Don't worry."

She hesitated, and I took advantage, nudging her out of my way as I entered the house. I went straight for Dominic's study located around back. A man stood at the door, but my presence clearly surprised him. I just grinned and walked right past him. I'd put my hand on the doorknob before I felt his hand fall on my shoulder.

I gave it a sideways glance, eyebrows raised, before meeting his gaze.

His eyes went wide, and the weight of his hand lessened.

He knew who I was. Good.

"Sir—" he started.

"Step back."

It took him a moment, and I didn't wait for him to decide. Instead, I turned the handle and pushed the door open to find Dominic, Roman, and my father sitting around the circular table inside.

They all turned at the interruption, my father and Roman surprised, Dominic furious.

"Isn't this cozy," I said, narrowing my eyes on Roman, the man I trusted most out of the three.

"I told you *nobody*!" Dominic roared to the man who'd stood guard and rose to his feet.

"Sir—"

The guard mumbled something, but I didn't care about that. Instead, when Dominic rounded the table, I pounced on him, grabbing his collar and dragging him backward until I had him pinned against the wall.

"What the—" my dad's voice came.

"Salvatore!"

Roman's shout registered, but all I could see were Dominic's eyes, the look in them both evil and proud, like the cocky prick he was.

He knew exactly why I was here.

"What did you want, taking Jacob?"

His grin widened. "Get your fucking hands off me."

"You scared the shit out of Natalie!"

"What's going on?" my father asked behind me.

"Nothing—" Dominic started.

"It's called fucking kidnapping, asshole!" I said before slamming him hard against the wall.

"Salvatore, get off him," Roman said, his voice the calmest of all. "Let him go."

"Yeah, Salvatore, get off me," Dominic mimicked Roman.

His face, his tone, they infuriated me. He didn't give a shit about anything or anyone. Not Jacob. Not Natalie, not anyone. "You fucking prick." I released him, and Dominic straightened, attempting to fix his collar, but as he did, I drew my fist back and struck his jaw so hard, his head slammed back into the wall, and he stumbled. "You don't even give a shit, do you?" I straightened him, and this time, drove my fist into his gut. "You don't give a shit about scaring that little boy. About scaring the crap out of your brother's wife."

It took three men and Roman to drag me off him, but before

they did, I'd landed one more punch on Dominic's jaw. He struggled to stand, his grin angry as he wiped blood from his lip.

"What the *hell* are you talking about, Salvatore?" my father demanded.

I noticed then how he stood back, watching, a weariness in his eyes.

"Why don't you tell him?" I said, fighting against the men who held me, watching Dominic, his expression pissed, bruises already coloring his face. "Tell him what you did."

"He's my nephew too."

"Fuck you, you've never cared about that."

"Enough!" My father's voice bellowed through the room. "Sit him down."

The men holding me shoved me into a seat and held me there. I watched my father stalk toward Dominic. I'd never seen him do that with him before.

"Did you hurt Jacob?" he asked, his tone low, threatening.

"I didn't hurt him. I took him toy shopping and bought him a fucking ice-cream cone!"

"You scared him. He's just a child. Your brother's son!" I said.

"Dominic?" my father asked, some of the color drained from his face.

I freed myself of the men who held me and stood. "I have just one message for you." My voice came low and deep. "Stay away from Natalie and Jacob, or God help me—"

"Dominic!" my father snapped.

I walked out, shaking out of the hold of one of Dominic's men. "I'm leaving. Keep your hands off me."

"Did you lay a finger on Sergio's boy?" I heard my father ask.

I didn't look back. I walked out the door and back to my car, satisfied with having beaten Dominic, but not quite trusting that my threat would keep Jacob and Natalie safe.

As I started the engine and turned the wheel, movement at

the front door caught my attention. It was Patricia. She glanced behind her several times as she made her way toward me. I rolled down my window.

"Mr. Benedetti." She was out of breath.

"Yes?"

"Your uncle asked me to give this to you." She slipped a note to me and quickly backed away from the car.

"Thank you, Patricia," I said absently as I unfolded it and read the brief, hurriedly written note: *Dominic visited Isabella DeMarco late last night, just before your arrival there.*

Dominic was there? I'd gone inside—well, I'd gotten as far as the foyer. Did Lucia know Dominic was there and keep it from me? And did this confirm my growing suspicion?

16

LUCIA

I woke suddenly, sucking in a breath, my throat incredibly dry.

Looking around, I remembered where I was, remembered the night before. I lay in Salvatore's bed, his scent still on his pillow, the indentation where his head had been now containing a small piece of paper.

Unfolding it, I read:

I need to take care of some business. I will be back this afternoon. I have Marco's phone, and I've programmed the number into yours in case you need anything.

Salvatore

I set it down and closed my eyes, feeling sheepish at what I'd done, dropping his phone into the toilet.

But now, I had to face the thing that had woken me, as unbelievable as it was. I wished I'd kept my father's note rather than throwing it away. At the time, I'd been so upset.

My father had committed suicide because he couldn't live

with the decisions he'd made. Because he hadn't been able to come to terms with the fact that when I turned twenty-one, Salvatore would claim me as his. Did he have any idea how that letter would make me feel? Did he know he laid more guilt on my shoulders with that letter than he had in signing the contract that bound me to the Benedetti family?

But there was something else. He'd said something I'd just remembered moments before waking. He'd blamed the Benedettis for destroying *both* his daughters.

I'd thought—when I'd heard the man's voice last night, I'd thought I'd recognized it, but it wasn't a familiar voice. I'd thought it was Dominic Benedetti. But what would he be doing at my sister's house? Isabella hated them more than I did.

But what my father had said...

"No."

I sat up and pushed the blankets off. I was naked and saw that Salvatore had carefully bandaged my knees and the heels of my palms from where I'd torn myself up, running from him last night. When he'd caught up with me, he'd been fierce but also tender. Caring.

I shook my head and got out of bed. Back in my own bedroom, I dressed in running clothes. Running always helped clear my head, and I needed my head cleared really bad right now. Once dressed, I headed out. I heard Rainey in the kitchen and someone vacuuming in another part of the house.

I started at a slow jog, trying to choose some music, but then I stopped, wrapped the earbuds around the phone, and tucked it into my pocket. I didn't want music today. I'd listen to the sounds of the forest.

Last night, when I'd asked him what he wanted, Salvatore had said he wanted me.

"At this moment."

The swell inside my chest deflated instantly at the memory. He had to have me. It's not like I was his choice.

I shook that thought aside. I needed to figure out what was going on. I needed to talk to Izzy, but how? How could I tell her I'd heard a man's voice without giving myself away? How offended would she be if I asked if Dominic Benedetti were at her house?

But what if it *was* him? What if she'd known him for far longer than I realized?

And what if she knew about what he'd done to that little boy, kidnapping Natalie's son like that?

"I took care of what you wanted done."

No. No way. Izzy would never have arranged for something as terrible as the kidnapping of a child. And I should be ashamed of myself for thinking it.

I pushed myself to run faster, even though I hadn't properly warmed up yet, and broke a sweat within a few minutes. I ran harder than I usually ran, but I needed more, needed to burn and exhaust my muscles, purge myself.

When did things get so complicated? Isabella and I were DeMarcos. We hated the Benedetti family. That was simple. It was black-and-white. But this? This attraction, this pull toward Salvatore? My yielding to him? It didn't make sense. And my questions about Izzy. About what my father potentially referred to in his letter. About having heard Dominic's voice in her house late at night.

I was running too fast on unfamiliar terrain and not paying attention, so when I tripped over the exposed root of a large tree and went flying, I shouldn't have been surprised. But when I tried to stand, I had to haul myself up with my arms. My left ankle was already starting to swell and hum with pain.

"Shit."

I looked back toward the house, but I'd run too deep into the woods to see any more than the decorative chimney tops. I forced myself to stand, leaning all my weight on my right leg. Holding on to nearby trees, I hobbled toward the house. It wasn't more than five minutes, though, before I realized I'd never get back there on my own, not with my ankle quickly doubling in size.

Fishing my phone out of my pocket, I unwrapped the earbuds and stuck one in my ear. I then scrolled down to where Salvatore had entered Marco's number and dialed.

He answered quickly, sounding like my call surprised him. "Lucia?"

"You know how you said to try and not get lost when I'm running?

He chuckled, audibly relaxing. "Are you lost?"

"No, that's not it. I'm not lost, and I didn't even have any music blaring, but—"

"What?" he cut me off, his tone anxious. "What is it?"

"I caught my foot on a tree root and fell. I'm trying to get back to the house on my own, but my ankle's swelling and hurts pretty badly."

"Get your weight off it, and elevate it if you can. I'm coming. Just pulling into the gates now. Do you know which trail you took?"

"I headed east, same as the morning you ran into me, but I've already passed the spot where we stopped last time."

"Okay, I'm on my way. Just keep talking to me, so I can hear you."

I heard the sound of stones beneath the car's tires. He really had just gotten back.

"Where did you go?" I asked, since he said to keep talking.

"To see my brother."

Could I tell him my suspicions? But he continued talking as he walked—the front door opening, him saying something to

Marco, sliding the glass doors open before the sounds of his footsteps crunching on the forest floor reached my ears as he hurried to me.

"My father, Roman, and he were in a meeting. Some days, I question my trust in Roman."

"You do? Trust him, I mean?"

"Out of the three, yes. Sergio did too. But I know if push came to shove, he'd take care of himself first."

"Was it Dominic who took Jacob? Did he admit it?"

"Yeah."

"I can hear you! I mean, not just on the phone."

"Hot-pink running shorts?" he asked.

I glanced down and smiled. "I guess it's a good thing."

"It'd be hard to miss you in those," he said, hanging up as he came into view. He wore his usual uniform: dark T-shirt and jeans. And he made my mouth water.

Salvatore scanned me from head to toe and knelt down by my hurt foot, making me flinch as he lightly touched my swollen ankle.

"Ouch. Hey, your hands!" His knuckles were raw and bruised.

He looked at them as if seeing them for the first time and smiled proudly. "You should see Dominic's face."

"You beat him up?"

He nodded, his attention back on my ankle. "I'm going to lift you up and carry you back. Just let me make a call."

He dialed, and I realized he'd called Rainey as soon as he said her name.

"Can you get Dr. Mooney out here for me? Lucia's hurt her ankle. I don't think it's broken, but I'd like him to have a look anyway."

"I don't need a doctor, I just need some ice," I said, but he pretty much ignored me.

"Thanks, Rainey." He hung up and turned to me. "Let's not take any chances."

He lifted me up in his arms, and I blinked back tears with the movement.

"Sorry."

"It's okay."

"This is getting to be a habit."

"You carrying me into the house?"

He nodded, navigating his way carefully through the forest so as not to hit branches with my hurt ankle.

"Can I ask you a question, Lucia?"

"Sure."

"How did I not see Dominic when I came to get you last night?"

How did he know?

"It was dark, but I'm pretty sure I would have seen him," he continued.

"I wasn't sure it was him. I overheard them from upstairs, but I never saw who it was."

"So I'm right, he was there."

"You mean you didn't know?" I looked at him, confused.

"Not one hundred percent."

"Why did you ask it that way, then?" He'd tricked me.

"Wouldn't you have tried to protect your sister rather than tell me the truth?"

We neared the house, and I saw Rainey waiting by the doors, a large bag of ice in hand.

"Answer my question, Lucia."

I looked into his deep-blue eyes, seeing not darkness, not rage or hate. I saw instead goodness, as much as one could be good in our world. "Probably," I answered honestly.

He nodded. "Thank you."

"Doctor will be here in twenty minutes. He said to keep it iced and elevated," Rainey said as we entered the house.

Salvatore laid me on the couch and rested my hurt ankle in his lap as he sat beside me.

Rainey smiled and handed me a cup of her homemade lemonade and two Advil.

"Thought you might need these."

I returned her smile as I popped the pills in my mouth. "Thank you. You're a lifesaver." Rainey went to wait for the doctor, and I took a sip of the lemonade, yelping when Salvatore tugged my shoe off. "That hurt."

"I'm sorry."

He gently peeled my sock off, inspected the swelling limb, then placed the ice bag on my ankle.

"How did you know about Dominic?"

"I've had men watching the house since the day I saw Luke there. Luke's involved in some dangerous things. I truly hope, for her sake, that Isabella isn't a part of those things, Lucia."

I didn't miss the warning, but Salvatore wouldn't hurt her. He'd promised.

Salvatore continued. "I guess I was surprised to hear it was Dominic who made a visit in the middle of the night rather than Luke. Is she sleeping with both of them?"

"Salvatore! You don't know that! *I* don't know that! She's not some kind of—" I couldn't say the word.

"I don't care if she sleeps with a hundred men in one night, Lucia. But I do care if she's fucking my brother."

"She wouldn't! She hates him. She hates all of you!" I tried to take my ankle off his lap, but he placed the palm of his hand firmly on my thigh.

"Who is Effie's father, Lucia?"

I looked at him, my breath coming in loud and heavy, my eyes watering with the accusation. It was like he was picking information from my brain. Things I hadn't yet come to under-stand, things I couldn't have be true.

"Why do you do this? Every time I feel like we're finally getting somewhere, feel like I maybe understand you, why do you have to fuck it all up?"

Two sets of footsteps came from the foyer. "This way, Doctor," Rainey said, ushering him in.

Salvatore and I had devolved into some kind of staring contest. I finally had to forfeit when a tear rolled down my cheek. I turned away.

"Dr. Mooney," Salvatore said. "You'll excuse me for not standing, but I think I'd only cause her pain to move her leg."

He did. He only caused me pain. Every. Single. Time.

17

SALVATORE

I stepped out of the room when I saw Roman's call come in and left Dr. Mooney to wrap Lucia's leg. I was right; just a sprain, but painful nonetheless.

"Roman," I said as I entered my study and shut the door.

"Well, you know how to make an entrance."

"He kidnapped Jacob from the daycare. This is after he'd gone to Natalie's house a few days ago, and she'd refused to let him in. He was sending a message, Roman. I wanted to be sure he received mine loud and clear."

"Well, your father was pissed. You were gone for most of that, though."

"Really? Franco Benedetti pissed at the son that's not me for a change?"

"Franco can be pigheaded sometimes, Salvatore. We both know that. He's tougher on you because he knows you'll be the one replacing him, but he can't ignore Dominic. Franco is more aware than you think of the potential threat Dominic presents, and this stunt with Jacob banished any doubts he may have still clung to."

"Finally," I said sarcastically.

"Either way, unless Dominic is stupid, he won't go near Natalie or Jacob again. Franco's gone out there himself to make sure she knows she and his grandson will have his protection."

"Neither Dominic nor I hold a candle to Sergio, even in death." I hated that I felt this pang of jealousy toward Sergio, as tiny as it was. I'd known this all my life, but it had never come between us. And I wouldn't let it now. "Never have and never will."

"The fact that Sergio is gone still hurts your father. He doesn't love you any less. He's just missing one child. He is human, after all."

I didn't comment.

"I want to talk to you about the DNA test, Salvatore."

"Go on." I hadn't yet had a chance to read through the rest of the report to get a clearer understanding of the results.

"When the results came back, disqualifying Luke as the father, I used a sample from myself. Family shares DNA, in some cases more than in others, but there is always something."

Roman had studied genealogy for a while and was in the process of compiling his family tree.

"What made you do that?" Was I ready to hear what he would tell me?

"A hunch. Effie DeMarco shares at least some of our DNA, Salvatore."

I sat down. Hearing it was different than thinking it.

"I'm obviously not the little girl's father, but I'm running more tests today. I took a sample from Dominic's home."

"What, did you swab him?" I chuckled, but there wasn't any humor behind it.

"Took the hair off his brush."

"When will you know for sure?"

"I'm hoping within twenty-four hours."

"Does my father know anything about this?"

"No. Nothing. He won't find out unless I'm one hundred percent certain."

I leaned back, exhaling. "So Dominic's been having an affair with Isabella DeMarco for five years?"

"That I don't know."

"Where do his loyalties lie, I wonder? And how does Luke DeMarco play into this? This just got a hell of a lot more complicated."

"Talk to Lucia. See if you can glean any information at all. She may not be aware herself, Salvatore."

"I think she's innocent." No, I knew it. And this knowledge would only hurt her.

"I'll get back to you as soon as I know more."

"Thank you, Roman."

I made one more call to check on Natalie, who had called in sick to work and was spending the day with Jacob at home. She knew my father was on his way, and although not pleased about it, she seemed reasonably calm and promised to call me once he'd left.

When I returned to the living room, Dr. Mooney was just packing up his things.

"Just keep it iced and wrapped. You'll be fine in no time. I've already ordered crutches. They'll be here hopefully within the next hour or two."

"How long will I need those?" Lucia asked.

"Only as long as you feel pain when putting any weight on your leg. I don't think long, a week or two."

"Thank you, Dr. Mooney." I extended my hand and shook his.

"You're welcome, Salvatore." He turned back to Lucia and shook her hand as well. "It was nice to meet you, my dear. Call if you need anything at all."

"I will. Thanks again."

Rainey walked Dr. Mooney out, and I took a seat beside Lucia.

"I don't want to talk to you right now."

"I didn't mean to upset you with my question, Lucia."

"But you did, Salvatore. That's the point. Ever hear the saying 'the road to hell is paved with good intentions?'"

"Let's go sit by the pool before it gets too hot."

"I said I don't—"

Ignoring her, I lifted her into my arms and carried her out. Lucia simply sighed.

"Can you bring my lemonade at least?"

"Sure. Would you like something to eat?"

She gave me a cautious look. "I think I smelled cake."

I had too. Rainey had been baking. "I'll be right back."

In the kitchen, I sliced two chunks of the still-warm cinnamon cake I found cooling on the counter and set them on a tray along with two fresh glasses of lemonade. Back outside, I handed one of the plates to Lucia and placed her lemonade on the table beside her lounge chair before taking the seat by hers.

"This is Rainey's signature cake." Not bothering with the fork, I picked up the fat chunk I'd sliced for myself and bit into it. "God, it's delicious."

"I'm going to get fat," Lucia said through her mouthful.

"I'll make sure you get enough exercise."

She glanced at me from the corner of her eye, then returned her attention to the cake on her plate in her lap.

"We need to talk about last night."

"I thought we had."

"About what you overheard."

Her wary gaze met mine. "She's my sister, Salvatore."

"Jacob was very afraid, Lucia. If Isabella had anything to do with that, I think it's important I know."

She rubbed her face with both hands then pushed her fingers into her hair and pulled at the roots. "I don't know, Salvatore. What happened to that little boy, what Dominic did, was cruel. I hope to God my sister wasn't involved in anything like that. The Izzy I knew wouldn't be. She'd never hurt a child. And I know he wasn't physically hurt, but taking him without his mom knowing? Freaking her out like that, and scaring the little boy? I just—"

She looked away and shook her head. When she turned back to me, her eyes glistened with tears.

"Thing is, I don't know her anymore. I've shut everyone out for so long that I don't even know who *I* am anymore. I thought this was black-and-white. I hated the Benedetti family. Period. But my sister involved in or even possibly orchestrating something like the kidnapping of a child?"

She shook her head again, her face lined with worry.

"She's a mother herself. How...what's happened to us?"

"Too much hate. Too much power," I said. "Too much of a lust for blood and vengeance. War never makes friends out of enemies. The opposite. It solidifies that hate. The war between Benedetti and DeMarco may have been fought in our fathers' time, but we inherit the hate, the bad blood. It doesn't just go away. It carries down generation to generation."

"I don't hate you."

"You have every right to."

"I don't. You're not like them, Salvatore."

But I was. I had killed. I had taken. I had lived off blood money. I'd shed that very blood with my own two hands. Standing up to my father after whipping Lucia, though, and then today—walking away, not giving a shit about what he thought—was I changing? Was I finally growing out of my father's shadow and casting my own?

And would mine be as dark as his?

"I asked Roman to run a paternity test on Effie, Lucia."

"I don't want to know."

She started to stand but then realized she couldn't without my help. Which was precisely why I'd laid her on one of the lounge chairs rather than sitting her on a chair.

I touched her arm. "You have to know."

She closed her eyes and reopened them after a minute but remained silent, waiting.

"Luke isn't her father."

From the look on her face, I had the feeling she knew that.

"She carries DNA from my family." Christ, was I saying this out loud?

A tear rolled down each of Lucia's cheeks, and I knew she knew.

"They're testing Dominic's DNA now. We'll know for sure soon whether Dominic Benedetti fathered Effie DeMarco."

It was a long moment before she spoke. I didn't know how Lucia would take what I told her. On the one hand, she'd seen enough evidence to suspect the truth. She'd seen it herself before I told it. On the other hand, Isabella was still her sister, and I was still the enemy's son. I was her keeper. The man who'd signed a contract, claiming ownership of her.

"What do you want out of this, Salvatore? When all is said and done, what do you want?"

I'd been straddling the seat and now... I lay back and looked out across the pool toward the forest. It was so quiet here. So still. So peaceful.

I turned back to her. "I want to live a quiet life. I don't want to look over my shoulder at every turn. I don't want to see an enemy in every set of eyes I meet, every hand I shake. I want the people I love to be safe. I want them be happy." Strange. Six months ago, I would have added 'I want my brother to be alive' into that list, but something had shifted. Somehow, I'd come to accept that he was gone. Not the cruelty or the unfairness of the act, but the knowledge that he was gone. And that my life lay here.

She cleared her throat and blinked her pretty, innocent eyes, casting them somewhere in the space between us. I didn't take my eyes off her.

Lucia was all the innocence in my life.

She was my redemption.

And I wanted her. Her presence here, us together, as tumultuous as it was, as wrong as I was for keeping her, it saved me. *She* saved me.

And that was why I would keep my promise and release her once I could. Once I knew she would be safe and out of harm's way.

"What do *you* want, Lucia?"

She met my gaze, shrugged her shoulders, and gave me a tiny but sad smile. "Same things, I guess."

"You'll have them. I promise."

Another promise to her. Another one I didn't know I could keep. But I would try. I would try every day up until my last breath to give her what she wanted. A life. Simple, peaceful, beautiful.

Like her.

It was in that moment I realized I loved her. Somewhere, somehow, I'd fallen in love with her.

But my debt to her was greater than anything I felt, any hurt or loss I'd experience. And because of that debt, I would never say those words aloud, not to her, not to anyone. She'd been locked away most of her life. All of her brief adult life. I was the only man she'd known—a cruel trick of fate. If I said the words, I knew what would happen. Lucia would mistake survival for love. Because right now, she needed me to survive. To survive my family. To survive the war that I'd mistakenly thought over. I would stay alive for her. I would fight for her. I would do every-thing in my power to save her. Nothing else mattered, not even my own life. Everything from this point forward would be for her.

"I want to make love to you, Lucia."

She looked at me, confused, although her body began to prepare. I could see it in the slight dilation of her pupils, the stiffening of her nipples, the parting of her lips.

"I want you to want it. I want you to give me the word. Up until now, I've taken it from you."

"Salvatore—"

I held up my hand. "I've taken it."

She touched my arm. "Salvatore—"

I moved to stop her from speaking. She combed her fingers into the hair at my forehead and tugged.

"You're so damn stubborn."

She leaned in to kiss me, her mouth soft, her tongue sweet as it probed my lips. She pulled back and looked at me, swallowing.

"I want it. I want you. Make love to me, Salvatore."

I wrapped her in my arms and kissed her, lifting her up as I stood, cradling her to me, carrying her to the door of my study. Our lips still locked, we entered. I took her to the couch, sat her on it, and kneeled before her between her spread knees. Her eyes on mine, she pulled first her top, then her sports bra off, her round breasts settling into place, the nipples already tight. I worked her other shoe off her foot and then slipped my fingers into the waistband of her shorts and panties. She lifted up a little, allowing me to drag them down and off so she sat before me naked.

"Spread your legs wider and lean back," I said, tugging my shirt off.

She did as I said, opening herself wide, leaning back,

offering me her pussy. With my thumbs on either side of her lips, I opened her farther and brought my mouth to her, licking her length once before taking her clit into my mouth, still watching her as she leaned her head back and closed her eyes.

"Fuck, Salvatore, I love that."

I sucked, pulling her toward me so her ass hung off the couch. I pushed one finger inside her, and when she tightened her muscles around it, I stopped sucking, licking her clit instead, teasing it. She opened her eyes.

"You like when I eat your pussy?"

She nodded and tried to drag my head back.

I smiled. "Greedy girl." I stood, rid myself of my clothes, and stroked myself, loving how she watched me, her hungry eyes never leaving me.

"I want to suck your cock, Salvatore."

Placing my knees on either side of her on the couch, I straddled her and brought myself to her mouth. She took my cock in her hands, sliding one beneath to cup me, and opened her mouth, licking the tip before taking me into her hot, wet mouth.

"Fuck, Lucia, I love you sucking my cock." I rocked my hips against her, moving slowly, relishing the wet heat of her on my swelling dick until I needed to fuck her faster. I pulled out then and lay her on her back on the couch before taking the leg she hadn't hurt and pushing it back so I could see all of her. "I love looking at you too, at your dripping pussy." I rocked myself into her, sucking in a breath as I did. "Knowing it belongs to me."

"Hard, please."

I shook my head. "Not yet." I moved slowly, taking my time, penetrating her deeply before sliding out, feeling every inch of her until she nearly screamed for me to make her come.

"Please, Salvatore!"

"I want something else today," I said, pulling out fully and going to my desk.

She lifted her head, her expression confused, annoyed. I opened one of the drawers and found what I wanted, a bottle of lotion.

She looked at it, then at me. "What?"

I took the lid off and squeezed some of the scentless cream onto my hand, coating my cock in it while she watched. It took all the restraint I had not to shoot my load right then and there while fucking my palm.

"What do I want?" I asked, smearing more of the lotion on myself.

She nodded. I pulled her good leg out, bent it at the knee, and pushed it toward her chest. I then squeezed half the bottle of lotion onto the flat of her belly.

"I want to fuck your ass."

Her eyes went wide, and she opened her mouth, but I stopped her, dipping one finger into the lotion and taking the tip of it to her asshole.

"I think you'll like it," I said, circling the tight, virgin ring, smearing lotion all over it. "But first, I'm going to fill your sexy little hole with this." I dipped my finger in the lotion again, and she watched, a slight flush to her cheeks, caution in her eyes alongside the curiosity.

After several times circling, I pressed against the hole, and she gasped as my lubricated fingertip penetrated. I waited, watching her face as she took it, relaxing enough a few moments later so that I could press deeper.

She sucked in a breath and gripped the side of the couch. I moved slowly until she was taking the length of one finger easily in and out of her tight little ass. I then pulled out to dip my finger into more of the lotion and repeated.

"You like my finger fucking your ass, Lucia?"

She made some sound and averted her gaze before giving me the smallest nod.

"No, look at me. I want to watch you take me." I slid a second finger in, causing her to tighten all her muscles again, her eyes wide on mine. "Take it." I thrust a little harder, then circled inside her, smearing lotion along her walls. "When I fuck your asshole properly, I'm going to watch you take me then too. I'm going to watch you when you stretch and come and I'm going to watch you when I fill you with my seed."

"Salvatore, I..."

"Wait, Lucia. Wait until my cock is inside you before you come." I pulled both fingers out and smeared the last of the lube onto them, dipping them back into her more easily now. "That's it, it feels good, right?"

She nodded.

"When your ankle is healed, I'm going to have you bend over my desk and bare your ass. You're going to like this so much that when I tell you to beg me to fuck your ass, you're going to do it. You're going to spread yourself wide and arch your back and beg me to fill your ass with my cock."

"I can't...I'm coming."

She closed her eyes, and the walls of her ass clenched around my fingers. I watched her come, watched her slide one hand to her clit and rub herself as she moaned, her pussy leaking, my fingers thrusting in and out of her ass.

"Bad girl," I said once she'd come down. I pulled my fingers out of her and lifted both her legs up, pressing them against her sides to make taking my cock easier. "I'm thicker than my fingers, but we'll go slow until you're ready."

She nodded.

"Touch your clit, Lucia. Make yourself come again, this time with my cock inside your ass."

She did as I said, rubbing herself slowly as I lined up the head of my cock against her asshole and slowly began to push into her, taking my time, stopping when her muscles tightened, watching her face, feeling her body to know when she was ready for more.

"Salvatore, it's too big. It hurts."

"Shh. Relax. Open for me." I moved in and out of her, one inch at a time, slowly rocking my hips, wanting to drive into her but holding back until she came again. I was about two-thirds of the way in.

"Fuck, Salvatore!"

This orgasm took her more violently, her walls clenching, relaxing, opening for me to fill her fully.

"God, you're so fucking tight." I held myself deep inside her for a moment, knowing I wouldn't last long. When I began to move, she cried out, her fingers still working her clit, another orgasm on the heels of the last until she called out my name. The sound of my name on her lips, the feel of her around me, took me over the edge until my cock throbbed and I emptied inside her, filling her, owning her, owning every part of her.

I SAT in the tub with Lucia between my legs, her bandaged ankle resting on the edge. We'd barely settled in when Marco barged into my bedroom, calling out my name, probably only stopping when he realized from the pile of clothes I'd dumped just inside the doorway that I wasn't alone.

"Shit. Sorry."

"Give me twenty minutes," I called out.

"It's urgent."

I glanced at Lucia. Marco wasn't one to cry wolf.

"I'll be right back," I said to her as I climbed out I settled her against the back of the tub.

"What's urgent?" she asked.

I dried off and wrapped a towel around my hips. "No idea." I went into the bedroom. One look at Marco told me this was bad. "What is it?"

He glanced toward the bathroom. I followed his gaze, then walked over closer to him.

"What's happened, Marco?" I asked more quietly, so Lucia wouldn't hear.

"There's been a shooting."

My entire body tightened. "Who?"

"Luke DeMarco. He's being airlifted to Bellevue Hospital right now."

"Fuck."

"What's happened, Salvatore?" I turned to find Lucia wrapped in a towel, hopping on one leg, leaning her weight against the wall.

"It's Luke." I went to her, put her arm over my shoulder, and propped her up by her waist. "He's been shot."

"Oh my God! Is he okay?"

"Not sure yet."

"I have to call Izzy. She wasn't there, was she?"

"I don't know."

"Shit, my phone is downstairs."

"Here," Marco said, handing her his.

She looked at him as if she were surprised, but took it and dialed.

A knock came at the door. Rainey peeked her head inside and held up the crutches Dr. Mooney had ordered.

"Already here," she said, her smile fading when she saw the looks on our faces.

"Thank you, Rainey," I said, taking them from her. "Maybe you can make us all a pot of coffee."

Lucia looked up at me. "I'm on my way, Izzy," she said into her phone. "I'll be there as soon as I can." She hung up.

"Salvatore, I have to go to them."

I nodded. "We'll get dressed and go."

Lucia blushed, and Marco and Rainey awkwardly left the room. I went into her bedroom and chose some clothes: a dress and a sweater in case it was cool at the hospital. I helped her get her clothes on before getting dressed myself. I handed her the crutches that had just been delivered.

"Thanks."

Since she had never used crutches before—and there was no time to practice—I ended up carrying Lucia down the stairs—it was just faster that way—and asked Marco to follow us.

"Did your sister know anything?" I asked Lucia once we were in the car and on our way.

"No. Only that he was in critical condition. He took two bullets, one to the stomach, the other in his shoulder. She's a mess."

I checked my watch. "It's about an hour's drive from here without traffic."

"Crap."

My mind raced with thoughts of who'd done it, and I couldn't shake the feeling the assailant was closer to home than I'd like once I'd learned the truth. But we'd deal with that if and when we had to. Right now, I had to get Lucia to the hospital and find out what the hell was going on.

18

LUCIA

Salvatore made call after call as he drove us to the hospital, first to his uncle, then to Marco who tailed us, then to Dominic. Dominic didn't pick up his call. He also arranged for security to be added to the hospital, for which I was grateful.

I tried Isabella twice but never got hold of her. With traffic, by the time we got to the hospital, it was well over an hour later. Salvatore's phone rang once more just as he parked the car. He checked the display, and I glimpsed the name. It was his father.

"I have to take this."

I nodded, opening my door and setting my crutches outside. What a time to sprain my ankle!

"Marco," Salvatore called out once Marco had parked his car. "Take Lucia upstairs, and stay with her until I get there."

Marco nodded and took my arm, helping me out of the car.

"I got it," I snapped, hating feeling helpless. I glanced at Salvatore, who walked away with the phone to his ear. Marco followed me into the hospital. At reception, I found out where they'd taken Luke. I went as quickly as I could to the trauma unit and found Isabella holding Effie's hand, her face one of frustration and worry, her eyes weary and red.

"Izzy."

She turned, a look of relief quickly replaced by surprise at my state.

"It's nothing, just a sprain. I fell while running."

She got up, and we hugged.

"Aunt Lucia, are you hurt too?" Effie asked.

"I'll be okay. It's just a sprain, kiddo." I gave her a hug then turned to Izzy, who was watching Marco talk to two other men I just noticed.

"Salvatore?" she asked, gesturing toward them.

I nodded. "He wanted security for Luke and for us.

She snorted. "He's probably the one who put Luke in here!"

"Wait. No, he was with me."

She rolled her eyes. "Don't be so naive, Lucia. All he has to do is give the word!"

"Mama?"

Izzy wiped away a tear and looked down at her daughter.

"Let's calm down." I touched my sister's shoulder, and she sighed.

"Sorry, honey. It's fine," she told Effie. "Everything's going to be fine."

"Uncle Luke is hurt," she said to me.

"I know. Hey, I saw a vending machine just around the corner." I dug into my purse and found my wallet, took out some dollar bills, and handed them to her. "Go get us some chocolate bars, okay?"

She looked at her mom, who nodded.

"Marco, will you keep an eye on her?" I asked.

"Of course."

Wow, this was a different Marco than the inflexible man I'd met thus far.

"Here, some sodas too." I handed Effie more money to keep her busy. She went with Marco. "Let's sit down. Tell me what happened," I said to Isabella once Effie was out of earshot.

"He was at the stupid bowling alley," she started, taking a crumpled-up tissue out of her purse and wiping her dripping eyes. "He always goes there in the mornings, so the bastards knew where to find him. He'd just gone to get a cup of coffee, and two guys came in and opened fire."

"Jesus."

"The owner who was working the bar took a bullet in his arm. He'll be okay."

"Anyone else hurt?"

She shook her head. "No."

"Any idea who?"

She shook her head. "They wore ski masks."

"I guess they would. Why do you think it was Salvatore's men?" I asked.

She shook her head with a flat look in her eyes. "Who else but someone from the Benedetti family." She turned her attention to digging for something in her purse.

"Dominic is part of that family," I said, watching her.

She glanced up, her lips narrow, her face tight.

"He was at your house the other night."

She stood. "This isn't the time, Lucia."

"What was he doing there?" I asked, following her, the crutches an irritating nuisance.

She kept her back to me, shaking her head, watching Effie push buttons on the vending machine.

"Izzy, what's going on?"

She faced me finally. "A big fucking mess, that's what."

"Are you having an affair with Dominic Benedetti?"

Izzy threw her arms up into the air. "There you go again,

another affair. First it was Luke, now it's Dominic? Excuse me, sis, but I'm not going to justify that with an answer."

"Ms. DeMarco?" a doctor called out, rounding the corner.

"Yes?" Isabella went to him, and I followed, hobbling behind her.

"Your cousin's injuries are very serious. We're operating now, but it will be several hours. I can't speak to the outcome just yet."

"He can't die," she started, her eyes watering, her voice desperate. "You can't let him die."

The doctor looked to be immune to her emotion. Probably so used to doling out bad news, it just didn't faze him anymore.

"Mommy, I got you a Snickers bar," Effie started, coming back toward us with the candy bars, Marco behind her carrying cans of soda, looking as much out of place following her as possible. It would have been comical if we weren't standing in a hospital waiting room with Luke in critical condition a few doors down.

"What did you get for me?" I asked, lifting her up and turning her away while Izzy wiped her tears.

"A Twix. Same as me."

"I love Twix. Good choice."

"I thought you might."

"I'll check in with you as soon as I have some information, but it will be several hours before he'll be out of surgery," the doctor said.

I watched them. Izzy nodded her head. When I set Effie down, she went to her.

"Here, mommy." She held out the candy.

Isabella took it then hugged the little girl. "I love you, honey."

"It's just a Snickers," Effie said, confused, and tried to squirm out of the tight squeeze.

Salvatore walked in just then, and I felt an immediate sense of relief. His expression, however, showed how preoccupied he was. Isabella glared at him, but he watched her with concern.

"What are you doing here? Not enough that you had to attend my father's funeral? You had to come see this too?"

"I'm here for Lucia."

She snorted.

"How is he?" Salvatore asked me.

"Critical. They'll be in surgery for a few hours."

"Mommy, is Uncle Luke going to be okay? I got him his favorite candy bar too."

"That was sweet of you," Izzy said, then looked up at me. "It may be best if Effie goes home. There's nothing for her to do here."

"I'll take her. You stay. Just call me as soon as you hear anything, okay?"

"I will."

"I want to stay with you, mommy."

Isabella hugged her daughter again. "I'll be home as soon as I can, but there's nothing for you to do here. Go home, and bake some of those cookies Uncle Luke likes. Then you can bring them with you when he wakes up, okay?"

"What kind of cookies?" I asked to distract Effie.

Effie studied her mom then gave her a tight squeeze, whispering something in her ear before turning away. A tear rolled down Isabella's cheek.

"It'll be okay," I said, hugging her while holding Effie's hand. "He'll pull through. He's almost as stubborn as you, after all."

She gave me a smile, then turned to Salvatore. "Are you staying with them at the house?" Her tone changed utterly when she addressed him.

"I'll take them there, and I've already got men stationed outside. I have to attend a meeting but will be back as soon as possible."

"Of course, another meeting. You see what comes of those meetings," she said, gesturing to the door the doctor had disappeared behind.

"Izzy," I leaned in close so Effie wouldn't hear. "Salvatore didn't do this. I promise you that."

"Take care of my daughter, and take care of yourself." She hugged me. "I have a gun in my bedroom," she added in a whisper. "Nightstand drawer."

I pulled back. She had a gun? By her bed?

"Here are my keys." She pulled her car keys off and handed me the ring. I took it, still not quite believing what she'd just told me.

"Let's go, Lucia," Salvatore said after giving Marco some orders.

"Call me if you hear anything. Come on, Effie."

Effie and I followed Salvatore to the elevator and out to his car. Once we settled Effie and my crutches in the backseat, we climbed in. I spoke with Effie as we drove to her house, which was about half an hour from the hospital. Although she tried to hide her unease, it was evident she was anxious and unsure. Salvatore said only a few words, preoccupied. Maybe grateful for Effie's presence, since that meant I couldn't question him.

Once we got to the house, I saw two cars parked along the curb with two men inside each one. Salvatore pulled up in the driveway, and we all climbed out, me last, since I had to figure out how to use the damned crutches, and putting weight on my foot made me wince every time. Effie held my crutches while I climbed out and watched me while Salvatore walked over to the men sitting in the cars by the curb and, I assumed, gave them instructions before returning to us.

"Ready?" he asked, closing the door behind me.

Effie nodded and walked ahead to the front door.

"What meeting are you going to?" I asked, not sure if I liked him going to any meeting after Luke had just been shot.

"Luke's shooting is just one of the incidents. Two of our businesses have been attacked as well."

"What businesses?" I knew they had several shops, and I didn't want to know what those shops fronted for.

"Doesn't matter," he said. "What matters is that what I feared would happen in time, what *Luke* was working on, is here now."

"Luke? But—"

"He's in the hospital, I know."

"Is it Dominic?"

His face changed, and he looked just beyond me. "I'm not sure, Lucia."

"What aren't you telling me?"

"That the time for war, it's dawning."

Salvatore's phone rang, and he reached into his pocket to get it. "I'll call you right back," he said and disconnected the call. "Let's get you inside and settled. I'd rather have you at home, but this will have to do for now."

We headed for the door. Salvatore slid the key into the lock and opened it. Effie went directly into the kitchen, leaving us alone for the time being.

"You'll be safe here. I'm leaving four men outside. They won't let anyone in."

"Or out, I'm guessing." He turned to me and took my face in his hands.

"Correct."

He looked at me for a long moment.

"This is one I really, really need to trust you on, Lucia. I don't have time to go looking for you, and I can't keep you safe if you disappear."

"I'm not going anywhere."

"Good, because if you do, I'll take my belt to your ass again, and this time, it'll be a month before you can sit down."

"I said I'm not," I snapped, not wanting that memory.

He nodded then kissed my mouth, his hands still on either cheek.

After walking him out, I glanced once more at the cars parked out front. One man sat inside each one. I wasn't sure where the others had gone. Probably around the house. I didn't care as long as they didn't come inside. I closed the door and went to the kitchen to find Effie had taken out flour and a big bag of M&M's, but even she wasn't snacking on them.

"I can't reach the other stuff," she said, her tone somber. "M&M cookies are Uncle Luke's favorites. Mommy has the recipe on her iPad."

I smiled and squatted down to her level, rubbing her arms. "The doctors are going to do everything they can to make sure he's okay, understand?"

She nodded, but her face remained serious. "He and mommy had a fight last night. I heard them."

"Their fight doesn't have anything to do with what happened. You know that, right?"

"I'm scared, Aunt Lucia. What if he's not okay? What if he doesn't wake up anymore?"

How could I answer that question, when I didn't know myself the outcome? I stood and looked around, finding an apron, my mom's, in the drawer she kept it in, neatly folded as if she'd just had it on yesterday. My dad hadn't gotten rid of anything of hers. In fact, I was sure the closet in his bedroom would still be full of her clothes unless Isabella had packed everything up. I hoped she hadn't.

I slid the apron over my head and tied the strings at my back. "This used to be your grandmother's apron," I said to Effie.

"She's in heaven," Effie said as she opened the same drawer

and took out a second, smaller apron. "This one is mine. I got it for my birthday."

"Oh, that's a pretty one. Shall I help you tie it?"

She nodded.

"Okay, let's get started. Where does mommy keep her iPad?"

"Here."

I followed her into the living room, where she opened a drawer in the coffee table and pulled out the tablet, punching in the code before handing it to me.

"It's 0-0-0-0." Effie shook her head. "I cracked that one in no time."

I ruffled Effie's hair and led her back to the kitchen, looked up the recipe saved in the Favorites tab, and we got to work. It took much more time than I expected because Effie insisted on using only the colors of M&M's that Luke liked best, and she patterned them into individual smiley faces. We spent the rest of the day playing in her room or watching TV, and I reheated lasagna I found in the fridge for dinner. At eight o'clock, I took her to her room and read her a story before putting her to bed, anxious that I hadn't heard from Isabella yet. When I'd tried her phone a few times, it had gone right to voice mail.

I dialed Salvatore, who answered on the third ring.

"Hey, it's me."

"Everything okay?"

He sounded rushed. "Yes, it's fine. I'm just wondering when your meeting will be finished."

He sighed. "I'm not sure, but I'll be there as soon as I can. Just lock the doors and go to bed if you're tired. Have you heard from your sister?"

"No, and she won't pick up the phone." Someone called his name, a man I thought might be Roman.

"I have to get back, Lucia."

"Okay. Call me when you're done. I don't care about the time."

"Make sure the doors are locked."

"I will."

"Be safe."

"You too." We hung up. I walked around the house for the fifth time and made sure all the doors were locked. The cars were still parked outside, and I spied one man in the backyard at the far end. Still, I didn't feel safe. I had no idea what was going on, and being here I felt exposed, like I was a sitting duck.

Shoving those thoughts aside, I made a pot of tea then closed the curtains on all the windows. From the bookshelf in the study, I found some old photo albums. Taking two of them, I settled on the couch to wait for my sister to call or come home.

That was when I heard the creaking of a door and footsteps coming from the back bedroom, the one my parents had converted on the main floor.

I turned my head. "Effie?" But it couldn't be her. I'd waited until she'd fallen asleep upstairs.

The hair on the back of my neck stood on end, and I watched the dark hallway as the steps grew closer. Terrified and unable to drag my gaze away from the shadowy space, I fumbled for my cell phone on the coffee table.

I knew who it was. Who it had to be. But still, when Dominic stepped into the light in the living room, I gasped, shocked, suddenly shaking when my gaze fell on the pistol he held at his side.

"Toss the phone, Lucia."

19

SALVATORE

I walked back into the meeting room at my father's house. About a dozen men were gathered around the table, all family, cousins and uncles. My father raised his eyebrows but didn't comment on my having left the room to take the call.

I hated leaving Lucia alone. She didn't know to what extent things had progressed in the last twelve hours. Hell, I was shocked to hear it all myself.

After I'd left Dominic's house, my father had apparently gone ballistic on my brother. Roman filled me in on the details. Franco had been furious with Dominic. So much so that he'd apologized to Natalie himself. I knew he was going to her house to make sure she knew he would protect her, but to apologize? That wasn't Franco Benedetti's style.

He'd also stationed men at her house when she'd refused to come to the city with him and stay at his house until things settled. She'd had no choice in the matter. He would do whatever he needed to do to protect his grandson.

And he had sent Dominic to the house in Florida to cool off. To *"get his head out of his ass"* were apparently his exact words.

The shooting of Luke DeMarco had surprised my father. It wasn't done on his order and obviously not on mine. The video footage only showed two masked men walking into the bowling alley and opening fire. It was a wonder more people weren't hurt.

Two of our businesses, one a restaurant and another, a bicycle shop, both of which fronted for money-laundering operations, had been attacked, but no one had been killed. Nothing of the businesses connected directly to us, so investigators would not find anything linking the crimes, but this was only the beginning. Money was taken from both businesses, but the amount of cash wouldn't have warranted the burglaries.

No, a message was being sent.

This was the prelude to a war.

But Luke DeMarco's shooting threw us off. He was working with the Pagani family. Why would he have been attacked?

That was the piece that gave us all pause.

"I feel real uneasy about this," I said. "They wouldn't have attacked DeMarco. Hell, if things had progressed to this point, DeMarco wouldn't have been at a fucking bowling alley. Something isn't right. It's someone else."

"Isabella?" my father asked.

Roman glanced at me.

"I saw her at the hospital. She's beside herself."

"You were at the hospital?" he asked.

I'd told Roman where I was, but not my father. "They're Lucia's family."

His lips tightened. "You miss the point of everything."

"By point of everything, you mean my treatment of Lucia." I knew. It wasn't a question. "If it's the fact I'm not a monster to her, then you're right, I miss your point. Maybe you should have given her to Dominic after all." The thought sickened me, but my saying it out loud to him, and in front of other members of the family, it only reaffirmed the fact that I would never allow that to happen.

My father made no reply, which surprised me. But it also strengthened me.

Every man in the room seemed to be holding their breath.

"Leave Lucia out of this. She's my concern and mine alone. Period. Let's talk about the damage done, who's behind it, and what we're doing about it."

He exhaled but turned his attention back to the task at hand. I assumed he'd deal with me later, but when that time came, he'd learn there would be no more dealing with me. My strings had been cut. I was no longer his puppet.

Maybe it took that contract to teach me that, to break me from my weakness, my cowardice when it came to Franco Benedetti. If any good could come out of something as terrible as stealing a life, this had to be it.

"Back to who is behind this," Roman began. "I believe the Pagani family is carrying out the attacks. I don't believe Isabella DeMarco would have her cousin assassinated. Assuming that was the intent."

"What else would it be? They put two bullets in him," I said.

Roman agreed. "Maybe Isabella is a bigger threat than we gave her credit for. Maybe Luke was an underling, a cover for her."

"Maybe the Pagani family is acting alone?" I added.

"No." My father shook his head. "I've spoken with the senior Paul Pagani."

Paul Pagani Sr., an eighty-six-year-old man who still refused to hand over the reins of the family business to his son. Although knowing the son, I understood why.

"He has not authorized any shootings, and he is aware of talks between DeMarco and his son. When he learned of it, he forbade any action."

"But his son could have gone behind his back," Roman added.

"And attempted to kill Luke DeMarco?" Stefano, one of my cousins, asked.

"There's something we're missing," I said, shaking my head.

I caught Roman's concerned look.

"Pagani has stated if it is his men who carried out the shootings without his permission, they'll be dealt with, but I'm not satisfied," my father said. His phone rang, and he looked at the display. "Excuse me."

He stood, and although he didn't leave the room, he turned his back to the table and walked a few steps away.

The men at the table continued to talk, but Roman and I remained silent, listening to the call.

"What do you mean?" my father asked, checking his watch. "That was hours ago." Silence on the line. "You've tried him? His driver?" Silence. "Fine. Reschedule it. And find him."

When he turned to us again, he immediately met my gaze and gestured to the door. Roman also stood, and the three of us stepped into the hall and closed the conference room door behind us.

"Dominic didn't make his flight."

"What do you mean?" I asked, alarm bells sounding.

"I mean that was the fucking captain, calling to say he was about to lose his time slot," my father snapped.

I watched him try to call Dominic, but the call went directly to voice mail.

"His driver is missing as well."

"Missing?" Roman asked.

My father placed another call and spoke into the phone. "Get Natalie and Jacob packed up and to my house. I don't care what you have to do to make that happen, but get them here now."

"I have to go," I said, pulling my phone from my pocket.

"Godamnit, I need you here, Salvatore!"

I stopped, took a deep breath in, and turned to face him.

"Dominic has always wanted what you have," my father stated. "What you will inherit from me once I am ready to retire. That's no secret, not for any of us."

I listened in silence.

"I don't like all of the things he does," he continued, the words obviously difficult to say. "I sometimes don't like who he is." He breathed in deeply. "But he is still your brother."

I shifted on my feet. My father didn't usually resort to making me feel guilty to do something I didn't want to do, and I wasn't sure that's what he was doing now, but what he said triggered something akin to guilt inside me.

"I was harsh with him when I learned what he did to Natalie," he said.

"No, not harsh," I disagreed. "It needed to be done. Dominic was the only person in the wrong on that one. Question is, does he realize it? Does *he* think so?"

My father ran his hand through his thinning hair and sat on the chair just beneath the window. Seeing him weary—it was strange, felt wrong. I'd only ever seen my father as strong. All powerful. And ultimately, always in control.

I always thought I'd celebrate his fall, his weakening.

I went to him and placed a hand on his shoulder.

"I'll look for him."

He sighed, nodded his head, then met my eyes and took my hand. "I'm too fucking old for this."

"Go upstairs, Franco. I'll handle the meeting," Roman offered.

My father looked at him, shook his head, and steeled his spine before standing. "I'll handle it."

Roman nodded. We both knew he couldn't not handle this one. It would be seen as ultimate weakness.

"Dominic is unsatisfied. Always has been," he said to me. "I've always pushed him to want more. It corrupted him in a way."

I wanted to tell him it wasn't his fault, but wasn't it? At least partially?

He put his hand on my shoulder and came to within inches of me. He tapped his forefinger against his head. "He's not right, not now. He can't accept his place. But remember, he is your brother. Find him, and bring him home. Do that, and I'll take care of him."

20

LUCIA

"What the hell are you doing here?" I asked, standing and leaning my weight on my crutches. I didn't feel half as confident as I somehow managed to sound. "How did you get in?"

He stood in the light just on the other side of the coffee table looking disheveled, his shirt untucked, his hair messy, his face bruised. He gave me a lopsided grin, and I really looked at him for the first time, the dimple on his right cheek disarming me momentarily. His eyes were a light blue-gray, the lashes thick and darker than his blond hair. He was tall, well over six feet, but he had a leaner build than Salvatore, although still muscular. Powerful.

I returned my gaze to his face, saw his grin widen. The darkness in his eyes reminded me who he was.

He tucked the gun into the back of his jeans before reaching into his pocket and taking something out.

I cocked my head to the side when he held it out to show me, not understanding right away.

"I have a key."

It dawned on me that he held a key to my old house. To the house where my sister and niece lived.

"Isabella gave it to me."

"I don't understand." But I did. I just hadn't come to terms with it yet. I studied him, taking in his features, comparing them to Effie's. Although she hadn't inherited his blond hair, she had similar eyes, although hers were warm, innocent. The rest was Isabella, but there was one thing she shared with Dominic: that dimple in her right cheek. That was from her father.

No.

I had to stop this. What was I thinking? I was talking about my sister here. And Effie's father could be anyone. It wouldn't be him.

What about the tests?

Nothing was definitive, not yet.

And the key. Why did Isabella give him a key?

"You're lying. My sister wouldn't have given you a key."

"Why not?"

"She hates you."

He snorted then went to the liquor cabinet and poured himself a drink. "Want one?"

"No."

He leaned against the cabinet and watched me as he brought the tumbler to his lips and swallowed the deep amber liquid. I hoped it burned on the way down.

"What do you see in my brother?" he asked.

"What do you want, Dominic? What are you doing here?"

"He's a puppet to our father. A weak little windup toy who does as he's told. Who humiliated you. What in hell do you see in him?"

"I see his heart. I see what's real behind the mask he puts on for you, for your father."

At that he chuckled and poured himself another drink.

"That's fresh. Now Sergio," he began, drinking deeply. "He was a man's man. A man to be respected, like me. Even Franco Benedetti respected him."

"And you think kidnapping his son makes you respectable? It makes you a monster. A weak, hateful monster."

He laughed and stalked toward me. I forced myself to stand my ground, even when he stood only inches away, breathing whiskey on my face as his gaze roamed over my body. He looked me in the eye.

"Well then, you may need to actually open your eyes and see the other monsters much closer to home."

A car pulled up outside, and I exhaled in relief. He stepped away just as a key turned in the lock, and Isabella walked into the house. She stopped in the doorway as soon as she saw him. They exchanged a look before she turned her gaze on me.

I watched her, then him, then her again.

And I was certain.

"What are you doing here?" she asked Dominic, her tone much too casual as she closed the door behind her.

"What, do you two compare notes or something?" he asked, finishing his drink and setting his glass down. "I'm hungry." He went into the kitchen, leaving us alone.

"Izzy? What the hell is going on?"

She plopped her bag down on the coffee table and rubbed her eyes with her hands. She looked defeated in that moment, and I saw through the tough facade she put on more and more.

"Luke's out of surgery," she said, heading to where Dominic had left his glass, filling it with the same whiskey and drinking it down. "He's going to make it."

She stood quietly a moment before her body slumped, and she broke into sobs. I went to her and embraced her, the crutches tucked awkwardly under my arms. I held her so tight that she finally surrendered herself, letting herself go, weeping, hugging me back.

"I thought...I thought...God, if he died?" She sucked in a loud breath and wiped her eyes, leaning back. "I prayed, Lucia. I haven't prayed in five years." She shook her head. "I love him. I love him, and all I've done is hurt him."

"Luke?" I was so confused.

She nodded, and we walked over to the sofa and sat down.

"He was adopted," she started, as if that was what I was concerned about. "We're not blood relatives."

"I know, Izzy. God, I know. It's okay. I don't care. It's fine."

"I owe you an explanation. Multiple, probably."

I nodded.

"Five years ago, more than that, actually, I met Dominic. It was accidental, nothing planned. I was seventeen. It was a party in the woods, and I didn't know who he was. Same for him. He didn't know me, and we didn't exchange last names. It was just Dominic and Isabella. That's all. We hit it off, and things got heated over the next few weeks. Months."

"You still didn't know who he was?" I didn't believe that.

"By then we knew. Hell, by our third date, we knew. But there was something there. I don't know what it was, maybe even the whole Romeo and Juliette with warring families and the romance of it all, the sneaking around, meeting in the woods, sitting under the stars. Just us. Together."

"You fell in love with Dominic Benedetti?"

She nodded her head. "He wasn't like this, not then. We were each other's firsts. First love, first..."

"Then you got pregnant."

"Yes. It was right around when things were coming to a head between the families. Dominic was going to tell his father. I told Papa."

"That's why he was so mad."

She nodded sadly. "I was pregnant with the enemy's child. Never mind that I was barely an adult and unmarried."

"He disowned you because it was Dominic's?"

"Yes. He couldn't accept it. It shamed him. Infuriated him. Looking at me pissed him off. I think I was the ultimate reminder of his disgrace."

"How long did he know before you left?"

"A month. He gave me an ultimatum. Abort the baby or lose everything."

"Abortion? Papa?" He was a devout Catholic. As old school as they came.

She nodded, her eyes glistening again. "I couldn't do that." She glanced up the stairs. "I'm so glad I didn't."

"Does Franco Benedetti know?"

"No. Dominic never told him. In fact, we stopped seeing each other as soon as I found out I was pregnant. Well, it trickled to a stop. But things were different then. He sent money, though, after I left."

"Well, isn't he a prince?"

"We were both kids, Lucia, and I've forgiven him. You don't have to, but this is between him and me."

"Does Effie know?"

She shook her head. "No one does."

"Well, I think Salvatore may." She opened her mouth, but I continued. "He and Roman suspected it was Luke, and Roman had DNA tests done."

"Fuck."

"When it came back that Luke couldn't be the father, Roman, who apparently had his suspicions, used his own DNA to test against it. Traces matched, and he's running Dominic's now."

"My fucking uncle is always sticking his big fucking nose where it doesn't belong." Dominic leaned against the entrance to the kitchen eating a sandwich, not bothering to hide the fact he was eavesdropping. "Not that it fucking matters. Not anymore."

Isabella stood, suddenly fuming, and went to him. "Was it you? Did you order the hit on Luke?"

He walked around her, biting off another piece, chewing like he didn't have a care in the world. "I didn't realize you *loved* him," he sneered.

She grabbed his arm, making him turn to face her. "We had an agreement! Goddamn you, we had a fucking agreement!"

"You're the one who wanted him involved."

"I couldn't meet with them, you know that!"

"Meet with who?" I asked.

They both looked at me as if they were surprised I still stood there.

"The Pagani family. Paul Jr., the old man's son and wannabe successor," Dominic filled in, stuffing the last of his sandwich into his mouth. "Fucking asshole."

"Old school. They won't deal with a woman," Isabella said.

"Deal with a woman over what?"

"What I told you when I first came to Salvatore's house."

"What, starting another war? Reclaiming our place as what, the biggest and baddest? The family who sheds the most blood? Izzy, what are you doing? I don't want this. You can't want it."

"I did, at first." She dropped into a chair. "But now, after what happened? After I saw him like that, Luke hooked up to too many machines to count, barely alive? Jesus, how could we…"

She stopped and turned toward Dominic, then stood and went to him. She poked a finger into his chest.

"Did you order the fucking shooting? Did you order them to kill Luke?"

"You're starting to bore me. What happened to my vengeful little bitch?"

"Fuck you, Dominic."

"Fuck you, Isabella." He took her glass and finished it before slamming it down on the coffee table. "You may be over it, but I'm not. No way I'm standing by and letting my father hand everything over to my half-wit brother. No. Fucking. Way."

The door flew open right then, and Salvatore burst in, his face a mask of fury as he slammed Dominic against the closest wall, his forearm crushing his neck. "How the fuck did you get in here?"

Dominic shoved him back and chuckled. "Check inside the house before you plant guards outside it, dumbass."

"Mommy?"

Effie's voice had all of us turning toward the stairs. The fighting had woken her up. She stood there, clutching her teddy bear and watching us.

"Honey!" Isabella ran up to her and took her in her arms. "Uncle Luke is going to be okay, baby!"

"He is?"

"He is."

"I'm so glad. Can we go see him?"

"He's still sleeping, but soon. I'll take you to him, and you can give him all those cookies you made."

"They're delicious, Effie," Dominic yelled up.

Salvatore's stood at Dominic's side, hands fisted.

"Thanks, Dominic."

Effie's relaxed familiarity with Dominic surprised me and, when I glanced at Salvatore, I saw that it surprised him as well.

"It's late," Isabella said over her shoulder. "Go home." She turned and walked up the stairs with Effie.

"Why was everyone yelling?" I heard Effie asking her mom as their voices disappeared down the hall. I didn't hear my sister's answer.

"Well, she always was good at dismissing anyone she had no use for," Dominic bit out.

"Fuck you. Dad's looking for you. Go home."

"You go home. And take your pretty little plaything with you before I decide to have a taste myself. Her sister was pretty good."

Salvatore reared up to punch him, but I grabbed his arm. "He's not worth it, Salvatore."

"Get out." Salvatore didn't look at me, but stood nose to nose with his brother.

"I wasn't planning on staying."

It was a moment before he walked out the front door.

Salvatore turned to me and took me into his arms.

"Are you okay? Did he hurt you?"

"I'm fine. He didn't do anything to me."

"He was right. I should have checked the house."

Salvatore stepped back and looked me over as if he wanted to see with his own eyes that Dominic hadn't hurt me.

"Stop. Nothing happened. And everything is out in the open now."

His eyes searched mine, and I touched his face with my hand.

"Take me home, Salvatore."

21

SALVATORE

Lucia sat silently beside me.

"What is it?" I asked after a few minutes.

"Effie is Dominic's daughter. Isabella confirmed it."

"I'm not surprised."

"They fell in love, Salvatore. They were young and just fell in love. You were right in what you thought. That's why Papa sent her away, disowning her. He gave her an ultimatum: abort or leave. She left."

I remained silent, understanding a little more of Isabella. I'd pegged her to be a hateful, power-hungry bitch. She might well be, but she was also stronger than I gave her credit for.

"Dominic was supposed to tell your father, but he never did."

I glanced at Lucia. "I can't say I'm surprised."

"He let her go all alone." Lucia looked off into the distance. "He sent her money, though." She rolled her eyes.

"Lucia." I don't know why I felt the need to defend Dominic. I wasn't, really; I just needed to explain how things were at our house. How my father was. "My father is a very domineering man. When we were kids, Sergio was the only one brave enough to stand up to him." She opened her mouth to speak, her expression unbelieving. "Wait. I'm not defending Dominic or what he did. I'm just telling you there is more to his story, another layer, like there is with your sister."

I'm not sure if she accepted that or not.

"Luke and Isabella, they're in love," she said, changing the subject.

"I heard he's out of surgery, and that he's going to make it."

"I'm so relieved."

"There are still too many questions, Lucia. This isn't over."

"Who shot Luke?"

I shook my head. "Unclear. Luke was working with the younger Pagani, Paul Jr. His father forbade any interaction once he found out what his son was up to."

"I think Dominic is more involved than you know, Salvatore."

"What do you mean?"

"He and Isabella, I think they have been working together. She said they had an agreement."

Fuck.

"I think she's wondering if Dominic ordered Luke's shooting."

"So my little brother is working with Isabella DeMarco and Paul Pagani to bring down his own family?"

Our gazes locked, but neither of us said more.

As we pulled up to the tall gates of the house, I fished my phone out of my pocket and dialed Roman.

"What are you doing?" Lucia asked.

Roman answered.

"Where are you?" I asked.

"At your father's. The last of the family is just leaving."

"Are Natalie and Jacob there?"

"Just got here. She's pissed."

"Well, don't unpack her."

"What do you mean?"

"I'm calling a family meeting. It's an emergency. I want you to bring Natalie and Jacob to my house. And I want my father and Dominic here."

"What?" Lucia asked.

"What meeting?" Roman asked. "What's going on?"

"Tomorrow morning, I want a second meeting with you, my father, Dominic, both Paul Pagani Sr. and Jr., and Isabella DeMarco. I want you to arrange it."

"Izzy?" Lucia asked, her eyes wide as I pulled the car to a stop at the front door.

"I'll give you an hour to get the family over here. Call the others for tomorrow morning. Seven o'clock. That should give them enough time to get here. This is going to end."

"Let's meet with the family first and discuss this, Salvatore. I think it would be wise for us to—"

"This is fucking ending, Uncle. Period."

I disconnected the call and turned to Lucia.

"Salvatore, you can't involve my sister."

"She's already involved, Lucia. She involved herself."

"No, I won't allow it!"

"You won't *allow* it?" I asked, getting out of the car and going around to her side. She'd already swung the door open and had her crutches on the ground, trying to climb out. I took the crutches in one hand and lifted her out with the other.

"Put me down. I can do this."

"I don't have time for this, Lucia."

"I said put me down!"

"Christ. You are the most pigheaded..." I set her down, and she leaned on me until she could get the crutches under her. "Let's go inside."

"You want my sister in with that room full of killers?"

"It will be a peaceful meeting." We entered the house, and I closed the front door behind us. "This is my house. I make the rules." I dialed another number on my phone. Once it started to ring, I covered the mouthpiece and turned back to Lucia. "Go upstairs to your room. You'll wait for me there."

"I am not a goddamned child!"

"Then stop acting like one."

Marco answered the call. He was still at the hospital. "Yes?"

"I need you back at the house. Arrange for two men to stay at the hospital. I'm calling a meeting for tomorrow morning. I need more men here. We'll have the Pagani father and son along with Isabella DeMarco. The Paganis will bring their own guard. I'm calling for no weapons, but I want the manpower here."

"I'm on it."

"Thank you." I could trust Marco to take care of things every time.

"You already sound like you're the boss of the family," Lucia taunted, still standing there, not having moved an inch.

I checked the time and tucked my phone into my pocket before turning to her. I looked her over, her dress rumpled, her eyes looking a little tired, but she was still too damn pretty.

"You need some time?" I asked, closing the space between us. "With me?" Sliding a hand to her waist, I tugged her close.

"Salvatore, this isn't—"

"Shh." I kissed her mouth and took one of the crutches away while the other one slipped out from under her arm as she wrapped it around my neck. "Let's go upstairs."

She gasped when I lifted her, cradling her in my arms. I carried her up to my bedroom. I sat her on the bed and tugged her dress over her head before pushing her to lie on her back. After stripping off my shirt, jeans, and briefs—all while Lucia watched with rapidly darkening eyes—I slid her panties over her hips and off her legs. I brought them to my nose and inhaled deeply.

"Salvatore!" She tried to tug them away, but I held them just out of reach.

"I like your smell," I said, leaning over her to kiss her, swallowing her moan in my mouth. She tasted so sweet, so innocent. I dragged my mouth from hers and trailed kisses down over her jaw and to her throat, across her collarbone and down to one breast, then the other, drawing out the nipples, making her cry out when I bit just a little harder than she liked.

I ran my tongue down the center of her chest and tickled her belly button before sliding it lower. I settling myself between her legs to take her clit into my mouth.

Lucia sighed heavily.

"You taste fucking amazing."

She curled her fingers into my hair and tugged. "Wait."

"Why?" I asked, looking up at her, her scent intoxicating.

"I want to taste you." She pushed herself up on her elbows. "Please."

I nodded and lifted her slightly, lying on my back and setting her on my hips so she straddled me. "Does it hurt?" I asked.

"Huh?" She seemed confused.

"Your ankle?"

She shook her head.

With my hands on her hips, I guided her folds over my cock.

"I want to taste you," she said.

"Patience." I smiled, liking her greedy, a little dirty. I'd corrupt her, and I'd make sure she loved every minute of it. "Turn around, and put your knees on either side of my face."

She hesitated only for a moment before turning, presenting me with her beautiful ass, then, her gorgeous, dripping cunt just over my face. She lowered herself to her elbows, and I pulled her to me, pausing to bite my lip when she flicked her little wet tongue over the tip of my cock before sealing her lips around it.

"Fuck, baby." I brought her to my face, tickling her with the little bit of stubble I needed to shave off. I dipped my thumb into her wet cunt before sliding it up to her asshole and pressing there, not penetrating, not yet, only holding it there as I tickled her clit with my tongue while she went to work on my cock.

I'd only ever been with experienced women. Having Lucia's innocent mouth on my cock made me heady. What she lacked in experience, she made up for with lustful enthusiasm: sucking my cock, licking it, taking me to the point she gagged, all while I teased then sucked her clit and slid another finger into her cunt while my thumb kept its pressure on her ass. She arched her back, moaning, as she worked me with her hand, like she'd watched me do, and sucked. My cock swelled even thicker. When my release was moments away, I closed my mouth around her clit and sucked hard, penetrating her ass with my finger as I did. She cried out, the sound muffled by my thick, throbbing cock, and she stilled when I came, emptying into her mouth while she throbbed around my finger, pressing herself into my face, squeezing every ounce of pleasure from my tongue.

A moment later, Lucia lay beside me spent, her hair splayed out on the pillow, some of it falling on my face. She turned to me and slid one leg between mine.

"I liked that," she said, kissing me.

"I'm glad, because I'll want your little mouth around me often." I checked my watch. They'd be here in twenty minutes. All I wanted to do was hold her, stay here with her, but I had to take care of business. "Go to sleep, Lucia." I climbed out of bed and covered her with the blanket.

She shook her head and rose up on an elbow.

"My sister, Salvatore."

"She'll be fine. But if she orchestrated Jacob's kidnapping, she'll need to answer for that."

"You're not going to let anyone hurt her."

It wasn't a question, but I answered it anyway. "No. I'll keep her safe. My intention is to keep everyone safe and end this."

"I want to be there with her."

"I want you to stay out of family business."

"My sister is my family."

I shook my head, my tone harder when I spoke. "Your sister is in over her head, and I want her out of it too. Can I trust you to stay here, or do I have to bind you?" I needed her to know this conversation was over.

She glanced at the restraints, perhaps remembering how easily I could do just what I said.

"You make me really mad," she said.

"Mad I can handle. I just need you safe."

She nodded.

"I need to have a shower. Stay."

"Can I at least call Izzy?"

"That's okay by me." I tossed her my phone and walked into the bathroom to have a quick shower before everyone got there. It was going to be a long night.

I WASN'T surprised when Dominic didn't show up.

I also wasn't surprised to find Lucia making her way down the stairs, dressed, clumsily working her crutches.

My father and Roman stood in the foyer watching her, my father looking at her with tired eyes rather that the contempt he normally showed. I walked up to her with a look that said I'd deal with her later, but when I tried to take her crutches and carry her down, she refused.

"I'm not an invalid. I just need to get used to these. Besides, my ankle can take a little weight." She flinched as she demonstrated putting a bit of weight on it.

"Pigheaded."

I walked the steps with her to make sure she didn't fall. By the time we got down, Natalie walked into the house with a sleeping Jacob in her arms.

"Father, Roman, why don't you go ahead into the dining room."

They both nodded and left. Everyone was tired.

Rainey went to Natalie and took the bag off her shoulder. I'd woken her to prepare a room.

"Natalie, I'm sorry to keep you and Jacob up so late, but I thought you'd be more comfortable here," I said.

"I'd be most comfortable in my own house," she said, glaring at my father's receding back.

Lucia giggled, then had the presence of mind to cover it up with a cough.

"This is Lucia," I said. "Lucia, Natalie. And my nephew Jacob."

Jacob stirred, opening his eyes then closing them again. I watched how Lucia looked at Natalie and saw Natalie with renewed eyes. I'd known her for so long, and she'd been so much like a sister to me from day one that I sometimes forgot how attractive she was, even with her long dark hair wound into a bun, wearing no makeup, and dressed in an old pair of pajamas.

"Nice to meet you," Lucia said. She then peeked at Jacob. "You probably want to get him to bed."

"And me too. It's nice to meet you. Salvatore's told me about you."

They both glanced at me.

"Should I be worried?" Lucia asked.

Natalie smiled and shook her head. "Not given the way he looks at you," Natalie said with a wink.

"Why don't you go up with Natalie and help her get herself and Jacob settled," I said to Lucia. I then pulled her in close. "And this time, stay up there," I whispered, squeezing her ass so she knew she'd pay if she came down again.

"Fine. I don't want to be around your father anyway."

I didn't offer to help her upstairs this time. She'd refuse anyway. Instead, I went into the dining room and closed the doors.

"Where's Dominic?" I asked.

"Don't know," my father answered.

"I thought he'd come home," I said.

"Why would you think that?" my father asked.

"Because I talked with him. He was at Isabella DeMarco's house."

My father's lips tightened. "What the fuck was he doing there?"

It wasn't my place to tell him about Effie. I'd let Dominic do that when he was ready. Strange. I realized just then how difficult these last five years must have been for my brother. He'd abandoned his child and a woman he'd at one point cared about all out of fear of my father's disapproval, his wrath. He'd wanted his acceptance, his approval, as much as I had. Maybe he still did. He was as much a puppet to my domineering father as I was.

Roman cleared his throat.

"Why do I get the feeling you two know more than you're letting on?" my father asked.

"Let me make a call. I think I may know where he is," Roman said, standing.

"It's important he's here," I said. "Critical, actually."

He nodded and made the call. My father and I waited in

awkward silence until Roman returned. Rainey knocked and entered with a tray holding a bottle of whiskey and several glasses. I poured for everyone and sent her to bed. She'd need to be up early to greet the remainder of our guests. It was only a few hours before they got here.

"I know who was behind things."

My father drank his glass of whiskey then pulled the bottle over to pour a second.

"Isabella DeMarco and Dominic have been working together with Pagani's son, Paul Jr. Luke was just the front man, acting on her behalf."

"I knew that fucking bitch would be trouble. Only good DeMarco is a dead DeMarco," my father said.

"That's enough," I said more calmly than I expected I could. "I called this meeting to put an end to this stupidity. This feud that's torn your own family apart. When will it be enough for you?"

"When I'm dead."

"Don't push me."

"Gentlemen, we're on the same side," Roman said, standing between us with a hand on both our shoulders. "I'm having someone pick Dominic up and bring him here."

"Where is he?" I asked.

"He has a bar he likes to go to."

Roman didn't expound on that, and I left it alone.

"He's got some explaining to do, that fucking bastard," Franco said. "Cancel the meeting. I'll deal with my son myself. You deal with the DeMarco cunt, and Pagani will deal with his son." He rose to his feet. "I'm fucking tired. You called me here for this bullshit?"

"Sit down," I spoke quietly, not rising but remaining where I sat, feeling more in control than I ever had in my life. I knew what I wanted, what I needed to do. It would all truly end tonight.

"Be careful, son," he said, but he lowered himself back down into his chair.

"We're dealing with this publicly. We're forgiving what's happened thus far and calling a truce."

"You're not boss yet, Salvatore. I decide, not you."

"I already decided, old man. Let it be."

"Franco," Roman started.

My father kept his eyes on me, but listened.

"Let's do this Salvatore's way and end this. It's grown too far out of proportion," Roman said.

"And how do you propose to get Dominic to agree?" Franco asked.

That was where we were all at a loss. He couldn't be given a property to manage, not as volatile as he was. He'd bring war wherever he went. He needed to be controlled, but I didn't know how. I was truly at a loss when it came to Dominic.

"I will talk to him," I said. I'd give him one more chance, talk to him like maybe I should have been talking to him all along. Maybe he'd have come to me five years ago when he was in trouble if I'd been a better brother to him.

By the time Dominic arrived, it was almost five o'clock in the morning. He stank of liquor and stumbled in making a lot of noise, propped up by two men who worked for my father.

"You called, brother?"

The lids of his eyes were drooping, and the bruises I'd given him earlier had colored a dark purple.

"Summoning me to your grand estate?" he said, slurring his words as he gestured around the house.

"Get him in the fucking shower."

"I'll make coffee," Roman said.

Marco had also arrived in the meantime, and men were

being arranged throughout the property. We had about two hours before everyone would get here. According to Roman, Pagani Sr., wasn't surprised by the call, which meant he'd already talked to his son. Good. The less surprises, the better.

Isabella was a different story. Roman had spoken with her and told her the reason for the meeting. Maybe it was vanity, a feeling of being acknowledged as head of the DeMarco family, because for all intents and purposes, she was. We just underestimated the DeMarco family's level of activity. It was stupid on our part. Isabella would be here bright and early, as anxious as me to put this behind her, now that she realized what she could have lost.

I had Dominic taken to a bedroom downstairs, knowing he'd raise hell wherever he was just because he was Dominic and he was piss drunk. Roman remained with my father while I went to check on Dominic's progress.

"You're not boss yet," was the greeting he threw at me when I walked into the bedroom.

"You at least smell a little better," I said, tossing one of my dress shirts at him. "Put this on." I'd changed too, wearing a suit minus the jacket.

"You want me looking respectable for those assholes?" he asked, but he took it.

"I know about Effie," I said, sitting down.

He met my eyes but remained silent.

"You haven't told anyone all these years?"

"What, that I knocked up a DeMarco? All while father hands you one on a silver fucking platter." He shook his head in disgust. "You're the golden boy, aren't you? First it was Sergio, then you. Fuck Dominic."

I wanted to punch him but had to remind myself why he was being defensive. "I'm sorry I didn't make it easier for you to talk to me."

"Don't get sentimental on me now." He said, then returned his attention to buttoning his shirt before continuing. "Does father know?"

"No. Only Roman and I. That's how it'll stay unless you decide to tell him."

He nodded, and I knew it was as close to an actual thank-you that I would get.

"Tell me about Luke DeMarco's shooting."

Nothing.

"Isabella and you were working together with Pagani, Jr."

He snorted. "He is a colossal fuckup. Fucking dimwit."

"That we can agree on. They'll be here soon, Dominic. We're all going to be in a room together. I would rather know the truth now, from you."

A knock came on the door.

"Sir."

It was Marco. "Come in."

He opened the door and glanced at Dominic but spoke to me. "Isabella DeMarco is here."

I checked my watch. "She's early." It was barely six a.m. "Does Lucia know?"

Marco gave me a short nod.

"Of course she does. Where are they?"

"Your study."

"All right. I'll be right there. Make sure they stay in there until I get there."

"I will."

He closed the door. I turned back to Dominic, who'd finished dressing and was now combing his hair, studying me.

"Last chance to tell me everything."

"Go get everyone under control, brother. I'll see you when it's time for the meeting."

"Suit yourself." I walked out of the room and directly to my study.

Lucia and Isabella sat on the couch talking in whispers when I walked in. Lucia at least had the grace to give me a meek smile.

"You shouldn't be here," I said to her.

"She's my sister, Salvatore."

"Why do I feel like I'm hitting a wall at every turn?" I asked.

"For once, I'm taking his side, Lucia. This is my business, and I don't want you involved," Isabella said, standing.

"I'm not letting you face those men alone."

"She's not alone. I will be there with her," I said.

"Luce, I did this. I brought this on us. I had Dominic kidnap Jacob. I ultimately was responsible for Luke being shot." She turned to me. "I'm so sorry about Jacob. I just, I wanted to scare Franco. I didn't even think about Natalie. It was all about sending a message to Franco. Everything. And every time I look at Effie's face and hold her in my arms, I keep thinking about Natalie. How she must have felt. How scared Jacob must have felt. I'm sorry. I was wrong."

Lucia squeezed her hand.

I nodded. "Is it over?"

"Yes. For me. But I'm not sure how much control I have or ever had. The burglaries—we'd talked about it but hadn't decided on anything. And Luke... I hope Dominic didn't order that."

"I don't know myself, but we'll soon find out."

Before I could say more, loud voices—two men yelling— interrupted us. Dominic and my father.

"Stay here," I said, rushing to the door and out. They were in the dining room, Roman, my father, and Dominic.

"You betray your own family!" Franco yelled, his face hot with fury.

"What was in it for me? What was ever in it for me? Why in

hell did you even have me?" Dominic countered, all drunkenness having left his system, the heat of his anger perhaps having burnt it out. "After Sergio died, it all went to Salvatore. What about me?"

"You're the youngest. I can't fucking help that."

"The backup to the backup."

"You're stupid if that's what you think!"

"So worried about your grandson. Everything is about Sergio. His boy. Taking care of Jacob."

"Like I would take care of yours!"

"Really?"

"Everyone calm the fuck down." I walked into the room, but neither my father nor Dominic noticed my arrival.

Isabella walked in behind me, her gaze locked on Dominic. When my father stalked up to her, she stood taller, and I stood beside her.

"You stupid little bitch," he started.

"Stop! All of you! What is this, fucking preschool? We're all going to sit down, and we're all going to talk."

"Salvatore."

Roman said my name and walked into the room. I just then realized he'd been absent.

"I just got off the phone with Paul Pagani, Sr. Neither he nor his son will be here after all. He's already addressed his son's responsibility and taken care of it. Jr. won't be a problem, he assures us. The moneys that were taken have been returned, and he's given his word his allegiance is to the head of the Benedetti family."

I nodded. "Then this will truly be a family meeting."

"Apart from this whore," Franco muttered.

The tension in the room was palpable. No one moved to sit, and it looked like either Dominic or my father would explode at any minute.

I sighed, shaking my head, but before I could speak, Dominic drew a pistol and held it at his side.

"She's the mother of your other grandchild, old man, but you're too fucking stupid to see it, aren't you?"

"Dominic, give me the gun," I said, shadowing him as he moved around the table to where my father stood, but it was like he couldn't hear me. Couldn't see me. Couldn't see anyone but our father.

"I was too much of a coward to tell you she was pregnant with my baby. *Mine*, you stupid fuck."

"Dominic," I started, cautious.

Franco watched him, glancing at Isabella for a moment as he finally understood. But Dominic wasn't finished.

"You never cared about me. All your love went to Sergio."

"That's not true," our father said. "He was just firstborn."

"Fuck firstborn! This isn't the fucking Dark Ages. It doesn't fucking matter."

"You betrayed your family. I accepted you as my own, and you betrayed me."

All heads snapped to my father then.

Roman approached Franco and whispered something into his ear. I turned to Dominic to see his face as he slowly understood what was being said.

"No, I'll tell this bastard who he is." My father shoved Roman away. "Son of a fucking foot soldier who thinks he should be head of *my* family."

"You're lying," Dominic said, raising the pistol.

"Dominic, give me the gun," I said, mirroring every move he made.

I heard a gasp at the door, and Isabella moved, shielding Lucia, who'd just walked in.

"Dominic, please, give me the gun."

"You all thought your mother was a saint. Died a martyr."

Franco snorted. "You didn't know her very well. None of you did."

"You're a fucking liar, old man," Dominic spewed.

"She whored herself out."

"He's not worth it," I said to my brother. "He's lying, and he's not worth it." But it was like he couldn't hear me at all.

"Don't you dare talk about her like that." Dominic wiped his face with the back of the hand that held the pistol.

"Like your bitch," Franco said, gesturing to Isabella.

That was it, it was finished. Dominic aimed, my father's face changed to one of surprise, of shock. I don't know if any of us thought he'd do it. Thought he'd actually pull the trigger.

I grabbed Dominic's arm, but he cocked the gun. My father's mouth opened, another taunt leaving it, pushing Dominic to the breaking point.

Gunshots never sound the way you think they should. They're louder, deadlier, and a hell of a lot faster than in the movies.

Lucia's scream was all I heard. Everything else was background noise. She drowned it all out with her scream.

I lunged between them, intending to push my father out of the way, to save him. To save Dominic from doing something he'd regret for the rest of his life.

But it never worked that way in real life either. Never like the movies. The heroes didn't walk away, arms raised, triumphant.

More often, they got hurt.

They got killed.

I did knock my father out of the way. Landing on him was softer than the damned marble floors I always hated. A second later, and I'd have been too late.

Or maybe I already was.

Lucia screamed again, dropping to her knees, her hands bloodied, her face splattered with it. Her crutches clanked to the floor near my head as she grabbed my face, looking over her shoulder, shoving someone away. Her tears kept dropping on my face, and she kept wiping them away again and again, talking, I think. Her mouth moved, but no sound came. No sound. Only pain. Only fire in my side.

When I put my hand to the place, it felt warm and wet, and when I reached to touch her pretty, pretty face, I covered it in red, smearing it down over her jaw, her neck, down until she faded from view. The last thing I felt was her hair tickling my face, her body pressing against mine, the movements desperate.

22

LUCIA

"Salvatore, no!"

I held his face with one hand and pressed my other hand to the place on his side that wouldn't stop bleeding. I kissed him. Kissed him and kissed him. When I tried to push the hair back from his forehead, I left blood in its place. His blood. God, there was so much of it. Too much.

"Don't die."

He hadn't promised me that. He'd made me three promises, but he'd never promised me he wouldn't die.

I'd never asked him to promise that. I'd never...

"Don't die," I whispered just to him.

He was too still, and when my sister touched my shoulder, and I looked up at her through the blur the haze of my tears caused, I sucked in a trembling breath. Her face, the look in her eyes, telling me it was bad.

"There's a helicopter on its way to take him to the hospital," she whispered, kneeling down beside me, holding me when I turned my attention back to him.

They would take him away. They would take him away, and I

would never see him again. Why did they do that? Why did they take them away? How could you hold an empty space? How could you say good-bye?

My lip trembled. I bent down to his face, his beautiful face so pale, so still. My hair made a curtain between us and the room, and I listened for his breath, tried to feel it on my skin, feel its soft warmth. I wanted him to call me pigheaded again.

I wanted to hear him telling me he would keep everyone safe.

He had. He'd kept that promise.

Why hadn't I made him promise to keep himself safe?

"I'm sorry," I whispered.

"Lucia."

My sister said my name, but I ignored her.

"I should have made you promise," I said, tears rolling from my face onto his. I smeared the blood with them, trying to clean him, remembering then that he had made one promise to me he hadn't yet kept. "You have to wake up, Salvatore," I stated, gaining some strength. He kept his promises. He wouldn't not. "You promised me you'd give me what I wanted. The life I wanted. You promised. You have to wake up now."

"Lucia," Isabella said again.

"Go away," I told her, still cleaning his face with my tears.

"Ma'am."

Other hands were on me, another voice was talking to me.

"Lucia, they're here. They're going to take him to the hospital. You have to let them see Salvatore."

I kept one hand on Salvatore's chest, trying not to think about the fact it was still. I looked up at the men, at the room around me, and I leaned away, letting them look at Salvatore. Letting them start their work.

Two other men lifted Franco Benedetti onto a stretcher.

Roman looked at all of us, his face one of shock, blood splatters marring it and ruining his perfect suit.

"Ma'am, we need to take them now."

"Which hospital?" Isabella asked.

"Bellevue."

"Come on," Isabella said, dragging me to my feet.

"He's not dead?" I asked, confused.

The paramedic gave me a cautious look. "We'll do what we can for him."

"Let's go," Isabella said again. "We need to get to the hospital. They'll be much faster with the chopper."

"What's happened?" Natalie asked from the doorway, her face crumpling when she saw Salvatore unconscious on the stretcher.

I looked around the room, searching for him, for Dominic. "Where is he?" I asked my sister. "Where is he?" Anger gave me strength, but my sister held fast to me.

"Salvatore got in the way between Dominic and his father," Isabella said to Natalie.

"Where the hell is Dominic?" I screamed to anyone who would answer.

"Let's go," Isabella said. "Salvatore needs you now."

That got my attention. I turned to her and nodded. I followed her to the front door, cursing the crutches and my damn ankle.

"He's so fucking stupid," I said to her as she drove too fast off the grounds.

"He wanted to save everyone," she modified.

"Why did they take Franco?"

"Heart attack."

A fresh onslaught of tears came, and I sucked in a loud breath. "He did it for nothing. He tried to save that horrible man for nothing."

Isabella took my hand and squeezed it, forcing me to look at her. "He's not dead yet. He needs you to believe in him, understand? You can't be weak now, not now, Lucia. He needs you."

I looked at her face. She looked much older than her twenty-two years all of a sudden, and her eyes—they held lifetimes of sadness inside them.

"How's Luke?" I asked, remembering.

She focused her attention back on the road. "No change."

"Where's Dominic?"

"He slipped out." She shook her head. "I saw his face. He just kept looking at Salvatore, lying at his feet. For so long, it was what he wanted, but then, when it happened..."

"Where is he?"

"His face, Lucia. I'd never seen him look like that before. Not ever."

But I didn't care about Dominic or what he felt or what his face looked like. I would kill him with my bare hands when I saw him.

My sister was right, though. Salvatore needed me now, and I would focus all my energy on him. He was a survivor. He would survive. He had to.

When we arrived at the hospital, he was in surgery. They'd brought him to the same unit where Luke had been.

Déjà vu.

Only this time, the doctor wouldn't talk to us. We weren't family.

"Fuck! I just want to know if he's alive!"

"Ma'am, you need to calm down," the doctor said.

"Lucia."

I heard a man's voice behind me. I turned to find Roman walking into the waiting room, his face cleaned of blood, although his shirt still had splatters of it.

"They're operating. There's nothing for them to tell." He

turned to the doctor. "Add Lucia DeMarco to the list," he said. "Keep her updated on Salvatore Benedetti's condition."

The doctor nodded and made a note of what I assumed was my name and walked away.

"Thank you," I said to Roman.

He nodded and sat down. Defeat was the one word I would use to describe him in that moment.

"What about Franco?" Isabella asked.

"Stable"

"Of course. Of course he's stable while his son is in there possibly dying." I sank down into a chair, and Isabella wrapped her arms around me.

"Shh. Remember, you have to be strong. He needs you now more than ever."

I nodded, wiping away tears and snot.

We sat in the waiting room for a long time. Isabella excused herself to make some calls, to make sure the sitter could stay with Effie longer, to check on Luke. Roman and I remained silent, lost in our own misery. All the while, my ankle throbbed.

"He should never have goaded Dominic like that. He'd sworn never to do it."

I turned to Roman. "What are you talking about?" I hadn't been in the room, not until it was almost the very end.

Roman glanced at me. "Franco isn't Dominic's father, but he loved my sister. Loved her enough to keep it hushed. To act like Dominic was his son all along. He had no right to tell him like this."

"You're worried about Dominic? He deserves to be the one in there, not Salvatore."

He met my gaze. "No one should be in there. Period."

"I may be a horrible person, but I don't agree."

He sighed. "You're nowhere near a horrible person."

He got up and left the room. I remained where I was. Isabella stayed with me until, almost four hours later, a doctor finally came out, looking for next of kin.

"That's me," I said, although it wasn't quite me. "Lucia DeMarco."

He checked his sheet of paper. Satisfied, he looked back at me. The space of that second stretched to an hour, and I dreamed the worst, thought I should prepare myself to hear it, but how did one prepare to hear something that terrible?

"Mr. Benedetti is an incredibly lucky man. And his will to live is tremendous."

I smiled, feeling a thousand pounds lift from me. "He's going to make it?"

"He shouldn't have, not given the route the bullet took, but he is. He's asking for you."

"I can see him?"

"Only for a few minutes. He needs to rest. We'll sedate him, but he's insisting on seeing you first."

"He's pigheaded," I said, wiping away fresh tears. I followed the doctor, a joy filling me that I'd never in my life felt before. Never knew possible.

I walked into the private room, where machines beeped and doctors and nurses worked around the bed where Salvatore lay, eyes closing, then opening, turning his head away from the nurse who tried to attach yet another tube.

"Salvatore!" I hobbled over to him and took the seat someone pushed behind me.

He opened his eyes and gave me a weak smile. He kept opening and closing his hand, and I placed mine inside it. He stilled then, lay back, and shut his eyes. I sat there and watched, not sure if he held my hand or I held his, not sure it mattered anymore. I watched him sleep, counted the needles in his arms, watched them inject something into the tube of one of the IVs.

"He will be out for a while. You can go home and get some rest. We'll call you when he's awake."

"No," I said, not taking my eyes off him. "I'm staying here."

"Ma'am..."

I felt Salvatore's tiny attempt at squeezing my hand and turned to the doctor. "I'm just as pigheaded, just so you know. I'm not leaving."

23

SALVATORE

I probably dreamed Lucia calling herself pigheaded, but it made me smile all the same. And every time I opened my eyes, there she was, sitting by my side. At first, she still had blood on her. My blood. Then she looked like she'd showered and changed. I saw Roman too, but she was my constant.

She'd remembered what I'd said. What I'd promised her. I vaguely recalled her voice, telling me I hadn't yet kept the promise to give her the life she wanted.

I had changed rooms. I knew it from the way the light came in the window. I wasn't sure how long I'd been in the hospital until finally, I opened my eyes, feeling a little less groggy, and the things around me didn't seem so like a mirage.

Was it a mirage? Was Lucia a mirage?

"Hey."

I looked up at her beautiful, smiling face. She still sat in the same place, holding my hand, watching me.

"Hey." It felt strange to speak.

"How do you feel?"

"Like I've been run over by a truck."

"Do you remember what happened?"

My mind traveled back to that morning. My father, Roman, Isabella, and I in my dining room. Dominic. Dominic with a gun. My father telling him he wasn't his son. Calling our mother a whore.

Something beeped, and the door opened. A nurse rushed inside.

I took a deep breath, and the beeping leveled, but the nurse gave me a warning look.

"It's good to see you're awake, Mr. Benedetti, but you need to stay calm, or we'll have to sedate you again."

I opened my mouth to tell her to fuck off, but Lucia squeezed my hand and spoke to her.

"It's okay. I'll make sure he stays calm."

"Thank you."

The nurse left, and I looked back at Lucia.

"They called you pigheaded," she said. "Well, I did actually, but they agreed."

I smiled, but it hurt to speak or move. And as much as I wanted to keep looking at her, my eyelids began to droop.

"Go to sleep. I'll be here when you wake up."

I did, unable not to, and when I woke next, I was in a different room yet again, this one less sterile-looking. Lucia again sat by my bed, talking to her sister, who sat on another chair, and Effie, who was watching TV with the sound muted.

"He's awake," Isabella said.

Lucia turned to me. "Finally. I didn't mean sleep for three more days."

This was surreal. "I want to sit up."

"Bossy already," she teased and handed me a remote control. "Here, push this button. Stop if it's painful."

I pushed, and the bed moved. Effie came over to watch, entranced by the operation.

"Wow! Can I get one of those, Mommy?"

"No," came Isabella's voice.

I smiled and came to a stop when the slight throb at my side became painful. "How long has it been?"

"Almost two weeks."

"I baked you some M&M cookies" Effie said, coming over with a tin. "They helped Luke, and he's out of the hospital now. If you eat these, you'll be out soon too."

"That so?" I asked.

Lucia took the cookie Effie had fished out for me. "I'll give it to him after his dinner, okay? We don't want to spoil his first proper hospital meal, after all."

I made a face, and so did Effie. She then turned to me. "Grilled cheese is the only safe thing," she whispered. "And no matter what you do, do not eat the pea soup."

I laughed but had to quit; it hurt too much.

"All right," Isabella said, taking Effie's hand. "Time for us to go." She looked at me. "I'm glad you didn't die."

"Thank you?" I guessed.

Lucia walked them out then returned to me. "Effie's a hoot," she said.

"Yes. And I'm staying away from that pea soup. I trust that kid." It grew quiet as our smiles faded.

"I thought you were dead. I couldn't feel you breathe, and you were so still. And the blood..."

Her eyes filled with tears.

I reached up to touch her face, although my arm felt sore even with that small movement. "I'm not that easy to kill off."

"I kept the clothes I was wearing."

"Huh?"

She shrugged a shoulder. "With the blood."

I must have made a face when I got what she was saying.

"I know, it's creepy."

"You can throw those away now. I'm not going anywhere. I have a promise to keep."

She smiled.

"Where's Dominic?"

She shook her head. "No one knows. He disappeared after that night. Good riddance."

"He's not my father's son."

"I know."

"He wasn't trying to kill me. You know that, right?"

"I don't care, Salvatore. He almost did."

I decided to drop it for now. "My father?"

"He had a heart attack, but he's fine. He's home already. Roman's been running the show apparently. Probably waiting for you to get well enough to take over." She snorted, her face changing, darkening.

"He had a heart attack?"

"I guess seeing one son shoot another was too much even for his cold heart."

A knock came on the door. We both turned to see Roman peek his head in.

"I heard he was awake."

"Come in," Lucia said and stepped aside.

"Where are your crutches?" Salvatore asked me.

"You've been out a while. Long enough, my ankle's mostly fine."

"You should use them—"

"Bossy."

"I need to talk to you," Roman said to me, glancing at Lucia.

"I'll wait outside," Lucia said, picking up her bag.

"You can stay," I told her.

She shook her head. "It's fine. I'll get some coffee."

"Thank you," Roman said.

Once she was gone, he sat in the seat she'd occupied and took a folder out of his briefcase.

"How are you feeling?"

"I've been better. What's going on? Fill me in."

"You know about your father's heart attack?"

I nodded.

"Well, Franco is home and recovering. He's not doing well, though, Salvatore."

I didn't reply.

"He wanted to come and see you, but the doctor advised him against it."

"Okay." Was he telling me that so my feelings wouldn't be hurt?

"He knows you saved his life."

"I didn't do it for him. I did it because I knew my brother would regret it for the rest of his."

"You have every right to feel the way you feel."

"I don't need you to tell me that."

He inhaled a deep breath.

"Where's Dominic?"

"I don't know. He disappeared after the shooting. No one knows. He didn't go home, didn't pack, didn't take anything with him. Just left."

"Is it true?"

Roman nodded.

"And you knew?"

"I'm the only one apart from your mother and father who knew. He regrets having told him."

"He should."

I cursed my father for having told Dominic like that. What purpose did it serve? It would only wound Dominic. Perhaps irreparably.

"Franco is no longer able to manage the family, the businesses, anything, Salvatore. I've been doing it until you're recovered."

We studied each other for a long time. I just couldn't tell what my uncle was looking for.

"I have papers here, things I want to go over."

A small knock came on the door. Lucia opened it.

"Not now," I said to him. "Just take care of everything for now."

"I can come back," Lucia said.

"No, you stay. Roman, thanks for your visit."

Roman took his dismissal with grace and left. Lucia sat back down in the same chair.

"Coffee is so crappy here," she said, setting the untouched paper cup on the table nearby.

Before we had a chance to talk, though, the doctor walked in to look things over and told me I'd be home in three days' time. Lucia vacated her chair and stood back and watched, giving the doctor room. Every time I looked at her when she didn't know I was, I saw the worry on her face. My mind traveled back to what I'd told her. What I'd promised her. Freedom, as soon as I was boss. Freedom, once I knew she was safe. A quiet life. Happiness. I wanted it for everyone I loved. I wanted it especially for her.

24

LUCIA

Salvatore moved into a bedroom downstairs while he recovered. I slept beside him, taking care not to touch the still tender spot the bullet had ripped into. I knew he felt pain, but he insisted on less and less medication, saying he could manage it. Within a day of being home, he could walk on his own to the bathroom, although it wore him out.

"I hate this," he grumbled a week later after one of his visits to the bathroom. "I hate being weak."

I tucked the blanket up to his waist. "You're getting stronger every day."

"Not fast enough."

"You hate having someone else take care of you. You're so used to taking care of everyone and everything and being in charge of it all but can't stand to be in a position where you need others yourself."

He studied me, then looked beyond me to the waning light outside the window.

"Let's sit outside."

"I'll get your wheelchair." I'd already stood to unfold it. He hadn't used it except for the time they'd rolled him in here in it.

"No."

I looked back to find him rising on his own.

"Jesus, Salvatore, it'll only take longer if you don't take care—"

"I said no,"

He leveled his gaze on mine, giving me a glimpse of the man I knew him to be—rough and tough and sexy as hell.

He must have seen the change in me too, because his expression softened, and his gaze rolled over my body.

I swallowed, my nipples tightening, my belly fluttering. Just one look from him, and I shuddered.

"Okay," I said, clearing my throat. Then, without asking his permission, I opened the bedroom door and called out to Marco. "He's too stubborn to use the wheelchair, and I can't support his weight, so maybe you can walk with him."

Marco gave Salvatore a look then glanced back at me. What he saw in my face must have trumped what he saw in Salvatore's, because he put Salvatore's arm over his shoulder and held on to his waist.

"Come on, boss."

Salvatore shook his head. "You'll answer for that later," he told me.

"Is that another promise?" I gave him a dirty grin and walked ahead, taking my time, knowing he was watching my ass as I led the way out back.

Once Salvatore was settled, Marco left us. We sat quietly, watching the light dance along the surface of the swimming pool. Salvatore held my hand.

"I've been thinking," he said, then stopped.

I glanced at him, but he looked straight ahead.

"I'm going to hand it all over to Roman."

"What?" I didn't expect that.

Salvatore looked at me. "I only have one thing to do as boss, then I'm walking away."

One thing. I knew what that was. It was what I had wanted.

"You're free, Lucia. I'll talk to Roman tomorrow, destroy the contract, and draw up a new one, so they can't touch you or your family ever again. You'll be free of me, of all of us."

Free of him?

I watched his eyes. Soft again. Like they'd looked the day we'd been forced to sign that terrible piece of paper. Gentle. I'd been wrong when I'd thought he was like them. A monster. This was the real Salvatore. It had always been there, lying beneath the fear.

Only thing was, I didn't know if I wanted to be free of him at all anymore.

I cleared my throat. "I can't leave you alone while you're not yet recovered."

"I'll be fine," he said, then looked away from me again.

"Salvatore—"

We started to speak at once, but he won. "I'll make sure you have enough money to set yourself up, buy a house, take some time—"

I pulled my hand free of his. "I told you before. I don't need your money." I turned the back of my head to him in case he saw me wipe away a stupid tear.

We were back to this.

He picked up my hand and squeezed, making me look at him. If he saw my eyes were wet, he didn't mention it.

"I'm going to take care of you, whether you like it or not, so just accept it as a part of life."

"Do you know what you're going to do?" I asked, swallowing a lump in my throat, not sure what else to talk about, needing there not to be any silence between us because in that silence, I would fall apart.

"Sell this house. Move. Look for Dominic. I don't know."

"You're worried about him."

"Yeah. He needs someone now, after everything. Not sure he wants it to be me, but I'm going to try."

"Can you walk away from it, though? Can you just up and leave?"

"I'm going to." There was a long pause. "What about you? Where do *you* want to go?"

"My sister is putting the house up for sale. I think it's a good idea to start fresh. She, Luke, and Effie are looking at Florida." For a moment, I thought I would go too, but then the thought of being without him made me stop. Didn't I want this? Didn't I want my freedom?

Strange, how priorities shifted. I thought I'd always want revenge for what they had done to my family, but that had all slipped away. All the anger, the hate, it just wore me down to think about it, and now, it was gone.

"Salvatore," I started, but again, we spoke at once, our voices and gazes colliding.

"If you don't know…it will take some time to sell the house. Maybe you can stay…" He trailed off.

I nodded. "That would be good. Izzy and Luke need their space, and I can help you get the house ready and make sure you're—"

He took my face in his hand and drew it to himself to kiss me, swallowing up the empty words.

"I want to make love to you."

"The doctor said—"

"I need you, Lucia. I've needed you for so long."

25

SALVATORE

I kept my promise to Lucia. Roman came to the house the following morning and handed me the initial contract she and I had signed. I set it aside and had him draw up another one. This one forgave any and all debt any DeMarco owed any Benedetti, real or perceived, and the two families were no longer bound in any way. And it could not be overturned at any time in the future.

I signed it and had a copy sent to Isabella. I would deliver a copy to my father personally. This insane vendetta was finished. I ended it as one of the two things I did during my hours-long rule over the Benedetti family before I gave everything—the reign, the rule, the power—over to Roman.

It was another week before I could move back upstairs to my own bedroom and another month before I was fully healed. All that time, Lucia stayed with me, caring for me like I didn't remember ever being cared for by anyone apart from my mother.

I also saw Natalie and Jacob. She came to give me the news she too was moving away, along with her parents. She didn't trust anyone but me, and with Roman now taking over and Dominic somewhere out there, she didn't feel safe. She promised to keep in touch with me, though, and I let her go, let her take my nephew with her. I would miss them. It was another piece of Sergio that was gone, but I knew part of him would always be with me, no matter what.

As far as the house, it turned out I didn't have to put it on the market. An anonymous buyer bought it outright, furnished, within hours of my talking to a real-estate agent. We needed to be out within two weeks. I let Rainey go with a hefty bonus to tide her over until she found work. I didn't need to worry about Marco. He would go to work for my uncle. Lucia and I simply had to pack up our personal things, and we were free to truly walk away.

Those last two weeks in the house were strangely more bitter than sweet. Lucia would go to Florida, where her sister had already gone with Effie, while Luke took care of the selling of their house. I hadn't yet decided what I would do. I couldn't think about it for some reason. And I still had one more person to see before I could close this long chapter of my life.

"Can we take the Bugatti?" Lucia asked, a glint in her eye when we got to the garage.

"No." That was my baby, and she was insisting on driving 'considering my injuries.' "We can take the BMW."

She pouted but picked up the keys.

"It's not that I don't trust you driving it," I started, "although I don't. But the less bumpy the ride, the better."

"My driving is just fine."

"We'll see."

"You nervous?" she asked.

"About your driving?" I joked, but I knew what she meant.

She only glanced at me as she pulled out of the garage.

"Not nervous, just want it over. I know he's my father, and maybe it's wrong, but I don't feel anything close to love for him."

"Have you forgiven him?"

I thought about it. "For being a complete and utter failure where it counted?"

She shrugged a shoulder, but her gaze was serious. "Regret sucks, Salvatore."

I knew she still had some of that.

"I actually have, I think. The way he's chosen to live his life—well, look at him. He's alone. He'll die alone. Roman will be there for him, but not us. I don't feel any anger toward him anymore. It's like it's sated or something. Not because I'm happy he's alone. I'm not. But he made his bed, and I'm making my peace. It's all I can do."

"You're good, Salvatore."

Once we reached my father's house, I climbed out of the car. I held the envelope containing the new contract. It was symbolic, nothing else, but it was necessary for closure.

"Ready?"

Lucia wound her arm through mine. We'd gotten used to each other's company, but when she did things like this, touching me like this, it still felt strange, special. It made my heartbeat quicken.

"You don't have to go in there." I watched her; she watched the house.

"I want to be there with you, Salvatore," she said, turning to me.

"Are you sure?"

"Yes."

We both took a deep breath and walked up the stairs and to the large, foreboding double doors. I rang the bell, and Roman opened the door, expecting us.

"Morning," he said, quickly hiding his surprise at seeing Lucia.

"Morning."

"Come in. He's waiting for you in the study." I nodded and took a step. Roman put his hand on my shoulder.

"Should I keep Lucia company—"

"No, thank you," I said, tucking her arm tighter to me.

He stepped back. "I'm glad you came."

I nodded, and we moved forward, neither of us speaking. Knocking once on the study door, I pushed it open, not expecting to find what I found. I heard Lucia's gasp, but I had schooled my face for so many years that masking my surprise came more easily than I thought it would.

"Salvatore," my father said after glancing at Lucia on my arm.

"Father." They'd moved a hospital bed into his study. It stood in place of his desk, which was pushed to the side. I remembered that desk, how I'd trembled on the opposite side of it when I'd been called in for this reprimand or that growing up. There had always been something he was displeased with.

"Don't just stand there, come inside. It's not contagious."

His bitterness held an edge of regret. I heard it clearly.

We both entered. He adjusted his positon, so he sat up taller. He looked so much smaller than the last time I'd seen him. So much older. Dark circles ringed his eyes, and his cheeks looked sunken. He must have lost about twenty pounds too.

"I came to say good-bye," I said, not wanting to delay this any further.

He once again glanced at Lucia before returning his gaze to mine.

"I assume you've seen the contract?"

"Roman showed it to me."

"Well, here's your own copy." I set it on the foot of the bed. "You were wrong to tell Dominic. He never needed to know."

He took in a deep breath, and his hand trembled, but his eyes remained fixed and hard.

"It was a mistake," he said. "One I will pay for until the end." No one spoke for a long moment. "Will I see you again?"

"No."

He lowered his gaze to the envelope then back to me.

"I forgive you," Lucia said, surprising me. "I forgive you for everything you did, all the hurt you caused."

He only stared at her, but I couldn't read his eyes.

"We never could please you, huh? None of us, not my brothers, not our mother, not really."

"I've never been an easy man, son. Don't think I don't know that. And don't think I don't know I've made mistakes. I only did what was best for my family."

"I believe you believe that."

I released Lucia's hand then and went to him. Leaning down, I kissed the top of his head. "Good-bye, father."

His eyes glistened when they met mine, and he nodded but didn't speak. I walked away and took Lucia's hand. Without a backward glance, we left the house, got into the car, and drove away.

It was silent for a very long time, and I wasn't even sure where I was driving to.

"I want to scrub my skin," I said finally, inhaling a loud breath. "I want to burn my clothes and wash with scalding hot water."

"Pull over, Salvatore."

"I want—"

"Pull over."

I did. Lucia reached over and wrapped her arms around me. I buried my face in her shoulder and wept like no man should weep. "I've never wanted to leave a place so badly. I've never wanted to leave a person—"

"Shh."

"So many lives wasted."

She held me, and I clung to her. A lifetime's worth of pain and sadness welled out of me. So much was lost for so many of us, all of it so pointless, so unnecessary. So much death, so much anger and jealousy and hate. So much I needed to purge until there was nothing left, nothing at all but this broken, exhausted body.

When I pulled back, I found Lucia's face stained with tears. She wiped mine away, just kept brushing my face with her thumbs, looking at me, looking at me, not letting me go.

"Don't leave," I said finally. "I don't want to lose you, Lucia. Not you too. You deserve so much better than this, than me..." She hugged me to her again, fresh tears pouring from her eyes. "I have no right..."

"Come with me," she said, pulling back. "Come with me now, and we'll start again. A new beginning."

I shook my head. "I shouldn't have asked...I'm—my world, Lucia, it's dark. It's so damn dark inside. You deserve light. You deserve carefree and happy and light. So much light."

"And you don't think you do? You stubborn fool."

She kissed me, a salty kiss.

"My brother—"

"Come with me," she said again, this time more firmly. "Right now. We'll drive. Come with me, please, Salvatore."

"I love you, do you know that?" How could a grown man weep like this?

"It's you who doesn't know I love you."

When she kissed me that time, something inside me shifted. I felt it like a physical thing in my chest, my gut. I squeezed my eyes shut and felt her, her body in my arms, her lips on mine, her tears wet on my face. I kissed her back, inhaling deeply, my tongue inside her mouth, my hands pulling her closer and closer because I couldn't be away again. I couldn't have her away again. And so, when we pulled back, I smiled and turned the car around, and I drove south, leaving everything behind and just driving away with the girl I loved beside me.

LUCIA'S EPILOGUE
SIX MONTHS LATER

We did it. We drove to Florida. We drove as far as we could from New Jersey and ended up on the very tip of Key West. We bought a modest old house with a strip of private beach and started again.

The renovations on the house would probably take us over a year to complete, but I liked it. It was built in the 70s, and the seller was the son of the sole owners of the place who had done zero updates since its build. It needed a lot of work, but work was a good thing. It kept us occupied, kept our minds busy, especially Salvatore's.

It was strange at first, as though he didn't know how to be without the Benedetti mafia behind him. Around him. Taking up all of his energy. Defining him. There was no one to take care of here besides us. Natalie and Jacob had settled in California. Roman took care of the family business with few questions for Salvatore. He'd been so involved when Franco had been boss that he was a natural fit. I didn't think Salvatore regretted handing everything over, but this life was very different than the one he'd had.

My sister and Luke lived south of Miami, which was just shy of a four-hour drive to Key West. At first, the tension between Luke and Salvatore had been high, but both men had something in common. They'd both nearly died. They both realized what was important, and that was family. I wished they lived closer. I wanted to be around my sister and Effie after having missed out on so many years, but this worked, and it was better than what I'd had for five years.

As happy as Salvatore and I were with the simplicity of things here, there was one thing that bothered him. Dominic's absence.

He'd hired several investigators but came up short at every turn. Dominic had vanished, and Salvatore struggled to come to terms with that.

I stood outside of our little house at the barbecue looking out at the beach, startling when I heard him.

"You smell like a steak," Salvatore said, suddenly behind me, his mouth on the back of my neck.

"Christ! How do you always sneak up on me?"

He'd walked around back where I was grilling two steaks. He'd been gone most of the day, picking up supplies.

He laughed and held out a bouquet of sunflowers. "You're too involved in your head, that's how."

I was too involved for a reason.

"I missed you." His mouth found mine.

"Me too." I kissed him back and took them. "These are pretty. Thanks."

"I'm glad you like them." He looked at the grill. "Early for dinner, isn't it?"

"I'm just hungry."

"Well, I'm not hungry for food just yet," he said sliding his hands down and into the back of my shorts. He squeezed my ass, kissing me deeply, his big body bigger, even more muscular since we'd started working on the house. His skin had darkened in the Florida sunshine. He seemed to smile more, and his face looked more relaxed. I didn't think it would be possible for him to be even sexier than before, but he was.

"I've been thinking about this all day."

He picked me up. I wrapped my legs around his hips and my arms around his neck.

"I haven't fucked you on the picnic table yet," he said, pushing my shirt aside and taking a nipple into his mouth.

"You are a dirty, dirty man, Salvatore."

"I think you like it, Lucia."

He set me on the table and continued to kiss me before pulling the peasant shirt over my head.

"Do you remember," he started, stripping his T-shirt off, "when we were in my study, and I fucked your ass for the first time?"

I felt my face blush as he pushed my knees apart and stood between them, his grin evil and his eyes dancing while he unbuttoned my shorts and pulled the zipper down.

I leaned in close. He thought he was embarrassing me, did he? Taking his hair in my hands, I tugged, turning his head to the side and licking his ear. "I remember I liked it. But who says I'm giving you permission to fuck my ass again?"

One hand raked up my back, pulled the tie out of my messy bun, and gripped a handful of hair.

"I need to ask permission?" he asked, closing his mouth over mine.

This kiss had a hunger to it.

"Don't you remember what I said you'd do the next time I wanted to fuck your ass?"

I shook my head, although I remembered perfectly. My hands moved to explore his chest. "Refresh my memory."

"Something about you bending over my desk and spreading yourself open. Something about begging me to do it."

"You think I'll beg you to fuck me?" I chuckled and slid my fingernails down his back to push my hands into his shorts and cup his tight ass.

"I do," he said, tugging my shorts off and dipping his head down. "I think I'll have you begging to be fucked in no time."

"Do you?" I asked as I leaned back.

He gave me a cocky grin and slid the crotch of my panties aside. Sparing one glance at my pussy, he returned his eyes to mine.

"Judging from this dripping cunt, yes."

He dove in, making me suck in a sharp breath, only taking breaks to taunt me.

"I think I'll make you wait too."

He tickled my clit.

"Make you bend over and spread yourself open while I watch. Hell, maybe I'll make a couple more steaks while you're begging."

I pushed his head into my pussy. "You talk too much."

Fuck, he could work his tongue. He could make me come in a minute or an hour, depending on how evil he felt. And today, Satan himself feasted on me.

"You're killing me," I finally said, refusing to beg, to ask him to make me come, but trying to drag his mouth back to me.

"Stay," he said, straightening. "Just like that, legs wide. And hold your panties aside. I want to see your cunt."

"I hate you," I said to his back but pulled the string of my panties aside, feeling all the more exposed for it.

"You love me," he answered, disappearing into the house.

I stayed as I was, liking it, out in the open, exposed for him. The backyard was completely private, but it thrilled me to think someone could walk around the house at any moment and find me like this.

He was back a few moments later, and I saw what he carried with him. A tube of lube.

"Good girl."

He was happy to see that I was still in position. He lifted me to stand, turned me around, and pushed me to bend over before sliding my panties down to midthigh and stopping.

"What are you doing?" I asked, glancing back at him as he stepped away.

"Reach back and spread your ass open."

"I won't beg you," I said and slid my hands back to my ass and did what he wanted. The expression on his face was worth my own embarrassment. I slipped the panties off to spread my legs wider.

"Fuck."

"What?" I taunted, wanting him but wanting him to be the one to beg. "You want?"

He rubbed himself over his jeans and approached me. He unzipped his jeans, took out his cock, and stroked it.

"You okay there, Salvatore?" I asked, arching my back and wiggling my hips before sliding a finger inside myself, then smearing the moisture up and around my back hole.

With a groan, he slid into my pussy. I put my hands back on the table when he gripped my hips, his eyes going dark as he watched himself fuck me.

It felt so fucking good, him slowly sliding in and out of me, thinking of him seeing me as I opened for him making me wetter.

But then he stopped moving, kept his cock in my pussy, and picked up the lube.

I groaned, and he grinned, uncapping it and squeezing out a

generous amount before rubbing it onto me. That was when he started to move again, his cock in my cunt, his fingers in my ass.

"This is not fair," I managed.

"Just ask for it, and I'll give it to you good and hard just like you like it."

"Fuck you."

He withdrew his cock and rubbed it through my folds instead, his fingers still working in my ass.

"I won't," I grunted, fisting my hands. "I..."

He leaned over me and tickled my ear with this tongue. "Just say please. Just once."

"Never!"

"Feels good and tight, Lucia. You're ready for a good, hard, ass fucking. You want it. I just need the word,"

"You'll never let me forget it."

"Think of it, of me pounding into that tight little hole. Think of how sensitive it is, how you're already so close." He pulled his cock away from my clit and withdrew his fingers. "But if you don't want it—"

"Please!"

"Please, what?" he whispered, cock ready at my ass.

"Please fuck my ass."

I swear I heard him smile.

"I told you you'd do it."

He kissed my cheek before straightening. He pulled apart my ass cheeks with one hand, smeared lube on his length with the other. How I loved watching him grip his cock. I could just look at that all day long. He grinned and slid the other hand beneath me.

"And you call me dirty."

I arched my back. "Fuck me already."

"Up on your elbows. It's going to be hard and fast."

I braced myself but couldn't have been ready for that.

"Good girls get rewarded, Lucia, remember that?"

"Fuck, yes!" His fingers worked my clit roughly while his cock thrust in and out, movements deep, slow at first but increasing in pace as I came, my first orgasm making me cry out, making him thicken inside me until, on the heels of my second orgasm, he thrust one final time and fell over my back, his cock throbbing as he came. He breathed hard against my ear and bit the edge of it just a little too hard, but that nip drew one final, smaller shudder from me.

We clung to each other, neither of us speaking as our breathing slowed. I don't think either of us took our time together for granted. I knew I never would, and I knew it would never be enough.

We showered afterward before sitting down to eat. I plated the steaks and carried the dish over to the table where Salvatore had just put two beers down. I took a seat across from him.

"You're really going to eat two steaks now?"

I nodded, ravenous, unsure how to tell him, happy myself but uncertain how he'd feel. We'd only been living together for half a year if I didn't count the time in New Jersey.

He watched me for a long minute, sipping his beer while I devoured the food. He pushed my untouched beer toward me. I met his gaze but popped another bite of meat into my mouth instead of going for the beer.

"Lucia?"

He could always read me like a book.

"I'm pregnant."

SALVATORE'S EPILOGUE
THREE MONTHS AFTER THAT

I married Lucia on the beach in our backyard. Lucia walking toward me barefoot, her belly swollen, wearing a simple, flowing white dress bound by golden thread just beneath her breasts and a crown of flowers in her hair, was probably the most beautiful thing I'd ever seen.

I'd never been so happy in my life.

We wrote our own vows, and she blamed hormones when she wept throughout the ceremony. Luke and Isabella were our witnesses and Effie our flower girl. That was all. No other guests apart from the priest who married us. Afterward, we barbecued and swam and talked about baby names and about Isabella and Luke moving closer. Effie spoke more to her little cousin inside Lucia's belly than to anyone else. She may have been as excited as Lucia and I were.

They spent the night and drove back home the next afternoon. We didn't have a honeymoon. There was nowhere either of us wanted to be but here. Together.

"We have everything," she said as we lay on lounge chairs, watching the night sky.

We did, and neither of us took a moment of it for granted.

"Will you tell your father?" she asked.

"In time."

"What's on your mind?"

I looked over at her and tugged the thin blanket over her shoulder. She'd filled out a little with the pregnancy, and she couldn't be more beautiful to me.

"Dominic. I'm worried."

"He'll turn up. He has a lot to process, and probably feels awful for what he did."

"He'd know by now that I'm fine. He'd know where we live. He just disappeared, and that worries me."

She touched my hand and brought it to her belly. I faced her to kiss her lips and rub the warm mound.

"He'll turn up when he's ready. Give him space."

"What if he's...hurt himself?"

"He's not the type. It's far more effective to torture yourself while living, Salvatore. You and your brother both—guilt is like a second skin to you. It's like you have to learn how to live, how to breathe, without it. You're learning, but you've got a good teacher," she finished with a wink.

"How did I end up so lucky?"

"You signed a contract, remember?"

She rolled onto her side, her back to me, and I pulled her in, holding her tight.

"Smart-ass."

"Don't forget pigheaded."

"Oh, no, you prove that on a daily basis."

She jabbed her elbow into my gut.

"Apart from my brother, my life couldn't be more perfect. It scares me a little." It scared me more than a little. "What if... I've done bad things, Lucia. I don't know if I deserve all of this."

"You've done good things too, Salvatore. You deserve all of

this and more. We're making up for lost time, you and I. It's time for us to be happy and carefree and walk in the sun with sand between our toes. It's past due, in fact."

She squeezed my hand, pulled it up to her heart.

"Don't be scared of losing this. Just be happy and grateful. That's what I've learned. I think that's what we're supposed to learn. It's so simple, but we make it all so complicated."

"My oracle."

"I am wiser than you, that's true."

"And not at all arrogant." I heard her smile.

"Good night, husband."

"Good night, wife." I kissed her neck and held her as she fell asleep, her body relaxing, her breathing soft and even. I looked up at the night sky, at all the stars, and listened to the sound of the ocean, knowing I held everything that mattered right here in my arms. Knowing she was right about Dominic, that he needed space, that he needed to figure this out for himself. She was also right about the guilt. I was very good at wrapping it over my shoulders, weighing myself down with it. Maybe I needed to learn that some of that didn't belong to me.

Lucia was wise and strong. I'd given her what I'd promised, a peaceful life, happiness. And while doing so, I had given the same to myself.

I may not be able to save my brother, but maybe it wasn't up to me to save him.

I squeezed Lucia tighter and closed my eyes, nuzzling my nose in her hair. Life was both crazy and beautiful, and out of the ugliness and hate, we'd made love. I would not forget to cherish that, to cherish her, forever.

DOMINIC: A DARK MAFIA ROMANCE

ABOUT THIS BOOK

Gia

I'm the daughter of a foot soldier. The sister of a snitch.

Monsters have been part of my life for as long as I can remember, but the morning I woke in that cold, abandoned cabin with Dominic Benedetti looming over me, I knew I'd met the darkest of them all.

He took me to break me. But I'm not so easy to break. And when he saw the mark on me, everything changed.

But I've never believed in fairy tale endings and happily-ever-after doesn't belong to people like us.

Some love thrives in the light.
Dominic and I, we belong in the dark.

Dominic

I'm the last-born son of the Mafia King.
The one with nothing to lose.

I walked away from my family. Turned my back on everything
that should have been mine and became what I was meant to be.

A monster.

Until the day I stood over Gia cowering in the corner of that
decrepit cabin in the woods. Until I saw the mark they'd put
on her.

It was then I understood something my father used to say. Keep
your friends close, your enemies closer.

My enemies had overplayed their hand.

It was past time I returned to the family. Past time I collected the
debts owed me. And long past time I punished those who
betrayed me.

1

DOMINIC

Fear has a distinct smell, something that belongs only to it. Pungent. Acidic. And at the same time, sweet. Alluring, even.

Or maybe only sweet and alluring to a sick fuck like me. Either way, the girl huddled in the corner had it coming off her in waves.

I pulled the skull mask down to cover my face. The room was dark, but I could tell she was awake. Even if she held her breath and didn't move a single muscle, I'd know. It was the scent. That fear. It gave them away every single time.

And I liked it. It was like an adrenaline rush, the anticipation of what was to come.

I liked fucking with them.

I closed the door behind me, blocking off the little bit of light I'd allowed into the small, dark, and rank bedroom. She'd been brought here yesterday to this remote cabin in the woods. So fucking cliché. Cabin in the woods. But that's what it was. That's where I did my best work. The room contained a queen-size bed equipped with restraints, a bedside table, and a locked chest holding any equipment I needed. The attached bathroom had had its door removed before my arrival. Only the bare essentials were there: a toilet, sink, and a shower/bathtub. The bathtub was truly a luxury. Or it became one at some point during the training period.

The windows of both the bedroom and the bathroom had been boarded up long ago, and only slivers of light penetrated through the slats of wood. Both rooms were always cold. Not freezing. I wasn't heartless. Well...I had as much heart as any monster could have. I just kept the rooms at about sixty degrees. Just cool enough that it wouldn't do any damage but it wouldn't be quite comfortable.

I walked over to the crouched form on the floor. She stank. I wondered how long they'd had her. If they'd washed her during that time.

I wondered what else they'd done to her, considering the rule of no fucking on this one. My various employers didn't usually give that order. They didn't give a crap who fucked the girls before auction. It's what they were there for. But this time, Leo—the liaison between the buyer and me—had made certain I understood this particular restriction.

I shoved the thought of rape aside. I didn't do that. Whatever else I did to them, I didn't do that. Some tiny little piece of my fucked-up brain held on to that, as if I were somehow honorable for it.

Honor?

Fuck.

I had no delusions on that note. Honor was a thing that had never belonged to me. Not then, not when I was Dominic Benedetti, son of a mafia king. So close, so fucking goddamned close to having it all. And it certainly didn't belong to me now. Not now that I knew who I was. Who I *really* was.

More thoughts to shove away, shove so far down they couldn't choke me anymore. Instead they sat like cement, like fucking concrete bricks in my gut.

I stepped purposefully toward the girl, my boots heavy and loud on the old and decrepit wood.

"Wakey, wakey."

She sat with her knees pulled up to her naked chest, her bound wrists wrapped around them, and made the smallest movement, tucking her face deeper into her knees. I noticed she still wore underwear, although it was filthy. That was new. By the time they got to me, they were so used to being buck naked they almost didn't notice anymore.

The three night-lights plugged into outlets around the bedroom allowed me to take her in. Dark hair fell over her shoulders and down her back. So dark, I wondered if it would be black after I washed the dirt and grime from it.

I nudged the toe of my boot under her hip. "You stink."

She made some small sound and dug her fingernails into the flesh of her legs, crouching farther into the corner, folding and withdrawing deeper into herself.

I squatted down, looking at what I could see of her too skinny body. I'd check her for bruises later, once I cleaned her up. Make sure there wasn't anything that needed immediate attention. No festering wounds acquired in transit.

"Did you piss yourself?"

She exhaled an angry breath.

I grinned behind my mask. There we go. That was different.

"Lift your head, so I can see your face."

Nothing.

I lay one of my hands on top of her head. She flinched but otherwise didn't move. I gently stroked her head before gripping the long thick mass of hair and turning my hand around and around, wrapping the length of it tight in my fist before tugging hard, jerking her head back, forcing her to look at me.

She cried out, the sound one of pain and anger combined. They matched the features of her face: eyes narrowed, fear just behind the rebellion in her hate-filled, gleaming green eyes. Her mouth opened when I squeezed my fingers tighter, and a tear fell from the corner of one eye.

"Get your hands off me."

Her voice sounded scratchy, low, like she hadn't spoken in a long time. I looked at her. Heart-shaped face. Full lips. Prominent cheekbones.

Pretty.

No, more than that. Aristocratic almost. Arrogant. Beautiful. Different.

Different than the usual girls.

She scanned my face. I wondered if the skull mask scared her. Fuck, it had scared me the first time I'd put it on. Nothing like death staring you in the face.

"Stand up," I said, dragging her by her hair as I straightened.

She stumbled, but I kept hold of her, tilting her head back, watching her process the pain of my fist in her hair. Teaching her.

Actions spoke louder than words. I always started my training from minute one. No sense in wasting time. She'd learn fast to do as she was told, or she'd pay. She'd learn fast that life as she knew it was over. She was no longer free. No longer human. She was a piece of fucking meat. Owned. Owned by me.

That first lesson was always hardest for them, but I was nothing if not thorough.

I guess you could say I'd found my true calling.

"You're hurting me," she muttered.

She swallowed hard and blinked even harder, maybe to stop the tears that now leaked from both eyes. This girl was a fighter.

She hated weakness. I could see it. I recognized it. This battle, she warred as much with herself as she did me.

"What's the magic word?" I taunted.

She glared, her gaze searching, trying to see through the thin layer of mesh that covered even my eyes. I could tell she was trying not to focus on the mask but rather my eyes. To make me more human, less terrifying.

Fear. It was the one thing you could always count on.

"Fuck you."

She reached up with her bound hands to grab hold of the mask, but before she could tug it off, I jerked her arms away.

"Wrong."

I spun her around and shoved her against the wall, pressing the side of her face against it. She pushed at the cheap, dark-paneled walls with her hands, her bound wrists just in front of her chest. Her breathing came hard, harder than mine.

I looked her over. Even beneath the layers of dirt, I saw the print of a boot turning blue on her side.

I was right. This one was a fighter.

Leaning in close, I let go of her hair and pressed my body against hers, bringing my mouth to her ear. "Try again. Magic word. And remember, I don't usually give second chances."

"Please," she said quickly before a sob broke out that she tried hard to suck back in.

I kept my chest to her back, holding her against the wall. I wondered if she could feel my erection. Hell, she'd have to.

"Gia," I whispered against her ear. I knew her first name, knew it was her real name when she sucked in a breath.

That was all I knew, but I wouldn't tell her that. It was all I wanted to know. Contrary to what my various employers thought, I didn't like training the girls. Or selling them. I wondered if I should. It was one of the things my father had done, my real father. He was a scum-of-the-earth asshole. I'd just been trying to live up to my heritage over the last seven years. Hell, I had to make up for lost time. Twenty-eight fucking years' worth. From the terror on the girl's face, I was doing a good job of it.

I hated myself a little more because of it every day. But that was the point, wasn't it? I didn't deserve any different.

"You belong to me now. You will do as I say, or you will be punished every single time. Understand?"

She didn't answer, but her body began to tremble. She squeezed her eyes shut. I watched as tears rolled down her cheek.

"Understand?" I asked again, trailing my fingernails up her back and splaying them beneath the heavy veil of hair at the base of her skull, ready to grip and tug and hurt.

She nodded quickly.

"Good."

I abruptly stepped back. She almost fell but caught herself. She remained standing as she was, her back to me, her forehead against the wall. Her hands moved, wiping her cheeks.

"Turn around."

It took her a moment. She moved slowly, keeping as much space between us as she could, keeping her bound hands raised so they covered her breasts.

Defiant eyes met mine, the green shining bright in contrast to her dirt-smeared face. There was something about her. Not once in the dozen girls I'd trained had I ever felt anything but emptiness, a space between me and them. The girls, they weren't even human to me. It was easier that way. They were things. A means to an end. That end being me sinking deeper into depravity, so deep I'd never see the light of day again.

I steeled myself and let my gaze roam over her. She shivered, and I knew it wasn't the cold that made her shudder.

"Raise your arms over your head. There's a hook there. There are many throughout the room."

I watched as she scanned the room. Her eyes would have adjusted to the dim light, so she'd see at least the outline of what I was talking about. Chains had been fitted to the ceiling in various spots. Overkill maybe, but like I said earlier, I liked fucking with them, and imagination was often worse than reality. Attached to these chains were large hooks, like meat hooks. When I needed to, I used them to secure the girls.

"You'll have to stand on tiptoe to slide the ring at the center of your restraints onto the hook. Do it."

Her chest moved as her breathing came in short gasps while her gaze traveled around the room again before finally coming to rest on the one over her head.

I walked over to the locked chest and took the key from my pocket. "I already told you, I don't like to repeat myself," I said as I bent to unlock it. I raised the lid, taking out what I needed. This was the usual. Gia was no different than the others. They always had trouble obeying at first.

I put the lid down and held the crop close to my leg so she wouldn't see it. When I reached her, I took one of her wrists and raised both arms to secure her on the hook.

"No."

She immediately started trying to free herself. It was futile, but what the hell. She could wear herself out. I already knew she'd be a slow learner. The fighters always were.

"Yes," I said, moving around her.

She tried to follow me but on tiptoe, she was slower. I wondered if she even saw the first strike come because at the sound of leather striking flesh—a sound my sick brain loved—she sucked in a breath and went stock-still.

"Do I have your attention?" She tried to turn this way and

that, wriggling to lean away. I raised my arm again and this time, struck the side of her hip.

"Stop!" she cried out.

I gripped her arm, turned her to face away from me, and brought it down three more times over her still panty-clad ass.

"Please! It hurts!"

"No shit, Sherlock."

I struck again, this time spinning her to face me and marking the fronts of her thighs.

She screamed. I wondered how much of that was shock, although the crop could sting like a motherfucker, and I wasn't being gentle. No sense in coddling them.

"More?" I asked.

"No!"

I laid one more stripe across her thighs anyway. "No, what?"

"No, please, no!"

"Well, hell. Maybe you're not as slow a learner as I'd pegged you to be." I tossed the crop onto the bed and adjusted the crotch of my pants. Her mouth fell open, and her eyes widened as she watched. "Now don't move."

I looked her over, checking for bruises, finding several, all of which seemed to be a few days old. No fresh cuts, nothing that needed anything other than time to heal. Although time was limited.

Turning her, I touched the imprint of the shoe on her side. She hissed when I pressed. "You must have pissed someone off." I chuckled.

"He didn't appreciate my knee in his crotch."

I laughed outright. "I like a girl with some fire," I said as I slid my fingers into the waistband of her panties. "These have to go."

She struggled violently until I smacked her ass with the flat of my hand. "I said don't fucking move."

"Please."

"That won't work every time, honey." I tugged them off, watching them drop to the floor. Gia squeezed her legs together, clenching her ass as she tried to get away from me.

"Please," she tried again.

I dug my fingernails into her hips to keep her still. "Do you need the crop to stop fucking moving?"

"No! Just don't...please don't—"

I felt her struggle to stop moving, and I knew what she was afraid of. I knew exactly what she was afraid of.

"Still." My voice came as a low, dark warning.

She shuddered in my grasp and hung her head, her breathing loud and uneven.

That was when my thumb rubbed against a thick scabbing of skin. It was about two inches all around and when I pressed against it, she sucked in a breath. I leaned down to have a closer look. The circular scar stood on the side of her left hip. It was an intentional marking, a burn.

"What's this?"

She just made a sound.

"What is it?" I asked again after smacking her other hip.

"He didn't exactly bother telling me when he fucking branded me." She swallowed a loud sobbing breath.

I straightened. It couldn't have been more than a few days, maybe a week old. I'd see what it was once the scab healed. In the meantime, I had work to do.

When I didn't hold her steady, she wobbled from foot to foot, unable to get any sort of a foothold considering her height. She couldn't be more than five feet five. She'd barely come to the middle of my chest when she'd stood on flat feet. I walked around her a few times, just circling, taking my time as she tried to follow my movements, her eyes watching me closely.

"You really do stink," I said, stopping to face her. "Did you piss yourself, or did they piss on you?" I couldn't help it. One corner of my mouth lifted at the question. At the callousness of it.

The girl's eyes narrowed. A brief look of shame flashed through them.

"Are you going to kill me?" she asked finally. "If you are, just do it. Just get it over with."

She wasn't begging for her freedom, or her life, for that matter. Hadn't offered a single bribe—they usually did. Offered all the money they had. Their families had. They didn't have a clue that what I'd be paid would far exceed what most families of these lost girls could earn in a year.

Lost girls. I'd come to call them that. This one, though, this Gia—she was no lost girl. No. She was different, and I wanted to know what it was that made her so.

"You're not here to die. You're here to train. We only have two weeks, which is less than my usual. And given your...unpleasant disposition"—I let my gaze travel over her—"it'd take anyone else double that time." I looked her in the eye and winked. "But I'm a professional. I'll make it work."

"Train?"

"Teach you how to behave—for the auction, at least. After that, you're not my problem anymore."

"What auction?"

"Slave auction. There's one in two weeks. You'll be there. Guest of honor. At least, one of the guests of honor. Let's get you cleaned up, so I can see what I've got to work with."

I reached up to free her cuffs from the hook, and she sighed in relief when her feet stood flat on the floor again. Holding her by one arm, I wrapped the other around the back of her neck and pulled her close. She planted her hands on my chest, keeping as much distance as she could between us.

"You want the cuffs off?"

She searched my masked face, focusing on my eyes, then nodded.

I reached into my pocket and took out two pills. "Open up."

She eyed them. "What are they?"

I shrugged a shoulder. "They'll help you relax."

She shook her head. "No. I don't want them."

"I don't recall asking you if you wanted them."

She slowly turned her gaze up to mine and gave me a one-sided grin, then opened her mouth.

"Ahhh."

Piece of work, this one. I would administer the sedative a different way next time, and when I did, she'd be begging me to take it orally again. But for now, I brought my hand to her mouth and tilted it. But before the pills could slide in, she opened wide and bit hard into the flesh of my palm, breaking the skin.

"Fuck!" I yanked her off but only after she'd drawn blood. My hand automatically rose to slap her, and she cringed, cowering before me.

In the moment I hesitated, she backed up against the wall, eyes huge, hands up, palms to me.

I lowered my hand and took hold of her arm instead, shoving her to the floor. "Down!"

My blood streaked her skin where I held her. She made a sound when her knees hit the hardwood.

"Pick them up."

She whimpered, muttering something senseless. I squatted beside her and gripped the hair at the back of her neck to force her to look at me.

"Pick. Them. Up."

Her terrified eyes shifted from mine to the two pills lying on the floor and back. Holding my gaze, she felt for them and closed her fist around them.

"Hold them out to me."

She did, her hand trembling, her eyes locked on mine.

"You want to swallow these, or do you want me to shove them up your ass?" I sounded calm, as if I had full control of myself. Little did she know that was when I was at my worst. When rage owned me.

She studied me, perhaps unable to speak.

"Ass it is," I said, making to rise and dragging her with me. But by the time we were standing, those pills had disappeared down her throat, and she gripped my forearm, trying to relieve the pressure on her hair. "Open."

She did, and I turned her head this way and that to make sure she'd swallowed. She had.

I released her, and she stumbled backward.

"I owe you one," I said, referring to a punishment, but from the look on her face, she didn't get it. I headed to the door.

"Wait."

I unlocked it and pulled it open. I'd bandage my hand while the pills did their work.

Gia moved toward me and then stopped.

"Go lay down," I told her.

She'd be out soon. The dosage was probably too high. She was a little thing. I'd guess maybe 115 pounds soaking wet.

"Please let me go," she managed.

I took her by the arm and walked her to the bed, picked her up, and placed her on top of it.

She pulled her knees into her chest, and my eyes fell again on the scab that had formed on her hip. Something about that worried me. I had a feeling I wouldn't like what I found once the wound fully healed.

I met her gaze again. Our eyes locked, hers searching, uncertain.

She reached for the blanket, pulling it toward her. Her

fingertips touched mine when I took hold of it and dragged it away.

Warmth was a privilege earned, and she had in no way earned it.

She shivered. "Please. I'm so cold."

I looked at her and shook my head.

"Don't fight me, Gia," I whispered. "You won't win."

2

GIA

I drifted in and out of sleep. There were moments of lucidity, and it seemed I'd just be gone for a while, as if I'd stepped away from the conversation, then picked it up again like it hadn't happened at all, like I hadn't just nodded off. How long did this go on?

I recalled my last night with Victor. I'd sworn to myself that I would not be a victim. I wouldn't allow him to make me one. The memory of it made me shudder.

Shit.

Shit, shit, shit.

Did they think I couldn't hear them? Did they think I couldn't hear the fucking fire crackling?

Mateo had fucked up. God, he'd fucked up so big, and he'd paid. He'd paid big. He was gone. And he'd saved me—he'd made sure I'd live.

They'd made me watch. Victor, fucking Victor, had made me watch. I glared at him sitting there now, all smug, in his perfect three-piece suit, adjusting his perfect cuffs, turning the gold links, that smirk on his face, the one I wanted to permanently wipe off. His hands were the bloodiest of all, even if he never raised a freaking finger to do the actual work of killing.

"Ready, boss," one of his masked soldiers said. I never did see their faces.

A whimper escaped me. I didn't want to make a sound. I didn't want to scream. To give him the satisfaction. But I pulled as far back as I could even though the chains made it impossible to move more than a few inches.

Victor stood.

"Last chance, Gia."

I glanced at the steaming branding iron—I wouldn't let my gaze linger, wouldn't let fear paralyze me. I wouldn't. I couldn't. But the orange glow, the smell, the heat—it scared the fuck out of me.

I turned frantic eyes on Victor. Could I pass out first? Could I piss them off enough that they'd hit me? Knock me out before they did it?

"What do you say?" Victor asked, standing close enough now to lift my face to his.

"Last chance to fuck you?" I asked, a slight tremor to my voice as the man holding the iron came so close I could smell it. And I could imagine the scent of flesh burned away by it. My flesh.

I would be strong. For Mateo. He'd been strong right up until the end.

Victor squatted down beside me and wrapped a tendril of hair around his finger, tugging. "What do you say?" His tone teased. He loved this. The fucking bastard lived for this.

"What do I say?"

He waited.

I looked him straight in the face, knowing I sealed my own fate but drawing all of my courage anyway. I spat. I spat right on his smug killer's face.

"I say, no, thanks. You'll kill me either way."

The back of his hand slammed across my face so hard, stars

danced before my eyes, but it wasn't hard enough to render me
unconscious.

He stood. "Stupid, arrogant bitch." He nodded to the man holding
the iron, and two other sets of hands turned me onto my side.

White-hot pain burned through me, and I opened my mouth and
let out a bloodcurdling scream. The sound of the iron sizzling, the scent
of charring flesh, were too much to bear.

I never did pass out, not during, not after, not once until Victor
slapped me again.

"I'll see you on your knees, Gia. God help me."

The mad grin on his face was the last thing I saw, his words a
mystery as I processed pain like I'd never felt before, welcoming the
blackness the back of Victor's hand across my cheek finally, thankfully, delivered.

I'd been sure Victor would kill me. Why hadn't he? Did I still
have Angus Scava's protection? Angus Scava was the boss of the
Scava family. I'd been engaged to his son. I may not have been
his first choice for a daughter-in-law, but he'd accepted me, been
kind to me even, for his son.

But would he have had me branded and sent me here? To
this psychopath? To do what? What had he said? That he would
train me. Train me for the slave auction.

Slave auction.

No. Angus Scava would not have ordered this. This was
Victor acting alone.

I blinked, trying to turn onto my back but unable to. It was
like I was too heavy to move. The pills must have been some sort
of muscle relaxer and the dosage too high. I guessed that was his
intention, though. To incapacitate me. It would be easier to
control me if I couldn't fight back.

I thought of my captor, the man in the mask. That horrible
mask. I couldn't even see his eyes apart from a hint of them, a
glint of color. Blue or gray. I couldn't tell for sure. I hadn't needed

to see them to know the wickedness there, the cruelty. But there was more. When he'd raised his hand to slap me and then had stopped—that was when I'd felt it. Then, and when he'd seen the mark on my hip. A momentary reprieve, a pause in the middle of madness.

I mentally shook my head at myself. I was grasping at straws, needing to hope. The man who had me, he was no better than Victor or any of his soldiers. He was readying me to be sold as a fucking slave. I had no doubt what that entailed.

I'd been afraid he'd rape me. When he'd pulled my panties off, I'd thought that was it. He was going to do it. Victor hadn't. He hadn't let his men do it either. Why? Why not let them? Wasn't that what he wanted? To break me? To—what had he said—*"see me on my knees?"*

Maybe it was his deal with Mateo before he'd killed him that saved me from the horror of rape.

I closed my eyes against the image of Mateo before he'd died, forcing it away. I didn't want to remember my brother that way. I needed to hold on to him as he'd been before—in life. Before he'd ever met Victor. Before everything had happened.

Why hadn't Victor let his men rape me? Why hadn't he done it himself? It made no sense. He wanted me. That was obvious. Had been for the two years I'd had the displeasure of knowing him.

Auction.

Slave.

When I woke next, I could roll onto my back and raise heavy arms just inches off the bed on which I still lay naked.

I had to figure out where I was. Who the man was who currently had me. He was going to train me, so he'd probably been hired by Victor. Train me for what, though? To not fight? I'd never stop. I'd never let them win. I'd never let Victor win.

I wondered if Angus Scava knew what he'd done. He'd kill

Victor if he knew, I was sure of it. I'd almost been his daughter-in-law, after all. I'd been engaged to James, his son. James had loved me. No way Angus Scava would ever allow this to happen to me.

I thought back to James. To how good things had been two years ago. Before he'd been killed. Before Victor had come into the picture. I wondered about my mom. Did she know about Mateo yet? Did she know we were missing at least, even if she didn't know he was dead? She was in Palermo, and although we weren't particularly close, surely she'd try to phone.

The deadbolt slid, the sound calling my attention.

For the first time in a very long time, I thought of the man who had promised my father he would protect my family. The man my father had worked for, and for whom he had died. He'd vowed to keep me and Mateo safe. Could he save me from this?

But that was years ago. And a promise to a foot soldier couldn't have meant a whole lot to a crime boss.

The door creaked open.

I blinked, lifting my head as much as I could, and watched as my captor filled the doorway. He was a foot taller than me and strong. I'd never physically be able to take him down. And if he kept me drugged, I wouldn't be able to do much at all.

Light outlined his body from the outside room, creating a sort of halo around his head. I squinted, used to the dark now, and when he closed the door, I saw his face again—saw that mask. A skull. Death. As if he were death.

I made a small sound, and my body instinctively tried to pull back. Tried. Nothing much happened, though. Nothing but him stepping closer, chuckling. He must have seen the attempt. He seemed to see everything.

He sat down on the edge of the bed, and when I saw the bottle of water in his hand, I opened my mouth, realizing how dry it was, how thirsty I was.

I couldn't pull away or cover myself when his gaze raked over me, but when he reached into his pocket and produced a key that he used to unbind my wrists, all I felt was grateful.

"Really need to get you washed."

He twisted the lid off the bottle, and I swallowed in anticipation. But then he brought the bottle to his lips and took a long sip, emptying half of it. I wanted to cry. I may have even, but I couldn't be sure.

"Thirsty?" he asked.

I blinked.

"I like you like this, you know? You're kind of sweet when you're not talking."

Then he raised my head and held it as he brought the water to my lips and gave me two small sips before setting the bottle aside and standing.

"All right."

He tugged his shirt off. It looked strange, his chest bare but him wearing that mask covering his face. In the dimly lit room, I saw he had a tattoo on part of his chest and down one arm. I couldn't make out the shape, though. It was just shadow.

"Let's get you cleaned up."

I barely had a chance to look at him before he hauled me up and carried me into the bathroom. My face bobbed against his muscular chest as he carried me, the skin soft, his scent clean, enticing even—or it would be if I wasn't being held against my will. There was something else too. The scent was almost familiar. Was it an aftershave someone I knew wore? I couldn't place it.

"This is probably going to be a little cold at first."

I gasped when he set me into the freezing tub, but my head lolled to the side, and I lay there, shivering, unable to move. He pulled up a chair from the corner and sat. I watched his eyes as he took me in, traveling over the length of me. I tried to cover myself, managing to place a hand over my mound—or close enough to it I could pretend I shielded myself.

"Now, now."

He turned on the taps. I tried to pull back at the rush of icy water that gurgled out. It sounded like no one had bathed here in a very long time.

"None of that," he finished, pushing my hand away. "We're going to get very intimate, you and I."

I groaned and half turned on my side. I watched as his gaze again fell on the scab at my hip where Victor had branded me.

The water warmed, and he closed the drain to let the tub fill up. He then picked up a washcloth and a bar of soap that sat on the edge of the tub.

I made some sound of rebellion.

"It's clean," he said, holding up the square of cloth. "Relatively."

I must have made a face because he laughed outright.

"Just kidding. Christ, lighten up, princess."

Princess. Victor had called me that a few times. He'd picked it up from Mateo. But the way he said it made my skin crawl.

"Stop," I said, the word coming out slurred.

"Look at you, got your voice back."

He lathered up the washcloth and started to rub me down. I had to admit the water filling the tub felt good. Warm, almost hot. It was so cold in the other room. Although it made me hiss when it reached the tender wound on my hip.

He raised each arm and scrubbed each finger, not leaving even a tiny square inch of skin untouched, paying special attention to my breasts until my nipples hardened.

"Pretty," he said.

I tried to slap away the cloth but he took my hand and shook his head as if he were chastising a child.

"Be a good girl, and I won't add on to the punishment you've already got coming for biting me."

Goose bumps covered me at his words, and I did as he said. I lay still while he cleaned me, his touch gentler than I expected, especially around the scabby, tender spot at my hip, as if he were taking care of it. Maybe he wanted to be sure he'd be able to read whatever it was.

My captor pushed my legs apart then, and, with his eyes on mine, dragged the soapy cloth between them.

I protested by closing my legs and pushing his hand away, realizing as I did so that I was regaining mobility a little at a time. But it wasn't nearly enough to make any difference when all he did was "tsk" at my efforts. This time, he held one knee wide, wider than he'd spread me before, and cleaned between my legs. My face heated—given he'd turned on the lights in here, I could see through the mesh covering his eyes—and I swear he smiled behind his mask. I hated him for it, hated him for his tender invasion, for the natural response of my body as he rubbed that very delicate spot over and over again, as if wanting to draw that very thing from me.

"There," he said. "Almost done."

And to my utter shame, he turned me on my side and cleaned me in the back too, taking his time again until he felt satisfied, before finally allowing me to lie back as he drained the tub.

"Let's get some clean water in here, so we can wash your hair."

He stood, his gaze sliding the length of me.

I pushed myself up a little, although I still needed the support of the tub, and cleared my throat.

He allowed me to sit up and refilled the tub, taking a seat again as he picked up a half-full bottle of some cheap shampoo. How many girls had been here just like me? How many had he washed like he was washing me? How many had he—I had to swallow hard not to choke on the word—trained? Sold into slavery?

I felt my eyes welling with tears. Was I just fooling myself? I was in so deep. After James, I'd kept out of things and had warned Mateo to do so too. I warned him not to get involved with the mob. With men like Victor Scava. But he had, and he'd paid the ultimate price. Would I now pay that too?

His thumb rubbed across my cheek, and I realized I'd started to cry. I watched his eyes as he wiped away my tears, expecting some rude comment, some sick joke about my future, but all I got was silence.

I turned my head away, and the moment was gone. *Poof.*

"Deep breath."

He had his hand on the top of my head as he said it. He barely gave me time to register the words though before shoving my head down under the surface. Water gurgled in my ears, and my scream turned to bubbles before fingers pulled at my hair and drew me back out.

I sucked in air, suddenly panicked, and all he did was chuckle.

"Nothing like a dunk under water to wake you up, huh?"

I spat water and coughed while he poured shampoo on my head.

"Told you to take a deep breath. Next time, you'll know to do it."

"Why?" I cried out.

"To shampoo your hair, silly."

"Why are you doing this?"

"Oh, that."

He rubbed until he got lather, his fingers digging into my scalp.

"Money. Why else? Why does anyone do anything but for money?"

I looked up at him, wanting to see his face, his eyes. Needing to in order to read him.

"Let me see your face."

He paused. Had he been expecting something else? "Going under again, deep breath."

I barely had time to think, gulping air before he shoved me under then, moments later, pulled me back up.

"Your name, at least tell me your name."

"Shouldn't you be asking different questions?"

He dunked me again, three times more before the suds were gone. He pulled the plug from the drain.

He took one of the two threadbare towels from the rack— again making me think of those who had come before me—and once the water had drained, he draped it over my shoulders and lifted me up to stand. He held on to me when he did so, maybe testing himself how much the drug had worn off. Not nearly enough, considering my knees buckled as soon as I stood upright.

Wrapping one of the towels around me, he carried me back into the bedroom and deposited me on the bed.

"Questions like what's going to happen to me once I'm sold?"

Leaving me there, he went back into the bathroom to return a moment later with a hairbrush. I noticed the hairs stuck in the bristles. Blonde and red and brown. I wanted to throw up.

He opened the towel as if unwrapping a candy bar and pulled it out from under me, then patted me dry before dropping it on the floor.

Goose bumps rose all over my body, both at the cold temperature in the room on my still damp skin and the thought of my future. Of the fate that awaited me.

"Or who will buy me, and what will my new owner expect of me?"

He sat leaning against the headboard and lifted me up so that he cradled me between his thighs, making me very aware of my naked back against his bare chest. At least he was warm. After towel drying my hair with the second towel, he started to brush it, his touch not quite gentle, but also not cruel. Not purposely at least.

"Will he fuck me himself, or pass me around to a dozen friends to initiate me?"

I wondered if he used that tone—quiet and unaffected—on purpose. If it was meant to scare me. If his breath on my face was to let me know I would have no boundaries. That nothing was mine anymore, not even the air I breathed.

Could he feel the quiet tremors breaking me apart inside?

Would he be so callous if he could?

"Or maybe something as simple as will they use lube?"

He chuckled at that, but there was no joy in his tone. In fact, he grew more and more despondent with each comment he made, his tugs on my hair working out the knots, becoming slightly rougher each time as if he paid less and less attention.

He left me to ponder that last one for a while, and when he was able to pull the brush through without a snag, he lay me back down and stood.

I shifted and rolled onto my side, the sedative slowly loosening its hold on me. The tingling in my limbs told me it was almost over. I'd be free of it soon.

But not soon enough.

"Maybe something more imminent, like what punishment can I expect for my earlier transgression?"

Punishment.

He rolled me onto my belly and pulled me toward the foot of the bed until my legs hung over the edge.

I tried to push myself over or off the bed, but that proved too difficult. When he saw my attempt, he snickered.

"You want to see my face?" he asked, his voice quiet.

He came around to where I lay, my right cheek pressed against the bed.

"I guess it doesn't matter."

He seemed to say that more to himself than to me. He squatted down so he came to eye level.

"Will it make any difference for you?"

He brushed a wet strand of hair off my forehead, the touch of his finger making me shiver.

"For me?"

His voice, his tone—it sounded so utterly hopeless, as if truly, it made no difference at all. As if nothing mattered at all.

"No, not really, not for you. And not really for me." He reached up to tug the mask off his head.

I watched, my eyes widening, and gasped.

Short dark-blond hair stood on end, static taking hold of it, making me think of a kid with a balloon, a boy giggling as his hair fanned out in all directions.

What had I expected? A monster. A terrible, horribly scarred monster. Maybe some deformity? What?

Whatever it was, it wasn't this.

Certainly not this.

He was...beautiful. Beyond beautiful. His face—it belied an innocence that did not belong to him. That I knew in my gut had never belonged to him.

Blue-gray eyes the color of coldest steel softened by the thickest lashes were set in the face of an angel carved in solid, unbending stone. Too beautiful. Too unbearably beautiful. Thick, blond scruff darker than his hair and spotted with gray dusted his hard, square jaw. His lips were full, as if swollen from kissing.

Kissing.

He had the face of a man who'd just stepped out of a magazine. But it wasn't only that—that cool, easy, deceptive beauty. There was more. So much more. And it hid behind his eyes, in that bottomless abyss of blue-gray. Looking at them now sent a shiver racing down my spine, making every hair on my body stand on end. He had the eyes of a man who'd taken more and who'd lost more than any one human being should. A man who'd learned terrible things. Who'd seen the worst mankind had to offer one another. A man who'd hurt.

No. Much more than hurt.

A man who'd done unspeakable evil.

I shuddered.

And he smiled.

He smiled a smile of pure evil, and the dimple in his right cheek disarmed me, or would have, had I not seen the darkness, the depravity, the cold, cold emptiness inside those steely, beautiful eyes, and I wished—and I knew he knew I wished it in that moment—I wished I could take it back. I wished he had never taken the mask of death from his face. I wished he'd never shown me this, this perfect evil, this perfect, cold beauty.

"You want to know my name?" he asked, rising, breaking into my thoughts.

I shook my head. He patted my hair as if he were a proud parent. He then unbuckled his belt and whipped it out of its loops. The sound made me gasp. He doubled it over, watching me as he set the buckle in the palm of his hand.

He moved behind me.

"I underestimated you."

The first lash of the belt seared my ass, making me scream.

3

DOMINIC

I have no delusions about the darkness inside my soul. It is a black abyss, a hole so deep and so dark, it could consume me.

It could swallow me whole. It will if I have anything to say about it.

After leaving Gia's room, I locked the door and set the mask on the kitchen table. I opened the fridge and took out a beer, popping the bottle cap off and drinking half of it down on my way to my bedroom. After whipping Gia's ass, I needed a drink. And a shower. Whipping was hard work. A workout, really.

And it made my dick hard.

Sick fuck.

In my bedroom, I stripped off my boots, jeans, and briefs, finished the rest of the beer, and switched on the shower. I stepped into the icy flow before the water even warmed, the cold not doing anything to alleviate my rock-hard erection.

I'd heard Salvatore describe me once. He'd been talking to Marco, his bodyguard—glorified foot soldier actually, but who was I to judge, considering. I'll never forget the word he used. That one word. *Monster.*

Thing was, he'd been right all along. The golden boy had hit the nail on the fucking head.

I was a monster.

Salvatore thought he must be one to do what he did to Lucia. I snorted at that. He was a fucking white knight compared to me. He did bad things. You couldn't not. I mean, it's the fucking mafia, and he's king. Or would have been, but he handed it all over to our uncle. I could still call Roman uncle. He was a blood relation. That should make me feel better, but it only made me sick.

Fuck them. Fuck the Benedetti assholes. Roman's allegiance was to them—my uncle whom I'd hated because of how well trusted he'd been now sat like king of the family. Well fuck him too.

I was never one of them. I didn't even come close to looking like my brothers or the man I'd believed to be my father for twenty-eight years of my life. Blind and stupid. Hell, I didn't even *look* like my mother except for the eyes. The color at least. The look inside them was all my father: Jake *the Snake* Sapienti. I was Dominic Sapienti, and I looked like my loser father. How in hell could my mother have fallen for him? I mean, once she'd gotten to know him? On the outside, I could see it. But the inside? Black as Satan's soul.

He'd aptly earned his nickname. He slithered from one loyalty to the next. Wherever the payout was, there he was. No friends to speak of, but too many enemies to count. A killer. Ruthless. Hateful. He did the work no one else would do. The jobs that no one wanted to take. Crimes that made even me cringe.

I'd learned from Roman that Franco would have killed him when he found out about me. About his wife's affair. She'd begged him not to, she said she loved him. And Franco loved her too much to hurt the man she loved.

Well, wasn't he the fucking romantic. A regular Romeo.

I turned my thoughts to Gia.

To her face.

Her eyes.

Her fear.

I gripped my cock and began to pump, leaning one hand against the wall while water sprayed my head and shoulders. I fucked my hand at the image of her bent over the bed. The sound of her exhalations, her grunts and screams, her drugged attempts to get out of the way of the belt. I thrust harder into my fist at the memory of her bare ass bouncing with each stroke, the welts turning a deep red. I imagined the heat of her ass if I were to spread her open and plunge into her warm pussy. I wondered if she'd be wet. If she'd be ready for me.

The thought made my cock throb. Some girls got off on it. Not the way I'd done it just now, maybe, but for some of the girls, there was something about getting their ass whipped. It made them wet. And even though I didn't rape them, I made them come after punishing them. It was a power play. That was all. I owned them—owned their pain and their pleasure.

I imagined Gia coming. Imagined kneeling behind her and spreading her open, feasting on her pussy—*fuck*—as she'd beg for me to stop. I threw my head back, water prickling like needles against my face as I blew.

She'd beg. I'd make her beg. I'd hurt, and then I'd make her body yield, make it surrender even as she fought its release, its yielding to me, to a man she would come to hate. I'd watch that betrayal work itself into her brain. I'd fuck with her. And I wouldn't stop. That's what this was. Training. She needed to learn, and pain taught. So did pleasure. It taught you who your master was.

I slumped forward, heart pounding, my cock still throbbing in my fist. I opened my eyes.

What I should have done, though, was come all over her instead of in the shower.

Degradation was a good teacher too.

I had time, though. Not much—two weeks until the auction. It'd have to do.

I washed my hair and scoured my body. I did that a lot now, scrub at my skin to the point it hurt. For the last seven years, it was as though I was trying to claw my way out from inside it. I hated myself. I guess I always had, but now I had a reason. Now I knew the stock I came from. The scum I was.

I climbed out of the shower and grabbed a towel, scratching the rough cloth against my skin as I made my way into the bedroom.

Had I intended to become what I was? A mercenary for hire? Taking the highest paying jobs, no matter the cost to my victims? Not consciously, no. Over the last few years, though, I had done everything I could to live up to my heritage. I was a mercenary. I went where the money was.

I didn't like training women, readying them for something like this. But I was good at it. And I wasn't sure there was another job on earth that would make me feel any lesser trash than this. Taking women and knowingly delivering them into the hands of other monsters like me. Worse than me.

I was well and truly a sick fuck.

I'd started taking these types of jobs two months after the night I'd learned the truth. After that night at Salvatore's house when my world had exploded around me, and left me holding the smoking gun. When I'd stood over my brother's—half-brother's—dying body.

He didn't die.

But that didn't matter. I'd felt Franco's hate. His revulsion. Had he always felt that way about me?

I sat down on the edge of the bed, as if needing the support.

Had I just always been too fucking stupid to see it? Too cocky? I'd been my mother's favorite. Her little prince. I knew why now. She'd loved my father more than she'd loved Franco Benedetti. And I was the living, breathing result of that love.

I shook my head. What would she think if she saw me now?

My throat closed up, and I stood. I had to forget. I just had to fucking forget. I could try to understand forever, and it wouldn't make any difference. It wouldn't change anything. I just needed to stop thinking about it.

I went to the dresser and opened the top drawer, taking out a fresh pair of underwear, jeans and a long-sleeved, V-neck T-shirt. Black. It was all I wore these days. Underneath was the photo I kept there. Taking it out, I touched the little face. The tiny smiling face. Effie. My little girl. She was eleven now. And I missed her. I'd been in her life off and on for her first three and a half years, but when she and Isabella had moved back to New Jersey, I'd seen her almost daily. I think that's why I missed her so much now, even after so many years had passed.

I was just Dominic to her, though. Not dad.

Dad.

I shook my head. *She's better off, asshole.*

Isabella—for some unknown reason—kept e-mailing me photographs. I printed the ones I was especially fond of. It was strange. I didn't think she'd want me in the picture at all. Did she feel bad?

No. That bitch didn't have a conscience. Or she hadn't until Luke.

She was the only one who knew how to get ahold of me, and I knew she hadn't told a soul. That was confirmation of her lack of conscience. She'd watched her sister and my half-brother search and search for me, and she never said a fucking word.

But even she didn't know about this cabin in the woods.

Even she could not forgive this.

I tucked the photo back into the drawer and got dressed. That was what I needed—to remember all the lowlifes in my life. To remember none of us had a conscience. Well, except maybe Salvatore. And fuck him. I was sick of thinking about him.

In the kitchen, I grabbed another beer and opened it, taking a sip and looking at the food supply. The cabinets would have been stocked before I got here. Part of the setup. I had several contacts, but only one man knew of the location of this cabin. And I only knew him as Leo. He got me my jobs. No one knew they were hiring Dominic Benedetti or Dominic Sapienti. Leo got the cabin ready and delivered the girls. I didn't kidnap them. I was purely a trainer. I spent about six weeks with them. I got them from here to the auction. And I delivered them submissive.

Like I said, I had no delusions about what I was.

I took out the eggs and bacon and switched on a burner. My thoughts went back to the girl. No sound came from the room. All cried out from her whipping, she was probably sleeping off the rest of the drug.

She was different than the others. She fought me; they all did to an extent. But they also begged for their lives. She'd done the opposite. She'd told me to get it over with if I was going to kill her. I wondered where she'd come from. Who'd had her, and who'd branded her. I wondered if her new owner would want that mark cut out. They usually liked them pure. Maybe he'd burn his own brand over top of whatever decorated her hip.

There was one thing that bugged me, though. That kind of nagged at me. When she'd bitten my hand, I'd gone to slap her but stopped. I'd never stopped with any other girl before. It was something in her eyes that had done it. Not the fear, but something else. Something almost familiar.

I lay strips of bacon into the pan and cracked two eggs beside them, the sizzle and smell making my stomach growl, and wondered who she was. It wasn't just her looks but the look inside her eyes. She was different than the others. She wasn't a random pickup off the street. And I had a feeling she was older than the usual girls by a few years. The girls I trained were between eighteen and twenty-one. I wouldn't take them younger. If I had to guess, I'd say Gia was twenty-four, maybe twenty-five. The buyers usually wanted young flesh.

Sick fucks.

Sicker than you?

I scrambled the eggs and told that voice to fuck off. Once everything was cooked, I plated it and set it on the table, grabbed my laptop out of its bag beside the door, and booted it up. I finished the plate of food as I checked my bank balance for the deposit—ten grand up front, the rest upon sale, the final price determined by the amount the girl brought in. Not bad money. But I guessed human trafficking brought in serious money. The auctions were always interesting. I enjoyed looking at the girls. Who wouldn't? But I more liked watching the buyers, who were mostly men, some couples, and a few single women. The same ones seemed to turn up at every auction. I wondered if they were growing their stable of stolen women or if they needed to replace lost or damaged goods.

That little bit of conscience that gnawed at me got shoved back down into its box and the lid locked down tight. I thought of the girl—the job—and how I could maximize my earnings. She was good-looking, even if she was older than the usual girl, but she had something most of the others didn't: that arrogance. Nothing like breaking a cocky girl. I just needed to somehow preserve that during her training, make her bow down with just that hint of indignation.

Once I finished, I cleaned up, then grabbed a granola bar and a bottle of water and headed toward Gia's room. The cold inside gave me a chill. I saw how she lay sleeping huddled into herself on the bed. I set the water and the granola bar down on the small bedside table and walked back out. Tomorrow I'd give her a chance to earn back the blanket.

4

GIA

I ate the granola bar and drank the water when I woke up. I couldn't remember the last time I'd had real food. Hot food. I had dreamt of bacon while I slept. I even thought I could smell it right now. It was like a mirage of water in the desert. I must be desperate.

No light came through the slats of the boarded-up window, so I knew it was late. How late, though, I couldn't be sure. And it was cold. Really cold. I was glad to have such dim lighting in the room. Sleeping on the bare mattress and knowing others had been here before me—well, I didn't want to know what I'd find staining it.

I stayed at the window for a while, knowing screaming would be useless. If anyone would have been able to hear me, he would have made sure to gag me anyway. This wasn't the first time he'd done this. I knew that much. But I tried anyway. I cried out the window, not caring if he could hear.

"Hello? Hello, can anyone hear me? Is anyone out there?"

Nothing. Nothing but the sounds of night. I went back to the bed and sat down, rubbing my arms to warm up.

I wish I knew exactly what would happen to me. My captor —what was his name? I decided I would call him Death. He looked like an angel of death. That death mask hid his angel's face.

I needed to find out more information. Try to figure out where I was. How far from civilization. I heard no noise, and trying to look through the window slats had proven useless earlier. The room smelled musty and old, like it hadn't been used in a while. The mattress and pillow—I didn't want to think about what those smelled like. But if I went close to the window, in addition to the freezing-cold draft, I could smell pine. We were in the woods somewhere. Question was, where and how far from civilization?

Death. He'd whipped me so easily. Hadn't even had to hold me down to do it, although he had had to adjust my position a few times. I'd have to figure out how to not swallow the pills next time. I couldn't be so out of control again. I needed to find an opportunity to run. But what if when I got that chance, it turned out there were more men out there? What if he wasn't alone? What if I did manage to get past Death and got out there, only to find a second man? Or third. Victor had so many at his disposal.

But did Death work for Victor? I guessed he'd have to. Victor would have to be making money off this auction. Was he doing this to me to keep his promise to Mateo? How cruelly he kept his word. How easily he twisted it.

Mateo had begged him for my life.

He'd been on his knees when they'd brought me in. He'd been beaten and bloodied, bound and kneeling in the middle of that horrible room with the scent of fresh blood, of death, overwhelming every other sense. When he'd seen me, God, his eyes when he'd seen me. The shock. The horror. Like everything they'd done to him up until that point was moot. Like me seeing him like that, Mateo, my older brother, my hero, the one who always took care of me, who saved *me* every time, me being there to see him on his knees had broken him in a way they hadn't been able to break him before.

He'd begged them, then. I knew he hadn't begged before. Victor said so.

Victor.

Victor had looked so smug upon hearing my brother beg.

I would kill Victor with my bare hands. I would do to him what he'd done to my Mateo.

I wiped hot tears from my face and steeled myself. But remembering...remembering what he'd made Mateo do to promise to keep me alive. What he'd made me watch.

I leaped off the bed and ran into the bathroom, making it to the toilet just in time as that granola bar made its way back up. I'd had nothing to eat in so long. I didn't even know how long.

When I stopped retching, I opened the medicine cabinet in search of a toothbrush. I did find one, a small travel-size one, but no way was I going to brush my teeth with a used toothbrush. And before he made me do it, I flushed it down the toilet. At least there was a tube of toothpaste. Squeezing some on my finger, I brushed my teeth as best as I could.

I needed to focus. To find some way out.

Using the night-lights, I searched both rooms again, and like the first time, found nothing. The chest where he'd kept the crop was locked tight, but I knew if I could get in there, there might be something for me to use, some sort of weapon. Something to use to escape, or at least to hurt him long enough to get out of here. He had to have a phone. I would take it and make the call to David Lazaro, Mateo's contact. I'd memorized his number. But was he in on it too? Had he set Mateo up?

It didn't matter, not right now. I needed to get out of here first. He had to have a car. I mean, if we were in some remote location—and I knew we must be—he'd need a car to get here. I could take the car. The rest I'd figure out. I just needed to get out of this room.

I didn't know how much time had passed, but I tried the door for the hundredth time, growing so frustrated that this time, I pounded on it with both fists, screaming out for him to let me out.

A light went on in the outer room. I scrambled backward to the bed, climbed on, and waited, my back pressed against the headboard.

The lock slid, and I found myself hugging my knees, hiding my face behind a curtain of hair. When the door opened, I lifted my head. Death stood there without the mask, wearing jeans and a long-sleeved shirt. His damp hair told me he'd recently had a shower. I guess he'd built up a sweat whipping me.

My ass hurt, and I shifted my weight.

He didn't close the door.

Without a word, he entered. I studied him.

He watched me, his gaze as effective as chains keeping me locked to the spot.

Then he changed direction and reached into his pocket for what I knew was the key to the chest. It was like as soon as he looked away, he released me. Like the bonds holding me stupidly to the bed while the door stood open had been broken, and I ran. I bounded up faster than I thought I could move and bolted straight for the door. I didn't trip, I didn't think, I just ran. It wasn't a big room. It would only have taken five or six steps to get to it. But I didn't make it. And I knew from the look in his eyes that he'd expected me to do just what I did. That he'd left the damn door open on purpose, testing me. I knew it the instant he shot his arm out and caught me just before I could set foot outside the door. Just a breath away from that other room, that brightly lit room.

Death wrapped an arm around my middle and slapped my ass hard before hauling me kicking and screaming back to the bed with the bare stained mattress.

"Let me go!"

He threw me with enough force that I bounced. I scrambled to get away from him.

"You're so predictable," he said, his voice calm.

I slid off the bed opposite him and planted my hands on it. I shifted my gaze from him to the door and back.

"Get on the bed."

We both danced from foot to foot, him mimicking my movements as I bounced left then right, looking for the opportunity to run.

"Just let me go! You don't have to do this."

"Get on the fucking bed."

God, he sounded bored of all things. Fucking bored.

"I don't know what you're being paid, but I can pay you more." It was a total lie. I had no money.

I took two steps, then stopped when he matched them, standing opposite him on the other side of the bed.

"No, you can't. Now get on the bed, and I'll take your obedience into consideration when it's time for your punishment."

My ass throbbed at the word. I shook my head and this time, went for it. I just went right for the door even though I knew I wouldn't make it. He was faster. He was bigger. And he was stronger. So when the door slammed shut almost catching my fingers between it and the frame, I wasn't wholly surprised.

I whirled around, feeling him so close. Close enough to knee? He hadn't locked the door yet. If I could—

But he must have anticipated it because he caught my knee between his thighs and pressed himself up against me, holding me tight against the door. We stood like that, watching each other, breath coming fast, my naked chest heaving against his with the effort to keep taking in air as he squeezed it out of me. I felt this strange sort of pull to him, this sort of...attraction? No, not that. He may be beautiful, but he was evil. He was no better, no different than Victor. The draw, though, I knew he felt it too. I saw it in the way he looked at me, now that he wore no mask.

But sexual attraction was a thing of the bodies, not the mind. Not the heart. If it was that, it was mechanic. That was all.

There was more. Something else. Something different.

Sometimes, things we can't remember carry emotion with them. That feeling—good or bad—it's the thing that's present between two strangers. And we were strangers. It's just, this feeling...no, I was confused. Maybe it was a sort of Stockholm syndrome, although it would be too soon, wouldn't it? When did Stockholm kick in? Maybe because Victor had held me for...how long had he held me? Days? Weeks? Hours? How long ago had I witnessed Mateo's execution?

No, I was confused. There was no emotion. No feeling. There was only confusion. Confusion and hate.

We stayed like that, our eyes locked, and I felt him, I felt his cock at my belly, hard and thick and ready. He was aroused. I knew he'd been aroused before too. After he'd whipped me, I'd seen how tight his jeans had stretched across his crotch.

"You get off on this." I said, my voice somehow a controlled whisper, wanting him to know I despised him. Wanting him to believe I felt repulsed by him. "You like it. You like chasing naked girls around this decrepit room, wearing your little mask."

He grinned and pressed his cock against me once as if to say yes, yes he did.

"I'm not wearing my mask now."

"You like scaring women half your size? Who could never stand a chance against you physically?"

In the next moment, he circled my wrists with his hands and drew my arms overhead. He leaned down, so his forehead rested against mine.

"I do, Gia," he whispered.

His eyes roamed over my face and settled on my mouth.

"I like it very much."

I swallowed and felt the hardening of my nipples against the fabric of his shirt and hated myself for it. Hated my body for it.

"I like a little fight too."

He brought his mouth to my ear, inhaling along my cheek as he did so.

"It makes my cock hard," he whispered.

He leaned his face down to where my pulse throbbed against my throat and slid his tongue over it, one long, drawn-out taste to tell me he knew I was terrified, he knew how my heart pounded, and he knew, despite the bravado in my talk, I was scared shitless.

But he didn't know that didn't mean I was done fighting.

He brought his face to mine again. His right cheek dimpled when the corner of his mouth turned upward as he looked at my slightly parted lips. He thought he'd won. He thought I wanted him. His eyes declared his assumed victory.

He leaned his head in and kissed me. He took my lower lip between his and moaned as he sucked on it, and I stood there, feeling my body go limp against his, letting it, using its traitorous reaction to my advantage. And when I tilted my head back and he kissed me full on the lips and slid his tongue inside my mouth, I struck. Even knowing full well I'd be punished, I struck. I drew my head back and banged it into his nose. A break would be painful enough to give me the second I'd need to get out.

I didn't break it, though. I knew instantly because his grip on

my wrists tightened and he slammed them hard against the
door.

"You're a bitch."

He lowered my arms and twisted them behind my back into
one of his hands, wiping the blood from his nose with the back
of his other hand. He turned me so he stood behind me, then
walked me toward the chest where, without a word, he unlocked
and opened it to take out three sets of leather cuffs similar to the
ones that had shackled me when I'd gotten here.

I struggled against him as he led me back to the bed. I didn't
ask for freedom. I didn't beg. But I fought because he was right. I
was a bitch. And I wasn't going to make this easy. Even if that
meant I'd pay.

He didn't speak either, didn't tell me to be still, didn't do
anything but keep his steady hold on me, tightening it a little.
When we got to the bed, he released my wrists and took hold of
one arm, pushing me to sit on the edge. I struggled against him
as he drew it out and attached the leather to the wrist before
fighting me for the other and binding them together. He met my
gaze afterward, and I knew this was a show of who was in charge
and just how in charge. And I hated myself for the little scream I
let out as he drew me backward on the bed to attach the cuffs to
a ring on the headboard. He was nothing if not prepared.

He released my arms and stood, looking down at me.

I tested the bonds, knowing they'd hold but needing to
anyway. I don't think I'll ever forget the clanking sound of it, of
metal on metal, of my louder scream, of the desperation in it as
he took one ankle and stretched it toward one corner of the bed
and bound it. His face remained empty of expression as he
walked casually to the other side, and I found myself mumbling,
muttering pleas as he stretched the other leg out and bound me
so I lay spread eagle, exposed, at his mercy.

He stood back and looked down at me, first at my face, my

eyes, then down over my breasts and belly and to my sex. There his gaze hovered and when he moved to climb between my legs, I screamed and I begged. I begged for him not to rape me. I begged for my life. I begged for mercy. And he just watched me, watched it, and placed his hands on my inner thighs, softly trailing fingertips up and up until tears streamed down my face. His fingers settled on either side of my pussy and spread me open.

"Please. Please don't."

He stopped then, and his gaze met mine. I thought he'd say something, but he didn't. He just watched me for a long time, as if he wanted me to know he held all the power. That he owned me. That he could do whatever he wanted to do to me. And then he bent his head and licked my pussy. He licked its length slowly and purposefully while his eyes remained locked on mine and my breath caught in my throat. He did it again, taking his time, tasting every inch of me, teasing the hard nub of my clit until I couldn't take anymore, until I felt my back arching, my body moving without my brain's permission. I couldn't look into his eyes because I'd see my shame there, see how my body yielded so quickly, gave itself so easily to this man, my captor. My jailor. My keeper. My tormentor.

I squeezed my eyes shut and lay there while he sucked on my clit and died a little when I heard the moan that came out of my mouth as he teased and taunted and tasted and made me gush, made me come so hard I thought I'd break apart. And maybe I did, maybe, in a way, I did.

He didn't speak when it was over, and I opened my eyes to find his locked on mine as he rose from the bed and wiped his mouth with the back of his hand. We stayed like that for a long time until finally, I blinked, turning away, humiliated, and he walked back out the door and locked it behind him.

I wept silently for so many things. For my brother. For

myself. For the shame I felt as cool air dried my pussy, dried where he'd licked me to orgasm. I cried, knowing I'd come under my enemy's tongue, knowing this was only the beginning, knowing there would be so many betrayals, so many concessions. I wondered who I'd be by the end of this. If I survived, that is.

And I hated myself for not wanting to be left alone anymore. Hated myself for my weakness. My fear.

5

DOMINIC

Eating her pussy didn't involve penetration. It wasn't the same as fucking her. Not that I didn't fuck the other girls. I did. Some. Not all. Only if they were virgins in any way. Well, that was *mostly* true. It would be better for them, easier, if I took that from them. I'd never eaten one out, though. I'd never wanted to. I'd played with them, I'd enjoyed fucking the ones I did, but it was just that, a fuck, a piece of ass. This was different. Maybe it was like kissing. Too personal.

And I'd kissed her too. Or tried to. Hell, I should have thanked her for nearly breaking my nose.

I don't even know what made me do it. Yes, my cock was already hard after our little struggle, but hell, that was the norm, and in the last couple of years, I'd gotten to know my fist pretty well. And when I wanted a woman, I paid for it. Anonymous sex, exactly how I liked it.

So why the fuck had I eaten her out?

And why couldn't I stop thinking about how she tasted? How she sounded when she came? How she thrust her hips at me, wanting more, even as she resisted me?

I'd felt it again, that strange sense of familiarity, when I'd walked into the room and she'd been sitting on the bed, watching me like that. It was those damned haunted eyes. Haunted? Or haunting. They'd seen evil. They saw through me and into my evil. She'd survived evil. But would she survive me?

Yet it wasn't just that. I knew those eyes. As ridiculous as it was, they were connected to some distant memory, something brief, something...better than this.

Hell, this was all ridiculous. I just needed to focus here and do my job, and if it meant I fucked her while I was at it—virgin or not—then so be it. Stupid fucking rule anyway, considering I trained them to become sex slaves. What difference would it make for them if I did fuck them? None, that's what. And I needed to remember this was a job. Any nostalgic feelings, any attraction to this girl—it would have to get gone. She was a fucking job. Granted, a job with a restriction: no penetration. But hell, if it happened, it happened. No one would give a fuck, not in the end.

I finished my coffee, closed the shutter letting the too-bright sunshine into the kitchen, and walked into her room. She lay awake, but the moment our eyes met, she blinked and looked away. I closed the door and locked it behind me, walked into the bathroom where I'd left the chair, and brought it into the bedroom. I set the blanket I'd carried in on it.

She eyed it.

"Chilly in here," I said casually.

She searched my face, my eyes.

"I'm thinking you need to use the bathroom?"

She nodded, her gaze settling on a spot just beyond me. I guessed she'd be embarrassed after last night's impromptu session. I hadn't intended to do what I'd done. I'd just meant to fuck with her a little. I'd been reading, and all her racket had been annoying, quite frankly. She had to know I wouldn't keep her somewhere she'd be found so easily, so why the screaming?

"Did you sleep well?" I asked, sitting on the edge of the bed and tracing the edge of one of her ankle cuffs.

"How well do you expect me to sleep in this freezing room bound and naked and fucking humiliated?"

Well, no elephant in this room, then. She was straightforward. I liked that. I brushed a strand of hair from her face, and she shook her head to rid herself of my touch. I gripped her chin and forced her to look at me. "Getting my cock sucked puts me out like a light. The way you came, I'd thought you'd have slept into next week."

Her face grew warm beneath my touch, and I had to smile at the blush creeping up her neck and cheeks.

"The least you can do is thank me."

"I hate you. You're the worst of them all."

"Worse than the men who branded you?" I raised my eyebrows, although truly, I didn't care. Fact was, she was right. I *was* the worst of them all.

"The worst," she spat out.

"Then we have no misunderstandings between us." I undid her ankles first. Then I unhooked her from the ring at the top of the bed but kept her wrists bound. "Go."

"With my hands tied?"

"Call me when you're done. I'll wipe."

I almost laughed when her face got so red I thought she'd explode. Truth was, it was an act, this flat, uninterested tone. Not that I cared, I just...that hint of conscience crept in through the cracks in the fucking walls of my chest. It seeped through the tiniest fissure, and it fucked with me. I didn't like it.

She walked into the bathroom. I noticed the bruises on her ass. I hadn't whipped her too hard, but hard enough they'd serve as a reminder to behave every time she sat down.

While she took care of what she needed to, I went to the chest, unlocked it, and took out what I needed: the collar and the crop. A few moments later she returned, wiping droplets of water from her face with her hands.

"I need a toothbrush."

"Isn't there one in there?"

She didn't hesitate. "No."

"Funny, I could have sworn..."

Her gaze fell to the things I held, and I could see the effort it took for her to stay in place.

"Would you like to earn a blanket?" I asked. "Maybe get some more water and food?"

"What do I have to do?" The question came out slow and cautious as a crawl.

"Kneel."

She studied me, distrust in her eyes, hesitation in the way she bit her lip. "What are you going to do?"

"Put this collar around your neck." I didn't feel like playing all of a sudden.

I could see her mind working, trying to figure out what to do, what was expected, perhaps what would earn her the least amount of pain. But slowly, she knelt. It surprised me.

I stood motionless, looking at her. She turned her gaze away, distancing herself perhaps. I cleared my throat and walked to her, collar and crop in the same hand. She remained as she was, but she looked at me again, her eyes turned watchful. I circled her once, looking down at the top of her pretty head, at the smooth flesh of her toned if not too skinny body. I'd have to feed her soon. For all I knew, that granola bar was all she'd eaten in days.

When I stopped behind her, she craned her neck to look back.

"Face forward unless you're told otherwise."

She gave me a wary look but did as I said. I smiled. Pain and pleasure, the threat of the former and the shame of the latter. Remarkable teachers, that pair.

I picked up the hairbrush I'd left on the nightstand, sat on the bed behind her, and set the crop and collar down so I could pick up her hair. I brushed the length of it, taking care to work out the knots, appreciating the weight of it, the shine when brushed. Once I finished, I braided it into one long, dark pleat down her back and secured it with an elastic wrapped around the handle of the brush. I got off the bed, squatted behind her, and took her in, appreciating how she knelt so quietly, so obediently, waiting. I wondered how hard her heart pounded, and when I swept the back of my hand over the curve of her neck, she shuddered.

I stilled.

I think we both held our breath.

I forced myself to continue and picked up the collar, raising it over her head to secure around her neck, locking the small lock at the back, one only I had the key to and the one she would wear until she was sold. I stood, with my hand on the top of her head and the crop held in the other, and circled to stand where she could see me.

She lifted her pretty gaze to mine, the green of her eyes bright, the pupils dark, dilated. There was a stillness about her. Her nipples tightened, and a scent—her scent, as I'd come to know it last night—hung in the air between us.

She was aroused.

I turned my hand into a fist and gripped the hair at the back of her head. She flinched but remained as she was, keeping her hands together on her lap. I brought her cheek to me, to the hardness just behind the fabric of the jeans.

"Men will want you." Why did the thought not please me? "They will pay to have you." In fact, the idea of it made the fist in her hair tighten. I only noticed it when the first tear slid from the corner of her eye, but I didn't loosen my hold because right now, all I wanted were her lips around my cock, her tongue licking its length, her sucking me off. What I needed was to shoot down her throat, and when she choked, to come all over her, to mark her as mine, to destroy her. Because that would decimate her, and that was what I needed to do. Take her to the point of breaking, but keep her just on this side of that abyss.

Beauty knelt at my feet.

And I would be the beast who would break her.

The monster who would destroy her.

Better me than another.

She'd be mine then, in a sick, unnatural way. In a sick, unnatural mind.

"What happened to you that you're like this?"

Her quiet voice broke into my thoughts, accused me.

"That you can do this?"

Our gazes locked. I felt the shift in my chest, a flashback of me as I'd once been. As Dominic Benedetti. A man with a place, a home, a reason to live. A man with the whole world at his feet.

And then the realization of how I'd lost it rushed in on the heels of that memory, dampening everything else, regret and loss smothering me.

"What?"

I wondered if in that millisecond, she'd seen a flash of emotion cross my face.

I felt hot, sweaty. I felt—

"I changed my mind. I want to know your name."

I blinked to dislodge this hold, this strange, new thing she held over me, but it didn't work.

"Tell me your name," she said.

My fist in her hair went limp. "Why? Why does it matter?"

"I don't want to call you Death."

I must have looked as confused as I felt.

"Your mask. The way you act. You try to be cold, like you couldn't give a fuck, but I know that's not it. There's something else. There's more there."

I tightened my fist and grinned at her pain. "Don't fool yourself. There's nothing else."

"Then it won't matter if you tell me your name."

"What are you going to do for it?"

"You can make me do whatever you want anyway."

"Making you and you choosing to are two different things."

"I get the feeling you'd like making me."

"You'd be right," I said, then squatted down so my face was inches from hers. I inhaled and searched her eyes, let my gaze drop down to her mouth, then back up. "Don't think my eating your pussy means something. It's just part of the job," I lied, then leaned in closer, close enough to trace the curve of her ear with my tongue. She shuddered. "I smell you, Gia," I whispered. "I smell your sex. And I bet if I slid my hand between your legs, you'd be wet."

She didn't blink, didn't breathe. I watched her, challenging her, and when she remained silent, I rose to stand, feeling victorious.

"If I—" She cleared her throat. "If I sucked your cock, you'd come too. It doesn't matter, doesn't mean you have some power over me. It's physical. That's all."

"You want to suck my cock?" I knew that wasn't what she meant.

"No. I was making a point."

"What point?" I asked callously. "I missed it."

"I hate you." It started out angry, but when she repeated the words, tears glistened in her eyes, and she turned away.

"So you've told me." I looked down at the top of her head, glad she wasn't looking at me anymore, glad she couldn't see my face right then, not until I collected myself. Remembered myself. "You should hate me." The words carried no emotion.

She pressed the heels of her hands against her eyes.

I stepped away and readied the crop. I needed to get my head in the game and move. I was overthinking things. Overthinking her. "Forward. Hands and knees. Doggy style."

"Wh...what?" The word seemed to trip out of her mouth, caught between tears and a sob.

"Forward!" I raised the crop, and she flinched.

"That's what you do, isn't it? You beat women. You tie them down and beat them until they're so scared and broken, they have no will left. No will to defy you."

I slid my fingers through the space between her collar and her pretty little neck. I hated what she said, but she only spoke the truth. "That's right," I said, tugging so she had to put her hands out in front of her or she'd fall on her face. "It's what I do."

"Fine!"

She tried to pull away, but I held her.

"You want to whip me? Fine. I've had worse. I've survived worse. You're nothing. You can't even tell me your name."

I brought the crop down on her ass, and she bit back a scream. "Crawl," I said, tugging her forward before releasing the collar, sending her scrambling to break her fall and striking again.

"At least I knew who Victor was!" She wept but crawled forward a little, pausing to wipe her face.

"I didn't tell you to stop!" I drew her forward again, and she moved, hurrying to get out of the way of the crop. "Faster!"

"I can't go faster, you sick prick." She fell forward, her bound hands hindering her progress.

"Are you hungry?" I asked sharply as I delivered another stroke.

She glanced at me, and I saw the answer in her eyes, heard it in the way her stomach growled.

"Then you'd better move. Are you cold?"

She sucked back tears and paused again to wipe her face.

I struck, aiming where she'd been branded.

This time, she let go of a scream and fell to her side, protecting her hip, watching me accusingly.

"You'd better get used to this. Get used to being treated like this."

"Like a fucking dog, you mean."

"That's a good way to think of it. This is obedience training, and you're my bitch."

"You're a coward. You hide behind a mask. You carry your weapons, against what? Defenseless, bound women who are half your size?"

"Fuck you, Gia."

"It's what you do. Own it. But you have to own what it makes you too. A fucking coward."

"How'd you get yourself caught, anyway?" I asked, gripping her collar and hauling her up to her knees. She fought like an animal. I leaned down so my face was inches from hers. "I'm getting the feeling you weren't some random pickup."

"Let me go. You're hurting me!"

"How? Tell me."

"I wasn't a random pickup you fucking prick."

She shoved at my chest, but she wasn't nearly strong enough.

"Piss off a boyfriend? He finally get enough of your bitchy mouth?"

Tears pooled in her eyes and spilled over onto her cheeks, a raw and complete pain intensifying the green.

"You don't know anything about me. Not a thing!"

"Tell me!" I shook her hard, lifting her to her feet and pressing her against the wall. I held her there by her throat.

Her face reddened, and she watched me. I wasn't sure if she was able to speak or not. Rage hotter than hell burned through me, and I squeezed her neck.

"Fucking tell me!"

She choked out a sob, and when I loosened my hold, she began to cough.

"Did he order your branding as punishment?"

"He wasn't my boyfriend," she choked out.

I released her, and she dropped to her hands and knees, still coughing.

"He's a murderer. A monster." She paused, turned her face up, and added: "Like you."

I narrowed my gaze, although we both knew she was right. The room stood strangely quiet, her on her knees at my feet, eyes red, cheeks wet with tears, hate spearing me.

"Just like you," she said again, sitting back on her heels and lowering her gaze, giving herself over to the tears that seemed unending. I watched like the monster she accused me of being. The monster I was. I just stood there and watched her come apart until she quieted, and then I pulled the chair closer and sat down, my gaze still on her, as if I'd never seen this before, never seen a person come unglued.

She sat up and wiped the last of her tears, the look in her eyes telling me hate fueled her now. Hate kept her upright.

"I normally don't give a shit about the girls that pass through here, but you're different. You're like me, Gia. You're filled with hate."

"I'm nothing like you."

I ignored her. "Maybe I won't bother taking you to the auction. Keep you for myself until I wear you out instead. Until there's nothing left."

She stared at me. Was it fear that left her mute? That pushed tears from her eyes?

"That's a scary thought, isn't it?"

"It would be if there was any truth to it, but you're a peon."

Her voice broke, betraying her panic. But she kept going.

"You're a nobody. You work for them. You don't get to decide. You don't get to choose what happens to me."

I swallowed hard. She was right. She was exactly right. She paused, and I wondered if she could read my face. I needed to end this, to take back control.

"You don't know anything about me," I defended.

"I think I do." She sniffled, wiped her nose and eyes. "And you're wrong. We may both hate, but I don't hate myself. I know who I am. I'm not evil. I don't hurt people. You...you're a monster. You hate yourself more than you could ever hate anyone else."

I swallowed hard suddenly, wanting my mask, needing it. She saw me, she saw right through me, and she said the words I was too fucking afraid of, too much of a coward to say myself. The words I was too weak to own.

I stood and kicked the chair out from behind me, sending it crashing against the far wall, making her jump, making her lean away from me.

"Turn around." I ordered.

She eyed the crop, and I saw her tremble as her red, puffy eyes searched mine.

"Turn the fuck around." Quieter now. Had she realized yet I was at my deadliest when I grew calm? I watched her think. I studied this girl who desperately needed humbling. This girl who burrowed too deep under my fucking skin.

Her eyes darted to the crop once more, and I set it aside. I didn't need that. There were other punishments. Pain wasn't the worst I could do.

Her throat worked as she swallowed, but slowly, she turned to face away from me. Her hair had come partially out of the braid. I reached to pull the elastic holding it together out. Gia startled but held her position. I ruffled the braid I'd so carefully pleated until her long hair hung down her back. I picked up the mass of it and set it over one shoulder. She remained tense, shoulders high, arms tight by her sides as I squatted down to trace my fingertips down the length of her spine. Her skin was so soft, her body slender, the lines long and straight, her narrow waist giving way to rounded hips. Her arms were toned, like I'd noticed her legs were. Apart from the bruising and that branding scar, she was flawless. Perfect.

I pulled my hand away like I'd been burned and stood.

"Put your forehead on the floor and raise your hips." My voice held a different tone, quieter, darker. My cock throbbed to life, hard and ready and wanting.

Wanting her.

She turned her head, just glancing behind her but not quite able to hold my gaze.

"Do it."

I didn't know what I would do. I could anticipate what she expected, why her face had twisted, and why she remained silent as she slowly leaned forward, her bound hands sliding along the floor, creating a cushion for her forehead as she did as she was told.

I waited, taking her in, slight and frightened and so fucking erotic. I wanted her. I wanted her surrender, her submission, but more than that. I wanted her in a way that was different. Not like the others. Not like the women before—in my former life.

She raised her hips slowly, and I sucked in a breath.

I'd seen her naked. I'd cleaned her. I'd touched her. I'd tasted her. But this, this presenting of herself to me, even if it was under duress, it felt different. And some part of me, it longed for her. Longed to have her. Possess her. Break her and own her.

It longed for this surrender, for her submission, to be real.

I don't know how long we stayed like that, her quiet and obedient, me in some trance, under this strange spell, watching like this was the first woman I'd seen like this. Wanting like I'd never wanted before. Feeling something almost pure wash over me, at least momentarily, before she sniffled, and I knew she was crying. Quietly crying. Afraid.

No.

Terrified.

Overpowered.

Breaking.

I took a step back, seeing as if for the first time this filthy floor in this filthy room. This terrible place where I would break her, break this beautiful, perfect creature and make her less. I would take everything away from her. That was what I did. What I had done to so many others.

I stumbled backward some more, misstepped, and caught myself.

Pure. I'd felt something pure washing over me. What a joke. What a sick, fucking joke.

I turned on my heel and walked out the door, slamming it shut behind me, locking it, locking her in. I grabbed my jacket and keys and stalked out of the cabin, breaking my own rule and leaving her behind. I climbed into my truck and drove through the narrow passage in the woods and out onto the open road. I didn't stop at the nearest town like I would have in the past. I didn't want a woman. And I didn't want whiskey. I just wanted to be out of my head. Out of my skin. I wanted to be someone else. Anyone else. Because the lowest scum of the earth had to be better than the filth that was me. Than the aberration that was me. This hateful monster who hurt, who broke, who took beauty that did not belong to him and destroyed it.

She was right. Salvatore had been right.

I was a monster.

I was the worst kind of monster.

6

GIA

He'd left the blanket behind. After washing my face and hands, I grabbed it and wrapped it over my shoulders, not caring how dirty it was, not caring about the stains or the smell. I just held it to me and climbed onto the bed and lay on my side, shivering, knees pulled in to my chest, clutching this foul blanket to me. And no matter how hard I tried, I couldn't make the tears stop. I wept like I had when I'd watched Mateo die. How could there be tears left inside me? How could more come, how could I not be dead of dehydration after all this fucking crying?

They'd shot him in the back of the head after they'd cut out his tongue. They'd made me watch it all. Watch him as he set his face before the block—a fucking tree stump stained with the dried blood of how many others? I'd watched as he had laid his tongue on the stump, his eyes wide, trying hard not to show his fear. Failing. I'd seen Victor's nod in my periphery, giving the order. Watched the ax come down and blood pour and Mateo fall over, a garbled scream coming from him. From my brother.

My vital, loving, crazy brother whom I loved so, so fucking much.

He'd done it to save me. To spare me. He'd made Victor promise. He'd made the deal. He'd offered his tongue in exchange for my life.

And then, after, was it a mercy then that they'd hauled him up to his knees and pressed his head back onto the block until he held it there, chin cushioned in his own dismembered tongue, in the pool of his own blood seeping into the stump of the tree. He'd looked at me once more before closing his eyes. That was the moment he'd given up hope. I knew it. I saw it. Victor pushed the barrel of the gun to the back of his head then. This time, the scream was mine.

There had been so much blood, an impossible amount. My brother's blood covered me as he fell over, gone, his savaged, beaten body murdered, his life stolen before my eyes, just inches from me while I stood powerless to save him.

He'd made Victor promise he wouldn't kill me. That was the deal. They'd have cut his tongue out anyway, but maybe they'd have done it after he'd died. Or maybe they'd force him. I didn't know. I didn't care. All I knew was that I'd never forget the sound of the ax coming down, the look on Mateo's face, in his eyes. And then that final, deafening sound of the gun being fired.

I'd read that in real life—as opposed to the movies—it sounded like a pop, but this was no pop. It was an explosion, an ear piercing, deafening explosion. Louder than anything I'd ever heard before. More horrible than anything I'd seen.

I'd never forget that day. I'd never forget what they did to him. And it was the one thing that kept me together now. The thing that had me gathering the pieces of myself. Because if I gave in now, then Mateo's death was for nothing. Victor thought he'd won. That Mateo and I were finished. But he was wrong. I had vowed vengeance for what he'd done. I had promised it silently to Mateo, to myself. And I needed to pull myself together, to collect my strength, because I knew now that I had a chance. I knew it.

I had fully expected Death to rape me. I thought...I thought what else could he want? I had taunted him—hell, maybe I wanted him to kill me, to end it all, to make the decision and take the responsibility of vengeance away from me. But that was weak. I knew that now. Hell, I'd known it then. And he, this man I called Death, he surprised me. He unwittingly gave me hope.

I was different to him. He wanted me. I could see it in his face, his eyes. He'd made a mistake, taking off that mask. He should never have done that. He didn't know me. He didn't know I would stop at nothing to avenge my brother.

Although he was right about one thing. There was one area where we were alike. We both hated. We'd both been hurt—no, we'd been battered. But neither he nor I had broken, and I wouldn't break now. He wanted to break me. It was his job. I had a suspicion, though, that that wasn't wholly true. His own conflicting emotions weakened him. But it would be good to remember that those exact things made him dangerous. They made him volatile and unpredictable. I needed to control him. I didn't need to search for a how. I knew how. I just had to come to terms with the fact that the idea of it didn't repel me like it should. The thought of his hands on me, his mouth on me, his cock inside me, it didn't turn my stomach. The opposite, actually. And that was what made me sick. That made me question who I was. How I could feel these things, feel this way. How I could not abhor this man.

Because if I did hate him, if I were repelled by him, I would still do what I had to do, and I would hate myself a little less for it. But as it stood now, as I felt now, I knew I had to be some sort of monster to be able to feel attraction for my captor. To come under his tongue. To want it again.

I'd lied when I'd said what I'd said to him about it being physical. It wasn't physical, not for me. It never could be.

He'd said he had two weeks to train me. To ready me for the auction. Well, I had two weeks, then. Two weeks to get under his skin, to burrow so deep he couldn't let me go. He'd have no choice but to keep me. Perhaps even to help me.

No, that I could not expect. I would kill him as soon as I could. It would be good training for when the time came to kill Victor. Because killing was new to me. I may have been born into a family of foot soldiers, men who'd worked for various crime families for generations, but I'd never even touched a gun, never felt the weight of one in my hands. I would learn, though. Maybe I'd even learn how to wield an ax when it came time to take Victor down.

I let hate fuel me while I gathered my courage and pushed the blanket off. I walked into the bathroom and, with my hands bound, switched on the shower. I didn't wait for the water to warm. Instead, I stepped into the tub and stood beneath a spray of icy water, not thinking about the dirt at my feet, the filth around me. I washed away my fear and willed myself to think of Mateo, of his strength right up until the end. I exchanged fear for strength and let the water wash away any weakness inside me. When I was finished, I returned to my room and waited there, ready for Death to come.

BUT HE DIDN'T COME BACK. NOT for the space of six meals.

A few hours later—I wasn't sure if it was hours, as time seemed to crawl by, so it could have been an hour or a day— when the door opened again, it wasn't Death who entered.

All my resolve, all the courage I'd thought I'd gathered, all the strength and drive I had built up, dissolved when that door opened and another man entered.

The only sound was that of my gasp. He was almost as tall as Death but built differently, his body almost paunchy although still strong. He had dark hair and black spots for eyes, his skin tanned and leathery. I'd guess him to be in his late thirties but for the look in his eyes, which seemed ancient. I couldn't see his face. He had a black bandanna draped over his nose and mouth.

I pulled the blanket to me.

"Don't flatter yourself." He stepped into the room and closed the door behind him, locking it and pocketing the key. He carried a tray of food and two bottles of water.

I started to salivate at the smell of rice and chicken wafting from the takeaway box. I sat up straighter, unable to drag my eyes away from it. My stomach growled, and the man chuckled. As he came closer, I inched away but stayed on the bed with the blanket covering me. His eyes remained hard as they watched me, and he set the tray down on the nightstand.

He then produced a fork. A real fork, not a plastic one. "You get one chance with this. If you think you can try to stab me with it or do anything else stupid, I'll whip your ass and dump your next meal on the floor for you to lick it off, understand?"

I swallowed, wanting the food, my gaze locked on the man's. I nodded.

He held the fork out to me. I hesitated, knowing this was a challenge from the way he raised an eyebrow.

I reached out, intending on grabbing the fork out of his hand without touching him, but he had other plans. As soon as I was close enough, he snatched my wrist and yanked me toward him, twisting my arm as he did.

I cried out in pain.

"I'm not playing fucking games, we clear on that?"

"Yes! You're going to break my arm!"

He tugged once more, smiling as he yanked another cry from me, then released me and set the fork down on the tray.

"Eat it all," he said. He turned around and walked back out the door like our exchange was the most casual thing in the world.

Once the door locked behind him, I picked up the box and fork and opened the lid. Chicken and rice and even a side of broccoli. How thoughtful to give me my veggies. It was bland but warm, and I ate every last rubbery bite, forcing myself to slow down so I wouldn't throw it up. My body needed this fuel. I needed it if I had any hope of surviving.

The stranger threw me. Was Death gone? Had he quit? Could you do that in his line of work?

I almost laughed at that last thought, drained the second bottle of water, and sat back, feeling better for having eaten. When was the last time I'd had something warm? How long had I been here, and how long had Victor kept me prisoner before turning me over to Death? How long ago had Mateo died?

For five more meals, the man with the beady black eyes came, checked that I'd eaten everything, took the trash and left me with new food. By the third delivery, I started to ask questions: what day it was, what time, where was Death? He never answered a single one. It seemed we were getting on a regular schedule, though, with the meals. Maybe two in a twenty-four-hour period? I couldn't be sure, but I was starving between them.

The delivery of the seventh meal changed everything. Just as I was starting to get more comfortable, even considering using my fork to do the very thing he warned me not to do, everything changed.

That was when Death returned.

He came when I was sleeping. It was night. No sunlight penetrated the slats of wood over the windows. I woke to find him inside the room, standing at the foot of the bed, watching me. I startled, screamed, and scrambled as close to the top of the bed as I could, the blanket bunched up in my arms, a barrier between him and me.

He wore his mask again. It took me a minute, but I knew it was him. I knew it from his body, from the way he moved. It was as though he screamed power.

"Didn't meant to startle you."

His voice mocked me. He walked around the bed, and it took all I had not to scream again, not to run to the other side of the room to get away from him. He'd changed. He was different. He was cocky, a bastard, like in the very beginning.

"We're changing how we do things."

He took hold of the blanket and tugged it from me. I fell forward and had to release my hold on the one thing that gave me comfort. But maybe it was good he took it. It gave me a false sense of security. As if somehow, everything would be okay. It would never be okay. Nothing would ever be okay again. How could I ever think it would? How could I ever think I could seduce him? That I could somehow win him over, make him want me enough that he didn't take me to the auction but would instead keep me for himself? That he would help me avenge my brother's murder?

"I heard you've been eating, doing as you're told."

I didn't answer, I couldn't. I just watched him, my gaze glued to that fucking mask as he folded up the blanket and set it on the chair in the corner.

"And that you didn't attack Leo with the fork."

Leo. That was the other man's name. What was Death's name? And why the fuck was he wearing that mask again? It worked as a barrier, shielding him from me, keeping him separate from me. And looking at it terrified me.

"I don't like the mask," I said, my voice coming out small.

NATASHA KNIGHT

"Don't you." It wasn't a question.

He unbuckled his belt and pulled it through the loops, holding it like he had that night he'd whipped me, with the buckle in his palm. He then raised his other hand and curled his finger, motioning for me to go to him.

"Kneel." He pointed to the spot by his feet.

I watched him, beginning to tremble, unable to take my eyes off that terrible mask.

"Gia."

"Take it off. Please, take it off." I gripped the rungs of the headboard when he placed one knee on the bed as if he were going to come get me. "Please, just take it off."

In an instant, he was on the bed, one hand fisting my hair and dragging me off and toward the floor.

"I said fucking kneel!" he roared.

I cowered at his feet, covering my ears as best as I could with my wrists still bound together, my heart hammering against my chest, tears spilling down my cheeks, screaming at the searing burn of the belt across my ass.

"When I say kneel, you fucking kneel!"

He lashed me twice more, his anger a palpable thing, his rage so real, so fucking terrifying, I did more than kneel. I crouched down at his feet, my forehead on the floor, then on his boot. I knew he was punishing me not only for disobeying his first command to kneel, but for the last time he was here, for what had happened then, for how he'd left, for his having stayed away. He was punishing me for his own weakness, his own sin.

When he stepped back, I kept my head down, whimpering, my chest heaving with heavy breath, my back and ass throbbing with the lashes he'd delivered.

"Up on hands and knees."

I obeyed, moving as quickly as I could, not earning a stroke this time. He took two more steps away.

"Crawl to me."

I did, I crawled. I covered the space clumsily with my hands bound, all of my limbs trembling, and when I reached him, he took another two steps back, then another, taking me in circles around the room.

"Now bend over the edge of the bed."

"Please don't whip me anymore. I'm doing as I'm told. Please."

"You're not doing as you're told now, are you?"

I swallowed and glanced at how his hand clutched the belt. I crawled to the foot of the bed and stood, then bent myself over it like the first night I was here when he'd whipped me.

"Spread your legs."

I did as he said, widening my stance while he stood behind me. I didn't know what to expect, didn't know if he'd whip me or fuck me or both.

"Don't turn around, whatever you do."

I didn't speak. I was unable to. It took all I had not to look over my shoulder.

It was quiet forever, and I knew he watched me until, an eternity later, his footsteps broke the silence, and he approached. I held my breath, the tears finally having stopped, and when he lay the belt across my back, I startled at the cool, heavy leather.

Fingertips touched me, hands on my ass, tickling at first, then pulling me open.

"Please," I begged, not sure what I begged for. Not expecting the thing that came, the soft wetness of his tongue on me, on my sex, licking me, tasting me, pulling me wide as one hand snaked toward my clit. He began to rub the hardened nub.

I fisted my hands and bit my lip. His tongue working me expertly, the pleasure unbearable as I fought against it, the battle lost when he slipped his tongue inside me, his fingers rubbing harder. I arched my back and pressed against him, squeezing the muscles of my legs and closing my eyes, drawing blood from my lip in an effort to mute the moan that preceded the orgasm while he sucked and rubbed. I gasped for breath and clawed the mattress, my knees giving out as I began to slide from the bed.

He caught me, and when he did, I turned my head to meet his eyes, discovering that the mask had been discarded somewhere on the floor. Blue-gray eyes shone back at me, the pupils big and dark. With one hand, he kept me pinned to the bed while with the other, he undid his jeans and pushed them and his briefs down. He took himself into his hand, and our gazes locked. He began to pump. I watched his face, his angel's face, his burning eyes, swollen lips parted and glistening with my juices.

"I like how you taste," he said, his body jerking a little.

I turned my gaze to the hand that held his cock, watching him pump hard and fast.

"I told you not to turn around, didn't I?" he asked.

I licked my lips, unable to tear my eyes away and was ready when he fisted my hair and drew me to my knees before him.

"Suck my cock, Gia." He shook me once. "If you bite, I'll fucking kill you."

I nodded. I had no intention of biting. I opened to take him into my mouth, his taste salty, the skin soft around his thick, hard cock. He pressed back too far too fast, making me choke, but when I tried to push him away, he only held me still and did it again, his eyes on mine, his gaze telling me he was punishing me.

"I told you not to turn around."

He fucked my face now, thrusting deeper and deeper down my throat, cutting off all breath until I thought I'd pass out and releasing me for an instant to draw desperate gulps of air before repeating.

"You'll learn to do as you're told."

His cock thickened impossibly larger inside my mouth, his hand in my hair so tight it drew tears from my eyes.

"Fuck, Gia."

He pushed me backward so my head leaned uncomfortably on the bed, and he stilled. I felt the first stream of cum hit the back of my throat. I choked, not ready, but he held me still, closing his eyes until I couldn't take any more. Then finally he pulled out, his grip on his cock tight as streams of cum covered my chest and my breasts, marking me as his, claiming me, owning me.

Only when he'd emptied did he release me. He pulled up his briefs and jeans and looked at me, his eyes strange, searching. He then reached into one of his pockets and drew out two little pills. I looked at them, at him, and shook my head no, feeling again the buildup of tears, those never-fucking-ending tears.

He only had to raise his eyebrows in warning, and I reached out my hands. He dropped them into my palms and watched me put them into my mouth and swallow. Made me open again so he could make sure I wasn't hiding them, and when he was satisfied, he picked up his belt and the discarded mask and walked back out the door, locking me in my room once again.

7

DOMINIC

I went into my bedroom while I waited for the drug to work. There, from inside the same drawer I kept Effie's photograph, I pulled out a small box and opened it. Inside was my ring, the one I'd worn when I was a Benedetti. The one all the Benedetti men wore. I sat on the bed and studied it, ignoring the desire to slip it on my finger. Shoved away the thought of how much I'd lost. How different my life was meant to be.

Isabella had called me late last night. I'd only spoken to her once after I'd left, when she'd called to tell me Salvatore had handed everything over to our uncle, Roman. She hadn't called when Effie had broken her arm. I'd only found out about that when I saw Effie wearing a hot-pink cast in one of the photos. She also hadn't called to tell me about her engagement to Luke. That too I'd seen when I'd spied the rock on her finger in another photo of my daughter. Not that I cared about her marrying Luke. They deserved each other. Where Isabella was concerned, I had no affection. She was the mother of my child. That was all. We'd always be connected no matter what, but that didn't mean anything more.

No, she'd called to tell me about a body turning up. The body of Mateo Castellano. I'd known Mateo. He'd done some work for my fa—for Franco Benedetti—a few years ago. He'd actually tipped me off about a deal being a trap, which had probably saved my ass, even though I hadn't acknowledged that fact then. Too fucking arrogant. We'd gotten along well. He'd become a friend even. But then he'd disappeared, moved on, I guessed. He, like I was now, was a nobody. He went where the money took him.

I didn't get the reason for her call at first. People in our line of work died all the time. A side effect of mafia life. Hearing about Mateo's death, though, had been a little like when I'd heard my brother Sergio had been killed. It made me pause.

There was more. Isabella said the killer had intended for the body to be found. It had been meant to send a message. Castellano had been worked over, which didn't surprise me, then shot execution-style: bullet to the back of the head. But there was one more thing. Two more things, actually.

His tongue had been cut out. He was a snitch.

I had told her callously that I wasn't totally surprised, considering he'd snitched before when he'd saved my ass. But she'd told me to shut up and listen. There'd been a mark on him. A brand. It was in the middle of his chest. She'd seen a picture of it. How she'd gotten her hands on a photo like that, I had no idea, although she was incredibly resourceful. Never underestimate Isabella DeMarco. Hadn't I learned that yet?

She thought the mark would be of interest to me. It was to Salvatore, apparently. The brand was a larger version of the Benedetti family crest, a generations-old symbol of power in our world, at least in southern Italy and the northeastern United States. It was an exact copy of the one I held in my hand. Mateo Castellano had been branded before his death, and someone wanted to get two messages out: one, that he was a snitch, and

snitches were dealt with mercilessly. Two, that it was a Benedetti
who'd done the dealing.

But this wasn't how Roman operated. It wasn't his MO. I
wouldn't put it past Franco, but he had a different sort of cruelty.
He was just as brutal but not medieval in his torture. I didn't
suspect Salvatore for a second.

That's why I'd given Gia the pills.

Mateo was my age, or close to it. He had a kid sister. I'd met
her once, a long time ago. I think I'd been seventeen or eighteen.
It was at a party, which my father had attended, where a secret
meeting had been held. He'd brought me along. When they'd
gone to talk, I'd wandered around the property, bored, annoyed
at not being invited into the meeting. A little ways from the
house, I'd come across a little girl backed against a tree by two
boys about twelve, I'd say. They were apparently trying to take
something from her, and she'd been putting up a hell of a fight,
but she couldn't have been more than seven. I'd told the boys to
piss off and leave the kid alone. She'd given me a look. It wasn't a
"thanks for saving me" or anything like that. It'd been a glare.
She'd been just as pissed at me as she'd been at those boys. I
remembered I'd laughed when Mateo had found us there and
told her to get back to the house and help their mother with
something. She'd spoken to him in Italian and thrown a sideways glance my way before running back house, the flash of her
angry green eyes from beneath those thick dark bangs now
unsettlingly familiar.

I didn't know Mateo's sister's name. I'd never asked.

And I had a suspicion I wanted gone.

I needed to check the mark on Gia's hip.

She'd be the right age. That party had been seventeen,
almost eighteen years ago. If I was right about the little girl
being seven, that'd make her twenty-four now.

Did I have Mateo Castellano's *sister* trapped in that room? If so, who the fuck had sent her to me? Did they know they were sending her to me? And why the Benedetti brand? I knew all the workings Franco had his dirty hands in, and human trafficking wasn't part of any of it. He did some bad shit, but he didn't sell stolen women.

That was why I needed her knocked out when I first saw the mark. I couldn't give anything away. She knew who had taken her, and it was personal. I'd never bothered to ask more, because I didn't give a fuck, and I didn't want to know. But now, having heard about the brand on Mateo Castellano, I needed to know.

After putting the ring away, I made myself something to eat, wanting to be sure she was out before I went back in there. After waiting over an hour, I took the key out of my pocket and unlocked the door. Light from the room I was in shone on her motionless form on the bed, tucked tight beneath the blanket. I made my way to the bed to make sure she was out. She was. From the locked chest, I took out a lightbulb and screwed it into the ceiling from where I'd removed it before Gia's arrival. I then switched on the light, not too bright but bright enough. Gia didn't stir.

Sitting on the edge of the bed, I pulled the blanket back, guilt gnawing at me when the scent of sex wafted off her. I hadn't meant to do what I'd done earlier. I'd wanted to let her know I was back, and I was in charge. But then, watching her like that... hell, I had wanted her.

I guessed she hadn't been able to shower before the drug had knocked her out.

She mumbled something and rolled onto her back.

Avoiding what I had to do, I went back to my room and returned with a clean washcloth, towel, and soap. Remembering the toothbrush I'd picked up for her, I set it, still in its packaging, on the edge of the sink in her bathroom. I then ran hot water over the washcloth and rubbed the bar of soap over it until it was sudsy. After ringing the excess moisture out, I went back to her and gently cleaned her face, chest, and belly, rinsing off the cloth twice more as I washed her thighs and her sex until the scent was gone. I patted her dry with the clean towel, all the while watching her.

I could tell myself all I wanted to that it was to make sure she didn't wake up, but I knew it was a lie. In a way, I felt something for her that I hadn't for any of the other unfortunate girls who'd lain in this same bed. I could usually put a wall up between myself and the job—whatever or whoever that job was. With her, though, I couldn't put my finger on any particular reason why that wall wasn't staying up. It had for all of five minutes when I'd entered this room the first time. Maybe it was the physical attraction, the pull I felt toward her. Maybe it was the mark on her hip. Maybe I subconsciously knew already, had felt already, that this was different. I didn't know. I just knew I needed to get on with it and see the damn thing once and for all.

After hanging both the washcloth and towel to dry in the bathroom, I went back into the bedroom and turned her onto her side, eyeing the scab that covered the healing brand. My heart pounded. I touched the rough skin. It had already begun to peel away at the edges, revealing pink skin beneath, a circle to contain the crest. Using my fingernail, I scratched away rough skin, exposing more and more, recognizing the ornamental *F* of *Famiglia*. Because to the Benedetti, family came first.

Fucking joke.

The scab became harder to peel away once the edges were gone, but I didn't need to go too much further. I saw what I needed to see. The ornamental *B* of Benedetti, the tips of the spears crossing at the top, protecting the *famiglia* beneath. I didn't need to see the face of the lion at the center of the crest. His mane took shape around the edges, and I had no doubt once the scar had fully healed, I would see the Benedetti crest branded into her skin.

I stood quickly, looking down at the girl. I squatted down again until my face was an inch from hers. I pushed the hair back from her cheek, tucked it behind her ear, and looked at her. At the pretty, unconscious woman lying in the filthy bed, eyes closed, lips parted, her breath shallow. I tried to remember the little girl from the party, but the only image my mind had held onto was those eyes. Gia had looked at me like that once, her glare from beneath her dark hair burning a hole into me.

But was she Mateo Castellano's kid sister? Had whoever killed him taken her? What had she had to do with anything? Although it wasn't like she needed to be involved at all. This was the Italian mafia, after all. Families thrived together, and they were destroyed together. Was this sleeping woman the girl I'd once saved from two overzealous boys at a party?

I stood abruptly and stepped away.

What did it matter if she was? She was a job. That was all. Just because I'd saved her from some idiot kids years ago, didn't mean we were connected, that I was going to be her savior again. I had to remember I was no longer a Benedetti. I no longer had an army behind me. I was Dominic Sapienti. A nobody. Even if I fucking wanted to protect her, what the hell could I do? It's not like I had the fucking money to buy her outright. I'd blown all the money I'd had when I'd bought Salvatore's mansion, lock, stock, and barrel. Everything in it now belonged to me, and it fucking sat there under seven years' worth of dust because it wasn't like I was ever going back there. I didn't even know why I'd bought it.

And even if I hadn't, what now? Buy her? Keep her?

Keep her.

"You're a fucking imbecile, Dominic," I muttered to myself. I stood, walked the few steps to the center of the room to unscrew the lightbulb from the ceiling, and plunged the room into near darkness again. It took a moment for my eyes to readjust.

Keep her, and do what with her? I'd question her about the brand. Find out who'd done it. Why they'd done it. Then what?

This was the drawback to my line of work. I never knew who hired me, and they never knew who they hired. An anonymous world of monsters.

I reached for the phone in my back pocket, closing the space between me and her, and began to dial a number I hadn't dialed in way too many years. I pulled the blanket back over her, taking in her sweet, innocent face—at least in sleep—and walked out of the room, locking the door behind me. I looked down at the phone display. One digit more and the phone would start ringing. My heart pounded, and my hands felt clammy. I hit End. I wasn't ready for that. Not yet. Instead, I opened up my laptop and took a seat at the kitchen table, where I typed in Mateo Castellano's name on the Google search field, already knowing what I'd find.

8

GIA

ight filtered through the slats of wood covering the bedroom window. My eyelids felt sticky as I blinked them open, my mouth like cotton, and my head heavy. A combination of the drug and life.

Sitting up, I dragged the blanket up and tucked it around myself. Why did he have to keep the room so cold?

I scratched my head. That was when a small movement near the bed startled me. I gave a little involuntary gasp.

Death sat somber in the chair, no mask, his eyes dark, his gaze heavy upon me. Watching me.

Every hair on my body stood on end, and my heart fell into my stomach. What was he doing here? How long had he been watching me sleep? Why? How would he torture me today?

I curled my fingers around the blanket and waited.

"Who sent you to me?"

I pulled my legs underneath me and sat on my knees, covering as much of myself as I could.

"Who branded you, Gia?"

I had to swallow several times to get my voice to work. "Why?" The question made me sound weak. Vulnerable.

"I know who you are."

I stared at him, at this man who held me prisoner. This cruel captor who gave and took as he pleased, who both scared the hell out of me and also drew me like no other. His face, an angel's face, was etched into the hardest stone, his eyes of steel, colder now, the pleasure he took in mocking me no longer glowing like embers of a dying fire. An anger, a hatred replaced it, and that fire was burning bright, ready to consume. To obliterate.

It was a terrifying thing to see.

"What does it matter, who I am?" I asked, my heart pounding, knowing the thin ice I walked on, waiting, watching to see what this brought.

His expression didn't change.

"Who sent you to me?"

It was as though he held his breath.

"Victor Scava."

This seemed to surprise him, because it took him a minute to continue.

"Did he brand you?"

I nodded.

"Under orders from whom?"

"I don't know. I don't know that he took orders from anyone."

"Why did he do it?"

Emotion coursed through me, memory and feeling and loss. Before me sat one of the men responsible for my suffering. I didn't know if he was involved with Mateo's torture or death, but I did know I owed him nothing.

Gathering my courage, I raised my head high.

"Why do you care? Why do you get to ask any question you like, when you won't even answer the one I've asked you?"

"You still want to know my name? It's that important to you?"

Maybe he was right. Maybe I should have been asking a different question. But I nodded and narrowed my gaze.

"Dominic. My name is Dominic"—hesitation, then— "Sapienti."

Even in the dim light, I saw his eyes shift when he said his last name, and I knew it was a lie.

"Dominic Sapienti," I said, watching him closely.

He nodded once, blinking as he did, and I felt sure I was right.

"He branded me because I wouldn't fuck him."

That seemed to catch him off guard. His forehead furrowed, and a crease formed between his eyebrows as he processed my information and waited for me to continue.

I raised my own eyebrows. "You seem to enjoy eating my pussy. I guess he wanted to too. So does it make you more of a monster, since you took it without my permission, when he could have but chose not to?"

"He chose to brand you instead. To mark you permanently. He then sent you to me, knowing what I'd do to you, what you'd have to go through before being sold to some animal. I'd say his actions trump mine in the monster arena."

"Fuck you."

"Besides, I don't recall you shoving me off. In fact, if memory serves, and it does, you were pushing your ass into my face for more."

I turned away. He was right.

He got up, approached the bed, and stood over me, his body a warning in itself. Taking my chin, he forced me to face him.

"I could have taken more. I may yet."

I wanted to say something, to challenge him, but every warning bell inside me went off, and I lowered my lashes instead. I had to be smart, and goading this man into hurting me was not smart.

"Tell me about your brother."

He released me and sat back down in the chair.

I snapped my gaze to his. How did he know about Mateo? What did he know? Was this part of his "training?" Fucking with my head now, because hurting me physically, making me hate myself for my reactions to him, wasn't enough?

"Is that why you're doing this? Why your boss sent me to you?"

"I don't work for Victor Scava," he quickly clarified, his lip curling in disgust.

"Then I don't understand. Why would he send me to you if you don't work for him?"

"I'm an independent contractor. Now tell me about your brother, Gia. Tell me what Mateo did to get himself killed. To get you into the kind of trouble you're in."

I studied him, hearing the change in his tone, his words, his whole way of being toward me. I didn't understand. "My brother was a good person who got involved with bad people, and when he tried to get out of it, they killed him."

"His tongue was cut out. That means one thing in our world."

My heart hurt at the mention. Would I ever think of Mateo and not remember that?

"*Your* world."

"No. *Our* world."

I looked down at my lap, exhaling. He was right. This was our world.

"How do you know what happened to Mateo?"

"His body turned up yesterday. It was left where it could be found. Whoever killed him is sending a message. Now tell me why they executed him."

"Why do you care?"

He stood, ran his hand through his hair, and looked away, shaking his head as if he were having some conversation, an internal argument. He then turned back to me.

"Just fucking tell me."

"Because he'd gone to the feds about exactly what you're doing to me now. He'd started to do some work for Victor. I'd told him not to. Told him Victor was bad news. He found out the hard way, and when he tried to do the right thing, they killed him. They tortured him, and they made me fucking watch." My voice broke, and I wiped away a rogue tear. "I think that was the part that broke him."

The room fell silent, and when I looked up, I found Dominic's gaze steady on mine, affected but silent.

"Did you have anything to do with that? With Mateo going to the feds?"

I shook my head. "I didn't know what Victor was doing. I didn't know he was selling girls, not until my brother told me."

"Why didn't Victor kill you?"

"Because he's a sick fuck?" I tried to make light of it, but a sob caught in my throat.

The buzz of a cell-phone message interrupted, and Dominic reached into his pocket to retrieve his phone, his gaze on me.

"You were engaged to Angus Scava's son, James?"

I nodded. "When he died, Victor came into the picture. He was next in line, since Mr. Scava didn't have any other kids."

"Mr. Scava? You say that with some tenderness, Gia. Scava is not a nice man."

"He was always kind to me."

Dominic shook his head as if what I said were unbelievable.

"How can you be so sure he didn't order this?" He gestured around the room.

"No. No way. James loved me, and he loved James. He wouldn't do this to me."

"You're a fool."

"You have no heart, no soul. I wouldn't expect you to understand love like that, a father's love."

Dominic recoiled as if I'd stabbed him with a knife. It took him a moment to recover.

"Love is changeable. Disposable. It's not everlasting, not in our world. Only a fool believes in happily-ever-after, Gia."

He turned his attention to his phone then. His face changed. Confusion and then alarm crossed over his features as he read the message.

"I'm going to kill him. I'm going to put a bullet in Victor Scava's head," I said.

He looked at me, his forehead creased, eyes dark. Then, without a word, he walked out the door and locked me inside, leaving me once again in this dark, dank room, confused but also, somehow, hopeful.

Mateo's body had been found. It had been left where it could be found. And its discovery had rattled my jailor.

9

DOMINIC

*R*umor has it one of Roman's men killed Castellano. *Franco's pissed. He'd sworn to protect the Castellano kids or some shit. Can you believe it?*

I had to read Isabella's message twice to understand. To remember.

Mateo's father had worked for Franco. He'd taken a bullet for him. He'd died saving Franco's life. I remembered now. I'd heard it later, heard him talking to Roman about it, about taking care of the Castellano family. Making sure everyone knew they were under his protection.

And Roman had Mateo Castellano killed? Why in hell would he have branded him? Why advertise that? Franco would fucking kill him. It made zero sense. If what Gia told me was true, did that mean he'd had his hands in human trafficking? Did the Benedetti family now sell women on the black market?

I took a seat at the kitchen table and pulled up Salvatore's number. It was time. Hell, it was past time.

I hit Send and listened to it ring. It took everything I had to not hit the End button this time. And when he picked up, his voice so familiar even after all these years, it took me a minute to reply. It took me that minute to get my heart to stop pounding, to get my voice working.

"Salvatore," I said and waited.

Silence on his end now. Then: "Dominic? Is that you?"

Hearing his voice, fuck, it brought back so many memories. So many emotions. "It's me," I said flatly.

"Jesus!"

If ever I could say I heard the sound of relief, now would be the time. As if he gave a shit.

"Where the fuck have you been? I've been looking for you for seven fucking years."

"I'm here. I'm fine." I paused. "How are you?" It was polite to ask, and I needed to be polite. I needed information.

"Fine. Good."

"I heard you have two brats running around and a third on the way."

"You've been keeping tabs?"

"Yeah."

"Two little girls. A boy due in six weeks." He paused. "They should meet their uncle sometime."

"Nah." Fuck. I stood, gritting my teeth. "Better this way."

"Better for whom?"

I ignored his question.

"And Effie?" he asked.

"Better for her too."

"No, not fucking better. Where are you? Are you okay?"

I hated the tone of his voice. The authenticity in what he said.

"I'm around, and I'm okay. I needed to go figure out who the hell I was."

"You're my fucking brother, that's who you are."

"Not so simple."

"I thought you were dead," Salvatore said.

"After what happened, I wanted to be." A long silence followed. The words *I'm sorry* may have fit here nicely. *I'm sorry for almost killing you.* Hell, they might even be true, but I couldn't go there. I hated the Benedetti family. I hated all of them. And that had to include Salvatore.

Quiet.

"I heard they found a body. Mateo Castellano. Did Roman order the killing?"

Salvatore sighed. "I think it's pretty obvious, don't you?"

"I thought the Castellano family was under Franco's protection."

"Me too. Father's pissed. Not sure how Roman will survive this."

Snakes always slithered out just when you thought you had them cornered. But this time, I was sure it wasn't Roman. "He's not being set up?"

"I don't know. I talked to him, but I can't be sure."

"Do you know any details?"

"I don't care about the details. That's why I'm here, in Florida, out of that life. Keeping my family out of that life. I've already been brought in for questioning twice, and I'll tell you what I told them. Roman and I talk twice a year. I called him about this for my own peace of mind. He claims it wasn't him."

"Do you believe him?"

He sighed and took a moment to answer. "Look, I'm not involved anymore. Period. And now I'm telling you that neither are you. Best thing you did was getting the hell away from our father."

"*Your* father."

"Yeah, well, maybe you should count your lucky fucking stars."

"It was a brutal killing."

"I know you and Mateo were friends once, but you can't get involved. You can't get back into it. Let Franco handle it."

Salvatore always had this way of beating you over the head with shit, especially if he thought he was doing it for your own good. That hadn't changed, apparently.

"I'm not really out of it, Salvatore."

"What the fuck are you talking about?"

"Mateo has a sister."

"Who disappeared a few days after he did, and who's probably dead."

"No, she's not."

"Shit, Dominic. What are you talking about?"

"Look, I just needed to know if Roman ordered the killing. Is he covering his ass now that the body's been found? Because that opens up a whole other can of worms."

"What can?" he asked tightly.

I knew he was waiting for me to fill in the blanks. I wondered if he knew I hadn't talked to Roman in over five years. And how did I tell him how I knew Gia Castellano was alive and that I had her here?

"I know for a fact it was Victor Scava who put the bullet in Mateo Castellano's head," I said.

"Scava? Angus Scava's nephew? What the hell would he have had to do with anything? The brand on Castellano's chest is the Benedetti family crest."

"Then you believe it was our uncle who ordered it?"

"I don't know what I believe, and I'm tired of thinking about it. I'm sorry Mateo was killed, but nothing will bring him back, and my knowing—or *your* knowing—won't change that. Stay out of it, Dominic."

"Victor Scava is involved in human trafficking. Mateo was going to turn over evidence. That's why he was silenced. Made an example of."

"Stay the fuck out of it," Salvatore repeated.

"Too fucking late for that."

"What are you talking about? How do you know all this?"

"I've got Gia Castellano. She witnessed the murder. Scava branded her too. Same mark." I paused, but I needed to tell him everything now. In a way, it was a sort of confession. Although I had no hopes of redemption. Hell, wasn't I way beyond wanting it? "She's due to go to auction in a week."

"Due to go to auction? What the hell does that even mean?"

He knew what it meant. It was the one thing the Benedetti were not involved in. One thing where Franco, his father before him, and his father before him, had put their foot down on. No human trafficking.

Fucking saints, the lot of them.

"Any chance Roman could be involved with Victor Scava in something like this?" I pushed.

"Human trafficking? No. No way. Where exactly are you, and why do you have the girl?"

"If he's not involved, then why would Mateo have been branded with the Benedetti mark? Why not quietly kill him and get rid of the body? I mean, we all know how to get rid of a fucking body if that's what we want to do. Scava was sending a message. I want to know what that message is, and how the Benedettis are involved."

"This is fucked up, Dominic."

"No shit."

"Roman knows—"

"And he doesn't give a shit. He's king now. You made him that, remember?"

"If he betrayed our father—"

I closed my eyes and pinched the bridge of my nose, counting to ten. I'd let this one slide.

The pause told me he realized his mistake. "Where are you, and where's the girl?" he asked.

"Vermont."

"Vermont? You hate the cold."

"I'm surviving." What, were we going to make fucking small talk?

"What do you mean with taking her to auction? You can't be involved in anything like that."

"I'm already involved." Nearly a dozen girls involved.

Salvatore sighed. "Tell me about the auction."

"Ten, maybe twelve girls. Enough buyers invited to make the bidding interesting."

"Jesus."

I snorted.

"Do you know who'll be attending?"

"No."

"Can you find out?"

"There isn't exactly a guest list to these sort of events."

Salvatore paused at my remark. "Has our uncle been to one before?" he asked, a note of caution to his question.

"Why buy the product when he's the supplier?" The more I thought about it, the guiltier Roman grew. The more I saw how he was always there, watching, silent, having earned Franco's trust like no one else had, not even his sons.

"No. No way. He's our fucking uncle, Dominic. Better than our father ever was to us."

"Your father. *Your* fucking father."

"Let it go already."

"You try finding out you're not who you thought you were for twenty-eight fucking years then *let it go already*."

Another long silence filled the space, "I'm sorry." He sighed. "Exactly how much do you know about the auction?"

"It's not my first."

"Are you buying girls?"

"Providing trained girls."

"Jesus."

Fuck. I hung my head, shaking it. What the fuck was I doing? How many lives had I destroyed? How many more would I crush? All to prove to myself and the world the scum I was? God. Fuck. Putting a bullet in my own head would have been better than this.

"Dominic?"

"Yeah," I said, wiping the back of my hand across my nose.

"We have to do something about the auction."

I heard the *we*. And I knew what I needed to do.

I stood.

"No. Not we. *Me.* You're not involved, not anymore, remember? You did good, getting yourself and Lucia out. Keep her safe now. Keep your family safe. Don't tempt fate twice." It had started out spiteful, but that last part, I meant it.

He paused, and I could almost hear him preparing to argue with me. But he didn't. His family came first. Just like it should.

"What are you going to do?"

"I don't know. I'm going to find out if Roman's involved first."

"It doesn't make sense, Dominic. He wouldn't be involved in something like this. You've already tried and convicted him in your mind. And you're on your own, remember that."

Meaning I had no backing. None.

"I won't be on my own."

"What does that mean?"

"Mateo's sister. She knows at least some of what's going on. And she wants revenge for her brother's murder."

"She's a woman. Untrained. Innocent, maybe. She's a victim. You can't involve her any more than she already is."

"Haven't you learned not to underestimate women with an agenda?" Isabella DeMarco's name didn't need to be said.

"Be careful with Roman," Salvatore said soberly. "He's different now. Harder."

"He was always like that. You just never saw it."

"I'll talk to dad," Salvatore said.

"How is he?" The question came before I could stop it.

"He's sorry," Salvatore said quietly. "He writes to me, and every time he says how sorry he is about how he told you. How he lost both his sons that night."

I bit my tongue not to speak. I didn't give a fuck. I. Did. Not. Give. A. Fuck.

Salvatore sighed. "He's older. Weaker. But he's Franco Benedetti. He'll outlive all of us. But if this is true, he'll skin Roman alive." He paused. "Do you have a safe place to go, to take her?"

"Yeah."

"Don't tell me where."

"I wasn't going to. I have to go."

"Check in with me. Please. And if you need me—"

"I won't. Go be with your family."

"I love you, brother."

Fuck. How could those words impact me now? Seven years later?

"I have to go." I disconnected the call before I said something stupid. Before I had to eat the words I'd fed Gia and stand the fool.

———

First thing I needed to do was get Gia out of there.

I had no delusions about what that would mean for me. I was stealing from Victor Scava. Possibly from his uncle, Angus, the head of the Scava family. Either would kill me for what I was about to do.

But according to what Gia told me, Victor at least knew where we were. He'd sent us here to this cabin. I'd used it before. Eight times, to be precise. So he'd been the one who'd hired me all those times. But did he know I was once Dominic Benedetti? If he did, would he have sent Gia to me with our brand marking her body? Or was it just that? Had he sent her, intending for me to find it?

For a moment I entertained the idea of taking her to Franco. Of reminding him of his pledge to keep her and her family safe. But then, I live in the real world. Family comes before any pledge and ultimately, Roman was family. He was his brother-in-law. Gia was the daughter of a dead foot soldier and the sister of a snitch.

Either Victor Scava branded and killed Mateo Castellano and left it to look like Roman's work, or he'd taken the order from Roman to kill him. Would Victor take an order from Roman? No. No fucking way. And no way Roman would tell him to brand his fucking name on the dead man. He was much too clever for that.

The two families didn't deal with each other. There wasn't a rivalry; they didn't share territory. But was there some sort of allegiance? A secret pact? And had something gone wrong for Victor to want Roman out badly enough he'd send a message that could make Roman's own family turn on him?

Ultimately, Roman wasn't head of the Benedetti family. How could he be if he wasn't even a Benedetti? When I'd found out Salvatore had handed the entire operation over to him, I'd felt so angry. The Benedetti throne did not belong to him. Hell, it belonged less to him than me. He was the usurper.

Then what the hell was I if he was that? I was cut from the same cloth. It'd be good for me to remember that. The Benedetti name did not belong to me either. And ultimately, I'd bring it down. I wanted to end the Benedetti crime family. End their rule. Shove their noses into the dirt.

But I had to admit, it still burned. The thought that he, my uncle, was head of the family I'd so wanted to rule. It fucking burned.

After packing my few things into a duffel bag, I chose a hoodie and a pair of sweatpants for Gia to wear on the drive. She'd swim in the clothes, but it was better than being naked. I'd get her something that fit as soon as I could. Right now, we had to move. I didn't know if Scava would come for her early. Take her to auction himself. Hell, fucking put a bullet in her head for all I knew. Victor Scava was a son of a bitch.

I entered her room and found her standing by the window, trying to peer out from between the slats.

She turned to face me, pressing her back against the wall when she did so, panic widening her eyes like it did every time I walked in. I studied her, trying to keep my attention on her face, not wanting to remember the things I'd done to her. Trying instead to focus on her eyes, her defiant, beautiful, sad, terrified eyes.

"Get dressed." I tossed the clothes on the bed. "We're leaving."

It took her a minute to comprehend what I'd said.

"Where are we going?"

"Away from here. Hurry up."

"Why?"

"Because I said so."

"I...is it time? Is the two weeks up?"

I was confused for a moment, then realized she thought it was time to go to auction. "No. We're leaving this place. I'm not taking you to the auction."

"Then where are you taking me?"

"Somewhere safe."

She studied me, uncertain.

"Let's go. Unless you want to stay here and wait for someone to come find you. It could be today or a few days from now when you don't show up at auction, but they will come, and I don't want to be here when they do. Now I don't mind you naked—in fact, I prefer it—but you might be more comfortable wearing clothes, seeing as how it's freezing out there."

"Why would you help me?"

She moved toward the clothes on the bed. I met her there and uncuffed her wrists, taking the restraints. She pulled the hoodie over her head. I watched it fall almost to her knees.

"Because you're going to help me. I don't like Victor Scava, and I think he's playing games." I left out the part about the games being played against my family. I did that for two reasons. First, I didn't want her to know who I was, and second, I couldn't figure out why I still considered the Benedetti family as my own.

Gia put the pants on and pulled them up. She had to bunch them up and hold them in place so they wouldn't slide off. She then stood there, looking at me, waiting.

"These will be too big, but it's just until we get to the truck."

She slid into the pair of boots I set on the floor. She looked a little ridiculous, but I liked her in my clothes.

I stepped aside and gestured for her to follow.

She moved, uncertainly at first, then more assuredly, in a hurry to get out of the room. Just as she passed me, I grabbed her arm and made her stop.

"Just one thing. You do as you're told or else. You need me to survive right now. I'm the only person who can keep you safe from Scava. Don't fuck with me. We clear?"

"I don't like you, Dominic, and I trust you even less, but I do know you hold the key to my freedom, so I promise not to fuck with you, okay?" she said, trying to free herself.

I tugged harder and leaned in close, close enough that the

scruff on my jaw brushed against her soft cheek as I inhaled, then cupped her face so we stood nose to nose. "You've got a smart mouth, but I like it better put to other uses."

She jerked her face from my hand.

"Don't mistake me for a pussy, Gia," I said, shaking her once. "I'm doing this for me, not for you."

I grabbed the duffel bag with my clothes and computer, and we walked out of the cabin.

10

GIA

Dominic drove the SUV with its black-tinted windows through a narrow opening out of the woods, leaving the cabin behind us. I looked back at it as we bounced along, shuddering at the feeling it gave me, like a decrepit, abandoned, haunted place. Maybe it was haunted. Maybe the ghosts of the girls who'd gone before me lingered in that terrible cabin.

I physically shook. Dominic glanced at me, his expression looking as if he were deep in thought, so deep my involuntary movement seemed to surprise him.

"The heating will kick in soon," he said, returning his attention to the dirt road.

He thought I shook with cold. No. It was terror that still gripped me with its long, icy fingers.

"What's changed?" I asked. What had happened between yesterday and today? And was he stealing from Victor now by taking me away from the cabin? What did that mean for him? For me? What use could he possibly have for me?

"What do you mean?"

"Why are we leaving? Why are you helping me?"

"I'm not. I'm helping myself."

"What game is Victor playing with you?"

"I don't know just yet."

"I don't understand."

"You don't need to understand. You just need to be grateful."

"Where are we going?"

"You ask a lot of questions."

"If you answer one, maybe I'll stop asking."

"Smart-ass."

"Bully."

"New Jersey. We're going somewhere Victor won't think to look for you. Because when he finds out you're gone, he's going to come looking for both of us."

"And he'll find out when I don't show up at auction?"

He nodded and turned the SUV onto a lonely paved road. I saw a sign for a highway twenty-six miles away.

"Franco Benedetti promised my father he would protect Mateo and I when my father died."

"Did he?"

Dominic didn't sound surprised. "Maybe I should go to him."

"Because he did a bang-up job protecting your brother?"

"You have a point." I was silent for a moment. "How many days until I would have gone to auction?"

"Eight."

"What's the date?" I didn't even know that.

"Eleventh of January."

"They killed Mateo the day after Christmas." They'd come for me that same morning. That meant I'd been held captive for more than two weeks.

Dominic didn't respond. We rode in silence, both of us lost in our own thoughts, until we merged onto the highway. It was still early morning, and there were only a few other cars on the road besides us. A sign told me there was a McDonald's at the next rest stop.

"I'm really hungry," I said. "Can we get some food?"

He glanced at me like food was the last thing on his mind.

"Please?"

He put on his blinker, and we took the exit. He rode slowly up to the drive-through window.

"If you try anything, Gia—"

"I won't. I already told you at the cabin. I want Victor Scava. I'm not fool enough to believe I can get to him on my own." It was true. I had to be realistic. Dominic's hatred of Victor meant we had a common enemy. He was taking me away from Victor. I didn't fool myself into thinking Dominic was good, not by any means, but as long as our goals lined up, Dominic was the lesser of two evils.

He nodded. "What do you want?" he asked when we got to the menu board.

"Everything." I felt greedy as I scanned the options. "But I'll settle for a sausage egg McMuffin and a big cup of coffee."

Dominic ordered, taking a sandwich and a coffee for himself as well. He gave me one more warning glance as we drove to the drive-through pick-up window.

I just held up my two hands and shook my head. I wouldn't do anything. Getting away from him may have been smart— getting to the police even smarter—but if I wanted revenge for Mateo's death, I needed to stick this out. I needed Dominic.

I watched the girl in the window when she saw him. Saw how her eyes widened and her smile grew, and for reasons I could not understand, I felt a jealousy in my core. An anger at her boldness. But when Dominic then began to flirt with her that anger boiled. I roughly grabbed the bags from him, and he made a joke to the girl as she handed him our coffees.

"I don't mess with her when she's hungry."

He winked at her as she gave me a sideways glance.

"She has sharp teeth and a sharper tongue."

The girl giggled like a fool. I only glared at him. Finally, we drove off.

"Why did you flirt with her?"

He bit into his sandwich. "Why do you care?"

"I don't. I just don't like being made fun of."

He shrugged a shoulder. "This is good. I haven't had McDonald's since I was a kid. My mother only allowed it when we went on vacations."

I glanced at him. It was hard to imagine him as a kid with a mother. The SUV bounced over a dip in the road just as I brought the cup to my mouth. The scalding liquid burned my tongue. Damn.

"How many girls have you sent to auction?"

He only glanced my way but didn't answer. Instead, he turned his attention back to the road.

"Let me ask you something else. This isn't Victor's first time hiring you, is it?"

He shook his head.

"Does his uncle know?"

"I don't know."

"He doesn't like him much." He didn't. Angus Scava could hardly stand Victor, but he had to put up with him. There was no one else to take over the family reins. "He'd been readying James to take over the family. But then James was killed."

"He was shot, correct?"

I nodded. "On his way home from a meeting he'd gone to in place of his father."

Dominic's eyebrows seemed locked in a permanent furrow, but he seemed to be a man used to shielding his thoughts. The momentary flash of vulnerability I saw in his eyes was gone like it had never been there in the first place.

"The Scava's are a powerful family. James' grandfather was killed much the same way as he was. He had a sister who died in a car crash. I know Mrs. Scava had miscarried twice. James was the only direct survivor. Bad luck."

"Not bad luck. They're a leading crime family. They have enemies. The more powerful you are the more hated you are."

"You seem to know a lot about this."

He glanced my way. "I've been around. What about your family?"

"The men have been foot soldiers for as long as I can remember. I don't think many make it past fifty. So fucking stupid. Such a waste."

"How did you meet James Scava?"

"At a party being used as cover for a meeting. My father had gone as Mr. Benedetti's bodyguard. I'd been invited to come along. Mateo hadn't been there. He'd been at school. He was getting out of the life, making a new start."

"Go on." he said.

I realized I'd stopped talking. I didn't know when I'd stopped missing James. He'd been so good, so caring, so protective of me.

"I'd just turned twenty. His birthday was one day after mine. He was thirty, older than I usually dated, but we hit it off."

"And you knew who he was, what he did, and still fell for him?"

"He shielded me from that side of things. So had my father. I never saw it. And it's easy to pretend it's not happening when it's someone you love whose hands are bloodied."

Dominic took a bite of his sandwich. "They never found his killer."

"How do you know so much?"

"It was in the news."

"Mr. Scava believed it was a rival family, but I wouldn't be surprised if Victor had his dirty hands in it."

"That's quite the accusation."

"It's not an accusation if it's truth."

"Be careful, Gia."

"It's a little late for that, isn't it?"

"Tell me how Mateo got involved with Victor."

"When my dad was killed, Mateo came back for mom and me. He wanted to be sure we were cared for, protected. He didn't listen to me when I told him to go back to school, that we'd be fine. And then he started to work for Victor. I wasn't sure at first. If I'd known what Victor was up to, I would have gone to Mr. Scava, but I didn't know until it was too late."

"Are you sure Angus Scava isn't already involved?"

"I'm telling you, he wouldn't have done this to me. He would never have let Victor..." I broke off, remembering those nights when Victor tormented me, scared the fuck out of me.

"Your mom, where is she now?"

"She was spending time with her sister near Palermo. I don't know how much she knows. I need to talk to her."

"No."

"What do you mean, no?"

"It's too dangerous."

"But—"

"Not now, Gia. Let me think this through. I'm sure she doesn't want two dead kids to bury."

That made me stop. He was right. "Victor was always jealous of James. I'd go so far as to say he hated him." I drank the last of the now lukewarm coffee and turned to him. "How long is the drive?" I didn't want to talk about this anymore.

"A few more hours."

"Then what?"

"Then I'm going to find out what the hell is going on."

"What about me?"

"You do as you're told, Gia, and I won't have to hurt you."

"Did you know Mateo?" I asked out of the blue, remembering that sense of familiarity, that moment I'd thought I'd met him before.

"No."

He wouldn't look at me. Why didn't I believe him? And why would he lie?

"You won't hurt me," I said, not sure why I said it.

"Sharing a common enemy does not make us friends."

"You won't."

"How do you know I'm not taking you to the auction? Don't you think it'd be easier for me to transport a cooperative *slave*?"

He gave me a moment to process that before continuing.

"Quiet now. I need to think."

Fine. I needed to think too. I needed to figure out how I would proceed. As much as I wanted to kill Victor outright, wasn't it smarter for me to use the evidence Mateo had collected and turn it over to the feds? I still knew where the copy of the recorded conversations were: safe and sound in plain sight. What then, though? Go into witness protection and live in hiding for the rest of my life? Could I trust Mateo's contact? Should I go to Angus Scava, or was Dominic right? That he could be involved too? That he could have ordered Mateo's murder, my kidnapping? Was I naive to think he'd stand by me rather than his own family, even if he did hate Victor? What was I to him? Nothing. Not now that James was gone.

I needed to think. To figure out what to do. How to proceed. How to make Victor pay and stay alive in the process.

I needed to figure out how to manage my captor, how to align his goals to mine, and ultimately, I'd need to figure out how to escape him. I had no doubt his hands were as bloody as Victor's, and I couldn't forget that, no matter how attracted I was to him.

11

DOMINIC

Gia fell asleep sometime in the next hour, leaving me in blessed silence as I drove toward Salvatore's house. My house.

All my thoughts led to the same place: I needed to figure out the extent of Roman's involvement, and he *was* involved. Everything in my gut told me so. Every instinct told me he and Victor were partners in this secret endeavor, at least to some degree.

But I needed to remember he was my mother's brother. He'd loved her. Franco trusted him. Sergio had too. Salvatore didn't trust anyone, and it sounded like the last seven years had only put distance between him and the Benedetti family. Me? Roman and I had a strange relationship. He'd known all along who I was—and who I was not. He'd been decent to me, to some extent. Roman was always good to Roman first, though. But hell, same could be said of any of us. Except maybe Salvatore.

Roman had helped to organize the buying of Salvatore's house, helped me sell off the cars and much of the furniture. He'd made sure the house was maintained, even though no one lived there. Why? Why would he help me after that night, when

I was out, finished? When I was no longer a threat? One more Benedetti son out of the picture.

Why not, though? Why raise my suspicions by denying me help? And couldn't he then keep better track of me? Keep me in my place, which was far from his.

I thought back to those years and wondered if he'd been a friend to any of us, really. Or did he manage each of us, his eyes on the prize all along—becoming head of the Benedetti crime family.

No, that seemed too far-fetched. Too impossible.

But maybe it wasn't. To be so close to the kind of power Franco Benedetti wielded and sit impotent at his side for so many years? I knew how that felt. I knew what it made of me.

Power corrupted. And Roman was corrupt. I'd bet my fucking life on it.

I slowed as I drove the final mile toward the mansion. Night had fallen, and a crescent moon illuminated a thousand stars in the clear night. Gia stirred beside me.

"Are we there?"

"Yes."

She rubbed her eyes and leaned forward to get a better look as we got close enough for the lights of the SUV to shine on the gates protecting the property.

I slowed the vehicle, and she took it all in.

The last few miles I'd been tense. Now, that tension had reached a new level. I hadn't been back since that night. I hadn't been in the dining room since the shooting, and I was about to face it all now.

"Stay inside," I told her, climbing out to punch in the code. I watched the gates slide open. The single change I'd made to the property after buying it was to have all the locks changed and a keyless entry system put in.

Once the gates opened, I drove the SUV through, then

stopped again to watch them close behind us. I'd change the code tomorrow. Roman also knew it. I hadn't thought twice about him having it, not back then.

Gia sat awestruck at what she saw as we drove the long drive toward the front door.

"What is this?"

"My house," I said, realizing it was. I'd taken over Salvatore's home, kept some of his furniture. And he didn't even know it.

I didn't bother trying to figure out my own twisted motivation.

"Your house?"

"Mercenary life pays."

"Can't pay this much."

I parked the car. Gia climbed out. I walked ahead to the front door and punched in the code. The number combination registered, and a click signaled the unlocking of the door. I pushed it open, memory of that last night flooding all of my senses as I stood on the threshold, gripping the doorknob to remain upright as the wave crashed over me, then, slowly, way too slowly, passed. I swallowed hard and reached a shaky hand to switch on the lights. The hallway illuminated immediately, and I moved aside to allow Gia to enter.

"Wow."

It was all she said while she turned around in a circle, her gaze up on the vaulted, frescoed ceiling. Salvatore had tacky taste if you asked me, but watching her take it in, to see her in awe, made me strangely, stupidly proud.

I cleared my throat and pushed the door closed, hearing the lock engage when I did. I moved swiftly through the house, turning on lights as I went, seeing the layers of dust covering the sheets protecting the remaining furniture.

"It'll need to be cleaned," I said, trying to avoid looking at the closed door that led into the dining room. Trying not to think of that night. Of what I'd find there. That was the one room I hadn't allowed to be cleaned. I wondered now how it would look —glasses left on the table now filled with dust, the whiskey having long since evaporated. Would the blood have seeped into the obnoxious marble floors? Splattered and stained the walls with permanent reminders? Would it take me back in time to that night, that terrible night, when I'd learned the truth and lost everything in the process?

"This room is off-limits," I told Gia, gesturing to the closed dining-room door.

She shifted her weight onto one leg and narrowed her eyes. She looked like she was about to say something smart, but then her expression changed, like she knew this was serious. Like she knew not to fuck with me on this. She nodded.

I walked over to the liquor cabinet and found a bottle of unopened whiskey. I took it and found a glass. She followed me into the kitchen, where I turned on the gurgling tap and waited until the water ran clear before rinsing the glass. I filled it halfway with the liquor. I held it out to her.

She hesitated but then took it and sipped, squeezing her eyes shut. I guessed it scorched the back of her throat. She then handed it back. I drank a long swallow and refilled the glass, appreciating the burn. Salvatore had good taste.

"Can I have a proper shower?"

I nodded and finished the glass, then led the way upstairs to Lucia's old room.

"Who's room was this?" she asked, eyeing the abandoned makeup, the lipstick on the vanity with its lid off, the discarded pair of shoes lying beside the bed.

"My brother's wife's room."

She looked at me, confused.

"It was my brother's house. He left it seven years ago. I took it over."

She searched my face, my eyes. Had she heard the story of the Benedetti brothers? Of how the one almost killed the other? No one knew what transpired that night, at least as far as the why of it. No one knew the secret Franco had told. No one but those who were here. As far as the mafia world was concerned, Dominic Benedetti was alive and well and had left after a family argument.

"Bathroom's in there. You'll have to deal with the dust. I need to make a call. Do I need to lock you in the bedroom, or will you stay put?"

"Lock me in?" She rested her hands on her hips, and her eyebrows rose high on her forehead.

I nodded. I didn't have time to deal with her right now. I needed to make a call. I needed to find out where Roman stood.

"I'll stay," she said, her tone irritated. "And I want this off," she pointed to the collar.

"Maybe we need to revisit some things." I went to her, took her by the collar, and walked her backward until her back hit the wall. She pressed against my chest, but I pulled upward, forcing her chin up. Her eyes went wide, angry but also fearful, like they'd looked in the cabin.

"You're still mine, you're still owned. When I took you out of the cabin, I stole you from Victor Scava. I did not release you. You do not give orders. You obey them. Understand?"

I felt her throat work as she swallowed. Her lips tightened, and her little hands fisted at my chest.

"I asked you if you understood."

"Yes," she bit out.

I gave her a grin. "Good." I released her. She took a full breath of air and stood against the wall as I left. I didn't lock the door behind me. I went downstairs to Salvatore's study. *My study.* There, I switched on the light and dragged the sheets off the chair and desk and sat down. Using my cell phone, I scrolled down to Roman's number and hit Send.

He answered on the second ring. "Dominic?"

"It's been a while, Uncle."

He exhaled deeply. "Yes, it has."

I hadn't seen him in almost seven years, and his voice told me Salvatore was right. He'd hardened in that time.

"I heard about the body," I said, getting right to business.

Silence, then, "And you want to know if I ordered Mateo Castellano's killing."

"I am curious why you'd mark him for everyone and their fucking grandmother to know it was you." I played dumb. Even if Salvatore had spoken with him after our call—which I doubted—he wouldn't betray me.

"I have enemies, Dominic. You know how it is for us. And snitches aren't tolerated. Period." He sounded stern, unmoved, like a real head of the family.

But he still didn't answer my question.

"He'd done work for us in the past. His father was a friend to Franco."

"Business is business. Where are you, Dominic?"

"West." I wasn't giving him anything. The more I thought about it, the guiltier Roman became.

"Do you need money? I can send you something. Franco won't know."

My lip twitched at his charity. His giving away the Benedetti money like it was his.

"No, Uncle. I don't need money." I could hear the hostility in my tone. Surely he could too.

Silence. "You're well, then? Do you want me to do anything with the house? Will you be coming back?"

"No. I just grew curious when I heard about the murder, the brand. It didn't seem like you."

"The body shouldn't have been found," he said flatly.

Again, not taking responsibility, although not quite denying it either.

"But it was left where it could be. Seems like quite the oversight."

"I need to meet with Franco, Dominic. Good to hear from you."

"Tell him I said hello." I hung up and leaned back in my chair. I had eight days until the auction. Eight days—at the most —until Scava would come looking for Gia and me. Eight days to figure out how Roman was involved.

A clanging sound stole my attention, and I stood. We were locked in the house. No one was here but us, no one knew about this place but Roman, and he didn't know where I was. I'd left my pistol in the SUV, but checking Salvatore's desk drawers, I found one there along with some ammunition. I loaded the handgun and opened the study door, listening. Another sound came, this time from the kitchen. I walked that way, scanning the large, open space as I went, the ghostlike lumps beneath the dustcovers eerie in the darkness of night.

The kitchen light was on. I could see it from beneath the door. Just before I kicked it open, I heard Gia mutter a curse from the other side.

I opened the door and shook my head. She stood beside the counter, sucking on the tip of her finger. She froze too, her gaze falling from my eyes to the pistol I held. I put the safety on and tucked it into the back of my jeans, then cleared my throat. I scanned her from head to toe.

"I found the clothes in the closet."

She wore an oversize lavender sweater that fell off the shoulder and a short, hip-hugging black skirt. On her feet she had on a pair of calf-length sheepskin boots that accentuated her slender, toned legs. She'd wound her long dark hair up into a messy, wet bun, and her face had been scrubbed of all the dirt from the last few days.

Gia shuffled her weight to her other foot and stuck the tip of her finger back in her mouth. "I guess I forgot how to use a can opener."

She looked so different than she had in the cabin. Everything about her seemed changed, now that she had proper clothes, a shower, a freedom of sorts. She looked confident. And fucking beautiful.

I cleared my throat. "There's probably a first-aid kit somewhere, knowing Salvatore." I started opening cupboards and drawers to search for it, doing anything possible to not look at her.

"Salvatore?"

I stopped. I'd given too much away. "My brother."

"And his wife, Lucia."

I looked at her sharply. "How did you know?"

"She likes to write her name in her books," Gia said with a smile. Then that smile vanished. "You're not lying, are you? She wasn't...a slave..."

I thought about Salvatore and Lucia's relationship, how it had started, how it was meant to be, how it had turned out. "No." Simple answer. "They're married and have two kids, a third on the way. They love each other," I added, confused why I added that last part.

I knew what lay beneath my anger over how things had been way back when, how I was last in line, the one who would only inherit upon the death of my two older brothers. I always knew, I just had never admitted it—not to myself, not to anyone—but I was jealous. I'd always been jealous, especially of Salvatore.

"Here it is," I said, finding the kit, unable to meet her gaze until I got the expression on my face under control. Too much fucking emotion in this house. Too much memory.

I held it out to her, and she took it, an awkward silence between us. I looked at what was on the counter. She'd cleaned the space and found pasta, an unopened bottle of olive oil, and a can of tuna. A pot of water rumbled to a boil on the stove top.

"Think tuna fish is still good after seven years?"

I shrugged a shoulder. "I guess we'll find out."

"The pantry's stocked. Mostly expired food, though," she said, sticking the edge of a bandage in her mouth to tear it open.

I took it from her and stripped off the wrapper, then took her hand, ignoring the almost electrical charge upon touching her, denying its pull, and held the bloodied finger under the water to clean it. After drying it, I wrapped the bandage over it. "There." I released her as quickly as possible.

"Thanks." She cleared her throat and busied herself with the pasta.

"You didn't stay in your room." I picked up the can of tuna and opened it.

"I was hungry. And don't worry. When I heard you talking, I walked on by and didn't go into the room you don't want me to go into." She rolled her eyes.

I peeked into the pantry to check it out. She was right. There was a lot of food, most of which would have to be thrown away, but it'd do for a couple of days. At least while I figured out what I was doing.

Reaching into a cupboard where dishes were stacked, I took two, washed them, and set them on the counter.

"Do you know what information Mateo had on Victor Scava?"

She glanced at me but returned her attention to the pot when she answered. That's how I knew she was lying. Women tried to look busy when they told lies.

"No. Not specifically."

I sniffed the tuna. "I don't think I want to take a chance with this." I dumped the can with its contents into the trash can. Gia kept her gaze on the pasta. I washed my hands and dried them, then turned to her. "You don't mind?"

She gave me a nervous glance. "No, you're probably right."

I took her wrist, squeezed a little, and made her look at me.

"What information did Mateo have on Victor Scava?"

She studied me, her expression cool, hiding any pain she felt behind her clever eyes as she weighed her options.

"He'd worn a wire and recorded some conversations."

"Why did you lie when I first asked you?" I softened my grip and turned her arm over to look at the soft inside of her wrist, so small and delicate, then returned my gaze to hers.

I squeezed again, hurting her.

She flinched.

"Why did you lie?"

"I don't know."

We locked gazes while water boiled over in the pot. "Do you have access to the recordings?"

Her jaw tightened, and I twisted her arm behind her back, standing so close our bodies touched, hers small and soft, mine wanting.

"Yes."

I waited, twisting again so that she cried out.

"You're hurting me!"

"Where?" My voice came clear and calm compared to her panicked cry.

"At the library where I volunteer."

"You volunteer at the library?"

"I like to read."

"Where exactly?"

Water spilled out from under the lid of the pasta, hissing as it fell to the stove top.

"Mateo saved the file on one of the computers. A public computer. No one will find it."

I smiled. "Clever."

"You're really hurting me."

As if I needed a reminder. Hell, she was the one who needed one. "I told you I would."

She didn't have a comeback for that. I released her, and she stepped back, rubbing her arm. I turned down the burner.

"Did you listen to the recordings?" I asked.

She shook her head. "He'd only done it the day before he disappeared. I found out the next morning when I went in for my shift and found an envelope tucked under the keyboard at my workstation with my name on the front. I recognized Mateo's handwriting and looked when I got a chance. It was a scribbled note with a file path. That's all. I didn't have time to download it."

"Why didn't you tell me before?"

"You didn't ask me."

"Omission is lying."

"This is a fucked-up situation. I don't know left from right, and you go from torturing me to...to..." she gestured around the kitchen. "To fucking playing house."

"We're not fucking playing house."

"No fucking joke. My brother is dead. He died because of what was on that recording. Excuse me if I don't give it up without a second thought to a man I called Death!"

I backed off, filled a glass with water from the tap, and drank, forcing myself to breathe, to calm the fuck down. "What were you going to do with the file?" I finally asked.

She shrugged a shoulder. "Depended on what was on it. I guess turn them over, get Victor arrested, sent to prison."

"That's naive."

"You think I don't know that?"

I know she tried to sound hateful, clever, but she didn't. She just sounded sad and a little lost, actually.

I shook my head and took the pot of pasta off the burner.

"Don't lie to me again," I said without looking at her.

She stood back while I drained then plated the pasta and poured olive oil over it. After wiping down the kitchen table, I carried them over and set them down.

"Utensils are in there." I pointed.

She looked as though she wasn't sure if the conversation was over or not.

I went into the living room and found a bottle of wine, picked it up, and took it and two glasses back into the kitchen. Gia was sitting by then, silent, her gaze on me.

"Hope you like red." After rinsing the glasses, I sat at the table, poured the wine, and started to eat.

Gia ate too, each of us silent, the clanking of forks and knives on the plates the only sound breaking the heavy silence.

"What now?" she asked when we'd finished. "I don't want to hide."

"I need to listen to those conversations. Where's this library?"

"Philadelphia."

"We'll go tomorrow. Does Victor know about the recordings? Does he know that you know about them?"

"I don't think he knows there's a copy. I know he had a flash drive he destroyed. He's dumb enough to think that's the only copy. When he questioned me, he didn't ask me outright about it, so I think Mateo told him I wasn't involved and knew nothing."

"Don't underestimate him." I didn't think Victor was a stupid man. An asshole, but not stupid. Although arrogance tended to give one blinders. I'd learned that myself. Maybe his arrogance would get him caught.

After eating, Gia took the dishes to the sink and began to

wash them. I watched her as I finished the wine. Neither of us spoke.

"I'm sleeping in Lucia's room?" she asked once she'd finished and wiped her hands clean.

I nodded.

"Where are you sleeping?"

"Not in your bed. Don't worry."

She gave me a smirk. "I'm going up to bed, then."

I watched her walk to the swinging door. "Gia," I called once she'd opened it.

She turned.

"Don't go anywhere else."

"Like where do you think I would go?" she asked, a hand on her hip.

I crossed one leg over the other and smiled, tilted my chair, and balanced on its back legs. "Like don't do anything stupid," I said, mimicking her.

"I wouldn't dream of it." She turned on her heel and left the room. I laughed outright, knowing she would do exactly what I told her not to.

I followed Gia upstairs half an hour later and walked into Salvatore's old bedroom. I had a shower then put on a fresh pair of briefs, opened the bedroom door a crack, pulled the cover off the bed, remade it with fresh sheets, and climbed in to wait. I hadn't locked Gia's door on purpose. I wanted to see what she'd do. She didn't trust me, which was wise, but I still needed her, and letting her go out there on her own would only get her in trouble. She most likely didn't believe that, but she didn't know this world like I knew it. Victor wouldn't just let her go. And if Roman was involved, he was not one to leave loose ends. Gia was most definitely a loose end.

I leaned my head back against the pillow and closed my eyes. I was tired and had just drifted off to sleep when I heard it: the whine of a door unused for too long opening. I blinked my eyes open and listened. She walked softly, but the house was old, and it creaked. A lot. I waited until she was on the stairs before throwing the covers back and getting out of bed. I didn't bother pulling pants on and left the pistol on the bedside table. Instead, I crept out of the bedroom and watched her in the dark. She stumbled once, righted herself, and moved toward the front door. She picked up the keys to the SUV I'd stupidly left on the hallway table, and when I saw her punch in the code I'd used to get us inside—sneaky little thing; she'd been watching—I sprinted down the stairs.

Gia turned at the sudden noise, and that second was what I needed. I caught up to her by the time she'd stepped outside the door. Catching her around the middle, I almost fell on top of her as we stumbled forward.

"Never put anything past a woman with an agenda," I said, hauling her back inside.

"Let me go!" she screamed. "You fucking asshole, let me go!"

She kicked and punched. I turned her, tossed her over my shoulder, and slapped her ass. The door banged shut behind us as I carried a fighting Gia up the stairs and into my bedroom, where I tossed her down on the bed. Looking at her flushed face, her hair splaying out on my pillow, her eyes wild with fury— wild like a feral cat—it made me fucking crazy.

She lay still for all of a second, then tried to push me off. I flattened a hand on her chest and shoved her backward, climbed on top of her, and with one knee between her legs, trapped one of her thighs between mine. I laid my weight on her, caught her wrists, and transferred them to one hand. I then lightly tapped her face twice with the other.

"Like I said before, you're so fucking predictable."

"I was out the fucking door before you got to me!"

I gripped her chin, pressed my knee against her crotch, and

watched her eyes darken. "Not far enough, though, considering you're in my bed now. You play, you pay, Gia."

She tried again to escape with her free leg, her torso, battling against me with every part of her she could move before I closed my mouth over hers for a quick kiss. I broke it long enough to warn her. "Don't fucking bite me again." I kissed her hard, devouring her, liking the taste of her, the fight in her. I forced her lips apart and bit down on one, not too hard but hard enough to taste the sweet, metallic taste of blood. I sucked.

Gia made some sound beneath me and, still keeping both of her wrists in one of my hands, I pushed the hoodie she had on up and cupped a breast, pinching her nipple through the bra and kissing her again, eating up her moan, my own, as I pressed my cock against her and slid my hand down to unbutton the jeans she must have switched into to make her getaway. I shoved them down, needing to free her wrists to grip the tight jeans with both hands and get them over her hips.

She pulled at my hair, but her eyes were closed and her mouth open, taking my tongue. I pushed my briefs halfway down my hips and gripped my cock, positioning myself between her spread legs, pulling back once to look down at her, at her pretty face, her lustful, panting mouth.

Her hands held onto my head, her fingers tangling in my hair, and when I fisted one handful of her dark mass and tilted her stubborn chin up, she reached to kiss me back, giving as good as she took, biting, her little teeth sharp as I brought my cock to her wet, hot entrance and met her gaze. I pushed into her, to the hilt in one thrust, eliciting a cry of pain from her, her fingers pulling at my hair again. I closed my eyes and kissed her again, moving inside her, her passage tight. She tilted her hips, wrapping both legs around me, and when I opened my eyes again, I found her watching me, her eyes dark and pupils dilated, biting her own lip as her pussy clenched around me, squeezing her pleasure from me. It took all I had to hold on until she released the vice-like grip of her thighs around my waist. I pulled out, my breath tight as I came on her belly, my cock throbbing between us, emptying, and finally, falling heavy on top of her, holding her beneath me, both of us spent, our breathing shallow gasps, her shuddering as I rolled off onto my back, one hand around her wrist, neither of us speaking.

12

GIA

Fuck.

I looked over at him. Dominic watched the ceiling, his breathing slowing down. Sweat covered his brow. His hard and damp tattooed chest rose and fell. I studied the artwork. Intricate drawings in color and black-and-white spanned his right-side upper chest and arm ending just below his elbow. I knew it wrapped around back too. Over his shoulder. I'd glimpsed the edges earlier.

Central to the design was a clock. Three-thirty-three. Heavy chains circled it, and a skull, a grim reaper, trapped a rosary between its grotesque teeth. Beneath it an eye, the blue-like crystal, watched, and around it, intricate dark designs of which I did not know the meanings bordered both clock and reaper. Within these were carved dates. The whole thing gave off a sense of regret. Of time having run out. Of doom and damnation.

Seeing this, the name I'd given him when I hadn't known his name fit.

Death.

And I'd just fucked him.

Or he'd just fucked me. Hell, we'd fucked each other. He hadn't had to make me. I'd spread my legs wide and gripped him hard, taking my pleasure from him, liking the taste of him, wanting it. Wanting him. Needing him inside me. Making sure he knew he wasn't taking anything from me.

I would not be a fucking victim. Not again. Not ever again.

Dominic turned to me, his gaze on my face.

"You fuck like you fight."

What was I supposed to say? Truth was, I'd never been like this with anyone else. And as much as I tried to convince myself that I did it in order to not give him power over me, I'd never wanted anyone like I wanted him. His darkness drew me as much as it should have repelled me. His loneliness, his secrets —they all worked like a magnet, making it impossible to ignore.

He slid off the bed and dropped his briefs on the floor. I couldn't help it; I let my gaze roam all over his body, his perfectly sculpted, powerful body.

"Up." He held out his hand.

I sat up, then stood, attempting to pull my jeans over my hips as I did, feeling the smear of him leak down my belly beneath this stranger's hoodie I'd found in the closet.

"No," he said, pulling my hand away. "Take it off. Take everything off."

I gritted my teeth, but my belly fluttered at the command.

"Off, Gia. Now."

I stripped, angry, pushing my jeans down and stepping out of them and yanking the hoodie up and over my head. There was nothing erotic in my disrobing as I tugged the panties off and threw them on the floor as I unhooked my bra, dropping it onto the soiled pile. This man had seen me naked more often than clothed.

Dominic looked me over. Having his eyes on me, as much as

I despised myself for it, only made me want. They made my
pussy ache. Again.

But they also made me want to understand the darkness
behind them.

"You look good wearing my cum."

"I hate you."

He closed his hand around the back of my neck and brought
his face to mine.

"I don't care," he whispered.

I believed him. He did not care what I thought, what I felt. I
wasn't sure he cared about much at all.

A shudder ran through me. He moved, leading me by my
neck into his bathroom. It was similar to mine but bigger, and
for all the white in mine, his was black. Droplets of water clung
to the glass wall and door of the shower. He reached in and
turned on the water.

"In."

I stepped into the stall, my belly to the spray. That was when
I felt him behind me, his naked body touching mine.

I turned, panicked.

"What?"

He casually ran his gaze down to my ass, his hands gripping
my hips. He leaned down, his mouth at my ear.

"I liked fucking you."

I froze when I felt him harden behind me again, and when
he rubbed himself against me as he leaned over me to pick up
the bottle of body wash, I stopped breathing altogether.

"I think you liked it too."

He squeezed some out onto his palm and began to rub it
over my belly, my breasts, down to my sex then back up as I
sucked in air. He turned my face and kissed me, his fingers
finding my nipples as he did so, the soap slippery as he kneaded

them. His tongue dipped inside my mouth, swallowing my moan whole.

He turned me so my back pressed against the wall, looked down at me, and spread my arms out to either side. His cock lay thick and hard and ready between us. God forgive me, but I wanted to touch it, to touch him, to kiss him, to feel him inside me.

"You're fucking beautiful."

He dipped his head to kiss my face, my neck, as the water of the shower rained down on us. He released one of my hands, and I brought it to his chest. He slid his hand down between my legs to first rub, then pinch my clit hard. Holding on to it, he leaned back to watch my face.

I grunted, an involuntary sound, and tried to reach up to kiss him, but he moved so his nose touched mine while he twisted and squeezed my clit.

"I should punish you for trying to run off."

He reached down and bite-kissed my lower lip.

"You won't," I said, closing my eyes as he squeezed harder. "Fuck."

"You like that?"

I curled my hand around the back of his neck and looked up at him, watching him watch me, knowing my vulnerability, knowing he saw it, the fact making me hotter. "Fuck, I'm going to come."

And beneath his gaze, I did, his fingers working as I panted and moaned, knees giving way so that he had to keep me upright, the orgasm quick after what we'd just done, and when he released my clit, I cried out, my eyes flying open to watch him lift me up only to impale me on his thick shaft.

It seemed the only word I could say was fuck again and again and again. Dominic chuckled, but his face grew serious as he took both of my wrists up over my head and brought his mouth to mine, his eyes wide open, fucking me harder, faster, until we both cried out with the release, my third, his second, the walls of my pussy clenching around the throbbing of his cock before he pulled out, again covering me with his cum.

I don't remember the rest of the shower. All I know is that by the time he tucked me into his bed and climbed in beside me, I was half gone, exhausted, thoroughly spent and empty. And when he turned to wrap his body around mine, I drifted off to the deepest, most restful sleep I'd ever had.

When I woke the next morning, Dominic was already gone. I got out of bed, shamefaced at the soreness between my legs, the memory of the previous night at once humiliating and arousing.

I'd wanted him. I'd wanted every inch of him. And I'd had it.

I picked up the clothes I'd worn on my getaway attempt— which had almost succeeded—and crept out the door and down the hallway to my bedroom. Mine at least for the moment. I chose clothes out of Lucia's closet, thanking my lucky stars she and I were similar in size so most things fit well enough. It felt weird wearing a stranger's underwear, but I did anyway. After choosing today's outfit, I went into the bathroom to dress. I wanted to check how the brand was healing, since the scabs had started to peel off.

Standing at the mirror, I turned to my side and looked at my hip, picking at the crusted, raised skin, hating the mark, this permanent brand Victor had burned into me. It would remind me always of that night. Of his power over me. I knew it was stupid to think of it as weakness. Me alone against him and several of his men? I'd had no chance. I'd fought anyway, though, knowing I'd lose. Knowing I'd pay. That's what had earned me all the bruises, which were mostly faded by now.

Victor was a bully. A thug. But it didn't mean I didn't feel shame every time I looked at the damned brand.

It was a circle containing what appeared to be a family crest maybe. I half expected it to be the Scava family crest, actually, and was surprised when it wasn't. I knew their symbol. It had been on a necklace James had given me after we'd been dating for a month. This wasn't it.

A *B* stood at the center of this mark, large and decorative. Spears protected that B and the *Famiglia* beneath. A lion's mane acted as backdrop and anchor of the design.

I leaned down to have a closer look, confused. What the hell kind of mark was this?

Would Dominic know? He seemed to know a lot about the mafia world. He'd called it "our world." He was an insider. I had assumed a foot soldier at first, then maybe a mercenary later, after I had gotten to know him a little more. He'd know what it was.

"Gia?" Dominic called out sharply from the bedroom.

I startled, grabbing a nearby towel and holding it up against me when he came into the bathroom, fully dressed in jeans and a tight-fitting, black-cashmere sweater. My eyes fell to the edges of the tattoo the V-neck left exposed. He stopped when he saw me, his blue-gray gaze sliding over me then rising to meet mine.

"What?" I asked once I could get my voice to work. I sounded annoyed, like him. It was an act, though. Was it an act for him? Did he act tough and cruel when he wasn't?

No. It would be a stupid mistake to think that.

"I want to go," he said, walking inside. He stopped, and it seemed to me he had to force himself to keep his gaze on mine even though he wanted to act like he didn't give a damn. Like he was unaffected. I knew he felt it too, this insane physical pull charged and sparking like a live wire between us.

"I just have to get dressed. Give me a minute."

His eyes narrowed a little, and I turned as he moved, keeping myself covered as best as I could, realizing the mirror exposed everything to him when his gaze slid to it.

"Please," I said, no longer able to help the dropping of my head. I needed to manage this, to figure out how to be around him. Fucking like we had last night, it didn't help. Only blurred the already fuzzy line.

He nodded, but I noticed how his gaze settled on my hip as if he too were trying to get a good look. I could ask him. I should. He'd know. But I pulled the towel over it instead. He turned to walk out the door, giving me room, letting me breathe as if he stole all the oxygen out of any room he entered.

I dressed quickly, brushed out the mess of my hair, pulled it into a ponytail, and headed out, stopping at the vanity in the bedroom to smear lip gloss on my lips and mascara on my lashes, not sure why I did. Not like I was trying to look good for him. He was my jailor. It'd be good if I could fucking remember that at some point.

Dominic stood in the hallway, keys in hand, impatience clear on his face.

"Can I eat something first?"

"You eat a lot."

"It's breakfast time."

He sighed, but his stance relaxed a little.

"I saw granola bars. They stay good forever, right? I'll just grab a couple." I walked away before he could stop me.

"Fine. Hurry up," he called out to my back.

In the pantry, I found the bars—dark chocolate and sea salt, my favorite—took two, grabbed two bottles of water, and went back out into the foyer, where I found him holding the door open for me. I walked toward the SUV. Dominic followed.

"I changed the code, so don't bother with another escape attempt."

"Wow, I warrant you having to change your security codes." I went to pull the SUV door open, but he pushed it shut, making me jump, making my heartbeat pick up. I looked up at him looming inches from me.

"I could just chain you to the bed if you prefer? Maybe I will, when we're back."

He stayed like that, his gaze burning into mine until I had to look away, conceding his win. Dominic pulled my door open and walked around to the other side without waiting for me to climb in. Once we were settled, he started the engine. A momentary panic came over me.

"What if someone's there? They see me?"

"Scava thinks you're at the cabin. No one's looking for you. I called already. Told them all was well. That we were on schedule."

I nodded as he drove out of the driveway, but my fear of Victor Scava—as nauseous as it made me to know I feared that man—was very real.

"Why didn't he kill me? Wouldn't that have been smart, in case I did know something?"

"You make a mistake if you think Victor Scava smart."

He made light of it, but then his face grew serious.

"He didn't want you fucked during the training either. The liaison was very specific."

"What?"

Dominic glanced at me as he navigated around the still opening gate. "What I said. And from what you told me, he didn't rape you. Did his men touch you?"

I shook my head. "He wouldn't let them."

"Why?"

"He was jealous of James. Maybe he wanted me for himself? He offered to spare me the branding if I fucked him. When I said no, he didn't force himself on me."

"And he sent you to me to train and sell off?"

"Maybe he planned on buying me himself."

"Sick fuck. I wouldn't put it past him. It would certainly return you...humbled."

"Let's talk about something else."

"Library address."

I gave it to him, and he programmed it into the GPS, studied the map, then turned the little machine off.

"I know where it is. It'll be a little over an hour."

I unwrapped one of the two bars.

"One of those for me?"

"No." As I brought the one to my mouth, he reached over and took it, biting into it himself.

"Don't be fucking rude, Gia."

"Fuck you, Dominic."

He grinned and shoved the rest of the bar into his mouth. "Shit. This is old."

I smiled, but my stomach fluttered, and my face heated. I had to turn and watch the passing scenery out the side window, unable to take his intense gaze. It felt like he read me like a damned book.

I focused on something else. On my mom. I wondered if she was planning Mateo's funeral. Wondered how worried she was about me. I didn't know if they'd trashed my apartment. They'd taken me when I'd walked out of a café after work. Did she even know I was missing? She had to by now, now that she knew about Mateo. She would get in touch with Angus Scava when she couldn't find me. It'd be the first place she'd go.

I almost asked Dominic about calling her but stopped myself. He'd say no. But this wasn't up to him. I'd make sure to get ahold of her or at least get a message to her that I was alive. I'd tell her to go back to Sicily. Hell, she was safer there than here.

At that, the thought that Victor would have hurt her crept into my mind.

No, he wouldn't have done that. He wouldn't have involved her. There was no reason to.

"Did he hurt my mother? Do you know?"

Dominic looked at me as if he hadn't heard my question. I repeated it.

"I haven't heard anything, but I haven't been looking for news. I'll make a call and find out."

To my surprise, he took out his phone and dialed a number then and there. It was to his brother, Salvatore. They spoke for a few minutes, Dominic asking for information and Salvatore, I assumed, promising to call back as soon as he found out.

"Thanks," I said. But that wasn't going to be enough for me. I'd make some calls myself once we got to the library and he was busy copying files.

13

DOMINIC

By the time we found parking and walked into the beautiful old library building on Vine Street, it was late morning. Traffic sucked, and parking was always an issue. I held Gia's hand. To anyone who glanced our way, we looked like a normal couple walking into the building.

Gia's hand felt clammy in mine, and I knew she was nervous. I didn't think she had any reason to be, although if anything did happen, we'd be unarmed, since I'd left my pistol in the SUV, assuming I'd have to pass through a metal detector.

"Lead the way," I said casually even though I looked at every single person in the place as we headed toward the long row of public-use computers.

"Hey, Gia. You missed your shift the other day."

A man came toward us, his face beaming at Gia. A frown replaced that stupid smile, though, when I moved in closer and put my arm around her waist, feeling much more possessive than I maybe should.

Of course she'd run into people she knew. She fucking volunteered here.

Gia tensed beside me.

"Smile," I told her.

"Hi, Ron," she said, her voice tight. "I wasn't feeling well. I asked my friend to call. She must have forgotten."

Ron's gaze kept shifting to me, and I almost laughed at his struggle to keep smiling.

"No, she never did. I covered for you. No worries."

"Thanks, Ron."

I cleared my throat. "Aren't you going to introduce me, honey?" I had to bite my tongue not to laugh outright at the look on Gia's face.

"Um, Ron this is...um...Donnie."

She recovered fast and relaxed. Even smiled. At least for a minute.

"Her boyfriend," I said, gripping her tighter and pulling her close. *Donnie? WTF?*

"Oh, uh, nice to meet you. I guess. I didn't know you had a boyfriend," Ron said, trying not to look at me.

"Yep," I chimed in. "Haven't been together long, but once you get a taste of Gia, well, nothing quite like it..." I winked at her mortified face. "We're on a tight schedule, though," I said, checking my watch.

"Nice to see you, Ron," Gia said, walking stiffly toward the public-use computers.

"Nice to see you," Ron called out.

It took all I had not to flip him off.

"What was that?" she asked in a sharp whisper. "How could you say that?"

"Donnie? What the fuck kind of name is *Donnie*?"

She stopped and turned to me, one hand on her hip, one eyebrow lifted.

"Did you want me to tell him your real name?"

"You couldn't come up with anything better than *Donnie*?"

She only grinned. "That one," she said, dropping the conversation as an elderly woman vacated a computer.

"Let's go." Someone else tried to take the seat, but I shoved Gia ahead and onto the chair.

"I have been waiting!" the woman said.

"Us too." Ignoring her, I watched Gia pick up the mouse and navigate to the file. Mateo had hidden it well while keeping it in plain sight.

"Here, this is it," she said.

I took the thumb drive out of my pocket and handed it to her. "Copy it."

She stood. "I have to use the bathroom. You copy it, and I'll be right back."

Before I could argue, she was gone. The woman we'd butted in front of was pointing at us and talking to the man at the counter, so I knew we had limited time. I took over, copying the file onto my thumb drive, hoping Gia wouldn't be dumb enough to try to run off. I didn't think she would, though. Not with this evidence in my hands now, not knowing I could copy then delete the file. Although I wouldn't. It was my backup.

"Sir."

The man who worked at the library approached my seat with the woman just as the file finished copying.

"That's him. He just butted right in front of me!"

I ignored them both, double-checked the complete file had copied onto my thumb drive, and ejected it.

"I'm done," I said, heading in the direction Gia had gone while looking for signs to the bathrooms.

But I didn't find her at the bathrooms. Muttering a curse under my breath, I walked fast up and down the aisles looking for her. I was going to kill her. My temper grew hotter and hotter with every step I took. And then I saw her. Talking to fucking

Ron behind a desk, a phone tucked between her neck and shoulder.

"Gia!"

All heads turned. Someone 'shushed' me and I sped toward her, walking fast without breaking into a run. I wanted to slap the phone away. I saw her talking and reached her just as she hung up.

"Donnie! There you are. Are you done? I couldn't find you."

"Yeah, I'm done. We're done," I said, grabbing her arm as she moved around the counter. "Let's go."

"Gia?" Ron called out.

"What the fuck was that?" I hissed through gritted teeth.

"I needed to call my mom. I knew if I asked, you wouldn't let me, so I didn't bother asking! She's worried sick!"

"Did you tell her where you were?"

"I don't even know where the house is, and no, I didn't mention the library. She's planning my brother's funeral, Dominic! I know you don't have a heart, but try, just try to be fucking human for a minute!" She wiped a tear from her face as we reached the car.

I bit my lip, wanting to shake her but feeling sorry for her and hating her—or wanting to hate her—for what she said. I mean, she was right. It's not like I had a fucking heart. Monsters didn't have hearts.

So why the fuck did her words sting? Why did I give a crap?

I slammed her door shut and took a minute, my fingernails digging into my palms as I got hold of my anger. I climbed into the driver's seat and pulled the SUV out of the garage, still so fucking mad I could hardly breathe. Gia sat staring straight ahead, and I could see her eyes glisten. She was trying not to cry.

"That was a stupid thing to do."

She didn't answer.

"Fucking stupid, Gia."

Nothing.

We drove in silence all the way back. Once we were back in the house, Gia slipped from my grip and ran upstairs to her room, slamming the door behind her. Fine. That was just fine. She wasn't going anywhere; we were locked in tight. I'd deal with her later. I wanted to listen to the recordings first, and I wanted to do it without her.

After grabbing my laptop out of the duffel bag, I headed into the study and closed the door behind me. I plugged the thumb drive into the port, hit the button to play and leaned over my computer, listening.

The quality was shit, grainy as fuck. Mateo's equipment either sucked, or he wasn't wired right. I could make out Victor Scava's voice, his laugh grating on me, his mood swings in the span of a few minutes giving me whiplash. The man was insane, clearly. He'd say one thing, then the exact opposite just a few minutes later.

Much of the conversation was useless, at least for my purposes. He talked about moving drugs. Moving money. I didn't care about those things. I wanted to know about the trafficking. I wanted to hear Roman's voice.

Mateo must have been recording for a good month. I wondered how they'd figured out he was wired. I thought of how they'd killed him. Right then, Victor laughed again. I fisted my hands.

"Sadistic motherfucker."

How are you different?

I shut down that voice and listened, replaying a piece here or there. It was only toward the end that things got interesting.

I never did hear Roman's voice. There was one time Victor talked on the phone with someone. Victor was pissed after that call. The conversation was about moving product. This particular product, I figured out, was living and breathing. Whoever he was talking to was tearing Victor a new one. Victor had fucked up apparently. Typical. After he hung up was when I knew who it was.

"That fucking asshole thinks he's the boss of me! Fucking imposter. He thinks he can tell me what to do. First old man Scava and now him."

"Take him out, boss?"

Static.

"No. Can't do that, not yet."

Silence. Static.

"If my pussy uncle found out—"

Static cut off the rest of the sentence. When Victor came back in, he was laughing and someone was getting hit.

"I have a much better idea. The fucker's gonna die, but it's not gonna be me to do it."

A struggle, someone grunting. More punches followed, the sound of furniture breaking.

I thought of Mateo watching the beating, maybe administering it. I wondered what had gone through his head then. He had to know what would happen to him if Victor found the wire.

"The Benedetti imposter's gonna get what's coming to him. I'll let my uncle be the one to do it, though."

"How, boss?"

"Thinks I'm fucking stupid. Thinks I don't know he's keeping me on as his fall guy, treating me like some fucking foot soldier and taking over what I started. What rightfully belongs to me!"

My heart raced. Static cut him off, but I had everything I needed.

"I'll let my uncle dig his and that asshole's grave."

Static again, then laughter.

"Two birds, one stone, and all that shit."

I checked the date on that recording. It was the twenty-third of December. Not a full twenty-four hours before Mateo had disappeared.

Victor Scava killed Mateo because he was a snitch, but he used Mateo's death to start a war. A war within the Benedetti family. He wanted Roman out.

Well, I guess that was one thing he and I could agree on.

With Roman out and no more Benedetti sons to take over, Victor Scava could move into Benedetti territory. Take it over. Hell, maybe he'd overthrow his own uncle in the process.

But if he thought I'd stand by and watch, he had another thing coming.

14

GIA

I sat in my room, waiting out Dominic's anger, figuring it was smart to just stay out of his way, at least for now. I picked through Lucia's closet, feeling like some sort of criminal to be looking through her things, snooping almost. She had a lot of books. I could read for a while.

I chose one from her shelf and sat on the bed, flipping it open. I didn't get very far, though. Not past the first blank page, where she'd made a sketch she'd then crossed out in angry lines. I recognized the drawing, but it took me a minute to realize why I knew it. I stared at it for a long time, knowing it was a drawing of the mark on my hip. I read the words *Benedetti Killers* she'd written beneath the drawing. I wondered about her. Those weren't the words of a wife in love. Had Dominic lied to me about that? Was Lucia as much a victim as I?

I didn't need to compare the sketch to my mark. I'd studied it. Hell, I'd memorized it. I knew it was the same. I just needed to figure out the connection.

Growing up, my father had shielded me from his work, but being the daughter of a foot soldier, there was only so much you could keep from your family. We were kids, Mateo and I, but we had eyes. We saw.

Mateo's introduction to the world our father lived in came on his eighteenth birthday. My family had a big birthday party for him, a gathering for extended family and friends we hadn't seen in years. There must have been three hundred people at our house that day with Franco Benedetti at the top of the guest list. In fact, he'd taken the opportunity to meet with several men, including my father, during the party.

I obviously hadn't been invited to the meeting, not only for the fact of my gender, but I was only seven. My father introduced Mateo to Franco Benedetti that day. Mateo had been given his first-ever job; something small, thank goodness. I remember how proud he'd been. How excited.

Franco Benedetti liked my father for some reason. He treated him differently than his other soldiers. My father considered it a promotion when he became one of Franco's personal body guards, traveling with him everywhere, coming home less and less often. Mateo had begged to join him so many times, looking at Franco like he was God almighty. He'd never been allowed, though.

It was during one of these trips that my father was killed. He died protecting Franco Benedetti. He'd saved Benedetti's life by sacrificing his own. That was why Franco had promised to take care of Mateo, me, and our mother.

I hadn't known Mateo was at the meeting, and I'd gone looking for him during the party. I wanted cake, but my mother said we needed to wait for Mateo to sing "Happy Birthday" first, so I'd decided to go get him myself. I remember I'd taken the envelope Mr. Benedetti had dropped off for him, Mateo's birthday gift. My mother had commented on its thickness, knowing it contained cash. She'd put it on the top of the refrigerator for safekeeping, but I'd climbed up on a chair and gotten it down, wanting to take it to Mateo, knowing how happy he'd be. I loved him. He was the best big brother. He was protective and even humored me by playing with my dolls when I begged.

Well, I hadn't found him and had wandered farther from the property, not realizing two older boys had seen me with the envelope and were following. They cornered me when we were far enough away that no one would hear and told me to give it up, give them Mateo's birthday gift.

No way I was doing that, and I told them so.

Well, they didn't exactly take no for an answer, and I realized that day how powerless I was without Mateo to save me. It pissed me off, actually and I readied to fight, knowing I'd lose, refusing to return to the house empty-handed. At least Mateo would know I'd fought for him.

But I hadn't had to because another boy had been there too. An older one, a friend of Mateo's. Or at least someone I'd seen with Mateo a couple of times.

That boy...I stopped breathing.

That's why I'd felt something, some sort of safety or protection around Dominic at the cabin. That's why the strange feeling of familiarity.

He'd been there that day. He'd been at my house. At my brother's birthday party.

Dominic Sapienti was Dominic Benedetti.

Dominic Benedetti had told those boys to take a hike and had given me the envelope back.

He had saved me that day, and later, his father had vowed to keep my family safe. Dominic knew this. If he didn't, I'd told him on the drive from the cabin to this house, and he'd said nothing. And now, I wore his family's brand on my hip, forever marked. They'd burned it into Mateo's chest before they'd killed him. Dominic Benedetti or his family had killed Mateo.

They had ordered my kidnapping, sending me to be sold as a sex slave. This from the man for whom my father had given his life.

I went downstairs to confront him, assuming he was behind the closed doors of the one room he'd told me I didn't have permission to enter. When I opened those doors, though, I stopped dead at what I saw. The splattering of blood on the walls, the residue of red where blood had seeped into the marble floor. The bottle of half-drunk liquor on the table. Glasses with the residue of whiskey and dust as if someone were drinking now. As if that room had been frozen in time.

I realized nothing was covered in the dining room. No dust-cloths, nothing. Two chairs lay on their sides, evidence of a night I knew about. Of the night that brought on the decline of the great Benedetti family. The night when one brother had almost killed the other.

I looked around the room and ran a hand through my hair, trying to make sense of this. I saw the large glass case to the side, and inside it, displayed and dusty, sat a book, the large, heavy tome of the Benedetti family. I opened the glass door and took it out, touching the carving of the family crest on the cover made of wood. I traced each of the grooves, every hair on my body standing on end. It took me a moment to open the book.

Generations of Benedetti were pictured inside. I didn't care about those long gone, though. I turned the pages, working toward the end of the book, noticing the binding, knowing it was a book that would grow with time, adding more and more members as old generations died and new were born. I saw ancient-looking certificates of birth, of marriage, of lineage. I recognized names, unions made to bind families together, making the Benedetti one of the most powerful, if not the most powerful, crime family in America.

At least the most powerful until that night. Until Franco

witnessed the battle between his sons and nearly died himself from a heart attack.

That was when things began to fall apart for the Benedetti family.

I turned the book over, laying it so I could get to the later pages. I saw the photograph of Sergio in his parents' arms. Saw the family grow with Salvatore's birth, Sergio as a toddler.

Knowing what I would find on the next page, I flipped past it, not wanting to see just yet. I got to the photograph of Sergio and his wife on their wedding day. She'd been laughing so hard her eyes were screwed shut in the picture. Then came the date he'd died. Then the one announcing his son's birth just months after his death.

He'd never even seen his son.

I flipped back the few pages I'd skipped, my heart racing, blood pounding against my ears, the noise unbearable. I found the page that pictured the third son. Dominic. His parents smiled, but I saw the strain in their faces, the effort it took. They didn't look like they had with the other two births.

The most recent photograph of Dominic had to be at least ten years ago. He'd have been twenty-five. He stood beside his father at a party, his arm around his father's shoulder, his grin cocky, everything about him carefree, as if he were the boy who would have it all. The girl by his side stared up at him, enamored with him, when he seemed barely aware of her presence.

Dominic Benedetti with his father, Franco. The man who'd pledged to take care of my family. Did Victor work for him? Was it a sort of rebellion against Angus Scava? He knew Angus didn't like him. But did that mean Victor did Franco Benedetti's bidding? It made sense. The brand screamed the truth. Mateo and I had been branded with the Benedetti family crest, not the Scava mark. Franco Benedetti had fucked us over, had promised my father he'd protect us then killed my brother and taken me prisoner. Dominic, a man I thought my ally in some strange way, was his son. I wore on my hip Dominic Benedetti's mark as if I were branded cattle, a thing owned, not a human life at all.

He'd lied to me.

He'd told me Victor was playing a game, but Dominic was the master game maker.

Fury raged inside me.

I'd been fooled.

I'd been played.

I'd fucked my enemy. I'd slept beside him, clinging to him, and I felt sick for it.

I picked up the first thing I saw and screamed, sending it crashing into the bloodstained wall, watching the glass shatter into shards on the marble.

I didn't stop.

15

DOMINIC

Something crashed to the floor in the other room. Gia screamed. I grabbed the pistol and jumped to my feet, running through the living room toward the open dining-room doors, where the sound of something else shattering had me cocking my gun, ready to fire.

Her scream came again, but I didn't hear fear in it.

I turned the corner and kicked one of the double doors open all the way to find Gia standing in the middle of the blood-stained floor, shattered glass all around her, her face the image of fury.

"You!"

She sneered at me, her lip curled, her eyes hard. No fear, not at seeing me. Not at seeing the pistol I held cocked and ready to kill.

"It was you."

She picked up the bottle that still sat on the dining-room table from that night. Franco and Roman had been drinking it. She raised it.

"What's going on, Gia?" I asked, holding out one hand, palm

flat, while I de-cocked the gun and slid it into the back waist-band of my jeans.

Déjà vu.

Except I hadn't disarmed the pistol that night.

She threw the bottle at me, rage burning her face as I sprang to the right. Glass shattered at my feet, sticky liquid staining my jeans.

"Calm down. What's going on?"

"He was your friend." She looked around the room for the next thing she'd chuck.

I moved toward her slowly, watching her take aim with one of the crystal tumblers on the table.

"My father took a bullet for yours. He was supposed to protect us! He pledged it the day my father died *for him*!"

She threw it. I sidestepped, and the glass smashed against the wall behind me.

"And you...you were Mateo's friend."

"Gia." I kept my voice calm, moving in closer, trying not to look at the stain on the marble floor, the splatters on the wall I'd ordered no one to clean.

"You like your little masks, don't you?" she asked, looking around the room, finding nothing left to throw and facing me again. "Tell me, was it you who branded Mateo? Was it you who branded me?" She sucked in a breath and pressed the heels of her hands to her eyes. "I never saw your faces. Everyone but Victor wore a mask." She looked at me again. "You sick fucking asshole."

"Gia," I said, close enough now to take her wrists as she tried to hit me. "Gia, stop."

"Did you kill him?"

"No."

"Were you there? Did you hold him down? Did you—"

A sob cut off her words, and she bowed her head into my

chest.

"Did you chop off his tongue?"

"No." *Christ. She'd seen that?*

"I know who you are. I know."

I let go of her.

She sank to the floor, her face in her hands.

"Gia." I squatted down.

"Don't touch me."

She shoved me away and sat with her back leaning against the blood-splattered wall. I sat across from her, watching her come apart.

"Don't..." she started, but her words trailed off to nothing.

"The brand was a setup. Part of Victor's plan, Gia."

"Mateo was trying to do the right thing."

She shook her head, not hearing me at all, her face scrunched up in confusion.

I noticed the book on the floor beside her then. The book of the great Benedetti family. Our family crest—no, not fucking ours! When the fuck would I get that into my head? When the fuck would I stop calling it mine?

"You knew all along," she muttered. She looked up, her eyes red and puffy.

But I had to look at the book again. At the open page. At Franco and my mother, standing there holding their second born, Salvatore. Sergio standing beside them, his hand in his father's. Dark wood paneled the background, and above it a painting of the damned crest. Franco stood taller, straighter, his face beaming, so fucking proud. The perfect fucking family.

"The blood, it's when you tried to kill your brother."

Her words broke into my thoughts. Forced me to hear.

"You think no one knows, but we all know. I should have recognized the names."

I turned my gaze to hers. I had no defense.

"You must have thought me pretty stupid, huh?" she asked.

"No."

"You're sick, Dominic. You're a sick, sick bastard."

I felt myself go still, my chest tightening. She was right. Every word she said, truth. My guilt must have been etched on my face, because Gia reached out a hand to shove me backward.

"You're a hate-filled monster."

She rose onto unsteady feet, and I followed, shaking my head but unable to speak, stepping closer to her as she pounded a fist against my chest.

"Sick."

I shoved her against the wall and closed my mouth over hers. It wasn't a kiss, it was to shut her up. I would eat her words, so I wouldn't have to hear them. Because what she said was true. I didn't deny the facts. But to have someone say them. To have *her* say them—

Her hands came to either side of my head, and she tugged at my hair, her body yielding just a little even as she tried to push me off. She turned her face to the side and spit, as if the taste of me repulsed her.

"You're a murderer."

I gripped her jaw and forced her face back to mine, looking at her, holding it tight enough she couldn't speak. I then wrapped one hand around her waist and lifted her, carrying her the few steps to the table, laying her on her back.

"Shut up," I said as I moved my hands to undo the buttons of her jeans.

"You betrayed your family."

"I said shut the fuck up." I tugged them and her panties down.

She grunted, pushing herself upright. Her hand came up, and she slapped me hard.

"What do they do to those who betray their own family?" she hissed. "A snitch loses his tongue. What do you lose?"

Everything. Every fucking thing.

I gripped a handful of her hair, tasting my own blood. I'd bit my lip.

"Again," I said.

She slapped me again, this time with the back of her hand. She was the only person to speak the truth out loud. To tell me what I was without fear of me.

My cock grew harder watching her, watching the raw fury burn her eyes.

"Again."

She obeyed, her palm open, colliding with my cheek. Blood splattered onto her face, but she didn't flinch and she didn't stop and I stood there letting her. Holding her in place by her hair, letting her slap my face until it went numb, until she grunted with the effort, until her hand tired. She stopped slapping and dragged her fingernails down both cheeks, drawing more blood. I smashed my mouth against hers again, set the pistol on the table, and unzipped my own jeans, pushing them down, trying to get between her legs, unable to with her tight jeans at midthigh.

"I hate you," she said against my mouth.

I licked her lips, then took one into my mouth and devoured it, devoured her, sliding her off the table to flip her onto her stomach and push her down over it.

"I hate you," she repeated when I gripped her hips and spread her open, bringing my cock to her wet pussy and thrusting into her.

I grunted, needing this, needing to possess her, desperate to be inside her, connected with her. Her breathing hitched as she said something else, something I couldn't make out, and with a hand in her hair I turned her face to the side and leaned down over her back, my mouth to her cheek, to the side of her mouth.

"Hurt me, Gia," I whispered, close to release.

She shook her head as much as my grip allowed. "No. I'm not going to hurt you. I'm going to *kill* you," she said, her eyes closing momentarily as her pussy tightened around my cock. "I'm going to fucking kill you, Dominic Benedetti."

"Do it. Kill me," I whispered as she sucked my lip into her mouth, then bit, and I held her to me, thrusting hard once more, coming like a fucking volcano erupting inside her, not caring that she didn't come, not even pulling out, emptying, emptying, my arms tight around her until finally, spent, my cock slid out, semen slippery between us.

I stumbled backward and pulled my jeans up. Gia straightened, turning to me, my pistol in her hand. I watched her and she me, and I knew what she wanted. I saw her hate; saw her need, her desire.

"Were you there? When they killed my brother?" she asked, cocking the gun. "They wore masks. They all wore masks."

"No."

"Were you there when Victor had me branded?"

I shook my head and dropped to my knees before her and gripped her hips, tilting them toward me, taking her clit into my mouth and sucking, my scent on her, my taste on her. Her free hand gripped the table at her back, and I spread her open, her pussy dripping, a mixture from both of us. I smeared it up along her opening with my fingers, sucking her clit harder, feeling her knees give away as she cried out, coming, the hand still holding the cocked pistol on my shoulder to keep herself upright, her body shuddering, her breath hitching.

I loosened my hold on her and looked at her face, her beautiful, soft, sad face. She slid to her knees, and we stayed like that, watching each other, enemies, lovers, pawns in a game.

"Kill me, Gia," I whispered, my voice failing as I took her hand, the one that held my gun, and set the barrel at my chest. "Kill me after I kill my uncle. After I kill Victor."

She watched me, and for a long moment, I wasn't sure what she'd do. All it would take was the quick pull of her finger, and I'd be dead. Out of my fucking misery.

I wasn't even scared.

But she shook her head and set the weapon down beside us and held onto my bloodied cheeks. She ran her tongue up along my face, then brought crimson-stained lips to mine and slid her tongue between my lips before kissing me, the taste of her mixed with that of my own blood.

"I want to pull the trigger on Victor. *I* kill him. Not you."

She barely took her lips from mine as she muttered the words.

I nodded and kissed her and remembered how I'd called Isabella my vengeful little bitch once. I grinned behind the kiss, holding onto Gia like she held me. Knowing we knelt on the very spot I'd nearly killed Salvatore, knowing I'd fucked Gia standing on the stain of his blood. Knowing I was truly a monster because I didn't find it wrong. I didn't feel guilt. Not anymore. And as I stripped Gia's clothes off her and spread her legs open to feast again, I felt good. I felt hungry. Hungry for vengeance. Hungry for her.

Gia was my match. My perfect match.

I was right when I'd told her she was like me. She hated like me.

And I trusted she'd do what she promised.

She'd end me once this was finished.

I'd help her get her revenge.

And then I'd be finished.

And I'd take all that was left of the Benedetti family down with me once and for all.

16

GIA

I kept Dominic's gun. I laid it beneath the pillow beside me and slept.

I wasn't sure if Dominic slept that night. I don't even remember getting upstairs and into bed after what happened in the dining room.

The scent of sex permeated my room. It was the first thing I smelled, his smell, my own, when I opened my eyes. I sat up in bed, rubbed my face, and picked up the loaded weapon.

I'd kill Victor Scava with this gun.

Then I'd kill Dominic with it.

He wanted me to. He'd asked me to. I finally understood him last night. I finally saw him. Really saw him. He'd been at odds all along, at once my cruel captor, then ally, then lover. I knew why now.

I got out of bed and walked through the door that connected our bedrooms. I didn't care what I looked like, that I was naked, unwashed. That his cum had dried and crusted between my legs. I didn't care.

I only cared about the gun in my hand.

Dominic walked out of the bathroom, a towel wrapped low around his waist, another in his hands, drying his hair.

"How long have you been hiding?" I asked.

He stopped and looked at me.

"You need a shower, Gia."

He resumed walking, tossing the towel he used to dry his hair on the bed.

"How long?"

He stopped and turned to me, paused, then walked right up to me and cocked his head to the side.

"Get your facts straight before you walk around demanding answers with a gun in your hand."

He easily wrapped his hand around the wrist that held the gun.

"You need a shower," he said again.

"Can't stand your own smell?"

His eyes narrowed, and he forced the weapon out of my hand.

"It's mine!" I followed him to the dresser, trying to reach around him to get it when he opened a drawer and set it inside.

He caught my wrists and walked me backward a few steps.

"You need to keep your shit together, and you need to have a fucking shower."

"It's mine," I said again, looking up into his eyes, blue-gray pools so deep, I could lose myself inside them if I wasn't careful.

"I'm not taking it away. It's yours. Come on."

His voice was quiet, as if talking down a child throwing a tantrum.

He walked me into the bathroom and ran water into the tub. The first time he'd bathed me came rushing back, and I pulled away. But he kept hold of my wrist and held me there.

"Relax. Do you want me to give you something to relax?"

"Your little pills? No, thank you."

"Then be a good girl and get in the tub."

I glanced at the tub filling up with water, saw him check the temperature and adjust it.

"In."

"I want this off too." I pointed to the collar.

"And I told you once before, it will come off when I'm ready to take it off."

"Why are you doing this?"

"Because I need you to keep your shit together if we're going to get the bastards who killed Mateo and branded you."

I took in his words, studying him, his face, his eyes. He gestured once more to the tub and released my wrist when I climbed in. And I remembered something.

"You have a daughter."

He stopped, as if that were the last thing he expected me to say. Then he nodded once and brought over a bottle of body wash and a washcloth. He sat on the edge of the tub, dipped the cloth inside, and rung it out before squeezing body wash onto it. He began to lather my neck and back.

"Effie. She's eleven now."

His face looked so sad right then. It was like the man I'd glimpsed last night, the one who hurt. The broken one.

"I haven't seen her in a long time. Almost seven years."

"Why?"

He looked at me, and for a moment, I thought he was going to say something other than what he said, but then, as if he'd just given himself over to it, the truth came out.

"Because I'm a coward."

He dropped my gaze, dipped the washcloth into the water, and brought it back to me.

"She's better off anyway."

"What happened that night?"

He knew the night I meant. There was no other night.

"I shot my brother," he said flatly. "I almost killed him."

He refused to look at me. I reached for his hand the next time he dipped the cloth into the water and held it, then reached up to cup his face, seeing the scratches I'd left yesterday, thinking I should have bandaged them for him.

Dominic met my gaze, the look in his eyes strange, dark... empty. As if he'd used the last seven years to create a gap so wide, a hole so big, he'd never be able to cross the chasm.

He shook my hand off and resumed washing me, his attention wholly on that as he spoke.

"Don't misunderstand, Gia. I'm not good. Being a father doesn't make me good. Missing my daughter doesn't make me good. When I say she's better off, I mean it. I know myself. I know what I've done, what I am. I know what I'm capable of."

He hated himself. I'd accused him of that very thing in the beginning, and it was more true than I'd realized then. And some part of me, hell, not some part, not any part. *My heart...*it broke for him.

"Tell me about that night," I said after a while, once he'd started shampooing my hair.

"Salvatore finally figured out what was going on. Roman— hell, Roman had been looking for shit all along, I have no doubt of that. Anything to discredit me. Although, it's not like I needed much help with that."

"From the beginning. Please."

"Salvatore and Roman figured out I was the father of Isabella DeMarco's little girl, Effie. The DeMarcos were our biggest rival then."

He paused, giving me a minute to absorb.

"We'd met when we were both young—well, she was young, and I was stupid. Didn't know who she was at first, and she didn't know who I was. She got pregnant, and the night we'd agreed to tell our families, I chickened out. She didn't. She told.

And then, she disappeared. It was either that or old man DeMarco wanted her to get rid of the baby."

"I remember the war between your families." It came back vaguely. I'd been too young to really pay attention all those years ago. "Lucia was given to Salvatore like she was restitution or something."

"Yeah, something like that."

"It would have been her older sister if you hadn't gotten her pregnant?"

He nodded.

"Well, they figured it out," he continued. "Luke, her cousin, an imbecile if you ask me, managed to get himself shot by another imbecile. It's what triggered everything. Roman, my fucking uncle," he spat the words, "tried to pin it on me, but Salvatore, my brother who can do no wrong, just wanted peace. Well, fuck peace. This is the fucking mob. You don't get to choose peace."

He stopped shampooing for a minute and looked off into the distance. I was glad for it. In his growing anger at his family, the massage had turned a little rough.

"You know what you get if you're the last-born son in a mafia family, Gia?"

I waited, eyes on his when he turned back to me.

"Nothing. You get nothing."

He picked up shampooing again, and I bit my tongue to keep quiet and let him tell his story.

"And if you're a bastard—"

"Bastard?"

"I was pissed that night. Salvatore, he could never be boss. Never. Hell, he didn't even want it. But he was getting it. He called a meeting at his house, and my uncle dragged me to it. I admit, I was half drunk when I walked into the dining room with a loaded gun." He shook his head. "Then my father called Isabella a whore. Called my mother a whore. I couldn't take it."

He swallowed. I watched his throat work.

"It was always about Sergio. About Sergio's kid. Well, he had another grandchild. It was time he acknowledged that." He shook his head. "But he had another card up his sleeve."

Dominic grimaced, his eyes distant as if he saw it all again.

"Always did have the last word, Franco Benedetti."

"What—"

"Turned out I wasn't his." He met my gaze. "I was the bastard son of a foot soldier and Franco Benedetti's wife."

Oh. My. God.

My mouth fell open. Nobody knew this. They only knew Dominic had tried to kill his brother.

He shifted his gaze to mine. "You see, I wasn't actually trying to kill Salvatore."

Dominic shook his head again, eyes glistening, at least for a moment.

"He just got between me and Franco and almost died for it."

Dominic dropped the washcloth he'd picked up into the bathtub. Water splashed, and he stood. He turned his back to me and ran a hand through his hair.

"Dominic," I started, climbing out, dripping wet, soap suds and shampoo clinging to me. I went to him, laid a hand on his shoulder, and forced him to turn around.

"I almost killed the only person in that family who is worthy of living, Gia."

He had a crazed smile, one I knew kept a surge of emotion at bay.

"You didn't, though. You didn't."

He pushed me away when I put my hands on his shoulders, but I refused to budge. I took his face in my hands and made him look at me, made him see me. See the present moment. See what was right there in front of his eyes.

"He was wrong to tell you like that."

"Leave it alone, Gia. Leave me alone."

"No." I kissed him even as he tried to walk past me. I just kissed him, trying to hold on to him.

His hands came to my waist, still trying to push me away, trying to make his way out of the bathroom.

"Gia—"

"You need to keep your shit together if you're going to get the bastards," I said, kissing him harder when he stopped, when he heard the words he'd used on me just a little bit ago. "Kiss me, Dominic."

He looked down at me, then turned his face to the side, his hands still on my waist, but no longer pushing me away.

"I said fucking kiss me."

This time, he didn't turn away and he didn't pull back. He kissed me, walking me backward out of the bathroom, his arms wrapping around me as his kiss became hungry, ravenous even. When the backs of my knees hit the bed, he pushed me onto it and stood back to drop his towel, his erection hard against his belly, eyes hungry as I lay back and spread my legs for him.

"Dominic," I managed as he knelt between them, then lowered himself onto me.

"I came inside you yesterday," he said between kisses.

"I'm protected." I kissed him back, our hunger matched. "And clean."

"Me too."

He thrust inside me then, and for the first time since we'd been together, we didn't fuck. We made love. Dominic moved slowly deep inside me and held me so close, there was never an inch between us. Our eyes were open the entire time, locked on each other. And when it was over and we lay spent, we still clung to each other, unable to let go, knowing, in a way, that we would be each other's savior. Knowing that as our enemies collected outside of this sanctuary, we had each other, only each other.

I wondered if we would die together, knowing I couldn't do what I'd said yesterday, not now, not anymore after knowing what I knew. I understood his self-loathing. His hate. His loss. I felt it from him. I felt it *for* him. It didn't make him good. It didn't clean the slate; didn't wash his hands of the blood he'd spilled. Nothing could ever do that. But it made him different. It made him human.

Ever since that night, he'd been trying to kill himself. And now, he had an end in sight. And after that end, he wanted me to kill him.

Well, I knew I wouldn't.

I couldn't.

17

DOMINIC

I sat in my study, listening to Leo's cell phone ring. It was the day before the auction, and I needed to check in. It was procedure. A day or two before the auction, I'd get the address for delivery. The auctions were held in different locations every time. Some at private homes, some in the woods. You just never knew.

"Leo"

He always answered the same way.

"She's ready to go," I said.

"Good. I'm sending you the address now."

"How many do you have?" I always asked this question, so it wouldn't seem out of the ordinary.

"Eleven."

"What about buyers?"

"Two dozen."

"Any names I should know?"

Leo paused. This wasn't on my usual list of questions.

"No," he said after a moment. "No names you need to know. The restrictions didn't cause a problem, I hope?"

He'd made a point of going over the "no fucking" rule when he'd delivered Gia to the cabin. Now it made sense.

"No. I am curious about it, though. It makes my job harder," I said.

"Buyer's request."

"She has a buyer? Why the auction, then?"

"It's a humbling experience, isn't it?"

I fisted my hand, fingernails biting into my palm. "Very." My phone dinged with a text. I glanced at it quickly. "I have the address." I already started to type it into google maps.

"See you tomorrow."

We hung up, and I zoomed in on the location.

"I want to go to the auction," Gia said.

My gaze shot up to find Gia standing in the open doorway. I hadn't heard her come down the stairs. She wore a dark gray knitted dress, the tight fit accentuating every curve, every soft swell, every sharp edge.

I cleared my throat and adjusted the crotch of my pants, forcing my gaze back to her eyes. The slight rising of one corner of her mouth told me she knew how she affected me. Told me she knew how beautiful she was. I knew too. Had seen it on day one, when she'd been huddled in a corner, beaten and filthy and stinking. But today, it was different. Today, she stunned; every part of her alive, charged. Her hair hung loose down her back, the thick fringe of bangs a stark contrast to her pale, creamy skin, intensifying the emerald eyes that seemed to shine brighter. Perhaps for her newfound mission, her renewed hate.

"No." I leaned back, folding my arms across my chest.

She leaned against the door frame and did the same. "Why not?"

"Because it's dangerous."

"Really? I hadn't realized that."

"Don't be a smart-ass, Gia."

"Why shouldn't I go? Victor will be there, right?"

"I don't know."

"He will. He's expecting me on the auction block, isn't he? Won't he want to see me humiliated? He told me when they branded me he'd see me on my knees. He swore it. I just didn't realize he meant it so literally."

I studied her. She was right. He'd likely be there to watch exactly that.

She walked into the study, casually scanning the books along the wall before sitting down on the couch. "Who was that on the phone?"

"Leo"

"Who's Leo?"

"The man who fed you while I was...away."

"Charming man."

"Dangerous man."

"What did he say?"

"He confirmed what you think, that Victor is planning on buying you back. He'll still take bids, but he's not planning on selling you. He wants to see you humbled, in Leo's words."

Her eyes narrowed infinitesimally, and inside them I saw her rage, raw and unrestrained. I'd need to make sure I had full control of her before letting her out of my sight. We needed to be smart about this. What I was planning would put a target on my back with too many men shooting to kill.

"I don't want to hide anymore, not from Victor, not from anyone."

"I understand," I said, scratching my head. I glanced again at the image of the large stable in the middle of fucking nowhere. It'd stink. I knew that already. This wasn't the first auction held in a barn, and old piss was the worst.

"What are you looking at?" she asked, coming around the desk.

I let her see. "Auction house."

She zoomed in but didn't say anything. I watched her face, saw her unease, the fear she felt that she tried hard to hide.

"You don't have to hide from me," I said.

"Hide what?" Her face closed down.

"Fear."

"I'm not afraid."

But she didn't quite meet my gaze when she said it.

"Of course you're not." I stood. "Do you know how to shoot the gun I gave you?"

She shook her head.

I smiled and pulled the weapon out of the drawer I'd put it in. "Figures."

"I guess you've had a lot of experience," she said.

I glanced at her. "More than you want to know," I answered, my tone deadly serious.

Her eyes searched mine as if she were deciding whether or not to ask the next question. She dropped her gaze.

No, she wouldn't want to know just how bloody my hands were.

"Bring the ammunition."

She looked inside the drawer at the two boxes, obviously not knowing which. I picked up the box and shook my head, leading the way out back. Gia followed.

I realized I'd left my cell phone back in the study when I heard it ring just as we reached the doors.

"I'll be right back," I said to Gia. "See if you can manage getting the gun loaded without hurting yourself."

She took the box and the pistol and gave me a smirk.

"I'll see if I can do that. I'm just a stupid girl, you know."

"Nah, not stupid. But definitely a girl," I said, taking her chin in my hand and tilting her face upward to kiss her mouth. Being around her, it made me want. It was like all I could think of was fucking her, how I wanted to fuck her. The many ways I still needed to fuck her. It was like I couldn't get close enough. Like being inside her was the only way.

The call went to voice mail, but whoever it was must have bypassed that to call back because it started to ring again.

"Persistent." I watched Gia swallow, her eyes wide on mine when I released her.

I went into the study and checked the display, swiping the screen to answer the call.

"Salvatore?" I hadn't expected him to be so quick with the information.

"I have some bad news."

His voice was so low and grave, my heart fell to my stomach.

"What is it?" I sounded normal, like myself, but it was like I stood outside myself, watching. Like it wasn't me at all who held the phone and listened to him tell his news.

"It's our...it's Franco."

I sank onto the couch, a sudden chill raising goose bumps all over my body.

"What?" It came out tight.

"He passed away, Dominic. Roman found him."

"Just a girl..."

I turned to find Gia coming inside, watched her smile vanish when she saw my face.

What? she mouthed.

"They think it was another heart attack," Salvatore continued.

I didn't care. I didn't care. I didn't fucking care.

"You should come to the house," he said finally.

"When did it happen?"

"More than a day ago. He'd sent his staff home. Stupid old fool. He'd sent them all away."

"He was in the house dead for more than a day?"

"Yes."

Silence. Gia knelt at my feet, her curious, worried face turned up to mine as if she'd draw information from my mind.

"Will you come to the house, Dominic?" Salvatore asked. "I'm on my way. My flight boards in a few minutes."

"What is it?" Gia whispered.

"I have to go," I said.

"Dominic," Salvatore started again, then sighed.

"I have to go," I barely managed before hanging up, shock having made a mute out of me.

"What?" Gia persisted.

I looked down at her eager face. "Franco Benedetti is dead. My uncle found him this morning."

No emotion crossed her face. She watched mine instead, waiting.

"I should be dancing, right?" I said wildly, standing swiftly, rubbing the back of my neck, walking a circle, not seeing her rise, not seeing anything. "I should celebrate."

"Dominic."

She touched my shoulder. I flinched, shrugging her off.

"Dominic."

She was more persistent this time, her touch more firm. "He was the only father you knew. It's natural—"

I looked at her, unable to speak. Not wanting her to see me, not now, not like this. Too much fucking emotion I should not be feeling. Too many memories flooding back, too much anger, too much rage, too much fucking goddamned regret.

"Go away, Gia."

"No."

"Leave me alone."

She shook her head.

Franco Benedetti was dead. And his last words to me had

been to deny me. To humiliate me. His last fucking words disowned me.

"Dominic."

"Fucking let me go, Gia," I snapped.

What she saw in my eyes frightened her. I knew it. I saw it. Hell, I felt it. She stepped backward, like she'd done in that room in the cabin. She kept her eyes on me, watching, as if she waited for her enemy to strike. To be prepared for when he did.

I ran a hand through my hair. I almost said something, but then I didn't. I walked out the door instead, fished the keys out of my pocket, made sure she was locked in the house behind me, and I drove off the property. I needed to think. To get these fucking emotions under control. He had made me weak in life; he would not do so in death. I wouldn't give him that power over me, not ever again.

I hated him.

I needed to remember that I hated Franco Benedetti.

18

GIA

Dominic's cell phone rang again. He'd left it in the study. I rushed back into the room and picked it up, reading the display before swiping to answer the call.

"Hello?"

Hesitation on the other end.

"Salvatore?" I asked.

"Who's this?"

"Gia. Gia Castellano."

Silence.

"Are you still there?"

"Where's my brother, Gia?"

"He just left. He wouldn't talk to me. I think he needs space to process what you just told him."

"Yeah, I can see that. Where are you? No, don't tell me."

I heard a final boarding announcement in the background.

"Look, I don't know you. I heard about your brother, though, and I'm sorry for your loss."

I snorted. Didn't people know it didn't help to hear that?

"But *my* brother needs someone right now. He probably shouldn't be alone, Gia. I don't know your relationship—"

"He'll be back."

"You sound confident of that."

"I am. And I'll be here when he is."

"If you can, try to get him to come to the house. The funeral will be tomorrow afternoon. It's probably good for him to say good-bye."

"I don't know that he's ready for that. I don't know the whole story, but from what I've seen, he's been running from this for seven years."

"I know. That's Dominic. Predictable. He'll always take the most extreme route."

It irritated me that he called Dominic predictable, but then, in the way Salvatore said it, I had to agree. My mind moved to something else. "Will the Scava's be at the funeral?"

There was a pause. "I assume Angus Scava will be."

A woman's voice came through, telling him they would be closing the doors if he didn't board immediately.

"Why?" he asked.

"You have to go. I'll talk to him. I'll make him come."

I disconnected before he could ask again. I had a feeling he knew at least a little bit about me. I paced the study, thinking, planning. The auction would take place tomorrow. But now, with the funeral on the same day, it changed things. I didn't know Dominic's plan about the auction, but the funeral opened up another door, another way in. Maybe a smarter way.

I went upstairs to Lucia's closet and found an overnight bag and began to pack. I found a black dress. I'd look stunning in it. It would be perfect for the funeral. And for showing Victor Scava he'd failed. That he'd now pay. Tomorrow may be Franco Benedetti's funeral, but it was my coming-out party. I didn't care about Benedetti. No, check that. I cared that the news held so much power over Dominic, considering their history. I knew now he'd truly done nothing but run, nothing but dig himself deeper into this black hole over the last seven years. A hole he would not be able to climb out of, not on his own. I saw it in his eyes, read it in his reaction. It was the same thing that I'd seen while he'd held me at the cabin. That hint of the humanity, the vulnerability behind all the hate and rage. Dominic Benedetti may be a monster, but he was a monster with a bleeding heart. That heart was in no way made of gold. It was more barbed wire and steel and sharp, deadly edges.

And those were the things that drew me.

Maybe it was because he wasn't the only monster in this strange thing happening between us. Maybe we had both truly met our match.

Love wasn't always beautiful. It wasn't always kind or sweet. Love could be a twisted, ugly bitch. I'd always known this was the kind of love I'd find. The only kind that could touch me. Because some of us, we belonged in the dark, and Dominic and I belonged in the dark.

After I finished packing my bag, I went into Dominic's room and found his duffel. He hadn't unpacked it since arriving. I emptied it to see its contents. Two pair of jeans, a couple of shirts, that was it. That and a small, worn-out envelope that fell out from the pocket of one of the jeans. I picked it up off the floor and opened it. I pulled out a worn photo of a little girl wearing a hot-pink cast on her arm and beaming into the camera. Dirt smeared on her face and wisps of hair stood wild, defiant, unwilling to be contained by her ponytail. She looked to be about nine years old.

I had to smile back at the little girl with creases across her face from the much handled photograph. Effie. I would have recognized her to be related to Dominic even if I didn't know about her. It was her dimple in exactly the same place as

Dominic's. But more so, her eyes betrayed her heritage. The color, the shape, the shrewd cockiness inside them. It was all Dominic.

How could he stay away from her? If I had a child, could I stay away from her? Walk out of her life? He loved her. I knew it from the way he talked about her. But it was his punishment, his self-flagellation. And it made perfect sense. Dominic hated himself for what he'd done. Hated himself for *who* he was, and more importantly, who he was not.

I tucked the photograph back into its envelope and went into the closet to find him a suit. I figured Salvatore's clothes were likely still there like Lucia's had been, and I was right. I wondered why he'd left in such a hurry. I'd have to ask him.

I realized he'd asked me where we were. He didn't know we were at his house? Well, Dominic had said it was his house now. I wanted to meet Salvatore, wanted to see the dynamic within the family. I wondered if Salvatore would recognize the suit I chose for Dominic. I grabbed Dominic's toiletries, finished packing his bag, and went downstairs to wait for him to return, knowing what I'd do while he was gone.

He'd left his laptop in the study, and the little flash drive I recognized as the one he'd used to copy Mateo's file stuck out of one of the ports. I sat behind the desk and listened, steeling myself, telling myself it would be over soon. That I'd have my revenge soon.

―――――――

DARKNESS HAD FALLEN when a car door slamming shut startled me awake. I lifted my head up off the desk and looked around, confused for a moment before remembering. I looked at the time on Dominic's phone. A little after two in the morning.

I ejected the flash drive from the computer and tucked it into my pocket then walked out into the foyer. Dominic stood just inside the door, his eyes looking as though he were a million miles away.

"Hey. You okay?" I asked.

"Why are you still up?"

"I was waiting for you. Thought you might need someone."

He seemed confused by my answer.

Shadows darkened his eyes, and his hair looked as though he'd been running his hands through it for the last few hours. "You don't look so good."

"What are those?"

His gaze fell on the bags I'd packed and set at the bottom of the stairs.

"I figured we'd need clothes for the funeral." I stood anxiously awaiting his response.

He studied me. "You can't go."

"You can't stop me."

"Scava will be there. Not to mention others who may be involved."

"I'm not hiding. I already told you that. I'm going to use this as my debut."

"A funeral for a debut." He chuckled, shaking his head. "You are one twisted girl."

"What difference does it make anyway? He's going to find out day after tomorrow we're MIA when I don't turn up at the auction. What better place to confront him than publicly within his own community?"

"There's more, Gia. More players. These are very dangerous men you're talking about."

"Ever hear of David and Goliath?"

"What are you going to do, take Victor Scava out with a slingshot?"

"Don't laugh at me. It's not always the biggest and the

baddest who wins. *I'm* going to win this round, and I'm going to win this war."

"I said no." He turned to walk toward the kitchen.

I chased after him. "You don't get to decide for me. Not anymore."

"No, Gia. N. O."

We walked into the kitchen, and I tugged his arm back, forcing him to stop. "You don't get to tell me no. Not this time." Anger fueled me. I would not stay back. No fucking way. "You know you owe me this. I have a right, Dominic."

"You have every fucking right, but you're going to get yourself killed. Let me go. I'm tired, and I'm hungry."

"Well, there's no food in this house that isn't seven years old! Turn around and talk to me." He freed his arm and opened the pantry door. "Look at me, damn it!"

"You don't understand how these men work. The ruthlessness with which they kill."

He kept his back to me, like he couldn't care less.

Well, I'd make him care. "Like you, you mean?" I said, stepping backward as his body tensed before my eyes.

Dominic turned then, closing the space between us. He stood facing me, all his fury focused on me.

I forced myself to hold my ground even as my mind worked frantically, wishing to somehow call the words back the instant they'd spilled from my mouth.

He gripped me by the arms and walked me as far back as the counter. My heart raced, sending adrenaline-charged blood pounding in my ears.

This was scary Dominic. This was loose cannon, wild Dominic.

This was the Dominic that made me wet.

And he knew it.

I saw the change instantly, saw how one side of his mouth

lifted into the smirk that said he knew his power, he read it on my face, he was used to it. Used to having women doing as he said. Used to them dropping to their knees before him.

Fuck him. I wouldn't kneel for him. Not for any man. Not again.

Wrapping one hand around the back of my neck, he thrust his other one under my dress and roughly up between my legs to grip my sex.

"You talk like you have a dick," he whispered. "But all I feel here is a dripping wet pussy."

"You're a sexist pig," I said, swallowing hard.

"I think you like this. You like fighting with me. It makes you hot, doesn't it, Gia?"

His grin grew wider, his cock hard at my belly while his hand began to work, fingers sliding inside my panties and finding my clit.

"Stop," I managed.

"Were you like this with your boyfriends?"

His eyes darkened when he said it as his finger thrust painfully inside me.

"No. Never."

"But you like it with me?"

I failed to contain the tremor that ran through me, but I forced myself not to look away. Not to let him win.

"You like it rough with me?"

He kneaded my clit, and I sucked in air. Fuck. I gripped his forearm, trying to pull his hand away.

"Stop."

"Make me."

He curled the hand at my neck into my hair and tugged my head backward.

"Make me stop, Gia."

His voice came dangerously low, a warning.

A challenge.

I watched him, hating the weakening in my legs as he slid his now slippery fingers inside me.

"Look at you. You're one woman. You're no match for me, and I don't have some twisted vendetta against you. How do you plan on fighting Scava's army off?"

"I'm going," I hissed through gritted teeth.

"I like your fight, Gia. I do. But you need to learn to listen."

"What are you going to do, whip my ass again to make me?"

He rubbed the length of his cock against me, and I felt every inch of his hardness even through the barrier of clothes.

"Maybe."

He kissed me hard before twisting my head so his mouth was at my ear.

"But I don't think I need to."

Fingers slid into my pussy, then traveled back toward my ass, smearing my arousal over it. I sucked in a ragged breath.

"I think, in fact, fucking your ass will be much more effective than whipping it, and I might like it even more."

He turned my face to his again.

"Why are you doing this?" I asked.

I had to close my eyes when he began to play with my clit again.

"You wanted my attention. You've got it."

He released my neck and tugged the dress up and over my head, tearing it a little as he forced it off me.

"You're playing with fire, little girl."

He threw the dress aside and looked down at me standing before him in borrowed bra and panties. He tore the bra away then met my gaze again.

"And if you're not very careful, you're going to get burned."

He reached down and took my nipple into his mouth while working my panties off.

"Stop," my voice came out weak. "I don't want this."

"I think you do."

He rose up again to look at me.

"You want me, Gia. As fucked up as it is, you want me."

"I don't." It didn't even sound convincing to me.

He grinned. "It's okay, though."

He leaned his face toward mine, licking away a tear I hadn't realized had fallen.

"I want you too. I want you to fight me. I want to make you. I want to hold you down and fuck you until you scream my name. I want to come all over you, so you know who you belong to. So you know who owns you."

He released me to tear his shirt over his head, baring his chest. He stood with his arms on either side of me, caging me in but not touching me.

"Touch me, Gia."

His low, deep whisper made me shudder.

I stared up at him. His pupils had dilated so that thin rings of blue-gray circled black. My breathing grew shallow, every hair on my body standing on end.

I moved slowly, tentatively, dropping my gaze to his muscled chest, the tattoo there, and down to his belly, to the trail of hair disappearing into his jeans. Hands shaking and with the lightest touch of my fingertips, I did as he said. I touched him, the tops of our heads coming together as we both watched my fingers move over hard muscle wrapped in soft flesh.

"You make me fucking crazy."

His chest rumbled with the rawness of his words. He gripped my wrist hard and laid my hand flat against his chest, over his heart. His other hand circled my hip.

"Feel this."

His heart beat a frantic staccato beneath my hand, and I found myself biting my lip when I turned my gaze to his, both our heads still bowed. He slid his hand over my belly and brought it to rest at my heart. He didn't speak the obvious, that my heart beat as loudly and as frantically as his. I didn't know what this meant. What he wanted. All I knew was that I wanted him. I wanted all of him.

"Take my cock out," he ordered.

I let my fingertips slide down over his belly, obeying, both hands working clumsily to undo his jeans and push them and his briefs down far enough to grip his cock in both hands. I held the hardness, wrapped my hands around it, and smeared the wetness at the tip.

"Get on your knees," he commanded.

I wouldn't do that. Didn't I say I wouldn't kneel for him? For any man?

Dominic's hand nudged my shoulder, and, weak willed, I slid down, the floor cold and hard against my bare knees.

He waited until I looked up at him.

"Suck my cock, Gia. Keep your eyes on me, so I can watch you take me. So I can watch you choke and cry when I fuck your mouth."

He gripped my hair, and I felt a drop of my own arousal slide down one thigh as I opened my mouth to take him, liking the salty taste of him, wanting him to make me, to do it hard, to hurt me a little maybe. He was right. I was fucked up. And as I took him deeper and watched his eyes, I knew he was too. We were both fucked up, and somehow, we'd found each other, and together, we became something else, something twisted but not ugly. Dark but deep and full, and I knew without a single doubt that when the time came to walk away, I would be leaving a piece of myself behind. A piece that no longer belonged to me.

I choked, and he thrust. He did this three times, until tears blurred my vision before he drew me to stand and kissed me, his mouth devouring mine as he lifted me only to impale me on himself, his thick cock calling a cry from me as I slid down over it, every inch stretching me wide, the touch of my clit against him making me cling tighter, wanting to be closer, to feel him, to feel.

"Fuck, Gia."

He kissed me, trapping me between him and the counter, fucking me. When he dropped to the floor, I wondered if his knees hurt with the impact of both our bodies, but he only pulled back to look at me, to untangle my limbs and turn me and push me down on all fours. He shoved my legs apart, and I arched my back. When he drew me apart and thrust into me again, I cried out. He thrust harder, his breath coming in short gasps and grunts. When he stilled inside me, his cock throbbing, releasing the first rush of semen, I came. I came hard, my pussy squeezing him as if it too needed to cling to him, needed to be possessed by him, needed to be close to him.

I would have collapsed, but he slid out of me and drew me backward to sit between his legs, my back to his chest, his back to the wall. The cold tiles felt good against my sweaty, hot skin. Dominic held me to him. His breath warmed my ear. Neither of us spoke for a long time. I wondered what he was thinking. If he was trying to figure out a way to keep me from going. He could leave me behind and go himself. He could make me do anything he wanted me to do. For all my talk, I knew he would decide. It came down to basics. He was bigger than me. He was stronger than me. He could make me do whatever he wanted.

"I want to go with you. Please, Dominic," I said.

"It's not safe."

"You'll keep me safe," I said, wondering who was more surprised by the words, Dominic or myself.

19

DOMINIC

I'd lost my mind, surely.

I glanced at Gia sitting beside me, her face closed off, both of us silent. A thick air of anxiety hung between and all around us, both of us tense for what would come. How would I be treated? How much did people know? And why in hell did I give a fuck? Why in hell was I going anyway?

The knowledge of Franco's death settled like a heavy black cloak around me, inside me, swallowing me up. I didn't know what I should feel. Hatred? Anger? But all I felt was regret. And a sense of loss like I'd never experienced before.

It was over.

He was dead.

There was no going back. No making amends. No saying sorry.

Salvatore told me he'd asked about me. Had he truly regretted what had happened? Had he regretted telling me like that? All those years, I'd thought he'd loved me. I had. It was maybe stupid, but I had believed it. Losing that love, I realized now, it had broken a part of me.

And through that break seeped a darkness that had oozed into my soul. Made me into a man I no longer recognized. But then I found Gia, bruised and afraid, huddled in a corner of that decrepit room. The moment she set her burning gaze on me, she saw me. She saw right through me. All the broken pieces of me. And now that she knew, now that I'd told her my story—the first time I'd ever done that—it was like those pieces slowly fused together again, even if it was inside out and backward, scar tissue barely covering too many razor-sharp edges.

I was no longer the man I had once been.

But I was stronger. I may be harder. I may be darker, but I was stronger. And I would never be fooled again. I would never be weak again.

Nerves twisted my gut as we neared the house in the Adirondacks. His favorite place. The last time I was here had been to celebrate his birthday.

I turned to Gia. "You do as I say. Every word, understand? You do not leave my side, and you do exactly as I say."

"You told me that already, and I promised I would."

Gia's gaze bounced from me to the road and back. And even as she acted tough as nails, the shadows beneath her eyes and the fact she'd refused to eat told of her anxiety.

"What about the auction?" she asked.

I grinned. That piece did truly give me joy. "I took care of it."

She tilted her head to the side, waiting for more.

"Watch them all at the funeral tomorrow. We'll see just who is involved."

I wouldn't say more yet.

We drove the last fifteen minutes in silence. As we neared the gates of the house, I saw several cars already lined the driveway. I parked behind the last one, recognizing several of the vehicles. I switched off the engine and took a deep breath. Gia's hand touched mine, startling me. She didn't say anything but looked at me with those eyes that seemed to know much more than spoken words.

I broke the gaze. "Ready?"

"Ready."

We stepped out of the SUV at the same time. I tucked a pistol into the back of my jeans, making sure my jacket shielded it. Gia had hers in her purse, although we'd run out of time for those lessons. Leaving our bags in the trunk, I went to Gia's side and took her hand. It felt cold and a little clammy. Strange enough, it made me stand taller, giving me strength enough for both of us.

"Whatever you do, do not show fear," I whispered.

She didn't deny she felt it this time. She simply nodded as we approached the foreboding double doors.

Without hesitation, I pushed on the doorbell. Last time I was here, I'd walked in, using my own key to enter. That key sat in my pocket today.

To my surprise, Salvatore opened the door, as if he'd been there waiting for me to arrive. We both stopped. His eyes scanned me from head to toe, and he gave me a small smile and a nod, holding out his hand.

I took it, meeting my brother's firm grip with my own as he pulled me in for a hug, patting my back.

"Good. You did good to come."

He released me. I looked at him, saw how much more gray was now mixed with the black of his close-cut beard, saw more lines around his eyes and mouth, not lines of worry or of a hard life. No. Lines of happiness. His skin glowed bronze, a byproduct of living happily under the sun.

Lucia turned the corner, looking tanned but otherwise just the same apart from her rounded belly protruding from the close-fitting dress she wore. She came to stand beside her husband, and I saw how his face changed, how his smile grew, how his gaze had brightened as he'd followed her path across the room.

How I felt, though—it was different this time.

It wasn't with envy that I looked at them. Jealousy had given way to something else. I didn't know when that had happened, but I was conscious of how my hand wrapped tighter around Gia's waist as I pulled her closer to me.

Salvatore's gaze moved to Gia while Lucia's found mine.

"Lucia," I said, giving her a short nod. "You look beautiful. Pregnancy becomes you."

"Dominic," she said, squeezing a little closer to Salvatore. "I'm glad you came. For Salvatore." There was no missing the meaning of her words. She hadn't forgiven me for what I'd done. For any of it. Not for abandoning her sister, her niece. Not for almost killing the man she loved.

I understood that and accepted my responsibility. It would take more than me showing up to win Lucia's favor.

"You must be Gianna," Salvatore said, studying Gia.

"Just Gia," she replied, taking his hand.

Lucia's gaze moved to Gia's clothes, a pair of jeans and a sweater. Gia stepped out of my grasp and did a little twirl.

"They're yours," she said to Lucia. "I was in a bit of a bind. I hope you don't mind."

"They look great on you," Lucia said. "I'm Lucia. It's nice to meet you. I'm sorry about your bro—"

Gia shook her head. Lucia stopped.

Salvatore's gaze returned to mine. "You came from Saddle River?"

I nodded.

"Was it you who bought the house outright?"

Again, I nodded, feeling embarrassed for the first time in a very long time.

He studied me but didn't say anything more about it. "Come

in. I think Roman has you staying in your old room. He didn't mention a guest."

"Gia stays with me." Even I heard the possessive tone of that.

Lucia and Salvatore exchanged a quick glance but stepped back to let us in.

"How are Effie and your sister?" I asked Lucia, feeling like an asshole actually. A real asshole. A father who is a no-show.

"Great. Luke has been great for both of them." Her delivery put me in my place.

"Lucia," Salvatore cut in brusquely, giving her hand a squeeze.

Lucia cleared her throat. "When Effie heard we'd see you, she wanted to make sure to send you some of your favorite cookies. I have a tin for you upstairs. Not that you deserve it."

"Enough," Salvatore said, wrapping his hand around the back of her neck in warning.

She turned her stubborn face to his, and their gazes locked. Salvatore must have squeezed a little because Lucia narrowed her eyes but bit her lip. Probably to stop herself from talking.

"She's right," I said. "I'm a shit of a dad. Lucia's just speaking the truth."

"We're not here to fight. We're here for a funeral. Our father's funeral."

"Not—"

"He raised you as his own. And he regretted that night. Put your anger aside, at least for now. The man is dead, for Christ's sake."

Salvatore and I locked gazes. Our hands fisted.

Gia cleared her throat as Roman walked out of the study. What Roman felt at seeing me, I didn't know. He'd long ago learned to conceal any emotion from his face. But when his gaze fell on Gia, I saw the infinitesimal change in his eyes, that spark of surprise.

No. Of shock.

"Dominic," he said, extending his hand to mine, drawing me in for a brief, cool hug. "I know Franco would be glad you came."

"You're looking well, Uncle." He did. His suit was more expensive than any he used to wear when he wasn't head of the family, and I didn't miss the Benedetti family ring on his finger. As if he had any right.

"I didn't realize you'd be bringing a guest."

He turned to Gia. He studied her closely but revealed nothing of how he felt.

"Gianna Castellano," Roman said, addressing her.

His mouth moved into a smile. It almost touched his eyes.

"I think you were this big when I last saw you." He gestured to his waist. "Franco would be pleased to have you here."

Gia shook his hand, betraying nothing even as I felt her tense beside me.

"You know my uncle Roman?" I asked her.

Her gaze flickered to mine, perhaps remembering what I'd said I'd do to him the night I made her promise to pull the trigger on me when it was over. When she had her revenge.

She cleared her throat and returned her gaze to his. "I vaguely recall the name, but I'm sorry, I—"

"I'd be surprised if you remembered me. You were a child," Roman filled in.

"Did you know my father?" she asked.

"I did."

I could see from Roman's face he did not expect or welcome Gia's questions.

"And my brother, Mateo?" she pressed.

I released Gia's waist to take her hand, squeezing a warning.

"Yes. I'm sorry for your loss."

"And I'm sorry for yours," she managed.

Roman nodded. "I'll have a room made up—"

"She'll stay with me. Have the maid send up extra towels," I ordered.

For the briefest moment, Roman's eyes went flat and dark, and for the first time, I thought I glimpsed the real Roman. But I'd always spoken this way to him. I'd always felt superior and never hid the fact.

"Of course," he said. A couple walked up the front steps just then, and he excused himself. The four of us stepped to the side, each of us watching every move anyone made.

"Did you bring your brood?" I asked Salvatore, not hearing any children running around.

"No. They're staying with Isabella and Luke."

"I don't like this," Lucia whispered loud enough in Salvatore's direction for Gia and I to hear.

"We'll be fine. Nothing's going to happen. We'll fly home tomorrow as soon as the will has been read," Salvatore said.

A maid came then, and Roman instructed her to take Gia and me up to our room.

"Why don't you go ahead? I need to talk to my brother."

"Lucia, maybe you can go help Gia," Salvatore started.

"I know when I'm being excused," Lucia said. "Come on. You look like you like this about as much as I do," she said to Gia. The two of them turned and followed the maid up the stairs.

Salvatore and I walked toward the dining room.

"A man named Henderson who claims he was a friend of father has requested a secret meeting with us," he said in a quiet voice. "He said it's urgent. He wants to meet before the funeral if we can. Definitely prior to the reading of the will."

"Why?"

"Another body turned up. I'm not sure if Roman is aware just yet."

"Body?"

"Same brand. Ours." He paused. "He was a federal agent. Henderson believes he was Mateo Castellano's source."

"A fucking federal agent? Branded with the Benedetti name?"

Salvatore nodded.

"Who is this guy, Henderson?"

"I'm not sure. He did some work for father over the last few months. Roman doesn't know about him apparently."

"Urgent meeting?"

Salvatore nodded. "I think we should go before the funeral. We'll leave together, the four of us, and meet at Henderson's home office. He was adamant no one would know. He seemed... nervous. Rumors are circulating, Dominic. The family has weakened, and with father's death, our enemies are becoming less and less subtle. The method of Mateo Castellano's death has brought unwanted attention to the family. And now, with a federal agent's dead body turning up, there will be more."

"I heard the recording Mateo made. At least what he got out before he was killed."

"And?"

"Scava names Roman. They were in this thing together. Roman is part of the human trafficking ring."

"How? Father would never have approved that."

"Maybe he was working alone. I know that was one thing the family did not dip their toes into. That's a whole other ballgame."

Salvatore nodded. Franco had always been adamant about that. I didn't know the reasons behind it but hadn't ever given it much thought.

"From what I could make out, Scava wants people to believe it was Roman who put the hit on Mateo. And now, I assume the federal agent as well. Why? If they were in on this thing together, why? Unless he wanted Roman out."

We looked over at Roman, who appeared out of another room just then, talking to an older woman with a bereaved expression on his face.

"Snake."

"Be careful, Dominic. Don't let on that you know. Although bringing Mateo's sister may have clued him in. Why did you do that? Not really your smartest move."

"No. But I wasn't going to leave her alone either. Victor Scava wants her. He's apparently already bought her. The auction is just a formality. A humbling."

Salvatore flinched, his mouth curling in distaste.

"She stays by my side," I added.

"If I didn't know any better—"

"She has my protection, that's all."

"What's going on with the auction?"

I grinned. "I'm guessing phones will start lighting up tomorrow around the time of the church service."

"You called it in?"

I nodded.

"Anyone know where the information came from?"

"No." I paused, and we both turned to watch our uncle. "Roman's involvement will be confirmed tomorrow."

"Let's go upstairs. I know Lucia doesn't want to be alone." He paused. "Memories of the last time," he said, his gaze sliding toward the dining-room.

I recalled and didn't miss the note of shame in my brother's words, in his face, or in his behavior.

"I just need to get our bags," I said.

"I'll help you."

Salvatore and I carried the two overnight bags upstairs and parted ways at my door. I watched Salvatore disappear down the hallway and into his room. After a brief knock, I opened my old bedroom door to find Gia standing by the window, biting her fingernail.

"Lots of people coming," she said.

"It'll just be family tonight. You don't need to look for Scava."

She picked up the tin of cookies that I assumed Lucia had given her.

"Here. These are for you. And there's a note."

I took the envelope and the tin out of her hand and sat on the edge of the bed, just looking down at the things on my lap. I touched the lid, tracing the brightly-colored pattern there. Then I opened it to find a pile of chocolate-chip cookies. I offered Gia one. She shook her head and watched me, one hand at her neck, her fingers rubbing her chin. I chose a cookie and bit into it. My throat closed up, seven years' worth of emotion I'd kept bottled up coming up now, threatening to choke me.

It took all I had to swallow the bite before I set the rest of the cookie back in the tin, not tasting a thing.

"I'll give you a minute," Gia said, disappearing into the bathroom.

I set the tin aside and took the letter out of the envelope. Her handwriting was pretty, very different to that of the small child who'd written in huge block letters way back when. Now, she wrote in a neat script.

Dear Uncle Dominic,

Thank you for all the toys and clothes and things you send me every month. When I heard Lucia would see you, I wanted her to give this to you.

Mom told me why you had to go away like you did. She told me the real story of what happened that night. I want you to know that I don't

think Salvatore is still mad at you. I know because sometimes I get up
for a drink of water and overhear things. Not that I'm eavesdropping or
something. I just overhear by accident. Besides, I think Uncle Salvatore
just misses you, and you should know that. No one is mad at you. We
all miss you, especially me. Well, maybe Aunt Lucia is a little mad, but
she just needs to get to know you like I know you, and the only way she
can do that is if you come for visits. You can even stay with us. And
maybe I am a little mad too, since you just up and left without saying
bye to me. But I'll forgive you if you come. Promise. Okay?

I love you, Uncle Dominic.
Effie

PS: I hope you like the cookies.
PPS: I got a phone for my 11th birthday. This is my number if you
want to call me.

I read the letter twice, memorizing the phone number, the surge of emotion as I heard her little voice through her words breaking my heart but also filling me with hope. How did she not hate me for having up and left? How could she forgive me?

How had I created something so good?

I had to smile at the eavesdropping piece. She was my daughter through and through. And I wondered at the gifts. I sent money monthly. I never sent things, though. Did Isabella buy them and say they were from me? She'd do anything for her daughter. She loved her fiercely. Would she even cover for my lack?

Gia returned from the bathroom and sat down beside me on the bed. I didn't pull the letter away when her gaze fell on it.

"Will you ever tell her the truth?"

"I don't know."

"She loves you. And she has a right to know."

I folded up the letter and tucked it into my pocket, rising to stand. "She's safer if my enemies don't know about her." I walked over to look out the window at the growing number of cars. "And after tomorrow, I will have enemies."

Gia came to stand by my side.

"This is only just beginning, Gia."

THE FOUR OF us left early the following morning, filling Lucia and Gia in on the way there.

"The agent, do you know his name?" Gia asked.

"David Lazaro. Ring a bell?"

"He was Mateo's contact."

"Roman will have found out by now," I said.

"No doubt. Henderson's house is here to the left." We parked around the corner of a beautiful, not too large house and climbed out, the early morning damp and chilly. We walked to the house in silence. The old man, Mr. Henderson, greeted us, obviously surprised by the presence of the women.

"Ladies, you'll stay here while we meet?" Salvatore said as if he were asking the question.

"My housekeeper will make coffee," Mr. Henderson said.

With that, we went into his office and closed the door.

"Thank you for coming. I know we don't have much time, so I'll get right to business. First, I'm sorry for your loss."

"Thank you."

Salvatore answered while I tried to keep my face hard and unexpressive as stone.

"I realize you don't know me, but I used to work for an agency where I had access to certain...things."

"What sort of things?"

"Surveillance. Video, audio, a few other things."

We both sat there, confused. "I'm sorry—" Salvatore began, but Henderson cut him off.

"We'll get to it. But first, the will. What will be read this afternoon will come as a surprise to your uncle. I know for a fact he is unaware of this last change made just days before your father's death."

"What change?" I asked. "And how do you know about it?"

"I stood witness. Your father trusted me."

"Mr. Henderson, I'm sorry, but I don't understand," Salvatore said.

"You will." Henderson turned to me. "Dominic, your father is naming you as his successor."

The words slammed into me. "What?"

"It was his wish that you become head of the Benedetti family."

"But—"

Salvatore put a hand on my forearm. "Everything has been decided already. I signed over power to Roman," he told Henderson.

He shook his head. "Your father was living when you did that. He has the final say. And he has spoken."

"You're going to take everything away from Roman?" Salvatore asked.

"Not me. Your father."

"Why me? I'm not even—" I started.

Henderson turned to me. "Franco Benedetti is named as your father on your birth certificate. You are his son, raised as a Benedetti. And you are named as head of the family."

"What happens to Roman?"

"He's cut off. He won't inherit a cent."

"Why?" Salvatore asked. "Why this sudden change?"

Henderson cleared his throat. "Because of me." He looked at each of us, his face grave. "I came across something some time ago, something I had to keep quiet for too long. Time came for me to go to your father with what I'd learned."

"Spit it out," I said. "What are you talking about?"

Salvatore didn't speak.

"The man who ordered the assassination of your brother was closer to home than you know."

No.

"Your uncle ordered the hit." He paused as if for effect. "And had you been there, Salvatore, as was planned, you would have died too."

"What?" I had to clear my throat. "What kind of proof do you have?"

"A phone conversation with a man named Jake Sapienti."

Time stopped. Apart from the pounding of blood in my ears, the room went completely silent. Henderson's eyes locked on mine as if giving me the time to see. Willing me to understand.

It felt like I'd taken a fist to my gut when I did see.

Salvatore glanced at me, and I knew he too knew the name of my father.

"Recording?" he asked.

Speech escaped me. I sat wordless.

"Sapienti's phone was tapped. Feds had been looking for information on his employers for a long time. Back then, they had bigger fish to fry than your uncle. And then evidence got old. Lost or forgotten."

"Lost or forgotten?" Salvatore asked. "How does something like that get 'lost or forgotten?'"

"We're human, and there are a lot of bad people out there, son. Your uncle wasn't the worst of them, not then."

"I want to hear it," I said.

Henderson glanced at me, and I wondered if all color had drained from my face.

"Are you sure?"

Salvatore's hand fell on my arm. I didn't look at him, though. I only nodded once. Henderson got up and fiddled with some ancient-looking equipment.

As soon as the phone connected, Roman's voice—laced with disgust—came through, the line clear.

"You're one short," he hissed.

Salvatore stiffened beside me. We both knew what he meant.

"Keep your money. You didn't tell me who he was. Find someone else to do your dirty work, rat. When Benedetti learns who ordered the hit on his son, you'll get what you have coming," Jake hissed.

"And you won't? He'd never believe you, and he'll kill you."

"If I had known who he was..."

Sapienti trailed off, his tone quieter.

I'd never heard Jake Sapienti's voice, but I had to first process the fact that the man who had fathered me, the man whom my mother supposedly loved, had killed my brother. Had shot down her beloved son.

"Mr. Sapienti's body turned up shortly after Sergio's assassination."

"How did you come by this recording?" I asked.

"The federal government hired the services of the agency I worked for. That's all I am at liberty to say on that," Henderson replied.

"Why now? Why go to my father after all this time?" Salvatore asked.

"And how do we know you're not fabricating this? Why do you give a shit what happens to the Benedetti family?" I asked, on my feet now, pacing to stand behind my chair and glare at the old man.

"Dominic—" Salvatore started.

"People don't do shit like this out of the goodness of their hearts, Salvatore. Get a fucking clue."

I turned and walked the length of the room, running both

hands through my hair, trying to make sense of what I'd just learned.

That my uncle had hired the man who had fathered me to kill my half-brother.

"Mr. Henderson, perhaps—"

"My son was the bystander who died that day along with your brother. He was a young man, engaged to be married in a few weeks' time. So you see, your uncle was ultimately responsible for his death as well."

"Why now?" I asked. "Why didn't you go to my father then?"

Henderson sat back in his seat and turned his palms up on the desk. "Because I'm alone now. My wife passed a few months ago. There's no one left who can be hurt or killed because of what I do now."

"And Roman doesn't know about the change in the will?" Salvatore asked.

"No."

He checked his watch and stood. "We need to go, Mr. Henderson. We'll be late for my father's funeral."

Henderson rose to his feet. I looked at the old man, tall but bent and tired.

"Why would he name me as successor, when it was my father who killed his most beloved son?" I wasn't sure who I was asking.

"It was his final act perhaps to do right by you. He did love you like his own, and he regretted that final night very much. In the short time I knew him, he talked about it often. About you often." Henderson walked around the desk. "Old age makes us see things differently, son."

He put a hand on my shoulder. I looked at that hand, unable to speak, unwilling to feel. I shrugged it off. Salvatore and I walked toward the door.

"One more thing, gentlemen," Henderson started. We

stopped and turned to him. He straightened something on his desk before looking at us. "The guards who will be at the reading of the will are loyal to your father."

I watched the old man's eyes. Heard his message.

Salvatore thanked him and said good-bye. We walked out of the room.

Lucia and Gia stood. Gia's eyes when she met mine turned angry, fierce even, and she shifted that anger to Henderson. Salvatore must have seen it too, because just as she took a step toward the old man, he intervened, taking her by the arm.

"Let's go. We're leaving."

She glanced from him to me and back.

"I said we're leaving," Salvatore said.

Lucia took Gia's other hand. "Come on. We'll talk in the car."

20

GIA

Lucia told me this morning that she'd worn the dress I wore now to her father's funeral so many years ago. That she'd only worn it that one time. We dubbed it the funeral dress. I decided I would burn it once I finished with it today.

While we waited for the men to return, she asked me about Dominic. Asked if we were a couple. I hadn't known how to answer that, so I shifted the conversation to her and her family. The way she spoke about Salvatore, I knew she loved him. And the way he looked at her, hell, he worshipped the ground she walked on.

I admit, I grew envious. I'd never had anything like that before. Not even close, not even with James.

Now as the men sat silent in the front seat of the SUV as we drove toward the church, I watched them, studying the physical differences, the light to the dark in physical appearance. But the thing that impressed me more was the similarity of the darkness inside each of the brothers. I knew the life they came from. Shrouded in shadow, they had seen and done terrible things.

Things neither would forget. Things perhaps neither should be forgiven.

I was a part of this world too. Their world. The day I'd seen Mateo tortured and killed had plunged me into its murky depths. We sat there now, all of us. The difference between Dominic and I, and Salvatore and Lucia, was that Salvatore and Lucia lived in the light. They could walk away. They had once and would again. In a matter of hours, they would shrug off the darkness and leave it behind, scrub it from their bodies before touching their children. But Dominic and I—I knew in every cell of my body there would be no walking away. He and I were embedded in dark. We would die in it.

"I don't want to stay for the reading of the will," Lucia said. "I don't want you in there either, Salvatore."

Her face had lost its shine and gone pale. Neither man had spoken since we'd gotten into the car, but she must have picked up on the thing vibrating off them just as I had.

Salvatore climbed out of the SUV and opened Lucia's door. They stood there then, just outside the vehicle, heads bowed together, talking in whispers, having such a private moment I felt like an intruder to watch but found myself unable to drag my gaze away.

Salvatore wiped her tears with his hands. They stood so close. It was as though they were one person. He then kissed her forehead and lay a hand on her belly. Lucia nodded, and Salvatore met Dominic's eyes, a signal passing between them.

"Let's go in," Dominic said.

My heart raced; my belly was in knots. Black sedans lined the street, the hearse already emptied, Franco Benedetti's body likely already waiting at the top of the aisle.

"Is Victor here?" I asked, clutching the bag that held the pistol.

"I don't know."

"Why didn't Lucia want Salvatore to go to the reading of the will?"

He shook his head, his mind obviously a million miles away.

"What is it? What did that man tell you?"

Dominic turned to me, but if he was about to tell me, he changed his mind.

"Let's get this over with."

He shifted his gaze to a point ahead, disappearing into thought, moving through the motions.

The organ began to play just as we entered the church. Everyone stood and turned. and I felt my face burn as every eye in the place landed on us.

The service was about to begin, but we'd interrupted. And now, we were the center of attention.

"So much for a subtle entrance," Dominic whispered in my ear, straightening, his body seeming to grow taller.

I looked up at him, seeing how he'd schooled his features to reveal nothing, seeing his strength, the cruelty in his gaze as he scanned each and every person in the place with cold, shuttered eyes.

I shuddered beside him, grateful that gaze did not fall on me.

He placed his hand around the back of my neck, pressing the cool collar into my skin; a symbol of protection. One of possession. He would have me and everyone know it.

Dominic Benedetti owned me.

And in some strange, sick way, I wanted to be his.

I told myself it was for now. A game, a role I would play. A necessary thing. But if I scratched lightly at the surface of that thought, I'd see the lie.

We walked up the aisle slowly, purposefully. Dominic cast his gaze down every row we passed, as if he were boss. As if he owned each and every one of the people here.

The first telephone rang, and Dominic checked his watch. I

looked up at him and saw the ruthless set of his eyes as he turned to the man who answered. Someone I did not know. Someone I felt sure he made a mental note of.

But then, in my periphery, I saw Angus Scava, James' father. My would be father-in-law and Victor's uncle.

I swallowed, unable to take my eyes from his. He cocked his head to the side, one corner of his mouth rising infinitesimally as he nodded as if to say, "well done."

Another phone rang somewhere behind us, but we walked on. And there, just two rows ahead of Angus Scava and directly behind the near-empty pew that awaited us, stood Victor, his face red with rage, his gaze burning into mine.

My first instinct wasn't fear. It was to laugh. He looked like he would explode.

Dominic's hand around my neck tightened, and I clutched my bag closer, feeling the hardness of the pistol.

I returned Victor's glare. Then, just like his father had done to me, I cocked my head to the side and narrowed my eyes, conveying to him my warning. War had come to his doorstep. An eye for an eye. A life for a life. He had killed my brother. I would kill him. Dominic would make certain of it.

Victor's phone rang. He broke our gaze to dig it out of his pocket, and when he did, we stopped walking. We'd reached the open casket.

One more phone was answered then. Dominic's uncle, Roman, quietly put his to his ear. Dominic glanced at Salvatore, whose eyes had narrowed. A silent understanding passed between them.

Dominic shifted his attention to me, turning my face to his, his blue-gray eyes looking for a moment like they had behind the death mask he'd worn those first days. But then, they changed, not quite softening, no, not that. Dominic burned too hot for that. They smoldered and burned instead, and in front of all those people and God and Franco Benedetti's open casket, he kissed me full on the mouth.

Women gasped, and when he abruptly released me, the entire church seemed to hold its breath.

I stood shocked. His gaze challenged me, dared me to make a move while warning me to be still. He glanced at the priest who watched this arrogance, this effrontery, this sin against God and man. Dominic didn't flinch. Instead, he looked once more over the assembly, satisfied with what he saw, before turning his gaze to the casket. His face betrayed no emotion, nothing, as if he were unaffected. I knew he was not. I knew Dominic felt. He felt deeply. He behaved as though he didn't give a shit, but inside, he was like a bubbling volcano of emotion, hypersensitive, and so, so well-schooled in hiding it all.

I waited with him, standing beside him until he was ready. I glanced at the old man in the box, feeling nothing myself.

Dominic turned back to me, eyes flat, and ushered me into the aisle so that I stood between him and his uncle. Roman's face had gone white. He tucked the phone into his pocket. Dominic leaned toward him.

"Urgent call, Uncle?"

Roman stood a few inches shorter than Dominic. His hands fisted as his throat worked, and he swallowed. He didn't have a chance to reply, though, because the sound of the priest clearing his throat rang out over the loudspeakers, and he began the service. All went silent apart from the man's booming voice, but I wondered how many in the room actually heard the service at all.

I FULLY EXPECTED to see Victor after the ceremony. Or at the very least, at the cemetery. But he'd left before the service ended.

Disappointment mingled with relief as I stood at Dominic's side while he greeted the mourners, shaking hands, making subtle comments about being back now. Nodding when anyone said anything about Franco Benedetti.

Behind us, calla lilies covered Dominic's mother's and Sergio's graves. I didn't miss the look either brother gave those two headstones.

Salvatore and Lucia stood in the same line and beside them, Roman, looking more anxious than grieved. My gaze traveled over the soldiers circling the gathered mourners, but when I heard the familiar sound of Angus Scava clearing his throat, I turned to look up at the older man.

"Gianna."

He took both of my hands in his, making a point of turning them over.

"Mr. Scava," I said. He'd always called me by my full name.

"You look well."

His gaze momentarily landed on Dominic before he touched my ring finger.

Did he think we were engaged?

"So soon after James' death," he added.

"James died two years ago, Mr. Scava."

"Scava," Dominic said from beside me, his arm circling my waist. "Where's your nephew?"

Angus Scava's face hardened. "He had to take care of some business."

"He took care of some business close to home, and I don't appreciate it," Dominic said, tugging on the cuff of his shirt.

"No. Nor do I. He will be dealt with."

"He kil—" I started, anger rising.

"I'll do the dealing," Dominic said, cutting me off.

They were talking about Mateo's death, about my kidnapping, like it was nothing.

Scava looked at Dominic. They stood the same height, eye to eye, two powerful men unafraid of battle. Beside them, Salvatore watched, dark and dangerous.

"Gentlemen," Roman began, placing a hand on each of their shoulders. "Now is neither the time nor the place."

Dominic's jaw tightened as he turned his face to his uncle. He no longer tried to hide his resentment of the older man.

Mr. Scava watched the confrontation, a small smile playing along his lips.

"What time is the reading of the will, Uncle?" Dominic asked through gritted teeth.

Roman checked his watch. "Within the hour. We should go."

Dominic nodded then turned to Scava. "This conversation isn't over."

"Certainly not," the older man said. "Gianna, pleasure to see you looking so...recovered."

Dominic's fingers dug into the skin of my arm.

"Let's go," he said.

Mr. Scava watched Dominic lead me away, the look in his eyes so different to how he'd looked at me before.

"Was James like his father?" Dominic asked as we climbed into the SUV, Salvatore and Lucia taking the backseat.

Why did it feel like a taunt? "James was nothing like him."

Dominic turned to face me. "He would have been boss of the family had he survived."

I shook my head, perhaps being naive. I didn't care. "He wasn't like his father."

"I'm like him," Dominic said. "Ruthless. Cold. Merciless."

I held his gaze, knowing he used his words as a warning. Knowing I would be smart to heed him.

"Not to me," I said instead. "Not anymore."

Dominic's surprise at my words showed up on his face. It was the slightest change, but I didn't miss it.

"Are you ready, brother? Roman is not going to be pleased," Salvatore said.

"He knows how to behave. I think he's very good at it in fact." With that, Dominic turned the SUV around and drove out of the cemetery and back to the house. We sat silent. Except for Lucia, who spoke with her sister on the phone, asking about the kids. When we arrived back at the house, I was surprised to see so many vehicles there. Had so many family members been requested to attend the reading of the will? It seemed strange to me. But then again, I'd never been to something like this. Funerals, yes. There was no getting around that in the line of work my father had chosen. But those who died around us didn't have the money to require a will.

Dominic parked the SUV and drew in a long breath, steeling himself, then nodded to Salvatore.

"Let's go."

"What's going to happen?" I asked, clutching his arm. "You know something."

"I'm going to be named head of the family," he said flatly.

My hand slid off his arm, and he and Salvatore walked away from Lucia and I and into the library, where about a dozen men had gathered. Two men stood outside. One of them reached to close the door, his jacket falling open, light bouncing off the pistol hidden in its holster.

21

DOMINIC

The attorney executing the will, Mr. Abraham Marino, a man who had worked for the Benedetti family for more than two decades, stood behind the desk. He addressed the collected family members requested to be in attendance, going over preliminaries. Roman stood beside him as if he owned the fucking place. Salvatore sat to my right. Two guards stood just outside the doors and two more at the back of the room. I wondered how they would all react once the will had been read, and I was named as head of the family.

I recognized all the people in the room. They ruled their own smaller families within the larger Benedetti umbrella. Some I hadn't seen since my youth, and some attended every event.

Realistically, Roman could attempt a coup. Hell, depending on how many men chose loyalty to him, he could win. My father was dead. He could force his way in. Although, without money and the accounts held in the Benedetti name, he'd struggle to pay them. In all my years both in and out of life within a crime family, I'd learned one thing: in most cases, loyalty was a flimsy thing. Money ruled. Loyalty generally leaned toward the side of cold, hard cash. And after the reading of the will, it'd be my cash. This house would be my house. The car my uncle drove would be my fucking car.

He'd hired my birth father to kill Sergio and attempt to kill Salvatore.

He'd betrayed my mother, his sister. He'd betrayed his nephew. He'd betrayed Franco. He'd betrayed the entire Benedetti family.

How in hell did Salvatore sit beside me now, revealing no emotion at all, not confusion, not even hate?

I'd been in my twenties when Sergio had died. For a moment, I wondered why Roman hadn't ordered my assassination too, but then I realized. He'd been playing my father all along. I was a bastard. My father already knew it. Roman banked on the fact that when Franco learned it was the man whose blood ran in my veins who had taken his sons' lives, he'd disown me, at the very least. Hell, maybe he even counted on Franco killing me.

I thought of Henderson's words: *"Old age makes us see things differently, son."* He'd said it didn't matter who my blood father was. I was a Benedetti according to my birth certificate. I was raised a Benedetti. There was some small part of me, something deep beneath the wretchedness, that smiled at that. That felt more happiness at that than I probably should.

Did Franco really regret that night? Did he feel sorry about what had happened? About telling me like that? Had he tried to find me? Roman had known where I was some of that time. At least in the beginning. Had he kept that information from Franco, knowing the old man wanted to reconcile? Had he wanted to reconcile?

I covered my face with my hands and rubbed my eyes.

I'd never know. That was all there was to it. I had to take it at face value. Franco Benedetti named me as his successor. He accepted me as his own in his final act. He was about to give me what I had wanted for so long—the rule of the Benedetti family.

And I felt heady with power.

Salvatore cleared his throat beside me, his gaze falling on me.

I straightened.

"Mr. Benedetti made a few changes to his will in the last days of his life."

Mr. Marino glanced at me.

I kept my face expressionless, but noticed Roman's eyes narrowed.

"This is his final will and testament, and it was his wish that no one should contest those changes but that they would be honored."

A murmur fell among the crowd. The attorney cleared his throat. Roman took a seat as the reading began. Mr. Marino went through mundane things first, small inheritances, moneys changing hands, debts being forgiven or passed on, mentions of family members, of children remembered. Then came the rewards of past and future loyalty.

"It was Mr. Benedetti's wish that I read this next piece as he wrote it, as if he were speaking to you now."

Salvatore and I exchanged a look.

"I realize in a family such as ours, there will be differences. There have been differences. But family is family, and for the Benedetti, family is first. It is our motto. It is our path. In life, I did my best for my family, for all of you. I know it didn't always seem that way, but I did. In death, I hope to amend mistakes I could not be forgiven in life."

It took all I had to keep my face a dull mask.

"Each family has been given a sum of money, which you will receive privately upon the end of this reading. Each envelope also contains a contract. If you accept the funds being offered to you, then your loyalty to the Benedetti family is renewed, the bond welded like steel and unbreakable. If you choose not to sign the contract,...well—"

He stopped abruptly to meet every eye in the room. I wondered if my father had given him that instruction too. It would be like him.

"I hope you do not choose that path."

My father. Franco Benedetti. He was my true father, not Jake Sapienti. Salvatore was right. Henderson was right. I was a Benedetti.

I sat up straighter in my chair.

"My son Salvatore has chosen to leave this life. He chose a different happiness, and I no longer hold that against him. He chose a path I did not. I could and would not. But I respect his decision and his family. My grandchildren shall receive trust funds..."

The attorney named the amount of the funds.

"Salvatore and his wife, Lucia, shall always have the protection of the family."

But no money.

I glanced at Salvatore, whose own mask stood firmly in place.

"To Roman, my once constant friend. Ah, Roman, my beloved wife's brother..."

I could almost see Franco shaking his head.

"You know the saying, 'keep your friends close, keep your enemies closer?'"

All eyes turned to Roman, who looked straight ahead.

"Well, friend, you kept me in your pocket, didn't you?"

Murmurs broke out, but the attorney held out his hand for silence and shifted his gaze to me.

"To my youngest, Dominic. I leave you what you have always

wanted. I leave the Benedetti family, your family, in your hands, son. Despite everything, out of all my sons, you are the most like me, aren't you?"

Roman stood. "This is..."

"Please sit down, Mr. Russo."

One of my father's personal bodyguards, a man I'd known to be around since I was a kid, walked behind Roman's chair and placed a hand on his shoulder. Roman sat. Two more soldiers loyal to my father approached the desk and stood behind it, their gazes on no one and on everyone.

"Now, on to those contracts. I have each of the envelopes here. When your name is called, please approach the desk. Mr. Benedetti?"

It took me a moment to realize he was addressing me. Once I met his gaze, he continued.

"Your signature is also required."

He gestured toward the chair behind the desk. Franco Benedetti's chair. My father's chair.

I stood, feeling all eyes on me as I made my way forward. I glanced once at Roman and then sat. Salvatore moved toward the door and took up a place where he could see each family as they were called up, their envelopes opened, and contracts placed before them.

I didn't know if this was custom. If after the passing of the father, old agreements were reinforced, renewed, reminded. I didn't know if he did it for me, to safeguard my position should anyone ever learn the truth behind my parentage. Should anyone contest my right to this seat.

The first man, Antonio Santa Maria, signed the contract. Antonio was a cousin, distant but powerful. His allegiance to my father had never been questioned. His sons, Gregorio and Giovanni, both in their late twenties, flanked him.

"Your father was a good friend. My loyalties have not before and will not now waver," Antonio pledged.

"Thank you, Antonio," I said. I turned to each of the sons and shook their hands, met their eyes, and nodded once. I wondered if they would remain allies or become enemies one day.

They walked out of the room.

The next man approached. Then the next. Each of them pledged allegiance. Each man signed. I took note of those who glanced in the direction of my uncle. These men knew to refuse to sign meant their death. I had no doubt Roman had supporters among them. No doubt they planned mutiny. But today, I would send a message. Today, my first day as head of the Benedetti family, I would send a very clear message.

Finally, almost an hour later, all the contracts were signed and only the attorney, four soldiers, Salvatore, Roman, and I remained.

The attorney packed up his papers, each of the contracts placed neatly into his briefcase. He then turned to me.

"I hope we will continue to work together, Mr. Benedetti," he said, extending his hand. "I look forward to being of service to the son of my friend."

Friend. Funny. But he was loyal. I extended my hand and shook his.

"Thank you, Mr. Marino. I'll be in touch soon."

He glanced once at Roman, then, without acknowledgment, moved toward the door, shook hands with Salvatore, and left.

"Make sure the house is cleared of guests," I told one of the men, my gaze falling on Roman.

"Yes, Sir."

"I want Gia in here."

"Do you think that's a good idea?" Salvatore asked.

"Get her for me, brother."

Salvatore's disapproval clear on his face, he walked out the door and returned a few moments later with Gia at his side.

She looked at the assembled men, her face betraying no emotion to those who did not know her. But I knew her. And I felt it coming off her.

She stood at the wall near the door by Salvatore's side.

I opened my father's top right-hand desk drawer. I'd been through it before, a hundred times, and I knew where he kept his pistol. Taking it out, I stood. I found the silencer deeper in the drawer and attached it to the barrel of the gun. I did this with a strange sense of calm, of peace. Like finally, for the first fucking time in my life, it was right. *I* was right.

Salvatore questioning whether bringing Gia in here was a good idea was a valid one, but she needed to see this. She needed to see justice for her brother, for herself. But she also needed to see me for who I was. I was not good. I would never be good. She needed to have no reservations, no hopes, no illusions. That last part, it was strange, but I knew who I was now. The clarity of it, of all of it, was undeniable. And Gia was part of that clarity. I knew what I wanted, and she was it. But I owed her truth, and what she'd witness today would be an absolute truth.

"Dominic—"

Roman started talking when I moved to the side of the desk and stood leaning against it, facing him.

"Silence, Uncle."

The guard behind him placed his hand back on Roman's shoulder.

Power. Fuck. A surge of it pumped blood through my veins.

"You hired Jake Sapienti to assassinate Sergio."

Roman flinched.

"Did he know who Sergio was? Did he know the mark?"

It took Roman a moment, but the cocking of my gun got his

lips moving. "No. He only knew the license plate of the car. He felt...remorse...when he found out who he'd killed."

"But you didn't." My uncle sat silent. "You would have killed Salvatore that same day had he been where he was supposed to be. You wormed your way into the heart of the Benedetti family to take what did not belong to you."

"Dominic, you and I, we're real family—"

I shook my head. "You are a traitor, Uncle." Distaste curled my lip. "You betrayed my father. You took his trust, his confidence, his friendship—he believed you to be his one true friend, but you never were anyone's friend, were you?"

"It's not—"

"You had his beloved son, your own nephew, murdered. Shot down like a fucking dog." A hot rage fired my words, and my chest tightened. "You used Sapienti to assassinate him. Why? Why would you do that? Why hammer another nail into an already sealed coffin? Why?"

"It was a mistake, Dominic. Just a mistake."

"You don't make mistakes. I know that." I paused, checking the chamber of the gun.

"Please, Dominic—"

"Where did your balls go, Uncle?" I looked at everyone assembled in the room. "What the fuck happens to these 'powerful' men when they sit facing the barrel of the gun rather than cocking it in the face of their enemy?"

No one answered.

"You've learned over the last seven years what it's like to exist just outside, Dominic. To not quite belong. To feel an utter impotence while standing beside the hand that rules the world. You now know what it was like for me all those years. You can't deny that you know."

"I have no reason to deny it. You're right. And you know what, it felt like fucking shit. But I didn't betray my family over the shit cards I'd been dealt. You played us. You played my father. For years."

"He's not your real—"

Someone cocked his gun. I turned to find Salvatore stepping forward, his angry gaze on my uncle.

"You listen, old man. You listen now, and show respect. Sergio didn't get to see his baby boy. He never got to say good-bye to his wife. To any of us. You took that away. You killed your own nephew," Salvatore said, rage slicing through the calm. "Now, you listen." The words were forced through gritted teeth.

Roman swallowed hard, his eyes glistening. Did he feel remorse?

Did it fucking matter?

"Before I kill you," I said, drawing his attention back on me, "I want to know your involvement with Victor Scava."

"Let me walk away, leave town, leave the goddamned coun-try. I'll tell you everything, just don't—" His voice broke.

Fucking coward.

"Don't what?" I probed, taunting. Hating him.

"Don't kill me," he begged.

"Get on your knees, and beg me not to kill you."

He looked around the room. He had to know no one would help him. Slowly, and with trembling legs, he dropped to his knees before me. Fucking fool. Fucking bastard, coward, fool. Did he really think I'd let him live?

I noticed the ring he still wore. "Take the Benedetti ring off your finger."

He looked down at his hand and then met my gaze. I think he decided this one he could concede because he wriggled the tight ring off and handed it to me. I set it on the desk.

"Please, Dominic, I'll tell you what you want to know, just let me live. Let my family—"

I pointed the gun at his shoulder and pulled the trigger. Roman fell backward, and Gia screamed.

"She stays," I said to the men at the door, my eyes on Roman.

"I'm not leaving," she said.

I glanced back at her but spoke to the soldier. "Make sure of it."

"Uncle," I said, looking at him again. "Get the fuck up. Back on your knees."

Salvatore remained silent but deadly beside me. He may have left the family, but this was what he came from. This wasn't the first time he'd seen something like this. Not one of us was clean, not a single fucking one. Not even sainted, dead Sergio.

But still. Loyalty ruled, and treason called for death. In this case, a slow and painful one.

"Victor Scava," I said.

Roman held his injured shoulder and glanced beyond me at Gia.

"I want a deal," he said.

"No fucking deal." I cocked the gun, ready to shoot again.

"Wait!" Roman cried out. "I have information for her."

I glanced at Gia, where Roman was also looking.

"About her brother."

"Don't fucking play games—"

"Wait, Dominic," Gia cried out, running to my side and griping my arm, the one that held the pistol.

I thrust it backward, holding her just behind me. My bullet would find its right mark this time.

Roman started to talk. "Angus won't give Victor the rule of the family soon enough. He wants to take it from him."

"Angus Scava is what...is he even sixty? Victor thought he'd just hand over the rule of his family?"

"Victor was gathering supporters."

"You being his number one?"

"No. My loyalty has always been to our family."

I aimed at his other shoulder.

"No!" He held up both hands. "Please!"

"You've always been loyal to you, Uncle."

"What do you know?"

Gia's voice stopped me from pulling the trigger.

"A federal agent turned up dead yesterday," Roman said. "He too was branded with the same brand as your brother. He was Mateo's contact."

"I don't understand," Gia said, her desperate gaze on mine.

"Talk faster," I told Roman.

"A deal," Roman said.

"Dominic, let's hear him out," Salvatore said.

"Deal depends on what you tell us, then," I said. "Start talking. If I even think I smell a lie, I pull the fucking trigger, understand?"

Roman nodded. "I stopped dealing with Victor about a month ago when Angus Scava got wind of what his nephew was up to. Victor wasn't very smart in how he did things. He underestimated Angus. He thought an alliance with me would give him the leverage he needed to take over the Scava family. I...made a mistake."

"Just facts," I said. I had no interest in his lies.

"I promised to help him in exchange for new territory. Then, once," he hesitated, choosing his words. "Once I took over, we would assassinate Angus Scava, who has no shortage of enemies, and Victor would take over as head of the family. I thought it would be easier to manage Victor than Angus. That's why I went along with it."

"How do the stolen girls fit in?"

He hesitated. "I took a percentage."

"You had no qualms about kidnapping and selling human beings?" I asked, disgusted.

He simply lowered his eyes to the floor, perhaps realizing it himself.

"My brother," Gia said.

Roman met her gaze. "Mateo was...uneasy with the girls. Beating up some asshole who doesn't pay what he owes is different than taking young girls—"

"Because he had a conscience," Gia cut in.

"He went to the feds, but he got unlucky. That agent happened to be on Angus Scava's payroll. That's how Angus found out. Needless to say, he was not pleased with his nephew's agenda, but he's family. He couldn't bring himself to kill him outright, I guess. And he smelled money. Angus Scava took over the operation. He left Victor in charge, at least for the sake of appearances, but he made all the decisions."

His eyes bored into Gia as if he would make sure she understood that part.

"Angus Scava wouldn't have ordered my brother's execution," Gia said quietly.

"He not only did that, but he ordered yours."

She shook her head beside me.

"No. I don't believe you."

"Victor was supposed to kill you."

"Why didn't he?"

"Rebellion against Angus. Lust. Who knows? He's completely unreliable."

"What about the agent? Why kill him?" Salvatore asked.

"All human life is expendable to Angus Scava. And there's more than one corrupt agent employed by the federal government. And now that Angus took over the operation, he wanted me out. He had no use for me, and that presented an opportunity to put the Benedetti family out of commission for good. Franco and/or I would be picked up, and that would be the end of us. Feds don't take the killing of their agents lightly."

"Angus Scava wouldn't have ordered my brother's execution. He wouldn't have ordered for me to be killed."

I glanced at Gia, who had her eyes squeezed shut, her hands on her face, fingers pressing against her temples.

"He did."

He said it so coldly. I raised my gun and pulled the trigger, putting a bullet into his other shoulder.

Roman cried out in agony.

"Get him up," I ordered the guard behind him, who lifted him back to his knees.

"A deal!"

"So before Angus stepped in, you'd agreed to help Victor overthrow his uncle for support for yourself, for money, for power, so when the time came that Franco Benedetti died, you'd be ready to take over more than the Benedetti share, the mourning *Consigliere*, a man like a brother to the fallen Benedetti whose sons deserted him."

"Mercy, Dominic," Roman begged. "I made mistakes—"

"You ordered Sergio's murder. You betrayed my father. Those things cannot be forgiven, Uncle," I spat.

"Please, Salvatore—" He turned to him, his final plea.

Salvatore remained silent.

"I can drag this out for hours, but because you gave me this, I'm going to show you that mercy," I said.

"Please, Dominic. Please, I—"

"I'm sending a message today, Uncle. I'm letting everyone know that if you betray me, you die. You die a very slow, a very painful death."

Roman sat on the floor in a bloody heap, crying like a fucking baby, begging for his worthless life.

I turned to Gia and held out the gun. "Do you want to finish him?"

She stared at him, never once looking at me. Tears ran down

her now alabaster face, all color having drained from it as she watched the horror before her. She shook her head and turned to me with a look of such utter desperation that I faltered.

"Take her away. I'll finish this," Salvatore said.

"I need to—"

Salvatore turned to me. "No, you don't. Take care of her."

I looked once more at my uncle, who now began to beg Salvatore. Tucking the pistol into the back of my pants, I took Gia and walked her quickly out of the room and up the stairs, lifting her into my arms and carrying her when she shook too badly to walk. I closed the door to my bedroom behind us and set her down in the bathroom, wanting to clean the blood that had splattered onto her bare legs, her shoes, her dress.

She trembled as I stripped her, talking to her, not sure she heard a word I said as tears poured from her eyes.

"He is partially responsible for your brother's death. You shouldn't feel sorry for him."

"I know."

She said it on a sob as I turned on the shower and waited for the water to warm.

"It's not that. I don't—"

"He killed my brother," I said. "He would have killed Salvatore."

"I know," she said again, clinging to me when I tried to move her into the shower.

I took off my jacket and set the pistol on the counter. Her gaze closed in on it. Her tears came faster. Holding onto her, I stepped into the shower with her. I stood fully clothed and forced her beneath the stream as she held me, as if she would fuse us together, as if she were unable to stand on her own.

"You needed to see, Gia."

She nodded, burying her face in my chest.

"You needed to know what I'm capable of."

"You think I didn't know?"

Her voice was full of anguish as she turned her emerald eyes to mine.

"Then...I don't understand. I thought you'd want to see—"

"I do. I owe it to Mateo. I swore it to myself. I just...I don't think I can do it. I don't think I can pull the trigger on Victor. I don't think I can keep my promise to kill him."

Something inside me broke open, and I held her tight to me, cradling her head, rocking her as she wept. Her pain, it had this strange impact on me. It made me feel. For the first time in my life, I *felt* another person's pain.

"You don't have to," I said in a whisper.

"I do. I swore vengeance."

"You'll have it, but you don't have to be the one to do it. You don't have to have blood on your hands."

She shook her head and pushed us out of the stream of water. "No matter what, the blood will belong to me."

"Shh. No."

"I'm weak," she said quietly, looking up at me, her hands on my cheeks now.

"Killing doesn't make you strong, Gia." I wiped the tears from her eyes and held her sweet face.

"I won't be weak."

"Maybe it's time you let someone take the weight. Maybe it's time to let go, and let me carry it. Let me carry you."

She pushed wet hair from my face and looked like she was about to say something, but then stood on tiptoe and covered my mouth with hers, her kiss soft and testing. I liked kissing her like this. Kissing her like we weren't battling as her hands fumbled with the wet buttons of my shirt until she pushed it off my shoulders, halfway down my arms. We kissed like we couldn't stand to separate, as if we needed to be touching while I lifted her and carried her into the bedroom, laying her dripping wet on my bed as I tore off the rest of my clothes and climbed between her thighs, her legs and arms wrapping around me, drawing me down to her, her mouth locking on mine again as I thrust into her, never letting her go, not once, not until we lay spent on the bed.

She knew who I was now. What I was capable of. And she didn't cringe away from me. She didn't fear me. It was the opposite. She clung to me. We clung to each other as if for life. As if for breath. As if without the other, it would no longer be possible to breathe, to live, to be.

22

GIA

The following morning, I woke alone in Dominic's bed. The sight of his uncle kneeling before him, cowering, begging, pleading for his life as Dominic coolly cocked and fired the gun, haunted me. I thought about Mateo. About how he'd died. Dominic wanted me in that room yesterday. He wanted me to see one of the men responsible for Mateo's murder on his knees, being brought to a different kind of justice —mafia justice—paying back what he owed: a life for a life.

I didn't feel sorry for his uncle. He deserved what he got, and not only for Mateo, but for all the rest. Dominic had told me the story, the whole story, after we'd made love last night. He told me what the old man, Henderson, had told him. Told me about the reading of the will, of the provision his father had made to have each of the families renew their pledge of allegiance to Dominic as head of the family. He told me of his uncle's betrayal. Told how his father—and Dominic now called Franco Benedetti father—sealed Roman's fate and had left it for his sons to mete out justice. And he told me why he wanted me in that room. Not only for Mateo, not only for me to see that Mateo's death would be avenged, but to see him. To see Dominic step so naturally, so easily, into this new role as head of a bloody family.

Dominic Benedetti now owned the Benedettis.

I touched the scar on my hip.

I guess it fit. He owned me too. Would he let me go once this was over? What we'd discussed that day in the dining room, that day I'd learned the truth of the brand, the truth of who he was, the day he'd fucked me in that bloodsoaked room when I'd been out of my mind. When he'd been out of his. The day he'd promised me he'd make sure my brother was avenged, and I'd promised him I'd kill him once it was over.

But it all had changed now. His father had left him everything in his final act of contrition. Dominic got what he had always wanted.

I wouldn't have been able to keep my promise and kill him anyway, but now I even wondered if he wanted me to.

Everything was different now.

Throwing the covers back, I got out of bed and went to the bathroom to have a shower.

Ironic, that. *Be careful what you ask for. You just might get it.* James would say that to me way back when I thought the mafia life glamorous. When I hadn't yet witnessed its dark, gruesome side. When I hadn't yet seen death.

Dominic's words came back to me. *"Killing doesn't make you strong."* He was right, I knew that. But to hold the gun that brings your enemies to their knees, it was heady stuff. The thought made my heart pump harder, made my blood run hotter. It made me feel powerful.

But then the image of the bleeding man impressed itself upon my brain, as if branding itself onto the insides of my eyelids, and I bowed my head. He'd looked much like Mateo had when Victor had brought him to his knees. Weakened and powerless and afraid. Mateo was no saint. I knew that. No one in this world could be. Not a single one. I did not have illusions on that note. I wondered if before it was through, once all was said and done, would I have blood on my hands too? Didn't I already, even if it wasn't me who'd pulled the trigger yesterday?

I switched off the water, shuddering at the memory of Dominic standing there so cool, so unaffected as the condemned man knelt before him.

He'd wanted me to see him like that.

I went back into the bedroom to get dressed and heard a car door closing outside. Dominic's room overlooked the front of the property, and I could see Salvatore loading a suitcase into the back of an SUV. Lucia stood beside him, one hand on her belly, the other on the door. She wanted out. She wanted to be gone. I understood it. But she and I were different. She was the mafia princess who'd been locked away in a tower and had never wanted any of this. Me, I was the daughter of a foot soldier, someone no one gave a shit about, and I was the one who ended up in the bed of the new king.

Question was, where did I want to be?

Who did I want to be?

Salvatore and Dominic spoke, hands clasped together like two powerful men making an alliance. They then hugged briefly, almost awkwardly. Dominic turned his attention to Lucia, who must have said good-bye before Salvatore opened her door, and she climbed in. No hug from her. To say she did not like Dominic would be an understatement.

Dominic stood on the front steps and watched the car drive off. He remained there until it disappeared down the thickly wooded road. He then glanced up at the window as if he knew I stood there. Our gazes locked, and my heart momentarily lost a beat. He turned to one of the men flanking him—of which there stood two, bodyguards I realized—and I stepped away from the window to dress and then went downstairs.

The door to the study stood open, and I heard Dominic speaking inside. I forced myself to walk into it, wondering if it would smell like it had yesterday—the metallic scent of blood mixed with fear and hate. But the desk had been moved, and the carpet was gone. Only bare floorboards remained.

Dominic looked up at me and told whoever he spoke with he had to go. After hanging up, he stood.

"Gia."

I looked for evidence along the walls, splatterings of blood, of tissue, but none remained.

"It's been cleaned," Dominic said, coming to my side. "You're probably hungry. Let's go have breakfast."

He spoke so casually. "Does what happened yesterday upset you?" I asked as he led me out of the room.

He paused. "I wouldn't say it upsets me, but it's not like I'm dancing with joy here, Gia. He was my uncle. He played ball with me when I was little. I don't remember him not being in my life."

"I'm sorry."

He didn't respond. We walked into the dining room, where a buffet of warm and cold foods sat waiting on the table. Dominic poured two cups of coffee, and I took one, not feeling hungry enough to eat.

"I thought I'd feel better," I said.

He set his cup down, took a plate, and began to fill it with scrambled eggs and bacon.

"You never do."

He spoke without looking at me.

"You just figure out how to go on." He chose a seat and began to eat. "Eat, Gia."

I picked up a plate and stood there, wondering if I'd ever have an appetite again.

"Tell me something," he asked.

I still hadn't moved to fill my plate.

"What do you want?" He leaned back in his chair and chewed on a strip of bacon.

"What do you mean?"

He studied me as if taking my measure.

"What they did to your brother, to you...What do you want?"

I understood what he was getting at, and I steeled myself, knowing exactly what I wanted, knowing who I was, what I could live with. I turned to the buffet and filled my plate, then sat down beside him to eat. He nodded and picked up his fork again.

"Salvatore and Lucia had to catch their flight home. They asked me to tell you good-bye."

"Did he..." I shook my head. I didn't want to ask. Of course he'd finished the job Dominic started.

"My uncle is dead if that's what you're asking."

"Do you believe what he said? That it was Angus behind it all?"

"Dying men are desperate men." Dominic looked at me. "But I'm not sure. I wouldn't be surprised and wouldn't put it past Angus."

"I want to meet with him."

"With Angus Scava?" Dominic seemed surprised at that. "What about Victor? We'll go up the ranks, Gia. Deal with them one at a time."

I shook my head. "This is for me. Your uncle, he owed you. But this is for me."

He considered this, narrowing his eyes, studying me closely.

"Are you sure you know what you're doing?"

"I know. I'm very clear, in fact." I picked up my fork and turned my attention to my plate.

23

DOMINIC

I watched Gia all that day and the next. Truth be told, her quiet was a little scary. I had expected her to be more frazzled, more like a woman, I guess.

Like a woman.

I sounded like an asshole. I'd never been attracted to weak women. In fact, only two women stood out for me in the string I'd been with. Isabella and Gia. Two strong women. Two women with an agenda. Two women you did not want to fuck with.

I meant it when I told her I'd do the dirty work of killing. I wasn't sure what she expected out of this meeting with Scava. She had to know she couldn't just walk in there and kill the motherfucker. We'd meet in a relatively public place, but we'd both be armed. And we'd have soldiers around us who were armed. But I didn't ask her what her agenda was. She was determined and had her own history with Angus Scava. I'd be there with her to protect her, but I'd let her do what she needed to do to make her peace.

"You're watching me."

She sat beside me in the back of the fortified SUV on our way to the restaurant.

"You've been watching me for the last two days."

"I'm curious."

"Are you nervous?"

I shook my head. "No. I do want to be sure you're going to get what you want out of this. If you told me—"

"No, Dominic. This is mine. This has nothing to do with you."

"Fair enough, but if I feel like you're overstepping—"

"It's mine. You told me you'd help me, and I just need you there with me. I need you to carry me a little, or at least let me lean on you. I'm trusting you with that."

We pulled up alongside the curb of the Italian restaurant, a place Scava owned. It was trendy and popular, and the food sucked, in my opinion. Angus Scava would be inside already. I saw two of his men standing beside his sedan parked at the end of the street.

I turned to Gia, taking in how the tight black dress hugged her, how the heels made her legs look longer. She'd let her hair loose tonight, and it hung down her back. Her eyes shown bright, seeming almost to dance tonight. Alive and buzzing as if adrenaline pumped through her even as we sat there.

I touched the flat of my hand to her heart.

"You're nervous."

"Will he know that?"

"No. Not unless he touches you like this, and if he does that, it'll be the last thing he touches."

That made her smile.

"You know how to keep your face impassive."

She nodded.

"I won't leave your side," I said.

"Thank you."

I knocked on the window, and the driver opened the door. I climbed out and saw that my men were already lined up, the number I'd brought matching the number Scava had brought. I didn't expect war, not tonight, but I knew from years of experience to never be caught unprepared.

I helped Gia out and led her toward the entrance, noting every eye on the street that turned her way, liking it. Liking that every man who passed wanted her on his arm. Knowing every woman felt a little pang of jealousy as they pretended not to notice her.

A man opened the doors, and we entered, followed by two of my men. The space was large and modern but completely empty of patrons tonight. Only a few staff I could hear working in the open kitchen, and Scava sitting at the far booth like he was fucking king.

"Why is it empty?" Gia asked.

I had an idea. "Privacy," I said, leaving out anything else I suspected.

Angus Scava smiled. He watched us enter, his gaze sliding over Gia as we approached. Sick prick. He was old enough to be her fucking father. Hell, he would have been if his son had stayed alive long enough to marry her.

I felt a note of possession at that. A hint of jealousy. Which was ridiculous, considering James was dead.

"Gianna." He stood when we neared. "Pleasure to see you." He took her hand and kissed her knuckles, then straightened. "You look enchanting. My son had wonderful taste."

She only looked on coldly.

I cleared my throat. Scava turned to me.

"Dominic."

"Angus."

He gestured toward the booth. "Please. I've taken the liberty of choosing the wine. I hope you don't mind."

"Not at all as long as you take the first sip," Gia said.

Angus chuckled as we sat, and the waiter poured. He made a point of picking up his glass, swooshing the dark red liquid around and inhaling before drawing a long sip.

"I'm still alive," he said to her.

She still didn't touch hers, but I picked mine up and sipped.

"My condolences, once again, Dominic. I hear your uncle passed not too gently last night."

"He was a liar and a traitor. He got what liars and traitors get."

He cocked his head to the side and raised his eyebrows. "You're as direct as your father."

"You did some business with my uncle?" I asked.

"He and my nephew were involved in some things," he said, his eyes catching Gia's as he sipped.

I felt Gia tense beside me.

"Where is Victor?" she asked.

"I didn't think you'd want me to invite him, considering."

"Can we just cut this bullshit?" she spat out. "You talk like we're all here having a friendly drink, but we're not."

I smiled. "She's direct too."

"You've changed, my dear," he said to her.

"You've opened my eyes," she replied.

Angus snapped his fingers, and we looked up. A door opened, and two men walked in, Victor between them. He wasn't quite standing on his own. Instead, he was hunched over their shoulders and being kept upright, his head lolling from side to side, his face bruised, his feet dragging as they walked forward.

Gia gasped. I held her hand under the table.

"My nephew made some poor choices," Angus said. "Concerning what happened to your brother, Gianna, you have my apology. And you'll have Victor's, well, you would except that he can't really talk at the moment."

"I'm going to be sick," Gia said.

"No, you're not," I told her.

"Not woman's work, this, is it?" Angus remarked. "Gianna, in an effort to make amends for what my nephew did to your brother, I'd like to offer you a gift. Would you like Victor's tongue?"

"You...you're sick!"

"No, only a man who punishes liars and traitors. You see, Victor thought it would be a good idea to try to save his neck by sliding a noose over mine." Angus' face changed, a look of disgust crossing it. "I don't like federal agents on my doorstep. Family business is family business, isn't it, boy?"

Victor's only response was to grunt when one of the men beside him jabbed his elbow into his ribs, which I assumed were broken. At least, considering the bruising on every visible part of him, I imagined they must be.

"I know it was you. I know Victor was no more than your foot soldier," Gia said.

"You know nothing."

"How could you do it?" she asked. "You knew me and Mateo. We've eaten at your table. I've slept in your house. I was engaged to be married to your son. How could you order his death? How could you order *mine*?"

"I never did like seeing you upset, Gianna."

"Are you so heartless? So inhuman?"

"I loved James very much, and had he lived, I would have accepted you as my daughter."

"Why me, then? Why order my execution?"

He didn't answer.

"You're a monster. You're a horrible monster," Gia said.

"I don't leave loose ends. You can't in my business. In

cleaning up my nephew's mess, I found he'd left quite a few. James didn't leave them either, by the way. I know you like to fool yourself into thinking he was somehow better than me, better than him—"

Angus pointed to me.

"But truth is, you're surrounded by monsters, Gianna. And you attract them like flies. What does that say about you? What's the expression? Like attracts like?"

"That's enough, Scava," I said, my eyes on Gia, who flinched at his words. I couldn't tell what was going through her head. If she was buying his bullshit. I'd made sure she came unarmed. I wasn't about to take a chance she'd do something as stupid as attempt to kill Angus Scava in the middle of his restaurant. "Get him out of here," I said, gesturing toward Victor.

Scava nodded for the men to take Victor away.

"I want to go," Gia said to me.

"You didn't answer me. Did you want his tongue—" Angus asked again.

She flew at him, knocking the bottle and our full glasses over before I caught her. Two men standing behind Scava drew weapons.

"Put those away for Christ's sake," Scava ordered, picking up his napkin.

Gia struggled against me, but I held her tight. "This isn't the place," I said.

"You're a sick, sick man," she told him. "You want to give me a gift? You know what I want? I want for you to turn the gun you'll use to kill him and put the bullet in your own head instead."

I handed her off to one of my men. "That's enough," I told her. "Take her to the car."

Angus sat there wiping at the bloodred liquid staining his clothes, his face, his hands.

"Let me down," Gia cried. "Let me go."

Once the door closed and Gia was gone, Scava looked up at me.

"I know you were involved, Angus. I know you're the one who ordered Mateo's killing and hers. Your nephew didn't do it, though, not out of the goodness of his heart, of course. He wanted her humiliated. He wanted the woman your son loved degraded." I shook my head. "Gia's right. You are a monster. But you're right too. We all are. You don't go near her again, understand? She's under my protection." I knew my choices. The realistic ones.

"She isn't a threat to me." He nodded and stood. "We go back to the way things were when your father ruled?" He held out his hand.

I looked at it. The thought of touching it meant I betrayed Gia.

I met his eyes, hard and flat, exactly the way I felt. I fisted my hands at my sides.

"No, old man. They don't."

24

GIA

We didn't talk on the drive back, and when we got to his father's house—his house now—I went to the stairs. Feeling Dominic's gaze burn into my back, I stopped two steps up and turned to face him, although I couldn't quite meet his gaze.

Angus Scava was right. We were all monsters. I'd seen what Dominic was capable of. And I knew James had been the same, no matter what I tried to make myself believe. And me, I wanted vengeance so badly I was willing to do what they'd done to me, to my brother, back to them.

An eye for an eye. A life for a life.

Who was I?

Seeing Victor like that, I thought it was what I'd wanted. I thought I would be satisfied. But it only left me feeling empty and ugly and sick.

"Like attracts like."

I was as much a monster as all of them.

"I want to go home." I'd go back to my mother's house, move back in with her until we could sell it, and move away for good.

Far, far away. Although I knew as hard and as far as I ran, I'd never be able to escape myself. My name. My skin.

Dominic nodded once, but I saw how his jaw tightened.

"I'll arrange it."

He took a step toward me, but I shook my head and backed up.

He stopped.

"When?" he asked.

"As soon as possible."

He seemed taken aback. "Tomorrow?"

I shook my head and took the two steps back down. "Now."

He looked surprised. "You need to pack—"

"Pack what? Clothes that don't belong to me?" I felt my lip tremble and my eyes fill with tears, but somehow, I managed to stop the shuddering that wanted to overtake me. Somehow, I held those tears at bay.

"What he said, it's not true, Gia. You're not a monster. You're not—"

"Please...just don't."

Dominic averted his gaze, then took a key out of his pocket. "Turn around."

I looked at it and touched the collar around my neck, which seemed to press heavier against my skin. I'd forgotten it. I'd forgotten all about it.

I turned and lifted my hair up. When his fingers brushed my skin, I shuddered. The sound of the tiny key sliding into the lock sounded as loud as a large iron key turning a Medieval lock, and then I was free. The weight was gone. I was no longer his.

I felt cold, and when I wrapped my arms around myself, Dominic took off his jacket and draped it over my shoulders. I let him and for a moment, we just stood there, watching each other. The draw to slide into his arms, to press against his chest and let him hold me was so strong, but I wouldn't do it. I couldn't.

He turned to one of his men.

"Take her where she wants to go," he said.

The man nodded and walked toward the door.

Dominic took out his wallet and opened it. "You'll need money."

"No. I don't want anything from you." It would only be another moment before the tears fell and drowned me. I needed to get out of there.

"If you ever do—"

"I won't."

"Gia." He started to reach out then changed his mind. "You'll be safe. You and your mom. Scava won't come near you."

I nodded. I couldn't speak.

I shifted my gaze down to my feet and clutched his jacket closer to me. I would keep it. I would keep this one thing of his.

"You'll always have my protection. Anything you need."

I looked at him one last time, memorizing his face, his eyes that studied me so closely, so carefully, eyes that seemed to want to draw words from me I could not say, not now, not ever. Eyes that saw the things I felt, the things I should not feel. That held a tenderness I only saw when their gaze fell upon me.

Without another word, I went to the door. The man opened it, and I walked out of the house. I didn't look back, not when he closed the car door, not when we drove away.

I didn't know if he watched me go but I knew he cared that I had left. I knew he hadn't expected that. But I couldn't think about those things. I couldn't. Not if I wanted to be able to go on.

25

DOMINIC

I went immediately into the study and shut the door. The house already felt different. Empty.

I took a seat behind the desk and opened my laptop.

It was better that she left. Better for her. What could I offer her? Life as my—what? Wife? I couldn't condemn her to that. Gia had been born into this world, but she could get out. She needed to get out. For all her talk of vengeance, she couldn't stomach it, couldn't take the reality of it. I knew that. I did. I think it's one of the things that drew me to her. As fierce as she was, inside her, the light of her innocence burned bright.

In a way, I sought absolution.

She was clean.

And I had no business dirtying her, no business staining her with my sins.

I opened the desk drawer and took out the letter Effie had written me, picked up the phone, and dialed. I only checked my watch after it started to ring and realized it might be too late to call her, since it was past ten at night.

But then she answered.

"Hello?" came her little voice.

I smiled, tears warming my eyes as my heart thudded.

"Hi, Effie. It's me, Dominic."

"Uncle Dominic! You called!"

I heard her elation, and it felt so fucking good.

"Well, you made those delicious cookies, how could I not?" I said. There was a pause. She didn't know what to say, how to proceed. "Effie, I'm sorry it's taken me this long to call. I'm very sorry, and you don't have to say you forgive me. I just want you to know I made a mistake, and I hope I can make it up to you now. I'm going to do everything I can to do that."

"Oh, Uncle Dominic."

I heard her sniffle.

"I've already forgiven you, silly. I just really miss you."

"Me too, honey."

"Where are you, Uncle Dominic?"

"I'm in New Jersey, but I am planning a trip to Florida very soon."

"You are?"

"Yep. I just have to talk to your mom to arrange some things. Maybe you can show me around?"

"I'd love that! And I'm a great tour guide. I know everything around here. Hold on!"

I heard Isabella's voice in the background, asking if she was still awake. Effie made up an excuse that she had to get a drink of water, and she would get back to sleep if her mom would stop interrupting. I laughed at that. A few moments later, she came back on the line. This time, she spoke in a whisper.

"Sorry about that. My mom thinks I'm a little kid."

"Well, you are a kid, and I probably called you pretty late. Don't you have school tomorrow?"

"Yeah, but no big deal. I'll be fine."

"I'm not so sure. I'll tell you what. Why don't we say good-bye for now, and you save my phone number and call me tomorrow after school. In the meantime, I'll call your mom and see if I can't arrange a visit."

"That would be great. I will call you at five minutes after three tomorrow when I get off the bus, okay?"

"I am writing it down in my agenda."

"Uncle Dominic?"

"Yes?"

"I'm not supposed to tell anyone, but I'm super excited and can't wait. Since you're so far away, it's okay if I tell you, right?"

"I won't tell a soul."

She giggled. "I'm getting a baby brother or sister soon," she whispered. "Mom told me last week."

Isabella was pregnant. I felt taken aback, left out almost. Like everyone was getting on with the living of their lives, and I was stuck here, in the past, alone.

"That's great, honey. I'm excited for you." I hoped she couldn't hear the effort it took me to say that.

"I'll be able to babysit her too. And I'm not doing it for free!"

I laughed. "Nor should you."

"Effie!" I heard Isabella's voice. "Give me that phone, young lady. You know you're not allowed to be on it after eight."

"Gotta go!"

She hung up. I smiled to myself, wondering when we'd finally tell her the truth. Tell her I was her father.

I held on to the phone, knowing it would ring in the next minute, and right on cue, it did. I answered.

"Why are you calling her at ten o'clock on a school night?" Isabella asked.

"Because I should never have stopped calling her."

WE MADE arrangements for me to fly to Florida the following week. Surprisingly, Isabella wasn't opposed to it. Maybe it was because we were in agreement that we wouldn't tell her until she was an adult that I was her father. It was just safer that way, especially now that I'd taken over the Benedetti family. I had enemies before, and I would have more now. And I wouldn't make her a target for those enemies.

Reuniting with Effie was more wonderful than I could have imagined. I needed her sweet innocence, her clever way of looking at things, and her carefree nature. I spent a week in a hotel nearby and took her to school and picked her up daily. Over the weekend, we drove down to the Keys to visit Salvatore and Lucia and meet my other nieces and brand-new nephew. Lucia tolerated my presence but was too tired to do much of anything but feed little Sergio, who was born weighing over ten pounds and had the exact same eyes of his namesake.

But all the while we were there, I felt like an outsider. Effie loved and accepted me. Salvatore too. But I didn't belong in their world. I felt like I cast a dark shadow on their doorsteps, and the fact disgusted me. I didn't want to be that.

When I returned home, I went to the house in the Adirondacks. To Franco's big, spacious mansion. For the next eight months, I took care of family business, keeping as busy as I could, but walked through the house like a ghost. I kept everything Gia had worn until her scent wore off the clothes, and even then, I packed up the duffel bag and set it in the closet beside my things.

I thought in time I would forget her. Or at least stop missing her. But I didn't. It didn't seem to matter how much time passed.

I kept track of her. She and her mother sold the house she'd grown up in near Philadelphia. Her mother moved back to Italy, where her sister still lived, and Gia rented an apartment in

Manhattan. I went into the city often, and each time I did, I got as close as the front door of the building before turning around.

She didn't need me in her life.

I decided I hated the house in the Adirondacks. It only held dark memories of times past, of hatred and jealousy and an old world I wasn't sure I wanted to be a part of anymore. All those years, I'd wanted nothing more than to be boss. All that time, I hadn't realized what it meant to be that. That my father would be dead. That anyone who mattered would be gone. I felt more alone than I ever had in my life, and in a way, as long as I stayed here, I knew I would be stuck in this cold, empty past.

It was on the morning I decided to put the house on the market that I saw the newspaper article. Angus Scava had been indicted on charges of drug trafficking, racketeering, and tax fraud, and was a person of interest in several murders, including that of Mateo Castellano. The key witness? Victor Scava.

I guess he wished he'd cut out his nephew's tongue now.

I closed the paper and stood. Going to the window, I opened it and inhaled a deep breath of fresh, cool autumn air. Summer was at an end.

I decided something else that morning too. I took the keys to my SUV and walked out the door, calling my attorney, Mr. Marino, the executor of my father's will, on the way. I gave him instruction to not only put this house on the market but Salvatore's as well. I also instructed him to find me a place in New York City. One that had never belonged to anyone before me. One that would be mine from the start. It would be the first step in my truly taking over the Benedetti crime family.

I didn't do this in anger. I didn't do it to retaliate. I simply did it because I needed to. I did it because I didn't want this anymore, not alone. I didn't want this empty house. This empty life. I wanted her. I wanted Gia.

A king needed a fucking queen. And I'd been a fool to let her think she could walk away.

I DROVE INTO THE CITY, arriving at lunchtime. I knew where Gia worked. She waitressed over the weekends while attending law school during the week. I walked into the restaurant, The Grand Café, and looked around the busy place, spotting her instantly.

"I want a table in her section," I told the host.

"Do you have a reservation, Sir?" he asked.

I glanced down at the stocky little man and took out my wallet. "Here's my reservation," I said, handing him some bills.

He cleared his throat, and I followed him to a table. She didn't see me when I was seated, and I opened my menu to wait for her. My heart beat frantically. Although I knew she had no boyfriend and hardly any friends, I wasn't sure how I'd be received. She kept to herself, and I imagined her existence to be as lonely as mine.

She came over, writing something in her tablet as she introduced herself. Then she looked up.

Our gazes locked, and she stopped midsentence. No, midword.

She had her hair pulled back into a messy bun, and she'd let her bangs grow out and had pinned the thick, glossy dark fringe to one side. She wore a white button-down shirt and black pants and the ugliest shoes I'd ever seen, and she couldn't have looked more beautiful to me.

"Wh…" Her voice caught in her throat.

"It's been a long time."

She broke our gaze and glanced around. "I…Dominic…"

"Sit down."

"What are you doing here?"

"I wanted to see you." *I needed to see you.*

She looked around the café. "I...You... I can't do this."

She quickly walked away, untied her apron, and disappeared through a doorway.

I got up to follow her, not caring that I almost knocked a trayful of drinks out of a waitress's hands as the door swung open and I entered the bustling kitchen.

"Sir, you can't be back here," someone said.

I saw the back of Gia's head as she disappeared out another door. I followed, ignoring everyone, and pushed through the door that led into an alley. The stench of the city and the trash containers overwhelmed my senses, and I wondered how the two standing across the way smoking cigarettes could stand it.

Seeing me, they quickly dropped their cigarette butts and put them out before going inside the door I'd just exited.

"Gia!" I called out, looking in one direction, then the other, where I spotted her leaning against a wall. Arms folded across her belly, the sunshine bounced off the natural red tones in her dark hair as she waited there for me, head bowed.

"You shouldn't be here," she said, looking up as I approached.

To be this close to her, to see her, hear her... "I should be right here," I said, reaching out to touch her, but pulling back, afraid she'd run off, disappear. "In fact, I should never have let you walk away. That was my biggest mistake when it came to you."

She watched me, confusion in her eyes.

"I made a lot of them, but that was the biggest. Letting you believe Scava, that you were somehow some sort of monster— that was another one. Making you watch that night—" I shook my head. "You're too clean for that. I should never have let you see—"

"Stop. I don't want to hear." She put her hands over her ears like a little kid.

"Gia—"

"You have to go," she said, cutting me off.

"Gia?" Someone opened the door and called out.

I took Gia's arms.

"You have customers," the woman said, her cautious gaze on me.

"Just a minute," Gia said, never looking away from me.

"You okay?" the woman asked.

Gia nodded. "I'll be in in a minute."

The woman went back inside.

"I've gone to see Effie," I said. "And I'm selling the houses—"

"You need to go," she said, cutting me off. She straightened and wiped her eyes, attempting to clear all emotion from her face. "You can't be here. You just can't."

The door opened again, and this time, the woman returned with two men.

"Gia," one of the men said, walking out. "Everything okay here?"

"Go, Dominic. I don't want you here."

The man came to stand a few feet from us. "You heard her. You need to leave, Sir."

"Gia." I reached out for her, but she turned her back and disappeared behind the man and back inside the building.

"Sir," the man said.

I glared at him, then saw the woman watching me from the doorway. I turned and walked away. But I didn't leave. Well, I walked out of the alley, but I didn't leave the city.

If she wouldn't have me, then I'd make her keep her promise to me.

I drove to her apartment building and rang random apartments until someone buzzed me in, anger and confusion and rejection circling like a hurricane in my head. It was easy to get into 4A, her shabby little place with its single bedroom, tiny kitchen, and living room barely as big as my bathroom. Light almost penetrated through the window, but not quite, not with the shadow of the building across the street blocking the sun. I looked around the space, opening every drawer, knowing I had no right, but feeling pissed off enough to not care. I'd opened my heart. Fuck, I'd poured it out. And she couldn't be bothered to give me the fucking time of day?

Well, fuck her.

I'd remind her of her promise.

I unscrewed the lightbulb overhead, took my pistol out of the back of my jeans, and set it on her coffee table. Then I sat back on the couch, watched the door, and waited.

26

GIA

I spilled drinks on three customers and dropped two plates of food after Dominic left. I'd never expected to see him again. I'd never thought he'd show up. I didn't bother wondering how he'd found me. He had resources. He'd probably been keeping tabs on me all these months.

It kind of pissed me off, now that the shock had worn off. How dare he walk back into my life, when I was just getting it back together? Scraping pieces of myself into something resembling some sort of normal.

After the day we'd met with Scava, I'd felt cold for a long time. Cold and empty. My mom and I had mourned Mateo together. I was pretty sure neither of us had really stopped grieving, but it had been time to move on. We sold the house, and she moved back to Italy with her sister. I moved to New York City and decided I would get my law degree and put assholes like Angus and Victor Scava away. It was what I could do to honor Mateo's memory.

I'd kept the flash drive with the phone recording. I'd only just turned it over a few weeks ago, in fact. I knew if I did it too soon, Angus would know it was me and retaliate. I'd sent it anonymously, and it had worked. They'd gone after Victor, and Victor was now their star witness against the bigger fish: his uncle.

Seeing Victor like that at the restaurant that night, beaten, his uncle threatening to cut out his tongue, it disgusted me. It made me see without a doubt that this wasn't who I was. Scava calling me a monster? I had believed him. And I guess I would have been one if I'd gone through with what I'd said I wanted.

The bus dropped me off a block from my apartment. It was almost midnight, and my feet and back hurt. I'd worked a double today, but I needed the money. My mom wanted to help me out, but she didn't have any more than I did so I lived in a shitty apartment in a shittier neighborhood and made my own way.

I climbed the apartment stairs and unlocked the outer door, then went up to the fourth floor. The hallway light was out, again, so I used the flashlight in my phone to slide my key into the lock and turn it. When I reached to switch on the lights in the apartment, nothing happened. I wondered if it was a building-wide outage. But then I saw the light coming from beneath the door of my neighbor's unit, and my heartbeat picked up. My eyes widened and I strained to see into the dark apartment just making out a shape in front of the window sitting on the couch.

Was it Scava's men already? Did he know it was me who'd turned over evidence? He wasn't stupid. Maybe I was for having done it.

"Don't fucking try to run."

Relief flooded me when I first heard Dominic's voice. But then, I remembered that afternoon. How I'd sent him away.

"Come inside and close the door, Gia."

I stood there as goose bumps covered my body at the sound of his voice. His command.

"I said come inside and shut the door."

He wouldn't hurt me. I knew that. But his voice sounded strange. Like it had once before on the night I'd found out who he really was.

"I didn't know you broke into apartments," I said, going for casual, walking inside and closing the door.

"You'd be amazed at what I can do."

He reached over and turned on the lamp beside the sofa. That was when I caught sight of the pistol on the coffee table and took a step back.

He stood. "I'm not going to hurt you," he said.

"What do you want, Dominic?"

He stalked toward me, and all I could do was watch him move, remembering how broad his shoulders were, how much space he took up. How being near him made my body feel.

"You owe me something, Gia."

He stopped when the toes of his boots bumped against my shoes. He wrapped a hand around my head and twined his fingers into the hair at the nape of my neck, making me gasp, making my heart pound.

"Domi—" But I never got the word out because he closed his mouth over mine and devoured the sound.

I'd forgotten the feel of him, of his lips. I'd forgotten the way he tasted, the way his body felt so hard and powerful, forgot how he tugged my hair and forced my face up to his. His tongue slipped into my mouth, and I closed my eyes, leaning into his hand as his other one slid up over my hip and waist to cup my breast and squeeze the nipple.

He broke our kiss and turned my head to the side to whisper in my ear.

"You owe me something, and I'm here to collect."

I pressed against his chest, squeezing the muscle beneath it, then moved my hands to his biceps and curled them around before I kissed him back, liking it when he bit my lip a little, liking the feel of his cock hardening at my belly.

Hearing the door lock behind me, I startled. Dominic's blue-gray eyes bore into mine, different than they'd been that afternoon. Harder. Like he used to look at me in the beginning at the cabin. Like he looked at me when he fucked me.

I stood there panting, my mouth open like some puppy, my eyes tearing as he tugged a little harder on my hair.

"Aren't you curious what you owe?"

He walked me through the small apartment and into my bedroom, dropping me on the bed before climbing onto it. It was my old bed from home. I'd had it for more than fifteen years, and it creaked beneath our combined weight.

"Your apartment's a fucking mess."

He pulled his shirt up over his head, the moonlight making the white clock face of the tattoo on his chest appear almost ghostlike.

"Shut up," I said, my hands on his chest, unable to get enough of his heat, his strength. I'd missed him. I'd missed him so much.

He ripped my shirt down the middle and pushed it from my arms. I would have been pissed if I wasn't so turned-on. He looked down at me and pushed the cups of my bra beneath my breasts. Taking one into his mouth, he sucked and then bit a little harder than he had my lip.

I groaned, arching my back.

He laid his full weight on me and looked at me, his face an inch from mine. Watching me, he took my hand and dragged it to himself, to his back, to where I felt the butt of the pistol I hadn't noticed he'd tucked into his jeans.

I gasped and yanked my hand away, or tried to, but he wouldn't let me.

"Take it," he said.

"No."

"Take it, Gia."

I shook my head.

"Fucking take it." He wrapped my hand around it and together, we drew it out so that I held the gun.

I looked at it, then at him.

"Do you remember what you promised me?" he asked, sitting up, trapping me between his thighs.

"Stop. I don't want this."

But he kept his hand wrapped around mine, so I couldn't let it go.

"I don't give a fuck what you want. I did, this afternoon, but you had me fucking dismissed."

"Dominic—"

He brought the gun between us and pressed the mouth of the barrel to his chest.

My heart pounded.

"You promised to kill me. You swore it."

I began to silently weep, heavy tears sliding from my face onto the bed. Dominic wrapped his other hand around my throat and squeezed. The tears stopped, and my eyes went wide as I gasped for breath. He cocked the gun, never taking his eyes off me.

"Pull the trigger, Gia."

I tried to shake my head, but I couldn't move.

"I'm an intruder. It'll be self-defense. Now keep your promise, and fucking pull the trigger."

He released my throat, and I choked and gasped for breath, my hand weak around the gun.

"I don't want to," I said, my voice coming out thin.

He tapped my face, small slaps that didn't hurt but that invaded.

"*I don't want to,*" he mimicked.

Dominic wrapped his hand back around my throat.

"You didn't keep your promise!" I cried out.

He kept his hand there, but his hold remained loose. I thought I saw the faintest hint of a smile play along his lips.

"You didn't fucking keep your promise!" I said again.

He let me pull my hand free from his, and I kept the pistol pointed at him.

"That's it. Get mad," he said.

He took the wrist of the hand that held the gun and pinned it to the bed and while he kept his gaze locked on mine, his hands worked the buttons of my pants, opening them, reaching inside to cup my sex over my panties.

"Get fucking pissed, Gia."

I closed my eyes, the feel of his hands on me again, of my own need, it fucking overwhelmed everything.

"You let him walk away!"

He slid his hand inside, fingers finding my clit, my slick, ready entrance.

"You let me walk away," I said more quietly.

Fuck. I closed my eyes and thrust up into his hand.

"I couldn't make you stay," he said quietly.

When I opened my eyes, I saw he'd leaned down over me.

"It had to be your choice." His voice came dark and husky. "But that was then and this is now and I changed my mind."

"Fuck me," I managed as he jerked my pants and panties down so I worked them off the rest of the way. "I need to feel you inside me, Dominic."

The pistol lay forgotten beside us as he used both hands to undo his jeans then push them and his briefs off.

"If I fuck you"—

His cock stood ready at my entrance.

"If you say yes"—

I opened my legs as wide as I could.

"You won't be able to walk away. Not again. Not ever again."

He thrust. He wasn't waiting for my answer, not really.

And I wouldn't have said no.

I cried out, and he held still inside me.

"Open your eyes, Gia. Look at me. I'm right fucking here."

I did, trying to move my hips beneath him but unable to.

"Hear me, Gia. You won't be able to change your mind. I won't let you walk away again. Do you understand me?"

I nodded, arching my back. "Please. I need—"

He pulled out and thrust again, I gasped, biting my own lip, tasting blood. *Blood.* With him, there would be blood.

"More," I said.

He smiled, pulled out, and impaled me again.

"You fucking left."

He was angry and furious and sexy as fucking hell.

"I won't ever let you walk away from me again. Fucking never."

I bit my lip again, harder, until I tasted more blood, and I came. I came with him watching me. I came watching him. My pussy throbbed around his cock, and he never even blinked until I'd squeezed every drop of pleasure from him, taking from him what he gave, knowing this sealed our pact, knowing that when he moved again, when he fucked me and I watched him come, that I was his.

I was his forever.

27

DOMINIC

"What did you have to do with Angus Scava's arrest?" I sat on a stool at the kitchen counter peeling an apple, watching her as she made coffee. Although she had her back to me, I saw her stiffen.

"Nothing."

"Liar."

She poured two cups of coffee out of the old-fashioned machine and set one before me. She sipped from her mug and stood on the other side of the counter, her eyes on mine. I could see her thinking as she worked out how to answer. Did she think I hadn't realized the flash drive with the recording had disappeared when we'd left for my father's funeral?

I picked up my mug and waited.

"Nothing," she said again, turning away.

I sipped from the mug. "Christ. What is this shit?" I looked at the dark-brown water in my mug. That's exactly what it tasted like: fucking dirty brown water.

"Don't be a snob. The coffee machine was here when I moved in. It's fine."

She took another sip, but even I saw how she had to force herself to do it.

"You get used to it," she said.

"I'm not getting used to it." I stood and walked around the aisle to the sink and dumped my mug down the drain before taking hers and doing the same.

"What are you doing?"

"Let's go get some real coffee." I shook my head as she tried to argue. "You're Italian, for Christ's sake. You can't tell me you like that crap."

"I didn't say I liked it."

She grabbed her purse and jacket, and we walked out.

Once outside, we walked two blocks to a small café. Inside, we took a seat in a corner away from the windows. Gia ordered a cappuccino and I ordered a double espresso. After they came, I asked again.

"Gia, what did you have to do with Scava's arrest?"

She shrugged a shoulder and kept her eyes on the flower design the barista had made out of her froth.

"I handed over the recording. I sent it anonymously."

I shook my head. "Do you think Scava won't know who sent it?"

"He'll think it's Victor."

"He might, but he might not. He will retaliate, you know that."

She met my gaze. "You'll keep me safe."

That took me back.

Yes, I would keep her safe, but I didn't expect her to say it, because saying it came with so much more.

"I couldn't just let him walk away scot-free, Dominic. Mateo died for that evidence."

"I know. But you put yourself in danger now."

"He's behind bars."

"He can run his entire organization from behind those bars. All he has to do is give the order."

"I couldn't not do it."

I drank from my cup. "I know. You'll come back with me today. You can't stay in your apartment."

"I have a job and school."

"You don't need a job, and you can take a semester off."

"I've already taken too many years off. I'm twenty-five, Dominic."

"If you're dead, you'll be taking the rest of your life off, won't you? You're studying to be an attorney. Which do you think is the better option?"

"Shut up."

"I'm putting both houses on the market, my father's and Salvatore's. We'll move to the city."

"We're just moving in together? Just like that?"

"You never once struck me as a girl for a long courtship with flowers and romantic walks on the beach."

"I'm not. But it's fast, isn't it?"

"I want you with me. I thought I made that clear last night."

"So I'll always be an available piece of ass for you?"

I sat back, confused now. "That's what you think?"

She didn't reply but watched me through hooded eyes.

"Gia, you're a bright girl. Do you really think I came after you after eight months being apart, spilling my heart out to you, because I think you're a nice *'piece of ass'*?"

"Do you consider what happened last night, what you said, to be spilling your heart out?"

Again, I felt taken aback. "What do you want? I've never been a flowers and romantic walks on the beach type either."

"Maybe I am after all," she said defensively, averting her gaze from mine momentarily.

I smiled, still a little confused, but understanding. I leaned forward and took her chin in my hand, raising it so she looked at me. "I love you. Is that what you want to hear?"

She only stared as if she didn't believe me.

"I love you, and those eight months without you were like a little slice of hell worse than the seven years I'd lived before I found you huddled in the corner of that rotten cabin. I have never in my life wanted someone as much as I want you. And as much as I love fucking you, what I mean is that I want you in my fucking life, not just my bed. I don't want to let you out of my sight again. I want you safe and close and—"

She cried and smiled at once.

"What?" I asked.

"You are a romantic, in your own weird way."

She leaned forward and kissed my lips softly.

"You don't have the smoothest way with words, but you have a bigger heart than you think, Dominic Benedetti."

She sat back in her chair, her hands still in mine, clutching onto mine as I did hers.

I felt flustered looking at her. I felt...unsure. I'd never told any girl these things before. I'd never felt them or even bothered pretending I did. With her, though, I meant every word.

"Maybe we should just get married while we're at it." I said it before I lost my nerve.

Gia laughed, then wiped away a tear before returning her hand to mine. "Are you proposing?"

"Are you saying yes?"

"I don't know. Aren't you supposed to get down on one knee or something?"

I looked around at the other people in the place. No one was paying attention to us, but they would be in a minute. I shoved the table next to ours out of the way—luckily it was empty—and got on one knee, her hands still in mine.

"You already have me on my knees," I said.

"Oh my God, Dominic, I wasn't serious! Get up!"

She looked around and tried to pull me up.

"No. Gia Castellano, I love you, and I want you to marry me. I'm asking you to. Here on one fucking knee."

Everyone was staring now.

Gia's face flushed red, and she looked from them to me and smiled wide and cried and nodded her head. "I will."

I got up and drew her to her feet to stand with me, wrapping my arms around her and closing my mouth over hers as everyone in the place started to clap and whistle.

She broke our kiss and whispered in my ear.

"That was so embarrassing, Dominic."

"If you want romance, you're going to get over-the-top romance." I cupped her chin and tilted her head back to kiss her again, a long, soft kiss.

"I love you," she said. "For a long time now. I don't even know when it happened."

"I think it was the first time I saw your eyes. When they were glaring at me," I added, making her smile. "Let's get out of here."

IT TOOK me two months to do the one thing I needed to do to close the door on the past before I could move on with my future.

"You want me to come with you?" Gia asked from beside me.

We had just driven through the gates of the cemetery and pulled up near my family's plot.

I looked at the gated-off area, at the three largest stones.

"No. I need to do this alone." I squeezed her hand.

She nodded, and I climbed out of the sedan with the bundles of flowers. My breath fogged in the brisk morning air, and all I heard was the lonely sound of leaves crushing under my feet. I made my way up the hill and through the headstones of countless other Benedettis until I reached theirs.

Squatting down, I cleared some of the weeds, then lay the flowers before each of the stones. First, my mother. Then my brother. And finally, my father.

That was when I paused, traced his name and the dates. I took a seat on a bench nearest his grave and glanced at the waiting car. With its tinted windows, I couldn't see inside and would have felt foolish for someone to see me, but I cleared my throat anyway and turned back to my father's grave.

"I should have done this when you were alive."

My eyes felt hot and damp. Death was so final and regret so permanent.

"But that night fucked with me, Paps. You telling me the truth like that, it fucked with my head. I wasn't like either of my brothers. Sergio felt duty bound, and Salvatore is just too good for this life. Me, I wanted it. Oh man, I wanted it so bad I could taste it.

"You're right, you know. What you wrote in the will about me being the most like you. You're right. Who'd have guessed it, huh, considering."

I wiped my hand across my face and stood, made a short turn, and kicked some pinecones away while I got myself under control. I didn't even hear her come up behind me until she slid her hand into mine and held it. Gia stood close but gave me space at the same time. This is what we'd become to each other. It was like we knew, like we felt each other's needs, and neither of us could stand the pain of the other.

Gia, a woman I'd hurt, one I'd been paid to break, had given me a part of her soul and stolen a piece of mine.

"Okay?" she asked quietly.

I nodded, and we walked back to the grave.

"I love you, old man. I miss you, and I wish I hadn't wasted the last seven years of your life. But you took care of me in the end, didn't you? You made sure I'd have the family's allegiance. And I forgive you for that night, for telling me like that."

Just then, a robin landed on my father's headstone.

Gia gasped beside me. The bird simply perched there, unmoving, and watched me for a long moment before it flew off and landed on a branch of the closest tree, still watching us. We remained silent until finally, it flew off into the sky.

"Wow," Gia said.

I exhaled a breath with a smile. "I don't think it's a sign or something."

"A robin symbolizes renewal, Dominic. Maybe it was your father—"

I touched the headstone one more time and turned to her, caressing her cheek, kissing the tip of her cold nose. "That's sweet, but it's just not really Franco Benedetti's style," I said with a short laugh.

I DIDN'T WANT Gia to know I was worried. If Angus Scava suspected Gia turned over evidence, he'd send men after her. He wouldn't need proof to do it. But I hoped with Victor coming forward as a key witness, he'd blame it all on his nephew. Victor would have had access to the recordings too, after all, and that recording was only a small piece of the evidence against Angus.

Gia quit her job, but she wouldn't quit school. So I moved in with her into her crap apartment for just over a month until I signed the lease on a condo in Little Italy. We fell in love with it the first time we saw it. It was charming with its exposed brick, reclaimed wooden floors, and huge windows. Gia and I had similar taste in furnishings: ultramodern, and it had nothing in common with any of the houses my family owned.

Moving in together felt so natural, as if we'd lived together our whole lives.

Effie flew up to New York to visit. Isabella let her stay with us over the Thanksgiving break, and she and Gia hit it off from the start. I liked seeing Effie so at ease, and as much as I wished I could tell her the truth, I knew it wasn't the time. I saw Gia watching me with her, and I hated the look of pity she sometimes got. We never talked about it, though.

Ruling the Benedetti family came with its challenges. Now that I was boss, things were different than I'd always thought they were. I had no one I trusted. Salvatore didn't want to have anything to do with the family business, and the taint of Roman's betrayal still tasted bitter on my tongue. I retained Henderson's services, but I had learned that everyone had their own agenda. I wouldn't be played again, not by anyone.

I married Gia over Christmas. We flew to Calabria, Italy, for the wedding. That house was the only one of the family homes I'd kept. I hadn't spent much time in it during my youth, and it didn't seem to hold the stain of betrayal in its walls. Salvatore and Lucia attended with all three kids. So did Isabella and Luke and their new baby girl, Josie. Effie was our flower girl, and Salvatore and Lucia stood as witnesses. Gia's mother and aunt attended, but that was all, and it was fine. I guess we were both loners. But together, just us, it didn't seem to matter.

I didn't show Gia the newspaper that arrived on our doorstep the morning of our wedding. I didn't tell her that Victor Scava had disappeared, along with all the evidence against Angus. I didn't mention the small box tucked inside the paper either. Angus Scava's wedding gift. A box containing Victor's tongue. Or what I assumed to be Victor's tongue. I guess it could have been Joe Blow's tongue, but I didn't think so. The card with it was addressed to the "happy couple" and wished us a long life.

I threw the box and the card into the fire.

This was mafia life. No rest for the wicked and all that shit. Both Gia and I had our eyes wide open, and we'd face whatever challenges came our way together. I'd keep her hands clean, though. I'd keep her pure and carry all the weight. All the blood.

I understood Salvatore for the first time in my life, then. I understood his decision to leave and respected it.

28

GIA

Dominic thought I didn't know about Angus Scava's release. He thought I didn't know Victor's disappearance most likely meant his death. I would let him believe it for now. This day was too important to spoil with talk of the Scavas. I was going to marry the man I loved. A savage beast of a man who'd been through hell and walked out on top of his world. I don't think he realized how lonely it would be at the top, not until he stood in his father's shoes.

But together, we weren't lonely. We fit perfectly, Dominic and I. It was almost as though we were the last two pieces in a puzzle, lost for years and found under the dusty couch. And once linked together, the empty space was filled and everything was complete as if it had never been empty at all.

When I was a little girl, I believed in fairy tales. Not the ones Disney tells. No, I believed the real ones. The scary ones. The ones where not everyone got to meet their prince in shining armor or got their happily-ever-after. I learned too young how fucked up life could be, how pain and suffering and death lurked behind every smile. But I never stopped believing in the power of love, and I always loved the beasts more than I did the princes.

Dominic was my beast. And somehow, I was his princess.

I stood along with Effie at the entrance of the ancient, tiny chapel where we'd be wed. I wore the antique-lace wedding dress passed down from my grandmother, clutching roses so red they almost appeared black. Two men opened the doors, and the small gathering stood. The scent of incense and time poured from the open doors.

I met Dominic's gaze through the net of my veil, and my heart thudded against my chest. For a moment, I wished I had accepted Salvatore's proposal to walk me down the aisle, because suddenly my knees grew weak, and I wasn't sure my legs would carry me the distance between us.

But then Dominic smiled, and I saw how that dimple softened his face, giving him a younger appearance, an innocent one. *An angel of death.* That's how I'd seen him at the cabin, where he'd been sent to break me. Now I knew it was true. He was my angel of death. But he would slay all my enemies, and he would protect and love me.

The organ began to play the wedding march: a heavy, dark gothic piece I'd chosen. One Dominic had raised his eyebrows at but accepted without question. Effie walked ahead of me scattering bloodred rose petals in her wake. I took my first step, standing taller as I did, meeting every eye in the church, knowing that even though Dominic and I may never be accepted by some, it wouldn't matter, not anymore. We only needed each other.

Dominic took the last steps to meet me, and with his arm around my waist, he led me to the altar. We stood before the priest. The music stopped playing, and he began the service. I didn't hear much of what he said. I couldn't stop looking at Dominic, and he seemed unable to take his gaze from me.

I realized then I was wrong when I thought the love I'd find would be an ugly and twisted thing. I realized that love itself would bend any ugliness into its own—sometimes strange—sort of beauty.

Because it had been in those darkest moments that love had crept in and tethered us together, tighter than any chains could.

It had been in that darkness that beauty seemed to want to find us most.

I'd always preferred night to day, and I'd never been afraid of the dark. And as Dominic and I stood hand in hand, promising ourselves to each other, I knew this was exactly where I belonged, where we both belonged. We'd come from ugliness. Suffering had put us on the road to our destiny. But Dominic had been wrong about one thing. Even in our world, our love would last forever. He and I, we would make our own happily-ever-after.

SERGIO: A DARK MAFIA ROMANCE

ABOUT THIS BOOK

I'm the first-born son of the mafia king. The favorite. Destined to rule, I'm a dangerous man, a ruthless one. But in my world, you have to be.

Then Natalie stumbles into my life. Wrong place. Wrong time.

Twice, fate put her in my path.
Twice, fate placed the innocent lamb at the mercy of the monster.

I gave her a chance to walk away. Told her it would be better for her if she did.
But she didn't listen.
And now it's too late.
Because I'm not good. I never wanted to be. And I won't let her go anymore. See, I'm not the hero. When I touch her, it's with dirty hands.

I know my reckoning is coming though. I know I'll burn for the things I've done, the sins I've committed. And I don't deny hell is where I belong, but I want my time first. I want my time with her.

She's mine.
Forever.
No matter what.

LETTER FROM NATASHA

PLEASE READ THIS BEFORE BEGINNING SERGIO'S STORY

Dear Reader,

Sergio's story wasn't one I ever thought I'd write. He was a secondary character in Salvatore and that was all. At least until late in 2017.

When a story starts to form in my mind, it's usually the hero who takes shape, whose eyes I see, who slowly grows into a living, breathing person for me. It's usually his voice that first sparks the story.

In Sergio's case, this started a few months ago with a song, Darlin' by Houndmouth. From the first moment I heard it, I thought this is it. This is Sergio. This is his song. Even as I write this, I can almost feel him, feel his arms around me, his body heavy as he moves slowly to the music, his breath warm at my cheek as he sings along.

I feel like Sergio was waiting his turn. Like he was patient and watched as the Benedetti world took form and grew layers and finally, he was up. He had a story too, and it had to be told, no matter what. And this is why I'm writing this letter. There will be a second one at the end of the book. Please do not read ahead.

This book is not a traditional romance and I know it will be upsetting to some of you, but I had no magic up my sleeve for this one. No tricks. No nothing. This is the only story I could tell for Sergio and I feel like from the first second I heard his voice, as much as it broke my heart, he knew it too.

I don't want to say too much more here. I don't want to give anything away. I just want to ask that you keep an open mind.

As always, thank you so much for choosing to spend your time reading my book. I am honored and awed, still, by this. I hope you fall in love and maybe even have your heart broken a little. I hope you feel every single thing the way I felt it and maybe when you play that song, you'll feel Sergio's arms around you too.

Love,
Natasha

PROLOGUE
NATALIE

"Wrong place, wrong time, sweetheart."

The words echo in my head.

I've done this before. Twice in my life now, I've been at the wrong place at the wrong time. Isn't there some sort of karmic balancing? Like isn't it enough to witness this kind of violence just once in a lifetime?

Last time was six years ago. I was fourteen and standing in front of the freezer of the convenience store down the street from my house deciding which ice cream bar I wanted. I remember the humming of the air conditioner. Liking the cool inside on that too hot August day. It was one of the few times my parents let me go alone. We didn't live in the best neighborhood.

The men came in so quickly, I barely registered the fact they were wearing ski masks before the first gunshot went off. I dove to the ground and shut my ears to the commands they shouted, but the man with the greasy shirt saw me. He came at me and I would have screamed if I could find my voice, but the others' screams muted me, and when he gripped me by my hair and hauled me to my feet, I followed where he led me.

Another gunshot was followed by another scream and I swear I saw red splatter the walls.

Blood.

But when he threw me to the ground in the last aisle and I registered what he meant to do, it all became surreal.

Gunshots and fists and screams all seemed in the distance. Like they weren't part of my reality anymore because my reality was about to change. My reality came down to him and me on the floor of this forgotten shop, with blood seeping from beneath the aisle divider. Fear in the voices of the others trapped here with me. Him with his pants undone. Him with his hands in my jeans. Me watching, mute. Trying to shove him away.

I remember the bell over the door going again.

Remember the sound of footsteps.

Someone cursing.

I remember the sound of a gun being cocked. Readied. How I knew what that little click meant I'm not sure, but it's an unmistakable sound. I remember the look on the face of the one between my legs as he registered cold steel on the back of his head.

We looked up at the man in the dark suit at the same time. He wore black from head to toe, a dark angel. His pistol shone bright in the blinking fluorescent light. The angel called me to go to him. I did. I scrambled to my feet and went. He glanced down to where my jeans were undone before meeting my eyes. He pulled me to him, put one hand on the back of my head, burying my face in his belly.

He told me to keep my eyes closed. To cover my ears. Said he'd try not to get blood on me.

I didn't think. I did as he said. Put my hands over my ears. And I swear I know what a bullet tearing through flesh sounds like now.

But all that I've managed to file away. Locked up in a box until now.

It's his words that play back over and over again. The sound of his voice that I recognize as now, so many years after that terrible day, I crouch behind the decrepit machinery in this abandoned warehouse and hide.

"Wrong place, wrong time, sweetheart."

Sweetheart.

I'll never forget that voice. Never forget the casual way he called me sweetheart. And I recognize it now. The man in the suit, my dark angel. The man who killed without flinching. The man who saved my life once. It's him. He's here.

And when he shifts his gaze in my direction, I swear he hears the pounding of my heart against my chest. Swear it'll give me away.

Except that this time, if he finds me, he won't be saving me.

1

SERGIO

F uck. I hate these fucking warehouses. Dusty and always frigid.

I'm flanked by two of my men. Four more soldiers trail us with a dozen more outside. It's to make an impression. Joe and Lance Vitelli have overstepped.

Lance. Who the fuck names their kid Lance in this business? It's no wonder he's acting out. Trying to prove he's not a pussy.

Our footsteps echo off the old machinery as I follow Roman, my uncle, through the main room and to the back where the brothers are being held. There's no door to that room and the glow of the single light bulb is a contrast to the pitch black of the rest of the place.

The sound of a fist connecting with flesh is followed by a grunt. The grunt, I know, belongs to either Joe or Lance. I pick lint off my sleeve and adjust the cuff of my shirt as we near the entrance. Roman steps into the room, stands to the side, folding his hands together. He takes in what's going on, then turns to me, gives a brief nod and waits.

I walk into the room, crack my neck. Slept bad last night.

The sight that greets me is not an unfamiliar one. The offenders are sitting in straight back chairs, but they're not bound. There's a splattering of blood on Joe's white shirt. It's fresh. I guess he's the one who took the punch I heard.

"That's disgusting. Get something on his nose," I say to one of my men.

"It's fucking broke," Joe whines, taking the wad of nasty cloth someone just shoved at him.

I go right up to him. Lean down to get my face in his. "You're lucky *you're* not broke. Be grateful or that'll change."

He breathes in a sharp breath and I know he's biting his lip not to reply.

"Sergio," Lance starts. Lance is the older brother. The slightly smarter one. Or the one with a healthier fear of death.

Of me.

I straighten, turn to him.

"Mr. Benedetti," he corrects.

I wait.

"My brother screwed up, but it's fixed. The girls are back home. No harm, no foul, right?" He attempts to smile but it fails and his lips droop.

"In whose territory do you live?" I ask. It's been a long fucking night already and it's not close to over. I'm tired, so I'll get to the point.

"Yours, sir," he answers.

"In whose territory do your families live? Mothers, sisters, wives, daughters."

Lance's face, which was pale when I got here, goes gray. "Yours, Mr. Benedetti. Benedetti territory."

I nod, shift my gaze to Joe. "To whom has your father pledged your family's loyalty, Joe?" His eyes narrow and when he doesn't answer right away, Lance clears his throat to, but I stop him. "I'm asking your fucking brother."

"Benedetti," Joe says through gritted teeth.

"DeMarco's were once loyal to us too, until they weren't," I remind them. What happened to that family should be enough warning. What is happening and still will happen to Lucia DeMarco, most precious daughter, should be enough. My father's right about fear. But there's more to it. Ruthlessness. It's what truly gets you respect in this business.

He is ruthless.

And I am my father's son.

"You have a sister, don't you?" I ask. "Anna, right? How old is she now?"

Lance just stares back at me, his eyes wide with fear.

I may not agree with how my father is handling the DeMarco girl, but I understand it. "Lucia DeMarco's age, am I right?"

"She's only sixteen, sir," Lance says, his voice a little quieter.

"Yeah, Lucia DeMarco's age when they lost the war they started with us." I don't need to say more.

"Sergio—" Lance starts. "Mr. Benedetti—"

I raise my hand to halt him. "Let's just be clear. I'm going to give you a warning. One chance, because I know your father. He's been a friend to my family. But if you overstep again, the consequences will be more...permanent."

Lance swallows.

"Benedetti's do not deal in flesh trade. Is that clear?"

"Yes, sir," Lance says quickly.

I look at Joe. If looks could kill, I'd be dead right now.

I grab a handful of Joe's hair and tug his head backward. "Is that fucking clear?"

One of my men cocks a gun and Lance whimpers like a fucking girl.

"You the tough one?" I ask Joe. "Sucks to always be in big brother's shadow, doesn't it?" He exhales, shifts his gaze away from mine, but not to his brother. I'm right. Like Dominic, my youngest brother, he knows he'll never be boss and it fucking kills him. "Am I fucking clear, Joe? Or do I need to make an example?" I squeeze the handful of over-gelled hair and if I twist just once in the wrong direction, I'll snap his neck. Quick and clean. No blood on my suit. And he knows it.

"Clear," he says.

I release him, wipe my hand on my pants and decide I'm not done yet. "Now, show me your loyalty. Your gratitude for my family's generosity in this unfortunate event." I step backward, giving him space. He knows what I want and it's going to kill him to do it.

But he's going to do it.

I wait. I'm patient.

"Joe. Just fucking do it," Lance orders his brother when a full minute passes and Joe hasn't moved.

Joe's face is a fiery red and his eyes are filled with rage. But soon, the leg of the chair scrapes across the concrete floor as he drops to his knees at my feet.

I look down at him. Give him more space. And my smile widens as he prostrates himself and his lips touch the toe of my shoe.

I want to kick the son-of-a-bitch, but I don't. I'm a man of my word. I will give them one more chance.

A sound comes from the metal ramp that runs along the perimeter of the large office forming a second level. I look at it. It must have been an observation deck to oversee the plant.

I don't know if anyone else heard it. A glance at Roman tells me he did, but the others haven't noticed. I nod to him. He steps out of the room and two men follow.

When I return my gaze to the spectacle in front of me, I'm very aware of my periphery. I want to catch any movement because that sound was too loud for a mouse.

"Get them out of here," I say to the two soldiers behind the brothers.

"Yes, sir."

I watch as Joe and Lance are walked rudely out of the room. After a few moments, I turn to my men. "Let's go," I say loudly. They walk out. I hang back, switch out the light, listen to the footsteps echo as they vacate the building. I reach for the handgun in its holster beneath my jacket and walk silently toward the direction from where the sound had come.

2

NATALIE

It's been silent for a while, but I'm too scared to move. I can't believe what I saw. What I heard. Benedetti. I know that name. And the one in the suit, the man who once saved my life, I think he heard when my boot caught the screw on the floor. Although I'm maybe overthinking it. He didn't say anything, just carried on with his business.

My knees creak when I finally dare to straighten. I've been hiding, crouched for too long. I'm holding my breath, my eyes wide. It's pitch-black here, but I'm too afraid to use the flashlight on my phone.

I take two steps, peek around the machine that shielded me from their view. The room is empty. I creep to the top of the stairs. My heart is still racing as I grip the ice-cold banister, my knees not quite steady as I make my way down. I tuck my phone into my purse. I'm at the bottom of the stairs, my foot poised to step onto the ground floor when I hear it. The cocking of a gun. Twice in my life now, I've heard a gun cocked at too close a range. It comes in the same instant as the arm that wraps around my throat, that presses my back against a chest of steel.

I scream as the light goes on and three men come into view. The older one in the suit. Two others. And the one who's got the barrel of the gun at my temple.

"Caught the mouse," he says from behind me, his voice a deep timbre.

None of the men smile. They're all looking at me. They each have a weapon in their hands.

"Warehouse is clear," one of them says.

"Should have been swept *before* the meeting," the one holding me says.

The arm loosens around my throat, is removed entirely, taking the gun from my temple. It's decocked.

I gasp for breath, stumble backward. The strap of my purse slides down my arm and the contents spill to the filthy floor. I drop to my knees. The man behind me, he walks around to my front and I'm hyperventilating. I'm looking down at the ground, at the tube of lipstick rolling toward his shoe. It's polished so perfectly I can almost see my own terrified reflection in it.

A hand fists my hair painfully and he draws me up to my feet, up on tip-toe. He drags me toward him.

"A sneaky little mouse."

It's him. The one in charge. Mr. Benedetti was what they'd called him. And the look in his eyes is dark.

"Sergio," the older man says.

Sergio. That's right.

He releases me from his gaze, but not his grip. I can't turn my head, but I shift my eyes to look at the older man.

"You're going to be late for the meeting. I'll take care of this."

Take care of this? By 'this' he means me?

Sergio returns his gaze to me again. He's blurry because my eyes have filled with tears. He tilts his head to the side and narrows his eyes.

"You deal with the meeting, Uncle. I'll deal with our mouse problem."

The grin he gives me coincides with the tightening of his fist. It forces the tears from my eyes.

"Do you want me to leave anyone?" his uncle asks. "A cleaner?"

Cleaner?

"I'll take care of it," my captor says, never looking away. I get the feeling he likes my tears.

"I'll see you tomorrow," his uncle says, and a moment later, we're alone as three sets of footsteps disappear out of the old warehouse.

"What's a cleaner?" I ask, my voice barely audible. I don't know why I ask it.

Sergio draws me into his chest. "Don't worry about that, mouse. What's your name and what do you think you're doing here?"

I'm going to be sick or pee my pants or both.

He's still studying me, his gaze is intense, like he's gleaning information just from looking at me. Then he does something that surprises me. He takes his thumb and wipes it across my face, smears my tear across my cheek and just looks at it for a long minute.

"Well?" he asks again, when he returns his eyes to mine.

"I...I..."

"I...I..." he mimics me with a chuckle, and releases me.

I stumble backward.

"Down," he says, his voice a low, deep command. He's pointing to the floor.

"Wh...what?"

"Your wallet. Give it to me."

I blink away, look at the spilled contents of my purse. I

remember how the other man had dropped to his knees at his command. How he'd kissed the toe of this man's shoe.

"Are you hard of hearing?"

I glance back up at him, confused.

He gives a shake of his head. "Your wallet. Give it to me."

I nod. I drop to my knees because I'm having trouble standing anyway. My hands tremble as I take my wallet and hand it up to him.

He opens it, takes out my driver's license and drops the rest back on the floor.

"Natalie Gregorian." He reads the address. "Asbury Park?" his eyebrows rise. "Far from home, aren't you?"

"My parents' house," I say stupidly.

"What are you doing in Philadelphia, Natalie Gregorian?"

"I go to school here. University of Pennsylvania."

"Ah." He looks at the driver's license again, then tucks it into his pocket and returns his gaze to me. "And what are you doing at this warehouse, in the middle of nowhere, tonight of all nights?"

"I have a project." I wasn't supposed to come tonight. I decided at the last minute.

Again, his eyebrows go up.

"Architecture. I was taking pictures." I hear myself start to babble. "One of my professors opens an internship slot for one student every year and I was hoping to get his attention with this." I have to force myself to stop.

Sergio looks really confused now.

"I heard the men come in and...I got scared and...I hid." *Shut up. Shut up. Just shut up.* "No one's supposed to be here," I add on, unable to take my own advice.

"Including you. It's a condemned building."

I stare up at him and the weight of what I witnessed is slowly dawning on me. "Please don't hurt me. I didn't see anything. Not really."

"Not really?"

I shake my head. Swipe the back of my hand across my nose before rubbing the tears from my eyes.

"Where's your car?"

"I took the bus. I don't have a car."

"Bus? You took a bus out here?" He's looking at me like it's the most unbelievable thing anyone has ever said.

"It stops four blocks away."

He checks his watch. "Hand me your phone," he says.

I do.

"What's your password?"

"0000."

He gives me an 'are you serious' look.

"It's an old phone." Not everything works like it should.

"Huh." He punches in the code and sits on one of the chairs. I look at him as he scrolls through my phone. My brief memories of him are nothing like the reality. He's tall, at least 6'4" if not taller, and big. His legs are spread wide and he's leaning forward with his elbows on his thighs. The suit he's wearing barely contains him. It strains at his shoulders and thighs. And I guess he's in his late twenties. Younger than I think he should be.

His gaze snaps up to mine and he turns the phone toward me. "Who's this?"

It's a selfie of Drew and me. Drew's my best friend. We've known each other since high school.

"Drew."

"Boyfriend?"

I shake my head, wondering why he's asking. He turns the phone back toward himself, scrolls through more photos.

"Just taking pictures for your architecture class?" he asks, turning the screen back toward me.

It's the single image I captured when the two men were brought in. I don't even know why I did it.

"That was an accident."

"How do you accidentally take that picture when you have sense enough to hide?"

I can't answer that. "You can see. There are a lot of the warehouse." I start to rise, to go to him and show him. But he halts me by raising his hand.

"Stay."

I do.

He drops the phone to the floor and stands up, puts his heel on the screen and crushes it.

"No!" I'm on hands and knees trying to grab it from under his shoe even as I hear it splintering.

His hand closes around my hair again and he draws me to kneel up. He crouches down so we're almost at eye level. I still have to look up, though.

"Sweetheart, you've got bigger problems than your phone right now."

Sweetheart. He says it casually, like before.

"Please don't hurt me. I really wasn't spying. I wasn't here on purpose. I..."

"Stop blubbering," he says, releasing me. He stands. "Get your shit together."

I nod. I sit back and I keep nodding.

He chuckles. "I mean get your *things* together. In your bag."

"Oh." I look at the spilled contents. I'm gathering my things and wiping my nose as tears are dropping to the floor as I consider what's going to happen to me. I never called my mom back yesterday. She'll be worried now. I should have called her. And dad. I don't remember the last time I talked to him. Shit. What will they think happened to me? Will they even find—

"Natalie," comes his deep voice.

He's got his hands on his hips and is looming over me.

"Please don't hurt me," I say with a loud sob. "I'm sorry. I'm so sorry."

"Christ, I believe you. Wrong place, wrong time."

I freeze. I think for a moment he remembers me, too, but I was a kid then. He couldn't. And when he speaks, I realize he doesn't.

"I don't think you'd be wearing a bright pink coat if you were trying to stay incognito. Blend and all. But you did overhear some shit."

"I won't tell anyone. I forgot it already. I don't even know what it was—"

He shakes his head. "Get up."

I reach for the phone, the last of my belongings.

"Leave it."

I look at the destroyed phone. It wouldn't do me much good now anyway, so I leave it and stand.

"Let's go," he says, taking my arm and turning me.

"Where to?"

"My house."

"Why?" I pull back.

He looks at me. "So I can figure out what to do with you."

3

SERGIO

The girl is sitting beside me wringing her hands in her lap. She's watching wide-eyed as we pass the exit into the city. She's quiet, like she promised she would be. It was either that or ride in the trunk. I didn't really intend on putting her in the trunk, but she doesn't know that.

She's scared shitless, but thing is, I believe her.

I don't think she was out there to spy. I would bet my life she doesn't even know who the Benedetti name belongs to.

My uncle suggesting a cleaner was dramatic, to say the least. But Roman is all about business. I glance over at her. If it was up to him, we probably would need that cleaner. There are some men in my business who take a sick pleasure for the job of punishing. Business is business for me. I'll do what I have to do. But soaking my hands in innocent blood doesn't get my dick hard.

I get off at my exit and Natalie sits up a little taller.

"Where is your house?"

"Chestnut Hill."

She nods. Is silent.

"Don't you have another question?"

"What are you going to do to me?"

Ah. There it is. The question that matters. Actually, I haven't decided what I'm going to do just yet. I need to make sure she doesn't talk. I need her scared for that.

"Punish you," I say.

"Punish me?" her voice falters.

I nod once while navigating the lonely, dark streets leading to my house. I don't normally have to deal with a woman like this and I'm not even sure why I'm bringing her to my house.

"Here we are," I say, pushing a button to open the tall iron gates as I turn onto the cul-de-sac where my house is one of three, each divided by a heavy stone wall. I wonder what my neighbors have to hide behind theirs.

I pull up along the circular drive and park the car. I get out, then go to her side. She's still strapped in, staring up at the huge stone structure with its intimidating pillars and oversized, hand-carved wooden front doors. I pull her door open and she jumps. I stand back and gesture for her to get out.

When she doesn't move, I reach over her, push the button to release her seatbelt and take her arm to encourage her out. She's pulling back, but thing is, there's nowhere for her to go. And still, the moment I release her and turn to the front door, she takes off. She's running back down the drive, back the way we came. Back to the now closed gates. They're twelve feet tall. She's not getting out.

But here's the thing with mice. I don't mind chasing them. Especially the pretty ones.

And so I do.

I chase my little mouse down the driveway, over the manicured lawn. Up the hill and toward the gates. I could overtake her easily, but I don't, not yet. I like this.

Just before she reaches the border of the property, I speed up and a moment later, I tackle her to the ground. She lands with a hard thud. It knocks the wind out of her and my weight on top of hers doesn't help her catch her breath.

I lean up on my elbows.

"Now look what you've done," I say, my voice low. "Dirtied my coat. Your clothes."

"Please don't hurt me!" Her voice is loud, it cuts into the night.

I look at her face. Watch her struggle. I let her. Let her tire herself out.

The ground is cold, frozen with the temperatures we've been having. I get up on my knees, keep her trapped with my thighs on either side of her hips. When she tries to push me off, I take her wrists and drag her arms over her head, transfer them into one of mine as I lean in close to her.

"Are you ready to do as you're told?" I ask.

She tries to pull free. Fails.

"Natalie? Are you ready to do as you're told?"

"If I go in there, are you going to hurt me?"

"If I were going to hurt you, don't you think I would have done it at the warehouse?"

She stops, considers that.

"Why bring you to my house? DNA and all?"

Her eyes widen at that.

"I'm kidding. Christ. And I don't *want* to hurt you, but I will if I have to."

She swallows, her eyes cautious on mine.

"We're going to go inside and get this done and if you do as I say, you'll be home in no time. You can make it easy or you can make it hard. Up to you."

She just keeps staring.

"Understand?" I ask.

She nods.

"Just to be clear, if you run again, that'll be making it hard, understand?"

"Yes."

I get to my feet and hold out my hand. She ignores it and gets up on her own and this time, when I walk up to the house, she follows.

The house is dark apart from one dim lamp in the living room and the light over the stove in the kitchen. I turn to my guest who's looking around in awe.

I guess it is an impressive house. Big, old, but completely renovated with an imposing staircase dead center, the kitchen to the left, living room taking up the back half of the house, my study on the right. All the windows are leaded, and it lends a dark, almost gothic feel to the house.

"It's pretty," she says when she turns to find me watching her.

"Thanks."

I take off my coat and hang it up then wait for her to give me hers. It's a puffer jacket and although I felt how small she was at the warehouse, she's almost petite when she's left in her Henley and jeans.

I walk into the living room and she follows. I go directly to the liquor cabinet and get the whiskey and two tumblers. She's standing at the entrance looking at everything, nervously pulling the sleeves of her shirt down to tuck her thumb through the holes at the wrists.

I carry the glasses and the bottle to the couch, sit and pour for both of us.

"Come here."

She hugs her arms, but moves toward me.

"Here." I hold one of the glasses out to her. She eyes it but doesn't reach out for it. "It'll calm you down."

"What is it?" she asks.

"Whiskey."

She takes it, drinks the smallest sip. Flinches when she swallows.

After draining mine, I pour a second glass and reach to turn on the lamp beside me. I sit back folding one ankle over my knee and stretching an arm over the back of the couch to get a good look at her. She was wearing makeup at some point but her earlier tears have smeared mascara across her cheek. Her eyes, a pretty almond-shape, are so dark, they're almost black. Her skin has a pale olive tone and she keeps biting her lower lip so it's bleeding a little. I can't tell how long her hair is. She's bound the dark mass into a messy bun.

"What did those men do?" she asks, surprising me.

I smile. "Don't worry about that." She's standing awkwardly and I'm thinking. "Do you know who I am?" I know she would have heard my name more than once.

She lowers her lashes and I wonder if she's contemplating lying, but then she nods once.

"Who?"

"Mafia."

"My name."

"Sergio Benedetti."

"Do you know my family?"

"Not really. I've heard the name, that's all."

"Drink your drink."

She takes another sip. "I have class tomorrow," she says.

I nod. Sip. Consider.

"What are you going to do?" she asks finally.

"I'm not going to do anything. You are. Get undressed."

"What?" She begins to tremble, shrinks into herself as she hugs her arms tighter to her.

"Get undressed, Natalie."

"Why?" her voice is a squeak.

"Insurance."

"Why?" she repeats, taking a step backward.

"Because I need to make sure when I take you home later, that you're not going to tell any of your friends what you saw or heard." I wait. Watch her process. "It's the only way to keep you safe," I add on, not really sure why.

"Safe? How will that keep me safe?"

"Trust me—"

"And safe from who? You?" Her eyebrows knit together. "You said you wouldn't hurt me."

"I said I wouldn't hurt you unless you made me."

"I already told you I won't say anything. I promise."

She wipes fresh tears from her eyes. I finish my drink, set my glass down and get to my feet. She takes a step away from me when I come around the coffee table.

"Remember what you agreed to outside." I reach her, take hold of her arms, rub them. "Just relax, no reason to get so upset."

"No reason? This isn't—"

"Now, what's going to happen next is you're going to do as I say and take off your clothes and I'm going to take some pictures."

"Pictures?" She's panicking. "Why?"

"You repeat yourself a lot, you know that?" I pause but I'm not expecting an answer. "Like I said, insurance. You talk and the photos get sent to your parents, your friends, are posted along the walls at school, etc..."

"Etcetera?"

"Trust me, this is the easiest way for me to do this."

"What's the alternative?" she asks as she pushes out of my grasp.

"The alternative would be...painful."

She swallows. She's wringing her hands. "I think I'm going to be sick."

"You'll be fine. It's just a few pictures."

She shakes her head, rubs her face. "No."

I point to the bathroom, and when she walks out of the room, I resume my seat on the couch. She doesn't come back for a full ten minutes, but when she does, her fear seems to have lessened, or at least it's well hidden behind eyes of fire.

She's pissed.

"You want dirty pictures?" she asks, spitting the words.

I casually shrug one shoulder. It's sort of funny to see her like this. I wonder about the pep talk she must have given herself to get so worked up because she's so mad she's practically shaking. "You think you're going to blackmail me?" She takes a step forward, then back again. "Huh? Pervert?"

She's bouncing from one leg to the other like a boxer. I chuckle at the image but it only makes her angrier. She finally stands still, fists her hands at her sides, her face going bright red.

"Well you can try and make me."

I lean deeper into my seat, consider her, wonder if she's realized how much more interesting she's just made this. Taking my time, I unbutton the cuffs of my shirt, roll the sleeves up to my elbow before I reply. "You sure about that, sweetheart?"

"Don't call me that."

"Are you?"

"Fuck you."

"And you seemed so sweet," I say, standing.

She spins to run from the room, but I catch her easily, my hand wrapping around her arm to halt her. I pull her into my chest. Cock my head to the side. "I was thinking I'd get a slow strip tease, but this will be much more fun."

"Let me go!"

I lean in close, inhale the scent of her. Smell the fear creeping back up to the surface. Make a point of doing so. "Just remember, you chose this. It could have gone easier."

4

NATALIE

He's too strong to fight off, but I try. I can't not fight. Thing is, I know he'll win. He'll get the pictures. But maybe I can hold on to one shred of dignity if he has to make me.

When I went to the bathroom, he must have taken his suit jacket off, and watching him roll up his sleeves a minute ago, seeing his thick forearms, it just made me realize how weak I am. I wonder if he expected this. Expected me to fight. Because he was ready for me.

The Henley's first. I hear it tear as he forces it from me and I stumble back when he does, hit the back of my knee on whatever's behind me. I fall backward. It's an ottoman. I fall onto the ottoman and Sergio Benedetti comes at me with that grin. It's wicked and dirty and makes his eyes shine bright. And when he drops between my legs and grips my boots, I kick at him.

He laughs. He's actually laughing.

"Stop, you're sick!"

He gets my boots off. Then kneels up, grips my wrists and

twists my arms. "Sure you don't want to give me that slow strip tease?"

"Go fuck yourself!"

"I'll be honest," he says, pulling me in close. "I like this better. I like it rough."

I don't know why but I'm shocked. Why would that surprise me, though? He's got my jeans undone and I slap at him as he tugs them over my hips, down my thighs, off my feet.

"Stop!"

"No."

He stands, pushes me backward so I'm laying on the seat of the chair behind the ottoman.

"It's enough. You can take pictures like this."

"No, not enough." He reaches down and with one flick of his hand, my bra is ripped in two and hanging off my shoulders.

I cup my breasts to hide them from view. "Stop! Please stop. I'll do it. Please!"

He leans down over me, holding me with one hand. "Too late, sweetheart," he says as he strips my panties from me and just like that, I'm naked. I'm naked and he's standing over me and looking at me.

I sit up. Cover myself as best I can. "You bastard. I hate you," I spit, but my voice is weak.

"He takes out his phone and snaps a photo. Then another. "Arms at your sides. I want to see it all."

I slide off the ottoman, but he comes at me with that stupid phone snapping away. Picture after picture.

I hit the wall, the corner. There's nowhere for me to go. "Please stop," I say. "Please." I wipe my face with the back of one hand. "I'm sorry. I just needed to see the stupid warehouse and it's not even going to matter anyway. I'm so sorry."

He ignores me and I cower, and only when there's no more flash do I dare look up. He's stepped backward, just one step, but he's still looming over me, all dark hair and blue-black eyes and danger. He can make me do whatever he wants. Anything he wants.

I'm hugging my knees, using my legs, my hair, anything, to hide myself.

He studies me, just watches me for a long time before snapping another photo.

I turn my face away simultaneously. Hide myself from him.

"Take your arms away," he says. His tone is different. Serious.

That shift in his mood changes things. I don't know why, but it does. I know there's no way out of this. Only through it. I've known it all along.

"Do as I say, Natalie."

And so, I do. I move my arms away and he takes a photo. I look at him. He's not grinning anymore. That cocky expression on his face is gone. He's not making fun of me as he does it. He's just taking pictures. I'm actually not even sure he's enjoying it.

"Stand up."

I do, but I can't look at him. Not at his eyes.

"Turn around and put your hands on the wall." I do that too. "Higher. Good. Walk backward."

I take two tiny steps, but it's enough. I know what he wants. My ass.

"Now look at me."

I shake my head once, feel my hair on my naked shoulders. Wonder when it fell out of its clip.

"Look at me," he repeats firmly.

I glance at him over my shoulder. I wonder if he wants my tears too.

"Good."

I see from the corner of my eye he's aroused. This could be worse. He could demand another, different sort of payment.

Who says he won't?

"Get on the couch. Hands and knees. Ass to me."

I want to weep. I want the earth to open and swallow me whole.

"Do it."

I do. But then his hand is on me, on my hip, and I jump. He slaps my ass, snaps a picture.

"Just pictures. You said—"

"It's just pictures." His voice comes out hoarse, like his throat is dry.

I crane my neck to look at his hand. At the ring there—something big and ornate and old looking. There's a dusting of dark hair on his arm and his watch is expensive. I can tell. It's what I try to focus on until, with just the smallest tug of his thumb, he opens me. And I don't know how or why because it makes no sense, but my belly feels strange and I'm holding my breath and when I look at his face, he's got his eyes locked on my ass. He looks different again. He's aroused, that's obvious, but there's more. There's something darker about it.

He's not taking pleasure in my humiliation. It's something else now. And the second he snaps the photo, he seems to hurry to shove the phone into his pocket and get away from me.

"Get dressed. We're done." He walks out of the room. I hear him go into the kitchen. Open a can of something. It takes me a long minute to move. My dignity is in tatters, like my clothes. I pull my underwear and jeans on. Tuck the ruined bra into my pocket and draw the Henley over my head. There's a hole at the seam. I finger it, try to think only of it. I don't want to think about what just happened.

I can fix this later. Sew it back up. It's not hard.

By the time I put my boots on, he's back and he's already got his coat on. He's holding mine out to me.

I can't look at him. I take my coat and put it on and zip it to my chin and, obediently and meekly, I follow him back outside. I get into the car when he opens the door.

"Where do you live?"

I give him the address. He starts driving and neither of us talk. Not during the drive. Not when he pulls up along my street. I live on Elfreth's Alley, a historic street in Philadelphia. Vehicles are restricted and I'm grateful for it, especially tonight.

When I reach to open my door, he finally speaks.

"Remember what I said will happen if you talk."

"I wasn't ever going to talk."

I slip out, my purse in my hand. I dig for my key in my pocket and he doesn't drive away until I'm inside and Pepper, my fourteen-year-old German Shepherd greets me, and I'm sobbing. Sobbing on the floor of my kitchen.

5

SERGIO

I go straight into my study when I get home. Even though I'm alone, I close the door out of habit. I sit with just the lamp on the desk turned on and I look at the photos. I scroll through each one. Study her face in them. I see her anger. Her fear. Her humiliation. I see it in that order. I study more too. More of her. And my dick's hard.

"I wasn't ever going to talk."

I knew that. I knew it all along. She's right. I am a pervert. Sick. Only a sick person would do this, would violate an innocent like this. It wasn't necessary to do what I did. I just wanted to.

But I came to terms with this darker part of me a long time ago. And I'm not psychoanalyzing it now.

The last picture, the one with my hand on her hip, has my attention. The Benedetti family ring is prominent on my finger, my hand big, masculine and rough on her softly curving hip. It's not even the gleaming pink of her pussy that's got my eye. It's how she's looking at me. Watching me with those dark eyes through that veil of hair. Like she's seeing me. Really seeing me.

I stare at them. I can't look away. What I see, it's not what I expect. Not hate. Not even fear. Something else. It has me curious. It's almost as if there's something familiar about her.

I can still smell her if I try. Was she aroused or is that just my sick brain at work? Making something up that wasn't there. I wonder if she's thinking about it now. If she's lying in bed with her fingers between her legs remembering my hands on her. My eyes on her. She'd hate herself for it, I know.

I scroll back to the first image. The one of her sitting on the floor, knees pulled up, hands covering as much of herself as she can. Her chin is bowed into her chest, her hair like a curtain hiding her face from me. But if I look close, I see her accusing eyes through that fall of hair.

There's something about this girl that I can't put my finger on. Something that's got me thinking about her long after I should forget.

"Insurance," I say to myself, standing. I turn on the printer and send all the photos to it. Listen to the slow hum and buzz as each one prints. Watch Natalie's face as each slowly slides out, stacks on top of the last. When they've all printed, I put them in a locked drawer of my desk before going upstairs to jerk off.

THE NEXT AFTERNOON, I go to her house. It's a little after four and the shadows are already growing long. Winter days are short. I don't mind them like most people do, though. I like the dark.

There's no doorbell so I knock on the crooked wooden door, peeking in through the lace curtains of the window beside it. The kitchen is empty but there's a light on deeper in the house. I knock again, louder this time.

"Hold your horses," she calls out as the lock turns and she

pulls the door open. She gasps, and the instant she sees me, she goes to slam the door shut.

I grip it, stopping her.

"Pepper!" she calls out.

I'm confused for a moment until I hear a lone, tired bark and the sound of a dog's nails clicking against hardwood floors. Pepper barks again, sticks her wet nose into the narrow opening of the door. She's old and not very ferocious from what I see.

"What do you want?" she asks. She's got her back to the door so I can't see her face, but feel her weight against it.

"I have something for you."

"I don't want anything from you."

"Let me in, Natalie."

"Why? So you can take more pictures? Freak."

"That's done," I say. "Let me in. Last time I'll ask nicely."

"I said no—"

Before she can finish her sentence, I give a shove and hear her small, surprised yelp as she stumbles forward. I step inside. The dog wags her tail and I get a look at the tiny, ancient kitchen, then at Natalie's startled face.

"You should close the door," I say to her, unbuttoning my jacket. "You're letting the heat out."

"What do you want?"

I reach into my pocket, put the box on the table. It's a brand-new iPhone.

"Here," I say. "Upgraded to the latest model."

She looks at it, confused, then angry. "I don't need you to give me a phone. I need you to get out."

She's wearing an ugly, oversized sweater and jeans. She doesn't have shoes on and her hair's wet like she just had a shower.

"I said get out!" she repeats, holding the door wider.

"Truce, Nat."

"Don't call me Nat. We are not friends."

"For Christ's sake," I say, taking the door and closing it myself. She backs toward the coat rack beneath the cabinets and reaches behind the array of coats, and a moment later, she's waving a wooden baseball bat at me.

"What do you want? Why are you here?"

"You're going to hurt yourself with that," I say, one eye on the bat while I pet the dog who's sitting beside me watching the spectacle. "Good girl," I say to her. "Not like your owner." I try not to laugh outright at Natalie with the bat, Natalie who has so obviously never had to confront someone like this before.

"She's not mine. I'm dog-sitting. And get out," Natalie says.

"Put the bat down, Nat."

"Fuck you."

"You told me that last night too. If you're not careful, I'm going to think it's an invitation."

Her mouth falls open and she has no response. I take the opportunity to reach for the bat. She tries to swing, but I catch it, tug it and her toward me, relieve her of the thing but keep hold of her.

"Truce," I say. "I'm just here to replace your phone."

"Why?"

"Because I broke yours and figured you might need a new one."

"I can buy my own phone."

"You always this stubborn when someone gives you a gift?"

"It's not a gift when you're replacing something you broke on purpose."

"You know why I had to."

"I needed those pictures."

"I'll take you to get new ones."

She stops. Gives a little shake of her head. "What are you doing here, really?"

I shrug a shoulder, release her and peek into the next room. "I've always wanted to see the inside of these houses," I lie. I could give a fuck.

I'm here to see her.

6

NATALIE

"You're here for a tour of the house?"

Sergio Benedetti, looking like a giant in my tiny kitchen, shrugs a shoulder.

I am so freaking confused. Yesterday he stripped me naked and took dirty pictures of me to essentially blackmail me into keeping silent, and today, he's here giving me a gift of a brand-new iPhone and he wants a tour of the house?

"I don't believe you."

"All right, a tour and coffee," he says.

"Is this a joke to you?"

"I'm not much for joking."

"What, you want more pictures?" I cock my head to the side, fold my arms across my chest. "Not enough material to jerk off to?"

He chuckles. "Plenty, actually." He winks, his eyes are practically glowing, the look inside them telling me he means exactly what he said.

I clear my throat and look away, embarrassed.

He mistakes my silence for an invitation and next thing I know, he's hanging his coat up beside all the others.

"You have a lot of coats," he says, looking through the collection.

"They're not mine. I'm house-sitting for friends of my parents while they spend the winter in Florida."

"Ah. Makes sense. I didn't imagine a university student could afford one of these houses."

"What I can or can't afford isn't any of your business."

He holds up his hands in mock surrender. "I didn't mean to offend you. Just an observation."

"Are you really not going to go until I give you a tour?"

"And coffee."

"Why?"

"I'm thirsty and I want to see the house."

He can't be serious. "That's all?"

"That's all."

"No strings?"

"No strings."

A voice in my head tells me that's not quite right. That there are strings. That there will always be strings with him. But I shove that voice aside. There's something about Sergio Benedetti. It's not that I like him. I don't. You can't like someone after they do what he did to me. I don't know what it is, though. I don't know why I'm not really scared he'll hurt me, even though I know who he is. He won't. And there's something else. Something about him that makes me want him to stay, as little sense as that makes. I wonder if it has to do with before, with the robbery. When he was the hero, not the villain.

"I want the pictures back," I say, knowing it's a long shot.

He shakes his head. "Can't do that."

"You can't ever share them. It'll hurt my parents if they ever thought—"

"Keep your end of the bargain and you have my word no one will see them." He picks up the phone. "Just a tour and a cup of coffee. No tricks. No hidden agenda."

I need the phone. I can't afford to buy a new one right now.

"Okay."

He puts the phone on the table and slides it toward me.

"This is the kitchen." I'll keep it short. I walk past him, my shoulder brushing against his arm when I do, feeling the solid mass of muscle. It makes my belly flutter. Makes me remember the feel of his hand on my bare hip last night. Makes me think of how he looked at me, and I swallow hard, feeling my face flush, grateful my back is to him.

"Come on, Pepper," I say, although she's not much of a guard dog when it comes to him from the way she's nudging her head against his leg.

Pepper, the German Shepherd who came with the property, lopes toward me. She's so old, she can barely see, but she's usually good about barking at strangers.

"She's quite the guard dog," Sergio comments, probably aware why I called her.

"Her sense of smell must be off if she likes you."

I catch his smile when I glance behind me.

"Living room," I say, pointing out the obvious. I love this house, love the charm, the creaks and even the ghosts I imagine on dark nights, but it is small and Sergio makes it look that much smaller.

"This is great," he says, touching the bookshelf, obviously appreciating the old wood and antiques. "How old is the house?"

I tell him, just talk to him like he's not who he is. Like last night didn't happen. It's awkward, but I try to ignore it. It'll be over soon. Coffee and a tour. He'll be gone in fifteen minutes.

He follows me through the living room, and I point out the bathroom downstairs before climbing the narrow staircase up to the second floor. Pepper stays at the bottom of the stairs watching us.

"She's too old to climb anymore," I say.

He nods. "Low ceilings." He has to duck his head.

"It's got more space than you'd think," I say, pointing out the two bedrooms. "This one's mine." I open the door to my messy room, walk in ahead of him and kick some clothes under the bed, close the dresser drawer that's still open and turn to him. He's checking out the fireplace.

"Can you use this?"

"I think so. I don't."

"Why not?"

"I don't want to burn down the neighborhood. You could say I'm accident prone." As if to demonstrate, I trip over a shoe on the floor.

"You're messy. That's why you're accident prone."

"You don't know anything about me."

He stands there watching me, and I see the shadow behind that light-hearted, entertained look on his face, in his eyes. He's dark. At his core, no matter how he tries to mask it on the surface, there's a darkness to him.

I shudder. Tell myself I have to remember this.

"I know you from somewhere," he says. Does he remember that convenience store robbery?

"Is that the real reason you're here?" I ask. I know he isn't interested in a tour or coffee.

Before he can respond, I hear the buzzing of a cell phone announcing a message. Sergio reaches into his pocket, reads the screen. He types something back then returns his gaze to me. His eyes, last night I'd thought they were black, but I see now they're midnight blue with specks of gold in them. Like stars. Like a clear night sky with stars.

I take a deep breath in. He's so close I can smell his aftershave.

Fuck. What the hell is wrong with me?

"Do I?" he asks.

He's studying me and my heart is racing. I wonder if he can hear it. But then he's reading another message. He's preoccupied. His phone buzzes a third time. After reading that message, he mutters a curse under his breath. Texts something. Pushes his suit jacket back to tuck his hand into his pants pocket.

That's when I see something glint, shiny and black in its holster under his arm.

"Do you have a gun with you?"

He doesn't reply, just narrows one eye, weighing how to answer my question perhaps. Or trying to steal my memory, to know why he feels a familiarity.

"Did you bring a gun into my house?" I ask again.

"It's not your house, remember?"

"Did you?"

"Would it scare you if I said yes?"

"You put one to my head yesterday."

"Before I realized you were...you."

"You scared me," I admit.

He pauses. Wrinkles form around his eyes for a moment as if this is a revelation to him. "Do I scare you now?"

I don't have to think about it. I shake my head. "No."

"Good. Besides, guns are more part of your life than you think."

"What do you mean?"

His phone buzzes again. It's irritating to have him read his messages while he's talking to me. He types a quick reply before giving me his attention, but I can see he's distracted.

"Second amendment, sweetheart. The world you live in is a violent one. You're just blissfully unaware."

"Maybe that's true for you, but not for me. I don't deal with guns or the mob."

"You'd be surprised." He steps back. "I have to go."

"Oh." I'm oddly disappointed when he gestures to the bedroom door.

"I'll take a raincheck on the coffee though."

My shoulder brushes against his hard chest when I walk past him and out the door. I don't look back as I descend the stairs, my heart still beating fast. In the kitchen, I look at the box containing the brand-new phone, wondering yet again how, twice in less than twenty-four hours, I find myself in a wholly surreal situation with Sergio Benedetti in the driver's seat.

He opens the front door and a cold gust of wind blows in.

"You have good locks on these doors, Natalie?" he asks, twisting the doorknobs, testing the lock.

"That's a strange question."

He turns back to me. "You're an attractive, young girl living alone in the city."

"Woman. Not girl. And I can take care of myself." His face tells me he believes otherwise, and I get that. Because last night didn't exactly make my case.

"The locks?" he asks again, ignoring my comment.

"They're fine."

He walks out of the house but turns back like he's about to say something. His phone rings this time and he steps out, but before answering, he mouths for me to lock the door.

———

MY MIND IS STILL in a daze when I get to the coffee shop to meet Drew the next afternoon. I walk inside to find him waiting for me at our usual table. He makes a show of checking his watch and I do the same on my new phone.

"I'm barely seven minutes late," I say, setting my purse down and pulling out a chair.

"Oh, nice," he says, taking the phone from me and looking at it. "What happened to your old one?" He sets it down. The phone, a rose gold, came ready to go and had one phone number programmed in it. Sergio Benedetti's.

No strings my ass.

"Long story," I say, not wanting to lie. Drew's my best friend. I've known him since I was a kid and we even dated through senior year of high school. But he was always more into boys than girls. Him coming out to me was the same day we broke up and I just remember feeling so happy for him that he knew, really knew, and was deciding to no longer hide it.

He was supposed to go to the warehouse with me, but canceled at the last minute. I'm glad now that he wasn't there.

"Rough night?" he asks.

"Is it obvious?" I wave to Mandy at the bar. I work here, and I pretty much never deviate from my double shot cappuccino, so she gives me a nod to let me know she's already working on it.

"Only because I know you. You went to that warehouse, didn't you? I told you to wait for me."

"I don't really want to talk about it." And I don't want to think about how things could have gone if he was there.

"Did something happen?"

Mandy calls out my name and I go to the coffee bar, grab my drink and hand her a $5 bill. "Thanks." Back at the table, I take a sip. "Can I ask you a question?"

His eyebrows rise. "Sounds serious."

"It is. Do you know a man named Sergio Benedetti?"

Drew all but spits out his coffee. "Benedetti?" he asks too loudly.

I glance at all the faces suddenly turned in our direction, and lower my voice. "Can you say it any louder?"

"As in son of Franco Benedetti? Next in line to take over the family business?"

"That's him."

"Why?"

"I kind of ran into him last night."

"You kind of ran into him? How do you kind of run into a man like that?"

"That's the long story."

"Nat—"

"Don't push. I don't want to talk about it."

"You mean at the warehouse?" His eyes go huge.

"Let's just say he was there conducting business."

"Nat—"

"It's fine. I'm fine." I'm not fine though.

Drew eyes my new phone. I should have scratched it up or something. He knows I could never afford a brand new, latest model iPhone.

"What exactly happened?" Drew asks.

"I really can't say, Drew. Please don't push me."

"Did you see—"

"Listen, I just want to know about his family. I tried to Google, but I can't find much about him. I know you hear stuff." Drew works at a gentlemen's club. It's a high-end strip joint and he's mentioned the clientele sometimes includes men from the local crime families.

"So you want to know about Sergio in particular, not the family."

I nod, bite the inside of my cheek.

He gives me a little history. "But this is where his story gets juicy."

"It's already juicy."

"Ever hear of the DeMarco family?" he asks.

I shake my head.

"Crime family. They were loyal to the Benedetti family, but then they weren't. Franco Benedetti, Sergio's father, took Lucia DeMarco, the youngest daughter, and essentially has her locked away at some nunnery until she's old enough to be *given* to Sergio."

"What?" My heart sinks into my belly. "What are you talking about?"

"It sounds Medieval, right? He took DeMarco's daughter to punish him. Make him pay for rising up against the Benedetti family."

"I don't understand. Who is Lucia DeMarco? What nunnery? And what do you mean she's to be *given* to Sergio?"

"She was sixteen when it all happened. That was two years ago. He literally had her sent to the nuns in some private school or something. She'll be a gift for Sergio." Drew looks almost mystified.

"What year is this? That's not legal."

"Tell that to Franco Benedetti."

"Will he marry her or something?" I almost choke on the word and can't figure out why I'm so bothered.

"He'll *own* her. I don't think finding a bride for his son was what Franco was going for." Drew waggles his eyebrows.

I feel a shudder run along my spine. Drew's phone rings and he gives me an apologetic look before answering. I'm too caught up in what I've just learned to care though. To do much of anything but digest this piece of information.

He hangs up. "Shit, totally forgot my meeting with the counselor." He stands, finishes the last of his coffee and stuffs his text book into his backpack. Drew attends University of Pennsylvania with me. "Speaking of, did you decide what you'll do with the Dayton internship?"

This is the reason I was at the warehouse to begin with. Professor Dayton owns Dayton Architecture, a leading firm in the Philadelphia area. I had a shot at a spot there for the summer, and ignored the stories about him being handsy with the interns. At least until I got a taste of it last week in a private meeting.

"Well, I'm not going to sleep with him for an internship and since I couldn't get the photos I wanted to work on, I'm guessing it's off the table."

"Prick." He zips his backpack, looks at me. "You can report—"

"Who'd believe me? He's too well connected. Besides, I'll find something else."

"I disagree, but it's up to you. You going to be okay?"

"Yeah, I'm fine." I wave him off. "Don't worry about me."

He leans down to give me a hug, but I catch his sleeve when he's about to go.

"Drew, is that all for real?" I ask. "The story about the girl?"

He looks at me for a minute, his expression becoming worried. "Nat, real or not, you can't get involved with someone like that."

I shrug a shoulder, break eye contact. "I'm not. It's just a strange story."

"I'll see you later, okay?"

"Okay."

I finish the last of my coffee and get up to leave. It's already dark out and the weather report had mentioned snow, which I really hoped would just be rain, but no such luck. I put my hood up and shove my hands into my pockets to walk the six blocks home all the while thinking about what Drew told me.

The story seems ridiculous, unbelievable and old-fashioned.

Would someone really do that? Lock away a girl of sixteen? *Own* her? What the hell does that even mean?

Flurries quickly turning into large, fluffy flakes blanket the ground. It would be beautiful except that right now, my brain's busy processing. I feel kind of stupid. Drew's right. I have no business thinking anything about a guy like Sergio Benedetti. I shouldn't even let him in if he comes back for that cup of coffee.

I'm not paying attention as I near Elfreth's Alley. The snow's coming down hard now and I'm rushing to stay dry. I'm digging my key out of my pocket when I turn the corner and bump right into someone.

"Oh! I'm sorry!" I think it's one of my neighbors but whoever it is rushes past me without an apology or even an acknowledgement. I turn to watch him go. I know it's a him because he's pretty big. "Jerk." I look down for my key, which slipped out of my hand. I need to get a keychain for it. It takes me a minute to find it in the rapidly accumulating snow and by the time I let myself into the house, my fingers are numb from the cold.

Pepper barks twice, lopes into the kitchen. "Hey Pepper." I pet her, remember what Sergio asked about the locks, then force him from my mind. "Want dinner?" I ask Pepper as I take off my coat and boots. I drape my coat over the radiator, and leave my wet boots on the mat by the door. I'm just finishing scooping out her food when there's a knock on my door.

I try to shove the first thought that pops into my head—the hope that it's him—out. It takes me a moment to get to the door and the knocking comes again before I pull it open.

Sergio Benedetti is standing outside my door, handsome and formidable.

His smile fades when I don't invite him in right away. "It's snowing out here."

I look around, let go of the doorknob and step back. The story Drew told me circles my brain.

I watch him stomp snow off his boots before stepping inside and closing the door to look me over. I look too. I'm wearing a sweater and an old pair of ripped jeans and thick wool socks.

"Weatherman was right for the first time in his career," Sergio says. He's studying me. He always seems to be doing that.

My mind is busy, too caught up processing what I learned today. "Are you going to keep showing up at my door like this?"

Pepper's nails glide along the floor and I know she'll go to him like she did last time.

He pets Pepper's head, but his eyes are on me. "You should wear a hat," he says, ignoring my remark.

I touch my hair, realize it's wet from my walk home.

"Why are you here?"

"Coffee."

"What?"

"Coffee. Remember?"

"Now?"

He looks at me like it's the most normal thing in the world that he showed up here for coffee.

"What's wrong with now? Besides, we never finished talking."

"I didn't realize we had anything to talk about. You said no strings, remember?"

"Make me some coffee, Natalie."

"Are you used to giving orders and having them obeyed?"

He stops, seems to consider this, then answers with a grin. "Yeah, I am."

I guess it was a stupid question. "I have a question first," I dare.

He cocks his head to the side. "You're a strange one, you know that?"

I ignore his taunt. "Who's Lucia DeMarco?"

7

SERGIO

"Ah." I watch her. I'm curious about her. She's torn, wanting to tell me to go to hell, but at the same time, drawn to me. "What did you do, Google the Benedetti family's sordid history?"

"I don't have to Google. Everyone knows."

"You didn't know until today." I step toward her, lift her hair off her shoulder, push it behind her ear before cupping her chin to tilt it up. Her mouth opens, and her eyes grow wider. "And who's everyone?"

She pulls back, turning her face the second she realizes she shouldn't have said that. "I didn't tell anyone about...the warehouse. I just said I'd run into you." She clears her throat, doesn't quite look at me as she answers and steps backward to put space between us. "I guess I want to know how you can own another human being." She folds her arms across her chest. Tries to look confident.

"What the hell are you talking about?"

"I know about Lucia. I know she was only sixteen when you locked her up."

"That so?" I ask. I look her over, walk a slow circle around her. I don't speak until I'm facing her again. "You know, you should really tell me right now to go to hell. To get out and never come here again," I say, I'm not one to mince words. Not one to play stupid games. Time is too valuable for that so I'm going to get this shit on the table. "Because you know I lied earlier. About the strings." I'm standing so close to her that she's trapped with me on one side, the wall on the other. She's not wearing any makeup and yet she's fucking beautiful. I wonder if she even knows how beautiful. I lean my face close to hers. "With men like me, there are always strings, Natalie."

She runs a hand through her hair, looks anywhere but at me.

"But you don't want to, do you?" I ask. "For some reason, you want me to be here," I say. "You liked that it was me when you opened the door."

"No."

"Huh." I scrape my lower lip with my teeth. Her gaze falls to my mouth momentarily. "So instead of asking me to leave, you want to know about Lucia DeMarco? You sure about that?"

She gives me one short nod.

"Okay." I step away, take off my coat and drape it over the back of a chair before sitting down. "Make me that cup of coffee."

She sighs. The table's too big for this space and she has to maneuver around it. I watch her fill the stove-top espresso machine with water and scoop out two heaping spoons of coffee. She stands with her back to me while the coffee brews. I wonder if she feels awkward but I don't mind the quiet. I like being here in this house. I like being with her.

When the coffee steams, she switches off the burner, pours two tiny cups of espresso out and sets one in front of me. She then pulls out a chair and sits.

"Thank you," I say, taking a sip. It's good. "Lucia DeMarco is my father's personal vendetta. For the record, I don't like what he's doing with her, but in order to punish the DeMarco family for their betrayal, he demanded something precious. The most precious things DeMarco has are his daughters, so..." I pause. "He took one."

"He just took one?"

I nod.

"People aren't things."

I shrug a shoulder.

"He took her for you?" she asks and I know this is what's got her wound up and I like it.

"Does that bother you?"

"What? No."

"You sure?" She opens her mouth, but I continue. "On her twenty-first birthday, she'll belong to my family."

"That's not legal. It can't be."

I give her a minute to think about that statement.

"But—"

"Shut up, Natalie. Just listen." Amazingly, she shuts up. "You want me to tell you Lucia DeMarco has nothing to do with me?"

She watches me, answers my question with her own. "What must she be going through? What's this like for her?"

"That isn't a question I can answer or even care to consider. There are consequences to actions. A price to be paid. That's all. And you shouldn't romanticize it."

"I'm not romanticizing it but she is locked away in a tower, isn't she?"

"She's at an excellent girl's school getting an excellent education. And I think that's enough on the DeMarco topic."

She stands abruptly, takes her cup to the sink. "What happened to your hand?" she asks with her back to me.

I look at it, notice the bruise forming there. "Nothing."

"Business?"

I have to admit, she's observant. When I'd had to leave so abruptly last time it was because of news about that idiot Joe Vitelli. Roman had thought I'd been too lenient. I've always known my uncle has a taste for blood. But this time, he'd been right. My talk with the brothers didn't quite set the younger one straight. Because Joe had a meeting I'm pretty sure his brother wasn't aware of with a family who is a very clear enemy of ours.

After my visit with the younger Vitelli brother this morning, though, he's not going to be talking to anyone for a while. In fact, he'll be lucky if he ever talks again.

The chair scrapes the floor when I push back. I'm behind her before she can turn. I reach around her, set my cup in the sink, and I look at her, turn her to face me. She grips the counter behind her.

"You asked me why I was here earlier. Well, I'm here because I want to see you."

Her eyes go wide, nervously searching mine.

"There's something about you that keeps drawing me back, so here I am. And I think you feel the same."

"I—"

"Now about the hand, do you want me to lie to you?" I ask.

She shakes her head.

"You know who I am. Who my family is."

"I need to remember it."

When she won't look at me, I make her. "I'm just a man, Natalie." She's silent. "Flesh and bone." I snake one hand up along her spine to cup the back of her head, curl my fingers into her hair and tug her head backward. "And you make me want."

Her throat works when she licks her lips. Swallows. "Wrong place, wrong time."

"What?"

"There was a convenience store robbery in my neighborhood

six years ago. I was fourteen. You said that after you shot the man who would have raped me."

I study her. Search her eyes. And slowly, it comes together.

I don't remember much about that day. Literally, I'd stumbled on the robbery. I'd needed to take a piss after a rough night of partying. Hell, I may have still been drunk. The two perps were stoned. Idiots. But when I saw the asshole trying to get the kid's jeans off, I lost it. Told her to shut her eyes and shot the fucker so he'd never be fucking anyone ever again.

I walked away before the cops came. Took that piss and left.

"You have a bad habit, then, of being in the wrong place at the wrong time." I lean down, touch my lips to hers. They're soft. And she doesn't push me away. I don't close my eyes when I kiss her. Take her lip between mine and taste her.

"You taste good. I knew you would."

She doesn't know what to say. I bring my mouth to her ear and inhale, touching the scruff of my jaw to her smooth cheek as I take in her scent. Smell her want. And when I lean my face down and push her sweater aside to kiss the delicate curve of her neck, she gasps, sets her hands flat to my chest, but again, she doesn't push me away.

I draw back. My dick is hard. She sees it pressing against my pants and swallows when she returns her dark eyes to mine, blacker now with her pupils dilated. Before she can say anything, I pull her sweater over her head and lift her up to set her on the counter. With my hands on her thighs, I push her legs wide and stand between them.

"I liked looking at you that night," I say. She's almost at eye level now. Just has to tilt her head up a little.

"What?" her voice wavers when she asks it.

"I liked it. Liked you naked. I liked opening you. Seeing you. All of you. And after I brought you home, I looked at your pictures. Memorized them."

I draw her closer, so her legs are dangling off the counter and she can feel me between them. Her bra is lace and not padded so I can see her pebbled nipples. I bring my mouth to one small mound, rub the scruff of my jaw against it, suck the nipple, liking the rough of the lace against the softness of her skin.

Her hands are on my shoulders. "I—"

She swallows whatever she was about to say when I pull back, touch my fingers to her chest, over her breasts, her nipples. Slowly, I lift her breasts out of the cups, tuck the lace beneath each and look at her. Meet her eyes again as I lift her off the counter and she stands before me. I slide one hand down over her belly, undo the buttons of her jeans, the zipper. I slip my hand inside, into her panties, and I cup her sex and when I do, she closes her eyes and sucks in a breath and she's wet and I smell her and I want her.

"Stop." It's a whisper.

I slide a finger inside her, feel her warmth. I watch her when I do. Her mouth is open, her eyes locked on mine. Desire burns inside them. The musky scent of it hangs heavy in the room between us.

"You're wet," I say, rubbing the hard nub of her clit between thumb and forefinger.

She closes her eyes, bites her lip. Presses her hands against me. "No."

I take that hard, little button and tease it and she's leaning the top of her head into my chest, one hand fisted there, the other pushing against me. Her breathing is coming in gasps and I think she'll come soon and I want to see her come. It's what I want most in the world right now.

She looks up at me. I grip her pussy, tug her toward me. I rub her clit again, watch her eyes when I do.

But then she moves her hands underneath my jacket and

she's feeling my chest, and I know the instant she touches the cold steel of my gun because she freezes.

Fuck.

I watch her. She blinks and that desire is turning into something else.

I clear my throat. "You should tell me to go," I tell her again, my voice hoarse. It's the right thing to do. I know it. She knows it.

I slide my hand out of her panties, my fingers wet with her.

She takes hold of either side of my jacket and pushes it back just off my shoulders and looks at the holstered gun, but she doesn't speak. Instead, she touches it. I watch her tentative fingers, delicate and fragile. But when she closes her hand over the handle, I take hold of her wrist and pull her hand off and push her away, turn my back to her as I lean against the counter, holding her at arm's length, needing a moment. Needing many moments. I adjust the crotch of my pants and when I finally look at her again she's watching me.

This time it's me who doesn't speak. Instead, I release her wrist. I adjust the cups of her bra and take one more look at her before I turn, pick up my coat. I don't bother to put it on before I open the door, even though it's icy out, and I walk out of the house without a goodbye.

8

NATALIE

I lay awake for a long time after he left and kept waking up throughout the night, remembering. It's the first thing I think of this morning.

He didn't say goodbye. And I didn't get a chance to say a word before he was gone. The door closed behind him and he vanished. Disappeared into the night like a ghost. Like he wasn't here at all.

And it's the strangest thing. The most unsettling feeling—something I can't put my finger on—but it's almost a premonition. Sergio here, then gone.

Just like that.

Like a ghost.

Pepper's barking alerts me that there's someone at the door. The doorbell's been broken forever. I get up, pull a hoodie on, and glance out the window. I know it's not Sergio. Pepper wouldn't have barked at him.

Three men are standing outside, two in black jackets with a logo I can't read at the back, and one in a long dark coat. The guy in the coat looks up, catches my eye in the window. He opens his arms as if to say 'hey, answer the door'.

I go downstairs, keep a hand on Pepper's collar when I open the door. I don't know these men.

"Good morning," the one in the coat says. He introduces himself. I only catch his first name. "Sergio sent me."

I'm confused. "What? Why? It's seven in the morning." I have class in an hour but still. I read the logo on the uniform of one of the men behind him. He's a locksmith.

"He said you need new locks. We'll get it done as fast as possible and be out of your way. Gentlemen." He puts his hand on the door to push it open, gesturing for the two men to enter.

"Hold on. You can't just barge in here and—"

"Miss, if you don't mind my saying so, these locks wouldn't keep a third-rate bum out."

My mouth falls open and he digs his phone out of his pocket, says a few words then holds it out to me.

"Here."

"What?"

"For you."

I am so confused. I take the phone.

"Good morning," Sergio says before I can say a word. I can almost hear the grin on his face.

"Are you responsible for this?"

"Yes. I realize it's early—"

"You can't just send someone to my house to change my locks. I don't even know you. It's not even my house. What's next, the windows?"

"Maybe. If you need it."

"No. I'm joking!"

"The owners will appreciate the better locks, Natalie. I guarantee that. I can break into your house with one hand tied behind my back."

"No one's trying to break into my house."

He doesn't speak for a minute and I think back to the man last night, the one who almost plowed me down on his way out of the street.

No one has tried. Yet.

"I just want to keep you safe. Young *woman* living alone and all. Want to make sure you're protected."

Woman. So he heard what I said.

"Nat?"

"I don't like people calling me that," I say.

"Natalie?" he amends. "Just do this for me and I'll get rid of the pictures I took."

"You will?"

"Yes."

"How will I know you did it?"

"You'll have to trust me."

"I'm confused."

"About trusting me?"

"About everything."

"We can talk about it later if you want, when I take you to get photos of the warehouse."

"I don't need those anymore."

"Why not? I thought they were for school."

"They are. Were." I shake my head. "I'm not taking the internship. The professor's weird anyway. He has a bunch of us volunteering at his firm and he'll choose one for the summer spot."

"What do you mean, weird?"

"Doesn't matter."

He's quiet but I know he wants to push. "Sergio?" I ask. I have a more pressing question.

"Yes?"

"Am I in danger?"

"What? No. No, nothing like that. Those are just shitty locks. Let me do this one thing for you."

"They're old, that's all."

"Right. We'll update them. A gift to the owners."

"Okay. But next time you talk to me first."

"I did. I told you they were shitty."

"I didn't think that meant you were going to replace them." I look at the clock. "Shit. I'm going to be late for classes."

"Eric will take care of everything. Go to school."

"Um, okay, thanks, I guess."

"Tell me about this professor."

"No. It's nothing." I'm worried suddenly. Sergio's not taking baby steps into my life. He's charging in and I have a feeling he'll shove anything he needs to shove out of his way without a second thought. "I have to go," I say.

9

SERGIO

It took all I had to walk away last night.

What I wanted, what I would have done with any other woman, was strip her bare, bend her over the kitchen counter, and fuck her raw. Take her to bed. Fuck her again. Then again.

And then I would walk away. Out the door never to return. Never to give a second thought.

With her though, it's different. With her, everything is different.

Wrong place. Wrong time.

Twice she's been put in my path.

I finish my coffee. Head out to the car. Sending Eric to take care of the locks means I won't have a bodyguard this morning. My father will have words with me when he finds out, which he always does. I need a bodyguard. We have enemies. All things I know.

Which brings me to Natalie.

If I'm not careful, she will become a target. And I feel very protective of her.

Those locks needed to be changed. They wouldn't keep anyone out and that dog's too old to protect her.

This professor she mentioned, I don't like the sound of him.

My phone rings when I get in the car. I check the display. It's my father.

"It's early for you, isn't it?"

"Heard the Vitelli boy is in the hospital."

"That's right." I glance at the bruise on my knuckle. I don't mind doing the physical work myself. Never want to be one of those men who's afraid to get his hands dirty.

"He'll be lucky if he can talk again," he says.

"My initial meeting didn't make the impression I hoped."

"Roman thinks it'll push old man Vitelli."

"Roman needs to learn his place."

"He was right before."

"I'm meeting with Vitelli Sr. today. He'll show gratitude for my restraint. My plan is not to incite another uprising like the DeMarco one. It's to garner respect and, perhaps more importantly, obedience."

"Power corrupts," he says.

"Absolute power corrupts absolutely," I say. "Where do we, the Benedetti family, fall in that? Or do we have no reckoning?"

There's a pause. "Just make sure you take Eric and at least two more soldiers with you. Roman too."

"I'll take the security, but my uncle can stay home this time."

My father would normally have handled this himself, but I've taken over some of the things he would do because with mom's illness, he's been preoccupied. As much as I trust Roman's loyalty to him and to our family, there are moments where he's ambitious, too much so. He's not a Benedetti. He's my mother's brother. He may be consigliere, but I am my father's son and successor.

"Sergio—"

"Is mom's appointment at Dr. Shelby's office?" I ask, even though I know. Instantly, I feel the shift in mood. Today's an important day. We find out if my mom's chemo worked. I know dad's scared shitless. It's actually the only time I've ever known my father to be scared.

"Yeah. At the hospital."

"All right. I'll see you then."

"One more thing before you go. I want Eric with you 24/7. It's why I pay him. You want to go fuck some girl, go fuck her, but he stays. I don't care where or how, but he stays, understand?"

The way he says 'some girl' grates on my nerves. "Relax, dad." I hear a door close on my father's side.

"Relax, he tells me," Dad says, but he's not talking to me. "Your uncle just walked in. Twenty-four fucking seven, Sergio. I'm not budging on that."

"Fine."

I ARRIVE EARLY at the restaurant where I'm meeting Vitelli. My men have already checked the place and I'm on my second espresso when Vitelli and two of his men walk in. I haven't seen him since a wedding eight months ago, but he hasn't changed much. Maybe a few more gray hairs, but he's got the same look on his face as always, the one that says he's owed something simply for the sake of a shared history, and I don't like it.

After my men are done searching them, Vitelli approaches the table alone.

"Sergio," he says in greeting.

We don't shake hands.

"Sit down." I signal the lone waiter. "What would you like?"

He looks at my espresso and orders the same.

"How's Joe?" I ask. It's unspoken who did the damage, but we all know.

"Recovering." His tone is flat. "Although it'll be slow."

I nod. Sip the last of my espresso as he gets his. Silence drags out, but it doesn't bother me. I want him to start.

"Look, Sergio, our families go way back. We were neighbors in Calabria."

"That was a long time ago."

"Yes, but we have history. Shared roots. My boys," he focuses his attention on the little espresso cup, and I see his mouth harden, see the rage behind it.

Violent men. It's what we are. He and I both.

He looks up at me. "My boys fucked up, Sergio."

"Yeah, they did. And Joe fucked up twice."

"My youngest is sitting in a fucking hospital bed with his face sewn together."

I study him, my expression even. Give him a minute to compose himself.

"You played together when you were little, for Christ's sake!"

"Like I said, that was a long time ago. I know you were unaware of their dealings, but I'm not sure that's an excuse. If you're unable to control your family..." I let my words trail off.

His shoulders visibly tense up and a moment later, he clears his throat. "It was an oversight," he acknowledges, knowing where I'm going. Knowing he can easily be replaced. Am I surprised he values his position over loyalty to his own sons?

"Will it happen again?"

"No."

"Because if it does, someone will be in a box rather than a hospital bed. Am I clear?"

His youngest got his eyes from him. The same arrogance fills them.

"You're clear, Sergio." He makes to stand, but stops halfway up. "How's your mother?"

I feel my eyes narrow, feel hate move through me.

"Your uncle mentioned she's finished with her treatments."

My uncle did what? He must see my surprise because I see that minuscule hint of victory in his eyes.

"Wish her well from my family."

"Goodbye, Mr. Vitelli."

I watch him leave, rage boiling inside me. How dare my uncle discuss our family's private affairs with anyone? Especially this.

Checking my watch, I get up and walk to the back door. Eric's beside the car. I get in, preoccupied now. This meeting didn't go as planned. As I expected. I'm distracted as we drive to the hospital but when we pull up and I climb out, I take a breath in, compose myself. I'll deal with Roman later. Right now, I need to be here for my mother.

When I arrive at the doctor's office, they're waiting for me. My mother and father sitting across from the doctor, my mom's head wrapped in a teal blue scarf. Roman is standing off to the side.

"Sergio," she says when she sees me. "There you are."

"Mom." She stands and I hug her, feel how much weight she's lost. And I think I already know what the doctor's going to tell us. I think she does too when she pulls back and gives me a weak smile. I wonder if all of this, if it isn't for our sake. If she isn't humoring us. Giving my father hope because she knows what will happen to him without it.

Another moment later, the door opens and my brothers, Salvatore and Dominic step inside. Salvatore spots me first, greets me, then our mother. Dominic goes directly to her and when everyone's said hello, she pats the chair beside her for Dominic to take. She keeps one of his hands in both of hers.

Dominic is different than Salvatore. Salvatore, I get. He and I are close. But Dominic has anger inside him. Rage even. Jealousy rules him and in a way, I understand. He's third born. If anything happened to me, Salvatore is next in line to rule. And to rule, to be king, is what my little brother wants most of all. I sometimes wonder at what cost.

Once we're all gathered, the doctor puts his glasses on and opens a folder on his desk. And from there, he delivers his news.

10

NATALIE

I haven't seen or heard from Sergio in three days. I'm confused, not sure what I should be feeling. Not sure I should be feeling anything at all.

If he's gone, it's for the best. Drew's right. I can't get involved with someone like him. What the hell am I even thinking? But why did he go without a goodbye? I don't understand.

It's past eleven at night when there's a knock on my door. I'm in the living room studying for a test. For a quick moment, I'm glad about the new locks on the doors, but shake myself out of it.

The knocking comes again, harder this time.

"Just a minute," I call out, zipping up my hoody. A damp chill clings to the walls of the house on these wet winter days. I understand why the owners leave until spring.

I look through the window beside the door and if he didn't have his face turned up to the streetlamp, I wouldn't have opened the door, but it's him.

I unlock and open the door. His hand is mid-air, ready to bang against the door, and I see right away he's in bad shape.

"Sergio?"

He looks at me like he's almost surprised to see me. He scratches his head. His coat is open and he's not wearing gloves, hat or scarf. His face is red like it's been whipped by the wind that hasn't stopped howling for the last hour.

"I was walking," he says. I can smell whiskey on him.

"It's freezing. You went walking tonight? Here?"

He makes some sound, looks beyond me into the house.

"Are you drunk?" I ask.

He returns his gaze to me, shakes his head, but I'm not convinced. He steps inside without waiting for an invitation. I close the door, shuddering at the cold.

"What's going on?" I ask.

"Long day." He stops, looks off in the distance, shakes his head. "Long fucking week. You have something to drink?"

"Coffee?" I ask, not surprised when he shakes his head.

"Something stronger."

"Um." I walk into the living room. He follows me. I don't drink whiskey, which I think is what he's looking for, but the owners have a stash of it. I open the cabinet, look at the various bottles, feel Sergio step close behind me. I turn to him, study his face. He's scanning the selection and a moment later, chooses a bottle from the back. He doesn't bother to pour it into a glass but drinks directly from it.

"Are you okay?" I ask carefully.

He looks at me, his eyes fierce in the dimly lit room. He drinks another swallow, sways on his feet. "I have a key," he says, producing a ring of keys from his pocket.

"Good for you," I say, not quite following. I reach for the bottle in his hand. "Maybe you've had enough."

He draws it back and shoves his keys back into his pocket. Drinks again. When he takes a step to the side, he knocks his shin right into the coffee table, and mutters a curse.

"Why don't you sit down," I say, taking his shoulders, turning him toward the couch. "And give me your coat." He reluctantly lets me take the bottle for the moment it takes him to slide his coat off. He flops onto the couch, taking the whiskey back from me to drink another swallow.

"What were you doing?" He picks up my notebook.

"Nothing." I take the whiskey from him, push the lid back on.

"Tell me about the professor."

"What? Oh." He means Professor Dayton. "Nothing."

"Tell me."

"Just he's another one of those men who thinks with their dicks. That's all. No big deal, nothing I can't handle."

"Did he touch you?"

"It's fine."

"Did he fucking touch you?"

"He stuck his hand up my skirt."

Sergio's hand fists. I watch him, study his eyes. This is dangerous ground. Dangerous for Professor Dayton. "Just forget it. It stopped at that. And I'm not taking the internship anyway. I'm leaving, in fact."

"Nat—"

"Please."

His eyes narrow, like he's thinking, and when he nods, I'm surprised.

"Did something happen tonight?"

He takes a deep breath in, then out, looks at me, takes my hands and holds them for a long minute. "Life is short, huh?" He releases me, runs both hands through his hair and leans back on the couch. For a moment, it's like he's drifted out of here, he looks so lost in thought. Then he returns his gaze to mine and just watches me for a long time. When he stands, he's steady on his feet, and he's got that same look in his eyes as the other night. My body understands it before my mind processes.

"Too short to waste," he says. He takes the zipper of my hoodie between two fingers and slides it down, pushes it off me and lets it drop to the floor. "Natalie," he says my name and stops, searching my face before his gaze moves to my bared shoulders and arms. "You're so beautiful, you know that?" He's slurring his words, swaying on his feet.

I watch him, and it's strange, the way he's looking at me. Intense and dark.

He takes the hem of my tank and draws it over my head.

"I want to see you. All of you."

"Sergio, you're drunk." I try to push his hands away.

"No, sweetheart, not that drunk. Hell, never that drunk." With a finger at my bare belly, he walks me backward.

"Wait, Sergio—"

"Shh." He touches my lips. "I just want to see." He leans in and kisses me, pressing my back to the wall, his cock is a thick rod between us. His eyes are burning when he pulls away.

Gripping my sweats with both hands, he slowly lowers to his knees, then drags my pants down over my thighs, off my feet. My socks are next so I'm barefoot, wearing only bra and panties. He gives me one glance before hooking his fingers into the waistband of the panties and dragging them off. I step out and when I do, he grips my thighs and forces them wider. Then he looks at me. Just looks at my bared sex.

My clit throbs beneath his gaze and he gives me a hooded glance before placing his thumbs on either side of my slit and opening me.

"Sergio."

"Quiet." He leans in, inhales deeply, then licks the length of me.

My gasp is a swallow of breath.

"I want you," he says, dipping his head low, licking me again, forcing my legs wider as he dips his tongue inside me before coming back to my clit and taking it between his lips to suck.

"Oh, fuck." I'm gripping him, his arms, his head and he lifts one leg up over his shoulder and devours me and when he takes my clit between his lips again and sucks hard, I fist his hair and grind against him and I come. I come so fucking hard I can't stand without him holding me. Without his hand on my belly pressing me to the wall, his other hand around my hip keeping me upright.

When I'm limp and gasping for breath, Sergio rises to stand, wiping the back of his hand across his mouth, a smile on his lips, a darkness in his eyes. He kisses me hard, mashing his lips against mine, lifting me in his arms and carrying me up the stairs. In my room, he flips the light switch and the dim lamps on either side of my bed go on. He sets me on the bed. When I try to sit up, he shakes his head, pushes me back down and draws my legs wide to stand between them. He leans down, grips my bra in both hands and rips it in two, arranging the pieces to either side of me, laying me out, displaying me, like he did the other night. He looks me over, up and down, keeping my legs wide with his between them, and draws his sweater over his head.

I catch my breath at the heavily tattooed arms and shoulders. I'd only seen the hint of ink on his forearms that first night. He's thickly muscled, his stomach ripped, and when he grips his belt to open it, my eyes travel to the trail of dark hair disappearing into his pants. I lick my lips and wait for him to push his pants and briefs down and off and I look at him, at his thick cock, the head already glistening. He lets me take him in and I want him, want more than his tongue on me. Inside me.

"You're soaked," he says, lifting my thighs, pressing my knees up, looking at me, at all of me. "You're fucking dripping."

I gasp when he touches his cock to me. When he smears himself over my sex.

"Sergio." Condom. We need a condom.

"Shh. I just want to feel you, be inside you. Just for one second." He slides into me unprotected and I suck in a breath and he stills and closes his eyes, and he lets out a long, deep moan and for a moment, I just watch his face and hold him inside me and it's not just about sex. Not just about coming. Not right now.

"We can't...condom," I force myself to say, even though all I want right now is him like this, warm inside me, and close, so fucking close.

He pulls out, leans down to kiss me, laying his weight on me for a moment before drawing away, keeping hold of my legs, keeping me spread for a moment longer before flipping me over and that intimacy, it's gone. It's sex now. It's about coming now.

"Up, Natalie. Elbows and knees."

I obey. Fuck, I want him. I want him to look at me. Want him to touch me. To lick me. To be inside me.

"Good girl," he says. "Now put your face down on the bed. "I want to see all of you." He takes my clit between two fingers when he gives the order and all I can do is moan and bury my face in the sheets. I feel his hands on me then, on my ass, spreading me wider, and then his mouth is on me again, closed over my pussy, licking and dipping inside me before sliding up toward my asshole.

I gasp. Tense up.

"Relax," he growls. His hand is on the back of my head keeping me down. "I want all of you, Natalie. Everything." I find myself arching my back then as he licks my ass, circling his tongue there, before dipping back to my pussy, devouring me, making me whimper as I come again. Come for a second time with his mouth on me.

I collapse on the bed when he flips me back over, climbing between my legs. He lays his full weight on me and kisses me.

"I like your pussy," he says against my ear. "And I like your ass. And I love watching you come. And hearing you come. It's the best fucking thing in the world."

I close my eyes, holding him to me, pushing his face into my neck so he doesn't see me. I'm embarrassed. I've never had anyone do what he just did to me. I've never come as hard as I do with him.

He draws back and pushes my legs wide again, and all I can think is I want him inside me again. I want to feel his heat, his hardness, his want. And when he slides into me, stretching me, it's exactly right, so fucking right. He lets out a groan and closes his eyes for a moment, an instant, seating himself deep inside me, opening his eyes again to lock gazes with me before he slides out of me.

He straightens, reaches into the pocket of his discarded pants and takes out his wallet. From inside, he retrieves a condom, unwraps it, sheaths his thick cock, then enters me. I close my eyes and arch my back as he stretches me.

I've never fucked with the lights on before. I've never fucked like this, faces inches apart, eyes wide open, the room filled with the sounds of our fucking, with the smell of it. Sergio's elbows close around my arms and he holds my face and he kisses me, just barely taking my lip between his before releasing it, neither of us blinking, not once. Our breathing is shallow, just gulps of air.

He makes a sound, something from deep in his chest, it's raw and base and I feel him thicken even more and I'm going to come. I'm going to come again and when he thrusts one final time, watching me, letting me watch him, I do. As he throbs inside me and I feel him come, I come too and everything about this moment feels so right. So fucking perfect.

And it scares the fucking shit out of me.

I close my eyes and feel, lose myself in sensation, in ecstasy. And when it's done, I'm spent. Empty and weightless. I blink my eyes open to find Sergio's still on me. His expression is strange, unreadable and I don't realize I'm crying until he touches his thumb to my face, wipes away a tear, smears it across my cheek.

He did that the first night too. At the warehouse. It's like he's mesmerized by my tears.

It's quiet, absolutely still, and he's still between my legs, still inside me. Still looking at me.

"Did I hurt you?"

I give my head a shake. It's all I can manage because right now, I can't speak. Can't form words.

But it's not that. He didn't hurt me. It was perfect. Right.

And too much.

He gets up, walks into the bathroom. I hear the water go on a few minutes later and he comes back wiping his hands on a towel. I draw the blanket over myself and sit up as he gets dressed. He looks at me all the while.

"You can stay. It's late."

He shakes his head and I can see from his expression he has something on his mind. "Why were you crying?" he asks, putting on his shoes before coming to sit on the edge of the bed.

"It's just a lot." I shake it off. I don't want to talk about it. I don't even think I can, not until I figure out what the hell is going on inside my head.

He studies me a little while longer, then stands, lays me down, takes the blankets and draws them up to my chin. He leans down and kisses my forehead before walking to the door.

"Why were you upset when you got here?" I ask when he reaches to switch off the lights.

He stops but doesn't turn around. He drops his head. "My mom's sick and she's not going to get better." He switches off the lights then turns to face me. I can just make out his face from the streetlamp outside my window. "I knew, but I guess I was hoping."

I sit up, holding the blanket to myself. "I'm sorry."

He rubs the back of his neck, nods, turns. He's lost in thought again, like he's right back to where he was before he got here tonight. I hear his steps as he descends the stairs. Hear the front door open and close. I don't get up to watch him go this time. I don't want to. The other night's departure still lingers in my mind and it makes me shudder.

It's an omen.

A bad one.

11

SERGIO

I walk in the door of my house, drop the keys on the side table, take off my coat and let it fall to the floor. I should have stayed with her. What I want more than anything right now is to lie down beside her and watch her sleep. Listen to her breathe. Hold this tangible, living thing. Hold it so fucking tight it won't vanish like everything does.

From the living room, I pick up a bottle of whiskey and a crystal tumbler. The lights are still off and I don't switch them on but make my way into my study instead. This house is so quiet. So still. The curtains in the study are always drawn. This is the darkest room of the house.

I move behind my desk and switch on the lamp. From underneath the desk, I take out the large, rolled up sheet of what looks to be ancient parchment. It's not. Just made to look that way. I unroll it, smoothing down the edges, looking at the black and white boxes, the gray, worn areas where I've erased and redrawn and erased and redrawn too many times. Where I've worn a small hole in one of those boxes.

This is why I came home. There's work to be done.

Without paying attention, I pour a glass of whiskey and set the bottle on one corner of the sheet, sipping as I move around to the next. I slide another edge beneath the table lamp. The paperweight flattens another corner as I take my seat. One more sip and my tumbler rests on the final edge and the parchment is laid out before me.

I don't have to look away to open the drawer and take out my pencils. Charcoal, for sketching. The callous on my middle finger is still dark from all the times I've held these.

The Benedetti family tree is all here before me from generations past. I wonder if anyone will continue to do this when I'm gone. When I'm one of the boxes that needs to be erased. Redrawn. The dates entered, finally.

I can't find the eraser right away and turn to rummage through the drawer. It had slid to the back. Taking it and my ruler, I erase the already smudged line around a cousin's box. I want it perfect.

No one's seen this little project of mine, not even Salvatore. It's morbid, I know. But it takes up so much of my mind, more and more as each day passes.

When I'm finished redrawing the box, I retrace the dates. This cousin was seventeen when he was killed. A car crash, not mob violence. Just too much alcohol and stupidity. We have those too. Life. Normal. Death.

When that's done, I drag my gaze to my father's box. Then my mother's. I touch hers with the tip of my finger. It won't be long before I add a date here.

I suck in a deep breath, rub the scruff of my jaw. If I don't shave soon, it'll be a fucking beard. I look away, look down at my brothers' boxes. My own. Funny, I've drawn theirs with connected empty boxes beside for their eventual wives. Their families.

I told Natalie time was a luxury, but so is family. Children. A fucking wife.

I swallow all that shit down, swallow the choking lump in my throat, bury it deep in my gut. I steel myself, look at my own name there. I'll be the boss of this family one day. It'll be when I've added a date to my father's box. It's not that I don't want it. I do. And it's not that I feel guilt over what I do. I don't. I'm very comfortable with who I am. It's just—it's always bittersweet, everything.

Someone always has to fucking die.

I line up the ruler, almost draw the link, almost add a box, but I stop. I can't do that because if I do, I'll be condemning her.

Instead, I take out a blank sheet of the same type of paper. This one's letter sized. I have it specially made—vanity, I suppose. I like nice things.

I set the sheet on top of the family map—our graveyard—and pick up the tumbler, swallow the rest of my whiskey. I pour another glass and get to work.

From memory, I start with her eyes. Almond shaped and so dark, they're almost black. Eyes are the hardest. Inside them is the soul. And I want to see her soul. I want it more than anything else right now.

It takes time, but I've got all night. My hands turn gray with charcoal as I smudge and erase and redraw again and again and again. I want to draw her like she was tonight. When she came. Soft and open and surrendered. Surrendered to me.

She didn't realize she was crying until I wiped away a tear. It's the strangest feeling, I have no word for it and I don't want to forget that, not ever. Memory is so fucking fragile.

When I finish with the eyes, I sit back and look at my work. I breathe from high in my chest, I've been holding my breath and didn't realize it. My hand reaches to find my glass but it's empty, so I drag my gaze away, stand to reach for the bottle, refill, splashing a few drops onto the family tree. I wipe them away with my sleeve and drink the burning liquid in one swallow. I wish it numbed me like it used to, but it takes a lot these days.

I push the sketch aside and look back at my box on the family tree, look at the line I started to draw to add a box, to link it to mine, and for one moment, I let myself imagine. I let myself dream the impossible.

And then I sit and I make myself remember.

Make myself count.

Make myself say aloud the name of every person here where a date had to be written in. Something that wouldn't be erased again. A box. A life. Another, different, sort of box. I count each one.

I do this every time I take this sheet out. Every time I feel sorry for myself because I have no right to. I'm not a good person. Salvatore, he has a conscience. I know his struggle. Dominic, not so much. He's a mean son of a bitch. But so am I. The only difference between my little brother and me is that I'm going to get everything I want and he's going to get nothing. That's my saving grace.

Although I'm not sure the word grace should be uttered by someone like me.

I sit. I run my thumb softly over the edge of Natalie's eye. Smudge it. I smear charcoal across the sheet of paper, like I smeared the teardrop across her cheek earlier.

I reach in my pocket for my cell phone and maybe I am a little drunk when my brother's groggy voice comes on the line and I look at the time. It's almost four in the morning.

"Sergio?" Salvatore asks, then with more urgency, "Is everything okay?" He must just realize the time.

"Yeah. Yeah, it's fine."

Pause. "You sure?"

I grunt. I can't drag my eyes from hers as I reach for the bottle and drink straight from it.

"Sergio. What the fuck? It's four in the morning."

"Listen." I don't recognize my own voice, it's so low. So quiet. So broken.

He hears it too, I know from the emptiness in the line. "I'm listening," he finally says.

"There's a girl," I start.

"A girl?"

"If anything happens to me, you'll have to make sure she's okay."

"What the fuck are you talking about? Nothing's going to happen to you."

"Just listen."

"Are you fucking drunk?"

"No. Yeah. Maybe a little. Doesn't matter." I smear charcoal on my fingertip. Smear it to Natalie's temple, create a shadow.

"Where are you?" he asks.

"Home."

"Alone?"

"Yeah. Alone."

"You need me to come over?"

"No, I'm fine. I just need you to shut the fuck up and listen now."

"Okay. Tell me about the girl."

I close my eyes, give my head a shake. What am I going to tell him? What can I say that will make any sense?

"Just make sure she's okay." Fuck. I'm definitely drunk.

"I'm coming over. You can make me fucking breakfast because it's not even the ass crack of dawn."

I chuckle. "No, it's fine. Salvatore, it's fine. I'm okay." I take a deep, sobering breath.

"Then tell me about the girl. What's her name?"

"Natalie. Natalie Gregorian."

He repeats the name, then chuckles. "Dad's going to give you shit she's not Italian."

"Yeah, well, fuck that."

"How long have you known her?"

"A couple of days."

He laughs. "She got you good, huh?"

"I like her, that's all. Just if anything happens—"

"Nothing's going to fucking happen to you so shut the fuck up. Don't be a goddamned ass."

I smile.

"Natalie Gregorian," he says seriously, and I know that's his way of telling me yes, he'll make sure she's okay if anything happens to me. "Why don't you get some sleep now, brother."

"Yeah." I get to my feet. "Listen, sorry I woke you. I know you need your beauty rest."

"Fuck you."

"Hey, the stuff with mom—"

"She's getting another opinion. Dad's calling in some specialist from Germany."

"Of course, he is." He's desperate. "It's shitty."

"Yeah it's fucking shitty. Listen, you can't think about it. You need to go have some fun. Take Natalie away for a weekend or something. Somewhere hot and sunny. You can't always be in this shit, you know? Not you, Sergio. You need a fucking break."

I know what he means, why he's saying this. I've got the family graveyard laid out in front of me. Drawn over years. This darkness, it's a part of me. And it's not that it belongs to me. No. *I* belong to *it*. Always have.

"I'll think about it."

"All right. Get some sleep."

"Good night." I hang up, set the phone down. I slide the large sheet out from under my new sketch and roll it up, put it away. I give Natalie's sketch one long look before switching off the lights and going upstairs to try and sleep, hoping for just a few hours of oblivion.

God, what I'd give.

12

SERGIO

Roman lives about an hour out of the city. We're not supposed to meet until this afternoon, but I want the element of surprise.

"Sergio," he checks his watch. "Did I confuse the time?"

"No, Uncle. I'm early."

"You didn't have to come all the way out here."

"I don't mind." I look around the elaborately decorated house. It's an older structure and dark, with wood everywhere. Not my style, but it's what he likes. "I have some business out this way anyway." It's a busy fucking day for me.

We walk directly into his study. Roman takes the seat behind his desk. I remain on my feet, studying the paintings along the walls. "This new?" I ask about a watercolor I haven't seen before.

"Yes. Bought it at auction a few weeks ago, actually."

"It's very nice." And quite expensive, I'm sure.

"Thank you. How are you holding up after the hospital?"

I face him, lean my back against the wall and fold my arms across my chest. I purposely don't take the seat before the desk. Before him.

"It's shitty news."

"Yes. Your father's very upset."

"Understandable."

"There are some meetings coming up that I'm not sure he'll be able to attend."

I nod. "I'll take his place."

"I can sit in as necessary."

"As his son and eventual successor, I'll take his place."

"As you wish."

"How did old man Vitelli know about mom, Uncle?"

Roman has been with my father for longer than I've been around. He has learned well to conceal any emotion. Mastered the art. It's not that I mistrust him, but there's something that's always niggled at the back of my mind with him.

"When we were talking about Joe's situation, it came up."

"Why were you talking to him about his son's situation?"

"I've known him a long time, Sergio. He had nothing to do with what his sons were arranging."

"It sounds like you're friends."

"You know as well as I there are no friends in this business."

"Does he know you would have dealt a harsher punishment than I had it been up to you?"

At that, there's a brief narrowing of his right eye. I only notice it because I've trained myself to watch people closely.

"What are you saying, Sergio?" he finally asks.

"I'm saying loyalty is of utmost importance, Uncle. Equal to family. Perhaps surpassing it."

"Are you questioning mine?" He's direct. We all are, I guess. "I'm your mother's brother, remember. Your godfather. Are you questioning my loyalty to you or your family?"

"Explain to me how it came up."

He raises his eyebrows. The chair creaks as he leans back. "I don't think the Benedetti family needs another war. Not right now."

I agree with him on that. The DeMarco war damaged us, at least a little. We won, but between that and my mother's illness, Roman is right. This is not the time for war. Vitelli—hell, any ambitious family—would use my mother's illness, see it as a weakness, an opportunity.

"I gave a little, to gain a little," he says. "I apologize if I overstepped."

"I don't like being caught off guard."

"And it wasn't my intention that you should be." He rises, walks around his desk and comes toward me. "Sergio, you're my nephew. My blood. And when the time comes, I hope I'll be of service to you as I am to your father." He gives a brief bow of his head.

I watch him do this, know what it takes to do what he's doing. He's right that we're blood. And to have to bow to a man almost thirty years his junior, whose only privilege is birth, must burn a little.

I nod, check my watch. "Anything new from the Vitelli boys?"

"No. Quiet as can be."

"Which we both know is not really a good sign." Silence always precedes an ambush. A deafening, deadly stillness.

"Yes, we do." He moves back behind his desk. Sits. "I'll keep my eyes on Vitelli."

"Do. I want to be kept up to date on any happenings. Let's keep my father out of this for now."

"I agree with that."

"Are you coming to Dominic's birthday dinner?" I ask to change the subject.

"Of course."

"I'll see you then," I say.

"You don't want to stay? Have something to eat?"

"No, thank you. I have some personal business to take care of."

"All right. I'll walk you out."

When I'm done at my uncle's, Eric drives me to my next destination, the Dayton Architecture offices. As in Professor Harry Dayton, the prick. He touched her, expecting her to fuck him for a fucking internship. Fucking asshole. I'm about to do this town a service.

As we near the offices, I wonder how she gets out here because she doesn't own a car. There's a bus stop a few blocks down. I'm guessing she takes the bus and although this isn't a bad neighborhood, the opposite, in fact, I don't like the thought of her walking on her own or waiting in the dark at the bus stop.

The office is a mansion that's been converted to serve as the Dayton Architecture firm. I admit, it's beautifully done. I've heard of the firm, too. When I bought my house, they were one of the ones I considered to do the job of renovating.

Eric and I walk up to the front doors together. I don't have anyone else with me, but I don't think I'll need much man power. When we walk inside, a pretty, young girl looks up from the receptionist desk.

"Good afternoon, gentlemen. How can I help you?" she asks, a smile on her lips.

"We're here to see Harry Dayton," I say, glancing around. There's a woman in the waiting room who's stopped flipping through the magazine on her lap to watch us and someone else peers up from her desk in an office at the back.

It's not like we stand out though, Eric and me. We're dressed well. Dark suits. Clean cut. But maybe we do. Maybe they can feel the aggression coming off us.

"Do you have an appointment?" she asks.

"Tell him Mr. Benedetti's here to see him."

"Professor Dayton's very busy, Mr. Benedetti." She pushes a few keys on her keyboard. "And I don't see you listed here."

"Upstairs?" I ask, ignoring her. "That his office?" Double doors at the top of the winding, elaborate staircase lead me to believe it is. Like a fucking king, he sits up there. Fucking pervert. "We'll see ourselves up."

"Sir! You can't go up there—"

Eric and I take the steps up at a brisk pace. I unbutton my suit jacket as I reach the first-floor landing and don't bother to knock but push the door open to find a very surprised, balding middle-aged man sitting behind a massive desk.

"What the—"

The girl from downstairs comes running into the room. "Professor, I'm so sorry—"

"That's alright, honey," Eric says behind me. I know he's urging her out. "We'll take it from here."

The door closes.

Dayton looks me over, rises to his feet, his face red with rage. "What the hell do you think you're doing?"

Eric walks toward the desk, then around it. He glances at the computer screen and chuckles as he puts his hands on Dayton's shoulders and pushes him to sit.

"We'll let you get back to your porn in a few minutes," he says. "This is Mr. Benedetti."

I sit, cross my ankle over my knee. Look around.

"Mr. Benedetti," Dayton says. From the look on his face, he knows who I am.

"I'm here about Natalie Gregorian," I say.

Color drains from his face.

"Recognize the name?"

"I...uh...she's a student of mine."

"You touch her?"

"I—"

"Did you fucking touch her?"

"She...no. What are you inferring?"

"You offer a coveted internship spot, don't you? You have special requirements for pretty, young students?"

He just stares at me.

"Let's make this simple. If she wants that goddamned internship, it's hers. The hours she's here, you won't be. If you happen to cross her path, you'll turn and walk—no, you'll fucking run—the other way."

"I...I...she's in my class."

"Then she better get straight fucking A's."

I stand, slap my hands on his desk. Dayton jumps, but Eric's hands on his shoulders keep him rooted in his chair and when I lean toward him, he shrinks back.

"Did you hear me?" I ask.

"Yes."

"Yes, what?"

"Y...y...."

Eric smacks him upside the head.

"Yes sir, Mr. Benedetti."

"Now we're getting somewhere. But just to be sure." I straighten, button my jacket, give Eric a nod and turn to walk toward the door. It only takes Eric a few minutes to make sure we're understood. He rejoins me by the time I'm halfway down the stairs, messaging Natalie that I'll pick her up for a late dinner.

13

NATALIE

I am fuming. It's late and I'm sitting on the bus and can't even see straight, I'm so mad.

My phone rings. It's Sergio again. He's been calling me for the last half hour. This time, I switch it off altogether.

I didn't get a look at Professor Dayton myself because he was gone by the time I got to the office, but the looks I got from everyone else told me his spur of the moment vacation plans had something to do with me. I'd gone in to let him know I was no longer interested in the internship. That I was withdrawing my application and no longer would be available to volunteer. But that didn't happen.

Lisa, the airhead receptionist, told me two men had come in to see Professor Dayton. That they'd been wearing suits and were good looking in a bad-boy, dirty kind of way. She'd sighed after saying it. She'd actually sighed. Of course, she couldn't remember their names. I'm surprised she remembers her own some days.

I knew exactly who she was talking about and texted Sergio that dinner was off. Told him I knew what he did.

I should never have mentioned the internship or the professor. I just didn't think it was a possibility he'd hurt him. But he must have had it on his mind all that time because he went behind my back and did what he wanted anyway completely ignoring what I said.

The bus pulls up to my stop about thirty minutes later. I get out, cursing the high heels I'm wearing. I had a presentation at school today, but I'd much rather be in an old pair of jeans, a huge sweater and comfy boots. Carrying my large, cumbersome portfolio along with my backpack and the few things I'd left at the office in a plastic bag, I walk the six blocks home. The streets are busy, it's the dinner hour, but for some reason, I find myself looking over my shoulder more than once, unable to shake the feeling I'm being followed. That's got to be Sergio's influence on my life. He's a mobster. What he does he proved tonight. He beats people up. Hurts them. It's what he knows.

Is it all he knows? With me, he's been so gentle. So generous.

I shake my head. Trying to reconcile these two sides of him is giving me a headache.

Elftreth's Alley is empty. No reason to be here unless you live here. The tourists usually come by during the day, not at night, at least not during the winter months. I dig my new key out of my pocket. The fact that I have these new locks—courtesy of Sergio who steamrolls to get his way—irritates me. I unlock the door and step inside. The first thing I do is slip off my shoes, leaving them as I walk to the kitchen table to set down the portfolio. I realize it's strange Pepper didn't greet me tonight. I'm later than usual and she's probably hungry.

"Pepper, I'm home. Sorry I'm late. You wouldn't believe my day." I walk around the table to open the cabinet under the sink and get her food. "Come on, honey. Dinner."

Nothing. Not even when she must hear the sound of food filling her bowl.

I stop. "Pepper?" My heart races. Shit. She's so old. What if...

I straighten, thinking the worst, and turn to head into the living room. I switch on the light and let out a scream because I'm not alone.

Sergio's here. Sitting in the middle of the couch, arms spread wide, eyes hard.

And right now, he looks like a fucking Godfather.

Pepper's on the floor, her head on his shoe, sleeping.

"I fed her." He's pissed, I can hear it in his voice, feel it coming off him. There's a half empty bottle of whiskey on the coffee table.

"What are you doing here? How did you get in?"

"She was hungry."

"How did you get inside?" I repeat. I can match his anger.

"I told you I had a key."

Fuck. That's what he'd meant last night. "You can't have a key. I never gave you one."

"You switched off your phone."

I walk over to Pepper, squat down to pet her. I don't look at him when I answer. "Because I didn't want to talk to you."

"When I call you, you answer."

"Doesn't work that way." I say, standing, spinning on my heel. I'm about to walk away when he captures my wrist, his grip firm, more firm than he's ever been with me. I make a sound, try to pull free, but he tugs on my arm, kicks my feet out from under me so I fall face down onto his lap. "What are you—"

He slaps my ass hard ten times in succession.

I'm gasping, instinctively reaching back to cover the spot. He captures my wrist, so he has both now, and holds them in one of his hands. I crane my neck to look up at him. He keeps his eyes locked on mine and rubs one hand over my ass, then spanks it again, ten more times on the other cheek.

"Stop!" It fucking hurts.

"When I call you, you answer, Natalie."

I tug at my arms, but his grip is vice-like.

"Do you understand?" he asks.

"Let me go."

"Do you fucking understand?"

"Yes!"

He gives me one more hard smack before releasing me, and I stumble to my feet. I feel hot, embarrassed, and I'm clutching my ass.

"I just want you safe." He gets to his feet.

I step backward.

He's wearing a suit, the jacket of which is hanging over the back of a chair. He gently moves Pepper's head off his foot before he walks toward me.

I'm mute as he approaches. There's a darkness to Sergio Benedetti. It clings to him, like a shadow. It's the one thing that scares me about him because I trust that he won't hurt me. And I believe that he wants me safe. I may not understand it, but I believe it.

But this shadow, it's not one he casts. The opposite. It seems to cast itself over him. To have a claim on him. Some strange, powerful hold over him.

"You shouldn't have hurt him," I say when my back's against the wall and he's standing inches from me.

"You couldn't protect yourself so I did it for you. Besides, this isn't important. That idiot isn't important."

"No, it doesn't work that way. I didn't want—"

"How does it work?" he asks, one corner of his mouth curling upward. He looks me over, leans his forearms against the wall on either side of my head. "Huh?" He dips his head closer, inhales, touches the scruff of his jaw against my cheek. "Explain to me how it works."

I look up at him, at his midnight eyes. I smell his aftershave, remember what we did last night. My body remembers too.

"How does it work, Nat?"

I hate the nickname. Always have.

"Huh?" he continues. "I stand back while some asshole intimidates you into his bed?"

"I didn't. I wouldn't. I'm not fucking stupid. And I don't need someone to protect me. I don't need some knight in shining armor and I'm not looking for a hero." Tears warm my eyes. I hate them, hate the weakness. But what I've said has made him stop. Confused him almost.

Then he laughs. "You think I'm trying to be the hero?" A moment later, he drops his head. His forehead creases and he's looking down for a long time before he shifts his gaze back up to mine, searching mine as if it holds the answers. "I'm not the hero, sweetheart. I'm the fucking monster."

When I don't reply, he grins. It's a sad, one sided thing.

"What do you think of that? Makes more sense, right?"

I push against him, but it's like trying to move a wall, and the look in his eyes, the dark desperation in his words, his voice, it scares me. "Let me go."

"No." He takes my wrists in one of his hands, draws them over my head, pins them to the wall. His other hand grips my skirt, yanks it up. "You're good. You're the only good in my life, you know that?" His eyes skim my bared legs, the stockings that reach mid-thigh. "And I want what I want," he finishes, dragging his gaze back to mine. "I should let you go. It's the right thing to do, I know."

I can't process what he's saying—it's almost like he's not talking to me but to himself. Like he's been thinking and thinking and he's just saying it out loud now.

He touches my face, my cheek. His thumb presses against my lower lip, forces my mouth open. "But I can't," he says finally.

"You have a key to my house." It's all I can say and fuck, he's so close and when he presses against me, against my clit, it takes all I have to not wrap my legs around him. Rub myself against him. Hump him like some animal. Because I do want this. Want him. It's not just that part of me, either. It's all of me. Even though I know my heart will shatter when it's finished. When he's gone.

He kisses me hard, not waiting for me to kiss him back. His fingers curl into the crotch of my panties, push them aside, roughly rub my clit.

"You're wet."

"This is too fast. We don't even know each other. Don't you see how strange this is? How not normal?" I'm just talking though. I don't want him to go. To walk away. Even if it is wrong.

Keeping me pinned to the wall, he undoes his belt, the buttons of his pants. He pushes them down and the smooth skin of his cock makes me moan as he rubs against my clit, between my folds.

"You should make me stop," he whispers into my ear, then bites my earlobe. It's like neither of us is listening to the other, though, because we're saying the same thing but we're both powerless to do it.

When he puts his mouth to mine, I open for him, our kiss wet, his tongue dipping inside my mouth as he sets my hands on his shoulders and lifts me up by my hips.

"Say no and I'll stop," he says, biting my lip, making me taste the metal of blood. "Say no, Natalie. Make me go. Make me walk away." He pauses, looks at me. "I'll let you in on a little secret." He whispers the next part: "It's better for you if you do."

He thrusts inside me, making me grunt, making me suck in breath. His thick cock stretches me and when he slides out a little, it's only to thrust in harder. He's watching me, eyes black but for the narrow ring of midnight, pupils dilated. He kisses me, but our eyes remain open. He's sucking my lower lip. I know he tastes blood. He must.

Again, he slides out a little, only to punish me with another thrust.

"Say it," he demands, a threat in his tone. "Say it now. Tell me to stop, this is your chance. Save yourself." He thrusts painfully and when I don't say what he wants me to say, when he speaks again, there's a violence to his words. "Tell me to fucking stop."

I gasp, cling to him.

"You know who I am. What I do," he continues.

It hurts, the wall at my back, his too thick cock driving into me, deeper and deeper, tearing me in two, tearing through to my core, piercing my heart.

"If you don't tell me to stop now, I won't. Not now. Not ever."

He stops moving, and I'm impaled. He takes my jaw in his hand again, makes me look up at him.

"Say it now. Tell me to stop. Tell me to go. It's your last chance."

I shake my head as much as I can with him gripping my face. Fuck. I'm going to come. I'm so fucking close, I just need...just one more thrust.

He smiles. He's got his answer. And that smile turns into a wicked grin a moment later.

"You want to come?" His voice is low, the words drawn out.

I make a sound, but I can't say the word.

"Say it."

I'm pressing against him, trying to grind against him. This isn't me. But he does something to me. Makes me something different. Makes me someone I don't recognize.

"Fucking say it."

"Make me come. Please!" I want him, and I can't get close

enough. I want to be filled up by him. Possessed by him. Fucking owned by him.

"Good girl," he says, kissing me, grinning wide, drawing farther out than before and thrusting so hard, I cry out. "Come, Natalie. Come on my dick. Come all over me."

That's all it takes, his command, his cock inside me, his eyes on me, watching me, seeing me, seeing me splinter and break. Seeing everything.

I squeeze my eyes shut and I come. I come so fucking hard I can't breathe, I can't think, and if he didn't have me, I wouldn't be able to stand. It's like an explosion, orgasm claiming my body as Sergio claims my everything, and when I feel him come, when I feel him throb inside me, feel him release inside me, I open my eyes and I watch him, clinging to him, wanting him, wanting it all.

My hands wrap around his shoulders, nails digging into his shirt, his back and he's coming inside me and I've never seen a more beautiful sight than Sergio's glistening midnight eyes. Sergio lost in bliss. In ecstasy.

I ADJUST the crotch of my panties, straighten my skirt.

"We should have used a condom," I say, because in my head, I'm counting days.

"I like coming inside you. I like knowing part of me is inside you." He zips and buttons his pants and buckles his belt.

"Sergio—"

"I'm clean, Natalie," he says.

"I'm clean too, but there are other things."

He seems surprised for the first time since I've known him. "You're not protected?"

I shake my head.

"Where are you—"

"I should be okay." I think. My period ended eight days ago. I still have a few days. "But we can't do that again. I mean without a condom."

He's deep in thought, suddenly. Not angry, just concentrated. Like something's just occurred to him. Something he's never thought of before. It's strange, the look in his eye. Unsettling.

"Our conversation isn't over," I say, simply to break into whatever is happening in his head.

"It's not?"

"You can't just hurt people in the name of protecting me."

He walks into the kitchen. "That prick deserved to be punished."

"That wasn't up to you." I follow him but he's not paying attention to me. He's opening a cabinet, taking out the coffee. "Sergio, I mean it." He's busy opening drawers, closing them, looking for a spoon, I assume. "Hey." I pull on his arm, make him stop. He does, turns to me, walks me backward until he's got me backed up against the refrigerator.

"Natalie."

I'm looking up at him, at his dark eyes. I smell aftershave and sex.

"I'm not going to let anyone hurt you. This bastard isn't important. We're wasting words. Wasting time."

I push against him. "This is too much. Too fast."

He studies me but doesn't reply. Doesn't budge.

"You have a key to my house. You beat up my professor. For what? An internship I wouldn't even take."

"What do you mean you wouldn't take?"

"I told you I didn't want it. You didn't think I'd work for him knowing what he'd expect, did you?"

"You withdrew willingly?"

"What would you do if I said no? That he disqualified me."

"That fucking—" he's suddenly so angry, that the shift in his mood is startling.

"See. This is what I mean! No, I withdrew. He wasn't even there when I got to the office. But see what I mean? You can't just beat up every guy who's an idiot."

"Why not?"

"I can handle myself."

"Nat—"

I put my hands on his face, wanting to make him hear me. "I can handle myself."

It takes him a moment, but he nods once.

"We're moving too fast." I say it because I feel like I have to. Not because I want to stop.

"No, we're not."

I blink, open my mouth, close it again. I'm not expecting that answer.

"I know what I want, Natalie. Do you?"

When he looks at me, his eyes are alive, searching and wanting more. More than I think I can give.

"I've never thought," he starts, speaking slowly, like he's choosing each word carefully. Purposefully. Darkness casts its shadow over him and he looks away, shakes his head, exhales before meeting my gaze again. "I've lost a lot of friends. Cousins. Uncles. Many of them too early. Most of them too early." He steps backward, releases me. "Time is a luxury, Natalie. One I don't think will be afforded me."

There's a sadness in his words. In his eyes. And that shadow, it seems to swell behind him. Always there. Ever present.

Ready to swallow him up and carry him away.

I shudder. "Sergio—"

"I won't waste it," he says. He steps closer again, this time, taking my jaw in his hand, tilting my face upward. He looks at me, my eyes and mouth, and then he kisses me. It's hard, there's nothing tender in this kiss. He doesn't slip his tongue between my lips. He isn't tasting me. He's laying claim to me.

When he breaks the kiss, he doesn't pull back. Instead, with eyes locked on mine, he reaches under my skirt, smears his hand over the cum drying on my thigh, slips his fingers inside my panties.

"I want my cum on you. I want it inside you. I want it to mark you." He rubs me, and somehow, feeling as raw as I do after that fucking, I'm aroused again. I want him again.

He grins. He knows it. He pinches my clit. It hurts and he knows that too, I can see it on his face, but he takes a minute to pull his hand out from under my skirt.

When he releases me, I have to grip him to remain standing because my knees are wobbling.

He wraps his hands around my arms. It takes me a minute to get my breathing under control. To straighten my legs. To process his words. To try to understand what he's saying.

I look up at him, but am unable to speak.

"It's not too fast. There's no such thing. I don't want to stop what's happening between us," he says, searching my face. "If I were a good person, I'd walk away, but I'm not. I'm not. I've done bad things. My hands are so fucking dirty. You need to know that. You do, don't you? You know that?"

I nod.

"Do you know what you want?" he asks.

I know this is important. I know he's important. But I can't say that. I'm still caught on his other words.

"Do you?" he repeats.

"What do you mean that time won't be afforded you?"

"I think you understand."

We look at each other for a long while, the only sound is that of Pepper's soft snores coming from the other room.

"Do you want me to go?" he finally asks. "I'll ask this exactly once so think hard."

I swallow, every hair on my body standing on end. Every nerve alive.

"Do you, Natalie? Do you want me to go?"

My mind is whirling, so much is happening so fast. I look away, down at my feet, at the cracked, old tile beneath them.

He squeezes my arms. "Answer my question."

"No."

14

SERGIO

We are moving fast but what I said to her is true. And even more true, more urgent, since I've met her. This feeling I've always had that my life would be a short one, it's on my mind more and more and I can't shake it like I could before. Maybe it's because of what's happening with my mother. The reality of the fragility of human life. My own mortality staring me in the fucking face. It's like everything is going at warp speed. Like what I said to my father a few nights ago about a reckoning—it's coming. It's coming for me.

My hands are dirty.

No, not dirty. That's too easy.

They're blood soaked.

Maybe that's why she draws me? She says she knows, but she doesn't, not really.

I think back to the night of the convenience store robbery. I remember telling her to close her eyes. She did without question, trusting me, a man—a stranger—with a gun. A man who leaves destruction in his wake. To whom darkness clings. She didn't see me take aim at the asshole who would have raped her. Didn't see me shoot, point blank, the terror in his eyes only fueling me. Giving me power.

No, I don't think she can imagine this. She may think she knows, but she cannot fathom the depths of the darkness that is my life. I am a monster. It's the beast I've created and fed.

Maybe in some way, I hope her innocence will absolve me. Even as I know that for someone like me, there is no absolution. I'm hell bound. I will burn for what I've done, for the sins I've committed. And I don't deny that's where I belong. But I want my time first. I want my time with her even though I know it's selfish. Even though I know I should walk away now before things get more confused.

Because they're already confused as fuck.

And when she mentioned the *other things*, the lack of birth control, I don't know what I was thinking. What I did before I left—rubbing my cum into her—in a way, what she said, the fact that a child is a possibility?

Fuck.

I don't even know what I'm thinking. What I'm doing. What do I want? To put a baby inside her? What the fuck is wrong with me? She's still in school. She's got her whole life ahead of her. And what if I'm right? What if I'm not around for long? What the fuck am I doing to her? How much more selfish can I be?

FOR THE LAST FEW NIGHTS, I've been determined to have 'normal' time with Natalie. Drinks, dinner and sex. A lot of sex. Tonight, I'm picking her up and bringing her to my house.

I park at my usual spot at a lot two blocks away, tipping the attendant generously. I get a text from my father.

"Why the fuck is it so hard for you to do me this one goddamned favor?"

I roll my eyes. I know what he's talking about and I'm going to have to talk to Eric. I realize he's on my father's payroll, but still.

I stop to text him back. *"I'm a big boy. I can take care of myself."*

My phone rings a moment later.

"You make sure Eric drives you. I don't like you out there on your own. We have enemies, Sergio. You fucking know this."

"Fine. Christ."

"Good. I'd hate to have to fire Eric. He's got a family to feed."

"I'll make sure he earns his money. I have to go."

"I mean it, Sergio."

"Me too, dad."

When I get to the tiny house, which I love but which I also know is something that is so not possible given who I am, I peek in the kitchen window. The lace curtains are open and I can see straight inside. I wonder if she realizes how much of her life is lived on display, with people always looking in. This is one of those things that gives me pause because I'm stealing that ease from her simply by showing up here, by inserting myself into her life. Because my enemies will become her enemies. And she doesn't even have a clue.

Without knocking, I unlock the door and go inside. At least she's good about keeping it locked.

"Nat?" I call out, walking through the kitchen, not bothering to take off my coat since we'll be leaving.

"You know I don't like anyone calling me that." Her voice comes from upstairs.

I smile, but before I can reply, a hairdryer goes on. There's a strange scent in the house today. It's familiar but I can't quite place it. It doesn't fit here and it leaves me with an uncomfortable feeling.

Pepper's lying on the floor beside the couch and her tail makes a thudding sound against the hardwood as she wags it when I approach. "Hey Pepper." I pet her, and she lays her head back down. She looks tired and I wonder how much longer she'll be around.

The blow dryer switches off and I hear heels click at the top of the stairs. "Hey, the bathroom window's stuck. Can you see if you can open it for me?" Natalie asks.

"Sure." I climb up the stairs. She's in her bedroom applying mascara. "You know you don't need that." I walk to her, meet her eyes in the mirror.

"I like it," she says, straightening, closing the tube.

That's when I realize what the smell is. Why it makes me so uncomfortable.

"What's that?" I ask, pointing to the chipped vase on the nightstand that holds a small bouquet of lilies. The flowers are pink and white and for as beautiful as they are, I can't fucking stand them or their stink.

"Oh," she glances at the flowers, then at me. "It was on my doorstep when I got here."

I go to it, and I'm holding my breath. "On your doorstep?"

"Yeah. I think it was Drew. He can be dramatic. I'm assuming they symbolize the death of the internship."

I glance at her as she rolls her eyes and returns her attention to her reflection, picking up a tube of lip gloss.

"So, no note?"

"Nope."

"Who's Drew again?" I vaguely remember the name.

She puts the gloss down and looks at me. "My best friend since we were kids," she says matter-of-factly.

"Did he tell you they were from him?"

"Is this a big deal? Are you jealous? He and I aren't a thing. I mean, we were once, but we're friends, that's all. Besides, he's gay."

I could give a fuck. "Did he tell you, Natalie?" I ask again, trying to keep the edge from my voice.

She picks up her phone. "Not yet. I texted him a little bit ago, but he hasn't read my message yet. Sergio, are you jealous?"

I'm not jealous, no. I glance out the window, look up and down the street. I should have put a man on her because I have a feeling these aren't from her friend. "I just don't like the stink of these."

"Most people don't."

"Throw them away. They'll smell up the house," I say, turning to her. "I want you to stay over tonight anyway."

Dominic's birthday is this weekend. I'm supposed to head up to the house in the Adirondacks tomorrow but suddenly realize I can't leave her here alone.

"Actually," I start, turning to her, deciding on the spot. "Come with me." She knows about the weekend, but I hadn't wanted to invite her before. I don't want her around my father, my youngest brother. Not yet.

"What?"

"My mom, she doesn't have much time." I shrug a shoulder and I'm not lying, I do want her to meet my mom. But that's not the reason I want to take her with me. "What do you think?"

"Isn't it a family thing?" She's obviously anxious about it.

"Yeah, but it's fine." I go to her, wrap my arms around her. "I really want you to come with me."

"Okay. I guess I can go. I'll ask someone to cover my shift at the coffee shop tomorrow."

"Good." I won't have to force her, then. "Do you have a duffel bag or something?" I open the closet, which is stuffed with clothes. "You're a mess, Natalie." I like things neat and organized and this drives me insane. From the top shelf, I grab a backpack. "This'll do."

"What about Pepper? She's so old, I worry—"

"We'll bring her too. She can stay at my house and someone will watch her."

"I can ask Drew maybe."

"Come on, I want to spend the night with you." I go to her, take her hands, draw her to me. "I haven't fucked you in my bed yet."

She grins, her eyes brightening.

I kiss her, then let her go. "Just toss what you need in there and let's go. I'll wait for you downstairs."

"Um, okay. I guess."

I take the vase with the flowers and head to the stairs.

"Wait, don't throw them away."

"The whole place will stink by the time you're back." No way this thing is staying inside her house. I fucked up. Shit, I hope I'm overreacting. Hope this Drew guy left them.

When I'm sure she can't hear me, I take my phone and call Eric. I tell him I want a man on her. One at her house tonight.

By the time Natalie comes downstairs, Pepper's waiting by the door and the flowers have been tossed into a neighbor's trash bin, vase and all.

"You're anxious," she says, setting the backpack down to get her coat.

I notice what she's wearing for the first time, a pretty wool dress that hugs her tight. It comes to just below her knees and pointy-toed shoes finish it off.

"You look nice," I say.

"Thanks."

I take her coat, she slips it on and we leave a few minutes later. I'm pretty sure she doesn't notice that I'm watching every person who passes us, memorizing their faces, looking for anything out of the ordinary. I don't want to bring up the flowers again, not until she gets confirmation from her friend. I'm hoping I'm wrong about them even though my gut tells me I'm not.

"Oh," Natalie says. She's reading a text message when I get into the driver's seat after settling Pepper in the back.

"What is it?" I ask, starting the engine and pulling out.

She types something back before turning to me. "Drew didn't know what I was talking about."

I nod, keep my eyes on the road. I want to be out of the city. Want to have her behind the gates of my property, safely locked away in her own tower.

"Maybe they were left there by accident," she says. "I wonder if they were for someone else."

Her phone dings and she looks at it again, shakes her head.

"Sergio, you were weird about the flowers."

I nod.

"Am I missing something?"

I glance at her, don't want to worry her, so I lie. "I just really don't like the smell. They remind me of funerals."

"That's cryptic."

"Death is." I merge onto the highway.

A weight settles alongside us in the car and the silence feels heavy. She'll see through my lie. I know it. But I don't want to have the discussion about the flowers. Not yet.

"Sergio," she finally says once we pull through the gates of my house. "Is there something about the flowers that I should know?"

I park the car, kill the engine. I climb out and the front door of the house opens as Natalie steps out of the car.

She looks at Eric and the man standing beside him, then at me.

"What's going on?"

I meet her worried gaze, shift my attention to opening the back door, lifting Pepper out and setting her on the ground. The dog's too old to hop out of the car on her own. "Let's get her settled." I take a step toward the house but she puts a hand on my arm.

"Sergio?"

I take a deep breath in, turn to her. "I don't think the flowers were left by accident."

15

NATALIE

"What are you talking about?"

I'm forcing in every breath I take, trying to stay calm.

"Let's go in," Sergio says, his eyes dark on mine when he takes my arm and walks us up the stairs to the front door.

I glance over my shoulder at the tall iron gates in the distance.

"In, Natalie. Now."

"Are we in danger?" I ask, Pepper loping beside us.

He doesn't answer but greets the men when we get inside. "Natalie, you know Eric. This is Ricco."

I glance at Ricco. He's big, kind of brutish looking, and he nods at me in greeting. I shift my gaze back to Sergio.

He's watching me, and I know he's weighing his words. "Ricco's going to keep an eye on you while you're at school."

I pull my arm free, step backward. Pepper's fur brushes against the backs of my legs. "What the hell does that mean?"

"Another man will be stationed at your house."

"What—"

"What that means is I intend to keep you safe." He turns to the men. "Eric, there's a bag of dog food in the trunk. I need you to get that. I'll meet you in the study in a few minutes."

"Wait," I start, but the two simply do as they're told and Sergio turns to me, and all of a sudden, he looks different. Bigger. Scarier.

"Nat." He takes my arm again.

"I told you I don't like being called that." But it doesn't matter. I don't care what he calls me right now.

"Come on," he says, tipping his head to the side, forcing a smile that doesn't quite make it. "Let's get you a drink."

"I don't want a drink," I snap, freeing my arm again. Or I try to, at least.

"Natalie."

"What's happening?" I hear how I sound, feel panic bubbling inside me, making goose bumps rise all along my body.

"Calm down. You're safe."

"Why would I not be safe?"

He studies me, wraps his arm around me, pulls me toward him. I plant my hands on his chest.

"Sergio, why—"

I stop because his fingers move up along my spine and his hand closes around the back of my neck. His eyes search my face. "You're with me now. Things are different. You knew that."

I glance away, shake my head. "I don't—"

"A drink, Natalie. Even if you don't want one, I need one." Without waiting for a reply, he walks me into the kitchen. He spins a stool at the counter and gestures for me to sit. I do.

From a cabinet, he gets a bottle of whiskey and two tall glasses. He brings them over to the counter and turns the stool beside mine toward me and sits. I watch as he sets the bottle and glasses down, then pours about three fingers full into each glass.

He closes his hand around one, pushes the other toward me with the knuckles of the same hand. His eyes never leave mine and when I raise my hand to the glass, it's trembling. Sergio sees it too.

"The flowers," I say, looking at the liquid, knowing it will burn when it goes down. "Were they a sign?" I pick up the whiskey, bring it to my lips, force a swallow. I hate this stuff but I take another sip because I need it right now. When I look up at him, he's still watching me. "You said they're funeral flowers." I'm processing my own words as I say them. But I've known this all along, haven't I? That knowing him, being with him, it puts me in danger.

He doesn't answer for a long time, just watches me like he's reading my thoughts, reading me.

Pepper lets out a bark from nearby and we both turn to her.

Sergio sets his glass down, gets up and opens a drawer, gets a bowl and fills it with water, sets it down in one corner and puts a second, empty one beside it.

"Why don't you get her fed. I'll be back in a few minutes. I'll cook us dinner then."

"I'm not hungry," I say, swallowing the rest of the whiskey and setting my glass down before getting to my feet, walking over to where Pepper's drinking the water. I kneel beside her, my back to Sergio, and pet her. She's so old, her skin and fur feel oily. I don't want to think about how much longer she'll be around.

Sergio sighs, but then he walks out of the kitchen and I assume he's gone to his study to meet with those men when I hear a door close.

I take a deep breath when he's gone, then get back up. Taking the bowl, I get Pepper's dinner then walk back to the counter, take the bottle of whiskey he left behind and pour myself some more. I drink and make my way to the living room.

Tonight, I feel like I have some rights here. Some authority. Because I'm realizing something. Something I've been processing since I met him. Something I still don't quite understand.

I haven't yet made the connection with what mafia life truly means. Not in the terms of real life. Of *my* life.

My mind wanders to what might have happened if Sergio hadn't changed the locks on my borrowed house. Would whoever left the lilies there have broken in? Would someone have been waiting for me inside when I got home? Waiting to do me harm?

No, that's not it. I don't think they meant to hurt me. I think they meant to send a message to Sergio.

I'm studying the photos in the living room when I hear the study door open. Sergio's saying something in Italian. I didn't realize he spoke Italian, but of course he does. A few minutes later, the two men leave, and Sergio walks into the living room. I turn to face him.

"It was a message for you, wasn't it? I don't matter. I'm just a vehicle to get to you, aren't I?"

He walks toward me but I halt him.

"Answer me, Sergio."

He considers for a moment, then answers. "Yes."

"Who did it?"

"That doesn't matter."

"Oh, I think it might matter."

His eyes harden a little. "I'll take care of it."

"Like you did Professor Dayton?"

He takes a deep breath in, lets it out slowly, and closes the space between us. I don't step back, but I want to. He takes the glass out of my hand and sets it aside. "I said I'll take care of it."

"Don't you think I have a right to know?"

He shifts his attention to my hand, takes it in his. He turns it over and pushes the three-quarter sleeve of my dress to my elbow. He studies the skin of my wrist, traces a vein up the inside of my arm. His touch sends shivers along my spine.

"These are my enemies, Natalie. Not yours."

"But if they're at *my* house, leaving *me* funeral flowers, they're *my* enemies too."

"I said I'll take care of it and I will."

"How?" Why am I asking? How much of this do I want to know?

"Don't worry about that. I'll fix it."

I shake my head, look down at his hand, at his fingertips light as a feather as they tickle my skin. He's watching too. Holding my small wrist in his big hand. It makes me feel vulnerable. Makes me think how easily it could be snapped. By whose enemies hardly matters. It would break all the same.

It's strange what I'm feeling for this man whom I've known for only weeks. Who is dangerous. Whom I know I should run from. But thing is, I can't imagine walking away. Can't imagine not having him in my life.

But I'm being stupid. I can't disregard what happened tonight, even if he 'fixes' it. I pull my hand free of his. "What about the next time? I'm guessing you have more than one enemy."

I reach for my whiskey, but he recaptures my wrist and takes my glass, swallows its' contents.

"Is this normal for you, Sergio? Normal life? Nothing out of the ordinary in someone leaving funeral flowers at your doorstep?"

He rubs the scruff of his jaw, the back of his neck. He's looking at me but he's in his head. I see him struggling with something. Maybe it's the same thing I'm battling.

It takes him a long time to speak. "I have many enemies. And

I don't want it to be your normal. I'm a dangerous man. It's dangerous for you to be with me."

"What are you saying?"

His eyes burn. There's so much inside them, conflict and rage and an intense darkness. An almost palpable violence.

He finally turns away, then answers. "Nothing. It doesn't matter."

I go to him, touch his shoulder. "You want me to leave? Walk away? Is that what you're telling me?"

He faces me, gives me a small smile, exhales loudly as he brushes a strand of hair behind my ear. "It's too late for that, sweetheart. I won't let you go. That's been the problem from day one."

"I don't want some man following me. I don't need a bodyguard."

"You don't have a choice," he says. "Not on this one."

"I do. I have to. This is my life. I get a say."

"Not when it comes to your safety," he says, his tone harder, his eyes darker. "Don't be naïve. You don't know this life. This is non-negotiable."

I try to pull free, but this time, he tugs me to him, making me bounce against his chest.

"Let me go." I try to push him off.

"No."

"You don't listen to anything I say when it doesn't suit you."

He cocks his head to the side.

"You didn't when you beat up my professor. Not when you changed the locks on my house without my permission, and now you're not listening either."

"Aren't you glad that I did change those locks?"

I stare up at him, and before I can answer, he puts the flat of one hand in the middle of my chest and walks me backward until my back hits the wall.

"I'm a modern man, Natalie, but I have my limits, and when it comes to your safety, I decide."

"And what, I do as I'm told?"

"That's ideal." He's trying to make light of it.

I try to push his hands off but can't. "Let me go."

"No. I already told you, I'm not letting you go."

"You don't get to decide for me."

"I won't leave you unprotected."

"I wouldn't be in danger if it wasn't for you being who you are."

"Enough!" He slams his fist into the wall.

I let out a small scream, and freeze.

There's an anger that's barely controlled when he next speaks, his voice low, a warning. "You went into this with both eyes wide open. You know it and I know it."

I shudder.

Is he right? I didn't know it, though, not like this.

But isn't that bullshit? And does it even matter? I won't leave anyway. That, I know.

He grips my jaw and tips it up, makes me look at him. "The first time we met, I had a gun aimed at the asshole hurting you. The second time, I had that gun pointed at your head. You've known from day one who I was. I've told you to stop me, to make me go. Told you I would if you told me to. But you didn't, did you? The other night when I fucked you , when I told you to tell me to leave, you didn't. Again. You. Did. Not. Well, it's too fucking late now, Natalie."

"I didn't intend..." I shake my head, try to clear it.

"What? You didn't intend what?"

But the words that come into my head make no sense.

"What?" he growls, this time slapping both hands flat on the wall on either side of my head, making me wince and cower, caging me in.

He must see my terror because he exhales, rubs his face with his hands. "Fuck." It takes him a few minutes but when he speaks again, his voice is controlled. "What didn't you intend?"

Someone clears their throat. Sergio takes a deep breath in, clearly irritated, and turns to Eric who's standing beneath the arched entry.

"You need to see something," he says, then adds something on in Italian.

Sergio walks over to him, and they both look at Eric's phone.

"Fucking bastard," Sergio mutters. "Give me a minute." Eric leaves and Sergio comes to me. "I have to go."

"Where?"

"I'll be back as soon as I can."

"Are you fixing it? Is this you *fixing* it? Will you come back with another bruise on your knuckles? Maybe blood on your shirt this time?"

His eyes narrow and when he steps closer, I take two steps back. "Don't fucking test me. Not now."

I swallow. He's warning me and for the first time since I've known him, I realize I don't know the lengths this man will go to, the violence he's used to. The violence he's caused. I thought I did, but I was wrong. To think you know something but then to really understand it, to feel it, those are two very different things.

He clears his throat. "Natalie—"

I look away, fold my arms across my chest. "Just go."

"There's some food—"

"I'm not hungry. Just go. Go fucking fix it."

"Trust me, Natalie."

I walk away. I don't want to hear anymore. I need to get Pepper settled. I find her in the kitchen eating the last of her dinner, oblivious to the shit storm in the other room. I don't turn around when I hear the two men speaking in hushed tones in the hallway. The front door opens and closes, and I hear a car's engine start. Pepper licks my face when I sit on the floor beside her. I don't know if I'm angry or hurt or scared or what. Sergio takes liberties, assumes things, and thing is, I know that's him. I know this is how it will be with him. Tonight is just a preview of what I'm signing up for.

Irritated with myself, I get up, take Pepper by the collar.

"Come on, let's find ourselves a bedroom." Because I'm not sleeping in his.

———

It's four in the morning when I abruptly wake up, bolting upright in the strange bed, gasping for breath.

The nightmare is gone as soon as my eyes open but it takes me a moment to remember where I am. Why I'm here.

Pepper's snore comes from the foot of the bed. I draw the covers back and get up. I don't want to sleep again. I don't want to go back to that dream.

Quietly, I walk out the door and into the hallway. It's dark, and I wonder if he's back yet. If I'm alone in this big, strange house. But when I reach the top of the stairs, I hear a sound. Music. It's muted, like it's coming from far away.

Barefoot, I walk down the stairs without switching on any lights. It's eerie this time of night. Old houses always are.

The music grows louder as I near the bottom of the stairs. It's coming from his study. I go to it and stop, and I hear him. He's singing along with the music. I recognize the song. *Darlin'* by Houndmouth.

I feel like I'm intruding on something very private so I knock once, quietly, before opening the door.

Sergio's sitting behind his desk. His jacket's off and his shirt's unbuttoned half way down, the sleeves rolled up to the elbow. His hair's ruffled, like he's been running his hands through it, and his eyes are bloodshot. I know why. The bottle on the corner of the desk is almost empty.

"You're back," I say, when he just sits there and looks at me. I realize the song is on repeat because it dies down then starts up again.

Without waiting for an invitation, I step inside and close the door behind me. It smells like him in here. Like his aftershave and whiskey.

I look down at what's on the desk. At the large parchment that spans the entire surface. He's holding two pencils in his hand. Charcoal. His white shirt has smears of it and so do his hands and forearms. The triangle wedge of a worn eraser sits near his glass.

He doesn't get up when I go to the desk. When I look down at the large sheet. It takes me a moment to realize it's a family tree.

I begin to read the names, the dates. There are symbols next to some of them—a small cross. It's the only thing that's not charcoal, but red marker. The crosses are the only permanent things, I realize. All the rest can be erased.

Sergio watches me as I study his lineage, follow the line from great-grandfather, to grandfather, to his father, Franco Benedetti. To his mother. To Sergio.

His brothers' names are beside his. Alongside those, I see lines drawn, boxes prepared for a second name. But next to his, where there was a line, it's now just smudged, erased. Just his birthday beneath with a dash. An eerie emptiness on the other side of that dash. A sort of permanence.

When I look up, I find him watching me. "Did you draw this?"

He pushes his chair back, rises to his feet, gestures for me to come to his side. I do and he takes my hand, draws me closer, stands me between himself and the desk.

Sergio closes his hands over the backs of mine, takes the pointer finger of my right one and traces a line up to his father, to another name I don't know. Presses it over the red cross—it's shaped like a cross from the days of the crusades. Gothic almost. Like he spent time shaping each one. Outlining each with darkest black, colored each in deepest red.

"The cross is a mob killing," he says. And, without a word, we trace ever single macabre cross on the sheet, he and I. I don't count. I lose track. I feel him behind me, feel the weight of his silence. The meaning of it.

When we get to his name, he traces the erased line. He's standing so close, I feel the heat of his body behind mine, the tickle of his warm whiskey-breath on the nape of my neck. The light kisses there.

"You know what I didn't intend?" he asks, picking up our earlier conversation, just before he'd abruptly left. "I didn't intend on falling in love with you."

The song begins again, the tone and lyrics dark and heavy.

It makes me shudder, makes an icy chill run the length of my spine.

I should be happy, right? Aren't these words every girl wants to hear?

Why does it feel like a cement brick has just landed in my belly?

"This one," he starts, releasing my left hand, wrapping his around my middle, pulling me to him, while using our right hands to point to the remnants of an erased box connected to his. "It's for you." His hand snakes up to cup my breast, squeeze it, then wrap around my throat, fingers gripping my jaw just a little too hard, like he wants me to look, to really see.

A moment later, he extends my right arm out, forcing us both to bend forward as he wraps my fingers around the edge of the desk, releasing my throat and taking my left arm to stretch it to the opposite side.

He pushes my hair off to the side and I lay my cheek on the drawing, knowing it'll come away smeared with charcoal. Maybe a little red, too.

"Stay," he says, his breath warm on my ear, lips soft when he kisses my cheek. He straightens, and I see him in my periphery, watch him loom over me, watching me. It's so dark, he's almost a shadow wrapped within a shadow.

His eyes glisten, and when the next part of the song plays, he sings along, the words cold and dark and wet make my heart hurt.

I hear him open a drawer, take something out, but I can't see what it is. His hands are on my back. Sliding down over my hips. Raising the oversized T-shirt I'm wearing high on my back.

Blood surges to my sex and I crane my neck to watch him. His focus is intent on his work as he drags my panties down over my hips, my thighs. Lets them slide to the floor and waits until I step out of them to stand between my legs. To take my ass in his hands to splay me open.

I swallow. He's watching me there, and a moment later, his thumb comes to rest against my asshole, presses lightly there.

When I tense, and begin to straighten, he squeezes his hands over my hips.

"I said stay."

I lay back down. He pushes the tip of his finger inside me. I realize what he took out of the drawer a moment later when I feel the cool drops fall on the cleft of my ass.

"Sergio," I start.

"I've been struggling ever since I met you," he says, beginning to rub the cream into me. It feels strange. Different, but good. "I know what being with me will mean for you and part of me is screaming to let you go. Not to condemn you to this life."

When he slides the fingers of his other hand to my clit, I suck in a breath. He keeps rubbing, and I hear the wet sounds of my arousal, hear his own breath coming shorter. And when he pushes a finger slowly inside me, I let out a moan.

"Natalie," he says, and I hear him unbuckling his belt, unzipping his pants.

I can't answer though, not when he's touching me like that.

"I need to be inside you. To come inside you."

I'm not protected. He can't come inside my pussy.

He's rubbing his cock between my folds, dipping into my wet pussy as a second finger penetrates my ass. It hurts, but it feels good too, and I want him inside me. I want him to come inside me. He's not the only one who needs this. Needs to be this close.

He sings louder with the refrain and he pulls out of my pussy and I look back, watch him pumping his cock with his hand, smearing cream all over it, watching me as he sings along, glancing away only for a moment to draw his fingers out and line his cock up to my asshole and when he pushes in, I gasp, and tense and arch my back and grip the edges of the desk hard.

It hurts, he's so thick, but he rubs my back, takes his time, stretches me slowly. When he strokes my clit, I find myself lifting to him, wanting him, and the sounds in the room, I think they're coming from me, short gasps, moans, and fuck I'm going to come and he's pushing deeper and deeper inside me and a moment later, I'm coming and he's watching me, burying his cock inside me, moving slow and deep until it's over, until the wave passes.

That's when he grips my hips and fucks me. That's when he really fucks me, drawing all the way out, thrusting back inside, the base sounds of an animal rutting coming from him, from his chest.

I know the moment he's going to release, to explode inside me and when he thrusts one final time, laying his full weight over me, his chest and face wet with sweat, and his cock throbs and I feel him release and empty and we're so close, so fucking close. Closer than we've ever been. And when he stretches his arms over mine and intertwines his fingers with my own and he's still throbbing inside me, I think I don't want this to end. I don't want to ever be apart from him. I don't want for him to ever go away. For us to ever leave this room. Because here, we're safe. Here, he's safe.

Sweat mixes with tears and when he finally pulls out of me, I'm spent. I have nothing left. My knees buckle and he lifts me in his arms and I just cling to him.

It's a long while later when we're upstairs and he's bathed me and put me in his bed when I ask him:

"Why, Sergio?"

It's that song, the haunting melody playing in my head. He had on repeat. I don't know how many times I heard it. Don't know how many times he'd heard it before I got there.

"Why don't you sleep at night?" I ask.

He doesn't look at me when he answers. Rolls over on his back instead, and stares up at the ceiling.

"Sergio?"

He turns his head. Studies me for a long moment before answer.

"Because time is running out."

16

SERGIO

Eric had managed to get video footage from a neighbor's security camera that showed the man who'd left the flowers on Natalie's doorstep. But people aren't stupid. He'd had on a hoodie with a baseball cap underneath, the rim pulled low over his face. It could be anyone and I didn't really expect whoever had done it to be waving their fucking hand in the air. This was to let me know they'd found a weakness. That they are not above using that weakness, hurting it—hurting her —to hurt me.

This is mafia life. No one is safe, not if you're the fucking boss, not if you're a foot soldier. Not if you have any connection to any of us. Because it's what I would have done, too. I'm not above exploiting my enemies' weaknesses, no matter how fucking innocent.

Karma. What goes around comes around. I guess it's coming for me.

And that's fucking fine. Me. Not her, though. She's clean. She's not part of this.

"Why are you so quiet?" Natalie asks. She's sitting beside me and we're driving up to my father's house for Dominic's birthday. I'm planning on spending the week up there, but Natalie needs to be back by Monday for classes.

"Nothing. Just preparing myself for the visit."

"You're making me nervous and I'm already a little anxious. Nauseous even."

Things are happening at break-neck speed for us. I know she's feeling a little swept up. And there's nothing I'd like more than to slow down time for a little while. Maybe take that trip Salvatore suggested, go away with her. Somewhere warm and quiet. Somewhere where it's just us.

Because time *is* running out.

Last night in the study with Natalie, that music, her, us together, it's haunting me. My own words keep repeating in my mind and I can't help but feel their warning. It takes all I have to keep it from dampening everything. From stealing the joy from everything.

It's dark when we arrive at the foreboding gates of the Benedetti family home a little before seven at night. They open as we approach, closing only once we turn onto the long drive leading to the mansion looming in the distance.

I glance at her, squeeze her knee. She's staring wide-eyed at the house. "Ready?"

She nods.

"Don't look so worried. I told my dad he'd better be nice to you." I wink, but she pales. "I'm kidding. Relax."

"I don't know why I'm so nervous. It's stupid."

"You're with me. Don't be nervous," I try to reassure her. "Oh, there is one thing. Dominic can sometimes be a dick. Just ignore him."

"Aren't we here for his birthday?"

"Yeah, more for my mom than anything else, though. And he's her baby. I know parents don't technically have favorites, but they do." As I open the car door she puts her hand on my arm.

"Sergio?"

One leg is already out of the car when I look back at her.

"How long does she have?"

I take a deep breath. "Hard to say. Months. She won't survive the year." I try not to feel anything when I say it, but that's impossible. "Come on, let's go in."

She opens her door and by the time she climbs out, I'm at her side, our bags on my shoulder. I take her hand and turn to the large wooden doors illuminated softly by the old-fashioned lanterns on either side. I love this house. Always have. And one day, it'll be mine.

The doors open as we approach and my father stands at the entrance. He barely glances at me. He's been waiting to see Natalie ever since I told him this morning that I was bringing her.

"Dad," I say as we climb the stairs. "Were you watching out the window?" I give him a hug and he pats my back.

"First girl you bring home? Yeah, I'm watching out the window."

Natalie stands tense beside me. My dad's not hiding the fact that he's looking her over from head to toe—taking her measure. He's gauging whether or not she's worthy of me. The real question is are *we* worthy of *her*.

"This is Natalie Gregorian," I say. "Let's try and not scare her off before she's inside, okay?"

My father's eyes are on hers and he lifts his chin a little. There's a moment of awkward silence before he extends a hand to her.

"Welcome, Natalie Gregorian."

I swear I hear Natalie swallow. My father can be overbearing, and that's putting it mildly.

"Nice to meet you, Mr. Benedetti," Natalie says, sliding her hand into his. He doesn't quite shake it, just holds it in his and I swear he hasn't blinked.

I look at him, try to see him as she is seeing him. Not like his son. His favorite son.

Dominic may be my mom's favorite, but I've always been my dad's. I almost feel sorry for Salvatore.

Not for the first time in my life, I see a coldness in my father's eyes. A ruthlessness. Is that what she sees? I wonder how much like him I am. Wonder if I should feel anything about that, because I don't.

Natalie finally drops her gaze and clears her throat.

"It's cold," she says to me.

I get the feeling she doesn't mean the weather. "Let's go in."

As the door closes behind us, voices come from around the corner. Salvatore and my mom. I'm doing the same thing now. Seeing them the way she must see them. My mom is the opposite of my dad. Warm and welcoming, her smile authentic and immediate.

Salvatore looks like a giant beside her, she's lost so much weight. He's a big guy, big as me, but that's not why she looks so small.

I shift my gaze to my brother, wonder what Natalie's seeing. If she recognizes the darkness that clings to him. That shadow of somberness. But maybe that's because it's hard not to think about the fact that this may be the last time we're here like this. With mom alive. Not in a goddamned box.

"Sergio," my mom says. I take her in my arms, feel the flesh and bone she's become. Curse the fucking cancer that's raging a war inside her.

"Mom. You look good." She's wearing a light pink headscarf.

"No, I don't, kiddo."

No, she doesn't. What I told Natalie is right. She won't last the year. She has months and I'm unprepared.

"Mom, this is Natalie. Natalie, this is my mom."

She shifts her gaze to Natalie, takes her outstretched hand in both of hers. "Natalie," she says, then pulls her in for a hug. "It's so good to meet you. We're glad to have you here with us."

The warmth of her reception is so opposite my father's.

"It's good to meet you too, Mrs. Benedetti."

"Sergio's never brought a girl home," she says, winking, pulling back to look Natalie over. She cocks her head to the side and studies her eyes for a moment longer than is comfortable. But then she gives her a nod. "I see what he sees in you."

I glance at Natalie, see her blush.

Dominic clears his throat and walks around the corner. My cocky younger brother is tucking his phone into his pocket and devouring Natalie with his eyes.

"This is my brother, Salvatore," I say, ignoring Dominic, knowing it'll piss him off to be introduced last.

"Nice to meet you," Natalie says as she and Salvatore shake hands.

"Finally, a girl who can stand my brother," he says.

Dominic clears his throat. "And I'm Dominic," he says.

I step closer to her, wrap my hand around the back of her neck. "My baby brother," I add on.

I see Dominic bristle at the introduction. He's so damn easy to fuck with.

"Go get Natalie settled. I'll see you in my study," my dad says before turning to walk away. "We have some business to discuss."

"Franco, I said no business," my mom starts.

But dad waves off her comment.

"It's okay, mom. I'll make sure he keeps it short."

I watch him go but I have to force the smile on my face.

"Your mom and Salvatore seem really nice," Natalie says once we're out of earshot.

I chuckle. "My dad's okay too. You just have to get to know him. This is my room."

We walk into my bedroom and I close the door. It's a spacious room, lavishly decorated in dark grays and blacks.

"Did you grow up here?" she asks.

"Here and in Philadelphia. My mom wants to be here now. It's her favorite place."

"It's a beautiful house."

"Thanks." I walk into the closet, switch on the lights to make sure the dress I ordered at the last minute is here. I didn't see anything in her closet for tonight's dinner. It is and it's perfect for Natalie. I switch out the light and return to the bedroom. "You okay?"

She nods. "My stomach just feels funny."

"Nerves. Why don't you relax. Have a bath if you want. Dinner isn't until nine. I'll go see what my dad wants, and I'll be up to get you."

"Okay."

"There's a dress in the closet for you. Wear it tonight."

"A dress?"

I smile, walk to the door.

"Sergio?" She asks when my hand is on the doorknob.

I turn. "Yes?"

"Um...It's nothing. Never mind."

"Sure?"

"Yeah, just a long drive. I'll go have a bath."

I nod. "I'll be back as soon as I can." I walk out, close the door behind me and don't like the feeling of leaving her alone. But I have to get this meeting with my dad over with. He doesn't know about the flowers at Natalie's house. I didn't tell him because it'll only worry him that someone would get that close to me. But I wonder if that's what he wants to talk about anyway. If it isn't the Lucia DeMarco situation he's more interested in discussing. In getting my acquiescence once and for all, especially now that Natalie's in the picture.

"Dad," I say, entering his study without knocking.

He's sitting behind his desk. "Pretty girl," he says, resting his arms on his desk and looking at me. "Close the door."

NATALIE

M y phone rings a moment after Sergio walks out of the room. I pick up my purse which I'd tossed on the bed and dig inside for my phone. It's Drew so I answer.

"Hey Drew."

"Hey. You there? At *the house*?"

I smile. "Yes." I plop down on the bed. "Weirdo."

"Well, what's it like?"

"Huge. Lavish. I wonder if it's haunted."

"Ha. Did you meet Franco Benedetti?"

"Yes."

"And?"

"And nothing. He's just like you'd expect. Cold. Sergio's mom's nice though. And one of his brothers seems okay."

"Yeah, well, what did *you* expect? I still can't believe you're with him."

"I know." I know Drew doesn't approve. He thinks I'm going to get hurt and I can see how he'd think that, especially given what just happened. I lied to him for the first time since I've known him, too. I told him the flowers were from Sergio. But I force that worrying thought from my mind. "How's Pepper?" He took Pepper for the weekend.

"She's fine, you don't need to worry about her."

"Thanks again for taking her on such short notice."

"Don't worry about it. Hey, I heard something about Professor Dayton taking a few weeks off."

Shit. "Is he?" I play dumb.

"Heard your boyfriend paid him a visit."

"Drew—"

"Just be careful, okay? These are dangerous people."

"He told me he loved me."

My comment is greeted by silence on the other end of the phone. "Did you tell him?" he finally asks.

"Not yet. But…"

"Nat, I'm worried about you."

"Don't be. He won't hurt me."

"It's not him hurting you that worries me. It's you knowing him putting you in danger."

I know this already. "I have to go."

"Shit. I'm sorry, I actually called to tell you to have fun. I don't want to be a shitty friend."

"You're not. You never could be."

"So go have fun."

I chuckle.

"And call me ASAP with any gossip!" he adds on, making me smile.

"You're worse than a woman."

"I know. Love you."

"Love you."

After slipping my phone back into my purse, I open the closet door, and walk in. There, hanging between several suits, is the most beautiful red dress I have ever seen. Beneath it on the floor is a pair of matching red pumps.

I touch the dress, feel the silky material, rise up on tip-toe to lift the hanger off the rack. The tags are still on the label, and I don't recognize the name of the boutique but I do know the Italian designer. I don't want to think about how much it cost.

I carry it back into the bedroom and walk to the ornate, full length mirror standing in one corner. I hold the dress up to myself. The long, layered skirts fall to mid-calf, and thick straps leave a wholly exposed back. The color is perfect, a deep, rich crimson. I love it.

Laying it on the bed, I walk into the bathroom. It, too, is large, and old-fashioned with a clawfoot tub set in the middle of the room boasting copper fixtures. I plug the drain and turn on the water, adjust the temperature and let it fill up as I wind my hair on top of my head and check out the soaps, shampoos and bath oils. I choose one that smells of jasmine, drop a few droplets into the rapidly filling tub and stand back to watch as I undress. I then climb in, letting the splash of water tickle my toes as I look out the window onto the dark, starry night.

This is why I don't mind the cold. The skies are clear then and out here, a million stars dot the midnight sky.

Midnight.

Like Sergio's eyes.

I close mine, and take a deep breath in and slowly sink deeper into the tub as I switch off the water with my foot. The scent of jasmine steams upward and I let myself relax, listening to the drip of the last few drops from the tap.

This weekend is important to Sergio for his mother's sake. I get the feeling this will be one of the last times they'll all be together and that she'll be healthy enough not to be confined to a bed.

I open my eyes and look up at the ceiling, follow the intricate pattern of the crown molding along the edges, around the light fixture. It's a mini-chandelier. I have to smile, shaking my head, wondering just how much money the Benedetti family has. It's a kind of wealth I don't think I can grasp.

But then I think of how they earn that money.

That thought sobers me. Reminds me where I am. And with whom.

I shouldn't get too comfortable. I can't forget what the last few days have brought. What it means for me. What Sergio Benedetti loving me means. Because he's right, I did walk into this—eyes wide open. And I'm not naïve enough to think Sergio's hands are clean.

I push those thoughts away and pull the plug on the drain. Water pours off me as I stand, grab a thick towel off the stack nearby and wrap myself up. I walk to the mirror, glance at my reflection, wonder how I got here, wonder how much I'm willing to ignore to be here.

Wonder who I am.

———

I'm DRESSED but barefoot and sitting on the floor in front of the mirror braiding my hair when Sergio walks in a little before nine. I meet his gaze in the mirror, but my smile falters. He looks strange, like he's got something on his mind, and in his hand, he's holding a tumbler of whiskey. He closes the door, stands just inside and watches me as he takes a sip of his drink and I wonder if it's his first. It doesn't look like it.

"Hey," I say quietly, returning my attention to braiding my hair, feeling my fingers disappear in the thick mass as I create a long, intricate pattern.

Sergio moves, he pulls a chair up behind me and sits, takes

another sip of his drink before setting it down. His legs are on either side of my shoulders.

"Okay?" I ask.

He nods. "You look good."

I finish the braid, but I don't get a chance to tie the end of it together before he puts his hands on the thick straps of the dress and pushes them off my shoulders. I look at myself, at the dress as it slips down to my waist. Look at my bared breasts. At how the braid is already beginning to unravel.

"Don't you want to get changed for dinner?" I ask.

Sergio reaches down and cups my breasts. Draws his fingernails over them. He takes the already hardened nipples between thumb and forefinger and rubs.

I swallow, my eyes locked on his in the mirror. "We're going to be late," I say weakly.

"Turn around," he says.

I kneel up, put my hands on his thighs and face him so I'm kneeling between his widespread legs. He touches his thumb to my lips, then smears the dark red lipstick across my cheek.

"What are you doing?" I ask quietly, beginning to rise as I touch the corner of my mouth. But he takes my hands and shakes his head.

"I want to mess up your face," he says, undoing his belt, the buttons of his jeans.

I watch, my heartbeat picking up when he pushes them down, takes his already thick cock into his fist.

"I want to bruise your perfect lips when I fuck your mouth. I want to come all over your pretty face."

He wraps one hand around the back of my head and draws me to him, ruining the braid as he pushes himself into my mouth. I open for him but it's not wide enough and when I try to draw back, he stands up, his fingers curling into my hair, fisting a handful of it.

"Just open," he says.

I'm looking up at him because he's got my head tilted upward. He bites his lip and I rise up on my knees, wrap my hands around his powerful legs.

"Good girl. Like that. Just open and let me fuck your face."

I want to slide my hand under my skirt but he's moving too fast, and I can't breathe when he pushes so deep, so I push against his thighs, try to pull back, but he won't let me.

"Shh. Relax, Natalie." He's not coaxing me. It's a command. "Look up. Look at me."

I do, and he nods his head and pulls out a little, lets me gulp in a breath, then slides his length back into my mouth.

"That's it, like that. I'm going to go deeper now. I want to watch you take my cock. Want to watch your face when I come down your throat."

He starts to pump and I panic when I can't breathe but he leans down and pets my hair and now he's coaxing me. Whispering something over and over again.

"Trust me, Natalie. Trust me."

I do. I trust him. And when I relax my mouth, my throat, he grips me so hard that I can't move, and thrusts in deep and I know he's going to come. I feel him grow even thicker and his eyes get that glow, that sheen, and a moment later, I feel the throbbing, feel his release, see it on his face as he empties down my throat and I swallow. I swallow and when he pulls out, I cover my mouth, but he doesn't release me. Instead, he crouches down.

"Natalie." He smiles at me, kisses me softly. "Sweet, pretty Natalie." He touches the scruff of his jaw to my temple. "You have to learn to swallow it all," he whispers, and smears what I couldn't swallow across my cheek, over the ruined lipstick, and kisses me, kisses me hard, his tongue where his cock just was, tasting his own cum, messing up my face, like he said he would.

"I love you," he says, holding me close, so close with his hand wrapped around the base of my skull, keeping me against him. "I love you and you're it for me. Mine. No matter what. Understand?"

I don't know how much he drank, but I taste whiskey on his breath and the way he's talking, the way he's holding me, it's strange. Too much. Too dark.

"Did something happen?" I dare to whisper. I don't want to pull away, to interrupt this intimacy. Because what he's saying, it's true. I'm his. I know it and I want it.

He draws back, his face an inch from me.

"Mine, Natalie. Always. No matter what."

18

NATALIE

Sergio and I are the last to walk into the dining room. Everyone is already seated, his whole family, and one other man who's reading something on his phone. I feel myself tense when he looks up and our eyes meet.

Franco makes a point of checking his watch as a waiter pours wine into his glass.

"Sorry we're late, mom," Sergio says, ignoring his father. "Natalie, this is my uncle, Roman."

Roman stands, extends his hand to me. I pause. Sergio rubs my back and I try to stop my hand from shaking when I extend it to his. Roman is the man from the night at the warehouse. The one who asked if Sergio needed a cleaner.

His uncle smiles. It's strange, like that night never happened. "Nice to meet you, Natalie," he says cordially, sounding very different from how he'd sounded at the warehouse.

I don't like him. I don't like him even one little bit.

Sergio pulls out my chair and I sit down. He squeezes my hand under the table.

"You look beautiful, dear," Sergio's mom says.

"Thank you, Mrs. Benedetti."

Mr. and Mrs. Benedetti are sitting across from me. Roman is on Franco's right and Dominic is beside his mother. Salvatore is the cushion between me and Dominic and I'm grateful for it. There's something about Dominic that makes me incredibly uncomfortable. Salvatore seems different. Franco and Roman outright terrify me.

Franco rings a bell and I'm startled to see a line of servants appear carrying dish after dish, and, beginning with Franco, serving him, then moving around the table.

Sergio gives me a wink when I glance at him, my eyebrows raised at this formality.

"My father can be elaborate. This is the first course so pace yourself," he whispers in my ear.

I suddenly look at the place settings, wonder if I'm going to be expected to know which fork goes with which dish. When it's my turn, I lean away as the servers fill my plate with a pasta dish that makes my mouth water.

It seems they all start talking at once then, Franco with Roman, Dominic with his mom, Salvatore and Sergio with each other as I sink backward in my seat. My stomach growls as I pick up my fork and am grateful for the fact that they're so loud that no one would have heard.

I'm trying to participate but I'm engrossed just watching them so when Mrs. Benedetti asks me a question, the table goes quiet before I realize she's talking to me.

"I'm sorry?" I set my fork down and wipe my mouth.

"Sergio tells me you're studying architecture."

"Oh. Yes. I'm at the University of Pennsylvania."

"I majored in architecture way back when," she says and smiles. I notice she's barely eaten a bite of her food.

I smile back. "I love it, love houses, especially older homes like Sergio's or this one."

"You know, the family has some contacts, if you need help finding work," Dominic says, shoving a huge mouthful of pasta into his mouth and watching me as he chews.

I feel like this is a test.

My gaze shifts to Franco, who's also watching me.

Sergio clears his throat. "I'm sure Natalie will have no problem finding a job on her own," he says, wrapping his hand around the back of my neck. He did it earlier too, when I first met Dominic. "If she needs anything, I'll take care of it."

He'll *take care of it*. He takes care of everything.

"I'm sure you will. Just want her to know her options, if she's becoming part of the family, I mean."

Mrs. Benedetti gives him a sideways glance and Dominic looks back innocently, raising his eyebrows, grinning, shoving more pasta into his big mouth.

Franco, who's now leaning in his seat, drops his fork on his plate and rings the bell. Servers return to the dining room and clear the table, pour a different wine into a second glass, even though mine is still full. Although a drink would calm my nerves, I feel like I should stay alert.

"Ignore him," Sergio says.

"Dominic, thought you were bringing a girlfriend," Salvatore goads his brother.

Dominic's face hardens. "We can't all be as lucky as Sergio, can we, Salvatore?"

The rivalry between the brothers is palpable.

Franco says something in Italian. Whatever it is has Dominic snort and Sergio tense. When Roman picks up the conversation, Sergio clears his throat. "Natalie doesn't understand Italian. Why don't we keep to English tonight?"

"It's rude, Franco," Mrs. Benedetti admonishes in a whisper.

I wish Sergio hadn't said anything because it feels like everyone is staring at me.

The awkward silence drags on until I clear my throat and speak.

"So that wallpaper is interesting," I say. It's strange, actually. Alice in Wonderland. Not a version you'd find in a child's room either. It's too dark for that.

Mrs. Benedetti glances behind her then she and Franco look at each other. "Franco had that done for me. And he absolutely hates it." She pats his back. He smiles and for the first time, there's a glimmer of tenderness in his eyes.

But I don't dwell on that because the smell of what the servers bring out next has me holding my breath. It's fish. Salmon. I love salmon, but tonight, I feel like I'm going to be sick.

"You okay?" Sergio whispers. "You're a little pale."

The server comes to my side then, and the large serving dish is practically under my nose. "Oh, just a little. Please." I don't think I can refuse it. I'll have to force it down.

"Hey," Sergio presses.

I turn to him. I wonder if I'm coming down with a bug or something. This isn't like me. "I'm fine." I force a smile. "Excuse me for a moment," I say, standing the instant the server steps away, touching my napkin to my mouth. "Where's the bathroom?" I ask Sergio, who's instantly on his feet.

He puts his hand on my low back. "Just go ahead," he tells his family and walks me quickly away. Instead of taking me to a bathroom downstairs, he practically carries me to his room, and the moment I'm in the bathroom, I just make it to the toilet and drop to my knees to throw up.

Sergio's beside me in a flash. I push my hair away as another wave comes. Sergio's hands pull the thick braid back.

"Go away," I groan, humiliated, sick to my stomach. "You don't need to see this."

"I'm not going anywhere."

Another wave and I think I'd rather die than puke. "I'm so sorry," I say, reaching up to flush the toilet, sitting back. "I think it's over."

"You don't need to be sorry."

"I must be coming down with something. I've been feeling funny for a couple of days."

"Come on, I'll get you in bed."

He's about to pick me up but I wave him away, stumble out of my shoes. I go to the sink to splash water on my face and brush my teeth. I don't do more than glance at my reflection.

Sergio hands me a towel. I take it, wipe my face. "Go back to your dinner. I don't want to ruin it."

"You're not ruining anything." He ignores my protests and picks me up, carries me to the bed where he strips off the dress, slides the T-shirt he discarded earlier when he changed over my head and lays me beneath the covers.

The nausea is gone, but I let him take care of me.

"If it's a bug or flu, I probably shouldn't be around your mom."

From the look on his face, he's already thought about this. "We'll figure it out." He tucks me in and sits on the bed. "Why don't you get some sleep."

"Please tell them I'm sorry. I'm so embarrassed."

He kisses my forehead. "Nothing to be embarrassed about."

"Go back to dinner, Sergio. I'm fine."

"You sure?"

"Yes. I'm just going lie here."

"Okay. I'll be back to check on you."

I watch him go, and shut my eyes, feeling so tired suddenly that all I can do is sleep.

WHEN I WAKE UP, the room is bathed in bright sunlight. I remember where I am, remember the embarrassment of last night, and although the other side of the bed is empty, I can see that Sergio had slept there. I don't even remember him coming back into the room.

It's almost ten in the morning and I get up. I feel better. Maybe it was a twenty-four-hour thing. But when I stand up, that nausea returns and I run to the bathroom, but nothing comes. It's just a dry heave, and it's gone. I splash cold water on my face and look at my reflection. I'm pale as a ghost.

With a groan, I turn away, and switch on the shower, strip off the T-shirt and panties and step under the flow. I shampoo and condition my hair, but don't spend too long in the shower. I feel better again, hungry even, so I get dressed in a pair of jeans and a sweater and step out into the hallway.

At the same moment, Dominic comes out of the room next door.

"Well, good morning," he says. His hair is wet from a shower and I find it strange how different he looks than his brothers. He's blond where they're dark, and although he's powerfully built, he's leaner than they are.

"Good morning," I say, knowing there's no way to avoid talking to him.

"You feel better? You look better," he gives me a smile.

"Yeah, it must have been a twenty-four-hour thing. I hope I didn't ruin your birthday dinner," I add on.

He shrugs a shoulder. "We're not really here for my birthday. We're here for mom and I know she's glad she met you."

I nod, thinking maybe I misjudged him. He's going to lose his mother soon. I open my mouth to say something, but he goes first.

"You know, a friend of mine had the same thing you had last night. The second she smelled fish, she turned green."

"What?"

"Turned out it wasn't a bug."

I'm confused, and I'm about to ask what he means but his cell phone rings and he fishes it out of his pocket, looks at the screen.

"What do you mean?" I ask as he swipes his finger across the screen and is about to walk away to answer the call.

He gives me a grin, starts talking in Italian into the phone, and pokes a finger in my belly. I feel my mouth fall open. Dominic's grin widens, he gives me a wink, turns and walks away, laughing at what the person on the other end is saying.

For a long minute, I stand in the empty hallway dumb-founded.

It's a bug. Just a bug.

I walk back into Sergio's room. I don't even close the door behind me but sit on the bed and I'm counting. But it's not possible. We've had unprotected sex once. We've been really careful. So careful.

No. Of course that's not it. I feel fine now. Dominic is just fucking with me. Sergio said he would.

I go back out into the hallway. I want to find Sergio. And get some coffee. Apologize to his mom for last night. I hear Dominic talking from what I assume is his bedroom. He must still be on the phone. Apart from that, the house is quiet as I soundlessly make my way down the stairs. I can't help feeling like a trespasser.

The large living room is empty, although soft music is playing from an ancient looking record player. Across the way is the dining room where we ate last night. It looks like there's a breakfast buffet arranged on the sideboard, but I bypass it.

I hear noise behind the swinging door on the opposite side of the dining room. It's the sound of pots and pans, of a woman giving the order to take a sauce off the heat before it's burnt. I turn and walk down the hallway toward rooms with closed doors. I wonder if Sergio's behind one of them and suddenly panic that he's not. That something happened and he left. I don't want to be in this house without him.

The thought makes me shudder, but then as I approach the farthest door, I hear him. Something tells me not to linger, but I do. It's not on purpose. I don't mean to eavesdrop. But when I hear Franco's raised voice, make out what he's saying, I freeze.

"I told you. I don't want the girl," Sergio says. "I have never agreed with what you're doing to her."

"The DeMarco's lost the war. This is their punishment. Consequences, son. Better get used to dishing them out, or they'll walk all over you when you're head of the family."

"Punishing an innocent girl doesn't sit right with me."

"It's a school. I'll educate her, at least," he says, leaning back. "She belongs to you. I don't care what you do with her. You know what's expected of you. You're first born."

"It's not the fucking middle ages. Give her to Salvatore. Or hell, don't give her to anyone!"

"No," Franco says a little more quietly, and I swear I can almost see the tight line of his mouth.

"Salvatore already signed the contract."

"I don't care who signed the goddamned contract."

"For the last time," Sergio starts, pauses. I know this tone of his voice. It's the one that says this is the end of the discussion. "I wash my hands of this. Of this contract. Of these particular consequences. Of Lucia DeMarco. This is finished."

Lucia DeMarco. She belongs to Sergio—according to Franco Benedetti. The jealousy I feel shames me. Lucia is a victim, she doesn't want anything to do with any of the Benedetti brothers, I am sure. She's a pawn. Like I am to Sergio's enemies.

So she and I, maybe we're more alike than I think.

Someone slams a fist on what I assume is a desk and I jump. I know it's Franco when I hear what he says.

"And for the last time," Franco begins, his words and tone similar to Sergio's and I imagine the two nose to nose, two powerful men doing battle. "Lucia DeMarco belongs to you. You'll be the one to collect her when the time comes. It doesn't matter who signed what and I don't give a fuck if you have that whore lick your floors clean day in and day fucking out. You do what you need to do with Natalie, but this is my final word. Am I fucking clear?" Franco demands.

I close my hand over my belly. I'm trying to process, to understand what the hell is going on. I mean, I do understand. But it's too impossible.

I step backward, stumble over something that wasn't there a moment ago. I spin as I begin to fall, see him standing there as tall as Sergio. As big as him. As menacing as Sergio can sometimes look.

Salvatore Benedetti.

He's right behind me.

It was his foot I tripped over.

He catches me, keeps his hands wrapped around my arms even once I'm steady on my feet. My mouth falls open and I can't look away.

He knows what I heard because he heard it too.

"Natalie," he starts, then stops and all I can do is stand there, mute and caught. "You shouldn't listen at closed doors. Especially with this family."

"I wasn't...I," I'm stuttering. "I didn't mean to." I realize how big he is, how that kindness I'd perceived earlier is gone. Did I imagine it? Because something else has taken its place. Something harder. Something darker.

He studies me. His eyes are different than Sergio's. Where Sergio's are midnight, Salvatore's are a cobalt blue. It's a striking contrast to his olive skin and dark hair, and I feel like, just as his brother can, he, too, can see right through me.

"Don't tell him," I whisper. "Please."

He doesn't react, not for a long time, but then he nods once. "Go back to Sergio's room and wait for him there."

"I really wasn't—"

"Natalie." He squeezes my arms, dips his head low, eyes bore into mine from behind thick lashes. "You shouldn't be here. You need to go. Now."

I blink, but as much as I want to run right away from here, I'm unable to move. I'm on the verge of tears, and I don't want to cry in front of him. But I don't move. I can't. Not until the study door opens behind me. Not until Salvatore has looked away, freeing me from the trap of his gaze. And the instant he releases me, I slip away, as fast as I can, back the way I came, my heels clicking as I go, as I miraculously don't trip and fall, and stumble back into Sergio's bedroom, like I was told.

Because I don't want to see Sergio. I don't want to see his father. I don't want them to know I've heard. To know I know. Because if I had any doubt, any delusions about anything related to the Benedetti mafia family, Franco Benedetti's brutal words obliterated them.

They showed me exactly the life I'll be walking into by being with Sergio.

19

SERGIO

"I think I should go home," Natalie says to me when I get up to my room. She's dressed and throwing things into her bag.

And I know she was standing just outside the study. I know what she overheard.

"I don't feel great," she adds on.

I don't bring up the fact that I saw her run up the stairs. Don't mention that the look I exchanged with Salvatore pretty much confirmed my thinking. I could kill my father. We've discussed this a thousand times. He knows where I stand. I'm not changing my mind. He knows me well enough to know he can't make me.

"I'm sorry," Natalie is saying when I tune back in.

She's not sick. She looks fine. A little paler than usual, but that's not flu. That's what she overheard.

"I'll take you home," I say.

She shakes her head. "No. You should stay with your mom. I can take a train."

"You're not taking a train. I'll take you home."

She stops, her back stiffening as she sucks in a deep breath, zips her bag and picks it up off the bed before facing me square on.

"Sergio, you need to stay here with your mom. I think you're right. I don't think you can take time with her for granted right now."

She's choosing her words carefully. Neither of us want to say out loud what we know she means.

"I'll be fine, and besides," she clears her throat, doesn't quite meet my gaze when she says the next part: "I don't want to get her sick."

That's the first lie Natalie has told me. She isn't sick—at least not with the flu. I study her, and she can't meet my eyes. I nod. "Okay."

"Okay?" She's surprised by my response.

"With conditions."

She exhales, waits, looks like she's on the verge of tears all of a sudden.

I go to her. "Are you all right? Really?"

She nods, but her eyes glisten.

I wrap my hands around her arms and rub them before pulling her into my chest. She sniffles, and I don't say anything when I feel the warmth of tears seep through my shirt.

"Remember what I said last night?" I ask.

She nods, keeps her forehead pressed to my chest. I weave my fingers gently into her hair, cup the back of her head, hold her.

"Mine. No matter what."

I hear her suck in a deep breath. Feel her shudder with it.

She pulls away, wipes the back of her hand across her eyes, her nose. She doesn't comment on what I've just said. "Conditions," she says instead with an attempt at a smile. "I would be surprised if you didn't have any."

"You know me well. One of our drivers will take you to my house."

She shakes her head. "I want to go home. To my house. It's easier with school work and all my things, and Pepper's more comfortable."

"That last part is bullshit but fine, your house with a guard. Ricco."

"Not in the house."

"I wasn't going to station him inside, but he will do a sweep."

She nods. "Okay."

"I'll drive back early. Come to your place—"

"Sergio," she cuts me off. I know what she's going to say. I see it in her eyes. "I need time."

I don't speak.

"I," she pauses, rubs her face. "I need to think."

"I know you overheard."

She looks down at her feet.

"Natalie, what you—"

"Please don't."

She turns away, puts on her coat. I bite my lip, forcing myself to remain silent as I watch her. When she's ready, I take her downstairs where I arrange for one of my father's men to drive her home and walk her outside. She turns to me, wraps her arms tight around me, tighter than I expect. For a long moment, she's clinging to me.

"I love you, you know. I do," she whispers.

There's a sadness in her words, a sort of finality. But when I draw back, she pulls away and slips into the backseat of the sedan. I close the door, tap on the front window and watch the car drive away, down the driveway and out the gates, disappearing from view.

20

NATALIE

The drive back home is long and I'm grateful to be alone. I'm thinking. Counting. Over and over again, I count days. And like an echo, Sergio's father's words keep repeating in the backdrop. I'm not paying attention to the scenery, the other cars on the highway. The man driving is stone-faced and the few times I catch his eyes in the rear-view mirror, I see a hardness inside them, and I know he's more than a driver.

"Accident up ahead. We'll have to take a different exit."

They're the only words he speaks to me. I'm startled by the intrusion and confused for a moment. But as the car slows and veers off toward an exit, I nod.

"That's fine. Thanks."

The sky is strange. Heavy clouds drop rain then briefly allow the sun to shine through spectacularly only to turn over another bucketful moments later. I turn on my cell phone—I'd kept it off on purpose—but Sergio hasn't called. I scroll to Drew's number, almost hit the button to call him, but change my mind and switch it off again. Tuck it back into my purse.

First thing I need to do is pick up a test. Confirm one way or another because maybe I'm not pregnant. Maybe I'm just late. Why am I letting Dominic's strange poke at my belly upset me so much? How would he know before me? He's just a jerk, like Sergio said.

"I don't give a fuck if you have that whore lick your floors clean day in and day fucking out. You do what you need to do with Natalie, but this is my final word."

Shit.

The way Franco Benedetti talks about Lucia DeMarco, the way he talks about me, what does he think? What does he envision for his son? That he'd be with me and have her too? In what capacity? And how firm is his word? Is Sergio bound by it?

We slow to a stop at a red light. There are no other cars around and the traffic light is useless. I don't know this part of the city at all. It's run down. Somewhere I wouldn't want to be alone at night or in the day.

There's a gas station on the corner. I glance into the main building. A man is standing behind the register, his attention on whatever is flashing on the little TV on the counter. A row of houses stands vacant across the street, graffiti on its walls, boards on its windows and doors. Black marks the upstairs walls and part of the roof is missing. Must have been a fire.

I wonder how much longer the traffic light will be red. It's a strange place, this.

A car pulls into the gas station on the other side of the pumps. It's old and the back door is dented. Something that fits here, but would stand out anywhere else. Both driver and passenger glance our way and even through the closed windows, I smell the cigarette smoke. When he kills the engine, the music abruptly stops.

Our light turns green, but we don't move. I notice my driver's eyes in the mirror. See him stiffen, reach into his jacket. I wonder if he's armed. He must be.

It's just when I'm thinking this that a car pulls up, speeds up, slams into ours. I'm wearing my seatbelt but I'm jolted. My heart is racing. Alarm bells go off in my head. We need to drive, but I don't think we can.

It's a black sedan with heavily tinted windows. I'm thinking how it stands out here when three doors open, the passenger side and the two back doors, and men exit the sedan. One is wearing a black suit. He's the one who catches my eye. The others are more casually dressed and before I can think, before I register what's happening, the one in the suit is pulling my door open and his hand is wrapped around my arm like a vice. He drags me out of the car and my purse falls off my lap, the contents spilling onto the floor.

My driver is scooting across the front seat, reaching for the passenger door because the driver's side door is jammed. He's got blood on his face. He must have slammed it against the steering wheel when the car hit us.

I scream and try to grab onto the back of the driver's seat, but I'm out of the car, falling to the ground. Pavement scrapes the skin of my knees open. Tires screech as a car speeds away. It's the old vehicle with the couple inside. They're hauling ass out of here, the gas tank still open, the hose ripping away, the scent of gasoline all I can smell.

The trunk pops open on the car that slammed into ours as the man in the suit drags me toward it. I'm fighting, one of my shoes is off my foot as I try to get a hold of something, anything, to stop him from taking me. The last thing I see before he hauls me up and drops me into the trunk is my driver finally stepping out, drawing a gun. But the others, they're ready for him, and one of them raises his weapon. He takes aim. Fires.

I scream again, watch as my driver hits the ground.

The man in the suit shoves me back down when I sit up and when I try to fight him off, he slaps me so hard, my head hits the edge of the trunk. I'm dazed, something warm slides over my temple, down my cheek. It takes a minute for him to come back into focus and when he does, he's grinning, and raising his fist and this time when he hits me, I don't open my eyes. I don't feel anything after the crushing pain on the side of my head. And all I smell is gasoline as he slams the trunk closed and I feel the car begin to move before I lose consciousness.

21

NATALIE

My head is throbbing and my eyes feel like they're glued shut. I can't move right away and I'm not sure where I am. I'm lying on my side, I know that because I feel a rough fabric on my cheek. It stinks and I want to vomit, I feel like I might. And maybe I already have. Maybe that's one of the scents I'm smelling. That and unclean bodies. Sex. The stench of it, of cigarettes and sweat and sex.

I turn my head, moan with the pain over my eye. Try to reach to touch it, but I can't. Something cold circles my wrists and they're bound up over my head. I force my eyes open and for a moment, the room spins. The threadbare blanket I'm lying on is a 1970's orange/brown combination. The walls are yellow but I think they used to be white. On top of a beat-up desk is an old-fashioned box TV and there's a jacket hanging over the back of the chair. It's the only nice thing in here. There's a can of Coke beside the TV and an ashtray full of cigarette butts. I roll onto my back and look up at the blobs of stains on the ceiling, then toward the large window with its curtains drawn shut. They match the blanket I'm lying on.

Footsteps outside, heavy ones, have me turning toward the door. My head throbs with the effort. It opens and a man I don't recognize comes inside. He's talking into a cell phone.

"Yeah. Got it." He gives me a grin and sits on the edge of the bed. "I'm not fucking stupid," he says and disconnects the phone, sets it on the nightstand. He never stops looking at me.

He's not the one in the suit. The one who grabbed me. Punched me. He's wearing a yellow T-shirt stretched too tight over his beer belly. It's got a stain on it. Tomato sauce I think. Or blood. Mine, maybe.

When he leans in toward me, I press my back into the mattress.

"You up, pretty girl?" he asks.

I don't react and try to pull away when he reaches out a hand and presses a fat finger into my temple. I suck in a breath and he smiles, digging deeper. Warm blood slides over my ear. He's opened a cut. I guess it happened when the suited man punched me.

"That's for puking on me," he says.

He rubs his finger on his shirt and my first guess was right. The stain I saw was tomato sauce because blood is much darker.

I look up at my hands, tug at my arms to test the handcuffs that are linked through the headboard.

"You ain't goin' nowhere," the man says, standing. He's tall. Really tall. And the way he looks, the way his eyes travel over my chest, my belly, my legs, it scares me.

"What do you want with me?" I croak. My voice isn't working, my throat is dry and I know I did vomit on him. I taste it.

He shrugs a shoulder, turns his attention to the TV and switches it on.

"Nothin' much," he mutters. "You ain't my type." He sits back down on the bed and is wholly engrossed in the channels he's flipping through. A pistol is tucked into the back of his jeans. "I like tits," he adds on, picking up his coke and slurping loudly.

I try to pull myself up to a seat, but my head throbs with the effort and when he turns and grabs hold of my ankle, I freeze.

"Where you goin'? Ain't nowhere you need to be."

I guess he's not as inattentive as I assumed.

"Where am I?"

He releases my leg, returns to flipping TV channels. Settles on a black and white cartoon. I feel like I'm caught in some time warp. Like this place is stuck in the past. A glance at the window tells me it must be nighttime, or I'd see sunshine coming around the curtains, I think. I listen, but either the room is soundproof, which I doubt, or there's absolutely no traffic outside.

"Where am I?" I ask again, a little louder this time as I manage to sit up a little, drawing my bound hands in front of me.

"Quiet."

"Can't follow the cartoon?" I ask.

He mutes the TV and turns to me and I realize how stupid that was.

"Want me to shut you up, pretty girl? I can do that right good and I'd like it," he says, getting up, walking around to my side. I cringe when he grabs my ankle and tugs me so I'm lying back down.

"I told you you ain't goin' nowhere, didn't I?"

I stare up at him, unable to answer.

"I asked you a question," he says, leaning his big face close, his stale breath on me.

"Yes," I say. "I just wanted—"

"Don't matter what you want. It matters what I want and I want you to shut the fuck up. Understand, cunt?"

I swallow. Nod my head.

He nods his, straightens, looks at me again, his eyes moving from head to toe. I watch his hand move toward me, toward that sliver of naked belly where my sweater has risen up. I make a sound when his fingers touch my skin, and when his hand fists the waistband of my jeans, I scream.

The door opens, slams against the wall and lets in a gust of cold wind. We both turn. Suit man is standing there minus his jacket. He looks pissed. Two others, these from the back of the car, flank him.

"Don't fucking touch her, fucking imbecile. You know the rules."

The man curls his hand tighter around the handful of material, lifting my hips off the bed. Although he's bigger than the man at the door, when the one at the door takes a step into the room, he backs off, releasing me.

"I just want her to shut the fuck up so I can watch TV."

The leaner man looks at me. "You think you can shut the fuck up so he can watch his cartoon?"

I nod.

"There," he says to the big guy. "She says she'll shut up."

"What if she don't?"

The man cocks his head to the side, looks at me. "I'll let you stick your dick in her big mouth. That'd shut her up, wouldn't it?"

I feel the blood drain from my face.

When I shift my gaze away from him, I see the swell at the crotch of the fat one's pants.

"Yeah. That'd shut her up good," he says, rubbing his stiffening dick.

"Fuckin' idiot," the man mumbles with a chuckle, picking up the jacket hanging over the back of the chair. He turns to the two men who are younger than the big one. "Remember the rules or the boss will have our heads," he reminds them.

"No problem."

Suit man heads back to the door but one of the guys stops him.

"When do we get the money?"

Suit man pauses and I see evil in his eyes. He's smarter than the others. He's manipulating them. "Tomorrow morning when I come back to pick her up."

The guy nods and suit man heads out the door, closing it behind him. I hear a car start and when I know he's gone, I look back at the three men I'm left with. The two younger ones walk through a door that I notice leads to an adjoining room. Fat guy picks up the remote and gives me a disgusting grin, his hand in his pants now, rubbing his erection.

I turn away and I shut up.

22

SERGIO

I know something's wrong when Ricco calls me at nine o'clock to tell me she's still not there. He's been waiting at Natalie's house and she should have been home hours ago. The driver hasn't picked up a single call and I feel like a fucking idiot for letting her go alone.

"Relax. We'll find her," Salvatore says. He's sitting beside me as we take the exit where the tracker equipped in the car that took Natalie says it's parked. Two soldiers ride in the car behind ours.

"I'm a fucking idiot."

"No. You're not. She wants space. You're trying to give it to her. Considering what she overheard—"

"No, she doesn't get to have space. Not anymore. Fuck!" I slam my fist on the steering wheel for the hundredth time. "I shouldn't have brought her to that house." I shake my head at myself as I speed down the deserted street.

"There," Salvatore says, pointing to the fencing around the abandoned cluster of buildings.

I slow as I pull up, stop at the closed gates. The place has been vandalized but a heavy lock keeps the lot sealed off so I can't drive any farther.

"We'll go on foot," I say, killing the engine, getting out of the car.

Salvatore is beside me and I hear the cocking of his weapon as we walk through a narrow opening that someone made by cutting the wire.

I spot the sedan in a far corner. It's out of place here where the windows of the buildings are broken or gone and even squatters won't occupy. The place is eerie. Haunted by the wretchedness of the people who lived and died here.

There isn't a single sound around us. If it's an ambush, they'll have us tonight. We should have brought more men. A fucking army. I've not only put Natalie in harm's way, but my brother too.

There's a low sound as we near the vehicle. I take my pistol out of its holster and exchange a look with Salvatore. While he goes around the back of the car, I move around the front to the driver's side. I hear the soft hum of music, I think it's country. The radio's on.

The driver's side window is open a crack. Although the windows are tinted, I should be able to see a form if anyone's in there and I don't. Still, I have my gun ready when I open the door. But the car's empty.

I reach in and pull out the keys, which are still in the ignition, killing the sound.

"Pop the trunk," Salvatore says, just as I peek into the backseat to find Natalie's purse on the floor, her belongings scattered. There's no blood at least. Nothing like that inside the car.

"Sergio. Pop the fucking trunk."

I glance at Salvatore whose eyes are locked on the closed trunk. I reach around, pop it and walk back at the same moment he decocks his gun.

"Fuck."

Fuck is right. The driver's body is inside. His face is bruised and there's a bullet hole between his still open eyes. On the lapel of his jacket is a note.

Keep your friends close.

Your enemies closer.

A name underneath the cryptic message. An address.

"What the—" Salvatore starts, taking it from me.

"Let's go. The address is Atlantic City."

We move quickly, driving the hour and a half to Atlantic City at breakneck speed. Salvatore is beside me. He's still studying the note, but there's nothing to learn from it.

"What the fuck does this mean?"

"It means someone's fucking with us."

"Vitelli?"

I shake my head. "No. No way. He'd be fucking stupid to after what happened with Joe."

"Then who?"

"Pick a number. We have enough enemies to choose from."

"DeMarco?"

"I don't fucking know."

Keep your friends close. Your enemies closer. It sounds like a warning.

We drive in silence, both of us thinking. If this *is* a warning, they won't hurt her. The plan was to take her. To show me they could. If it was to kill her, she'd be lying in that trunk with the driver.

It's almost five in the morning by the time we near the cheap motel outside Atlantic City limits. It's not operational and was probably looted months ago. I park the car a block away and we walk. This part of town is nearly empty. Any streetlights that once illuminated these dark streets were busted long ago. There's a traffic light flashing red about two blocks down and just past it is the motel. Twelve rooms from what I can see. The building looks like it's going to cave in any second and at the very last room, a truck is parked outside.

"She's got to be in there. You three go around back."

Salvatore nods and disappears behind the building and I walk to the last door, fury making me fist the pistol hard.

As I approach the second to last room, I know from the lights flashing through the split in the curtain that someone's watching TV in there. But they know I'm coming. Whoever took her left the fucking address. This is too easy. It reeks.

Salvatore and the two soldiers turn the corner. I signal for them to listen at the door of the room next to the one where the TV's on. A moment later, he nods. I put up three fingers and count down: three-two-one.

Both doors splinter as they're kicked in. Natalie screams. For a moment, I'm caught. I see her lying on the bed, arms over her head, cuffed to the headboard. A huge man moves much faster than I think he should be able to considering his girth and he's got his gun pointed at me before I know it. I'm still faster though and the bullet he shoots ricochets off the wall behind my head when mine catches his gun arm. He stumbles backward, his pistol flying through the air, landing three feet from him.

More gunshots go off next door and Natalie's screaming again, climbing to her knees.

"Stay down!" I call to her as I stalk to the giant who's fallen to his knees to retrieve his weapon. It's stupid. He could take me— or try to. We'd be matched.

"Close your eyes, Natalie." Déjà vu. I've told her exactly this before. The past is repeating itself.

I cock my pistol and taking aim at the back of the big guy's knee.

I pull the trigger and he screams, falling over onto his side, clutching his shattered kneecap. Although there's a silencer on my gun, it's still deafening. The sound of a gun firing is always that.

I stand over him, put my foot on the bloody crook of his arm and press. I know this idiot isn't the one responsible for taking her. He's a hired gun. Expendable.

"Who the fuck hired you?"

He screams, blubbers like a fucking girl. I hear footsteps behind me.

"There were two in the next room. Both down," Salvatore says.

"I want to know who hired the fuckers," I spit at the man without looking at my brother. When he doesn't answer, I cock the pistol again.

Natalie's crying. I hear her. She must know I'm readying to murder this guy.

"Watch him," I say to Salvatore, going to her. I look her over. She's messed up, a bruise at her temple, a cut that will scar. I'm getting more and more pissed off as I sit down, touch her. "Are you okay?" I say, trying to level my voice.

She shakes her head no, fresh tears starting.

"Physically. Are you okay?" I need to know. The other shit I'll deal with later. Right now, I need to know she's not physically hurt. But she just stares up at me, sobbing. "Natalie, look at me. Did he hurt you anywhere else?" I barely get the words out. "Did that fucker touch you?"

She stares at me, registers my meaning, shakes her head. "I want to go home."

I nod. Look up at her binds. I need a key. "Close your eyes," I say, cupping the back of her head and tucking it against my belly before shooting at the rung of the headboard through which her cuffs were woven. I hold her hands, cradle her.

"It's okay. You're going to be okay." I turn to one of the soldiers. "Get the car." He nods and runs out the door. "Find me the goddamned keys for these," I tell the other one, gripping the cuffs that bind Natalie.

A few minutes later, one of the men hands me the key.

Natalie turns her gaze up to Salvatore, who's standing nearby, watching. "You're safe now," he says to her.

She turns her attention to my hands which are undoing her cuffs and when they're off, I rub her wrists.

"Sergio," Salvatore says, eyeing the big guy on the floor.

I don't want her to see what's about to happen. "Give me a minute."

The soldier I sent for the car returns.

"Put her in the backseat," I say, standing, bringing Natalie with me. She's shivering. In shock maybe. "And stay with her."

"No," she says clinging to me. "No. I just want to go home. I want you to take me home. You."

"I need you to wait in the car for me. I need to take care of this before I can take you home."

She shakes her head, her nails dig into the back of my neck. Her eyes are saucers, her terror palpable.

"Nat." I know she hates being called that, but she doesn't even acknowledge it. Her gaze keeps bouncing to the man I'm going to hurt and each time, more tears well inside her eyes. "I need to take care of this. I need you to wait for me out in—"

"Do it," she says. She locks her eyes on the man and there's a darkness inside them that wasn't there before.

"You don't want—"

She shifts her gaze to mine. "I want you to do it."

I study her. She doesn't even blink, but returns her gaze to the man. She knows what I'm going to do.

"Look away," I say.

"No."

"Natalie, there are things you can't unsee."

"Don't you understand?" she asks, looking up at me. "I want to see. I need to."

Her eyes are stone.

I nod. Salvatore's watching us. I read what he's thinking on his face. This is fucked up.

When I walk to the brute on the floor, I take out my pistol and cock it and, without a word, I shoot his other knee. As loud as his scream is, I still hear Natalie's over it.

She wants to see.

She wants to see what I'm capable of.

What a monster I can be.

"Sergio," Salvatore puts a hand on my shoulder. "I can finish this."

I shrug it off. "No." I crouch down next to the man. "You want to die slow or you want to die fast? Because you're dying tonight. It's just up to you how."

"Please. Please. Mr. Suit. He hired me to watch the pretty girl. I didn't touch her. I didn't touch her. It's the rules."

I know he's mentally not all there, but I don't give a fuck. See, this is what makes me a monster. I have no compassion. Not when someone takes what's mine. Not when someone hurts what's mine.

"What's his name?"

He shakes his head, confused. "Mr. Suit."

I'm losing patience. I grip his filthy T-shirt. Drag him up by the collar of it. "What the fuck is Mr. Suit's name, asshole?"

He starts crying, sobbing. "Mr. Suit," he says over and over again.

"Fuck." I stand up, turn to look at Natalie.

She's immovable, sitting on the foul bed, fisting the filthy blanket. I don't think she's blinked or taken a breath.

I turn back to the guy, take my pistol and point it between his eyebrows.

I don't hesitate.

She wants to see. She'll see.

I pull the trigger—once, twice—twin holes in his forehead, between his eyes.

Overkill. but it's quick. My form of mercy. He's dead in an instant.

"Call a fucking cleaner." I holster my gun and, with blood on my hands, gather Natalie up into my arms, and she doesn't resist. I carry her to the car, cradle her in the backseat. Salvatore slides into the driver's seat and a moment later, we're driving away.

23

NATALIE

Two weeks have passed since that terrible night. My mind is in chaos but I won't stop to sort through the thoughts. To see again what I saw that night. I won't think about what happened. I won't feel the man's hands on me. Won't hear the sound of a silenced gun fired. I close my eyes against the picture of Sergio standing over the man, gun in his hand, cocked. Aimed. Fired. Not once, but twice. With perfect precision.

Did he even notice the blood that stained his coat? His hands? The blood he smeared on me when he held me.

I shudder.

The sound is strange, the silencer not quite silent enough. One millisecond and a life is snuffed out.

I don't feel sorry for that man or for the others who died that night.

I think about the driver who was killed because of me, and even him, I keep thinking that he chose this. He chose this life. Does that make me like them?

The image of Sergio that night, furious like I've never seen him, is burned into my eyelids. Cruel and lethal. So fucking lethal.

He tried to send me away. Didn't want me to see. But I wanted to see. I wanted to know exactly. Needed to.

What I heard in his father's house, it pales in comparison to what I witnessed that night.

"Miss."

I blink. The man behind the counter looks annoyed. "Sorry." I empty my basket of things I don't need—magazines, candy, cold medicine—not to bring attention to the one thing I do. The pregnancy test.

I'm sure now. The test is extra. I'm late. My body feels different, more achy and tender. And I can't keep food down morning, noon or night.

The clerk tells me the total as he bags my things and I pay him in cash, take my change and leave. I don't even say goodbye. The drug store is two blocks from my house and Ricco and another man whose name I don't remember are following a few paces behind me. They're not subtle, but I manage to ignore them. Besides, I don't think they're meant to be subtle. Sergio wants anyone who may try to take me again to think twice.

He calls me each night but I don't know where he is and he hasn't tried to come over. I thought he would. I can guess what he's doing. The damage he did the other night was only the beginning. He'll punish whoever was responsible. Am I supposed to feel guilty about that? I don't. And again, the same question comes up: *what does that make me?*

I told him what I could remember about the man in the suit. Told him I thought the others were set up. That the leader knew Sergio would come. Knew what he'd do. I was always meant to be rescued. Another message, a louder one than the funeral flowers left on my doorstep.

I unlock the front door, my fingers icy as I push it open. I'm wearing knitted fingerless mittens. Not a smart choice for the temperature, but I'm lucky I got shoes and a coat on before leaving the house. I haven't brushed my hair in days. My brain is mush.

After locking the door behind me, I set everything down, give Pepper a pat and head upstairs. I don't look at the instructions. It's pretty self-explanatory. Pee on the stick, of which there are two in this box.

I pee on that little stick and set it on the counter. I'm looking at the image on the back of the box, the one with the two pink lines as if I need it to know what they mean. But it's faster than I expect. It doesn't take a full minute before they appear on the stick.

Strange, I thought this official confirmation would feel different, but it doesn't.

I toss the test, the one I already took and the second, still wrapped one, into the trash can along with the box. I touch the dark shadows under my eyes, take out a tube of concealer and smear it on. Apply generous layers of mascara, too much so my lashes clump together. Looks like spider's legs—like the morning after a really long night. I don't care though. I drop the still open tube on the counter, watch it roll into the sink, and go into the bedroom.

There, I toss the things from the bag I'd packed for the weekend with Sergio into the laundry bin without looking at them, and put in two pairs of jeans, some sweaters and under things. A pair of running shoes. I switch the TV in the bedroom on, for Ricco's sake. From the bathroom, I get my toothbrush. I sling the bag over my shoulder and carry it downstairs, put on my coat and boots, and, taking Pepper, I walk out through the back door. Ricco and the other man are on the front side. There's no way to post a man back here unless he's in the backyard and I refused. I walk around to the neighbor's yard and through the door of our shared fence. Pepper follows easily, she's familiar.

Mrs. Robbins comes to the window of the back door before I even have a chance to knock.

"Natalie, what a nice surprise." She's about seventy years old and watches Pepper occasionally.

"Hi Mrs. Robbins, how are you doing?" I ask, walking inside. I'm attempting upbeat, but it sounds strange. Forced.

"I'm good, honey. Cold in this drafty house, but what else is new? You? You look tired, dear. Everything okay?"

I smile but it feels foreign. "Yeah, just school is busy. I was actually dropping by to ask if you'd mind watching Pepper over the weekend? I'm thinking of paying my parents a visit and Pepper doesn't do well on the longer bus trips. I know it's short notice—"

"Not at all," she says, smiling to Pepper who's already beside the old woman. "I'd love the company, honestly. Besides, it'll force me to get myself out of the house and get some exercise. It takes a lot to keep all this in shape, you know." She winks, patting her generous hip.

I smile. "Thank you so much. You have the number?"

"Sure do." She points to the fridge where my parents' home number and address are stuck with a magnet from the last time I went away a few months ago. "Spend as much time as you like, dear. It's nice you still visit them."

A pang of guilt has me shifting my gaze to Pepper.

"My boy, well, you know how boys are." She shakes her head and I feel sorry for her. I should drop by more often. Her son has visited exactly once the whole time I've been next door and he lives about a ten minute car ride away.

"Thanks, Mrs. Robbins. Maybe when I'm back we can go get lunch or something."

"I'd like that."

I say goodbye, give Pepper a big hug and walk back out into the yard. I take the exit opposite the one to my house which leads to the alley behind our street. From there, I put my hood up and walk quickly away from the house, taking the long way to the bus station. I buy a ticket to Asbury Park, where my parents live.

The bus doesn't leave for another hour so I order a cup of tea at the café and wait. I don't bother to call my parents because they're not home. They always spend this part of winter with my aunt in Arizona. The house will be empty, which is what I want.

I watch the passing cars on the drive and when I get to the bus station, I take a taxi to the house. It's too far to walk and the drive takes twenty minutes. My parents live right on the water, it's a beautiful small cottage they bought a few years ago. I pay the taxi driver and carry my bag around to the back of the house, unlock the kitchen door, walk inside. I set my bag down and the familiar smell washes over me and it feels safe here. It's silent, completely still, and I don't switch on the lights as I walk upstairs to the room I stay in when I visit. There, I turn on the lights and close the curtains looking out onto the street. I get sheets from the linen closet and make the bed and, after brushing my teeth, I lay down to close my eyes. Maybe I can finally rest. Take a reprieve from what my life has become.

Because I need to figure things out.

Because I'm pregnant with Sergio Benedetti's baby.

And as much as I love him, as much as it will hurt to walk away, how can I bring a baby into this sort of life?

I roll over onto my side, feel a tear slide over the bridge of my nose.

Am I foolish to think he'll let me go, though? He's the most possessive man I know. From day one, he owned me.

No, he won't let me go. Not if he finds out.

He can't ever learn about the baby. I can't ever see him again. *"Mine. No matter what."*

I have to keep this secret from him because I will be more his than ever if he ever finds out about this baby.

24

SERGIO

I thought Vitelli was behind Natalie's kidnapping. Either the old man or his sons. But it's not them. Too fucking obvious and they're not that stupid. The DeMarco family? They've essentially been castrated. Lucia DeMarco's father being made to watch what he watched, as sick as it was, it was effective. So who the fuck else would dare?

My father was outraged. Roman immediately started to list names. Make calls. But it's fucking killing me not to know. Not to wrap my hands around the throat of whoever ordered her kidnapping. To squeeze. To watch him gasp his last breath when I choke the life out of him with my bare hands.

I'm parked in my usual space at the garage and see Ricco sitting in the café at the end of her street. He can see her house and keep warm—weather's been icy this last week. I give him a nod as I walk past. The house is dark but for her bedroom window. I knock and slide my key in at the same time. She's been avoiding me but that's changing tonight. I want her to move into my house. I don't want her here on her own anymore. And I need to get her to talk about what happened. To tell it to me so she can get rid of it. So she can stop seeing it because I know she does every time she closes her eyes. She has to tell it to me so she can stop being afraid.

The TV's on upstairs. Not even Pepper comes to me, which is strange. But maybe she's upstairs with Natalie. I take off my coat and head up.

I call out. When she doesn't answer, I wonder if she's fallen asleep. But when I get to her bedroom, it's empty. Her bed is unmade but that's not unusual for her. The TV's on, but she's not here. I switch it off and the house is plunged into utter silence.

"Nat?" I call out, taking my cell phone from my pocket and dialing her number as I peek into the other bedroom.

I hear her phone ring nearby and red flags go up.

The sound is from back in her bedroom and it's on the night-stand, a book lying face down on top of it.

"Fuck!"

I disconnect and call Ricco. Tell him to get his ass over here now. I walk into the bathroom, see her makeup on the counter, the tube of mascara still open lying in the sink like she just walked away in the middle of putting some on. That's when I notice the box in the trash can.

"Boss," Ricco's boots are heavy on the stairs.

I reach into the bin and take out the box. An unopened pregnancy test falls out. Falls next to the used one. My heart thuds against my chest and I reach in and pick it up. See the two little pink lines. Look at the box in my other hand to confirm what it means.

"I didn't see her leave," Ricco starts. "Fuck. I've been watching the front door all fucking day! She ran to the drug store, came back with a full bag and the TV went on. I figured she was staying in."

I should have had Eric on her. Not this idiot.

But my mind is on what I'm holding. My eyes locked on those stripes. Pink. Delicate. Vulnerable.

I stick it into my pocket and turn to Ricco. "Where's the dog?"

"Not here."

"Why are you alone? Where's the man I put with you?"

Ricco shakes his head, shift his gaze. "He had something come up."

"Fuck that something. I'm fucking paying you imbeciles. Get his ass back here now. Get Eric here. Get a fucking army."

I shove past him, down the stairs. He was watching the front door, which means she must have gone out the back.

The pregnancy test is burning a hole in my pocket as I step out the back door and into her tiny garden. I go to the only door in the fence, open it, hear the startled yelp of an old woman in the doorway of the house next door as a motion detector shines a light on me.

I stop, put my hands up, try to smile. Pepper gives a bark but comes to me. She was in the opposite corner of the garden doing her business. The woman exhales.

"Hey Pepper," I say, making a show of crouching down to pat the old dog. Natalie wasn't taken. She left. I need to find out where she went.

"Who's there?" the old woman asks.

I look up at her. She's wearing a long nightgown and a heavy, ragged sweater on top.

"I didn't mean to scare you, ma'am. I'm Natalie's friend. I wanted to drop some of her schoolwork off, but she wasn't home. She must have forgotten I was coming."

"Oh, that's not like her. She's not here. Gone for the weekend. Maybe longer. She's sweet to still visit her parents."

"That's right. She mentioned she'd go see them. Shoot. I need to get the books I borrowed back to her. She needs them for a test."

"They live clear out in Asbury Park, honey. Best to leave it all for her for when she's back."

"I don't mind driving out there. You want me to take Pepper with me?"

"Oh, no. Pepper hates long drives."

"I can't remember the exact address of her parents' house. You don't happen to have it? I can call Natalie." I take out my phone, start to press some numbers.

"I have it right here. Give me one minute."

A moment later, I have Natalie's parents' address and am driving to Asbury Park.

She left. She clearly wanted to get away from me, but that wasn't happening before I found out she was pregnant and it's not happening now.

The sleepy town is dark when I arrive. I wonder how many residents leave in the winter. This close to the water and the weather can be icy. I do like it here though. It's charming and the quiet is so opposite my life.

Natalie's parents live on a cul-de-sac. Street lights give a dim glow to the otherwise pitch-black night. I park the car on the curb in front of her parents' house. All the houses, including this one, are perfectly dark. I get out of the car and walk to the front door of the quaint yellow house, realizing how late it is as I climb the porch steps to ring the doorbell. But nothing happens when I push the button. Not a sound. I wonder if it's broken.

I try the doorknob, expecting it to be locked, and it is.

Glancing around, I go down the porch steps and head around back. The backyard isn't fenced off and it's sandy back here. I can hear waves breaking on the beach and turn my collar up against the bitter wind.

Three steps lead up to the kitchen door. I knock on the window but no one's inside. It's dark. I jiggle the doorknob and it's locked. I don't want to break in, but seeing no alternative because I'm not about to go searching under freaking pots of plants for a spare key, I do. With my elbow, I bust the glass in one of the four panes, hear the clinking of it as it drops to the kitchen floor. I reach in, twist my arm to find the lock, turn it. I open the door and step over the glass and into the house.

No one seems to have heard my entrance. I make my way from the small but cozy kitchen to the dining room. I peek into the empty living room and turn and head up the stairs. They're wooden and I'm careful so they don't creak heavily. Four doors are closed on the landing. I open the first one to peek inside. It's the master bedroom and, to my surprise, it's empty. I push the door wider, confused. The curtains are open, the bed stripped bare, two pillows and a thick comforter folded neatly on top.

I step back out into the hallway to try the other door. It's a bathroom. Drops of water cling to the rim of the pedestal sink and a towel lies askew on the rack. A toothbrush sits on the glass shelf just below the mirror. Natalie's.

A sense of relief washes over me when I see it.

She's here.

I step back into the hallway and try the next door which is the linen closet. I pause at the final door before opening it quietly, see the shadow of a form lying in the bed, back to me. The curtain is closed but there's just enough light coming in from the split between the panels that I can make out her dark hair. I push the door wide, not caring to muffle the creak, and stand there, watch her startle awake, turn. Watch her face as she sits up, gasps, and I'm angry. So angry that I let her be afraid for a minute because she can't see my face. It's too dark where I'm standing. The pregnancy test weights heavy in my pocket and I'm fucking furious that she left, walked away, now. After everything.

I switch on the light and she blinks at the sudden brightness.

The blue bruise on her temple sends a pang of guilt through me but the burn of anger dissipates that.

"Sergio."

Her black eyes are huge, her face pale, gaunt almost. Darkness shadows the skin around her eyes.

I step inside. Her breathing is labored as she watches me approach.

"You left," I say.

"What?"

I reach into my pocket. Take out the test. She watches me lay it on the nightstand before I take off my coat.

"You left," I repeat.

She blinks up at me. "I—"

"Mine. No matter what. Remember?"

She's silent. I'm angry at her for not talking to me, for shutting me out. For leaving. For hiding the fact that she's pregnant.

For refusing to wait in the car that night.

For wanting to see.

To see me like that.

Ruthless.

Brutal.

Deadly.

I'm pissed at myself for letting her. I should have made her leave.

"I shouldn't have let you watch." I pull my sweater over my head, toss it aside. I don't take my eyes off her. I step out of my shoes, go closer to the bed. Rip the blankets away.

"Sergio—"

"That was a mistake. I shouldn't have let you see."

I look her over. She's wearing a tank top and panties. I set a knee on the bed, grip the collar of the tank. Rip it down the center.

She lets out a surprised scream.

"I shouldn't have stayed away. Hell, I never should have let you leave my father's house."

She's covering her breasts. My gaze slides down to her belly, pauses there before moving to her panties.

I shift my gaze back to hers. Push her backward on the bed.

She doesn't resist. Not then and not when I take her wrists and stretch her arms to either side of the bed and wrap her hands around the rungs of the headboard.

"Keep them there," I tell her.

I release her wrists. Look at her. It's like she's splayed out on the cross. Like a sacrifice. Like my sacrifice.

But that's not what this is. I'm not here to make an offering.

I undo my belt. "I should whip your ass. I would. You fucking deserve it."

She's watching me, mouth open, eyes like saucers. She swallows.

I rip her panties off her, look at her pussy. It's mine too. She doesn't understand that yet, though. I thought she did, but I was wrong. I hook two fingers inside her cunt.

"You're hurting me," she squeaks.

"Good."

"Sergio—"

"Who do you belong to?"

She squirms, grips my arm to pull me off.

With my free hand, I take her wrist and draw it back out to the headboard. "I told you to fucking keep your hands here. Do I need to tie you down?"

She shakes her head.

"Grip it," I say when she hasn't yet.

She obeys, silent but for her eyes. They betray her fear. But something else too. She does know. She does understand. She just can't accept it yet. I have to make her accept the fact that she no longer belongs to herself but to me.

"If you let go, I swear to God I will take my belt to your ass."

My face is stone as I undo my pants, push them and my briefs down far enough to free my cock.

She shifts her gaze to the stick I laid on the nightstand earlier.

I take hold of her ankles and spread her legs wide. Bend her knees and push them up. I've got her attention again and when I do, I look down at her cunt, the lips spread open, pink and gleaming.

My fingers dig into her legs and when she makes a sound, I don't soften my hold. I intend to hurt. To punish. I do it when I drive into her too. She's not ready for me but I don't care.

"Look at me."

She makes a sound, her forehead is creased when her eyes meet mine.

"You don't get to fucking leave. You don't get to walk away. We established that."

I draw out and thrust hard, slap her ass when I do. The sound of flesh hurting flesh bounces off the walls.

She grunts. I pull back, twist her body a little, slap her ass again. Twice. Harder. Before I drive into her. She's turned her head away, is squeezing her eyes shut.

With my cock buried inside her, I grip her jaw, turn her to face me. "Open your fucking eyes."

She does. A tear slides from the corner of one eye.

"What did I say to you that night at my father's house? What did I tell you?"

"Stop."

"No. That's not it. What did I fucking tell you?"

Tears are coming from both eyes now.

I watch her cry. She's so fucking pretty when she cries. I can't stop looking at her. It's sick, I know, but it's like her fucking tears mesmerize me. I'm deep inside her and it's warm and wet and I slide my hands up over her arms and close my hands over hers. She's still gripping the headboard like I told her to. I pry them off, interlace my fingers with hers.

"Natalie. What did I tell you?"

"I'm yours."

"That's right. Mine." It's a savage sound. Wild and untamed. "Always. No matter what."

Our eyes are locked and I thrust twice more and she hasn't come yet and I don't give a fuck because that's not what this is about. I bury myself inside her and throb and empty and fill her up and she's so fucking warm, all I can do is lose myself there for just a minute. In her eyes. In her cunt. In her.

25

NATALIE

Cum is sliding out of me and Sergio is looming over me. His gaze shifts to between my legs and he's got me trapped so I can't move, can't cover myself. He sits up. Pushes my legs wide. Watches his stuff spill out of me. Watches until it's finished before returning his gaze to mine.

"The test."

He pauses, and I wait wordlessly for him to continue.

"Is that why you left?"

I cover my face, rub my eyes. "What are we doing? What kind of world am I going to bring a baby into?"

"We," he says, his face like stone. "Not I. We."

"But that's the point."

He lies down on his side. It's like he knows what I mean. Thinks it too. "I shouldn't have found out the way I did."

"I just found out myself," I say, but it's not true. I've known. I've just been too afraid to face it.

He touches my face, turns it so I have to look at him. "I don't like it when you lie to me."

I don't deny the lie.

"How long have you known?"

"I took the test today."

"How long have you known."

"Since that weekend at your father's house."

If he's surprised, he doesn't let on. "How far?"

"Maybe six weeks." It's quiet. "I thought it was a bug. It was your brother who said something that made me wonder if it wasn't. That made me count."

"My brother?"

"Dominic. He caught me in the hallway. Made some comment about a friend vomiting at the smell of fish and how it turned out she was pregnant."

"He was fucking with you." We fall silent again. Sergio's watching me, his midnight eyes heated. "You can't leave, Natalie. Whatever you're thinking, get that out of your head."

"Your father, what he said about Lucia DeMarco…"

"My father can say what he wants. Lucia isn't for me. Period. She belongs to Salvatore and I don't want to hear her name again. End of that discussion, understand?"

I nod.

"Where are your parents?" he asks.

"Arizona."

"I busted the glass on the kitchen window."

"You broke in. Of course, you did." I feel my face darken. He's a criminal. A mobster.

The image of him standing over the man with the gun comes again. I close my eyes against it. I don't want to see him like that ever again. I should have listened to him when he told me there are things you can't unsee because that I wish I'd never seen.

He touches my cheek. I open my eyes. "You know who I am. What I'm capable of. You wanted to see and you did. You saw what I'll do to protect what's mine. How far I'll go when what's mine is taken. Hurt. You and the baby are mine, Natalie. I will protect you, always. I love you and I can't let you walk away, no matter what. No matter if it's wrong. I won't."

"I don't want to."

26

NATALIE

Two weeks later, I'm back at Franco Benedetti's house. Already, Sergio's mom looks worse. Feebler. Even as she tries to smile while pinning a veil to my hair.

"I wore it. My mother wore it. Her mother before her. It's a family tradition," Mrs. Benedetti says.

The veil is yellowing and there's a hint of something ancient that clings to it, a scent. A feel.

"We'll have a big ceremony in the winter. It's so pretty here with the snow," she prattles on, and I don't know if it's the thought that she won't make it to winter or something else that sits like a stone in my belly. But I smile back at her reflection. I refuse to let anything dampen the joy of this day.

"With a huge dress," I say.

"The biggest."

The plan is this small wedding today. And once the baby's born, we'll have a proper ceremony in a nearby chapel.

"There," she says, tucking one rebellious lock of hair behind my ear. It's pinned up with baby's breath tucked into it beneath the yellowing veil that reaches to the middle of my back. "You look beautiful. Glowing. My son is a lucky man." She squeezes my shoulder.

"He's a good man," I say. I feel like I have to say it. And when I do, her eyes darken a little, worry creeping into them.

She pulls up a chair and sits and takes my hands into hers. "This is a difficult family. A difficult life to marry into. I don't know that you would have chosen it had you known."

"I love Sergio." It's my only reply because she's right. I would not have chosen this if I had known. Although, as I think back, did I ever really have a choice? Or were Sergio and I destined to be together? To find each other? Even the way we did. Fate put me in his path not once, but twice. That means something, doesn't it?

"I won't be here for very long—"

"Don't talk like that," I cut her off, but she squeezes my hand, continues.

"But Sergio will protect you. And so will Franco. You'll be his son's wife. The mother of his grandchild. And they'll need you, too, Natalie. Once I'm gone, they'll need you, all of them, but especially Sergio." Her eyes are watering.

"Mrs. Benedetti—"

"I know it's a lot to ask, but I need to know that he'll be safe too. That you'll protect him, too."

"I will," I try to reassure, but she continues.

"Whatever you do, whatever happens, don't let him forget his humanity." She takes in a deep breath, straightens her spine and looks taller, stronger. "He is his father's son, Natalie."

I watch her as she says it. She's trying to relay a message. She wants me to understand this. And to love him in spite of it.

"I believe he's good. I do."

A knock comes on the door and we stand as it opens. But when Sergio peeks his head in, his mother gasps.

"It's bad luck to see the bride before the wedding," she walks to the door, trying to shield me from Sergio's view.

Sergio steps inside, smiles at her, then shifts his gaze to me, looking me over from head to toe. "Silly superstition," he says. He smiles.

I smile back.

"Your dad's waiting at the bottom of the stairs whenever you're ready," he says. "I'll seat my mom." He walks her out, then glances back at me. Smiles wider.

When he's gone, I take one final look at my reflection. I'm wearing a satin sheath. I was aiming for simple, but that wasn't happening with Sergio. The dress is beautiful, soft against my body while hugging it tenderly. The back is cut seductively low, the neckline at the front straight across my collar bones. My breasts already feel swollen and the dress looks prettier for it. A white cloud of satin floats all around my sandaled feet.

I touch my belly. I'm not showing yet but everyone knows why we're rushing this ceremony with a bigger one planned for after the baby's birth. I was fine to wait until after, but Sergio wouldn't have it. He wanted the baby born to us as husband as wife. Between that and his mom's health, I didn't fight it.

Taking one deep breath, I draw the front of the veil down over my face and pick up the bouquet of antique pink roses wrapped in a wide, pale blue ribbon. That's my something blue. Something old, something borrowed, the veil fulfills those. Something new, my dress.

It will bring us luck. I've done it right. All of it. We'll have good luck, Sergio and I.

I force my eyes from my reflection when they get watery, take a deep breath in and walk out the door and down the stairs where my father waits, still confused at this rushed ceremony, still trying to process the fact that I'm pregnant. And that I'm getting married to a man he's only just met. Who is next in line to rule the Benedetti mafia family.

I guess we're all trying to pretend like this is normal.

Only immediate family and Drew are gathered in the living room. Drew is sitting beside my mom. The Benedetti family is sitting across from them, Mr. and Mrs. Benedetti and Dominic. I don't look at Dominic. I don't need to to see the one-cornered smirk of 'I told you so'. I also don't look at Sergio's uncle. His ruthlessness terrifies me almost more than Franco Benedetti's.

What a turn of events.

Salvatore is standing beside his brother. I have no maid of honor. A priest I don't know waits, bible in hand. The pianist begins the wedding march again. I realize I missed the first cue. Sergio clears his throat when I still don't move.

I look up at him. He's not smiling. He's just watching me. Waiting.

"Mine. Always. No matter what."

And I'm doing this.

I take the first step and my father squeezes my hand and we walk down the aisle toward my destiny. My future. With this man who is as good as he is brutal. Who has killed with the same hands with which he has made love to me. This man whose baby is growing inside my belly. The man I'm bound to. Was bound to from before I ever set eyes on him.

27

SERGIO

For a minute, I'm not sure if she's going to do it. If she's going to take those steps down the aisle. Down to me. She's in her head and I know she's hasn't been sleeping. I see it in the shadows beneath her eyes.

I don't know what I'll do if she turns and runs.

I know I can't let her go. I won't.

But I don't want to chase her. I don't want to make her.

And a moment later, when the pianist begins the wedding march again, I'm glad I don't have to. Her lips move into a small smile, and, eyes locked on mine, she comes to me.

I've never felt relief like I do in that moment.

Does she deserve this? Me? My family? No, she deserves a hundred times better. I will live and die with that knowledge. I will live and die knowing I loved her too much to let her go. It's selfish. But I guess I'm selfish. And what I feel for her, it overwhelms me sometimes. It swells and surges and takes me under so I can't breathe.

She is breath. She is life. She is everything.

She reaches the altar and I take her flowers from her, hand

them to the priest because I don't know what to do with them. I lift the veil from her face and her eyes glisten with tears. I know they're not all tears of joy and I lean close to her, touch the soft skin of her cheek and bring my mouth to her ear.

"You're beautiful."

With my thumb, I wipe away a tear and we just stay like that for a minute and I breathe her in and I want to make this moment last forever.

"I'm happy," she whispers, more tears sliding down her cheeks.

I close my hand over the swell of one hip and draw back to look at her. I know happy isn't all she is. I know she's scared. I want to tell her not to be afraid. That I'll protect her. That I won't ever let anything happen to her. To us. That I'll take care of everything. But I can't do that. And I don't. And all I can do is smile at her words.

Someone clears their throat. Fucking Dominic. I want to kill him. I want to kill my bastard brother. But Natalie pulls back and we turn to the priest and he begins the ceremony and, a short while later, Natalie Gregorian is Natalie Benedetti.

My wife.

28

SERGIO

"I'm going to miss being in the city," Natalie says. We're a few blocks from the house on Elfreth's Alley where we just handed over the keys to a house-sitter I hired so Natalie and Pepper can move in with me.

"You'll appreciate the quiet. Although you will have to learn how to drive a car."

"I can drive a car. I just haven't in a while."

"If you always drive like you did tonight, you're going to take some lessons."

"I'm just rusty. And your car goes too fast. I'm not used to it."

"Right." I'm glad she can't see the expression on my face. "This is my favorite Italian place in the city," I say, changing the subject as we round the corner and I push the door to the tiny restaurant open.

"I've never even seen this place and I must walk by here four times a day," she says once we're inside.

I smile. It's loud in the restaurant, even though there are only seven tables. Italians are loud though, and everyone here is Italian.

"It's a well-kept secret," I say, hanging my coat on the rack by the door before helping her get hers off.

The owner nods his greeting from behind the bar where he's pouring two glasses of wine.

"This way," I say, my hand at Natalie's low back as I lead her to a table at the back corner. I pull out her chair then take mine. My back's to the wall so I can see who comes and goes. But this place is safe.

"Do people always stare at you when you go places?" she asks. "Are they going to start staring at me now?"

"If they're staring at you it's because you're fucking beautiful."

"I wonder if you'll still be thinking that when I get big and fat with this baby." She picks up her menu so she's not looking at me.

I take her hand to make her look at me. "I don't care if you weigh four-hundred pounds. You will always be beautiful."

She rolls her eyes but is smiling.

"I'll order for us, if you don't mind," I say.

"I can decide for myself, thank you," she says.

"It's not an infringement on your rights, you know. It's just dinner, especially considering—"

"No, thank you," she says.

"Suit yourself."

The owner walks over with an open bottle of Chianti and a bottle of water. "Sergio. It's always good to see you here."

"Good to see you, too. How are things?"

"Quiet. Thank you."

I nod. He raises the bottle to pour for Natalie but she stops him. "Just water for me, please."

He looks at me and I give him a nod so he pours a glass of wine for me and water for Natalie.

"Usual?" he asks in his broken English, setting both bottles down on the table.

"Natalie?" I say.

"Um," she's still looking at the menu, which by now she's realized is in Italian and I know she can't understand a word. "This one." She points to something.

He reads out what she ordered and I have to grin. I can't wait to see her face when her meal arrives. After handing her menu over, she clears her throat and sits back.

"Usual for me," I say.

He nods and walks away.

"So, what did you order?" I ask. From the look on her face, I know she has no clue but she's way too stubborn to admit it.

She picks up her water. "I'll surprise you."

"Didn't know you read Italian," I say, picking up my wine, holding it up. "Cheers."

"Cheers."

I drink, then put my glass down and watch her.

"Do you have to be gone for three nights?" she asks. I know it's been on her mind. It'll be the first time I'm away since we got married. She's not comfortable in the house yet and she's still fighting me over the bodyguard trailing her when she's not home or with me.

"It'll go by fast. Dad isn't focused right now. Not with mom like she is."

"Salvatore can't go alone? Or Dominic?" She can't say his name without making a face.

"Salvatore's coming with me, but it has to be me. It's important."

"I know, it's just I wish you didn't have to go."

A waiter comes to the table holding two steaming plates with the edge of a towel. He sets them down and I see from Natalie's face she did not expect what she gets.

I can't help my smile, but when she looks up at me, I pick up my fork and bring my full attention to my plate. I stick a fat gnocchi into my mouth and chew, but when I look up at her, I shove another two in to keep from bursting out in laughter.

"What did I order?" she asks, her face slightly pale.

"Liver and onions," I say with my mouth full.

"Oh my God."

I can't help it now. I shove my napkin to my mouth and try to swallow so I don't spit out my mouthful when I laugh.

"You jerk. It's not funny."

I shake my head, wipe my eyes because I'm laughing so hard, I'm crying. "No, it is funny. Your expression is hilarious, in fact."

She gives me a glare, sets her fork down, puts her napkin on the table. When she makes to stand, I capture her hand.

"Come on, you have to admit, you are so damn stubborn. You should have let me order for you."

She eyes my plate, picks up her fork and pokes a gnocchi. She shoves it into her mouth and closes her eyes. "Oh wow."

"Told you so," I say.

She opens her eyes and sticks her tongue out at me.

I take her plate and push mine in front of her. "Eat."

She looks down at the gnocchi. "You don't have to do that." But she doesn't offer to swap back.

"It's fine. Eat."

I keep hold of her hand for a minute and she meets my eyes, gives me a warm smile. "Thanks."

"You're welcome."

I TOOK Eric with me to the meeting where I sat in for my father. Salvatore was to have joined me, but he's come down with some bug and I didn't want Dominic there. I don't care that I'm alone. I prefer it.

This is what it will be like when my father's gone. Me in the back of the car. Me, alone. I'll leave Natalie as far out of this as possible. Keep her safe.

The baby, in a way, I hope it's a girl. I wonder if my father thought about that when mom was pregnant with me. If he wished for a daughter so as not to have to pass this legacy on to his own. I wonder if, to some extent, there's a part of us that knows that the inheritance of the first-born male is a condemnation. A daughter can't rule. Not in our family. Sexist, I know, but her husband would take control when the time came.

I'm thinking about this when Eric slows the car.

"Need to refuel," he says. The kid who was supposed to make sure the car was ready before we left the city hadn't show up. Probably hungover somewhere is my guess.

"It's fine," I say. I need to stretch my legs anyway. Meeting was in Manhattan and I've been sitting for too long.

I climb out of the car and dial Natalie. It's late, but she said she'd wait up.

"Hey." Her voice is soft.

I can hear her smiling. It makes me smile. "Hey. Were you sleeping?"

"Nope."

"Dozing?"

"Maybe."

"Did you eat dinner?"

"A grilled cheese sandwich," she says. "Two, actually. I'm trying to get to that four-hundred pounds so we can see if you still think I'm beautiful."

I chuckle.

"Are you almost home?" she asks, a note of worry creeping into her voice.

"About thirty minutes away. Go to sleep. I'll wake you when I get home."

"No, I'll wait up," she says through a yawn.

"I like waking you up," I whisper. She knows what I mean.

"You're dirty, Sergio Benedetti."

"You like me dirty, Natalie Benedetti."

She snorts, then her voice turns serious. "I miss you."

"Me too. This was the longest three days of my life, but I'll be home soon." The pump clicks, and Eric takes the nozzle out. "I gotta go. I'll see you soon."

"You promise?"

"I promise, sweetheart."

We disconnect.

There's no screeching of tires as two SUVs pull into the station, their windows tinted black. There's no rush. They just slow as they turn into the lot. I'm tucking the phone back into my pocket when it happens. When I feel something isn't right.

Silence is supposed to precede an ambush.

Silence always comes before devastation. It's what I've always believed. How I've always thought it would happen.

But when I hear the first round fired, it's like slow motion. I turn and watch Eric's body fling backwards. A dark red spot appears on the front of his shirt. It begins to spread in a perfect circle feathering along the edges like a snowflake. That's what I think of when I see it. A fucking perfect snowflake.

He'd left his coat in the car. He doesn't have his weapon. Not that it would do any good. They've come prepared.

Fuck. We shouldn't have been out here, in the open like this. Unprotected and vulnerable.

Instinct has me gripping my weapon and I take aim and shoot at the driver's side window, even though I can't see for shit because even the windshield is black. I hit the driver though. I know it when the SUV speeds up, crashes into a parked car just outside the twenty-four-hour market.

The first bullet hits me at the back of my arm. It's my gun arm. But I know the sound of an automatic. There's more to come.

It's time.

My reckoning.

I know it. I'm sure of it like I'm sure of little else.

For as much as I think about death, for as aware as I am of its eternal presence, it's cold, bony fingers, like claws, shadows trailing me, clinging to me, for as much as I am aware, when it comes, when it is inevitable, it's still somehow unexpected.

I manage to turn. The cowards put a bullet in my back, below my shoulder blade. It burns. Sends me to my knees. I look at the passenger side window. It's rolled part of the way down. I can see a flash of hair, a quick glimpse of blond or gray. But the bullets are still coming. Six, I think. Seven. I'm on my back and something warm is sliding up to my neck, down over it.

And all I can think about is her.

Her face.

Her eyes.

The baby inside her.

My baby whom I'll never see.

My wife. I've had her for so short a time.

I won't keep my promise to her tonight. This will be the first time I don't keep a promise to her.

I think of the box on the family tree with my name on it. The date of birth. Who will fill in today's date underneath my name? Who will color in the red cross. Will that task fall to her? No. It can't. I can't let it. It's too heavy for her. Too dark.

There's screeching now. And sirens. One SUV is flying out of the gas station. They shoot one more bullet but this one misses.

Not that it matters. One less won't make a difference. Not for me. Not anymore.

"Nat."

It always pisses her off when I call her that and I almost smile at the memory of her face when I do.

Something gurgles up from my throat. I open my eyes for a moment to see a stranger's face.

And then I'm watching. Just watching.

Nothing hurts. It did, the first bullet. It fucking burned. The second, too. And the one that ripped into my heart.

Now, nothing.

One leg is bent underneath me, the other stretched out. Blood pools all around me. The ambulance is here, and the sirens are fading. All noise is fading, I realize. Their screams. Their words. I hear nothing. And it's not like I think it would be.

I want to see her again. One last time. I need to. I will myself to. To be home. To lie beside her. To touch her just once more. To brush my fingers across her cheek. To lay my hand on her belly. Hear her laugh. Feel her curl into me. Feel her breath on my cheek.

To tell her I'm sorry.

And maybe it's my reprieve. Maybe some time in my life, I did one good thing, and this is my reward. Because I'm here with her. And she's sleeping. She's wearing my T-shirt. It's so big on her. And she's holding my pillow to her and her hair is fanned out all around her and she's so beautiful.

I want to scream to her, but I can't. I will the sound, but nothing comes. Nothing. I want to touch her, but I can't feel her. I can't fucking feel her.

Fuck. Fuck. Fuck.

I'm screaming, but there's nothing. Nothing but silence. Utter silence.

She stirs. Blinks. I stop. And for a moment, I think she's looking up at me. I think she sees me.

But then she closes her eyes again and rolls onto her side and she's asleep. Peaceful still.

She doesn't know yet. She doesn't know yet that I'm gone. That I won't be able to keep my promise. That I won't wake her tonight or any night.

She doesn't know yet that I died.

29

NATALIE

I haven't been inside the study in the four weeks since the night Sergio didn't come home. I've barricaded myself in this house, which I never had the chance to make my home. I wanted to. After everything, I wanted to make it a home. Our home.

I know it's too early, but I think I feel the baby moving inside me. Feel the little swell of my belly. Ever since that night, I swear I've felt it. Him. It'll be a boy. I know that too.

Sergio won't see my belly swell as his baby grows. He won't be there when his son comes into the world. Won't get to hold him. I wonder if he'll look like Sergio. In a way, I hope he doesn't because I think it will break my heart over and over again and I'm not strong enough for that.

The house is silent. All the lights are out except for the one over the stove in the kitchen. Standing at the study door, I take a deep breath in, because there's something I have to do. Something I have to finish.

I set my hand on the doorknob and turn it, hear the creak as I push the door open.

Instantly, I am overwhelmed by memories of him. By the scent of him. His aftershave. His whiskey. Overwhelmed by the weight of the life he carried. The shadow that clung to him, that kept him in its clutches. I remember all those moments when I'd felt that strange sensation that he wouldn't be with me for long. That he was a ghost. That this thing would claim him. I'd pushed those thoughts away then. They were too terrible to deal with. But the reality, it's worse because it's just that—real. And final.

The skin around my eyes is wet again, but I ignore it and walk inside, partially closing the door behind me. Make my way to the desk from memory. Switch on the lamp. His chair is pushed out like he just got up from it. I touch it, the leather cool but soft and worn and comfortable as I sink into it.

The tumbler he last drank from still sits on the desk. The half-empty bottle beside it. I wrap my hand around the heavy crystal glass and bring it to me. To my nose. I inhale. I remember. And tears slide down my face and into the glass and I bring it to my lips and drink the last swallow of whiskey and the choking sound that comes, it's my own. It's my grief and I can't swallow, my throat closes up. I want to throw up. But I don't remember the last time I ate. I have to eat for the baby. I know.

I force a deep breath. Feel myself shudder with it. Feel the whiskey burn when it does, finally, go down. It reinforces me and I steel my spine because I have work to do.

Setting the empty tumbler down, I reach beneath the desk and feel for the scroll. I pull it out, unroll it, mechanically open it on the desktop and set the bottle on one corner, tuck the other beneath the base of the desk lamp.

I survey the images, the boxes, scanning the names as I open the drawer and take out his pencils, dulled by use, the eraser worn to a nub. I rub my thumb over it. Try to feel him.

Dragging my attention from the sheet, I search deeper in the drawer for a ruler. That's when I come across the other sheet there. This one lies flat. I take it out, set it on top of the parchment so I can study it under the light of the lamp.

It's me. My face. At least a partially sketched image. I see smudges from his effort to perfect what he saw, and I swear, I see it too. Like I'm laid bare here. Like he drew my soul.

I set my thumb over the print of his bigger one and smear it across my cheek, like he has before, and the moment I do, every hair on my body stands on end and all at once, he's here. He's here with me. Behind me. Holding me. One hand closed over mine, his thumb on mine, his other arm wrapped around my middle, hand flat on my belly, and that's when that sobbing begins again except that this time, he's holding me. He's holding me as I fall apart. As I weep loudly, with a voice not my own, with anguish that can't belong to me. That I don't want.

"It's not fair."

It's stupid, but it's all I can say. Because it's not. We were supposed to have time. We were supposed to have a little bit of time.

And I feel his arms squeezing me, cradling me against his chest, holding me so tight that for a minute, I just close my eyes and imagine it's real. Imagine he's real.

"Come back," I sob.

He can't, though. I know that. I watched them put him in the ground.

The high-pitched wailing is me, I realize. And even as I feel the feather light kisses on my temple, even as the hair on the back of my neck stand on end at his touch, I wail. Because this is it. This is goodbye.

I hear his words inside my mind. The whispered "I love you." Feel one final squeeze of his arms, the flat of his hand on my belly. The scruff of his jaw on my cheek.

And when I'm able to breathe again, I whisper those words

back as he slips away. Sergio gone. Sergio gone from me. Gone from this world forever.

I don't know how long I sit there in the near dark staring at nothing. My face sticky from tears. My vision empty. It's when I hear the lock of the front door open that I move. That I shift my gaze to the partially closed study door.

"Natalie."

I startle. They sound so alike.

Footsteps approach the study and a moment later, the door is pushed open and Salvatore stands in the doorway and I realize the night is over because the warm glow of the morning sun surrounds him. It's strange. Like a halo all around him.

He looks at me. I almost have to smile at what he must see. I haven't showered in days. Haven't brushed my hair in that long. I'm still wearing one of Sergio's T-shirts I'd dug out of the laundry hamper.

Salvatore takes in the contents of the desk. Eyes the empty glass of whiskey. He steps inside.

"You don't look so good, Nat."

The way he says it, leaning against the door, taking off his gloves, one eyebrow raised and one side of his mouth quirking into a lopsided smile, it makes me smile, actually.

"Is that yours?" he asks, gesturing to the whiskey.

I shake my head. "It's his." I touch the pattern on the crystal. "Was his," I correct.

He takes off his coat, sets it and the gloves over the back of the chair.

"You're not drinking, are you? He wouldn't want that. With the baby and all."

"I'm not drinking."

"Good. When's the last time you ate?"

I shrug a shoulder.

"Called your parents? Called Drew?"

I shake my head. I don't know. I know they've called. I've seen the countless messages but I switched off my phone a few days ago.

"Drew called me this morning. Said you haven't been to school."

"I don't think school matters right now."

"Well, it does." He shifts his gaze to the parchment, steps closer to get a better look. Gives a shake of his head. "Fucking Sergio. Leave it to him to draw a fucking graveyard."

When he reaches out to touch it, I put my hand out, stop him.

He looks at me. "Have you been outside since the funeral?"

"What are you doing here? Why do you have a key?"

"Because my brother made me promise something. One thing. If anything happened."

Fuck. I'm going to lose it again.

Salvatore sits down, and a darkness shadows his features. "He called me one night after you two had met and told me if anything happened to him that I was to take care of you. Make sure you were okay."

"He did?"

Salvatore nods.

"I think he knew. I know he did." I say through sobs and tears. "He told me once that time was a luxury. One that he wouldn't have."

"Yeah, well, you know Sergio."

Knew. Not know. Sergio is no longer present. He can never be spoken of in the present tense again.

"He was always a little dramatic," Salvatore continues when I don't speak.

He's trying to make light of it. "Yeah. I guess."

"What are you doing in here in the dark?"

"I have to finish it."

"Finish what?"

I point to the place below Sergio's name. Just beneath his box. The day of his birth. The dash. The empty space.

Salvatore nods. He stands and comes around the desk. "Let me do it."

I roll my chair away. I let him. And I watch when he takes up the pencil and writes in the date.

He stares at it for a while and I look at him. At Salvatore Benedetti.

He'll take Sergio's place now. Next in line to rule.

Next in line to die?

"Do you ever get scared?" I ask.

He shifts his gaze to me.

"To die. Like he did," I add. Again, my face crumples beneath the pain and I'm struggling to breathe.

He considers this for a long time. Takes in a deep breath. "Yeah. Sometimes. But then I think don't I deserve it? I have blood on my hands, too."

I know he does. I know after Sergio's murder, the Benedetti family unleashed their wrath. They took vengeance for the death of the first-born son. And what a vengeance it was. What a brutal retribution.

"Did he really do that? Call you? Tell you to take care of me?"

Salvatore nods. "Drunk in the middle of the night." He chuckles.

The silence that follows is awkward, suddenly. I shift my gaze to the sheet. Reach over to take the red marker. To draw the cross.

"Mob killing," I say. And somehow, I don't cry. I draw the cross carefully. Perfectly. I color it in. I take my time because once this part is done, there's no erasing. Not that there ever was a going back. I know that.

"What are you going to do now?" he asks.

I look up at him. "Leave. I want nothing to do with your family." I don't apologize for it.

He nods.

"Will he let me go? Now? With the baby?"

He knows who I mean. "If what you want is out, I'll make sure you're out. I'll protect you. I gave Sergio my word and I intend on keeping it."

"Even against your father?" Because that's what this would be. Franco Benedetti has no intention of letting me take Sergio's baby and disappearing.

"Even against my father."

30

NATALIE

One and a Half Years Later

I f it wasn't for Salvatore, I wouldn't be here, in my own house in Asbury Park, right now. Franco was hell bent against me leaving. Against me taking his first grandchild away from him, taking that last piece of Sergio with me.

I understood something in these months and I'm glad for it. Franco mourned Sergio. He was devastated by his loss and it made me see a different side of him. A human side. Still cold. Still manipulative and all powerful, but human. This is the one thing Franco Benedetti and I have in common. We're both hurting over the loss of Sergio.

So we came to an agreement. Franco Benedetti will still be a part of my son's life, but he won't be in it, not now. Not yet. I'll deal with the future later.

I named my son Jacob Sergio Benedetti. And when he looked at me the first time, I was grateful that he did look like

Sergio after all. It hurt, but it also reminded me of him. And I don't want to forget Sergio. I don't want to forget a minute of the little bit of time we had together. And the baby we made, the love I feel for him is sometimes overwhelming.

It's almost eleven at night when the doorbell rings. It's Salvatore. He usually visits once a month, but I'm not expecting him for a few weeks, and when he comes, he usually comes early in the morning to spend time with Jacob. Although, we've become friends since Sergio's death and I like him. He struggles with the life he's now bound to lead. It's strange, he thinks of things so differently than Sergio did.

Something's up, though, because Salvatore called not twenty minutes ago to see if I was home. Asked if he could come.

"Hey, Salvatore," I say, opening the door.

He's preoccupied. It takes him a minute to even say hello back.

"Come on in," I say, opening the door wider.

"Why is it so quiet?"

"It's late. Jacob's asleep."

"Oh." It's like he didn't realize the time. He steps in, stops. Shakes his head with a snort as if he were continuing some conversation in his mind.

"What's going on?" I ask when I close the door.

He navigates around the toys to sit on the couch. "You have something to drink?"

"Sure." I get him a whiskey, take the seat beside him and pour myself a tumbler, too. I started to drink the stuff in the last few months. Just a little now and again. It still burns, but it's Sergio's favorite brand and it reminds me of him, of us sitting together while he drank a glass. The smell alone will do it, but the burn, it's what I crave some nights.

Salvatore takes a swallow then focuses his attention on swirling the amber liquid around.

"I have to claim her," he says.

"What?"

He looks at me. "Lucia DeMarco. Her time's almost up."

I just watch him. Watch the furrow between his brows. Salvatore's relationship with his father is different than Sergio's. Sergio could manage Franco. He was the favorite son. Salvatore and Franco, though, their relations are strained, at best.

He swallows the rest of his whiskey. "Not quite half a year left, and I have to take her. Show the world how powerful the Benedetti family is." He gets up, pours himself a second, generous glass full. Drinks half of it before turning to me. "I'm to break her. Destroy her."

"There's no way out—"

"No." He cuts me off with an ugly snort. "There's no way to do anything," he spits, finishes his drink. Pours another glass and swallows that too. "In six months' time, I'll own the DeMarco Mafia princess. I'll take her from her tower, bring her to my home, and I'll punish her for being born a DeMarco. I'll bring her to her knees to bury her father's nose in the dirt."

I go to him. "Salvatore," but what can I say? I have no advice, no comfort to offer. I know the DeMarco bargain. It's a devil's bargain made by Franco Benedetti, to be executed by his succeeding son. "At least it's not Dominic," I say.

He looks at me. Shakes his head. "Do you know what he did to her? What my father ordered when the girl was sixteen? Fucking sixteen years old. A child."

I don't want to know.

"He had her tied to a cold steel table. Had her legs pried apart and had a doctor confirm that her virginity was intact."

"Christ."

"While her own father was made to watch."

"Salva—"

"While I stood by and did nothing," he spits, his tone harder.

"Not a goddamned thing. Fuck. I couldn't even look at her. It made me sick. Or it should have. But you know what?" He walks away, so his back is to me. "It made me hard. It made me fucking hard."

I watch his back, big broad shoulders, muscular arms. He's built like Sergio. Powerful.

"I am my father's son. A monster. Like him. Maybe worse."

"No. No, that's not true." I try to take the drink from him, but he won't let me.

"I'll be *her* monster."

"Salvatore, you don't have to—"

"Yes, I do," he says too loudly. "I do have to. That's the point. I will take the girl. I will break the girl. It's my duty."

The monitor goes off then. Jacob's fussing. He probably hears us, his room is just down the hall, and Salvatore isn't being quiet.

"Shit," Salvatore says, realizing. "I'm sorry."

"It's okay. He's been waking up at night," I lie. I don't want him to feel any worse than he already does. Jacob lets out a long cry. "I'd better go settle him down."

Salvatore nods. I realize he hasn't even taken his jacket off. I go to Jacob, pick him up out of his crib, cradle him, kiss the top of his perfect head, kiss the soft dark hair there.

"Shh, baby. It's okay. Shh."

It doesn't take him long to fall asleep again. And when he does, I lay him back down and tuck him in, but by the time I return to the living room, Salvatore's gone.

31

NATALIE

I don't dream of Sergio often. I wish I could. But the nights I do, I wake up crying. Tonight's one of them. Maybe it's because Salvatore was just here. Maybe it's what he told me. Maybe it's just the mention of Lucia DeMarco's name.

And it's strange, although I can't remember the dreams themselves, I do remember feeling safe, even with the bitter-sweet edge. Even knowing I'll miss him that much more the following day. Jacob keeps me busy and I'm so grateful for him. I'm not sure I'd survive this if it weren't for him.

It's four in the morning when I wake up with tears on my cheeks. I switch on the light and get up, knowing I won't be getting any more sleep tonight. I go to the dresser, open the drawer where, at the back, I keep a box. I carry it to the bed, open it. Inside are just a few things. Memories. The first is the ring. His ring. The Benedetti family crest dark and proudly displayed. I always notice it on Salvatore's finger too.

I slip it onto my finger. It's so big and heavy, I have to hold it in place to look at it.

I'm to give it to Jacob when he's sixteen. It's part of the agreement. I'm not yet sure I can, but it's what Franco expects.

But I'm not above going back on my word with Franco Benedetti. I don't want Jacob involved in this life. I don't want him to die the way his father died.

Slipping it off my finger, I set it back inside the box and smile at the next thing I see. An 8X10 of us on our wedding day. Sergio is holding my hand and smiling so wide. And he's just whispered something into my ear that made me laugh so hard, I'm almost doubled over.

It's strange, if you look at my face, all you see is the happiest bride in the world. And I was happy in that moment. I remember the nagging feeling of something not quite right, and I know now that it was a premonition, but still, in that moment, I remember feeling happy.

I set the box down and put the expensively framed photo on the nightstand. And it feels right. Something inside me tells me this is right.

I've grieved for over a year. Sergio is gone. But I have Jacob now. And I have my memories. I'll take them. Take the bad, the sad, with the good. And in a way, time has been kind to me. Time is making me remember the good ones. Even though I never forget the sad. The feeling is always there, always along the edges of those happy moments, but it's manageable, more and more as time passes. I'll always love Sergio. He'll always be the love of my life. And I'll honor him. I'll raise his son to know him. Know his father as I knew him. Devoted and full of love.

That's what Jacob will know of Sergio.

Because that's who Sergio was.

2ND LETTER FROM NATASHA

Dear Reader,

I told you at my opening letter that Sergio had a very strong voice in my mind during the writing of the book. Well, that was true for most of it. By the time the last scenes came, he'd quieted. I know that he knew what had to happen. He went into it eyes-wide-open, too. And I think that takes courage. My heart broke to write this book. It's breaking now to write this letter. But I'm glad I did it. Sergio deserved to have his story told and I love his and Natalie's story so very much. I even love the heartbreak of it.

Thank you so much, again, for spending your time reading my books. You don't know how much that means to me.

Love,
Natasha

WHAT TO READ NEXT

KILLIAN: A DARK MAFIA ROMANCE

"A re you scared?"

She goes rigid. I know she can feel my breath on her neck.

"Answer my question."

"Yes." It's a squeak.

I walk around her, resume my position facing her. "At least one of you is honest. But what kind of message would I be sending if I let your brother walk out of here? If I don't punish him?"

She drops her head, wipes her nose on her shoulder.

"It wouldn't be good for business," I say.

"What are you going to do, then?" she asks, her jaw set when she turns her face up.

"Break a leg. Maybe two." I shrug my shoulder as Jones starts blabbering some nonsense. I realize he's probably stoned.

"I can pay you." Her voice breaks and she can't hide the fact that she's crying now.

I step to her, reach out to touch a tear with my thumb. She gasps.

"This isn't about money, sweetheart."

"Please don't—"

"Shh, Priscilla." I turn to Jones. "Get up."

She obviously thinks I'm going to break his legs right here, right now, because she throws herself forward, crashing into my chest. I catch her when she bounces backward to stop her from falling.

"I'll do anything!"

I'm still holding her by the arms and she's trembling.

"Please, please, just let him go. It was just a stupid—"

"Since when is stupidity an excuse?"

"Please. I'll do anything you want."

I let silence hang in the air between us, watching her. "Anything?"

She pulls back and turns her face up and suddenly, I want to see her eyes. But then, she nods. Three quick, nervous little nods.

I touch her face, smear a tear down over her chin, her throat, to the hollow between her collarbones, the skin of her chest. She's holding her breath as I drag my finger down to where her blouse has torn a little, feel the softness of her breast. "Are you offering to fuck me, Priscilla?"

She draws back sharply. I watch her struggle to come to grips with what she's just done. I walk behind her and touch the ropes binding her wrists. "I'll have to see what's on offer, of course."

She makes a sound and I know she's crying again.

Slowly, I untie the rope and the first thing she does is reach up to her blindfold. I grip both wrists from behind.

"Don't do that," I whisper in her ear. "Not if you want to walk out of here."

Her hands shake but she nods and slowly sets her arms at her sides.

I move to stand before her.

"Show me."

"Wh...what?"

"Show me what it is you're offering."

Her mouth falls open like she can't believe what I just asked her to do. I don't actually expect her to do it. To strip. I can tell she's not that kind of girl. But when her trembling hands reach to draw her coat off her shoulders, I'm surprised. Hugo's watching her too but her brother's head's bowed. I can't believe he'd let his sister go through with this. Fucking asshole. When I'm done here, I think I'll break his arms too.

Priscilla's coat drops to the floor and she reaches for the buttons of her blouse. Tears are sliding down her face, but I can't stop watching as each button is slipped through its hole and she pulls open her blouse, then drags it off, letting it drop to the floor on top of her coat. She's wearing a pretty little white bra and I can see her hard, pink nipples through the lace.

Her hands move back and it takes her a minute to get her skirt unzipped. Once she's done it, she pushes it down over slender legs. She's wearing skin-colored thigh high stockings and I can see the neat mound of dark hair through the white lace of her panties.

She sets her hands on either side of her. I guess she thinks she's done.

"Continue."

"I...will you..." she's starting to hyperventilate.

"Your brother's a piece of shit. You sure he's worth this?" I can't help but ask. She reaches up to her face and I grab her wrists again, hold them between us. "U-uh." I don't want to have to hurt her. It doesn't feel right. "Get dressed and go home. Let your brother deal with the consequences of his actions."

"I can do this. I—I just need a minute. I just—"

"Cilla." It's Jones. We both turn to him.

"I—" Cilla starts, but stops.

"Go home, Priscilla. You don't belong here," I say.

"Please, I just..."

"You just what?"

Nothing.

I look her over. Something about her makes me curious.

"One month," I hear myself say.

"W...What?"

"You're mine for one month."

"I—"

"I own you for thirty days," I make very clear.

"I don't understand."

"I think you do. You have one minute to decide."

"What do I have to do?"

"Anything I want."

She knows my meaning.

I catch Hugo's eye because suddenly, there's nothing I want more than this. Her. One month. Her to myself. Mine.

When I give Hugo a nod, he cocks the gun. She jumps.

"Yes! Yes. Okay. One month. What you said. Please don't hurt him. Please."

Jones is quiet. I look away from her to him, grip a handful of his hair. "You going to let your sister do this?"

"I said yes!" his sister cries out. "Leave him alone!"

"Nothing?" I ask Jones.

He whimpers. Like the fucking coward he is. I take a deep breath in and lean in close so he and I are eye to eye. "I just need to know one thing before I take your sister to my bed."

His bloodshot eyes finally glide over to where she's standing beside us.

"Here, Jones. Focus here." I tug on his greasy hair until he looks at me. "Who put you in touch with the buyer?"

Nothing. Nothing but fear.

"Let me help you out. Was it my fucking cousin?"

He doesn't have to answer. I see the truth in his eyes. I release him and he falls backward.

"Please don't hurt him!" the girl cries out again. I turn to her. Pull her toward me so her chest is touching mine, so my cock is pressing against her belly. So she can get a feel for what she can expect. Her hands come up between us, a barrier. One I easily push aside.

"Pretty Priscilla," I start, reaching to undo the blindfold, dragging it slowly from her eyes. "So concerned for your brother. But aren't you afraid I'll hurt *you*?"

One-Click the discounted box set containing both Killian and Giovanni's stories here !

ALSO BY NATASHA KNIGHT

The Devil's Pawn Duet

Devil's Pawn

Devil's Redemption

To Have and To Hold

With This Ring

I Thee Take

Stolen: Dante's Vow

The Society Trilogy

Requiem of the Soul

Reparation of Sin

Resurrection of the Heart

Dark Legacy Trilogy

Taken (Dark Legacy, Book 1)

Torn (Dark Legacy, Book 2)

Twisted (Dark Legacy, Book 3)

Unholy Union Duet

Unholy Union

Unholy Intent

Collateral Damage Duet

Collateral: an Arranged Marriage Mafia Romance

Damage: an Arranged Marriage Mafia Romance

Ties that Bind Duet

Mine

His

MacLeod Brothers

Devil's Bargain

Benedetti Mafia World

Salvatore: a Dark Mafia Romance

Dominic: a Dark Mafia Romance

Sergio: a Dark Mafia Romance

The Benedetti Brothers Box Set (Contains Salvatore, Dominic and Sergio)

Killian: a Dark Mafia Romance

Giovanni: a Dark Mafia Romance

The Amado Brothers

Dishonorable

Disgraced

Unhinged

Standalone Dark Romance

Descent

Deviant

Beautiful Liar

Retribution

Theirs To Take

ABOUT THE AUTHOR

Natasha Knight is the *USA Today* Bestselling author of Romantic Suspense and Dark Romance Novels. She has sold over half a million books and is translated into six languages. She currently lives in The Netherlands with her husband and two daughters and when she's not writing, she's walking in the woods listening to a book, sitting in a corner reading or off exploring the world as often as she can get away.

Write Natasha here: natasha@natasha-knight.com

NATASHA KNIGHT

sexy dark romance with heart

www.natasha-knight.com

THANK YOU!

Thanks for reading *The Benedetti Brothers Trilogy.* I hope you enjoyed it and would consider leaving a review at the store where you purchased this book.

Made in United States
North Haven, CT
13 May 2025

68822915R20446